Catherine Mangan grew up in Ireland before embarking on her own Italian escape. She studied languages at University College Cork before moving to Italy (briefly) with friends, which was the start of a life-long love affair with the country. She now divides her time between Ireland and Silicon Valley. *The Italian Escape* is her first novel.

Under another name, Catherine is an award-winning Irish entrepreneur and creator of a language-learning app, which has users in 175 countries.

Catherine Mangan

The *Italian Escape*

sphere

SPHERE

First published in Great Britain in 2021 by Sphere

1 3 5 7 9 10 8 6 4 2

A CIP catalogue record for this book
is available from the British Library.

ISBN 978-0-7515-7985-7

Typeset in Baskerville by M Rules
Printed and bound in Great Britain by
Clays Ltd, Elcograf S.p.A.

Papers used by Sphere are from well-managed forests
and other responsible sources.

MIX
Paper from
responsible sources
FSC® C104740

Sphere
An imprint of
Little, Brown Book Group
Carmelite House
50 Victoria Embankment
London EC4Y 0DZ

An Hachette UK Company
www.hachette.co.uk

www.littlebrown.co.uk

To Tom,
For being by my side

Chapter One

There are ten thousand and eighty minutes in a week. That is exactly how long Niamh Kelly has been feeling depressed. Well, not in the true clinical definition of the word, obviously, but at the moment anything else felt like a massive understatement.

Her iPhone vibrated on the kitchen table in front of her – more concerned friends checking in, no doubt – but she couldn't muster the energy to respond. She was tired of talking about it. She slumped back into the chair, tied her long, dark hair up into a knot, flicked the phone to silent and opened her thesaurus app. Surely there was a more appropriate word to describe her current state beyond just sad. But not even the app could offer much in the way of useful alternatives, proffering options such as 'Bereaved' (no one had died so that was totally useless), 'Forlorn' (sounded like someone from medieval England) and 'Lugubrious' (that sounded promising but she had no idea what it actually meant).

'How are you feeling today, Niamh?' she asked herself.

'Lugubrious,' she replied with an exaggerated sigh.

'Are you talking to me, love?' her mother asked from across the room.

'No, just talking to myself, Mam.'

'Oh, right,' her mother replied over the sound of the television.

'Lugubrious,' she whispered to herself, tapping the screen on her phone. The definition read 'mournful or gloomy'. Definitely accurate, she decided, but none of her friends would know what it meant, either, so she wouldn't be able to use it without sounding pretentious, so rather disappointingly it was another useless option.

She had gone to the trouble of calculating the number of minutes: twenty-four hours, times sixty minutes, times seven days. She couldn't do that kind of calculation in her head. Mathematics had never really been a strong point, not that she'd ever really cared enough to try. She'd never understood how Pythagoras' theorem would benefit any aspect of real life, or why anyone was forced to learn long division when calculators had already been invented. It all seemed like a massive waste of time when there were so many more interesting things to be learned. So tonight Niamh felt entirely justified that in just a few seconds her calculator app could tell her the exact number of minutes that she had been in this sad mental state, without the need to rely on mental mathematical gymnastics.

'Ten thousand and eighty-one now,' she sighed under her breath as she spun the iPhone on the kitchen table and topped up her glass of wine.

'What's that, love?' asked her mother from across the room, her eyes glued to the television screen.

'Nothing. Just talking to myself,' she mumbled.

'Nina, why don't you come over here and sit by the fire?' her mother asked, patting the sofa alongside her.

'No, I think I'll go to bed,' she muttered, examining a cluster of split ends in her hair.

'Bed? It's only nine o'clock. It's still bright out. It's a beautiful summer's evening,' her mother argued, tearing her eyes from the television programme. 'Will you, for God's sake, stop picking at your hair? Do you have lice or something?' She stood up slowly, rubbing her knee, and crossed the living room towards her daughter.

'What?' Niamh asked through the bottom of her wine glass.

'Why are you picking at your hair? There's an epidemic going around you know – of lice. And they can hop from one head to another so it's easy to get them.'

'Jesus, Mam, no, I don't have lice. I'm not dirty. It's just split ends,' Niamh cried, pulling on some strands of hair that had come loose.

'They like clean hair, actually.'

'What? Who likes clean hair?' Niamh asked, now utterly frustrated with the conversation.

'The lice do. They like clean hair. That's why they hop from one head to another,' her mother declared confidently, as if she had just eked out this nugget of medical certainty from the gospel that is the *Reader's Digest*. All of her facts and strong opinions originated from the *Reader's Digest*. Someone had once told her that if she subscribed to *Reader's Digest* she would be able to have a conversation about anything because it taught you a little about everything. Mrs Kelly had been a regular subscriber for eight years now and quite fancied herself as a great conversationalist. 'Anyway, it looks like you have lice or something when you pick at it like that. You don't want people talking about you, do you?'

'They already are, Mam,' Niamh sighed. 'I've provided plenty of fodder for the neighbours lately. No shortage of gossip this week. Niamh Kelly, thirty-three years old, newly single, no, wait ... dumped, in fact, and jobless. No man. No job. What a disaster.' Her voice was rising now. Her father lowered his newspaper a couple of inches. His glasses peered over the top momentarily, gauging the situation as he glanced from wife to daughter, but he quickly retreated back behind the temporary invisibility that the newspaper afforded him.

'You do have a job. There's nothing at all wrong with that job, Nina, and as soon as you're feeling better you'll go back to it. There's no harm in taking a week off. You were due a break anyway.'

'I'm not going back to it. I *can't* go back! How can I go back there?' She knew she was starting to sound hysterical now but she couldn't stop it. 'How can I go back and face him every day? I'd be the laughing stock of the place.'

'I'm sure there is a way to avoid him, love. You shouldn't have to give up your job just because you broke up. That's not right.'

'A, there is no way to avoid him, Mam. PlatesPlease is a startup – actually, even worse, it's *his* startup, so there's no avoiding him. And B, we didn't break up. I was dumped. Remember? Dumped, dropped and discarded, like it all meant nothing. Like the past four years meant nothing. What a dope. How could I not have known? You know everyone will say that I must have guessed something, known something . . . How could I not have known?'

'But you didn't know and that's not your fault. Sometimes things just don't work out. People change. You don't know what was going through his head, but if he could treat you like that then you're better off without him,' Una Kelly said, emphasising her words by jabbing her index finger on the table.

'I'm nearly halfway through my thirties, newly single and no job. How did I end up here? Seriously, how is this my life?'

4

Niamh asked, shaking her head. She poured the remainder of the bottle into her glass and watched as it reluctantly released its last few drops.

The theme tune to the Friday-night chat show – a Friday-night ritual in every Irish household – hummed along on the television, signalling the end of any other possible conversation and the urgent need to make tea. Parents and 'young marrieds with children' around the country were gathering in front of the television and the fire, settling in for the next two hours, happy to be entertained. It would be the usual rollout of minor celebrities promoting their new movie, losers who had found God, turned their life around and had now written a book to help all the other losers out there do the same, and some twenty-something-year-old who had rejected meat and dairy and embraced veganism the previous year, had started making granola in their kitchen and had just sold the company to Kellogg's for several million. At the end of the two hours, one half of the country would be motivated to fix or change their life and the other half would be depressed because their lives were just ordinary by comparison.

'Is the kettle on?' Niamh's dad asked from behind the paper. He wouldn't put it down until the programme started and it was safe to come out from behind it.

'I'm putting it on now,' replied her mother, opening a packet of biscuits. 'Will you have a cup?'

'I will so.'

Niamh smiled despite herself at the nightly exchange about the cup of tea that they drank religiously, and the easy way that her parents had with each other. She wondered then if relationships got easier with time and if, after so many years, you could just anticipate the other person so that there was never any need for angst or arguments. Did you just know the other person so well that you knew instinctively what they would or wouldn't like, what they would or wouldn't do, and so navigate conversations and situations easily, armed in advance with that knowledge?

'Night,' she said quietly, getting up from the table.

'Night, love,' they both replied at the same time, heads already directed towards the television.

'Have a good sleep,' her dad offered as he folded down the newspaper and stood to throw a log on the fire.

She picked up her phone and it flashed 21.10. This time last week she had been having dinner with Rick at the new tapas restaurant. Rick preferred to eat early in the evening so they always made an early dinner reservation.

'It's better for the digestion to eat early,' he would say whenever she questioned the need to race to a restaurant by seven o'clock. 'Plus, some places have an early-bird special before seven, so it's an added bonus. See, Niamh, there is value for money everywhere if you look for it,' he would recite smugly.

She was probably having dessert right around now, this time last week, in her new navy dress. Now that she thought of it, this exact time last week she was less than twenty minutes from being unceremoniously dumped and she was happily tucking into her tiramisu.

She hadn't noticed anything unusual about his behaviour. He had been distracted over dinner, but not more than usual. He was in the middle of raising another round of funding for the business. He was always stressed when he was fundraising, so she had assumed it was purely work related.

'Why do you think they have tiramisu on the menu if this is a tapas place?' she had asked.

'What?' he had asked, scrolling through emails on his phone.

'Tiramisu is Italian. Why does a Spanish tapas restaurant have tiramisu on the menu?'

'Niamh, I have no idea. Maybe the Spanish don't have that many desserts. Do you have any idea how many calories are in that thing?' he retorted. 'There are over six hundred calories in one slice of tiramisu, Niamh. That means you'd have to run for an hour and fifteen minutes just to burn that off,' he snapped as he stuck his phone back in his pocket.

'So I'll walk to work every morning next week.' She shrugged, and scraped the bowl.

'Niamh, I don't have time for this now. I have to work tomorrow.'

'But tomorrow is Saturday!' she whined.

'Entrepreneurs are always on, Niamh, you should know that by now. It's intense. We can't all saunter into the office five days a week at nine o'clock like you do.'

Niamh leaned heavily on the edge of the sink now, shaking her head. She sighed to herself, thinking back on the series of events last Friday night. She should have seen it coming, but she hadn't. Or maybe she had just refused to accept that there had been more arguments than smiles over the past few months.

She rinsed her glass in the sink and snuck two of her dad's night-time cold and flu tablets from the medicine basket over the sink, swallowing them with lukewarm water from the tap. Apparently they weren't addictive and they definitely helped knock you out at night.

She shuffled towards the kitchen door, thinking that she would have to burn that navy dress, but she couldn't burn it right now, even though the fire was perfect. It was roaring up the chimney, resembling a miniature towering inferno in the grate. But if she came back downstairs with the navy dress and tossed it into the fire, it might be too much for her dad. He would either abandon his current position on the armchair and flee from the room, not wanting any part of the madness (missing his show in the process – and she'd hear about that until next Friday's episode), or he'd think she had lost her mind and would start to worry about her.

She didn't need anyone else to worry about her. She certainly didn't need to have her dad offer any critical life advice. It was enough to deal with her mother and her *Reader's Digest* nuggets of wisdom. One thing was sure, however – she would never wear that navy dress again. It would always be the dress she got dumped in. Shame, really, because she thought she looked kind of skinny in it. Well, not *skinny* exactly, but slim, or at least slimmer than she looked in real life. Kind of like a sartorial magic wand.

'Waste of sixty euros,' she sighed, heading towards the stairs.

Chapter Two

She could hear the high-pitched whine of the vacuum cleaner downstairs. The postman dropped some envelopes through the door and the dog went nuts.

'Mother of God, it's eight o'clock on a Saturday morning,' she groaned from under her duvet. She wasn't hungover, exactly, but her head ached behind her eyes and her tongue felt like chalk.

What was it about small dogs that they always had to start a fight? It was like they were always on the defensive because of their size. Niamh had refused to walk Marty any more because he was completely out of control. He was a small, hairy little thing, a cross between a wheaten terrier and something else – no one knew exactly what. Her dad had taken him in when the neighbour's dog got knocked up for the second time in a year and had another three puppies. They were all headed for the local shelter but everyone knew that the shelter had a seven-day kill policy, so the Kelly family had come to the rescue. Her mother had refused at first to have anything to do with it.

'If you bring him in here, Paddy, you'll have to take care of him.'

'Ah, would you look at him. Sure he's a lovely little thing,' her father replied, scratching his chin. 'He'll be no bother at all.'

After a few disastrous attempts to walk him, Niamh refused point blank to take him out again. 'He'll just have to get his exercise in the back garden,' she announced, coming in through the front door and opening the back one. 'It's mortifying to try to walk him. Honest to God, if there is a German shepherd in sight he's heaving and straining at the leash, frothing at the mouth, trying to attack him, and he wouldn't even reach the German shepherd's knees. I think he has a Napoleonic complex or something. He definitely has issues of some sort.' From then on Marty was sent out into the back garden to run around and get a bit of exercise.

'Get *out*, Marty,' she heard her mother roar over the sound of the vacuum cleaner. 'Niamh, are you up?' she shouted up the stairs. Her mother only ever called her by her proper first name when she was admonishing her.

'No! Can you turn off the hoover, Mam? It's only eight o'clock in the morning! That noise is torture at this hour!' Niamh roared, despite her headache. She heard footsteps coming up the stairs. Clearly she wasn't about to win this one.

'The day is half over at eight o'clock in the morning,' her mother said, throwing open the bedroom door. 'Look at the state of this place, and it smells like a brewery. The window cleaners will be here in an hour so you better get up and get dressed.'

'My curtains are closed, Mam! And they'll only be washing the outside of the windows,' Niamh argued, rubbing her temples.

'It's not right having those men outside your window and you inside in bed. Sure they'll know full well that you're inside in it if you have the curtains closed.'

'Jesus,' Niamh mumbled into the duvet. 'All right, I'm getting up.'

'Stop swearing, Niamh. And your sister Grace will be here any minute to drop off the boys for a few hours while she gets her hair done.'

Niamh didn't know why her mother always referred to her as 'your sister Grace', but she did. It was never just 'Grace'. It's not like she had another one and might get them confused.

'All right, I'm up, I'm up.'

She'd need something to dim the headache before the boys arrived. The sound level went up tenfold when Blake and Ben landed. Blake was a year older than his brother, but Ben was the mad one. No shortage of personality there. Niamh always felt that Grace should have swapped their names once she discovered their personalities, as Blake was way too weird a name to give any Irish boy. He'd definitely get beaten up over that in the future. Ben could have handled it as he was a bully already at only two years of age, but Blake was a quieter, more sensitive little thing. He was still terribly loud, but sweet and gentle. She'd have switched the names before anyone got too used to them.

'Do we have any more of those dissolvable things in the red box?' she asked as she padded slowly down the stairs in her pyjamas.

'Did you drink too much wine again last night?' her mother asked with a disapproving tut.

'No, I think I'm getting a sore throat,' Niamh lied. That was the only way to extract any sympathy, as hangovers were not tolerated. In fact, between herself and Grace, she was pretty sure that they had each only once ever made the rookie mistake of admitting to a hangover. Every other occasion for painkillers was the certain onslaught of strep throat, migraine or the flu. That way you stood a chance of getting tea and a blanket.

'You should go to the doctor and get yourself checked out.

You're getting a lot of sore throats lately. Now go up and fix yourself, will you? Look at the state of you. They'll be here soon. Oh, and dress the bed so the window washers don't think we're a bunch of tinkers.'

Now that Niamh thought of it, she probably hadn't washed her hair since last Friday. The Friday that she wore the new navy dress and went to the new tapas restaurant. The Friday she was dumped. She hadn't seen a mirror yet today, but she knew that her hair would be standing up in clumps from its unwashed roots. She might have hidden it under a baseball cap for the day to avoid the chore of washing and drying it, but she knew her sister would waft in wearing something expensive and looking like she'd just stepped out of a salon, even before she'd had her hair done. She always smelled expensive, too. Niamh had tried her perfume once to see if she could smell expensive as well, but it just smelled like bottled, overripe fruit on her skin.

Her sister was the successful one. She had a shining career as an architect, two perfect, if loud and berserk, toddlers and a doting husband. He was starting to lose his hair early, which Niamh was certain freaked her sister out. She wouldn't be surprised if Robert showed up with hair implants one day to maintain the outward veneer of perfection, because who wants to show off their balding husband? Otherwise he was fine, though, and they seemed happy together.

She was tall, too, in the way that successful people are. Niamh had read once (in one of her mother's *Reader's Digests*, of course) that successful people are, for the most part, tall. Someone did a study of the most successful men and women in the USA and something like less than 1 per cent of them were short. That particular week had been especially tough at work, so the article had made her feel better about herself.

Good to know that she could now righteously blame her five foot, four inch height for her professional shortcomings. In fact, she felt sure that the term 'professional shortcomings' was most likely coined by a successful, clever, tall person for short people everywhere.

She heard them before she saw them. The front gate was flung open with a clatter and both sets of little feet thundered down the gravel path. It always amazed her how much noise such small people could make. They were babbling in through the letterbox before anyone could even get to the front door. It was nine o'clock exactly. That was another difference between Niamh and her sister – Grace was always on time for everything. Niamh pulled open the kitchen door and scooped them up, one in each arm.

'You two monsters are getting heavy!'

Blake called her 'Nee' but Ben hadn't quite worked out his words yet so he just roared random sounds at people. Apart from 'Mama' and 'Dada', the only name he'd got a handle on was 'Granda', which came out like 'Gah'. It drove her mother mad, of course, that he could say 'Granda' but not 'Nana', so every visit was like a warped speech therapy session, with Nana repeating her name slowly in Ben's face any time he would stand still.

When he wasn't eating, he preferred to stomp on things and kill anything smaller than him, like random spiders or any sort of bug that had the misfortune to move in the back garden. He was the sort of silent but deadly type. Not even Marty was safe, and he knew it, retreating with a kind of terrorised screech whenever he saw Ben coming.

Grace was putting the kettle on in the kitchen. 'I brought croissants from the French place you like, Niamh,' she said giving her a hug.

'Sympathy croissants?' Niamh asked with a grimace. She was pretty sure that Grace hadn't allowed a croissant to pass her lips in over ten years. 'So is this tea and sympathy with a pity croissant thrown in for good measure?'

'It can be if you like, but they're bloody good croissants.' To Niamh's surprise, Grace pulled off a corner and stuffed it in her mouth. 'So, what kind of mental state are we in, here? What stage in the grieving process – depressed and dejected, mad as hell, or sad and mopey?'

'Definitely sad and mopey.'

'So, what happened exactly? Did you do something to piss him off or is he just having an early mid-life crisis?' Grace asked, pouring three mugs of tea.

'I didn't do anything!' Niamh insisted. 'We went out to dinner like I told you and when we got home he just said something like he didn't "want to do this any more".'

'What *exactly* did he say, Niamh?'

'He said, "Niamh, I don't want to do this anymore. It's not working. We're going nowhere. There's no point."'

'Sounds like a mid-life crisis to me. He's a knob, Niamh. You're better off without him.'

'That's easy for you to say. You're not the one who's turning thirty-four next birthday and newly single.'

Grace leaned against the kitchen table. 'Are you telling me that you'd rather be in an average relationship than be single? Will you listen to yourself for a minute? That's an absolute travesty! Women burned their bras for freedom in the sixties and there you are wishing you could hitch your wagon to some aspiring entrepreneurial loser.'

Mrs Kelly paused her attempt to scrub last night's casserole dish. 'No one burned any bras in the sixties. That's a myth.'

'Mam, everyone knows that feminists burned their bras in

the sixties. That's known all over the world,' Grace countered confidently.

'Well, anyone who thinks that is wrong. It's a myth. The demonstration that created that myth was the 1968 protest of the *Miss America* contest when loads of women threw bras, stockings, girdles – all sorts of underwear – into a rubbish bin, but it was never set alight. Psychologists call it the Rashomon effect, where different people have contradictory accounts of the same incident.' She rattled this off with gusto and resumed her scrubbing.

'*Reader's Digest*, Grace,' sighed Niamh. 'I'd just take that one at face value and leave it at that if I were you, or we'll be here all day.'

Grace rolled her eyes. 'So when are you going back to work? You can't loll around here for ever or you'll go out of your mind.'

'I'm not going back to that place. I can't!' Niamh whined.

'What? That's ridiculous! That's a fine job and you were good at it. Of course you're going back.'

'I can't. I'll be such a pity party. I'm mortified. Thirty-three years old and rejected by the man I thought I was going to spend the rest of my life with. God, what a mess.' Niamh put her hands over her eyes. 'Anyway, it's his company, Grace, so it's not like he's going anywhere. I should never have gotten involved in it. I can't believe I let him talk me into it. "Help me get started, Niamh ... Let's build this together, Niamh ..." I gave up that great job at that restaurant PR firm for the chance to work at a startup. I thought I'd be at the forefront of everything, pitching to the media and arranging press evenings. Then off Rick goes, raising money and doing media interviews, while I'm left running payroll. Wanker.'

'Language, Niamh!' Mrs Kelly said into the sink.

'Well, he is, Mam, to be fair,' offered Grace in support. 'Look, you're not actually losing your job; you are choosing not to go back to work. That's different. That's quitting. Or you could just pull yourself together and go back to work – how about that? You don't have to lose your job over this. It's not like you see much of him these days at work, or he's directly in charge of you or anything. Don't let him win. Fuck him. Just go back to work with your head held high.'

'Language, Grace!'

Grace rolled her perfectly made-up eyes. 'Or get another job.'

Marty let out a howl from under the table.

'Ben! Get off of him!' Grace shouted under the table. '*Off!*' Ben was sitting on Marty who was, at this stage, flattened to the floor.

'Ugh. Get another job?' Niamh dropped her head into her hands. 'What do I tell them at the interview? Oh yeah, my boyfriend dumped me, and I worked for him for the past four years, helping him build his startup, so I've gained no real experience apart from buying birthday cards, processing invoices, trying not to die of boredom overseeing payroll, and making sure the company cactus doesn't shrivel up and die. Did you know it's almost impossible to kill a cactus? It's that sort of killer knowledge which makes me employee of the year material. They'll be lining up around the block to hire me.'

'Yeah, you sound like a bit of a sad, co-dependent loser when you put it that way.'

'Thanks. Oh God. I'm mortified,' Niamh said, cringing. 'How did this happen? What am I going to do? I can't stay out on sick leave for much longer. I already sent in one fake doctor's note.'

'How did you manage that?' Grace asked, breaking off a second piece of croissant.

Niamh threw a look in her mother's direction and lowered her voice. 'I just wailed and bawled and talked about not loving myself under these circumstances, until he gave me a note to say I was incapable of work right now.'

'But you've been out for a week. You made one claim of having lunatic tendencies and you got a sick certificate for a whole week?'

'Yes, all I had to do was think of everyone talking about me at the office and I worked myself up into a right state. I can't claim that I wasn't actually a bit of a nutcase in the doctor's office.'

'Well, the longer you leave it the worse it will be. You're still on sympathy leave right now 'cause people feel sorry for you, but if you stay out much longer then they'll think you've actually become a bona fide nut job over this. Is that what you want?'

'Of course it's not what I want. I didn't want any of this. I wanted to get married and live happily ever after.'

'Well, that's shot to shit.'

The dog gave another screech.

Mrs Kelly sighed. 'For the love of God! I'm up to my elbows in suds here. Will one of you please rescue that creature and put him out in the back garden?'

Grace grabbed Marty and shoved him out of the back door. Ben gave a roar, which was intended to mean, 'I want to go out, too.'

'Use your words, Ben. I can't understand you if you don't use your words! O-U-T. Say *out*.' Ben gave another roar and she shoved him out through the back door too.

'What was it he said, again? That he can't do it?' she asked Niamh as she closed the back door.

'"I don't want to do this any more."'

'That's so pathetic. Who says that? I mean, what actually was wrong with him? Do you think there's someone else?'

'I don't know. I mean, no I don't think so. I think I freaked him out.'

'How so?'

'Well, I had been dropping hints about moving in together and stuff like that and the last time I was over at his place I left some *Homes & Gardens* magazines lying around. Plus I had been hinting about the new batch of apartments being released next month, you know, the fancy ones on the canal? Then I asked him if he wanted to take a spin to IKEA on Saturday, just to have a look around. I think it all freaked him out. Are you going to eat the rest of that or what?' Niamh nodded towards the mostly uneaten croissant.

'No, you can have it.'

'''Tis no wonder you have such a good figure, Grace,' Mrs Kelly said as she folded up her rubber gloves. 'I wish I had your discipline.'

'Marvellous,' Niamh said, rolling her eyes. 'Oh well, I might as well add chunky and undisciplined to my list of offensive character traits.' She stuffed the remainder of the croissant into her mouth.

'You're not chunky, Niamh. Stop being so hard on yourself. You've just been comfort-eating for the past week and you feel like shit. It's a thing, you know. People comfort-eat when they are sad, then you put on a little weight and feel even worse about yourself. Look, shitty things happen, relationships end. It's just really, really bad luck that you worked with him, too, so you've got a double dose of crap to deal with, but honestly, Niamh, you are better off without him. He's self-obsessed, vain and hell-bent on world domination with that little food app of his selling subscriptions to people who can't cook. You just need a bit of distance, that's all,' Grace said emphatically as she sipped on her tea.

'It's not a *little* food app, Grace. It's doing really well, actually,' Niamh said with an indignant huff. 'Our early customers were people who couldn't cook so those subscriptions that deliver a box of ingredients to your home were useless because you still have to actually cook the meal, but in the last few months we've started getting real traction with people who are entertaining at home. They order the PlatesPlease meal that they want, it shows up fully cooked, and they serve it as if they had cooked it themselves. That's what is so unique about the product and that's where the real growth opportunity is, so that's where our focus . . .'

Niamh's voice trailed off. She leaned forward in despair, resting her head on her folded arms. 'Our focus . . . I just said "our focus", but it's not, is it? It's all his. I'm out,' she groaned, banging her forehead on the table for emphasis.

'You need to get out of here,' Grace declared as she stood up from the table, brushing crumbs from her cream-coloured pants.

'She can't go anywhere. The window washers will be here any minute and she'll have to deal with them because I have to run to the shops.'

'Not *now*, Mam. Not right this minute. I mean you need to get out of here – your routine, this house. Get out of town.'

'Right. I'll just grab my overnight bag and head to the airport. Catch the next flight somewhere exotic with . . . oh wait . . . with no one. You mean a "sad and alone" trip for singles?' She knew she was being mopey and dramatic again, but her sister always thought there was an easy solution for everything. Her life was always nice and breezy. She just

19

coasted through life with salon hair and perfectly groomed eyebrows.

'No, come with me next week to Italy!' she exclaimed with a wide smile, as if she had just solved one of the world's more pressing concerns.

'What are you doing in Italy?'

'I'm going to a conference. You know the one I go to every year? It's just three days but I'm staying on for the weekend too. Come on, it'll do you good. It will be fun!'

'Grace, I haven't left the house in a week!'

'That's precisely why this is a great idea. You need to get out. You need a distraction.'

'No, I can't. I'm just not up for it.'

'Oh, come on. It'll be fun. You won't have to do a thing – it's all organised. All you need is a flight. Everything else is sorted.'

Una Kelly turned from the sink to face her daughters. 'Sounds like a lovely invitation to me, Nina. It might do you good.'

'I dunno . . . I haven't been to Italy for years,' Niamh mused.

'I'll send you my flight details. Just book yourself a flight. Do you think you can get another nutcase certificate? Buy yourself another week off work?'

Niamh giggled for the first time in a week. 'Trust me, it doesn't take much to go from my current resting nutcase state to extreme lunatic. All I have to do is think about my life right now and I'll lose my mind all over again. What day are you going? And where?'

She realised that she was considering this trip without knowing the first thing about it. Maybe she did need to get out of town.

'I'm on the morning flight to Milan on Monday. The

conference is Tuesday to Thursday and I fly home Sunday. Robert is looking after the boys for the weekend and the nanny is going to do full-time during the week. We're not staying in Milan, though. I have a driver picking me up and taking me to the hotel in Liguria. We're staying at the Grand Hotel Miramare. It's part of the Leading Hotels of the World group. It'll be fabulous!'

Niamh could feel herself perk up already. She couldn't remember the last time she had made a decision so quickly. 'Shit, today is Saturday. I need to go buy some new outfits.'

'You can go after the window washers leave,' Mrs Kelly protested. 'But I think that's a great idea. A week away will do you the world of good. You can get your head straightened out and you'll be well able to deal with all of this nonsense when you come back.' She nodded approvingly.

'And for the love of God will you get something done with your hair today?' sighed Grace. 'You don't want to frighten the Italians.'

Niamh ignored the snarky comment, mostly as she had to agree that something needed to be done to tame her hair. 'I'll get an appointment for this afternoon.'

'OK, I'll text you all the details. Mam, I'll be back by lunch to pick up the boys.'

'All right, love. See you later.'

'And Grace?' Niamh said as she stuck her head into the hallway after her sister. 'Thanks!'

'It will be an adventure,' Grace replied with a wink.

Chapter Three

The air was different. It didn't just smell different; it felt different, different to the air back home in Dublin. It felt lighter. Maybe it was just drier and not as damp, but it felt good. It was warmer than it was back home, too. Not yet hot, as it was still only May, but warm enough that Niamh didn't need her jacket. She felt like a creature shedding a layer of skin that it no longer needed as she slipped it off. She had seen snakes do that on *National Geographic* documentaries on television and always thought it looked cool.

Grace had told her more or less what she should pack. Niamh had asked her some very specific questions about the kind of clothes she should bring, as she suspected that she and Grace took very different types of holidays and she didn't want to look like the hired help accompanying her more glamorous sister. Grace was a bit of a pro by now, as she travelled to Italy twice a year – once for the annual conference and once a year on holiday with Robert – whereas Niamh hadn't been in years.

'I know you think that my clothes are fancy and that I overdress for certain things, but you have to take my advice on this, and don't think I'm exaggerating.'

'OK,' Niamh responded slowly.

'Pack for your most glamorous self because you'll still feel like you look like a homeless person next to these Italian women. Honestly, I don't know how they do it. It's like they have an innate sense of style, or some internal gene that allows them to look effortlessly elegant all of the time. *All* of the time, I swear. And they are all skinny as rakes!'

'What about all the pasta and wine?'

'I don't know. Maybe they just eat it at lunch or something, 'cause honestly they all look fabulous.'

'But Italian grannies all look tubby and round.'

'Well that's just it – they are all skinny and fabulous until they hit fifty or so, then they all get the midlife spread. I think they just actually stop caring at that point, because they're married and can now eat pasta for dinner every night. I don't know, but every Italian woman under fifty looks amazing.'

'You've just convinced me that nothing I own is suitable, so basically I'm going shopping for a new wardrobe for the week. I just hope they've got summer stuff in the shops already,' Niamh sighed.

'A few cute dresses and some wedge sandals and you'll be fine,' Grace said with a shrug.

As they waited for their luggage, Niamh texted their mother to tell her they had landed safely in Milan. The orange beacon atop the luggage carousel started to flash along with a siren sound that was so unnecessarily loud it could warn of a threatening invasion. Niamh wrestled with her case and tried to heave it off the carousel without maiming anyone. She had definitely overpacked, she thought, as she hurled it to the floor. She probably should have used the smaller one, but she hadn't been able to decide on what to pack. This one had been labelled 'heavy', with a frown at the check-in desk in Dublin, and it was certainly not easy to manoeuvre as it only had three good wheels.

Grace always checked in a suitcase when she travelled as she always packed so many cosmetics and sprays that she couldn't possibly qualify for the carry-on luggage requirements, but she had one of those sleek, hard-shelled RIMOWA cases that seemed to roll all by itself. She spoke pretty good Italian and she certainly seemed to know her way around the airport. She had called the driver as they were walking from the luggage claim area. She was speaking Italian on the phone to him and laughing. It wasn't easy to laugh in another language. Niamh had studied French and Spanish for five years in school and couldn't remember a single conversation that had made her laugh. They say you've really mastered it if you can make someone laugh in another language.

The driver stood holding a sign reading GRACE QUINN, and greeted them with a wide smile.

'*Ben arrivata, Signora Quinn. Sono Vincenzo,*' he said, shaking her hand warmly before reaching for her suitcase.

'*Ciao, Vincenzo. Grazie,*' Grace replied, as she twirled her sleek RIMOWA suitcase around to face him.

Niamh hesitated for a moment, rooted to the spot, as she'd never been met anywhere by a driver. Was she supposed to hand him her suitcase, too, or was that only for the person who actually made the booking? She wondered if he could even drag both suitcases? He looked pretty old.

'*Buongiorno, signora,*' he said, leaning towards her and grasping the handle.

She watched as he strode away, her old black suitcase with the rickety wheel bouncing behind him.

Grace turned to face her, shaking her head. 'Seriously, Niamh, the charity shop wouldn't accept that thing if you tried to donate it.'

Niamh rolled her eyes. 'I didn't realise that my luggage was going to be judged too. "Niamh get your hair done, Niamh buy some new clothes, Niamh make sure to use your Louis Vuitton suitcase,'" she said in a mock whiney voice as she skipped to keep up with Grace.

Grace seemed to navigate the clusters of people easily, but then Grace, older by two years, always seemed to manage things with ease.

'I still can't believe you took Robert's name and changed your last name to Quinn,' Niamh said, jogging alongside her sister.

'That's a random statement, even by your standards.'

'No, the driver had a sign saying "Quinn" back there when we arrived. I almost forgot that you're no longer a Kelly. I couldn't imagine having another name – that would be weird.'

'Are you kidding me?' said Grace defensively. 'I couldn't get down the aisle fast enough to drop Kelly and take Quinn as my surname. You didn't have to deal with being mocked and called "princess" at school! I wasn't sorry to see the back of Grace Kelly!'

The two of them followed the driver through the terminal towards the waiting car. Niamh felt bad for the man. He must have been her father's age and he was dragging the two cases in his black blazer and black hat. Her father wouldn't be seen dead in that hat. It didn't seem to cost Grace a thought, though, as she pulled her sunglasses from her handbag as they stepped out into the sun.

'Of course, they were just sitting there conveniently at the top of your handbag,' Niamh muttered to herself as she rooted through her oversized bag. She bumped into an impossibly tall, elegant Italian woman.

'*Attento!*' the woman exclaimed. '*Porca miseria!*'

25

She didn't know what the second part meant, but it sounded mean.

'Wow, what a cow!' Niamh said incredulously. 'It was an accident!' she growled over her shoulder at the woman.

The woman made a hand gesture at her that she'd seen Italians do in movies. Even that looked effortless and elegant. She'd have to find out what they each meant.

Grace breezed ahead of her in layers of pale grey and cream. She seemed to have this great wardrobe of monochrome pieces that all worked together effortlessly. By comparison, everything Niamh owned was either black or brightly coloured. She decided that she'd have to try the monochrome look and see if it would make her feel any more elegant. She might talk to Grace about it and maybe they could go shopping together while in Italy.

Grace slunk into the back seat of the car, whipped out her phone and started dialling.

'*Allora, signora, siamo pronti?*' the driver asked, looking in his rear-view mirror at them both, wondering if they were ready to go.

Niamh nudged Grace.

'*Scusi, sì, grazie, Vincenzo.*' Grace nodded in his direction.

'Off we go,' he said in a strong accent, making it sound like 'Off-ah we-ah go'. He caught Niamh's eye in the mirror and winked.

Niamh leaned back into the cream leather seat. There was plenty of room for her legs, she noticed, much more so than the regular taxis back home. She placed her handbag on the ground next to her feet. She should have polished her shoes before she left, she thought to herself, peering down at them. They looked scruffier than normal against the cream interior of the car. There was a box of tissues on the ledge behind the passenger seats, little bottles of water in the compartment between them and a magazine tucked into the pocket on the back of the two front seats. She plucked out the one on her side but it was in Italian. Still, though, she could flick through the photos, as it looked like an Italian edition of *Vogue*.

'This is unreal.' She grinned at Grace. 'Do you always travel like this when you go for work?'

'Every time. The company pays for it,' Grace replied casually.

'Wow, I'd be on a bus by now, or trying to find a bus if I was doing this myself. This is the way to travel! It's no wonder you don't mind travelling as much as you do.'

'Don't mind it? Are you mad? This is what keeps me sane. I look forward to these trips away. I love the boys, but they are full on and demanding, and these trips give me a couple of days to be myself, or actually allow me to be the person I used to be before I became a mother.'

Grace's phone rang and she launched into a work conversation. Niamh rested her head back against the headrest and stared out of the window. She realised that the two of them had never been away together before and she had just had a previously impermissible glance into her sister's life. Her mother did always say that travel broadens the mind. She smiled, thinking that for someone who had lived her entire life in Dublin and had only ever travelled outside the island of Ireland twice, her mother knew a lot about a lot.

The car had tinted windows, which was just as well as she hadn't managed to find her sunglasses. She must have packed them in her suitcase.

'That was pretty stupid,' she sighed as she rummaged one more time through her handbag. It was a two-and-a-half-hour journey from Linate airport to their hotel in the town of Santa Margherita. Niamh had looked up the hotel online and didn't think she had ever stayed anywhere that looked more glamorous – and that was just from the photos, which everyone knows never truly do a place justice, except for in those package resorts where she normally went on holiday. They always had great photos of sprawling swimming pools and when you got there you wondered if you were even looking at the same thing. They looked massive in the photos, but the photographer was obviously using some lens trickery. It shouldn't be allowed, really, as it gave a different impression of what you actually got in reality. The truth was that she had never yet met a swimming pool in real life that exceeded the opinion she had had in advance, based on the photographs.

Niamh had never been to this part of Italy. She had been to Rome years ago for a weekend in August and, between the heat and the crowds, she swore she'd never go back. It wasn't as hot this time. The first half hour of the drive was the usual nondescript, grey scenery you encountered in most countries as you left the airport and navigated a series of ugly highways. The more developed the country the worse the initial drive seemed to be upon leaving the airport. Everything seemed dull and industrial – the roads, the fields, just a series of flat shapes alternating grey and green as they flashed by, interrupted by the odd, ugly factory.

She thought about Rick as she watched the signposts for Genoa whizz by. He'd like it here, she thought to herself. She wondered why they had never travelled like this together, on an adventurous sort of trip. They had always booked package holidays and usually returned to the same few places in Spain or the Canary Islands every year. They had gone to Turkey one year, to a city on the coast called Bodrum. She had thought it sounded exotic and adventurous, but when they got to the place they were staying, it was just a small resort with a couple of swimming pools and two restaurants. It was just like all the other places they had been, except for the food. The food was definitely more exotic. She remembered telling her mother about it when she got home.

'They grill their lamb there, Mam, and it's served pink in the middle!'

'What do you mean pink in the middle? It can't be pink in the middle, Nina, sure that's not even properly cooked!' her mother had exclaimed, horrified.

'I swear, Mam! It's pure pink in the middle. It was good, too.'

'You won't find me there, so then,' her dad offered from the armchair. 'Sure that's half raw.'

Niamh had felt quite sophisticated, regaling the two of them with tales of all this foreign food. Her dad was the classic meat and potatoes kind of man. If the dinner didn't have potatoes, then it just wasn't dinner.

'And we had whole grilled fish. It was delicious. First I thought it was a bit weird, 'cause it was the whole fish, but I covered his head with a bit of lettuce so I couldn't see his eyes and then it was grand.'

'What do you mean you could see his eyes?' her father asked.

'Yeah, they serve it whole. It's supposed to have more flavour, Dad, if it's cooked on the bone and served whole. Rick didn't mind it, but I had to cover his eyes so he wouldn't be looking at me while I ate him.'

'We definitely won't be going there, so! I couldn't eat him if he was looking up at me. Did they throw him on the grill too when he was still alive?' Her dad chuckled. He was a pretty good cook and he liked to cook fish (her mother didn't like the smell of fish cooking, so that was her dad's job), but it was all neatly filleted by the time he brought it home from the fish shop.

The drive was starting to get prettier now. The countryside was spectacular. Every so many kilometres there were little clusters of villages, each chock full of autumnal-coloured roofs and tall church steeples. The fields were littered with farming outhouses and only a scant number of cows or sheep from what she could see. Grace spent most of the journey talking or typing on her phone.

'You're missing the views, Grace!' Niamh admonished as she craned her neck to see out both sides of the car.

'Seen it all before.' Grace smiled, continuing to type with fury. 'The more I get done now, the less I have to do when we get there and it's almost time for cocktails, so we've no time to waste!'

'Ooh, cocktails! Fun!'

'Even better – cocktails Italian style! *Aperitivi*, right, Vincenzo?'

'*Sì, Signora Quinn! Sempre una buona idea,*' he laughed. 'Always ... how you say ... the good idea,' he said over his shoulder to Niamh.

She could feel herself getting excited. Her tummy had that little knot of butterflies as the car turned off the main road and onto a smaller one. They passed a sign for the Grand Hotel Miramare on the side of the road.

'Even the sign for it is posh looking,' she gushed.

'Honestly, you'd swear you'd never been out of the country before, Niamh!' Grace laughed, although secretly she was pleased to see her sister smile. She'd never admit it to Niamh, of course, as God forbid she'd remind her that she was supposed to be in some sort of relationship-mourning state. She'd just retreat back into a cloud of moping. This trip was the perfect opportunity to shake her out of her miserable, self-indulgent, sad reverie and point her in the direction of 'get a grip'. She was mad as hell at Rick, but she refused to indulge in the usual 'what if' type conversation with her sister. All that did was encourage more obsessing over the 'what might have been' scenarios and prolong the inevitable. Rick knew exactly what he wanted out of life and he always had done. He had simply decided that, for whatever reason, that no longer included Niamh. It was time for Niamh to get over him and move on.

Chapter Four

The car followed a winding road lined with a series of tall, exotic palm trees on both sides. The footpaths were gloriously wide and paved with a series of perfectly even grey flagstones. Niamh couldn't help but compare them to the footpaths at home, which were small and uneven. She had read about the Italian tradition of *passeggiata* – when the locals took a stroll before dinner each evening. It all looked so pleasant from her vantage point in the car that she could even imagine herself taking a leisurely stroll in the evenings. She turned to suggest the notion to Grace but she was still engrossed in her phone.

Everyone seemed to walk more slowly here, too, as if they were really going for a stroll and enjoying it. She had been to New York once and remembered being amazed at how everyone there walked insanely fast, but this was the opposite. Everyone looked so elegant, too. She hoped she had packed enough nice things. She'd have to ask Grace what she should wear before she changed for dinner tonight.

Every now and then she got a glimpse of the water, sparkling an iridescent turquoise. Little sail boats bobbed up and down and larger yachts sat imposing and immobile but for the fluttering of a flag declaring ownership or place of origin.

'*Allora signore – Santa Margherita Ligure,*' Vincenzo announced with a little flourish of his right hand as they approached the town.

'Wow,' Niamh gasped as they rounded the bend and the sea presented itself fully, lapping up just underneath the wide footpath on the right.

The road narrowed into a two-lane street with a smattering of shops along the left side. All of the façades were a similar shade of white, the only differences being the colours of their shutters or the signs that hung outside each shop.

The car slowed and turned left into the driveway of the hotel.

'*Signore, siamo arrivati,*' Vincenzo said, proudly announcing their arrival.

Even with no Italian, Niamh was able to work that one out.

'*Arrivati . . . arrivati . . .*' she repeated to herself quietly, as she rolled down the window and took a deep breath of air. She liked the way the words felt on her tongue.

The hotel stood imposingly at the foot of the driveway, with the sea curving to one side and behind it. Lofty trees, tilted to one side from years of strong sea breezes, lined the driveway. Teal-green shutters flanked the tall, narrow windows, with some offering their residents pretty wrought-iron balconies beneath them.

After pulling up beside the entrance, Vincenzo got out and opened the door for each of them. Niamh was fairly certain that she'd never had anyone open a door for her like that before. She'd have simply got out by herself but her door was locked, so she had no choice but to wait for him to round the side of the car and open it for her.

'*Grazie,*' she said, feeling a little self-conscious. She could smell the sea on the breeze and turned her face up to the sun, closing her eyes and soaking in the warmth.

'*Prego, signora*,' Vincenzo replied, with a smile and a nod.

A bellman had already rolled a shiny brass cart in their direction and he quickly whisked their luggage from the car.

'*Benvenuti al Grand Hotel Miramare, Signore Quinn*,' the bellman said, welcoming them as he loaded both cases onto the cart.

'I thought you said you hadn't been here before,' Niamh whispered, leaning in towards Grace.

'I haven't, why?' she responded giving her an odd look.

'Well, how does he know your name then?'

'The driver radios in advance to let them know when we're almost there. Didn't you hear that in the car? That way they can greet each guest by name. It's kind of a nice, personal touch.'

'No, I didn't hear that, but then again I don't speak Italian so how would I know what the driver was saying?' Niamh retorted.

'Oh right, that's right,' Grace said distractedly. She was back on her phone again. 'I'll have to get the Wi-Fi code and check in with the office before we get changed.'

'Why, where are we going?' Niamh asked. She was trying to keep up with Grace, but was trailing behind, her eyes darting in every direction.

'Nowhere. We're not going anywhere, we're staying here, but there's a cocktail thing starting at five o'clock. I just told you that in the car, Niamh!'

With a mounting sense of panic, Niamh got the sense that she was included in this cocktail thing by default. Grace had mentioned cocktails in the car, but Niamh had assumed that it referred to the drinking of them, not an actual official event. She had expected that they would go to some nice restaurants, have some nice meals and do a little exploring. She had packed for that, but she hadn't reckoned on anything that involved actual cocktail attire. In fact, she wasn't sure that anything she owned would qualify for cocktail attire, at least not in her sister's eyes.

'You didn't tell me that we were going to a cocktail party, Grace,' Niamh hissed as they followed the bellman.

'Oh relax, Niamh, for God's sake. It's not a cocktail party, it's a reception.'

'Oh right, that's fine then, it's just a reception,' Niamh responded sarcastically. 'What the hell is the difference? Not that it matters, 'cause no matter what the difference is I don't have a cocktail dress conveniently stuffed into my suitcase.'

Grace rolled her eyes. 'Look, it's just a welcome reception for the people who are going to the conference. It's basically just a drinks thing. You don't have to go if you don't want to but you're not allowed to sit in your room and be mopey. You're here to have fun, so stop brooding over Rick and cop on to yourself. You're in Italy. Just throw on a cute dress if you want some free drinks. It'll be over by about seven o'clock and we can go for dinner then.'

'I'm not being mopey! I haven't thought about Rick in at least an hour! And a "drinks thing" I can definitely get behind. It'd be rude not to go and leave you all alone, especially when there are free drinks,' she said, grinning.

The interior of the hotel was opulent but not fussy. The foyer rose up into a lofty, cavernous, cathedral-style roof. The walls were a soft white that was almost a light grey, and the mottled glass in the tall, narrow windows diffused the light so it had an almost velvety quality to it. The floor tiles were massive slabs of old stone and had the same lambent grey-white hue as the walls.

Their footsteps echoed softly on the stone floor as they entered through the double doors, following the bellman across the hallway, which was flanked by six-foot-tall floral displays on each side. It was easily the most beautiful hotel she had ever seen.

Their room was equally impressive, with original parquet flooring and two queen-sized beds covered in crisp white linens and a stack of pillows so lush that they could probably induce fatigue in the most die-hard insomniac. Double doors led to a panoramic balcony overlooking the *Golfo del Tigullio* and a light sea breeze came through the open windows, bordered by white linen curtains that felt as light as gauze.

Grace changed into a simple, fitted red dress that fell just to her knee, and wore a single strand of dark grey pearls.

'Wow, you look fab!' Niamh said admiringly, as she tugged on the material of her shirt. 'There isn't an ounce of fat on you!'

'You won't be saying that by the end of the week.' Grace laughed as she leant towards the mirror to put on her earrings. 'I'll be properly chunky after a week of pasta, pizza and wine!'

'There's no hope for me, so. They'll be rolling me onto the plane on Sunday.'

She winced at the thought of home and all the awkwardness and messiness that awaited her there. She'd much rather forget about it entirely for the week so she decided there and then that's what she should try to do.

'OK, I'm heading downstairs,' Grace said, picking up her purse. 'This meeting will only last about an hour and then the drinks thing starts at five o'clock on the balcony. See you in a bit!'

'OK, bye.'

Niamh showered and wrapped up in a large, fluffy white

robe that was about four sizes too big for her, but enveloped her in a delicious softness. She sat on the balcony transfixed by the view. The sun wasn't yet ready to set but the light was beginning to soften. The Gulf was flat calm and a few stray, thin clouds diffused the light onto the surface of the sea below. She watched a parade of tiny sailing boats, like minuscule versions of themselves, moving slowly on the horizon. She'd never been on a sailing boat, just a ferry from Dublin to Wales once. She imagined the silence all the way out there, with only the sound of the breeze and the water slapping against the boat. There were mountains to the left, a series of grey and black shadowy mounds that both fell into and sheltered the Gulf below. Church bells chimed and seemed to echo across the water, only adding to the perfection of the scene.

'Oh shit!' she cried, realising that the bells were signalling five o'clock. 'Dammit! I'm not even dressed!'

She stared, horrified, at her hair in the mirror. She must have been outside for more than half an hour and her hair had dried slowly in the sea breeze. It stood in different directions on top of her head.

'Fuck! I'm like a goddamn scarecrow.'

She teased her hair as best she could and sprayed it with enough hairspray to freeze a bird in motion. She slipped on a pale blue dress that she had bought just two days before. She had decided that Italy wasn't ready to see her pasty, white legs so this dress was perfect as it fell below her knees. Grabbing her wallet, she gave a cursory glance in the mirror.

'You'll have to do now. You're late enough as it is.'

The elevator opened onto the first floor. She followed the corridor towards the restaurant, off which was a large terrace overlooking the extensive gardens and the Gulf beyond.

There must have already been a hundred people in little clusters, chatting easily and laughing softly. A table was laid out at the entrance with dozens of name cards. Running her finger down the line with H–L she found hers, and pinned it to her dress.

She felt awkward walking in alone, and scanned the crowd for Grace. Waiters stood with trays of champagne on either side of the doors and there was a bar to the left and another to the right. She made her way to the bar on the far right, hoping that the barman spoke English.

'*Buongiorno*,' she offered slowly.

'*Ah no, signora, buona sera*,' he corrected her with a warm smile. 'After five o'clock is *buona sera*.'

'Oh sorry, yes . . . I mean, *sì, buona sera*.' She could feel her face start to flush.

'No problem, *signora*. My English is so bad it will make you cry,' he replied with a grin. 'Now, what would you like?'

She hesitated, looking at a group of women to her left. Each one of them was holding the same orange-coloured drink.

'What's that drink?' she asked nodding in their direction.

'Ah, is an Aperol spritz, *signora*. Is perfect for *aperitivo*!'

'OK then, *sì*,' she smiled.

She scanned the crowd as he mixed her drink. She knew they were largely an international crowd as Grace had talked a bit about the conference on the plane. They were architects from all over the world who converged in a different part of Italy each year to network and discuss advancements, challenges and opportunities in the industry. They were a well-dressed, elegant-looking bunch. The women were without exception stylish and slender.

'Must be a money thing,' she mused under her breath, "cause they're all successful and loaded – and every one of them is skinny.' She tugged self-consciously at the waist of her dress, willing it to sit lower.

'*Ecco, signora,*' the waiter said as he handed her the Aperol spritz.

She retreated behind several clusters of people and made her way towards the balcony. There was still no sign of Grace. She had no interest in making small talk with a bunch of strangers with whom she had nothing in common. Grace would show up eventually and force her to meet some people, but for now she was content to be alone in the crowd. The view was transfixing and she stood, motionless, staring at the horizon.

Her straw started to make noise at the bottom of her glass. She turned to make her way back to the bar and accidentally reversed into a waiter directly behind her, carrying a tray of Aperol spritz drinks. He in turn was propelled into the man walking past him, toppling one of the drinks over the side of the tray in the process.

'*Dio, io,*' the waiter exclaimed, and was suddenly surrounded by two other waiters brandishing clean white cloths and attending to the man in the suit.

'Oh God! Oh my God, I'm *so* sorry!' Niamh exclaimed in horror.

The man's pristine white shirt had a large orange stain spreading across the front. It was like a scene in a movie when someone gets shot and the blood starts to expand in a fast-growing puddle, except this one was bright orange alcohol.

'I'm *so, so* sorry,' she offered again, mortified as she watched his shirt change colour.

Her sister would kill her. Please God let him be a stranger that she doesn't know. The waiter mopped it off as best he could, apologised again in Italian, glared at Niamh and slunk away.

'It is fine. After this I go home,' the man said in a strong Italian accent as he stared down at his shirt.

'Jesus, your shirt is ruined. I'm so sorry!' she said again, her face flushed.

'It is fine. No problem. Perhaps now I should have a drink.' He smiled, signalling a passing waiter. 'You will have another, no?'

'Well, you're wearing one, thanks to me, so you might as well. I'm really sorry . . . and yes, I'll have another. I promise I'll stand back here,' Niamh said, backing up to the balcony.

'I am Giorgio,' he said, smiling as he extended his hand to her.

'I'm Niamh.' She was utterly mortified at the massive orange stain on what was clearly an expensive white shirt. He attempted to say her name but paused and made a sound not unlike the one Blake made when he called her.

'Nee . . . No, you must say that again for me. My English is not so good,' he said, shaking his head.

'Oh, sorry. It's Niamh, like "nee-uv",' she said, trying to pronounce it phonetically.

'But your name tag, they have written it in the wrong way?' he asked, frowning at the name tag.

'No, it's spelled correctly,' she responded, staring at it upside down on her dress.

'But where is the M? I did not hear an M. It sounds like you said a V sound.'

'Yeah, sorry, I know. It's Irish. Some Irish names completely freak people out 'cause they can't pronounce them. Like Saoirse, you know, the Irish film star?'

'No, no, I don't,' he said with a classic Italian hand gesture. He nodded towards her name tag. 'What is Kelly? This is also a girl's name, no?'

'That's my last name.'

'So, this would be similar if my name was Giorgio Francesco or Giorgio Alberto? Two men's names,' he said with a laugh, his dark brown eyes never leaving hers.

'I never thought of that before,' she said, mirroring his laugh. She couldn't help it. His laugh was contagious. 'I wasn't able to pronounce Niamh when I was small so I called myself Nina until I was about four. Bit of a late bloomer, apparently.'

'What is a bloomer?' he asked, a confused look on his face.

'A what? Oh sorry, umm, it's someone who starts late or grows late, you know like a flower that takes a long time to bloom.'

'No, I don't know what you mean still,' he replied, shaking his head. But ... Nina! *Perfetto!* This is much easier for me.' He extended his hand and switched to Italian. '*Piacere*, Nina. I am pleased to meet you.'

Niamh smiled shyly. '*Piacere*, Giorgio,' she said, hoping she hadn't totally butchered the pronunciation.

She noticed that he wasn't wearing a name tag. Hopefully he wasn't part of the conference group and her sister wouldn't know him.

A waiter came over with a tray of Aperol spritz. Giorgio took her empty glass from her hand and picked up two more drinks.

'*Ecco. Salute!*'

'*Ecco. Salute!*' she replied.

'No.' He laughed. '*Ecco* means "here", or "here you go". *Salute* means "cheers!"'

She could feel herself flush again.

'Oh, right, sorry. I don't really speak Italian.'

'Nina, do you always apologise this way for everything that you say?' His English was fairly good but his accent was ridiculously strong. He sounded like an Italian trying to speak English in an American gangster movie. Or like someone from *The Sopranos*.

She had never thought about it, but now that he mentioned it, she did say sorry a lot. Maybe it was an Irish thing? Or maybe it was just her. She couldn't be certain, but she didn't want to feel any more foolish than she already did tonight.

'No, it's an Irish thing. We say it a lot,' she lied.

He nodded, seeming satisfied with her answer.

'Are you an architect too?' she asked, in part because she wanted to change the subject and in part in the hopes of confirming that he had nothing to do with the conference attendees and her sister would never have to know of the unfortunate drink incident. If he was the CEO of some big fancy architect firm, she was dead.

'No, no, but I know many of these people here. I do some work with them.'

Christ, I hope my sister isn't one of them, she thought to herself.

'Oh? What kind of work do you do?' she asked, trying to sound casual.

'That depends if you mean for my work or my real life,' he replied with a smile and a shrug of his shoulders. 'For my work, I am a lawyer. I work with architects and engineers, so many of these people here are my clients. I like my work, but it is just my job, not my real life. My real life begins every evening when I leave the office and all weekend until the sun comes up again on Monday. Here in Italy, we work to live, unlike many other places where they live to work.'

She plucked another Aperol spritz from a passing tray. This was her new favourite drink, she decided. She had downed the last one in seconds. It must have been the shock of ruining this gorgeous creature's shirt. She watched him as he turned to wave at someone across the room. She liked how his eyes crinkled at the corners when he smiled.

'So do you work to live or live to work, Nina?' he asked with a grin. She noticed that he tilted his head slightly to one side every time he asked a question.

She hesitated and looked down into her drink. She wasn't sure what she was doing at present – faking a mental break-down, taking time off from her job, running away from her life to Italy for a week. She definitely didn't live to work. Work was grand and she never minded going to work, but she didn't *live* for it. But she also didn't work to live in the way he meant. She liked her life in Dublin, but it was kind of small in a way. They never did anything much besides go on a sun holiday abroad every year for two weeks and take a few weekends away around the country. 'They' . . . she caught herself auto-matically referring to a 'they' that she no longer had a right to, or a claim on. She felt her face flush and took a sip of her drink, hoping to hide momentarily in the glass.

'Well, I . . .' she started.

'Giorgio! *Andiamo!*'

Niamh's head turned to follow the Italian voice. A tall, slender, dark-haired woman in a figure-hugging, cream satin dress waved her arm in the air from the door of the terrace.

'*Sì, cara. Arrivo subito,*' he called back with a wave of his hand.

'I am sorry, Nina,' he said turning back to Niamh. 'But if I don't go now I will be in trouble.'

'Oh, sorry, of course. No problem. My sister will be here soon anyway, and we have dinner plans.' She frowned, real-ising she was rambling on to this stranger. Why did she feel the need to babble on like that?

The brunette weaved her way through the small crowd

and came to a stop alongside them. She hooked her right arm through Giorgio's in a gesture that looked overtly possessive to Niamh.

'*Amore, andiamo*,' she implored in a low, honeyed voice, without making eye contact with Niamh.

'*Certamente*,' Giorgio responded with a smile.

Niamh thought that he was just about to introduce her to the sultry Italian woman, when she leaned in the direction of the door, tugging on his arm. Giorgio shrugged his shoulders as if in resignation.

'Now, I must go,' he said to Niamh with a smile. 'Nice to meet you, Nina.' He placed his glass on the table next to them.

The brunette gave her a small smile that didn't quite reach her eyes.

'You too, and sorry again about your shirt,' she replied sheepishly.

'Ah! Now you are apologising again!' He laughed. '*Arrivederci!*' He smiled and headed for the door.

She looked over the balcony and watched as they exited from the door downstairs, noting that they were still arm in arm.

'Figures,' Niamh mumbled into her glass.

'Who was *that*?' Grace asked as she came up behind her and leaned over the balcony. 'He was divine!'

'I spilled a drink on him. Well, not "spilled", actually, but sent one flying in his general direction. That gorgeous creature is his wife or whatever,' Niamh replied as both sisters leaned over the balcony and watched them walk away together. 'She's like something out of a Pantene shampoo commercial with that hair.'

'Yeah, and that dress. The Italians are so stylish, aren't they?' Grace replied.

'She came to rescue him, obviously, before I caused him any more harm.' Niamh sighed. 'Cold as ice she was, too. And he was so friendly. I don't know what he's doing with her, apart from the obvious.'

Grace gave her a nudge. 'Maybe she thought you were a threat!'

'*Ha!* My little blue Zara dress can't compete with that! Where the hell have you been, anyway? I'm starving!'

'Sorry, I got stuck with that group over there just inside the door. I did some work with them in the past and they are trying to hire us again. Anyway, I could see you chatting to that guy so I figured you were fine!' Grace laughed. 'I'm starving, too. I'm done here. I'll be seeing enough of this lot for the next few days. Let's go find a bowl of pasta the size of our heads.'

'Grace, do you think we say sorry too much?' Niamh asked as they made their way through the crowd in search of dinner.

Chapter Five

The next morning Niamh got up early with Grace and pored over her guidebook at breakfast, trying to plan her day. Grace had been surprised to see her get out of bed so early.

'Niamh, it's only seven a.m.'

'I know. I couldn't sleep – bad dreams,' Niamh replied with a sigh. 'Anyway, I bet the breakfast here is divine and I'm determined not to be sad and gloomy in Italy. I'm not going to waste another minute moping over that moron back home.' She sounded more determined than she felt.

'Good girl!' Grace said with a smile.

'I don't know what I'm going to do, though. I'll have to get a map so I don't get lost.'

'You won't get lost, Niamh. Just pick a spot on the map and ask the concierge to map out the directions for you. It doesn't matter where you go, everywhere is fabulous,' Grace said, as she tucked her long, brown hair up into a neat bun.

'I think I'll go to Portofino, that's not too far away. It's where all the fancy yachts are. Sounds lovely.'

'Lucky duck!' Grace responded, getting dressed into her conference-appropriate outfit. 'Don't do too much 'cause I'll want to go exploring too once this conference is over on

Thursday. You can be the advance team and bring me back anywhere absolutely fabulous that you discover!'

'I will. I'll take notes.'

'I definitely want to go to Portofino, it looks beautiful from what I've seen online and I've heard there are some amazing restaurants.'

'OK, I'll go there today and see what it's like. Then if it's fabulous we can go back together,' Niamh replied, rummaging through her selection of dresses. 'Will this be OK for daytime?'

'Yeah, that's cute. You don't want to be the same as all the other tourists in their ugly shorts and T-shirt combos, do you? It's Italy, for God's sake.'

'Yeah, that's what I was thinking,' Niamh said, pulling on a short, khaki sundress.

Horrified at the cost of taking a taxi from one town to another, Niamh quickly discovered that the easiest and most cost-effective way to get around was by ferry. It was also the most picturesque way to travel as it afforded views of the mainland and the various towns along the way, from the perspective of the water. From March to September the ferry ran all the way from Santa Margherita to Portofino and continued up the coast to Genoa. She was dying to get to Genoa as it was rumoured to be a crumbling, authentic maritime city, but she had limited time and that trip required the commitment of an entire day. There were numerous other little towns along the coast begging to be explored and the hotel was so beautiful that she planned to hang out and read in the sun, poolside, for a few afternoons.

This morning she opted to explore Portofino, as it was an easy fifteen-minute ferry ride. She would have lunch, wander around and take the ferry back in time to meet Grace for drinks at six o'clock. She had asked the concierge for some recommendations for the area and he had mapped out a series of day trips along with recommended spots for lunch, coffee and gelato along the way. He had given her a list of restaurants for Portofino and had recommended one in particular that he proclaimed was the best in town. She took a peek at the menu on her Foodie app and recoiled in horror at the prices.

'I could buy a week's groceries for the price of that fish!' she exclaimed as she adjusted the app's filters to highlight other travellers' recommendations. 'Ah, that's more like it. This fish is priced like it was just pulled from the sea, not from some special intergalactic space mission. What is wrong with people? Who pays that kind of money for fish?' She shook her head and, with a few taps on her phone, made a reservation at the highly recommended and totally affordable local option.

A crowd had already gathered on the pier waiting for the ferry, and judging by the outfits they were almost exclusively tourists. Most of them wore trainers, ill-fitting T-shirts and oversized cameras. She wondered if they all knew how to work the cameras properly or just fancied themselves as professionals while taking mediocre point-and-shoot photos.

There was an excited buzz of chatter on the pier, with everyone eager to head off for the day and explore the various towns along the route. She heard three or four different languages, one of which she couldn't even identify. The ferry pulled in and a man stood on deck announcing 'Portofino' at the top of his voice. The crowd crushed forward, everyone eager to get what they thought was the best seat. She moved along with the swell of the crowd and handed her ticket to a man balancing with one leg on the ferry and the other on the pier.

'*Grazie*,' he said taking the ticket and extended his hand to help her on board.

'*Grazie*,' she replied with a smile. How gallant! she thought to herself.

She couldn't imagine why anyone would choose to sit in the enclosed bottom deck unless it was the depths of winter, so she skipped lightly up the steps to the top deck. The sun was full in the sky and she could feel the air warming up already.

She leaned over the side and watched the crowd board the ferry. She noticed that the man didn't extend a hand to other men, only the women, but she supposed that the men would be too proud to take his hand, even if they thought they might slip between the wobbling boat and the pier. It was most likely a testosterone-driven decision.

The engine revved and the ferry turned and headed straight out into the bay. Portofino was directly south of Santa Margherita on the map, but the ferry headed out in a westward direction before making a loop and heading south. It was an easy, fifteen-minute boat ride, with stunning views along the coast. The sea was calm and the wind was light. She sat back and closed her eyes, her face up to the sun. She always thought it was amazing that a two-hour plane ride could transport you to such a different climate. Despite being so close to home, southern Europe had proper summers and not much rain from May to the end of September.

Niamh thought that if you grew up in these climates in Italy, Spain and France, it must be very hard to get used to miserable weather in places like Ireland and the UK. Back home you could never be guaranteed a good day and anything planned outdoors always had to have a backup plan. Hardly anyone she knew had a barbecue as there was just little point, given the usual state of the weather. Grace had

had one once. They had bought it when they bought the new house and had invited the family over for a barbecue one Sunday. It had rained solidly all day and Robert had spent two hours standing under an umbrella trying to keep the coals alive while he grilled a bucket of sausages and chicken. They had had to concede to the rain and eat indoors. It had all seemed a bit pointless, really, not that Niamh ventured that thought out loud, after Robert had spent the afternoon in a damp shirt. Still, though, sitting at the kitchen table eating sausages and chicken skewers was hardly exciting.

Her thoughts were hijacked by someone speaking English with a loud, foreign accent. She opened her eyes and squinted in the direction of a young man in a short-sleeved, crisp white shirt. He carried a clipboard and was surrounded by a cluster of American tourists. Niamh wondered why he carried the clipboard. In this day and age surely all of his information could have been accessed digitally. Unless maybe it was provided by the tour guide company to make him look official. She decided that he definitely looked the part, and even though he had a strong accent – which she presumed to be Italian – he spoke pretty good English.

As the ferry started to turn to the right and make its way south, the tour guide pointed out some impressive-looking properties dotted among the trees along the cliff top. As they rounded the headland and made the turn in towards the town of Portofino, Niamh was provided with a free guide to the various celebrity houses visible from the water. He talked of celebrities who had holidayed there in the past, including Rita Hayworth, Liz Taylor and Clark Gable and some more recent, less dead stars, like Robert de Niro.

She gazed at the expansive homes and wondered if she'd bump into anyone famous today. She'd never met a celebrity.

The closest she had come was seeing the girl from the SuperValu ad on television cross the street in St Stephen's Green, but she didn't think that that really counted as she wasn't a celebrity in the true sense of the word. She hadn't looked as skinny in real life, either, and Niamh had decided there and then that professional hair and makeup made all the difference to a person. The SuperValu girl was living proof of that.

She heard her free tour guide say something excitedly about 'the Curse of Tutankhamun'. She remembered something about Tutankhamun from school. He had been an Egyptian pharaoh of some sort, but that was about all she remembered and she certainly didn't remember that he had a curse named after him. But apparently he did, as did all the other dead pharaohs, according to her adopted tour guide, who was gesticulating wildly with both hands. She squinted in his direction, wondering why on earth he was talking about an Egyptian pharaoh on the coast of Italy.

'According to the legend, the curse of the pharaoh is cast on anyone who disturbs the mummy of an ancient Egyptian person, especially if it is a pharaoh,' the tour guide said to the rapt attention of his little audience of American tourists. 'They don't care whether you are an archaeologist or just a thief,' he continued, 'but if you disturb the body you will be cursed.'

'Oh my God, I'm totally never going to Egypt,' one older American woman drawled loudly, as she blessed herself with the sign of the cross.

'Well, you can go to Egypt, but you must not disturb any mummies, that is all.'

He had a bit of an alarmed look on his face as if worried that he had terrified the woman and would get a bad review for his tour guide skills.

'So who died from Tutankhamun's curse?' asked an American boy, clearly fascinated with the idea.

'According to the legend,' the tour guide continued, 'a man called George Herbert, who was the Fifth Earl of Carnarvon, was present at the excavation of the tomb. He was the financier of the project, and when they opened the tomb in 1923 he was bitten by a mosquito and he died four months later. This was the villa that he lived in.' He gestured to a sprawling property overlooking the bay.

The American woman blessed herself for the second time. Niamh rolled her eyes, got up and made her way down the steps.

'Someone was obviously desperate for a good story back in 1923,' she muttered to herself. 'Imagine getting a mosquito bite and blaming a dead pharaoh because you died four months later.'

Still, though, she decided that she'd refrain from telling her parents that story as her mother already had strong feelings about mosquitos. In fact, ever since they were blamed for carrying and transferring the Zika virus, Una Kelly had sworn she'd never again leave Ireland.

'Thank God 'tis too cold and damp for them things here,' she had said in horror one night, having watched the nine o'clock news divulge the latest Zika virus epidemic stories. 'That thing is from Africa, you know.'

'What thing, Una?' her father asked from behind his newspaper, beating Niamh to the question.

'The Zika virus. They say it originated in the Zika Forest in Uganda and they can trace it all the way back to 1947.'

'Is this another nugget of wisdom from *Reader's Digest*, Mam?' Niamh asked, adjusting the strings on her pyjama bottoms.

'Be careful and don't spill that wine down my good sofa,' her mother admonished, glaring at Niamh on the sofa in her pyjamas with a glass of wine in hand.

'You'd think they'd have come up with a cure for it if it's been around that long,' her father offered.

'You'd think so, wouldn't you, but no, there's no cure.'

'God, that's terrible. But you can't get it here, can you?' he asked, dropping the newspaper a few inches and looking over it at the images of mosquitos on the news.

'No, you can only get it in hot places where they have mosquitos. Out foreign, you know? It's too cold for them here.'

'Out foreign' was a term reserved for faraway countries that 'normal' tourists didn't visit on holiday, and included anywhere on the continents of Asia, Africa or South America. The United States, Australia and New Zealand were considered foreign, certainly, but civilised enough not to be in the same classification as other places 'out foreign', most likely something to do with the fact that those countries all spoke English.

'Thank God for that. We'll be staying here, so,' her father said in closing, retreating back behind his newspaper, happy in the knowledge that Zika wasn't something he had to worry about any time soon.

Chapter Six

Portofino grew larger in front of Niamh as the ferry inched its way towards the pier. The bay narrowed into a channel with mega-yachts and sailing boats moored on the left and just in front of the little town that curved around the water's edge in a large semicircle. Wide pedestrian streets led from the water to an expansive piazza, at the back of which stood four- or five-storey buildings, each of them variations of muted, warm pastel colours. The buildings were tall and narrow and huddled together as if they had gathered conspiratorially for a clandestine meeting. The shops were a collection of luxury brands, offering everything the discerning, wealthy client never knew they needed. She strolled past shop after shop with wide, glittering window displays.

Even the mannequins are glamorous here, she mused, and insanely skinny.

It quickly became apparent that this was tourist central, but for a very specific type of tourist – wealthy. The Italians appeared to be outnumbered by tall, leggy blondes speaking Russian and toting multiple shopping bags. They were the fancy, cardboard kind of shopping bags that only posh shops used to send you on your way with your newly acquired luxury goods. She heard Eastern European languages that she couldn't identify. In fact, the only Italians, as far as she could see, were those working in the various cafés or restaurants.

She followed the path as it curved along the water's edge to the right. The street narrowed and it appeared to have less tourist traffic, as it was quieter and sat in the shade cast by the buildings that flanked it. She liked the fact that the crowd had dispersed a little and she chose a quiet café with a blue and white striped awning.

'*Buongiorno, signora.*' The waiter smiled and handed her a menu.

'Oh. Umm ... *buongiorno. Caffè?*'

'*Un caffè o un cappuccino, signora?*' he asked.

'Oh, *sì, un cappuccino,*' she corrected herself, following his lead.

'*Subito.*'

She didn't know what *subito* meant. Couldn't even guess. 'Sure?' she wondered out loud. It kind of sounded like it, but she'd have to check with Grace.

He took the menu from her hand, smiled at her again and disappeared as quickly as he had appeared. Minutes later he was back with a small hand-painted cup and saucer and the most perfect cappuccino she had ever seen. He shooed away a pigeon pecking near her feet and placed the cup and saucer in front of her.

'*Ecco, signora.*'

'*Grazie.*'

She sat back in her seat, savouring the warm creaminess of the froth and the tease of the strong coffee underneath. This was nothing like the kind of cappuccino you'd get back home, she thought. She'd even tried the Starbucks version in the new place near the office, but the cups were the size of her head and the foam took up half the cup and felt like she was drinking air.

'The office,' she sighed, slumping down in her seat. She immediately thought of Rick. It was Tuesday morning. She was an hour ahead in Italy but he would already be at his desk back in Dublin. He always got there before everyone else and would already have put in forty-five minutes at the gym.

'Bloody overachiever,' she muttered into her cappuccino foam. It made her angry that she had allowed him to crawl unannounced into her thoughts. One thought of the office back home and he had slithered right back in there. 'Fuck you, anyway.'

A lady at a table nearby turned her head slightly in her direction but didn't make eye contact.

Shit. Inside thoughts, Niamh, inside thoughts. She wondered if Italians swore like the Irish did. 'Probably not, but even if they did I wouldn't be able to understand them, so maybe they are swearing all day long but I just don't know it,' she muttered angrily. She sat quietly, engrossed in her thoughts for a few minutes and then waved at the waiter, giving the universal hand-signature-in-the-air gesture for the bill.

'Holy shit! Seven euros for a cappuccino? That's mad,' she blurted out loud. The lady nearby turned her head again. OK, Niamh, time to move on, she said to herself as she poked out coins from her purse. You clearly can't afford to drink leisurely cappuccinos in this town or at this rate you won't be able to afford lunch!

The shock of the overpriced cappuccino had banished all thoughts of Rick from her mind. She strolled along the narrow streets, admiring the clothes in the windows, but she had no interest in even entering one of the shops. The price of the cappuccino was evidence enough that she could barely afford to have breakfast in this town, let alone look at clothes. All the top couture brands had shops here, along with some Italian brands that she was unfamiliar with. The most glamorous of all was a shop called Brunello Cucinelli. She had never even heard of it. The window display had waif-like mannequins draped in soft, muted shades of beige, cream and grey. She could tell that it was expensive as it was obvious from her side of the glass that the materials were exquisite. All the pieces seemed to flow without any obvious structure.

'If I was rich, I'd shop here. Brunello ... Brunello.' She repeated the first word as if lodging it in her memory. She would have to tell Grace about this store but she knew she wouldn't be able to pronounce the second part of the name so she took a photo surreptitiously on her iPhone.

The sun got warmer as the morning slipped by. It was easy to pass the time here, wandering the narrow streets and ducking into the non-couture shops. She bought a fridge magnet for her mother and two cute Portofino T-shirts for the boys. She wandered aimlessly, enjoying the fact that the only thing she had to do was show up for her lunch reservation at half past twelve.

She sat on the low wall surrounding the marina, staring in amazement at the massive yachts moored in the bay. She had seen many marinas before, at home in Ireland and on various holidays, but they had always run the gamut from small fishing vessels to bigger yachts with sails. She had never seen anything like these boats. Some of them were the kind of glamour yacht that you'd see in the movies, but some of these boats were so large that she wondered if they ever left the marina. There were two in particular that were enormous, almost the size of a supermarket back home. Both were black.

One appeared to be deserted, but the other had a number of bikini-clad girls on the deck. They were, without exception, blonde and skinny.

She wondered what women like that did when they were in a place like Italy. She and Grace had talked about that very topic the previous evening at dinner.

'I mean, how do you not eat the pasta here when it's so good?' Niamh had asked her sister as she dipped a slice of crusty bread into olive oil. 'What are all the models and skinny people supposed to do – just ignore all the pasta and eat vegetables and fish? That's so sad! Imagine not being able to eat what you want?'

'I don't know, I suppose if they are models or whatever and they make their money from being skinny and looking a certain way, then they have to be disciplined.' Grace shrugged as a plate of steaming *spaghetti alle vongole* was placed before her. 'Mother of God, this looks divine.'

'Thank God we're not models.' Niamh sighed as the same dish was placed in front of her. 'You can't possibly eat a load of pasta and stay skinny, so I don't know what all these skinny people do, but I feel bad for them right now. God, this smells amazing. I don't think you can get clams at home, can you? I don't think I've ever seen clams for sale back home.'

'I don't think I have, either. Maybe they just don't grow in Ireland. Maybe only mussels grow in Ireland for some reason, I don't know.' Grace shrugged and twirled her fork in her bowl of spaghetti, spearing a clam at the same time.

'Do mussels grow?' The question was out of her mouth before she had a chance to stop it and pull it back.

Grace stopped twirling her fork to look up at her sister. 'What? Are you seriously asking me that question, Niamh?'

'No, I mean, I know they grow, but like ... when they

are born, or whatever, are they like seeds and they just grow, or what?'

'I swear, Niamh, sometimes you have the weirdest mind.'

'No, but really . . . I mean I know they don't grow on a bush or anything. They grow in the sea.' She giggled. 'But, like, are they actually born like the tiny fish are born in *Finding Nemo*, or what?'

'*Finding Nemo?*'

'No, wait. This is starting to sound weird, but all I asked was how do they, you know, become mussels like we know them? Like, for instance, are there male mussels and female mussels?' She tried to rescue the conversation and make it sound like it was a completely rational question to ask. 'Do they start off as little seeds or eggs and if so then how do they all attach themselves to rocks where we find them in the wild? Do they each cling to a rock for dear life and grow there until one day a human comes along and tears them off it and eats them? Kind of a sad existence, isn't it?'

'Honest to God, Niamh, sometimes I worry about you,' Grace said, shaking her head. 'I've never spent much time wondering about mussels so I'm afraid I can't answer your questions. Google it when we go home. Now, shall we get another bottle?'

'Honest to God, Grace, sometimes I worry about *you*,' Niamh said mockingly. '*Yes* would be the answer to that question. If I ever say no to that question that's when you should start to worry!'

She was smiling to herself now, thinking back on the conversation about mussels. She still didn't know the answers. She leaned back on the wall, her arms supporting her from behind, and wondered if the skinny girls on the boat in front of her were happy. They looked amazing, but they obviously weren't having spaghetti for every meal. She couldn't imagine not being able to order whatever she wanted off the menu – especially here.

'This is why you are chunky, Niamh, and why you are not exposing yourself to the world in a bikini,' she said quietly to herself. 'A burka would be more appropriate based on the amount of food you eat – and it is usually not salads.'

'I'm sorry, are you talking to me?'

She turned to see a young blond man sitting directly behind her on the wall. She had been so intent upon the boats that she hadn't noticed him sit down.

'Oh, no, sorry! I was just talking to myself,' she replied, hoping he hadn't heard what she had said.

'No problem,' he said with a smile. 'I do it all the time.'

His accent sounded American, but not like the strong American accents she had heard earlier that morning.

'You here on vacation?' he asked.

'Um, yeah. We're staying in Santa Margherita. I just took the ferry here this morning.'

Hopefully the change in conversation meant that he hadn't heard her berating herself about the lack of salads in her life.

'Ah, smart move. Traffic around here is nuts. The ferry is the way to go. That's a nice town.'

'It seems nice. We only got here yesterday so I haven't really seen much of it. I was dying to see Portofino so I thought I'd come here for lunch.'

'Good idea. There are some amazing restaurants here. Some of the best around, actually.'

'Have you been here long?' It sounded like he knew quite a bit about the area.

'A few months.' He shrugged. 'I'll probably just stay until the fall.'

Definitely American, Niamh thought, noting the use of

'fall' instead of autumn. She also noticed that he said 'prob-ably', which meant that he wasn't here to do something practical and finite like build a bridge or open a new hotel or something – probably another American just off around the world to find themselves and do something utterly useless in the process until they were summoned back home by the call of a real job. She couldn't tell what age he was but he was most likely in his mid to late thirties.

'That must be nice,' she said. 'I'm only here for a week.'

She wondered what it would be like to be able to gallivant around like that and decide when you might want to leave. He must definitely come from money, she decided.

'It sure is. I'm making the most of it while it lasts,' he said with a grin as he stood up. 'I'm going up to the little square there for a coffee. Would you like to join me?'

'Oh, that's kind but I actually have a lunch reservation in a few minutes so I have to get going.'

It was a bit of a lie as she still had half an hour before her reservation, but she wasn't about to get into a conversation about her disaster of a life over an overpriced coffee with a privileged American stranger who was just killing time in Liguria until he buggered off again to do something else, somewhere else. She figured a white lie was a safer bet.

'Where are you eating?'

'Um, Da Puny?' she said it in a hesitant voice, as if it were a question. She frowned, wondering why she always did that when she was shy or nervous.

'Excellent choice! It's a great local spot,' he exclaimed, turning to face the piazza. 'Well then ... Da Puny: one; Jeffrey: zero. My loss is their gain.' He smiled.

She returned his smile shyly, thinking that he was obviously a complete charmer and wondering if women really fell for those kinds of lines. She faked a laugh, as she didn't know how to respond to that. '*Ha!* Thanks, bye,' she said as he turned to walk away. She pretended to look busy on her phone.

'Bye, Niamh. Nice to meet you. Enjoy your lunch!' He grinned and walked away.

I didn't tell him my name, she thought, frowning again as she watched him go. *Fuck!* He *did* hear me rabbit on about bikinis and salads. She felt her face flush. Jesus, Niamh, the one cute, friendly foreigner you meet ever in your life thinks you're a nutcase talking to yourself in the middle of town. Excellent way to improve upon your disaster of a life.

She stood up from the wall, brushed off her dress and made her way in the direction of the restaurant. She couldn't tell if he had been flirting with her or if he was just genuinely nice and well mannered. Her flirting radar had become obsolete from lack of use. He was definitely cute though, she thought to herself with a smug little smile as she crossed the cobbled streets in search of her restaurant and her lunch.

Chapter Seven

The restaurant was at the very back of the piazza, facing out in the direction of the marina. It had a large covered terrace out front and was surrounded by pretty, dark green trellises, with a creeping plant of some description making its way up and around the latticework. It was the second of six restaurants in a row and was by far the busiest. A few doors down she could see the restaurant that the concierge had recommended and decided that she had definitely made the right choice. It was the kind of place that you could judge based on the clientele and how they were dressed.

Definitely dodged a bullet there. I probably couldn't even afford the bread basket in a place like that, she laughed to herself as she made her way towards the restaurant that she had booked.

The young woman who stood at the check-in podium out front couldn't have been more than her mid-twenties. She was statuesque and strikingly beautiful, Niamh thought as she walked towards her. She must be a model when she's not working here, she mused.

'Eh . . . *buongiorno*,' she said hesitantly.

The young woman greeted her with a wide smile. *'Buongiorno, signora.'*

Perfect teeth too, Niamh thought. 'Eh … I have a reservation for half past twelve. Under the name Niamh Kelly.'

'*Scusi*. For when, madam?'

'Umm … for twelve-thirty?' She heard herself saying it as if it was a question again. She stood up taller and pushed her shoulders back and her chin up. The woman still towered above her.

'Ah, OK. And what is the name again please, *signora*?'

'Niamh Kelly. I've reserved a table outside.'

'OK,' the woman said, in a lilting Italian accent. 'Is your entire party here now?'

'Umm, no. It's just me.'

'But the reservation is for a party of two, *signora*.'

Niamh knew she was probably imagining it, but she could almost feel the entire piazza go quiet and tune in to the conversation. She felt her face begin to flush. 'Well, no, it should only be for one.'

'Hmmm.' The young woman frowned and shook her head. 'No, *signora*, I'm sorry but the only reservation we have for Niamh Kelly is for a party of two.'

'OK, well, there is only one of me so what do you suggest I do?' Niamh asked shortly, feeling a rush of colour make its way up her neck.

The hostess raised one eyebrow and stared down at her. '*Signora*, I can see that we have a table for Niamh Kelly reserved for the outside, but it is for a party of two. We don't seat singles on the terrace.'

'Excuse me?' Niamh asked, incredulous. This bitch was actually going to argue with her because she was a single?

'We might have a table inside available in an hour or so, but we are very busy, *signora*.'

'But I have a reservation, *signora*,' she replied emphasising the last word.

'Madam, you have a reservation for two, not one.'

'Are you telling me that I can't sit here because I'm on my own?'

'Yes, madam, exactly.'

She could tell that the hostess was beginning to enjoy this now.

'That's ridiculous. What kind of a discriminating policy is that? You mean single people can't eat here?' She knew she was getting angry now and she should just walk away, but she was humiliated and she didn't want to give in.

'No, madam, single people cannot eat on the terrace as we only seat parties of two or more outside. And you made a reservation for two, but you are only one, so I cannot seat you outdoors.'

'This is ridiculous. I made the reservation online and the system probably just automatically booked it for two people. It's not my fault if the operating system defaults in favour of happy couples as the norm.'

Niamh was fuming and was just about to make one final smart comment and storm off when she heard someone speak behind her.

'Excuse me,' the woman said in a deep voice. She stood alongside Niamh at the podium and placed a hand lightly on her right arm.

'Monica, darling, apologies for being a little late,' she said to the hostess in a posh British accent. She turned towards the back of the terrace and waved towards the grey-haired, impeccably dressed man who was rushing towards her. 'Giacomo,' she said kissing him on both cheeks.

'Emilia, *piacere*,' he replied, bending to kiss her free hand.

'Giacomo, I'm late. Please forgive me.' She spoke slowly and enunciated her words beautifully.

'Emilia, is never a problem,' he insisted in a strong Italian accent. 'Please do not worry. We have your table ready for you just here, just as you like,' he said, indicating to a corner table alongside the trellis.

Niamh could do nothing but stare at her. She was meticulously put together. She wore a three-quarter-length, off-white jacket with matching Capri pants. Beneath, she wore a high-necked black top that looked like it might be cashmere, and black sling-back heels. Her blonde hair was knotted in an elegant chignon and pinned at the base of her neck. She finished the look with massive, oversized dark sunglasses, perched on top of her head.

'Marvellous. *Grazie*. Oh, and one more thing. Could you please help my friend here ...?' She turned and looked directly at Niamh.

'Niamh?' Niamh replied with a question, as she wasn't sure what was happening or what she was supposed to say.

'My friend Niamh,' the woman continued. 'There seems to be some confusion with her reservation and she would like to sit outside.'

'Certainly, *signora*,' Giacomo replied with a deep nod of his head. He threw a warning glance in Monica's direction. 'Any friend of yours, *signora*, is a friend of ours.'

He reached out and shook Niamh's hand. '*Piacere, signora.*' He glanced down at the reservation book and saw that she did indeed have a reservation. He glared one more time at Monica. 'My apologies for the confusion, *signora*,' he said to Niamh with a smile. 'We have a lovely table for you outside, just as you requested. *Un momento.*'

The blonde lady winked at Niamh and smiled, patted her

arm twice, then turned and drifted in the direction of her designated table. Giacomo fired off a rapid stream of Italian and a bow-tied waiter appeared by Niamh's side and escorted her to her table. The second place setting was whisked away as the waiter held her chair for her. Niamh's heart was pounding. She had no idea what had just happened or who that lady was, but she certainly had some serious influence in this restaurant.

She gazed around at the diners, each of whom was elegantly dressed. They all chatted quietly together over the chinking sounds of cutlery and crockery. She was glad that she had worn a cute dress, as she didn't think she would even have approached the bitch-in-heels at the podium if she were in her usual shorts and T-shirt holiday attire.

Her heart rate had returned to normal and she was relieved that none of the other diners seemed to be paying her any attention. She could see the profile of the lady who had rescued her in the opposite back corner, engaged in animated conversation with three other diners. 'Emilia,' she said to herself. 'What a pretty name.'

'*Allora, signora.* May I offer you a menu in Italian or you would prefer English?' The waiter who had seated her had returned with menus in hand.

'Oh, English would be great, thank you.'

'*Certo, signora.*' He smiled and placed it in front of her with a flourish.

He no sooner had left, than Giacomo reappeared at her side. '*Signora,* may I offer you a glass of prosecco?'

She hesitated, not knowing if he meant offer in the sense of 'offer on the house', or in the sense of 'Would you like it?' If the price of the cappuccino was anything to go by she should probably decline.

'As my gift, *signora*,' he continued, sensing her hesitation, 'for the earlier confusion.'

'Oh no, that's fine, honestly,' she said waving her hand.

'*Signora*, it will be my pleasure,' he said with a smile as he poured her a glass. 'Enjoy. *Salute!*' And he was gone again.

She spied the other tables to see what everyone was ordering. It looked like people were having either pasta or fish. The menu was dazzling and she suddenly realised how hungry she was. She had read that their *pasta pescatore* was one of their most famous dishes. It was a seafood spaghetti dish in a light tomato sauce. She spotted at least two other people with a dish that looked like it could be just that, which is always a good sign. It was thirty-two euros, so she figured that it had to be a life-alteringly good bowl of pasta. She reached out for a sip of prosecco but realised it was gone. She had obviously drained it in the flush of embarrassment of what had happened.

'Well, that's just classy, Niamh,' she muttered to herself. 'Eh, *scusi*,' she called to a passing waiter. 'May I have the wine list, please?'

'*Certo, signora, subito.*'

'*Subito, subito*,' she repeated quietly, exaggerating the pronunciation and enjoying the sound the word made. Italian words with their big vowels seemed to roll about in her mouth. She had no idea how to spell it but it sounded wonderful. '*Subito ... subito*,' she continued. She stopped abruptly when she realised that the lady at the table next to her was staring at her. She caught her eye, mortified. The lady gave a kind of small, sympathetic smile. The kind of apologetic, fake, half smile you'd give to a person with no legs who was sitting, begging on the street and had turned to catch you staring at them. Her face flushed. 'Great, you look nuts again, Niamh,' she muttered under her breath.

'*Ecco, signora,*' the waiter said with a big smile. 'Here are the wines by the glass.' He pointed to the first and second pages of the menu.

It's probably frowned upon to order an entire bottle for yourself, especially as a woman, she guessed, as she ran a finger down the list. 'Singles don't eat outside and they certainly don't drink a whole bottle of wine with lunch,' she muttered quietly as she munched on a breadstick. She ordered a glass of Pinot Grigio, even though she could easily have polished off an entire bottle. 'Best not to push one's luck!'

The waiter took her order and suggested that she have the minestrone soup as an appetiser. 'Is very good, *signora*, and is light.'

'OK, sure.'

Her glass of wine was poured at the table. She thought that was a nice touch, rather than just plonking an already-poured glass of whatever it might be in front of you. This way you got to see the bottle and you actually knew what you were drinking. She was given a taste first. It was nicely chilled. '*Grazie,*' she said, and she nodded her approval.

No sooner had the wine waiter left then a plate of tiny bruschetta was placed in front of her.

'From the chef, *signora*.'

There were three pieces of bruschetta, each piece no more than two inches long. The tomatoes glistened with oil. She bit into the first piece and decided that she had never tasted anything quite as good. The toasted bread was warm and crusty on the outside but gave way to a softness in the centre, not like the hard crusty things you got at home that resembled croutons more than this softly yielding, melting creation.

That feeling of intense satisfaction continued through the other courses as she sat surrounded by a happy hum of sounds. She hadn't felt this content in a long time, she realised. The food, the wine, the warm air, the foreign sounds all worked together in a happy little harmony. It was a perfect blending of sensations, tastes, sounds and emotions. She ordered a second glass of wine. The bruschetta had indeed been a precursor of great things to come, as she had never in her life had anything like the seafood spaghetti dish. It had mussels, clams, shrimp and squid all melded together in a light tomato garlic sauce.

'Insane. Insanely good,' she murmured to herself contentedly. She would have to tell Grace about this place, although she wasn't sure she would have the courage to come back and face the bitch-in-heels again. She scraped her fork quietly along the bottom of the bowl, trying to scoop up the last of the sauce.

'How was your lunch?'

She looked up to see Emilia towering over her, with her oversized handbag slung over one arm.

'Oh my God, divine.'

'Yes, it's good, isn't it?' She smiled.

'And thank you for ... you know ... earlier.'

'Oh, don't mention it, darling. It was good to take that wretch down a notch or two. She has the most God-awful superiority complex. Good to bring her back to earth every now and then.' She laughed. 'Now, I don't want to disturb your lunch ...'

'No, I'm finished. Um, would you like to join me for a drink or a coffee? It's the least I could do. I think this food might have changed my life and I would have been having a slice of pizza elsewhere if you hadn't rescued me.'

'Well, when you put it like that, how can I refuse?' Emilia laughed a big laugh again and pulled out a chair.

There was a rush of waiters to the table. One helped fix her seat, while another dusted off the table with a napkin. Giacomo appeared at her side almost immediately.

'*Signora*, what can we get for you?'

'What are you drinking, darling?' Emilia asked, nodding towards Niamh's glass.

'Um, the Pinot Grigio.'

'Well, that won't do, will it, Giacomo?'

Giacomo smiled. 'An Arneis, perhaps, *signora*?'

'Two please, darling.' She turned back to Niamh. 'The Pinot Grigio is fine, but the Arneis is divine.'

'Excuse my ignorance, but what is the ... what was the name of the wine?'

'It's pronounced *ar-neys*. It's from Piemonte, in the north of Italy. Have you heard of Barolo wine?' she asked without any hint of judgement.

'Yes, of course.'

'Well, Barolo is from Piemonte, as is Barbaresco, another famous red wine. And it so happens that the region produces the most divine white wine called Arneis.'

Niamh didn't recall even seeing it on the list of wines by the glass. She'd certainly have wondered what it was as it was such an unusual name. 'It doesn't sound very Italian. Would I have seen it on the list?'

'No, they don't serve it by the glass, only by the bottle, which is normally not a problem, but given the amount of wine I've already had it would be a little precarious to dive into another entire bottle.' She laughed her big laugh again.

Niamh didn't think she could imagine the lady diving into anything, especially not wine, as she seemed so elegant and refined. She also guessed that pouring Arneis by the glass was another concession made without hesitation in her favour. Who on earth is she? she wondered.

'I'm Niamh, by the way, as you already know from earlier,' she said, extending a hand.

'Oh my, how rude of me. That's right, we haven't been properly introduced. Forgive me. Emily,' she said shaking her hand firmly.

'I thought they called you Emilia earlier?'

'They did. The Italians will find an Italian version of anything if they can get away with it. Though Lord knows what they'll do with Niamh. Irish?'

'Yes. Are you British?'

'Yes, I'm from London. Or at least I was. I live here now.'

The waiter reappeared and poured two large glasses of white wine. Niamh couldn't help but study the man as he stood over them.

'So how come all the waiters are in black tie if this is a casual, local place?'

'It's a cultural thing here. The black ties don't necessarily mean that the restaurant is fancy,' Emily explained. 'It's just the traditional uniform. They are mostly always men too, the waiters that is. It's actually viewed as a real career here. They call them career waiters – absolute professionals who spend their whole lives in restaurant service, and more often than not at the same restaurant.'

'Really? At home it's something that people do temporarily while they're trying to figure out what to do next, or life in general.'

'Yes. Not the case here. They take great pride in their work and they tend to stay with the same company or restaurant for years.'

'Hmm, that makes sense. I was in Paris once and I noticed

the same thing – all the waiters were men. I bet it's the same career waiter sort of thing. This is divine,' Niamh said appreciatively, as she tasted the wine.

'It is rather, isn't it?' Emily agreed.

'Do you live here in Portofino?'

'Good Lord, no. I couldn't handle all these tourists.'

'Yeah, I did think it was a bit touristy when I got here this morning. It's beautiful though. So pretty.'

'Yes, awfully pretty, but far too many people. Most days I find that people are overrated.' She laughed. 'Are you here on holiday then?'

'Yes, we're staying in Santa Margherita.'

'And who is the other part of your "we"?'

Niamh laughed. 'I'm here with my sister. She's here for a conference and we're staying at the Grand Hotel Miramare.'

'Wonderful property, and Santa Margherita is a nice town – very grand.'

'Where do you live?'

'Not far from here in a small fishing village called Camogli.'

'Called what?' Niamh asked.

She spelled it out. 'C-A-M-O-G-L-I, but the g is silent. It's pronounced *Cam-ohl-yee*.'

Niamh found it hard to imagine this lady in a fishing village. She seemed so elegant and worldly and almost larger than life.

'You absolutely have to visit it. It's the most divine little village, very Italian. Small and quiet but with an abundance of wonderful restaurants.'

'I've never heard of it.'

'That doesn't surprise me. Most people who live there, and even those who visit religiously every year, tend not to talk much about it. It's almost like an unspoken pact. We want to

73

keep it just as it is and not have it overrun with tourists like some other towns nearby.'

Niamh hesitated. Portofino was quite stunning and this restaurant had been amazing, so she found it hard to see how another place could be even more perfect.

'You'll understand when you get there. It's as if no one wants anyone else to know about it. It's that wonderful.'

'I'm intrigued. I'll go with my sister at the weekend when she's done with her conference.'

'Marvellous idea,' Emily said, as she finished her wine.

Niamh was relieved to finally meet someone else who drank as fast as she did. All she got back home was criticism for it.

'Now, I must be off. My driver has been waiting for half an hour for me, poor man.'

'Oh, I thought that Camogli was one of the little villages on the coast.'

'It is, yes, why?'

'You don't take the ferry?'

Emily laughed. 'Darling, I haven't been on a ferry in twenty years! Now, must run. Here's my card. Call me when you get to Camogli if you would like to. I'll tell you where to eat and such.'

The card just had her name and phone number. It was made of heavy paper stock and her name was embossed: EMILY DRAKE. Who *was* this woman?

Giacomo and a waiter appeared at her side as she stood up from the table. She shook Niamh's hand and waved goodbye before she disappeared in the direction of the restaurant entrance, with Giacomo escorting her by the arm. Niamh motioned to a waiter for the bill. Giacomo reappeared minutes later with a tiny glass of limoncello. 'For you, *signora*, as a *digestivo*.'

'Oh thank you. I mean, *grazie.*'

'And the bill, it has been paid, *signora.*'

'Sorry?' she asked, looking up at him.

'Signora Drake has taken care of this. She said that you are a friend, no?'

'I ... oh ... what? Wow. Thank you.'

'Don't thank me, *signora*. Signora Drake is a kind and generous woman. You are lucky to have a friend such as this.' He smiled and disappeared, leaving Niamh to her thoughts.

She could feel tears sting the backs of her eyes and blinked furiously to ward them off. A random act of kindness, she thought, incredulously. Who does that? I want to be like her when I grow up. I want to be that woman who walks into a restaurant and spots someone who clearly needed to be rescued at some level and just say, 'I've got this.' How cool is that?

She leaned against the back of her chair. This was definitely the nicest thing anyone had done for her in a long time and she marvelled at how subtle it had all been. She slid her credit card back into her wallet and drummed her fingers on the table. It was hard to put an age on Emily. She was one of those women who had clearly aged well and life appeared to have been kind to her. She barely had a wrinkle on her face but she must have been in her early fifties.

Kind of like Nicole Kidman, she mused. She always looks amazing, not to mention skinny. I know she's loaded and wealthy women always look good – except the ones who've had too much Botox – but still, she looks amazing for fifty-something. Julia Roberts too – she still looks amazing. Oh and Sandra Bullock! She's fabulous. *And* she dumped that loser American actor after he cheated on her. Imagine being stupid enough to cheat on someone like Sandra Bullock? Isn't she still single? And then she adopted a black kid? These women have it all together. I really need to make more of an effort and get my life back together – and this time on my own terms.

She decided then that Emily must be in the same age range as those actresses. 'She's about twenty years older than me and is in better shape than I am,' she sighed. 'You really need to get your shit together, Niamh. A diet wouldn't be a bad idea, for starters. Maybe tomorrow you can make it through one meal without devouring an entire basket of bread?' she berated herself as she wove her way through the clusters of tables and out into the streets of Portofino.

Chapter Eight

I feel like a fraud, Niamh thought as she studied her reflection in the full-length mirror. She had read about something called imposter syndrome in one of her mother's *Psychology Today* magazines – essentially self-sabotage over irrational feelings of inadequacy. I wonder if that also applies to wearing someone else's clothes to fit in at a fancy restaurant, she thought.

'Hmm, maybe maxi dresses are the way to go, though. That actually doesn't look too terrible on you, Niamh, and it hides any evidence of years of doughnuts having been a preferred breakfast choice,' she said smugly, turning to look over her shoulder. She had borrowed a dress from Grace for tonight's dinner. They had a reservation at an elegant restaurant up in the hills behind Santa Margherita. 'Thank God Grace packed a few loose, floaty numbers,' Niamh mumbled to herself as she rummaged around in her bag for earrings.

The past couple of days had flown by. Niamh had surprised even herself at the extent of her wanderings around the peninsula. She had walked the length and breadth of Santa Margherita, happily ordering pasta at every meal. She had even explored the nearby beach cove of Paraggi and made a point of telling Grace that she'd tried spaghetti and sea urchin for the first time in a tiny seaside trattoria. Although, if she was being totally honest, that was really only because she had ordered the wrong thing and was in fact expecting spaghetti with shrimp.

Grace had an important presentation this afternoon and, as a result, she had been stressed and preoccupied for the past couple of days. Niamh was hoping that tonight her sister would finally be able to relax and get into holiday mode – and stop picking at her in the process. As a result of Grace's stress, nothing Niamh had packed had been deemed suitable enough for their dinners every evening.

'Honestly, Niamh, I told you this would be a fancy trip. Did you really only pack those three dresses?'

'Well, I didn't think I'd need to dress for royalty every night.'

'Don't be such a smart arse. We're here for a week so you should have packed an outfit for every evening. All the restaurants are fancy around here, especially at night.'

Niamh rolled her eyes. She didn't mind the idea of getting dressed up a couple of times, but having to wear a dress and heels every night was not exactly her usual style.

'Can I not wear flat sandals with this dress?' she had asked Grace earlier that evening.

'No. You'll look like a hippy. Do you want to look like a hippy? Put on a pair of wedge sandals at least, for God's sake. And don't be late. I'll meet you at the bar at seven o'clock.'

'I won't be late,' Niamh retorted, rolling her eyes. 'Good luck with the presentation!' she shouted from the bathroom, as Grace left for the afternoon.

Now, standing at the bar in Grace's maxi lemon chiffon dress, she felt like an entirely different version of herself, but it was easier to wear the damn thing than to listen to her sister moaning about her inappropriate choice of outfit again.

She ordered an Aperol spritz as she waited for Grace to arrive and was hoping that she would be easier to live with now that the conference was over. She had tried hard to put on a front and be cheerful all week, but her mind had wandered often to Rick and the situation back home. She must have worn her thoughts on her face one evening earlier in the week, as Grace had jumped all over it. She grimaced now, as she thought back on the conversation and the realisation that her relationship with Rick was definitely over.

'What's the matter with you? What's with the face?' Grace had enquired.

'Nothing. I was just thinking, that's all.'

'Don't tell me you are moping over that loser back home, are you? You're better off without him, Niamh. Honestly I wish you'd just get over him and move on.'

'Way to go there, Grace, with that large bucket of patience and understanding,' Niamh replied snarkily, as she chugged the remainder of her glass of wine. 'It's only been two weeks, you know. Give a girl a break, will you?' She reached for the bottle and poured two more glasses. 'I thought you were taking me away so I could feel sorry for myself and wallow in self-pity and self-loathing?'

'No, I brought you away so you could see that there is more to life than "Rick the Dick" and pull yourself together. You don't think he's sitting at home moping over you, do you?'

Niamh had been quietly checking her phone twenty times a day. She had secretly hoped that he might have regretted his decision and had been waiting for him to call to say that it had all been a giant mistake, but she refused to give in and contact him in any way.

'No, of course not.'

'Well, he's not. So the sooner you move on the better.'

'What do you mean by that?'

'Nothing, nothing,' Grace replied, looking down at the menu.

'Do you know something?'

Grace hesitated and sipped her wine. 'Well, it's just that I saw something on Facebook, that's all. But it's probably nothing.'

'What did you see on Facebook?' Niamh could feel the colour drain from her face. She had deleted him in a rage but had forgotten that her sister might still be friends with him on social media. Shit, she thought, this was a missed opportunity – I could have been stalking him on Facebook on Grace's phone this entire time, damn it.

'Nothing, just a photo, just forget it. There's no point.'

'Hand me your phone, please.'

'I didn't bring it with me to dinner.'

'That's a flat-out lie. That device is *never* not on your person. It's like an extension of your arm. Hand it over, please. Unlock it first.'

Grace sighed and reached into her bag. She tapped out her four-digit code and opened the Facebook app. She scrolled for a few moments and then stopped. She hesitated for a second before handing the phone across the table. 'Just don't freak out, OK? Don't make a scene. I had to beg to get this table.'

Niamh took the phone and stared at the photo in front of her. It was Rick, looking handsome in a dark suit, with a young blonde woman sitting on his lap. She looked vaguely familiar. She was sitting on one knee, with her hand on his other thigh.

'They look cosy,' she said slowly. 'Wow, didn't take him long, did it?'

'Give it back to me,' Grace said, waggling her hand across the table.

'Who is she?' Niamh zoomed in to get a better look at her. 'I don't believe it . . .' her voice trailed off as she frowned at the screen.

'What? Do you know her? Don't tell me you know her,' Grace replied.

'I don't believe it . . .'

'Not helping, Niamh! What?'

'That's Boobra.'

'Who?'

'Boobra from Sales.'

'Who's Boobra? What does that even mean?' Grace asked, her hands spanning out at her sides.

'Barbara,' Niamh offered, still not looking up from the screen. 'Her name is Barbara something-or-other. She's kind of new. I don't remember her last name, her dad's Vietnamese or something and I've no idea how to pronounce it. I don't really know her, I just know she works in Sales.'

'At PlatesPlease?'

'Yes. She went to Slovenia or Slovakia or somewhere like that in Eastern Europe last year for a cheap boob job. They had some promotional thing going on – some two-for-one special – two people, not two boobs, obviously – so she went with a friend.'

'What? What kind of dope goes for a discounted boob job?' Grace asked, aghast.

'This clown did. But in fairness, she did have boobs like fried eggs. I saw a before and after photo. Anyway, she wanted to go up two cup sizes but when she woke up the surgeon was standing over her saying that he had a surprise for her. He said that as he was doing it he decided that she would look fantastic with even bigger boobs, as she was so lovely and tall. So he went up three cup sizes while she was unconscious.'

'What? Are you serious?'

'Deadly. Now they just look ridiculous, as is clearly evident here.' Niamh, with the beginnings of a grin, turned the zoomed-in photo around for Grace to see.

'Ah come on, you're making that up!'

'I'm not, I swear. So now she has these obviously fake, massive boobs, hence Barbara became Boobra.'

'Did she sue him?'

'How could she sue him?' she exclaimed. 'She couldn't afford a full-priced boob job in the first place, let alone the cost of a lawyer to sue a plastic surgeon on the other side of Europe.'

'But that's absolute malpractice surely,' Grace said incredulously.

'I swear, Grace, you're the only person in my life to not see the funny side of this. Come on, it's hilarious – going for a discount boob job and waking up with more than you even wanted? It's like God poking at you for messing with plastic surgery in the first place!'

'That poor girl. Give me back the phone,' Grace said, waggling her hand in front of Niamh.

'I don't know her that well but she's not the brightest of sparks, to be honest, and what the hell is Rick doing with her, anyway? She didn't wait long for me to be out of the picture, did she?' Niamh pushed the phone back across the table towards her sister. 'They deserve each other!'

'Don't go all mopey and make me sorry I told you now. I thought seeing this might actually help you get all self-righteous and be all strong feminist-type and realise that you're better off without him. Please don't go wallowing, for the love of God.'

'I *am* better off without him, but allow a girl a moment to react to something as shocking as the visual of Boobra implanting herself on his lap – no pun intended,' said Niamh with a giggle.

'What?'

'Implanting herself ... nothing, forget it. Is there more wine in that?' she asked, tipping her head towards the bottle in the ice bucket.

Grace drained the bottle into their glasses and motioned for another. 'I'm sorry that you had to see that. I hope you're not all upset and just putting on a brave face for my sake, but you really are better off without him. I know that's a cliché and all, but it's true.'

'No, maybe I'm actually really in shock or something, but now I feel like a complete gobshite for wasting a minute feeling sad over him. I've been hanging out mentally in Loserville for the past two weeks and he's been getting his rocks off with Boobra. And she's not even pretty!' Niamh fumed. 'She's just skinny! Oh, but she has enormous boobs.'

'No, she's a bit of a dog, actually. Flat nose. Looks like she got whacked in the face with a frying pan,' Grace said, pouring two large glasses from the new bottle.

Niamh giggled at the idea of being whacked in the face with a frying pan. 'Yep, he's really dredging the bottom with that wench. Well, she can have him. She'll find out soon enough. The man has no stamina in bed. He leaves it all on the gym floor and whoever he's taking to bed gets seconds.' She held up her glass in a fake toast. 'Your competition isn't other women, Boobra – it's the bench press. Good luck with that!'

The two of them laughed uproariously. It might have been just the kind of release that Niamh needed because, for the first time in weeks, she slept like the dead that night and woke up without feeling anxious. Whopping headache, of course, but that could be easily cured and it had been worth it. An anxious heart isn't as easy to fix and she was grateful to wake up feeling some level of peace, at last.

She shook her head, dispersing the memory of the Boobra conversation that night at dinner with Grace and sat now quietly at the bar. She twirled her glass of Aperol spritz, keeping one eye on the door as she waited for Grace to finish her presentation, so the holiday could really begin. She regretted having lost her cool and gotten so emotional about the whole situation, but in hindsight it had been coming for a while. She couldn't believe that had only been a couple of days ago. It seemed like weeks ago, now, looking back on it, and she felt mentally exhausted from all of the emotional energy of the past couple of weeks. It was almost as if seeing the photo of him with that wench cemented everything in her mind. It was clear that he was moving on, and it was as if that photo had given her permission to do the same. She had decided that there was no point in mourning someone who doesn't want you any longer. So instead she had focused the next few days on exploring, pasta and plenty of wine.

'Well? How'd it go?' she asked Grace as she finally saw her approaching. She was relieved to see her with a smile on her face.

'It went great! But I'm so glad it's over. Now we can plan some stuff for the next few days. Where should we go first? Two whole days of no work, just play. Fabulous,' Grace said, plucking Niamh's glass from her hand and taking a sip. 'Cheers!'

'Well, you had said that you wanted to go to Portofino, and I'd like to go to that place the lady who rescued me is from – Camogli.'

'Do we take a boat there?'

'Yes, to both of them, they're both on the same route from

here. Portofino is the first stop, then the ferry continues on to Camogli.'

'Well, you've already been to Portofino, so why don't we go to Camogli first and wander around, have lunch and all that and then we can stop off in Portofino for a drink on the way back?'

'Good plan. Let's go in the morning, then.'

'Did she give you the names of some good restaurants for lunch?'

'No, she gave me her card and just said to call her if we were going and she could recommend some places.'

'Oh God, that doesn't mean we have to meet her, does it? I know she rescued you and all that, but we only have two days. I don't really want to have to have lunch with a stranger and make polite small talk. Is that mean? Sorry if that's mean, but I've spent the past three days talking to people so I'm kind of over it.' Grace grinned.

'No, that's fine. I don't have to call her. I'll look up some recommendations online later.'

The next morning started later than planned. Three bottles of wine might have seemed like a good idea at the time, but they rarely do so the next morning. The girls struggled down to breakfast before it finished at eleven o'clock.

'Do I look as bad as I feel?' asked Grace at the breakfast table.

'Yes. Woof. No offence.'

'God,' she groaned. 'Did we finish the third bottle?'

'Yes, and ordered two limoncellos, 'cause we still hadn't had enough.'

'I don't even remember getting home.'

Niamh plucked bits off her croissant. The large bottle of sparkling water in front of them was a telltale sign of chronic overindulgence the night before. 'My head is pounding,' she moaned, her chin resting in one hand. 'I don't think I can have a cappuccino yet. I'll have to have black tea. Here, take these.' She handed two painkillers across the table. 'They're the ones you dissolve in water. They work the fastest.'

'Thanks,' Grace replied, looking up at her. 'You still have makeup on from last night.'

'Oh God, I didn't even look in a mirror before coming down.'

'That's probably a good thing. You would never have left the room.'

'Are you serious? Am I a state?'

'You look like a racoon. You have eyeliner or mascara or both smudged a solid inch below your eyes.'

'Oh, Jesus. No wonder the waiter looked at me funny. Why didn't you tell me, Grace?' Niamh shrieked, sitting up and wiping her fingers beneath her eyes.

'Stop shouting,' Grace moaned, her head face down in her hands. 'I feel like roadkill. Will you pour more water please? I'm so stupid, I swear. I wish I could remember the night before just how bad I feel the next morning so I could trigger some kind of stopping action, but no . . . I just keep on going. Ugh. I need to eat something.'

Copious amounts of sparkling water and carbohydrates later, they made their way back to their room and lay on their beds.

'There's a ferry in an hour. We should try to make that one. It gets us to Camogli by about one o'clock,' Niamh said, hoping that the room would stop spinning soon.

'I just hope the sea is calm, that's all.'

'We can go up on top, that way we'll have a breeze. That will wake us up a bit, then we can have a nice late lunch.'

'How can you talk about lunch? I've just inhaled enough carbs to feed a small family. How long did you say it takes those tablets to work?'

'Usually twenty minutes or so. Come on, get up and take a cold shower. That will help.'

'OK. If I'm not out in fifteen minutes I may have just slipped down the plughole, so come rescue me,' Grace moaned as she stumbled towards the bathroom.

'I'll look up some restaurant recommendations while you're in there. A glass of wine will do you good. That will fix you – hair of the dog and all that!'

'Shoot me,' was all she heard in reply as the bathroom door closed.

Chapter Nine

It was the most perfect palette of colours, Niamh thought, as the ferry rounded the edge of the promontory and made a right turn in the direction of Camogli. They were still a few miles out from the town as they turned and faced into the bay, but even all the way back out here the town looked like a warm orange glow at the foot of a lush, dense green hill. The buildings were taller than in Portofino and they stretched far left and right beyond what looked like the beach and the pier.

The strong sea breeze had helped shake off some of the overindulgent cobwebs, and Niamh was starting to feel a bit more human. Grace was still unusually quiet and sat back against the railing with her eyes closed and face tilted up to the sun. The ferry continued steadily towards the village of Camogli, the burnt orange buildings getting larger as they drew closer.

The bay was protected by massive, overgrown cliffs on the right side, dotted here and there with pretty villas. To the left was Genoa, resembling little other than a white Lego town in the distance, and straight ahead of them sat Camogli. As the ferry slowed and made its approach, it veered right and followed the still waters around the pier, into the marina. The difference in the boats at this marina was notable. These were fishing vessels and small pleasure boats, nothing like the hyperbolic statements of wealth and affluence she had seen in Portofino.

The coloured collection of buildings stood five or six storeys tall in front of them. Many of the windows had been flung open, as if to invite in the warm, early summer air. Lines of laundry flapped in the breeze. Not uniformly starched, white linens but rather a more domestic, honest kind of laundry of underwear and towels. The ferry chugged to a stop, pulling up at one of two piers, and began to disgorge its passengers along a narrow wooden plank.

'Are we there?' asked Grace as she stood and followed Niamh down the stairs.

'Yep. Let's go find a coffee.'

'Definitely.'

They followed the long line of passengers along the pier and up towards the town. Everyone ambled along, with no one appearing to be in any particular hurry. Niamh noticed that they hadn't heard any English spoken since they had left their hotel earlier that morning.

'Oh look!' Niamh gushed as she pointed at one building after another.

'Can we please just get a coffee first? I promise I'll be more human then. Just a large injection of caffeine and I'll function much more normally,' Grace said quietly, as she hid behind a wide-brimmed hat and oversized sunglasses.

'There's an Illy coffee sign right ahead.'

'Best news I've heard all day,' Grace mumbled, following Niamh through the meandering clusters of people.

The crowd splintered once they had left the marina and they made their way easily up into the town. Cafés, restaurants and gelaterias were clearly in abundance. A narrow street sloped up into a piazza with commanding views of the marina and the bay. From there the street climbed higher to a wide pedestrian promenade. It was late Friday morning now, and the promenade was getting busy, but everyone looked and sounded Italian.

'They can't all be Italian, can they?' Niamh asked, as they pulled up two white chairs outside the café.

'Why not? We are in Italy, after all. What were you expecting? Arabs?' Grace asked sarcastically.

'God, I had forgotten how pissy you get when you're hungover. I'm going to stop speaking to you now until you have mainlined some caffeine and normal levels of human decency back into your system.'

Niamh ordered two cappuccinos and a couple of biscotti in the little café. The girl behind the counter clearly didn't speak English and so the short exchange was conducted solely in Italian, with strong support from hand gestures. The girl motioned for Niamh to take a seat, indicating that she would bring the coffees out once they were ready.

'The coffee is so good here, isn't it?' Grace said, sipping her cappuccino. 'Why does everything taste better here?'

'Dunno, it does though. Are you up for a walk around before lunch?'

'Yes, I'm starting to feel human again. Sorry for being such a witch all morning. My headache is starting to ease now, too. Good biscotti!' Grace wiped crumbs from her mouth.

'Ooh look, Grace! An estate agent's. Let's take a look. I'd love to know what a place here would cost. You know the way people stick things on their fridge for motivation? Mine could be an apartment here in Italy. Ooh! Maybe we could get a place together and I could just live here and you could come on holidays with the boys.'

'Are you sure you're sober?' Grace asked, draining the end of her cappuccino.

'Yes, why?'

'Umm, because last time I checked I already had a mortgage and you were recently out of a job. Reality check, perhaps?'

Niamh slumped back into her chair. 'Since when are you so negative on everything I say? You're the one who dragged me here, remember?'

'For a week, Niamh! We've got this glorious week to enjoy and then come Sunday we get back on the plane and go home. That's how it goes.'

'OK, OK. I just wanted to take a look. You're the one always telling me I should invest in a place of my own.'

'I meant in Dublin, Niamh, where you'd have a hope of working to actually pay for it! Now, what's next on the agenda? Where's lunch?'

'I got some recommendations from the concierge this morning for some local places here in Camogli. He said we wouldn't need reservations here at this time of year. Apparently it doesn't get really busy until the height of summer.'

'OK, what are the options?'

'Well, two of them require another boat ride, and one is right here in town.'

'I don't think I'm up for another boat ride just yet. What did he say about the one in town?'

'Just that it's one of the best seafood restaurants in town. It's a bit pricey, though, for the fish dishes, at least.'

'Ah, who cares?' Grace shrugged. 'We've only got two days left. Two lunches and two dinners … how badly crippled financially can we get in two days? Plus this place feels more casual than Santa Margherita, so it's bound to be less expensive.'

'It definitely feels more casual than Portofino, and this cappuccino was only three euros. That's less than half what I paid in Portofino, so that's a good sign.'

'What's the restaurant called?'

'Da Paolo. It's a local seafood restaurant. It's down a tiny alley somewhere.'

'OK, we'll keep an eye out for that. Let's go wander,' Grace said.

They gathered their things and left the café.

The village of Camogli was built on two levels and locals referred to them as the upper and lower streets. The lower street was mostly pedestrianised and bordered the bay, with a long, wide promenade overlooking the beach below. In typical Italian fashion, the beach was dotted with a series of private beach clubs providing loungers, changing and bathroom facilities. They were all closed for the season, poised to reopen the following month, and so the beach was deserted, save for a few locals walking their dogs along the water's edge.

They walked the length of the lower level, and climbed the steep steps to the upper level, pausing halfway up to catch their breath, pretending to be taking in the view of the bay.

'I swear, I think that little granny up ahead with her bag of groceries is going faster than we are,' Niamh huffed.

'How many bloody steps are there?' Grace asked as she doubled over and placed her hands on her thighs. 'This is not a recommended activity for people in a delicate condition like us.'

'At least it's not raging hot. Look at the view, though!' said Niamh, pointing behind them at the glistening bay. She watched a solitary sailing boat bob along on the horizon. 'It's beautiful!'

They continued to the top of the steps and stood to catch

their breath again. The upper level had a hip-height wall that ran the length of the village. It was larger than they had first imagined. Upon arrival to the pier, it looked as if the entire village was contained on the level along the beach and promenade, as the upper level was neatly tucked away out of sight. They could see now that this was the true local heart of the village, with little fruit and vegetable markets, a small grocery store, a post office and everyday kinds of services on offer. They wandered the length of the street slowly, looking in shop windows along the way. Smaller, narrower streets ran off this main thoroughfare, deeper into the village.

Local women wore housecoats and headscarves as they swept the footpaths outside their shops or houses. Old men wore flat caps and dark suits as they went about their daily business. Mothers fussed over children as yet too small to be in school, and a couple of skinny stray cats darted from one side of the street to the other in search of their next meal. Without exception everyone nodded or smiled a greeting as Niamh and Grace passed by.

The sun beat down on them warmly as they wandered the narrow, cobbled streets happily.

'I haven't seen that restaurant yet. Have you?' Grace asked, tilting her head upwards to admire the small church in front of them.

'No, but I kind of forgot to look for it, to be honest, I was so busy just looking around. Should we ask someone?'

'We better, it's almost two o'clock and we're lost. Will you do it? I don't have the energy to speak Italian.'

Niamh stopped to ask the next housecoated lady where they might find the restaurant, but clearly failed to pronounce it correctly. She pulled out the note that the concierge had written and showed it to the lady.

'*Ah, sì*. Da Paolo,' said the woman, correcting Niamh's poor attempt at pronouncing the name. '*Giù.*'

'*Giù?*' Niamh asked not understanding.

'*Sì, sì, giù,*' the woman repeated, indicating furiously with her arm to the level below.

'OK. Down. *Grazie.*'

'Oh well, at least it's down and not up again,' Grace laughed. 'We'll have worked up an appetite for lunch anyway, that's for certain.' She started to walk in the direction the lady had pointed, but Niamh remained leaning against the wall, gazing out at the bay. 'Come on, who knows how long it will take us to find this place.' Grace grabbed Niamh's elbow. 'What are you doing? Come on!'

'It's just so beautiful, isn't it? So peaceful.'

'Yes, it is. I'm starving. Come on.'

They turned back in the direction they had come and made a right turn onto a narrow side street. They passed another minuscule vegetable store with its crates of vegetables stacked carefully outside on the footpath, a fabric store of some sort, with linens, aprons and tea towels on display in the window, and a pharmacy.

'Is that the third pharmacy we've passed or do we keep passing the same one?' Grace asked, confused.

'No, we haven't been here before. I think the steps down will be at the end of this street, though. What a pretty street.' Niamh sighed as she admired the flaking, colourful buildings flanking them on either side. They could see the bay sparkling in the sun at the end of the street, which meant that they were at least going in the right direction. 'It's like something out of a movie back in time.'

With that the church bells began to chime out their hourly announcement. They reverberated somewhere

94

overhead, echoing against the buildings and seemingly surrounding them. Niamh tilted her head up to the sky, breathing in the clear air and the melodic chiming sounds. 'Magical.'

She rushed to catch up with Grace. 'Grace, look!' she exclaimed, stopping suddenly and peering through the window of a shopfront.

'What?' Grace asked, turning back to face her.

'Look, isn't this just adorable?'

'It's closed. As in, shut down, closed down.'

'I know, but look at it. Isn't it sweet?'

'I suppose it used to be at one time. It's a bit of a mess now.'

'No!' Niamh urged again. 'Look at the tiles and the little counter. It's so cute. It must have been a restaurant or a café or something. Look at the tables back there in the corner.'

'Dunno, come on. I don't want to be late.'

Niamh put her hands up to create shade around her eyes and pressed her nose to the window. She didn't know if it was the bells, or the warm air, or the feeling of contentment that she felt here, but this little town had captivated her imagination. She peered through the window of the dilapidated, abandoned building, imagining what it used to be in its past life. And then she saw the sign.

AFFITTASI, followed by a phone number.

It was handwritten in thick black ink on a piece of card, tucked on the inside bottom corner of the window. Niamh's breath caught in her chest and she glanced from the sign into the interior of the room and back to the sign. She didn't know exactly what it meant as she didn't speak the language, but she knew it wasn't a for-sale sign, as she had seen those around town – VENDESI, which looked similar to the French version that she knew. 'It must mean that it's for rent,' she whispered against the glass.

Grace had reached the end of the street by now, either oblivious to, or choosing to ignore Niamh's stalling.

'The steps are right here. Come on, hurry up, will you?'

Niamh drew her breath to tell Grace what she had seen, but hesitated when she turned and saw her, hands on her hips, impatient to get to lunch. Deciding against it, she whipped out her phone and took a photo of the handwritten sign, dropped her phone back into her bag and jogged the length of the narrow street. She glanced up at the corner, noting the street name because, without it, given her appalling sense of direction, she may never make her way back again.

'Via dei Limoni,' she whispered under her breath.

After a couple of wrong turns, the girls found the restaurant, housed in an old stone building. You couldn't access it from the main road as it was tucked away down a three-foot-wide alleyway. The only indication that there was anything at the end of the little alleyway was a small wooden sign, hanging overhead with the name of the restaurant etched on it. They followed the alley one behind the other as it wound around in a wide curve, ending in a tiny courtyard with eight outdoor tables.

From the courtyard, they could see in through the back door of the restaurant. Two female cooks were busily stirring and chopping inside. To get to the front of the building, and the main entrance of the restaurant, the girls continued along the alley and circled around to the other side of the building. They were greeted with warm smiles and shown to a small table inside. It was dark and cosy with tall, lofty ceilings, and the place was already packed with diners. Ceiling fans whirred overhead, attempting to regulate the heat being generated within the thick old walls of the building.

Relieved that their waiter spoke a little English, they asked if they could order a bottle of wine.

'White or red?' was all the waiter had asked. There was no wine menu.

They asked for a bottle of white wine, and a few moments later he presented them with a bottle of crisp Vermentino. 'Is from the hills nearby,' he explained in a strong Italian accent.

There was no lengthy ceremony and no tasting, instead he simply opened the bottle and placed it on the table. '*Salute!*' he said with a smile. He returned and handed them a menu. 'English is OK?'

'Yes,' Grace giggled. 'English is fine.'

The translations left a lot to be desired – 'head of shrimp' and 'white fish, cooked' – so they scanned the room to see what other diners had before them. Almost every plate that they could see had a version of the same thing. They couldn't make out what it was, but it was some tiny, silvery fish that had been flattened and was served with either lemon or tomato.

'Ah, *alici*,' the waiter replied loudly when they asked him what everyone was eating. 'Is a local speciality!'

The girls exchanged glances, neither one of them wanting to admit that they didn't know what kind of fish it was.

'Ah-lee-chee' Niamh repeated slowly.

'*Sì, signora*, Camogli is the best place in Italy to eat *alici*!' he exclaimed, with no small amount of pride.

'OK then, we will have that … them, please,' Grace decided. 'And the fish in salt, is that a good—'

'*Certo, signora!*' he responded excitedly. 'Is the best dish. I bring you the fish.'

He returned moments later with a large platter of

just-caught, shiny, fresh whole fish. He advised on one in particular to share, and when they nodded their agreement he was gone again.

'Well, I'm not sure what we're actually going to be eating, but that was easy enough,' Grace laughed. 'Cheers!'

'Cheers! It all looks amazing,' Niamh replied, watching the various dishes come out from the kitchen.

A basket of warm bread was brought to the table and local olive oil was swirled onto a small plate. The sisters chatted happily as they awaited their first course. The overindulgences of the previous night were quickly forgotten as they enjoyed the local wine in earnest.

'I could just die happily here with this bread and oil. It's so good,' Niamh sighed.

'I know. Why is it so hard to get good bread like this at home? Although, to be honest, everything tastes better here. All the food is just so much better, not just the pasta, which is totally amazing. Everyone seems to be happier or more easy-going, too, don't they? I don't know, they don't look as stressed out as people back home. I wonder if it has anything to do with the weather or the *dolce vita* that Italians talk about all the time?'

'Well, in fairness, Grace, you'd be a lot happier too if you could eat like this every day, not just for one or two weeks a year on holiday. I could live here . . . I think I could actually live here, you know?'

'Of course you could, until you ran out of money and had to go to work!'

'No, seriously, people do it, Grace. People move to new countries all the time and start over.'

Grace smiled across the table at her sister. 'I think everyone engages in the fantasy of running away from life and starting over in some exotic new place at some point in time, but then reality crashes in around you and you realise that you have to actually work to make a living, and you get back on the plane and go home.'

'Yeah, I suppose ...' Niamh responded quietly.

The waiter interrupted the conversation on their Italian life commentary by placing a plate in front of each of them. They had thought they had ordered the same thing, but he brought out two different variations of the seafood appetiser; one was prepared in olive oil and lemon and the other in olive oil with thin slivers of tomato. They ate in silence for a few moments, savouring the light flavours on their tongues. The fish was so delicate it seemed to melt in their mouths.

'I have to ask him what this is,' Niamh said, halfway through the plate. 'Do you want to swap and try this one? It's divine.'

'Sure, so is this,' Grace replied, passing her plate across the table. One dish was as delicate and delectable as the other.

'*Alici, signora,*' the waiter replied when he heard Niamh's question.

'But what is that in English? What kind of fish?'

'Anchovy, *signora.*'

'Anchovies?' they both repeated in unison.

Grace stared down at the remaining few fish; they were about three inches long and flattened out in the middle so they lay like butterflies. They were silver grey and glistening under the oil. 'These are anchovies?'

'He must have the wrong name in English. They can't be the same thing. I'll have to look it up,' Niamh said. She pulled out her phone and found Google Translate. 'He's right,' she continued, looking up at Grace.

'I wouldn't touch an anchovy at home with a barge pole.

Those ugly, salty, crumpled-looking, hairy things,' Grace said shaking her head and enjoying the last morsel. 'How can this be the same fish? See? Even anchovies taste better here.'

'Have you really never thought about living anywhere else?' Niamh asked, topping up their glasses of wine.

'Of course I have. I have thoughts of running away from my life on a regular basis. Particularly on a Sunday night and Monday morning.'

'But you love your job,' Niamh frowned.

'I do, but it's just hard sometimes with the two boys and all the rushing around, and Robert is away a lot for work, which is a pain. I always thought I'd like to live in America, actually, and work for a great big architecture firm, but it's so hard to get a visa.'

'What about in Europe?'

'Nah, Robert and I both make good money at home, so we have a decent quality of life. The only way we'd move at this point is if one of us landed a big corporate gig in the States and they were throwing gobs of money at us. God bless the Americans and their big corporate salaries!'

'Yeah, I suppose you're right,' Niamh replied distractedly, twirling her fork between her fingers.

'Look,' Grace said quietly, as she leaned across the table and put a hand on Niamh's arm. 'You're going through a lot and you've got a whole load of things to figure out. Change is hard, so don't try to solve everything at once. I'm not worried about you, Niamh. You'll figure out what's next, you'll find another job – a better job. Lord knows you were underappreciated at Rick's company. You'll find something better, you'll get a lovely new apartment and you'll start over. Everything will work out – it always does.'

Niamh was saved from any further conversation about her future as the waiter delivered their main course to the table. The fish was encased in a massive, hard mound of salt, which he hacked at carefully. The salt came away in large chunks, revealing the whole fish inside.

'It kind of looks like the lumps of ice you hack off when you're defrosting the freezer at home,' Niamh giggled.

The waiter freed the fish from its salt casing and divided it into two halves, placing two fillets on to each plate. Another waiter brought a plate of potatoes sautéed with garlic and lemon and another of green vegetables.

'I think this might be the most divine piece of fish I've ever had in my life,' Grace mumbled, not taking her eyes off her lunch.

'I don't understand what is happening in my mouth! Unreal,' Niamh agreed.

When they had finished, they ordered two espressos. The waiter brought them, along with a plate of almond biscotti.

'You stay here in Camogli?'

'No, we're staying in Santa Margherita,' Grace answered. 'We're taking the ferry back later this afternoon.'

'Ah, but you must stay for the sunset. Here in Camogli is the best sunset in all of Liguria. The sun – she looks you in the eye as she says goodnight,' he said, drawing circles in the air with his hand. 'It will be a little after seven o'clock tonight.'

They looked at each other across the table and Grace shrugged. 'Why not? We're not in any hurry, as long as we're back in time for dinner. We have a reservation at that place near the hotel tonight.'

'OK. Is there somewhere we can go and get a drink to watch it?' Niamh asked the waiter.

'Yes, you must go to La Terrazza. Is in the hotel at the other end of the pier. You have seen the hotel, no?'

'Oh, yes, I saw it as we came in on the ferry earlier,' Niamh said, nodding.

'*Va bene* – OK. You will go there before seven o'clock, no? It will be the most beautiful thing you will see in Italy, *signore!*' he said enthusiastically.

'How do we say no to that?' Grace said. 'How about a limoncello?'

'Well, now that we've got a few hours to kill that's not a bad idea at all!'

Chapter Ten

They left the restaurant sated and happy and spent the next few hours exploring Camogli, popping into bookshops, small boutiques, churches and markets. A little after six o'clock they made their way towards La Terrazza. The streets were quieter now, with only small clusters of children playing in alleyways. Boats approached the pier, ready to tie up after a day of fishing. A couple of scraggy cats sniffed around in corners near restaurant bins, and new batches of laundry were hung out to dry from apartment windows.

As they walked along, Niamh wondered why he had sent them to that particular place to watch the sunset. They passed dozens of places right on the promenade, overlooking the bay on the way to the hotel. The air was getting cooler now and she pulled a wrap from her bag. They strolled in silence, each of them lost in their own thoughts. She saw the ferry leave the pier, heading back in the direction they had come from this morning. She wondered if there was a second one servicing this stretch of the coast, as she watched it make the turn from the marina out into the bay. If not then this one would deposit its passengers in their towns of choice and then turn around in Santa Margherita and come back to pick them up. The thought of it made her smile, as if it would be coming back especially for them.

They entered the hotel and were greeted by front-desk staff with friendly smiles. They asked for directions to La Terrazza and were escorted by a smartly dressed, slender young woman down a long corridor and through a series of double doors. Her chestnut-brown hair was neatly tied up in a huge bun and she was immaculately made up. Niamh instinctively pulled her wrap around her and vowed to lose a few pounds, watching the woman's waistline as she walked ahead of her. The hotel corridors were quiet but they could hear strains of music playing as they approached the entrance to the terrace.

The brunette stood to the side and opened the right-hand door for them. '*Ecco, signore*,' she said with a smile.

No sooner had they stepped onto the terrace than they were greeted by a smiling man in a black waistcoat and bow tie. '*Buona sera, signore.*'

'*Buona sera.*' Grace smiled in return, taking in the scene in front of them.

The double doors had spilled out into the centre of a protected terrace, shaded from the breeze by tall, white walls on either side, with only the front remaining open and unobstructed. From their vantage point they could see that the terrace swept wide left and right and directly ahead, and the Golfo Paradiso seemed to arc around them. They were high enough not to have the beach or the beach clubs obstruct the view of the bay and the horizon, flanked on one side by the massive, lush green hills and on the other the colourful town of Camogli petering out and continuing in a series of villages all along the bay as far as Genoa. It was truly the most spectacular view that either of them had ever seen.

The waiter escorted them to the last free table on the far right and he and another waiter held their chairs as they sat down. Neither of them had said a word since they stepped onto the terrace. The waiter just smiled, as if he recognised this look of awe, and gave them a moment to take it in. The terrace was full of well-dressed couples and small groups of people chatting quietly, everyone facing towards the bay and the horizon. The sun was still high in the sky, but it was as if everyone had gathered for the screening of something special, and the show was about to commence.

'Do you think anyone would mind if I went out to the front to take a photo?' Niamh asked, standing up.

'I'm sure not, but you know you'll look like a total tourist if you do. Can't we just pretend to fit in here for a minute?' Grace said, rolling her eyes. 'I want to feel like I belong with all these beautiful Italian creatures, and not like some moron who just dropped in for an hour and would soon scurry off to her lowly hotel.'

'Fair enough.' Niamh smiled and turned to sit down.

'Ah, so you came after all!' Niamh heard the voice ahead of her but the sun was in her eyes. 'I wondered if you would flee the normal tourist-trodden route and venture further afield.'

Niamh shaded the sun from her eyes. It was Emily.

She flushed momentarily, embarrassed to have been spotted in Camogli and not having called her, especially as she had been so kind to her at lunch in Portofino. Emily crossed the terrace to their table, oblivious of the stares of people around her. She wore a long, off-white, buttoned dress that fell to her ankles and high wedge sandals in a similar shade. She looked like she had just stepped out of a Dolce and Gabbana advertisement.

'Hello, I'm Emily,' she said graciously to Grace as she shook her hand. 'Welcome to Camogli.'

'Grace, this is the lady who rescued me at lunch the other day, the one I told you about.'

'Oh wow, hello! It's nice to meet you.'

'I'm sorry I didn't call, but we just decided to come here last minute. It wasn't really a proper plan,' Niamh said sheepishly, glaring at Grace.

'Plans are usually overrated and lead to unrealistic levels of expectation, darling. You are far better off travelling on instinct rather than sticking to a rigid plan. Good Lord, you really can't see anything back here behind this wall. Come and join me at my table, won't you?' She motioned to a table all the way at the front, alongside the little terraced wall. 'Unless you like being tucked away back here with the masses, that is.' She laughed.

Niamh threw a quick glance at Grace and could tell that she was intrigued. 'We'd love to, thank you.'

Emily turned and motioned to the waiter who had seated them. 'Gianni, they are going to join me at my table.'

'Certainly, Emilia. *Prego.*'

Niamh recalled the quiet fuss that was made of her in Portofino and wondered if Emilia was treated this way at every restaurant and terrace bar she ever visited. She had an easy elegance about her, such that the expectation of excellence that she so naturally assumed seemed fitting. It suited her demeanour but it was all done effortlessly, warmly and graciously. It was very impressive. With a flurry of waiters, the three women were escorted to the front and seated at Emily's table.

'Oh, there's a lovely breeze here,' Grace said, smiling. 'This view is really incredible.'

'Yes, I don't know how anyone can bear to sit back there. It's stifling,' Emily said in her strong British accent. 'Now, drinks.'

Gianni reappeared at the table with a platter of various

little *aperitivi* for them to nibble on. 'Orange happiness, *signora*?'

'Yes, Gianni, *grazie*. Ladies, what would you like to drink?'

'What did you order?' Niamh asked, leaning into the table.

'I'm having an Aperol spritz, just like most people out here, as you can see. It's the drink of choice for *aperitivo*.'

Niamh had to agree that almost every table on the terrace had Aperol spritz, the only exception being a couple sipping on two tall beers.

'Germans,' Emily said with disdain, rolling her eyes in her head. 'No class whatsoever.'

'But what did you say to Gianni when you ordered the drink? He called it something else but I couldn't catch it. Is there another name for it?'

'Oh, no!' Emily sat back and laughed. 'It's orange happiness. Orange happiness in a glass, darling! I called it that the very first time I ordered it on this very terrace and I've been calling it that ever since.'

'That's cute,' Niamh said with a smile.

'It's true, darling. You sit here with this incredible view, on this lovely terrace, in this quaint little village and life slows all around you, and then as you watch the sun set you drink the most perfect drink of the same bursting orange colour. I mean, it's perfect. What else is there?'

'How long have you lived here?' Grace asked, taking the first sip of her orange happiness.

'Not long enough,' Emily replied ruefully. It was the first time they had seen her without a smile since they'd sat down. 'When you live somewhere like this, or move to a place like this, at least, then you almost resent any time you wasted elsewhere. It's that powerful. This place can put a spell on you quite easily, if you let it. I moved here ten years ago and now

107

my life in London feels like eons ago, and terribly superficial and small. I know that sounds like a contradiction in terms, but it's not. It was superficial as it was mostly about exterior pleasures, not pleasures of the soul, and small because everyone has a permitted circle of people and places, and people are mostly creatures of habit. If we let it, our lives can become small without us even knowing it, and we become smaller people as a result.'

'Don't you miss anything about it?' Niamh was intrigued.

'No, I get back often enough to satisfy whatever needs I might have for big city life, but honestly, darling, you can get that in Milan, too – and much more elegantly.'

Niamh thought about her life in Dublin. It wasn't superficial, but it was definitely small. What did she have back there apart from her family? It was always the same people, same places, same restaurants, same boring routine – yes, definitely small. She wasn't sure when it had become so rote. She had always had plans to travel and see the world, get an exciting job, earn good money, go on exotic holidays, wear great clothes, but along the way she had settled for less. She had met Rick and they were happy – or at least she had thought that they were. She had tried at first to keep things interesting, given that they worked together. He was a workaholic and a bit of a gym addict. Now that she thought about it, he did have a bit of a compulsive personality.

They had each had their own routine. Thursday night was Chinese takeout at home with a bottle of wine (he wasn't a big drinker but one bottle was never enough for two, so she always made sure they had a second stashed away on standby). On Friday night they would go to a restaurant in town and go for drinks afterwards. They'd usually have sex when they got home, and when she wasn't completely wiped out after the week, she'd make a big effort to be sexy and wear her fancy, matching underwear. On Saturdays Rick went to the gym – he went religiously six days a week – and she shopped for the week's groceries. Then they might go to a movie or get takeout pizza and watch something new on television. On Sundays he played rugby with the lads and she'd clean the house and then go visit her parents.

Niamh had always cooked a traditional Sunday dinner of roast chicken, beef or lamb because Rick loved that kind of food. She had been passionate about food and cooking since she was three years old, helping her mother bake pies and cakes, and dropping chopped vegetables into a large soup pot that would simmer for hours. The traditional Sunday dinner was something she could whip up in her sleep, and it was always the same, but Rick didn't like it when she tried to do something inventive and, frankly, it just wasn't worth the ensuing argument. After several disastrous dinners she had given up and resigned herself to Sunday nights of Irish recipes created in the 1960s.

Instead, she'd entertain herself by lighting candles to make the place look pretty and open a bottle of wine. The only night Rick would let loose at any level was on a Friday night and he wouldn't have more than two glasses of wine on a Sunday night. Two glasses felt to her like she was just getting warmed up, so she'd open a bottle and have a couple of glasses while she was cooking dinner, to get a head start.

'Niamh! Hello?' Grace said in a sharp hiss, conscious of being on a posh terrace where the only other sounds were of clinking glasses.

'Sorry, what?' She hadn't realised that she had drifted miles away.

Grace shook her head. 'Emily was asking if you wanted another drink.'

'Do we have time? What about the ferry?'

'Oh, the ferry runs until late, don't worry about that,' Emily said with a wave of her hand that both dismissed the thought of bolting for the ferry and summoned another round of drinks at the same time.

The sun sank lower and moved quickly, casting orange and pink shadows across the clouds above it. The terrace grew quiet as the bottom round of the sun dipped into the sea at the horizon and continued to sink below it. The hues of orange, red and pink grew stronger and wider, and then suddenly as it disappeared below the surface of the bay, they softened and dissipated. It was like a theatrical production. Niamh felt as if she should applaud.

Chatter resumed on the terrace and at their table and Gianni reappeared with a bottle of bubbles and three glasses.

'I have an unspoken rule, you see,' Emily explained. 'One cannot drink Aperol spritz once the sun has set. Luckily, the Italians have a wonderful alternative to champagne called Franciacorta.'

They chatted easily for the next hour. Emily talked about her life in Camogli, Grace talked about her boys and her work and, to her surprise, Niamh heard herself talking about her recent disasters back home. She suspected that the various drinks might have something to do with it.

'I should call and cancel our dinner reservation. We'd have to leave here in the next twenty minutes to make the ferry in time for dinner. You're not ready to leave, are you, Niamh?'

Niamh turned and looked at her distractedly. 'No,' she said quietly. 'No, let's stay here for ever.'

Grace stepped away from the table to call the concierge back at their hotel. Emily raised her glass to her lips and looked across the table towards Niamh. 'It's easy to decide to stay, isn't it?'

'Hmm?'

'Here in Camogli … I can understand why you would decide to stay. I mean, why bother going anywhere else? Right now, where else is there?' she asked, raising a glass in a silent salute.

'I don't know, actually. I don't think I've ever felt further away from everything and everyone in my life, and that's not a bad thing right now.'

'Separation creates distance and distance can bring either peace of mind or heartache, it just depends on your perspective. If you know where you are going, then there are no wrong decisions because you are following your true north.'

'We're not talking about me deciding to stay here for dinner any more, are we?' Niamh smiled.

'We never really were, darling,' Emily replied with a wink.

Chapter Eleven

'I'm not leaving.'

'Agreed,' mumbled Grace. 'How on earth are we supposed to make it to lunch today? I'm not even sure I can make it to the bathroom safely, my head's spinning that bad.'

'No, I mean I'm not going back.'

'Back where?' Grace asked, swearing under her breath as she tripped over the dress that she had hastily discarded on the floor the night before.

Niamh took in her sister's dishevelled appearance in the bathroom mirror. It was comforting to know Grace still had the capacity to look terrible.

'Back home. Back to Dublin. I'm staying here.'

'What? Don't be ridiculous, Niamh. You have to go back. You have a job.'

'I quit.'

'What? When?'

Niamh turned to face her sister. 'Last night.'

'Last night after a bucket of orange drinks and three or four bottles of wine?'

'Yes,' Niamh replied, dropping two soluble paracetamol into a glass.

'Niamh, you know I don't function well when I'm hungover,

so I really don't have the energy to deal with this *Eat Pray Love* shit right now. It's like all my patience and tolerance seeps out through my pores and is replaced with clouds of alcohol fumes,' Grace sighed, sitting down heavily on the edge of the bath.

'I'm serious, Grace.'

'Why did I mix my drinks last night?' Grace sighed. 'I'm such an idiot.'

'Grace, I'm not joking.'

'Sure you're not. Well then, you know what? I'm not going home either!' Grace retorted, now losing her cool. 'I have a few slivers of freedom when I get to travel for work. My normal life is an intense, full-time job, two toddlers who think I'm a mess-mopping, toy-fixing, walking snack machine and a husband who moans that I work too much but has no problem blowing through the second wage on rugby weekends. So, here's an idea. Why don't we both just run away and move to another country?'

'God, you get so ratty when you're hungover,' Niamh replied, rolling her eyes. 'I'm not being all *Eat Pray Love*—'

'In fact,' Grace cut across Niamh, 'I'm going home to tell my husband that I'm leaving him and moving to France because last year I went to Cannes for a conference and thought it was the most fabulous place I'd ever been. I'm going to drink rosé every day, live on baguettes and Niçoise salads and live happily ever after.' She fixed Niamh with a superior and satisfied stare that said 'point proved'. 'Now, come on, let's go to breakfast. I need coffee.'

'GRACE!' Niamh roared, exasperated. 'I'm deadly serious! I sent an email last night officially handing in my notice.'

'What the fuck, Niamh? You can't just quit. You were drunk.'

'Actually, I can. And, yes, I was a bit, but I still feel the same today, just with a wicked headache.'

'This is madness. Even if you do want to quit your job, you have to do it the right way. You have to go home, hand in your notice . . .'

'Since this is all sort of Rick's fault he can deal with the details. It's not as though we have an HR team. His problem, not mine!'

'Oh, for Christ's sake, Niamh, this is insane even by your standards. I know it sucks right now, but shit happens, people break up. You have to face reality, move your stuff out of Rick's apartment, move *on*. Get closure! You can't just decide you're not going home.'

'I've already taken all my stuff from Rick's apartment. Everything is back in Mam and Dad's place again.'

'Fine,' said Grace, exasperated, and changing tack. 'Say you do stay here, what's the plan?'

'Well, I don't have all the details figured out exactly but I did have one idea about . . .' Niamh hesitated, reluctant to share her thinking with Grace and have it dismissed as utter nonsense. 'I mean, I don't have it all figured out exactly, but I know I want to live here. Well, not here in this hotel, obviously,' she said, gesturing around the hotel bathroom. 'But I want to live in Italy. I know that much. I want to do something crazy, Grace, something different.'

'You want to do something crazy? Well, this qualifies. And you'll live where, exactly?'

'In Camogli. I—'

'But you've only been here for a week!' Grace was pleading now. 'You don't know the area, you don't know anyone, you don't know the *language*. What will you do about money?'

'I have savings that I can live off.' Niamh was very grateful

114

she'd been working this plan out over the past couple of days, and that she wasn't having to field this inquisition on the hoof. There was a strong chance her head might have exploded. She walked back into the bedroom hoping distance would deter Grace, but she followed without drawing a breath.

'What do you mean you have savings? Like what? What are we talking about here?'

'I have about twenty thousand euros in the bank.'

'You have *what*? How the hell do you manage to have twenty thousand euros in the bank?'

'I'm good at saving.'

'Holy shit, I'll say. I have about two thousand euros in savings and my credit card has a constant revolving negative balance that I treat as a second source of income.'

'Well, I didn't have much of a life with Rick in Dublin. I didn't do that much, so it was kind of easy to save.' Niamh shrugged.

Grace stared at her in disbelief. 'So, what am I supposed to tell Mam?'

'Tell her that I'm grabbing life by the arse, like she always told me to do.'

'I don't think that quitting your job and extending your vacation indefinitely in an Italian fishing village was what she meant, Niamh. I mean, spoiler alert, but Mam never was a massive fan of Rick so I think that her advice more likely related to dumping that mopey cretin in the first place, getting out from under his feet at work and getting out there on your own. That's the type of life she was talking about grabbing by the arse – one that was *yours*. Not one cooked up over a bowl of pasta.'

'You know what? I always do the right thing.' By now Niamh was pacing the bedroom and her voice was rising. 'I always do what I'm supposed to do, what everyone thinks I should do, or what I think they expect of me. And where has it gotten me? Nowhere. For the first time in my life, I'm going to do something that makes no sense to anyone else, but it does to me. I'm going to do what I *want* to do for a change – even if it's a mad idea.'

'It *is* a mad idea, Niamh. It's a totally mad idea that you will regret. Why not just stay for another couple of weeks? You don't have to quit your job. Call them and tell them you've made a mistake, get your job back and just take a couple of weeks out. Rick owes you that. I'm sure he'll figure out a way to get you some more paid time off.'

'No, I'm not changing my mind. I can't face going back there. Anyone can get another job, Grace. What I actually want is another life. One that I build for myself, one that I actually like, the one you say Mam wants for me. Even if you think it is a mistake.'

'You're being ridiculous, Niamh, completely and utterly ridiculous. This isn't some movie, you know, where you get to drop your real life and create a new one in a foreign country where you don't speak the language. This is your life and you are being totally juvenile about it.' Grace was furious now and flung some things into a bag. 'I'm going to breakfast and then for a walk. We have a lunch reservation at one o'clock. Text me if you come back to your senses and want to join me.'

The door slammed behind her. Niamh winced from the noise and grabbed her bag. She checked the ferry schedule for Saturday morning. The next ferry was in thirty minutes. She had four hours before lunch. She grabbed a croissant from the breakfast buffet and headed out to the pier. She dialled the number from the photograph on her phone as she walked.

'*Pronto?*' a deep male voice answered.

'Oh, hello. Umm, *buongiorno*. I'm calling about the café.'

'Sorry, you have the wrong number.'

The phone cut off.

Niamh frowned as she pulled up the photograph on her phone again and compared it to the number she had just dialled. It was the same number. 'Idiot.'

She dialled again.

'*Pronto?*'

'*Buongiorno.* Hello? I'm calling about the café for rent in Camogli. On Via dei Limoni? I saw the advert in the window,' she said in one quick rush.

'The café?'

'Yes. I got this number from the notice in the window.'

'You are calling about the café?'

She rolled her eyes. Who was this idiot and why was this so hard to understand? 'Yes, can I speak to someone about the café, please?'

'You can speak to me, *signora.*'

Marvellous, she thought sarcastically. 'Is the café still for rent?'

'Yes. Yes, it is.'

'OK, can I see it?'

'*Certo,*' he said slowly. 'When do you want to see it?'

'Is this morning possible? I can be there in an hour.'

'Today? *Signora*, it's Saturday.'

'Yes, I'm aware of that but I'm supposed to get on a plane tomorrow to go home to Ireland and I want to know if this crazy idea I have of renting a café is even a remote possibility.' She spoke hurriedly, afraid he might hang up again.

There was silence.

'So you are here on holiday and you want to rent the café?'

117

'Well I don't know, I mean, I think so, but I would like to see it before I throw everything else away. Would that be possible?'

He hesitated again and sighed. 'OK, I can meet you in one hour. You know where it is?'

'Yes. OK, thank you. I'll see you in an hour.'

'*Va bene*,' he said, sighing again as he hung up. He hadn't even asked her name.

She arrived a few minutes before 10.30, feeling quite proud for having only got lost once along the way. She had tried to retrace her steps once she got off the ferry but was confused when she reached the upper level of the town. The fact that she had zero sense of direction was no help. She checked Google Maps on her phone and stuck it back into her bag, leaving the bustle of the main promenade and followed one narrow little cobbled street after another, until she'd made her way back to Via dei Limoni.

She hadn't paid much attention to what was around her last time she was here, as Grace had been in such a hurry to get to the restaurant to inhale carbs. Checking the time to make sure she wasn't late, she wandered the length of the street, stopping to peek in through the windows of the shops along the way. There were all kinds of artisan shops, one selling leather gloves, another showcasing embroidered tablecloths and linens. There was a tiny place with wooden crates of limoncello displayed outside the door, and dried red chillies pinned, in bunches, to the doorframe. She put her hands to the glass and peered through the window of a shop with a sign that read PROFUMERIA. The shelves were laden with minia-ture glass bottles, each with their own tiny handwritten sign.

'A perfume shop,' she sighed quietly to herself, her breath fogging up the window pane before her.

Finally she reached the old café. It looked so forlorn in its dejected state, compared to the other pretty little shops further down the street. She stared through the window, admiring the original tile along the window sill. It was in worse shape than she had remembered, and this time she noticed more splintered wooden shelves and chipped counter tiles than she had done previously. She paced up and down outside the café. There was no sign of anyone.

Maybe it's for the best, she thought, still pacing. Maybe Grace was right and this is just a mad idea. What was I thinking? I don't even speak the language!

She sat on the window ledge outside the café and put her head in her hands.

She could feel her heart beat louder in her chest and a nervous swell in her belly. Have I made the right decision? Is this really nothing more than an unrealistic fantasy? she wondered. Maybe I could call the guy and tell him I had made a mistake and I'm sorry and now you don't have to waste your time showing me the café on a Saturday. She massaged her temples as she stared down at her feet with a classic case of buyer's remorse, even in advance of making any significant financial commitment.

But it was my idea. I know it's not for everyone, and Mam and Grace wouldn't understand, but I'm doing it for me. It makes sense to me, even if the details are marginally terrifying. So just don't think about the details. then, Niamh . . .

She closed her eyes, took a deep breath and placed both her hands on her knees. 'Stick to the plan. Be brave!' she whispered to herself.

'*Signora*, you are speaking to me?'

Startled, she whipped her head up and stared into the sun.

'No, sorry. I was just talking to myself.' She was mortified as she stood up.

'It is you again.'

She stopped in her tracks and looked up at him again, her jaw dropping slowly. This can't be happening, she thought as she stared up him. He's divine! He looks like he stepped off the pages of Men's *Vogue* and I'm not even wearing mascara.

He took off his sunglasses and smiled at her. 'Yes, I am right. It is you. You are ... umm ... Nina, no? Why are you here?'

'I came to see the café,' she replied slowly. She had forgotten how handsome he was.

'Yes, but I thought you stay in Santa Margherita, at the hotel.'

'I do. At least until tomorrow. After that I'm not sure.'

'But you are thinking of renting this café?'

'Well, yes, I had been. I saw it yesterday and wanted to come back and see inside. How is your shirt? Did you get the stain out?'

'The shirt, it will never recover. It died that evening, but there are many more shirts. Don't worry,' he said graciously, as he put the key in the door. 'Be careful, *signora*, is very dusty. Everything is dusty. It has been closed for a long time.'

'Oh, why? What happened? Why did the owner close it?'

'The owner is my brother. His wife was the one who ran the café but she died.'

She put a hand to her mouth, horrified. Can you not just for once in your life keep your mouth shut and your stupid, nosy questions to yourself, Niamh? she admonished herself silently. She took her hand down from her face. 'Oh my God, I'm so sorry. I shouldn't have asked. I'm really sorry.'

'Is OK, it was a few years ago. She died in a car accident.

They were married only one year. So he closed the café and he left Camogli.'

'Oh my God. That's awful. How sad.'

'Yes, this is why I was surprised to get your call this morning. I had not thought about the café for many years.'

'But is it actually for rent?'

'I think, yes. I will have to check with my brother if you decide that you are interested, but I think yes. It was a great place. She was a great . . . how do you call it . . . hostess? And she was a very beautiful woman. Everyone in the village came here. It always had a heart if you understand what I mean. When she died he moved to America. He wanted to be far from Camogli. He is a doctor so he . . . how do you say . . . he made a transfer to a hospital in Chicago. He wanted to start over with a new life.'

'I know that feeling.'

He looked at her curiously. 'You have this sadness in your life, too?'

'Well . . . no, not like that. Nothing like that, thankfully, but something else that is making me want to run from my life.'

'Perhaps you run *towards* something, not *from* it? You never know in this life until you try it. Perhaps you don't run from something, but this something, whatever or whoever it was, is no longer for you and something else is for you, but in another place that you must find.'

His English was broken and it wasn't expressed in the most perfect way, but the sentiment was powerful and sent chills down her spine.

'*Allora*,' he said changing the subject. He turned the key in the door and leaned against it. It was wedged stuck in the doorframe and wouldn't budge. It took two shoves with his shoulder

121

to release it. '*Ecco il caffè.*' He gestured with his right arm around the room as a small cloud of dust settled around his shoulders.

Niamh stepped in behind him. The place was a mess. It wasn't just dust, but also damage from years of neglect. There was mould on the tiles, sagging timbers, a broken countertop, chipped floor tiles. It was in a terrible state, but it was still beautiful. The woodwork was a deep mahogany and the tiles were a pretty blue and yellow pattern. She could imagine just how charming it once might have been.

'How much is it?'

'I do not know,' he said, shaking his head. 'We never had to think about this.'

'No one ever enquired about renting it?'

'No, *signora*, the people from the village would not do this out of respect for my brother and his wife, and we do not get so many crazy tourists here in Camogli,' he said as he shrugged his shoulders.

'There isn't, like . . . a bad omen or anything in the place, is there?'

'What is an "omen"?' He frowned.

'I mean, if no one from the village would ask about renting it, it's not like there is a curse or anything on it, is there? Is that a bad question to ask?' she asked, grimacing.

'Ah, OK. Yes.'

'Yes?' she replied, horrified.

'No, I mean, yes I understand now your question. I am sorry for my English.'

'Oh, no it's fine. Sorry, it was a weird question to ask.'

'No, *signora*, there is no curse. It was just a sad ending and the building has been in my family for many, many years so my brother did not have to worry about needing to rent it, so it stays like this. As for the price, I can ask my brother.'

'Oh right, yes, of course. How long will that take?'

'I don't know. I will call him but it is now very early on Saturday morning or late on Friday night in Chicago. If he is working at the hospital then he will not have his phone, of course.'

'Yes, of course. It's just that my flight back to Dublin is tomorrow.'

'I see, and when you will return to Italy?'

'Well, that's just the thing, you see – I saw this place and thought I could stay, and, you know, fix it up and maybe open a café here.' She heard the words come out of her mouth and realised just how insane she must sound to him.

'*Un momento.* I don't understand. You are here for a holiday and are thinking to not go back tomorrow, yes?' He was staring intently at her and she couldn't read his face.

'Yes. That is what I am thinking.' She realised that she was beginning to speak in broken English now, too. 'But now, if I don't know how much the rent will be then I don't know if I can afford it. So it's more complicated.' She sighed.

'Ah, I see.' He rubbed his hand across his chin. He wore dark stubble, whereas last time she met him he'd been clean-shaven. She wondered if she had dragged him from bed with her phone call, or if he always sported a casual look at the weekend. 'I will call my brother now and leave a message. Then we wait. If he does not reply soon then we think of something else, yes?'

'OK.'

Niamh nodded as she watched him pull out his phone. She wondered what his idea of 'something else' might be, but hoped irrationally that this would be straightforward and his brother would just answer the phone in the middle of the night and give him a figure for the rent. She listened to him rattle off a stream of Italian.

'He was not there,' he shrugged. 'Now I must go. I must meet a friend at eleven o'clock. We can meet back here at noon, no?'

'Sure. I can come back. Do you think he will call back?'

'I don't know for sure, *signora*, he is in America and sometimes he calls back at crazy times because he works crazy hours, but you are out of time, no? We must think of something so that you can make your decision.' He locked the door and gave her a wave. 'See you in one hour. *Arrivederci*, Nina!'

He made it sound straightforward, as if a Plan B was something that could be conjured up, giving her some momentary relief. What were the chances that his brother would be awake, get the message and call back within an hour? She decided then that she would leave it to fate. If it was meant to be then she would have her answer in an hour and, if not, she'd forget about the whole thing, catch the ferry back in time to meet Grace for their last lunch and say nothing of the morning's misadventure. Satisfied with her decision, she made her way down the steps to the lower level of the village and walked to the little café on the pier that she had visited with Grace to pass the next hour.

Chapter Twelve

Niamh was so busy stirring and staring into her cappuccino that she didn't notice the blonde woman walk in.

'Back so soon?'

She looked up from her reverie to see Emily grinning down at her from behind yet another pair of massively oversized sunglasses.

'Exactly how many pairs of sunglasses do you own?' Niamh asked as she looked up at her.

'I can't say I know,' Emily replied, pausing to think. 'Quite likely a dozen, I'd say, if I were to venture a guess. What on earth are you doing here this morning?' She pulled up a seat and joined Niamh at her table. 'An espresso please, Massimo,' she said in the direction of the owner behind the counter.

'It's a long story,' said Niamh.

'Well then, get started.' Emily nudged her and smiled.

'I don't want to go back.'

'I know.'

'You know? How do you know?'

'I could tell last night. It's easy to recognise something in someone else when one has already experienced it, my dear. I'm not talking about the usual end-of-holiday blues, but something close to absolute distraction at the thoughts of having to extract yourself from your current existence here and reinsert yourself back into what used to be your life before. I'm afraid, once you reach this point, darling, nothing will ever be the same again.'

'So you don't think it's a mad idea?'

'On the contrary! I think it's a solid idea. It's mad, certainly by normal people's standards, but solid. All that awaits you at home is depression or embarrassment, if not both, based upon what you have told me, and how could any sane person with a shred of self-respect ever go back and try to continue a professional career in the company of a maggot like that? It's just unthinkable.' Emily stirred two sachets of sugar into her espresso before she continued. 'By all means, go home, but be realistic about it if you do. Everything will have to change. Everything will be different. You will have to find a new job, as you won't be able to stand working in such close proximity to him and, let's face it, most of your friends are probably shared friends at this point. Am I right?'

'Yes.'

'Awkward! And you are back at your parents' house full time? Darling, that's enough to force anyone out into the back garden to dig a very large hole in the ground and want to sit in it in perpetuity.' She knocked back the espresso in one shot. 'If you stay here then all you've got to figure out is what to do with yourself. One problem, not three.'

'What do you mean?'

'Look, if you go home now then you'll have to figure out a new place to live and that will likely be determined by your next job, so you're stuck at your parents' house until you figure out the job part. Plus you're going to have to make new friends because it will become immediately apparent to you that you're going to lose some in the "divorce", as it were.'

'What do you mean?' Niamh asked in a confused tone.

'Well, it's my experience that when a couple splits, friends take sides. Right or wrong, friendships are just another casualty of a breakup. Your true friends will be staunch defenders and fiercely loyal. They'll stand by you, but some will skitter off, as they won't want to be stuck in the middle of any awkwardness. You just have to accept it for what it is. By comparison, if you stay here then you have no friends to start with, apart from me, of course, so any new addition will be a plus, not a minus. And this place is so small that it really doesn't matter where you live in terms of your work location.' She sat back, clearly pleased with her detailed diagnosis.

'I've figured out the work part. I think.'

'Well, don't keep me in suspense, for heaven's sake.'

'I'm thinking of renting the old café up on Via dei Limoni. I have to meet the owner's brother in about twenty minutes to see if he knows what it will cost. I can't make the decision until I know that much and he called his brother when we met earlier.'

'Lena's old place? Good Lord, that place must be a shambles. It was closed up in a hurry and hasn't been touched since. How on earth did you stumble upon that?'

'We were just wandering around yesterday before lunch and I saw it. Was Lena the brother's wife?'

'Yes, her actual name was Elena, or Helena, or something like that, but everyone called her Lena. She was from Milan originally. What a beautiful woman.' Emily sighed. 'I think she used to be a model at one point. Anyway, she fell in love with Marco and when she moved here she opened the little café. It was the heart of the town at one point, not least because of her charm. It must be in a terrible state now, though. I'm pretty sure it has been abandoned since she died.'

'Yeah, it's pretty rough, but it's still charming. It kind of seemed like it was waiting for me or something – I don't really know how to describe it. I know that sounds really wishy-washy, but I thought it looked beautiful, even in its current state. To be honest this whole place kind of . . . I don't know how to say it without sounding like I'm on *Oprah* or something, but it kind of spoke to me.' Niamh stared down into her coffee cup. 'What made you decide to move here in the first place?'

'What's not to love? Life is more pleasant here, more relaxed, darling. There is truth in that well-worn Italian expression, *la dolce vita*. Life is simply sweeter here: the antiquity of it all, the countryside, the seaside, the views, the food, the wine, even the language. I came here not really speaking any Italian but it just sounded so melodic to me. English is just so . . . I don't know . . . mainstream or pedestrian by comparison.'

'I know,' Niamh said. 'It's honestly just so beautiful here.'

'Don't get me wrong, London is marvellous, but you'll find that most people who live there do so out of necessity. It's where they work, or where their children are schooled. Then, they get into a routine and it becomes familiar, it's what they know, so it's easy and it just becomes the place they live. For most people it would be difficult to up and move, even if they wanted to.'

'I suppose I was kind of forced into the decision, given that everything was pulled from under me at home,' Niamh mumbled into her cup.

'Don't underestimate yourself. Not everyone is cut out for moving abroad, Niamh. It's not for everybody. It takes a lot of work to make it work. The language is an obvious challenge, as is the bureaucracy and the logistics of it all. The act of moving abroad is not unlike the notion of wanting to write a book, actually.'

Niamh squinted in her direction, wondering where this was going.

Emily tilted her head in feigned exasperation and continued. 'People read a book and say, "I could do that, I could have written that," just as they look at someone who has uprooted their life and moved to another country. But they don't, do they? They don't write the book. They don't relocate elsewhere, they just talk about it and are quietly content in the knowledge that they could if they wanted to. Niamh, darling, these honestly are the most frustrating conversations ever, as one is forced to listen to these self-imposed excuses for not doing ... well, anything. frankly.' Emily shook her head and rolled her eyes in mock frustration.

'What did you do there, in London, I mean?'

'Same as I do here, just more of it.'

'You work here? I didn't know that.'

'Very few people can afford to just sail off into the sunset and not work, darling. Plus I think one would soon get bored of the idea of infinite free time. If all we had was free time then where's the joy in it? One relishes it all the more when it's limited, rather like most of the good things in life.'

'I suppose,' Niamh responded, reluctantly. 'Although I think it would take a long time for me to get bored of infinite free time. I can think of a long list of things I could do! So what do you do, exactly?'

'I'm an interior designer. I just charge more for it now because I'm more discerning about which clients I choose to work with. I ran a very successful business in London for years while I was married. Then I changed my life and moved here.'

'You were married?' Niamh asked, unable to mask her surprise.

'I don't like to talk about it. I'd prefer to scratch it from memory entirely if I had the opportunity. It's so long ago now that it seems like someone else's life.' Emily turned her head in the direction of the horizon, her eyes narrowing almost to a squint. Her face seemed to take on a hardened expression, clearly practised from years of actively trying to eliminate any memory of this man or her life with him.

Niamh's jaw was actively disengaged from the rest of her face in absolute shock.

'What? How come? What happened? Am I allowed to ask that?'

'Oh, it's terribly predictable, I'm afraid,' Emily replied, with a small wave of her hand. She turned back to meet Niamh's wide-eyed gaze. 'He was the kind of man for whom one woman was not enough, but sadly I was blissfully unaware of the fact for years.'

'He was having an affair for years and you didn't know it?' Niamh asked, her mouth falling open.

'Precisely.' Emily lifted her cup to her lips. 'She was an artist, apparently. Very creative and wildly inspiring – his words, not mine.'

'He told you that?'

'In so many words, yes. We even had two of her paintings hanging in our home in South Kensington. I never liked them. He just showed up with them one day. I thought it might be some client ... you know, that he felt obliged to support. They always struck me as being rather angry looking, but apparently I just didn't appreciate her talent and it was a reflection of her wildly expressive nature coming out on canvas.'

'What did you do? I hope you kicked his cheating ass out immediately?'

'I called my lawyer an hour later and had divorce papers drafted in a matter of days.'

Niamh stared across the table at her new friend, shaking her head. 'I can't believe someone treated you like that and you had to go through a divorce because of it.'

'I didn't.'

'You didn't what?' Niamh asked with a confused frown.

'I didn't have to go through a divorce.'

'You didn't end up divorcing him? OK, now I'm confused.'

'I didn't have to, as it turned out. I had his whole sordid affair publicly announced at his club. He was a member of the British Bankers Club – a very exclusive members-only, mahogany-and-dark-leather furniture sort of place, where successful, wealthy, executive types engage in verbose, self-congratulatory, hubristic conversations. He had been a member for years and had a standing Thursday evening drinks appointment with some of his cronies. Anyway, I lost all rationale and drove a very large Wüsthof chef's knife right through the centre of both of her angry paintings and had them delivered to him at the club, so it was clear to everyone in the room that I knew and that I was not about to take it lying down.' She smiled a small smile.

'How totally badass of you!' Niamh said with a laugh.

'Well, that was about the only satisfaction I got and, in the face of the humiliation and the deceit, it was fleeting.'

Niamh stared at her in disbelief, trying to reconcile the image of this angry, revenge-seeking woman-scorned with the kind, gentle, generous woman she had come to know in the past few days.

'I hadn't counted on the shock factor. You see, most of

them – his cronies that is – are, or at least, were, still married. Divorce is not something that the super-wealthy like to engage in. It's messy, undignified and far too public. The wives too buy into it, because they don't want their lives to change. They have large homes, expensive cars, high-profile social lives and social circles. Divorce means downsizing and airing one's dirty linen in public, so many couples choose to remain together, despite irreconcilable differences in the marriage. Many of them cheat, of course, or have mistresses, and still others have a whole other relationship that their partner is aware of, but chooses not to oppose or challenge. The women are often guilty of the same behaviour, of course, and are not without blame.' Emily paused for a second and her gaze shifted slightly, as if moving elsewhere momentarily. 'I think I knew of two couples who seemed genuinely happy together. But, then again, I thought we were doing OK, so what do I know?'

'I can't believe someone could just turn a blind eye to the fact that their husband has a whole other relationship!' said Niamh. 'I've never heard the likes of that!'

'Oh, trust me, there's a lot more of it goes on than you'd rather think,' Emily said with a slow shake of her head. 'Anyway, I was never certain if it was the shock of the threat of divorce itself, or the mortification of having his affair so spotlighted in such a public manner at his club, but, as it turned out, I never got the chance to ask him. He stormed out apparently and went back to his office, presumably to make some calls to get his legal team on standby. He never came home that night. He went to the artist's house in a rage. Of course I heard all of this after the fact – even the wealthy love to gossip. The following day he suffered a massive stroke and collapsed. He died in the hospital two days later.'

Niamh sat and stared at her in shock. 'I actually don't know what to say. It sounds like a scene from a soap opera!'

'Indeed,' Emily said, raising one eyebrow. 'Another coffee?' she asked Niamh as she motioned for the waiter.

'*Si, signora?*'

'*Altre due, per favore,*' she said, pointing at the two cups in front of them.

'*Subito, signora,*' he replied, with an almost imperceptible nod.

'The real tragedy was that I never even got to mourn him. If the bastard had dropped dead a week earlier I'd have been none the wiser,' Emily continued. 'As it was, I had to act the part of the grieving widow in public, all the while fuming at the thought of the deception and the lies.'

'Did you ever meet her?'

'The artist? God, no! What good could ever come of that? Once I heard that he had died, I shredded the divorce papers and instructed my lawyer to stand down, as it were. So, it turns out that dying was the only decent thing he had done for me in years.'

'Wow – so you ended up getting everything,' Niamh said in quiet admiration.

'Yes, I did.' Emily gave a defiant tilt of her jaw. It was evident that she had had to justify or defend that reaction previously. 'Word got out, of course. His balding, simpering cronies couldn't help but spread word of what had happened at the club that night. Don't for one minute think that gossip is the pursuit solely of bored housewives. Once their respective wives got hold of the story it quickly became fodder for the finest salons across London. I stuck it out for four months as I got our ... *my* affairs in order, and then came here.'

'But did you know about this place before that?'

'Yes, we had spent many summer holidays in Portofino, so

I knew it well. He had always loved the glitz and the ostentatious glamour of Portofino, whilst I had preferred the quieter comfort of Camogli. He would play golf or whatever and I would come here, alone, for hours at a time, drinking in the sounds of local Italian village life and wandering happily amongst contented people, so much so that when the time came to leave London, this was an easy and obvious choice.'

'Crikey. I'm actually stunned,' Niamh said. 'What an unreal saga! It's honestly like something you'd read or see in a movie.'

'Quite. My life as a Hollywood blockbuster – except that no one would believe it. They'd say it was too far-fetched a notion!'

'Yeah, probably,' Niamh agreed, sipping her second cappuccino. 'So you ended up being married to a nasty piece of work and you're the one who had to give up the life that you knew and start over?'

'Well, everyone has their own struggles. Life may look simple or perfect from the outside, but everyone is dealing with something. My "somethings" just all came barrelling down on me at the same time. Some things in life you can fix, change, improve, but sometimes you just have to accept them and move on.'

Niamh thought for a moment about her own situation and her current longing to stay in Italy and start over. The circumstances were different, of course. Rick had ended the relationship, after all, but the hurt was the same. She had been rejected and had taken herself and her wounds off to another country. Now she found herself not wanting to return. She frowned as she thought how different it might have been had she stayed in Ireland, hoping for a second chance but instead being brutally shut out of Rick's life. She still thought he might reach out, that she might have heard something from him, but she hadn't heard a word. She felt a sudden sadness at just how cold and decisive people could be when it came to deciding that they no longer wanted you in their life.

'I'd never thought of it like that,' she said quietly, picking the errant, sticky-up piece of skin on her left thumb. There was surely a more clinical name for it, but she was damned if she could think of it now.

'Anyway,' Emily said abruptly, brushing nothing in particular off her white pants. 'I don't like to talk about it or dwell on it, for obvious reasons, so let's please change the subject. And please do me the favour of not bringing it up again.'

Niamh watched her adjust her posture and her expression simultaneously as she prepared to once again bury the memories and the unresolved pain. 'Wow, so the "stiff upper lip" British thing is actually a thing!' she exclaimed. 'Sorry, that was supposed to be in my head, but I just watched your expression change as you changed the subject. I didn't mean to cause offence.'

'None taken,' Emily said with a small smile. 'And yes, it is in fact a thing! I'd rather wear an exterior, glossy appearance of inner contentment any day, than wallow for ever in a large vat of gloom and self-pity, exuding strains of misery such that no one would come anywhere near me. Wouldn't you?'

Niamh shrugged. 'Yes, I suppose so,' she replied, wondering if she herself would have the grace and resolve to compartmentalise and banish her grief and anger in similar circumstances.

Emily stood, picking up her purse and adjusting both her sunglasses and her composure, looking nothing like a woman who had just poured years of pain and sadness onto the little round table that sat between them.

'I have to go and meet Giorgio again to see if he has any answer about the rent. Do you want to come with me?' Niamh asked.

'Why not? I quite like the idea of escorting you to what might potentially be your next life adventure. Onwards, Niamh,' she said linking Niamh's arm with hers.

Chapter Thirteen

'So you've already met Giorgio, then?' Emily asked, raising an eyebrow as they strolled towards the abandoned building.

'Yes, I met him this morning when I went to see the café, but I had met him last Monday night at the hotel in Santa Margherita. He was there for the cocktail thing, at my sister's conference. I think we talked about that last night – the architects' conference.'

'Sounds vaguely familiar, darling. I think you'll need to repeat much of what was said late last night – at least the important bits.'

'It was a bit embarrassing this morning, actually. I accidently toppled an Aperol spritz all over him that night, then I called the number to see the café this morning and he showed up. I was mortified all over again,' Niamh replied, shaking her head at the memory of it.

'Ah, yes, it makes sense that he would have been at that conference. Some of those architects would be his clients. He's quite a fine individual of a man, wouldn't you agree?' Emily asked, looking sideways at Niamh as they walked towards the steps.

'He's gorgeous, yes. He seems nice, too – friendly – but I'd say he's kind of quiet . . . is he?'

'He wasn't always quiet. Poor man has had a rather rough time of it. After Lena died, his brother was devastated, naturally. He tried to carry on with his life but he never got over her. So, he put in for a transfer and a year later it came through so he moved to Chicago. They had always been close, so Giorgio missed having his brother around. Then their father died suddenly – while Marco was in Chicago. He couldn't come home because of some visa restriction, so he missed the funeral. Giorgio had to be the rock for their mother and try to carry on with his own life, changed as it was. After all that, his fiancée – Giorgio's, that is – left him for another man about a year ago. She said that he had changed drastically after everything that had happened and was too sorrowful and he wasn't fun to be around any more. She claimed he had lost interest in her, but that just wasn't so, she was a terribly selfish individual. She got bored and didn't want to play the role of supportive partner. She wanted some diversity, so she found someone else and just left. He was devastated, and I'm not sure that he has got over it yet. To be honest, he shouldn't have bothered being so overwrought over her – the fiancée, that is – because she was really not a good person,' Emily continued. 'She was incredibly beautiful and I think she felt that her beauty was enough to endear her to anyone, including Giorgio. He fell for it. Then, once things got tough she took off. So now, with his brother in America, it's just him and his mother here in Camogli, and you know how close Italian men are to their mamas.' She rolled her eyes.

'He doesn't live with his mother, does he?'

'Heavens, no. He's more sophisticated than that, darling. In fact, he has the most gorgeous house up in the hills behind Camogli, but he takes care of her and they're very close. He's all that she has now that her other son, Marco, lives abroad.'

'But what about the woman I saw him with at that party?' Niamh asked, with a small frown.

'Ah, yes. They've been good friends for many years and I think it was perhaps a case of turning to a close friend for comfort in a time of need. I never thought they were the right fit, but then they surprised me and ended up as a couple. Then again, given my track record with men, I'm hardly qualified to pass comment on anyone's relationship.' Emily laughed.

'That's not the impression I got,' Niamh said, as they rounded the corner onto Via dei Limoni. 'She was kind of glued to him.'

'Wouldn't you be, darling, if you had been invited in to live life by his side?' Emily replied with raised eyebrows. 'One would hardly need a second invitation!'

'No, I suppose not,' Niamh agreed.

They arrived outside the café and Emily peered in through the window. 'It's in a worse condition than I thought it would be. Good grief. Are you sure about this?'

'Well, it depends on the price. I have no idea what he's going to say, to be honest. It's entirely possible that I won't be able to make it work.'

'One thing I've learned in life, darling, is that no matter what it is, if you want it to happen badly enough, you can make it happen.' Emily frowned as she scanned the room through the dirty glass. 'You just have to make sure it's what you really want. Are you sure this is really what you want, Niamh? It's going to take an awful amount of work.' She shook her head.

'I don't mind about the hard work. The only thing I'm uncertain about is whether I can afford it or not. Where the hell is he, anyway?'

'Giorgio?' Emily asked standing, up straight. 'Oh he's

always late for everything. I don't think he has ever been on time for anything in his life!' She laughed. 'It's a bit of an Italian trait, but he's particularly talented in that aspect. If you live here you will have to get used to that.'

If you live here . . . Niamh repeated in her head. The words sent chills down her spine with excitement and anticipation.

Giorgio rounded the corner suddenly, talking on his phone and carrying a bundle of files. The blazer of his dark grey suit was unbuttoned. He wore another pristine white shirt, she noted, and his body was lean and taut beneath it. He stopped a few feet from them and wrapped up the call with multiple frustrated repetitions of *sì* and *va bene*.

Niamh's breath caught just a little. His hair looked dishevelled, as if he had just run his hand through it.

Christ, you're gorgeous, she thought, instinctively wanting to reach out and flatten out his hair.

He greeted Emily with a smile and kissed her on both cheeks. '*Ciao, Emilia.*'

'*Ciao, Giorgio, come va?*'

'*Bene, bene, grazie,*' he said. He pulled the keys from his pocket and dropped them to the ground. '*Ciao,* Nina,' he said, looking up at her with a grin as he stooped to retrieve them.

'Working on a Saturday, Giorgio? That's most unlike you,' Emily said, playfully.

'No, no. I just help a friend with a problem. On Saturday I don't work. *Sicuramente, no!* OK, we go in,' he said, jiggling the key in the lock.

The door was sticking in the doorframe again so it took a couple of shoves to get it fully open. As he gave it a final shove there was a loud crack. He peered around the other side of the door to see that one of the panels had cracked. He shrugged his shoulders and looked at Niamh. 'You want to rent this?'

He dropped the keys on the dusty countertop and went to lean against it. He hesitated, wiped it with a hand and shook his head, deciding to remain standing upright. '*Allora* ... ' He placed the bundle of files on a small table near the counter. The leg buckled under the weight and the whole thing collapsed to the ground. 'You want to rent this?' he asked again, shaking his head.

'See – even Giorgio thinks you are mad,' Emily said, waving a hand in an effort to dispel the small cloud of dust that had risen from the collapsed table.

'What did he say? What did your brother say about the rent?' Niamh asked. She tried desperately not to sound overly concerned, but she wasn't sure she could take much more generic conversation without knowing what the actual outcome was going to be.

'My brother, he did not call me back. I think he must be working.' Giorgio shrugged.

'Shit,' Niamh said. 'Well, I can't just stay here indefinitely.'

'No. I understand. So this is what I have done. I cannot speak with my brother right now, so I called my friend who has a ... *come si dice* ... a shop that sells and rents the houses?'

'An estate agent?' Emily offered helpfully. She was clearly used to interpreting meaning and intent from poor attempts at English and converting them into proper English.

'Ah, *sì*. Yes ... this. I called my friend who has this kind of shop in the next village and asked him what would be a fair price for a small building such as this one in his village. Don't worry, his is a normal village like Camogli, just slightly bigger. It is not a very large expensive place like Santa Margherita or not a very fancy place like Portofino. There you cannot afford to rent anything! So I asked him what he thinks. He told me that there is one café similar in his village, maybe a bit smaller, I don't know. So, he tells me that this café, in his village, he rents for three thousand euros each month, but it is new, no?'

Niamh looked around in dismay. She had no idea what it might cost to get this place in working order, but it surely wouldn't be cheap.

'So, I think this is what we can do. You pay half of that rent and we sign an agreement for six months. If my brother does not like the agreement, you can make a new one with him in six months, but this way, you can know what you must do and you know that this building will be yours for six months, so you have chance to see if you can make a good start, no?'

She nodded slowly, thinking that half the rent was a pretty fair deal. 'But what if your brother freaks out? Can we have an agreement that he can't cancel the contract for the six months?'

'*Signora*, I am a lawyer. Yes, I can create the right agreement,' he said with a smile. 'So, do you want to rent it?'

She looked around at the dust, the broken furniture, the neglected counters and shelves and the chipped tiles. 'Yes, I want to rent it.'

It made no sense, that much she knew, but whatever uncertainty she had about this impulsive project, she knew that she couldn't go back home tomorrow. At least this way, with a six-month guarantee, she could defer the ultimate decision and give this a real shot.

'OK, when would you like to start the rent?'

'Right away, please. I mean, it's available immediately, isn't it?'

'Yes.' He shrugged again. 'Obviously it is available. We have done nothing with the building since my brother left. He didn't think that anyone would want to rent it, but he cannot do any work to improve it, so you must rent it in the condition that you find it. This is OK with you?'

'Yes,' she nodded. 'This is OK with me.'

'I will do one thing more,' he added. 'I think there is a lot of work to be done here, no? So, we can sign the agreement in my office on Monday, but you will start to pay the rent only in one month. You must pay the money to ... how you say ... *come si dice ...* '

'Renovate it?' asked Emily.

'*Sì, grazie!* Yes, to renovate it. So, for this I will offer you first month free of rent. This is OK with you?'

'Yes, that is very fair.' Niamh beamed.

'Oh my God, you are out of your mind, darling,' Emily said with a laugh, peeling a dangling cobweb from her hair. 'Giorgio, she's not signing anything today. Between now and Monday I'm going to try my best to talk her out of it.'

'*Va bene,*' he said, smiling. He turned to Niamh. 'If Emilia has some success then I don't see you on Monday. If Emilia has no success then I see you on Monday morning at ten o'clock at my office. *Ecco.* Here is my card.'

She took his card and smiled at him. '*Grazie.* See you Monday.'

'Don't count on it,' Emily shouted over her shoulder as she dragged Niamh from the dusty interior into the sunlight.

'*Arrivederci,*' Giorgio said with a nod. As a lawyer he dealt with people in challenging situations all the time and he knew determination when he saw it. He was pretty certain that he would be seeing this Irish woman again in his office at ten o'clock on Monday morning.

Chapter Fourteen

She was late getting back to the hotel. She had texted Grace to say that she was coming back for lunch but probably wouldn't get there until about 1.30. It was now a quarter to two. Grace had already been seated at their table and was tapping away furiously at her phone. Thank God she has a glass of wine in front of her, Niamh thought, as she was ushered through the restaurant to the window table. That's about the only thing that has any chance of keeping her calm and patient.

'Sorry, sorry, sorry!' she gushed as she sat down.

'It's fine, as long as I have wine for company I'm never alone,' said Grace with a shrug. 'So, where were you?' She pulled the bottle of white wine from the ice bucket and poured Niamh a glass.

'I went back to Camogli.'

Grace rolled her eyes. 'To the café?'

'Yes, I met the owner's brother to see how much it would cost to rent it.'

'Jesus, I was hoping that this was just a mad notion that you had yesterday and that it was powered by alcohol. So you're actually serious about this?'

'Yes, I am. Very.'

'I don't know what to say. I've never heard anything so

naive or ridiculous in my life – running away from your life and your problems like that.'

'Well, Grace, I'm staying, for better or for worse, so you can decide how this goes. Do we spend lunch arguing over it because you don't approve of my decision or do we talk about it like normal people? It's up to you.'

She surprised herself with her assertiveness and, judging by the expression on Grace's face, she had surprised Grace, too.

'Well, first of all, "normal people" don't make rash decisions like this and toss the return portion of their ticket and just not go home. They deal with their problems instead of fleeing from them, but fine, yes, we can talk about it. I'm not going to argue with you. I just think you are insane, that's all.'

'Think what you want, but for the first time in my life I'm terrified and excited about something. I've never been terri-fied of anything, ever.'

'And that's a bad thing?'

'Well, don't you think it says a lot about my life back in Dublin? It was boring and safe. I never made any of the decisions; Rick did. He was in charge of our lives and he was the one who made plans and forged ahead with his career. He was doing well, I was just happy to follow along like some kind of sheep on a leash.'

Grace remained quiet and let Niamh speak, which in itself was unusual.

Niamh looked down into her wine glass as if looking for inspiration of some kind. 'It was a small life, Grace. He was in charge and I just limped along like some sad individual, grate-ful to be included in his plans. He didn't mean any harm – it wasn't intentional, or anything. I mean, I was happy to go along with it all, but that's what I was doing. I was just going along with everything. He made all the plans and big decisions. I just decided what to make for dinner every time I stood in front of the butcher counter in Tesco. He had the great apartment that I kind of half lived in, but didn't own. He made more money and paid most of the bills, so he always had the final say in where we went on holiday, or which hotel we picked. He never compromised on his football or rugby, no matter what else was going on. It was always a priority, even over me, sometimes.'

'But you never had a problem with it before, did you? Why didn't you say anything?'

'I didn't even realise it, Grace,' said Niamh in a loud whisper across the table. 'I know this is going to sound soft, and like something you'd hear on a *Dr Phil* show, but it's like I was living it ... in it ... and so I couldn't see it. I had no perspective. I didn't know that there was anything else. I didn't want to know or need to know, because that was my life and it was safe – or so I thought. God, how wrong can a girl be?' She shook her head and continued. 'I never went anywhere on my own before. I never travelled without him, so it's as if any time we went anywhere, he was kind of in charge and I was happy to follow along. Grace, this is the first time in my life that I've been out of the country and not with a boyfriend. This is the first time in my life that I've gone and done stuff on my own in another country, like when you were at the conference those few days. I only ever went on package holidays, or a weekend to London. I never got off a plane in another country with no plan, only to have to figure it out myself. This is the first time in my life that I've felt like I've been on an adventure and it's not as if this is Nairobi or Madagascar or somewhere mad and exotic. It's Italy, for God's sake.' She gestured with her right hand, her glass of wine in her left. 'And I feel like I'm in charge of me for the first time in my life!' She leaned forward and hauled the bottle from the ice bucket, draining it into their two glasses.

'Oh, sweet Jesus,' Grace said quietly. 'This is my fault. Mam is going to kill me. It's all my fault. I brought you here. I plucked you from your safe, quiet little life that you were happy with. I insisted you come here with me and now you don't want to go back.' She motioned to the waiter to bring another bottle of wine. 'This is going to be a two-bottle lunch, I can already tell. We should order some food.'

'It's not your fault, Grace. It was my decision. Now, granted, if you had brought me to some other place like Romania or something I mightn't have been as fast to decide to change my life, but I love it here, and why the hell not?'

'Doesn't matter,' Grace replied, her two hands covering her face. 'Mam's going to think you've lost your mind and will blame me for dragging you here in the first place! Where is that waiter?' She gave a small laugh. 'I need a drink.'

They continued chatting for another hour over lunch. By the time they had finished, Grace was resigned to the fact that Niamh had made up her mind.

'All right. I still can't believe you are doing this, but I will accept the fact that you are not coming home with me on one condition.'

'What's that?'

'You have to call Mam and tell her before I get home. There is no way in hell that I am getting off that plane having to explain this to her. She'll lose her mind as it is, so it has to come from you.'

'OK, fine.'

'But you can't call her now. You can't be drunk talking to her or she'll think it was a mad idea based on too much wine, not just a mad idea all on its own merits.'

'Fair enough.' Niamh giggled. 'Do you really think it's a mad idea?'

'Yes, completely and absolutely insane. But kind of badass

too, in a way.' Grace smiled from behind her wine glass. 'Not, to be clear, that I condone it in any way. But if you had to pick some place to drop out of life then I suppose Italy would have to be top of the list. Just don't go falling for some randy Italian. If you are going to do this then make it your own adventure. You've been somebody else's project for too long. Be your own for a while.'

How is it that other people always seemed to have good advice for your own life and how to improve it, but from the inside it was hard to see what was even wrong, let alone put together a cohesive plan to fix it, Niamh wondered as they left the table.

They spent the rest of the afternoon wandering around the elegant town of Santa Margherita. The weather was a perfect mix of bright sunshine and light sea breeze. They strolled, stopping for a gelato, neither of them mentioning the fact that only one of them was returning home tomorrow. They were both in denial for different reasons.

On returning to the hotel, the concierge handed them a message. It was from Emily.

> Hello darlings,
>   I know that tonight is Grace's last night and I wondered if you two had plans for the evening? If not, a friend of mine owns one of the best restaurants in town – Sara's – and tonight they reopen for the season. It's always a marvellous affair! If you don't have plans then I would love you two to be my guests.
>   No need to call if you are coming. Just meet me at La Terrazza at six and wear something absolutely fabulous!
>   (Oh, and bring a wrap. We're going on the water!)
>   Ciao darlings,
>   Emily

Niamh read the note over Grace's shoulder.

'Jesus,' said Grace, turning to her sister. 'How do you refuse an invitation like that?'

'Umm, you don't?'

'Absolutely. OK, I've got to go see what outfits I have left to wear. If Emily says to wear something absolutely fabulous, then that's about as glam as I've got.'

'Well, I'm trotting behind you in the fashion stakes, so I may need to go back into town to those boutiques.'

'Let's just do that then. Come on,' Grace said, grabbing Niamh by the elbow.

Three boutiques and six shopping bags later, the girls returned to their hotel for the third time that day. They had an hour to get ready before the 17.30 ferry departure. By the time they were ready to leave an hour later, the room was filled with a cloud of steam, perfume and hairspray.

They opted to sit inside on the short ferry journey to Camogli so as not to demolish the hair creations so carefully sculpted just minutes earlier. The ferry ride was easy, and less than thirty minutes later they pulled up to the pier in Camogli. The two sisters made their way to La Terrazza to find the place completely packed. Apparently opening night at Sara's – wherever it was – was clearly cause for celebration, and half the town had turned out to kick off the evening at La Terrazza.

They made their way through the throng of people. The terrace was standing-room only tonight and the air crackled with excitement and laughter. Niamh stayed close to Grace as they weaved through the crowd, feeling more than just a little bit intimidated.

'What are we doing here? Who are all these people?' she asked Grace nervously, as she scanned the elegant crowd. 'I feel like I'm in some kind of movie or something.'

'I don't know. This is nuts. Just smile. That's what I do when I'm in a large group of people I don't know. It helps make you look more confident.'

Niamh planted a small smile on her face, hoping it looked more authentic than it felt. Emily was holding court alongside the pop-up champagne bar and waved at them to come join her. The crowd was very well dressed and everyone was drinking champagne served in old-fashioned coupe glasses instead of the usual Aperol spritz cocktail routine.

'Wow, what *is* this?' Niamh asked Emily above the cacophony of laughter and chatter.

'It's opening night, darling! Tonight marks the first night of the season and Sara's is one of the best restaurants in town. It's not something one can get on the list for – rather, it's strictly invitation only, and the way Sara thanks her local and loyal customers for their patronage and support during the season. But she's a dear friend of mine, so I throw an annual opening-night party here at La Terrazza before we go to her restaurant.'

'Crikey, this is your party?' Grace asked as she looked around and took in the crowd.

'Yes! Isn't it fun?'

'I'll say,' Grace said in agreement, as a waiter in a white waistcoat offered her a glass of champagne.

'I'm glad we shopped, Grace,' Niamh said, hissing into her sister's ear. 'I'd have looked homeless if I'd shown up tonight wearing anything in my suitcase!'

'Me too. Can't let the side down, you know? Especially as you're going to be living here now. You've got to represent!'

Just hearing the words sent shivers down Niamh's spine. She looked around at the glamorous crowd and her stomach flipped with both anxiety and excitement. She felt giddy as she realised that she might actually live here from tomorrow on. It wasn't just about tonight, with its glamorous setting, elegant outfits and champagne party. If she were to be honest, that was a little more intimidating than it was enticing right now. But rather it was more about this place here, these people, the snippets of Italian conversation that she couldn't possibly understand. This might actually be her real life from tomorrow.

'What did you mean in your note about going on the water?' Grace asked.

'Ah, yes. Well, the restaurant is not here. This is just the gathering point. From here we take a boat to Punta Chiappa.'

'We just passed that on the way here, didn't we?'

'Oh yes, that's right, you would have done coming from Santa Margherita. Punta Chiappa is the stop before Camogli. Look.' Emily pointed with one slender arm towards a cluster of tiny lights in the distance.

Both sisters looked in the direction she was pointing. The cluster of lights was at the base of the lush mountain range that ran along the left side of the bay. Niamh had seen Punta Chiappa on the ferry timetable but hadn't taken much notice of it on any of her journeys to Camogli. Emily explained that it was so small that it didn't even qualify for village status and was really just a little hamlet. There were two restaurants, a church and a cluster of houses, and it could only be reached by water or by a vertiginous hike through the lush mountain range. There was no road access, which only added to its sense of remoteness.

The restaurant clientele arrived either by ferry or at the end of a one-hour hike (not possible at night), and the wealthier clientele arrived by private water taxi or, better still, private boat or yacht.

'In the summertime there is the most spectacular collection

of antique *gozzo* boats and gorgeous yachts moored out in the bay. The owners swim and sunbathe and then have lunch at one of the two restaurants in Punta Chiappa. They are both great restaurants, but tonight is the opening of Sara's. So grab another glass of champagne and we'll get moving in about twenty minutes or so.'

'Are we taking the ferry to the restaurant?' Niamh asked, as she plucked two glasses of champagne from a passing waiter.

'Darling, I don't do ferries,' said Emily, laughing loudly. 'Giorgio is taking his boat over and I've hired a few of the local water taxis for people. They're much faster than the ferry and far more fun.'

'Oh, Giorgio is going?' Niamh asked, sipping her champagne.

'Anyone who is anyone is going and, yes, he said he was. He should be here somewhere, but I haven't seen him yet.' Emily craned her neck to see around the terrace. 'Then again, he's always late for everything.'

'I feel like I'm missing something here. Who is Giorgio?' Grace asked with a raised eyebrow.

'Oh, he's the guy who I'm renting the café from. It's his brother's place.'

Grace narrowed her eyes and stared at her sister. 'What are you being all coy about? You're not the coy type, Niamh.'

Niamh rolled her eyes. 'I'm not being coy, Grace. I don't think I'd know how to be coy if I tried.'

'So, what then?'

Emily grinned and gave Niamh a nudge. 'Go on, tell her . . .'

'Nothing. It's just that when I showed up to meet him at the café it turned out that he was the guy I'd met at your cocktail thing that first night.'

'Ah! The guy you threw a drink at, on the terrace?' Grace said, with a shriek of laughter.

'I didn't throw a drink at him, Grace. It was an accident,' Niamh said defensively.

'I bet he stands well back from you tonight,' Grace replied, giggling, prompting another eye roll from Niamh.

'As you two are my guests this evening, you should come on the boat with us. The mayor is a friend of Giorgio's, so he and his wife will be on it, and a couple of other friends from town. I'll introduce you to everyone later on.'

'Oh, lovely, that sounds fabulous,' Grace said appreciatively. She turned and leaned in towards Niamh. 'Where on earth have we landed? Who are these people and what is happening?'

'I know, it's weird, isn't it? I mean, in a good way obviously. It really feels like a small village and everyone is so friendly.'

'If this is anything to go by then getting integrated here isn't going to prove too difficult,' Grace said, looking around and taking in the crowd and the setting on the terrace. 'You might be on to something, Niamh. I might be dropping out of my life and turning around to follow you back here! Is that him? The guy with the café?' She was pointing at a tall, well-dressed man who was making his way through the crowd on the terrace.

Niamh followed her gaze and saw Giorgio greet Emily with a wide smile and a kiss on each cheek. 'Yep, that's him,' she said, looking him up and down.

'He's divine looking. Is he single?'

'Umm ... no. Emily said he's involved with someone. I didn't get all the details. I don't really know him. I've only met him briefly a couple of times. He's pretty hot though, isn't he?'

'That's an understatement, Niamh.'

'Actually, he has a kind of sad story.'

'Jayzus, why is it that they are either gay or have some kind of sad sob story? Are there no non-screwed-up hot straight guys any more?' Grace asked, plucking another glass of champagne from a passing tray. 'Thank God I don't have an early flight tomorrow. This is way too much fun to pass up!'

'No, I don't believe there are, but you are probably asking the wrong person, given my train-wreck history with men.'

'Fair enough. He's handsome, though. I'm pretty sure I could help him get over his tragedy, whatever it was. It could be my personal pet project,' she said, gazing in Giorgio's direction. 'He doesn't seem too distraught or sad right now,' she added.

Niamh looked in his direction. He was laughing along with Emily and another couple.

'By the way, did you call Mam today?'

'No, I'll do it in the morning.'

'Niamh, you better call her! I swear to God I'm not dealing with this when I get home. She's going to lose her mind completely over this, so I need to make sure that she has enough time to stress about it in advance before I get there and have to listen to it.'

'I know, I know. I'll call tomorrow, I promise. Drink up, it looks like this party is moving out.'

Both girls downed their glasses of champagne as Emily ably corralled the crowd towards the exit. The sisters strolled to the marina arm in arm as part of a larger contingent slowly snaking their way through the town.

'I feel like I'm in a Christmas nativity play, you know, that scene from *The Little Drummer Boy*,' Niamh giggled, as she glanced over her shoulder at the crowd behind them.

'I can't believe I have to go home tomorrow and you get to stay. So unfair!' Grace cried.

'I know, it's a bit weird just thinking of it. Oh, and if you don't want to pack all your stuff you can leave any cute pieces you want here with me.'

'Nice try. I'll need them for when I come back to visit you.'

'I'm starving.'

'Me too,' Grace agreed, as the two of them reached the top of the marina. 'Let's wait here for Emily. We don't want to miss that boat, wherever it is.'

Emily and Giorgio were the first to reach them.

'*Buona sera*, Nina.' He smiled as he stood alongside them. 'Emily tells me that you ladies need a . . . *come si dice* . . . a lift to the restaurant?'

'Yes, please!' Niamh grinned, and introduced her sister.

Giorgio led the way down the steps to the pier and stepped lightly onto a classic mahogany-panelled motorboat, extending a hand first to Emily and then the two sisters. 'Take a seat. We wait for a few more people,' he said as he readied the engine.

'Wow, this is a beautiful boat, Giorgio,' Niamh gushed.

'*Grazie*. Yes it is old, but very elegant. It is a traditional wooden boat that you find in Italian bays and around the islands. Perfect for sailing.'

'Everything about this evening is elegant,' Grace whispered to Niamh. 'Look at us, sitting on this gorgeous boat, waiting for the mayor and his wife and then zipping off to a restaurant opening! I have a feeling that this is going to be epic!'

'Me too. I'm beside myself right now. I think I've pinched myself twice already!' Niamh agreed excitedly, as the last guests stepped aboard and Giorgio revved the engine.

Chapter Fifteen

There was already a crowd at the restaurant as their boat pulled up and docked at the little pier in Punta Chiappa. Before they were able to see anyone, there was no mistaking the sounds of a party in play. Giorgio's boat had sped across the bay in less than twelve minutes, the sky backlit orange with the setting sun. Emily was first off the boat, followed by the mayor and his wife, and the two sisters, with Giorgio staying behind to tie up the boat safely. It was only a short walk from the pier up the winding path, through a grove of trees to the restaurant.

The entire place was lit by strands of tiny fairy lights, strung from the eaves of the restaurant roof to the palm trees and olive trees lining the bay side of the terrace. White linen tablecloths and simple silver candelabras decorated the two long tables, each of them seating twenty-four people. Bowls of cream and white wild roses were placed at every four seats down the length of each table. A string quartet decked out in black tie played classical pieces in the corner, and a pop-up Franciacorta bar stood ready to serve the evening's invited guests.

Everyone appeared to know each other and the two sisters stood quietly, taking in the view back across the bay towards

Camogli. Emily was nowhere to be seen; presumably she had dashed inside to greet their host and her friend.

'I can't believe I passed this place on the ferry from Portofino,' Niamh commented as she leaned on the wall and stared down into the crystal-clear water in the bay below.

'It's like something out of a movie. I've never been to a more stunning restaurant setting,' Grace gushed.

'Ladies, you do not have a drink. You will have champagne, no?'

The two sisters turned around to find Giorgio coming up from the pier behind them. 'It is not a party without champagne, and tonight it must be a party, no?'

'Yes, please,' they replied almost in unison and walked with him to the pop-up bar. The bottles of Franciacorta were displayed in oversized vintage wine coolers and had been perfectly chilled.

'Ooh, isn't this what we had the night we met Emily on the terrace?' Niamh asked, with an excited clap of her hands as she turned to face Grace.

'Probably, yes,' Giorgio interjected with a smile. 'If you were with Emilia then I am sure you were drinking Franciacorta. Tonight will be a feast.' As he talked, he poured them each a glass. 'Sara is a wonderful chef. I am sure that you would have . . . how do you say . . . found your way to her restaurant during the summer, but to be here tonight is special.' He held up his glass. '*Salute!* To the start of summer.'

They clinked glasses and drank to the start of summer.

'*Allora*. You must excuse me as I must go now to find our host.'

And with that he was gone again.

'There's something kind of elusive about him, isn't there?' said Grace, as they watched him walk away. 'I mean, he's divine, obviously, and friendly and all that, but he's kind of distant too.'

'Yeah, maybe he's just quiet or shy,' Niamh commented, as she too watched him go.

They could see a tall brunette in a flowing red silk dress make her way slowly through the crowd in the distance.

'Don't tell me that's the owner,' Niamh muttered to Grace. 'For the love of God, she's stunning. She's like a model.'

They watched as Giorgio greeted her warmly with a kiss on each cheek, followed by a hug.

'He's not quiet and shy now,' Grace commented from behind her champagne glass.

'She looks familiar,' Niamh said, squinting in her direction. 'Wait a second! She's the woman who was at your cocktail thing the other night. The woman who came to pull Giorgio away.'

'The night you destroyed his shirt?'

'Yes, that's her. Emily said they've been friends for years and they're an item now.'

'They look good together. Imagine what their kids will be like.'

'Yeah, like "the Clooneys: the sequel",' Niamh muttered in reluctant agreement.

They heard Emily introduce their host to some people nearby as the 'illustrious and accomplished Sara Rovella'. She looked like a film star or a model and must have been at least five foot eight.

'That's definitely her,' Niamh sighed. 'How does one person get to be so stunning and obviously talented and successful as well? Talk about winning the life lottery.'

'Yeah, but didn't you say she was kind of mean to you that night?'

'No, not mean exactly, just didn't really acknowledge my existence . . . whatever.' Niamh shrugged as she looked around in awe at their surroundings.

Emily waved in their direction and approached the two sisters.

'Niamh, Grace, please meet my friend Sara, our host for the evening. Sara, these are the Irish girls I was telling you about.'

'It's a pleasure to meet you,' Sara said, shaking both of their hands.

'Likewise, and thank you so much for inviting us this evening,' Grace said.

'It is my pleasure,' Sara said, in almost pitch-perfect English. 'Which one of you is Nina?'

'Oh, that's me.' Niamh smiled. Grace looked sideways at her but she continued uninterrupted. 'It's a real pleasure to be here. We've heard such wonderful things about your restaurant.'

'That is kind of you to say. I understand you are about to embark on your own adventure, and you will open a café? Camogli has captured your heart and your imagination, no?'

'Yes, it has.' Niamh nodded in agreement. 'I've never been anywhere like this.'

'I understand how you feel. The same happened for me when I came to visit from Rome. I never went back. That was many, many years ago.'

'Yes, I have to call my mam tomorrow and explain that I'm not coming home.'

Sara and Emily both laughed.

'Sara had a similar dilemma,' Emily said, smiling.

'Yes, except it was my husband at the time who I had to call,' Sara said with a strained expression. 'He wasn't very understanding. It was quite a difficult phone call, as you can

159

imagine. But I hope that your phone call to your mother will not be as dramatic.' She frowned slightly and put a hand to her mouth. 'You look familiar to me. Have we met before?'

'Oh, yes, at the drinks thing, em . . . cocktail event at the hotel in Santa Margherita,' Niamh said hesitantly.

There was no doubting the change of expression on Sara's face as she registered having met Niamh a few days earlier.

'Ah yes, that is right. Well, you must excuse me as I need to put on my apron and continue my work, or no one will eat tonight.'

She nodded her goodbye and turned in the direction of the kitchen.

'She is the most delightful person,' Emily said as Sara turned and left. 'Now, just wait until you taste her food and you will wonder if there is nothing that she cannot do.'

Niamh wasn't sure she'd describe Sara as 'delightful', based on the two brief encounters she had had with her, but thought it wise to say nothing for now.

'What happened with the husband?' Grace asked.

'She left him that time and never went back. He raised his hand to her once and one belt in the face almost fractured her jaw. That was what it took for her to come to her senses and leave. She wasn't exaggerating when she said that she never went back. This is home to her now, and we are her family.'

'God, that's terrible. Imagine having something like that happen to you. I'd run a mile and never look back if any man did that to me. That's inexcusable,' Grace said in horror.

'Indeed,' was all that Emily said in response. 'Come, let me introduce you to some people. Remember, Niamh, these people could be your customers in a few weeks,' she said with a wink.

'No pressure, Niamh, just don't cock up any of these

introductions tonight,' Grace said wickedly. 'Your whole future career could depend on it.'

'I'm glad to see that my notion to open a café is such a source of entertainment to you,' Niamh replied, as they followed Emily up the slanted walkway to the main terrace.

'Oh, wait,' Grace said, once Emily had left their side. She turned to face her sister. 'Why did Sara call you Nina? What was that about?'

'Oh yeah, Giorgio thinks my name is Nina, or actually, he'd prefer if it was as he thought Niamh was too difficult to pronounce.'

'That's interesting.'

'Why? It's just because of the spelling of Niamh and the V sound and I told him that as a child I used to call myself Nina so he just started calling me Nina, that's all.'

'Well, she said she had heard about the Irish girls and then asked which of us was Nina. I presumed Emily had told her about us.'

'Well, of course she did, she's the one who brought us here so she'd have had to.'

'But Emily calls you Niamh.'

Niamh hesitated and frowned.

'Yes, Emily calls you Niamh,' Grace continued, 'so Sara must have heard about the Irish girls, and in particular the one called Nina, from someone else.'

'Did you notice her expression change back there?' Niamh asked her sister quietly.

'I did. What was that all about?'

'I don't know, but that was definitely weird.'

'It's opening night. Maybe she's just stressed.' Grace shrugged. 'Don't give it another thought.'

The next hour passed in a blur. Waiters proffered platters of tiny hors d'oeuvres as dozens of bottles of Franciacorta were popped. The sun had set entirely now and Camogli was a cluster of glittering lights in the distance. The last of the guests had trailed in by eight o'clock, just as the waiters got ready to seat everyone at the long tables. Emily pointed them in the direction of two seats next to each other towards one end of the long table. Niamh and Grace turned to make their way through a group of eight or nine people, with Grace saying '*Scusi*' as they did so.

'Hello again,' came a voice from behind in a soft American accent.

They both turned to face the blond man who was grinning in their direction. Grace's face remained blank as she glanced at Niamh. Niamh frowned. He looked vaguely familiar in the way that a bit-part actor in a film you had seen once a long time ago might look familiar.

'You don't remember me, do you?' he asked Niamh directly.

Grace glanced at her again inquisitively.

'Umm, well . . .' she stuttered, racing through facts and places in her mind to place this man who stood before her, certain that she knew him somehow.

'It was a pretty wild night, so I'm not surprised you don't remember,' he offered. 'It is Niamh, right?'

Niamh stared at him blankly. 'Shit, he does actually know me,' she said quietly to Grace as he made his way towards them.

Grace had stopped fully in her tracks by now and was staring in amusement at the situation developing in front of her. 'Niamh, aren't you going to introduce me?' she asked, grinning. She couldn't remember when she had last been so entertained by her sister's infamously poor recollection of faces and names.

Niamh was racing through her internal mental filing

cabinet and coming up with nothing. What the hell kind of night was this man talking about, and when? 'Well, I . . . umm, this is my sister, Grace.'

'Pleasure to meet you Grace. I'm Jeffrey.'

'Jeffrey,' Niamh said aloud in the hope that it might trigger some sort of memory. 'Jeffrey.' Suddenly recognition lit up her face and she slapped him on the arm. 'You're Jeffrey the American, from Portofino,' she shrieked. 'You had me quietly freaking out there trying to remember what wild night I met you.' She laughed with relief and felt her face flush.

'I'm sorry. I couldn't resist it. It was clear that you had absolutely no idea who I was and, as crushing as that was, it was even more fun to tease you.'

'Jesus, don't frighten a girl like that, will you? I was wondering what kind of wild night you meant.' She turned to Grace, who was still watching with amusement. 'I met Jeffrey the day I went to Portofino for lunch. He caught me talking to myself at the pier and was gentleman enough not to comment on it. Gentleman until now, that is. You just lost that status!'

'Yes, I'm sorry. That is all entirely true,' he said, shaking Grace's hand. 'It was the middle of the day and I tried to buy her a coffee but she was not to be persuaded. She was intent upon her lunch date and she stuck to her guns. You are wrong about the American part though,' he said turning back to face Niamh. 'I'm Canadian.'

'Oh, sorry. I just assumed you were American. I can't tell the accents apart. What are you doing here?' Niamh asked, hoping for a change in conversation.

'Here in Liguria or here in this restaurant?'

'Well, both I suppose.'

'I've been studying at the university in Genoa for the past two semesters as an international student and, apart from a few inconvenient exams in a couple of weeks, I'm just about done. And as for this restaurant, well, my friend is on the guest list and I'm tagging along for the free food.'

'Oh, right. You did say you were here for the summer or something like that.'

'Aha, so you do remember,' he said, smiling.

'The conversation is coming back to me now. What are you studying?'

'Law and international business. I've been working my tail off for the past few years and when I go home I have to take up a placement with one of the big law firms in Canada or the US, so I'm planning to take the summer off. I figure it might be the last chance I have to do something utterly irresponsible and selfish.'

'What better place to do that?' Grace offered. 'I'm beginning to feel like I'm the only person here who is not changing her life in some way and choosing Italy. It's really all a bit depressing. I may need another drink.'

'Allow me,' he offered without hesitation. 'Franciacorta? Two?'

'Yes, please,' they said, again in unison.

Jeffrey made his way to the champagne bar as people were starting to take their seats at the tables. Grace turned to her sister and raised both hands in the air. 'What are you out here? Who are you? Some kind of man magnet? What the hell is going on?'

'What? What do you mean?' Niamh asked in a high-pitched voice.

'First Giorgio with the café and the boat and now this Canadian taking the summer off and just hanging out here. I mean, who are these people and how do you know them all? This is not the quiet Niamh from Finlay Place in Dublin that I know, the one who orders Chinese food every Thursday night of her life without fail. Who the hell are you and what have they done with my predictable sister?'

Niamh giggled. 'Grace, I just met this guy sitting on a wall at the marina in Portofino. He asked me if I wanted coffee, just like he asked you if you wanted champagne just now. That's it. That can happen to anyone. It's nothing more than that. Before he walked up to us here I had spent an entire three minutes in his company in a piazza in Portofino. I have no idea what he's doing here at this opening night thing or who he knows to score an invitation from. And, as for Giorgio, his brother owns the café and his fiancée ran off and left him for another man, so he was sad and depressed and apparently hooked up with that goddess in the red dress. It's not like either of them are here hanging off my arm or dancing with me under the stars. You're exaggerating this like you always do everything! It's like you have this vision of me slotting into life here, finding the perfect man and living happily ever after.'

'Well, of course I do. Then I can come visit and stay in your fabulous villa! I think it's a perfect life plan for you.'

Jeffrey returned with three glasses of champagne. 'Where are you ladies sitting?'

'Over there in those two seats,' Grace said, pointing to the chairs Emily had indicated.

'My friend's not here yet. Mind if I join you?'

'Sure!' Grace answered before Niamh had a chance to draw her breath. 'As long as there is a free seat.'

'I'll make sure that there is. This is a much better idea than trying to follow a conversation with someone else in Italian. I've been here six months and my Italian is still pretty awful.' With that, he took off in the direction of the tables and their allocated seats.

Chapter Sixteen

Jeffrey had somehow managed to shuffle the place cards so that he was able to sit next to Grace and across from Niamh. Sara had changed from her red silk dress into her chef's whites as course after course came out from the kitchen. She came and introduced each of the courses as they were served, describing the ingredients and the preparation of the food. The sommelier did the same as the wines changed with each course. It was a study in Italian fine dining, an exquisite meal from beginning to end.

Jeffrey and the two girls chatted and laughed easily across the table. He was very good company – charming, witty, self-deprecating and utterly easy to be around. Emily sat a few seats from them and checked in after the first course was served to make sure the girls were having a good time. She needn't have worried. Niamh couldn't remember the last time she'd had such a wonderful evening and she was pretty sure that Grace felt the same way, judging by the constant grin painted on her face.

The sky had grown black and the stars sat like splatters on a canvas far above their heads. Cicadas creaked and croaked in the bushes and a light sea breeze slapped minia-ture waves against the cliff face beneath them. It was heady and intoxicating.

After dinner the string quartet resumed as a display of desserts was set up on one side of the terrace. Coffee and after-dinner drinks were served along with more champagne, and the festivities carried on for hours.

'So you two are here with Emily tonight?' Jeffrey had asked in a break between courses.

'Yes, we're her guests. What about you? You said you were here with a friend?'

'Yeah. My buddy from law school in Genoa is Sara's younger brother. He asked if he could bring a friend, so here I am.'

'So where is this friend?' Niamh asked looking around. She hadn't seen him with anyone else all evening.

'Well, I took the ferry here from Genoa earlier today. I wanted to wander around and have lunch before going on to the restaurant, but my buddy decided he'd take his own boat. His own, very old boat, that is now sitting somewhere out in the Golfo Paradiso waiting to be tugged in to shore.' He sat back against his chair laughing. 'In hindsight, the ferry wasn't such a bad idea after all.'

'Oh no, his boat broke down?'

'Yep. He's fine. I mean, the coast guard people, whoever they are, have already been in contact with him and they are arranging for a tug, but he just has to sit there and wait until the tug reaches him.'

'But do you know anyone else here?' Grace asked.

'Nope. He just told me where to go and said he'd meet me here if he got towed in to the port in time.'

'Oh God, the eejit! Imagine missing a party like this because his boat broke down.' Niamh giggled.

'Excuse me? What's an "eejit"?'

'Oh, it's an Irish word for idiot or gobshite.'

'Gobshite?' Jeffrey looked even more confused.

Niamh giggled again. 'Sorry, another Irish word for idiot.'

'"Gobshite." I like that. It's very emotive. I'll have to use that one. Oh, speak of the devil!' he continued. 'Hey, Franco! Over here!' he said, waving furiously at his friend. 'You're just in time. Dinner is over!' All four of them laughed.

Sara came out and hugged her brother, rattling off a rapid stream of Italian and gesturing towards the kitchen.

'If you will excuse me, my dinner has been saved for me in the kitchen,' Franco said with a faint American accent.

Once he had been fed he rejoined the group at the table and regaled them with the story of being stuck in the middle of the bay with only darkness and the odd jumping fish for company until the coast guard came and berated him for being so stupid in the first place.

'I thought they had come to rescue me, not to yell at me,' he said in perfect English. 'I was happier in the bay in the darkness before these men showed up to tell me how reckless I had been.' He laughed, and sipped his wine.

'Your English is excellent,' Grace said appreciatively.

'Oh, thank you, that's kind of you to say. It's the result of years of international schools. My father was in the military and wherever we lived, we were educated in international schools, with English being the common language.'

'Where do you live now?' Niamh asked.

'Well, my family are all in Rome, except for my sister Sara. I've been studying in Genoa for the past few years and that is coming to an end this summer, so I guess I have some decisions to make.'

'Did you study law, too?'

'For my sins, yes, and now I embark on a legal career, but not until the end of summer. Right, Jeffrey?'

His accent might have almost been American, but he looked very much Italian.

'Amen to that. One perfect, lazy summer coming up,' Jeffrey replied, raising his glass in salute.

'God, I'm so envious of you all! I can't imagine an entire lazy summer anywhere, let alone in Italy,' Grace said, draining a bottle of red wine into her glass.

'I think I know where she stocks that,' Franco said with a smile, nodding to the bottle of wine. He got up and moved out past them towards the kitchen.

'I'll give you a hand,' Jeffrey said, and he stood up to help his friend scout out more wine.

'I can't believe I have to go home tomorrow,' Grace said, twirling her wine glass and watching the legs roll down the inside. 'I'm depressed at the thought of it.'

'Well, if it's any help, I won't be having a lazy summer. I'm about to get up to my ears in God knows what crap to fix up a ramshackle café and try to make a living from it.'

'Fair enough.' Grace grinned. 'Hardly the glamorous life, but still, it is Italy.'

'Yep, that's true. I'll have to learn some Italian in a hurry, though, or I'll be lost before I even start.'

'Well, how many weeks do you think it will take you to get the place ready to open?'

'I don't know – a few weeks, certainly. It needs a bit of work, and not just cleaning.'

'Well then, just apply yourself to learning Italian at the same time. You'd be surprised at how quickly you'll pick up the basics.'

'Yeah, good idea. Maybe I could get a tutor or something?'

'Is that code for lover?' Grace asked mischievously.

'Grace. The last thing I want is a man. I'm just getting over the last one.'

169

'Well, you know what they say about the best way to get over a man . . .'

'No, I don't, and I don't think I want to know,' Niamh said firmly. 'I'm here to fix my life, remember? Not complicate it further by adding another man into the mix. Give me a break!'

'Fair enough. Suit yourself, but celibacy is overrated. Just look at the number of nuns leaving the church. They're running screaming from convents looking for a penis.'

'Grace! That's disgusting! You can't talk about nuns like that!' Niamh was horrified.

'What's this about nuns?' Emily asked from behind them. 'I haven't spoken to you two all evening, but by the looks of things you were having a fine time.' She smiled.

'Oh, so much fun! Thank you so much for inviting us, Emily. What a fabulous evening,' Niamh gushed.

'Now, tell me, where are you going to stay until you get yourself settled? Have you thought about it?' she asked Niamh.

'Well, I took a look online and there are all kinds of Airbnb options in Camogli, so I rented one for the next month. It's a little one-bedroom apartment on the third floor of one of those old buildings on the upper level of town. It's small but really cute. Plus, I get a discount for renting it for a month, so I'm checking out of the hotel tomorrow.'

'Good idea. I think that's a smart move. It reduces your overheads significantly and in the meantime you can decide what you want to do on a more long-term basis.' Emily nodded in approval. 'And that will give you enough time to get the café up and running, and you can fix up the place upstairs at the same time.'

'What do you mean the place upstairs?' Niamh asked with a frown.

'Do not tell me that she's going to be able to live over the café?' Grace asked, turning to face Emily. 'If it all works out this perfectly I swear I'm just going to shoot myself.'

'Well, of course, darling. What did you think was upstairs?'

'I didn't know, I mean … I didn't think that the upstairs went with the café!'

Emily sighed. 'Niamh, darling, you are renting the entire building. That means the bottom half and the top half.'

'Sweet Jesus, she doesn't even know what she's renting.' Grace shook her head. 'Emily, will you please keep an eye on her when I'm gone?'

'Of course, darling. But Niamh, you had to know that you were renting the entire building, surely?'

'I didn't think about it. I only saw the downstairs, and I haven't seen the contract yet, so I've seen nothing in writing. I just looked around the café and thought I could make it work, I never thought about the upstairs,' she replied, feeling entirely foolish.

The two boys returned with a bottle of champagne and two more bottles of red wine.

'Oh, marvellous! I'll have another glass of red wine please, Franco,' Emily said, handing him her glass, 'and then cut me off or I shall die tomorrow. And welcome back, darling! We haven't seen you in Camogli in ages.'

The group continued chatting for the next hour, with Franco entertaining them with story after story. Niamh was relieved to have someone change the subject, until Giorgio suddenly appeared by their table with Sara by his side.

'I'm sorry to interrupt, but I must take the boat back soon,' he said, more to Emily than to anyone else. 'The mayor and his wife have already left, so we have room for two more if you boys want to return to Camogli on the boat.'

'Well, given Captain Franco's adventures earlier today, I'd be delighted to take a ride back with you, that's very kind,' Jeffrey said, grinning at Franco.

'Yes, as I am without a boat, a lift back to Camogli would be great, thank you, Giorgio,' Franco said graciously.

'Oh, boo, must we break up the party so early, Giorgio? It's only half past midnight,' Emily said feigning a sulk.

He laughed. '*Sì cara*. I'm afraid so. Tomorrow I will sail with some friends in the morning and must be up early to get the boat ready. You will thank me for this tomorrow, no?' He nodded in the direction of the collection of empty wine bottles.

'Yes, I suppose I will,' Emily sighed. 'Sara, are you coming back with us?'

'No, my dear, I must stay here. Tomorrow is my last day off for the season and we reopen to the public on Monday, so it will be a busy day.'

'Spoilsports, all of you! Now, Giorgio, I have a question for you—'

'Don't!' Niamh insisted, but Emily continued, unfazed. 'The building that Niamh will rent from you ...'

'Who?' asked Franco, confused. 'Who is Niamh?'

'Oh, for goodness' sake, these names get very confusing after a few glasses of wine, Niamh ... Nina ... I'm referring to the building that she will rent from you. Is she renting only the ground floor, or the entire building?'

'I don't understand the question, Emilia,' Giorgio replied, sounding confused.

'You quoted her a price to rent the building, to open the café again. Is that for just the ground floor or does it also include the upstairs?'

'It is the whole building, of course.' He turned to Niamh. 'You did not know this?'

'Umm, actually, no, I didn't realise … I mean, I hadn't thought about the upstairs …' She faded off quietly, realising that everyone at the table was now staring at her. She felt herself begin to blush.

'So, you think it was a good price for the lower half, no?'

'Yes,' she agreed.

Giorgio threw his head back and laughed. 'So now, is an even better price, no? Because you get the upstairs half for free, no?'

To Niamh's mortification, he found this hilariously funny and roared with laughter, causing her to blush a crimson red.

'So glad that I could provide the entertainment tonight,' she grimaced.

'Don't worry, I can show you tomorrow, when I return from the sailing. I will be back by lunchtime and can show you in the afternoon.'

'OK. Grace has a car picking her up at noon, so I could make my way to Camogli then.'

'Don't remind me,' Grace groaned. 'The holiday is over and back to the grind I go.'

'Very well. I have your number. I will text you in the afternoon to show you the other half of your building,' Giorgio said. '*Va bene?*'

'OK, yes. *Va bene.* That sounds good,' Niamh said quietly, mortified at her mistake.

'See you all at the pier in twenty minutes,' he said as he walked off with Sara. Niamh watched as she accompanied him down the slope to the pier.

Niamh found herself feeling irrationally envious of Sara. She had hardly spoken to her during the evening, but it was clear that she was a very talented chef, had her own successful business, as well as being tall, slender and beautiful – the kind of woman who could pull off a long red silk dress. Sara seemed to be a woman for whom life had come together, but there was definitely something cold and aloof about her that wasn't in keeping with the kind and generous descriptions Emily had shared of her. And then there was the fact that she was accompanying Giorgio down to the pier to say goodbye, alone . . .

Niamh sighed and turned her gaze towards the glittering lights up in the trees.

'What's the matter?' Jeffrey asked her quietly.

'Oh, sorry, was my sigh that loud?'

'Yep. Was that one meant to be in your head?' he asked, turning his head sideways to look at her.

'I suppose so. Sorry, there's nothing wrong. I was just thinking, that's all.'

'That's a dangerous pursuit and not one that I'd recommend. You'll never find contentment if you are constantly thinking and weighing up your life.'

She looked at him, wondering if he had read into her sigh and guessed correctly what was going on in her head, or if he had just said the right thing by chance.

'You're right,' she smiled. 'Sometimes I get stuck in my own head so much I don't even know if I'm thinking or speaking out loud. Gets me into all sorts of trouble!'

Jeffrey threw his head back and laughed. 'I bet.'

'All right, you lot,' Emily said, corralling the five of them towards the pier. 'Giorgio is always late for everything but he hates it when others keep him waiting. One of life's ironies, I'm afraid, but it's either him or call a water taxi, and I, for one, don't plan on missing this ride.'

They made their way to Giorgio's boat. He kissed Sara and hugged her before stepping aboard. The rest of the little group thanked Sara again and said goodnight, stepping onto the boat one by one. As Niamh, last in line, stepped on board, Giorgio turned and offered her a hand, but Jeffrey had been standing, waiting to do so. Giorgio directed his attention back to the controls and turned some dials. Emily looked from one to the other of them, then patted the wooden deck alongside her and indicated for Niamh to sit.

'Hold on tight. He likes to go fast in the dark!' Emily said, as Giorgio reversed out from the little pier towards the open bay.

The boat took off and the blast of cool air was intense. No one said a word. It would have been hard to shout above the engine and instead each was lost in their own thoughts as they powered towards the marina. An exhilarating ten or so minutes later they slowed down to round the bend and enter the still waters of the marina, backlit by streetlights glowing orange along the pier.

Emily said goodnight to the group and goodbye to Grace and headed home.

'Come back and visit us soon!' she threw over her shoulder to Grace.

Jeffrey called a taxi for Niamh and Grace as they had missed the last ferry going in the direction of Santa Margherita. Minutes later a car pulled up and Jeffrey opened the back door for them, telling the driver in Italian where to take them.

'Meet me for lunch tomorrow,' he said quietly to Niamh, as she went to step into the car.

She hesitated and looked up at him. 'I don't know. I . . .'

'I heard you say that you're coming here anyway tomorrow to see the upstairs that you didn't realise you had.' He grinned. 'Look, no pressure. It's up to you. But it's just lunch and you have to have lunch anyway, you know?' He shrugged and waited for her answer.

'Yes, OK. You're right, it's just lunch. I can probably be here by about one o'clock, after Grace leaves.'

'OK, I know exactly where I'll take you. Meet me right back here at one o'clock then.'

'Right here?'

'Yes, it's as easy a place as any, right?'

'OK.' She smiled as she got into the car.

'*A domani,*' he said closing the door and tapping on the roof.

Chapter Seventeen

The next morning the two sisters awoke reluctantly to the sound of church bells ringing out throughout the town.

Niamh stumbled out of bed first, rummaging through her bag for headache tablets. 'Ugh,' she groaned. 'How can they possibly be gone? I brought two boxes.'

'They're in the bathroom,' Grace mumbled through sheets in the next bed. 'I took some last night.'

'Smart. I should have done that. Ugh, I've a red-wine head-ache,' Niamh moaned, padding into the bathroom.

'Well, we were also drinking champagne like there was an alcoholic drought forecast and we might not see a drink for six months. Mixing is the worst—'

'Can we not talk about it please, Grace? It's not helping.'

'What time is it?'

'Ten. I counted the bells just now. I can't find my phone.'

'Oh God, I need to get moving, my car comes at noon.'

'Do you want to get breakfast first or pack first?' Niamh asked, before chugging back a glass of misty-coloured dis-solved medicine.

'Breakfast. I can't pack now. My head hurts. I need carbs. Bread, toast, butter ... everything that is bad for me. Do you think they'd make spaghetti carbonara for breakfast?'

'Probably not. Let's get some bread and tea and things. You'll feel better once you've eaten.'

The two of them moved slowly, rooting through bags for suitable clothes – nothing too tight, too short or too bright. If they could have gone to breakfast in sweatpants they would have, but it just wasn't that kind of place.

'You know, if Jennifer Lopez was staying here, or one of the Kardashians, they'd rock down to breakfast in a pair of sweatpants and still look hot,' Niamh grumbled, as she threw on a loose, lightweight shirt.

'Well, first, they'd be wearing some four-thousand-dollar version of sweatpants, and, second, they are all skinny as razors and would have some amazing crop top showing off a perfectly toned midriff, so no one would be focused on the sweatpants, even if they had cost four thousand dollars,' Grace mumbled matter-of-factly.

'Fair point. Are you ready yet? If you're not ready then I'm going to have to lie down again. Standing up is hard work this morning.'

'No, I'm ready. Let's go.'

They stumbled their way quietly through breakfast, downing black tea and sparkling water. As they got back to the room, Grace turned to her sister, squinting back the headache that sat behind her eyes and said, 'OK, I'm going to pack and you are going to call Mam. I'm not getting on that plane if you haven't dealt with this, and you've just run out of time. Got it?'

'Oh God, I was hoping I wouldn't have to do this with a hangover.'

'Niamh, I—'

'All right, all right, I'll call her now,' Niamh groaned. She retrieved her phone from under the bed and stepped out into the corridor to call home.

'Hello?'

'Hi, Mam, it's Niamh.'

'Oh, hello, love. Well? Have you two had a great week?'

'Yeah, great. It was fabulous.'

'You sound tired. Are you all right?'

'Oh yeah, I'm fine. Just a bit of a sore throat, I think.'

'Was the hotel lovely?'

'Gorgeous. Very fancy, actually, but not pretentious, if you know what I mean.'

'Oh, that's lovely. Are you all set for your flight tonight?'

'Actually, that's why I'm calling.'

'Oh, before I forget to tell you, the internet is gone out here so you won't have any when you get home. The man is coming out to look at it tomorrow but he said he mightn't get to us until the afternoon, but I said that would be fine. I don't know what happened to it, but it went out two days ago, and sure, I hardly use it so I kept forgetting to call about it.'

'That's fine, it doesn't matter, actually.'

'Now what time do you two land tonight?'

'Not until about midnight.'

'Oh Lord, that's very late. Are you coming straight home or will you stay at your sister's place?'

'Well, actually, that's why I'm calling. I won't be going home.'

'No problem. I thought you might stay at Grace's anyway tonight because I knew the flight was landing at some late hour. Sure, there is no hurry anyway. You're not going back to work tomorrow, are you?'

'No, Mam, I'm not going back to work tomorrow.'

'Good, you can have a bit of a rest so when you get home. Oh and your dad said to tell you that your magazine arrived during the week.'

'What magazine?'

'The new one your dad got for you. The cooking one.'

'Oh. Right.' Niamh rolled her eyes, hoping this wouldn't be an extended segment of the conversation. She had completely forgotten that she had signed up for a new *Food & Wine* subscription weeks earlier. Her dad had read out an advertisement from his fishing magazine about a special offer.

'You should get that, Niamh,' he had said, explaining that he thought it would be good for her. 'You could try new recipes and they teach you about wine, too. That sounds like something you'd like, doesn't it? And it's only twelve euros for the whole year. Sure that's great value.'

She had agreed that it was and he had filled in the coupon and pulled it out of the fishing magazine. 'Una, will you post that tomorrow for her? If I ask her to do it herself it'll end up at the bottom of her bag, or will be stuck on the fridge for the next month and the special offer will be gone. It says that it expires at the end of the month, so get it in the post.'

'I will,' her mother had replied, rooting in the drawer for an envelope. 'And she can be cooking all kinds of weird things for you to try. Won't you, Nina?'

Niamh shook her head, jolting back to the present conversation.

'Mam, it doesn't matter about the magazine,' she said, interrupting her mother's banter. 'I'm not getting the flight home tonight.'

'What? Is something wrong? Did something happen?'

'No, nothing happened.'

'What about your sister Grace? Is she coming home tonight? Was your flight cancelled? Is there a problem?'

'No, there is no problem, and yes, she is still on the flight tonight.'

'Grace is coming home, but you're not? Why on earth aren't you coming home? Have the two of you had a fight or something?'

'No, Mam, it's nothing like that. It's just ... I don't know how to explain this so it won't sound ridiculous, but I've just decided to stay.'

'For how long? Another week, or what? What are you talking about, Nina? What about work? When are you going back to work?'

'I'm not going back, Mam. I quit.'

'Quit?' her mother gasped. 'What do you mean, you quit?'

'Mam, I can't go back there. I just can't. I can't face going into work every day and seeing him there. It's just not going to work.'

'Jesus, Mary and Joseph, she's after quitting her job, Paddy. Your father is coming to the phone now.'

'Mam, will you stop? Look, it's this simple. I'm not going back there to work. I don't want anything to do with him or that bloody place. I have savings so I'm fine. I got here and it's just fabulous, really fabulous, and I know it sounds crazy but I just feel right at home here. The people are lovely, the place is stunning, the food is amazing, I just love everything about it.'

'But, love, you're on holidays. Everything is supposed to be lovely, but then at the end of it you're supposed to come home. I know that the breakup was hard, but you can't just abandon everything you've worked for. You're just not thinking straight.'

'What I've abandoned or given up is nothing, Mam. The job was an average job, I never loved it, and to be honest it was just a job that paid the bills. I won't miss it and I won't miss going in there every day. I'm thirty-three years old and I've never done anything that I've actually loved. You're always telling us to grab life by the arse and get out there and do something with our lives, so that's what I'm going to do.'

'Jesus, Mary and Joseph,' her mother recited again. 'So now you're going to take my advice when you're off out in a foreign country? You never took it at home when I meant that you should get another job or go back to school.'

'See, well, I'm doing it now instead ... and no, I never listened to you before and nothing ever changed. All I ever did was the same thing, day in and day out, boring, reliable, uninteresting Niamh with a boyfriend who clearly didn't give a toss about her in the end. Well, that stops now. I'm going to stay here and give it a shot.'

'What on earth are you going to do? And where are you going to stay? You can't afford to stay in that fancy hotel, surely?'

'No. I found an Airbnb for a few weeks until I get settled.'

'A what?'

'Airbnb. It's like an apartment that you rent for a few days or weeks at a time. You know, short term rentals. I rented it for a few weeks until I figure out where I'm going to live.'

'Good Lord, no, I've never heard of it. And what about work? Money?'

'I'm going to rent a little café. It's a place in the village that needs some work. I'm going to fix it up and open with a simple menu – you know, sandwiches, salads, stuff like that. It's nothing fancy, not a restaurant or anything, it's just a small place, but it's cute and I got it for a great deal.'

'Good God, but you don't know anything about running a café. I don't know what to say. Your father wants a word.'

She could hear mumbled chatter as her mother handed the phone to her father.

'Niamh?'

'Hi, Dad,' she replied, grimacing and bracing herself for his response.

'Are you all right?'

'Yes, I'm fine, Dad. I'm grand, honestly.'

'And what's going on? You want to stay there, is that it?'

'Yes, I'm going to stay here and open a little café. I've already found one, Dad, a small place in town.'

'When did you decide all this?'

'Earlier in the week. Grace has seen it too, and the village that I'll be staying . . . I mean, living in. And I'm moving into an apartment later today, after Grace leaves.'

'I see. And is everything else all right?'

'Yes, everything's grand, Dad. Why, what do you mean?'

'Do you need money?'

'No, I have savings. I have enough to do this and live for about six months.'

'Good girl. I'm glad that you saved while you had that job. No woman should ever be dependent on anyone else, or any man, for that matter. Your independence is everything, Niamh, that's your freedom. If you have that, then you can stand on your own two feet and you don't need anyone. I'm glad you have that, that's good. Good girl.'

She felt her eyes sting with tears. She hadn't expected him to get mad, but she had thought that he might not understand her rash decision and instead think she was crazy to throw away 'a good job', as he put it. She could hear her mother gasp in the background and could imagine her trying to pull the phone out of her father's hand.

'Sure you couldn't go back to that job and face that little fecker every day, not after the way he treated you. So, if this is what you want to do then just go for it, but do it right. It's a big decision to walk away from your job, so make sure you do something properly, not half-arsed. Do you hear me?'

'Yes, I do,' she said quietly. She bit her bottom lip and

blinked back tears, trying not to let her emotions register in her voice.

'Well then, that's that so. Sure, you're only in Italy. It's not as if you're moving to Australia. Isn't that right, Una?' Niamh could hear him chuckle. 'Right, I'll put you back on to your mother. She's huffing and puffing here next to me, but don't worry, she'll calm down eventually. At the end of the day you have to try new things, otherwise what's it all for? Isn't that so? You'll be grand. Here's your mother, bye now,' he said as he handed the phone back to his wife.

'Yep. Thanks, Dad. Bye.'

'Well, I don't know what's gotten into him,' her mother huffed. 'He must have been reading one of my psychology magazines, because normally he'd be a raging lunatic at the thoughts of you giving up a fine job.'

'It's no longer a fine job, Una,' Niamh heard him retort in the background. 'That prick ruined it for her and she's better off without him, if you ask me. If I got my hands on him I'd give him what's what, the little runt. Now, will you let the girl alone and let her get on with her life?'

'Lord God Almighty, it's like I'm living with Gandhi suddenly,' her mother said sarcastically. 'I'm just worried about you, Nina, that's all. I'm not trying to ruin your fun, I just want to make sure that you're not making a mistake, that's all.'

'I know, Mam, and I'm not. Or, if I am, then I'll just come home. I just want to try it, that's all. I've never done anything like this in my life and it just feels right. I just want to get settled in here and then I'll come home in a few weeks and get more of my clothes and stuff.'

'Well, this is quite a surprise. Tell your sister that I'll want to see her when she gets home to get the whole story. And you're sure that everything else is all right?'

'Yes, Mam, I promise. Everything is good. I'm fine, honestly.'

'All right so then, well, mind yourself and call again in a few days to let us know how you're getting on, will you?'

'I will. Thanks, Mam.'

'All right, love. Chat to you soon.'

'OK, Mam. Bye.' Niamh heard her mother begin her chant of 'Jesus, Mary and Joseph' as she took the phone from her ear to end the call. No doubt this conversation would go on for a while yet in the Kelly household this evening. Niamh was relieved that conversation was over and grateful that they had tried to be somewhat understanding. She was most surprised by her dad's reaction. Who knew that he'd be the supportive one in all this? she thought as she waited for Grace to zip up her bag.

The car was waiting for them downstairs.

'Being hungover actually helps with goodbyes, I think. It's hard to focus on anything 'cause my brain is fuzzy on the inside, so I won't get all sad and weepy,' Niamh joked.

'Just be grateful that you're not travelling in this condition for the next seven hours. What was I thinking?' Grace moaned out loud. 'Good luck with everything and don't sit and dwell on stuff too much. You've made your decision so just get stuck in. Everything else will fall into place as it's supposed to.'

'OK, thanks. And sorry in advance for the Spanish inquisition that you'll get at home.'

'That's all right. I'll just avoid them for the next few days. Call me during the week, OK?'

'I will. Bye!' Niamh waved madly as the car turned and made its way down the long driveway.

Chapter Eighteen

Niamh sat on the top deck of the ferry, her head hanging out over the side. She figured she probably looked like a dog with its tongue hanging out and its head stuck out of the window of a car, but she didn't care. The air felt good. She had raced to get her luggage packed up and stored with the bellman before checking out at noon and she was already regretting agreeing to meet Jeffrey for lunch. That had definitely been the wine talking. She barely knew him, she generally didn't like meeting new people, she was sleep deprived and the last thing she wanted right now was to get involved with a man at any level. Those were four solid reasons not to show up as planned on the pier, but she felt bad about standing him up. She wouldn't like it. 'Do unto others, Nina . . . ' She could hear her mother's words ringing in her head.

She got to the pier at two minutes past one and made her way to the spot where they had disembarked the night previously. She frowned and looked around. There was no sign of Jeffrey. She sat on the low wall at the pier's edge and dangled her legs over the side, staring down into the water. She pulled out her phone and texted Grace to see how she was doing. She checked the time. She strolled to the end of the pier and back, snapping some shots of the boats in the harbour. She checked the time again. It was quarter past one.

'Am I in the right place?' she muttered, before she noticed Giorgio's boat moored just a few feet away. 'Yep, you're in the right place, Niamh, but he's not here. He stood me up!' She fumed. While she was busy working herself up into a small, quiet rage, she also acknowledged that, while she was pissed off, she was actually a little relieved to not have to sit through lunch with a practical stranger. 'Who does that!' she huffed, and headed back in the direction she had just come, making her way up the steps and walking briskly to the far end of the promenade.

The restaurants were already busy with families and groups of friends out for Sunday lunch. She walked to the last restaurant at the opposite end of the pier and did a quick scan of the crowd. Perfect, no familiar faces, she thought as she stood in the entrance.

'*Allora, signora, buongiorno,*' the host said, as he came to greet her.

'*Umm . . . Buongiorno, solo uno per favore,*' she said, raising one finger as if it weren't clear enough that she was alone. Jilted, party of one! she thought to herself.

'*Ah, brava. Un momento, signora.*'

'Did he just say "brava"?' He did. He just congratulated me for dining alone, and on a Sunday too,' she muttered, shaking her head. 'How very Rosa Parks of me it was to venture out alone to have lunch. Niamh Kelly, single, radical and fearless – not afraid to eat alone in Italy in public on a Sunday. Her actions might just change the world for singles everywhere,' she mocked. 'Clearly not the done thing in Italy.'

The waiter sat her at a corner table and she scanned the other tables to see what people were eating. The menu made her mouth water just by reading it. A basket of warm bread was placed to her left and another waiter appeared and poured her a glass of something bubbly. She looked around again and realised that all the tables had glasses of bubbles. Must be a Sunday thing, she thought appreciatively.

She ordered a glass of local white wine, caprese salad and a bowl of *spaghetti pomodoro*. She moved her chair so she wasn't facing directly into the sun, and adjusted her sunglasses to sit up high on her nose. She spent the next two hours luxuriating over bread, wine and food, and all with the most perfect views of the bay. She sent a photo of her lunch to Grace by text.

Jealous! I'm still in the car, ravenous and queasy at the same time.

She ordered an espresso and replayed the conversation with Jeffrey in her head. She tried to convince herself that she wasn't too bothered, but it actually had stung a little to have been stood up. Even though she was glad that she hadn't had to feign interest in any kind of conversation or make small talk, she couldn't help feeling rejected for the second time in a matter of weeks. Maybe he had changed his mind in the cold light of day? Maybe he'd forgotten? It didn't matter, she decided. The chances were she might not even see him again as he lived in Genoa. Anyway it was best not to complicate things right now.

She got to the café early and waited for Giorgio. He was late, as usual. Her phone buzzed and a message flashed up from an Italian number. It was Giorgio. He apologised, explaining that he was delayed and directing her to where a key was stashed outside, telling her to let herself in if she was there already. She fished the key from the hanging flower basket that held the remains of some dead weeds and dried, crumbling earth and unlocked the door. It felt different being here alone. There wasn't a sound to be heard, except for her footsteps on the old tiles.

She stood behind the little bar and ran her hand along the counter, leaving a trail in the dust. There was all manner of boxes stashed behind the counter, some unopened and others in disarray. The coffee machine was thick with dust and grime and what she suspected might be a coffee grinder had spider's webs running from its lid to the coffee machine, making a footbridge for the tiny spiders that called the place home.

She wandered down the narrow corridor behind the counter. The last time she was here she had assumed that it led to a bathroom and nothing more. This time she noticed a second door, which revealed a staircase behind it.

'OK, that's why I didn't see any stairs. Well, at least you're not entirely thick, Niamh,' she muttered to herself. 'It's not like there was a staircase staring you in the face that you just completely missed. Anyone could have missed this!' She felt marginally vindicated from not having realised that there was an upstairs to her building.

She made her way upstairs, the steps creaking as she went. The small landing at the top gave way to three rooms. The first door at the top of the stairs revealed a bathroom. Like the rest of the place it was dusty, but she couldn't help but admire the original pedestal sink, the old mirror on the wall and the antique glass doorknobs. The floor was tiled with vintage dusky pink and black tiles and a similar colour scheme complemented the walls. The other two rooms had clearly been used as storage rooms as they contained dozens of boxes – again, some unopened, and some with all kinds of paraphernalia spewing out like entrails from the inside and onto the floor.

One of the two rooms faced onto the narrow street below, while the other faced west and looked out over rooftops towards the bay. 'Not only did I not know I had an upstairs, but I have an upstairs with a sea view!' she exclaimed, as she threw open the two windows and leaned out. She took a picture of the rooftops and the glistening bay in the distance and sent it to Grace.

Where's that? came the immediate text response.

That's my upstairs! Can you believe it?

Holy shit, that's fabulous! Can you live there?

I don't know, I suppose so. I'll have to ask Giorgio. There might be rules about the use of the building.

OK, keep me posted. I'm getting ready to board here soon. Will text you when I land and I'll call tomorrow!

OK, safe flight!

'It is quite a view, no?' Niamh jumped and dropped her phone, whipping around to see Giorgio standing in the doorway. 'Damn it, Giorgio, you can't just walk up on someone like that. You frightened the life out of me.'

'Oh, I am sorry. I thought you heard me come up the stairs.'

'No, I didn't,' she said, bending to retrieve her phone from the floor. 'Jesus, my heart is pounding.'

'I am sorry. I did not mean to frighten you. I see you have found the upstairs.' He grinned, still enjoying the fact that she hadn't known she was renting the top half of the building. 'I have not been up here for a very long time. It is . . . how you say . . . a big mess?'

'Yeah, but it just needs a good cleaning, to be fair. What was this place used for?'

'It was never really used for anything. My father bought the building a long time ago and the café was downstairs, but this was always just used for storage.'

'Did anyone ever live here?'

'No, I don't think so. At least not since my father

190

bought the building.' He crossed the room and sat on the window ledge alongside her. 'What are you thinking to do up in here?'

'Well, given that I didn't even know that it existed all along, I haven't really thought about it,' she said, shrugging. 'Are there any usage restrictions?'

'No, this building is old. It was built before any usage rules were created, so there are no restrictions for what you can do inside. Outside you have to maintain the building as it is – no changes are allowed.'

'OK, that's cool,' she said, looking around. 'And what should I do about all this stuff? Does someone want it? Or should I put it somewhere?'

'I think if it has been here for so many years, then no one even remembers that it is here, so you can just get rid of anything that is in your way. Some of these things might be helpful,' he said, standing up and turning some boxes so the labels faced him. 'Some were for the café, so you can use them if you like. Some are just rubbish.' He gestured to the open boxes with their contents spilling onto the floor.

'OK, what do I do with rubbish? I mean the big stuff like these boxes?'

'There is a place to take it to but you need a car or . . . *come si dice, un camion . . .* '

'A truck?'

'*Sì*, yes, a truck. You need a truck to get there. If you move the things that you do not want and put them inside the door downstairs, I will have someone come to take it for you.'

'Oh, that would be great, thank you.'

'Just let me know when you are ready and I will send someone. Now, I must go. *Ecco* . . . these are for you.' He reached into his pocket and handed her a set of keys.

'I'm getting the keys already? But I haven't signed any-thing yet.'

Giorgio smiled. 'Nina, what are you afraid that you will do? I am not afraid, so I give you the keys. Don't worry so much . . . is bad for you. Tomorrow I will come back with the agreement for you to sign. You will be here tomorrow, no?'

'Yes, I'll be here first thing in the morning. So you don't want me to go to your office?'

'No, no, I come here to you. Is easy for me. This time I will make more noise so I do not frighten . . . what did you say . . . your life out of you?'

'Something like that, yes.' She grinned.

'*Arrivederci,*' he said, with a small nod of his head. '*A domani.*'

She hadn't intended to get stuck into any real work, but as she poked through some boxes it became clear that most of them would need to be dumped. She spent the next few hours opening boxes, labelling those that she might use in the future and stacking them in a corner. Any open boxes containing stuff that was of no use to her were shoved to the landing at the top of the stairs. She found a roll of black bin liners and filled six of them with pieces of old paper and cardboard, old paper cups, receipts, magazines and newspapers, lugging them down the stairs one at a time.

Several boxes contained foil packages of coffee beans. She would have to ask someone if they were even any good any more or if coffee beans had a shelf life. She couldn't even guess how long they had been stored there, and they had no expiration date on them.

'You don't want to go poisoning your first customers with dodgy coffee beans,' she grunted, as she shoved the boxes into another corner of the room. She had all the windows open upstairs to let in some fresh air and every now and then she would pause to listen to the church bells ring out over the village.

The only indication that it was getting late was that the light had begun to change. 'I've been here for four hours!' she gasped, as she checked the time on her phone. 'I really must get a watch some day.' She calculated the time it would take to get to the ferry and decided that, if she hurried, she could make the 19.30 departure. That would get her back to the hotel by eight o'clock, to collect her luggage and take a taxi back to her new apartment. 'Yeah, after you've scraped the layers of grime off of you,' she muttered as she turned to lock the front door. She stopped and looked around the room downstairs. 'Congratulations, Niamh, it looks like you've made the place worse than it was, not better.' She rolled her eyes and locked the door, walking lightly down the deserted, cobbled street towards the steps to the lower level and the marina. Still, not a bad day's work, she thought, pleased that she had at least gotten started. More tomorrow, she reminded herself, resolving to get an early start and begin her new life as she meant it to continue.

Chapter Nineteen

Niamh was spending every waking hour at the café. She was completely absorbed in the renovations and had lost all track of time. She had bought cleaning supplies, gallons of paint, paintbrushes and rollers, and a stepladder at the local hardware store. To her relief, she realised that the walls didn't need to be painted – a good cleaning would suffice – but the skirting boards, doors and cupboards were scuffed and chipped and would definitely benefit from a refresh. Niamh was on her hands and knees behind the counter when he came into the café.

'*Ciao*, Nina? Hello? You are here?' Giorgio asked, his head poking through the door.

'Yes, I'm here,' she shouted from underneath the counter. She stood up and brushed her hands on her jeans. 'Hi.'

'Ah, *buongiorno*. You are busy.'

'No, it's fine, I'm just cleaning,' she said, aware that she looked like she had just crawled out of a dumpster. She tried in vain to beat the layers of dust from her sleeves and her jeans.

'I just bring you a copy of the agreement,' Giorgio said, placing the document on the countertop. He was wearing a navy blue suit and another stunningly crisp white shirt. She wondered exactly how many white shirts he owned.

'Oh, great, thanks. Your brother was OK with everything?'

'Yes, he is just surprised that you wanted to rent it, I think.' Giorgio looked around at the chaos. By the look on his face she guessed that he too was surprised.

'I just made some coffee. Would you like some?'

She watched as his gaze went to the large espresso machine behind the counter.

'Nina, is not possible to make coffee with this machine in this condition.' A look of horror flashed across his face as he wondered for a moment if she had used the machine in its current disgusting state. 'How can you make coffee like this?'

'No, this coffee,' she laughed, putting a steaming French press on the counter. 'Will you have some? It's freshly made.'

'What is this?'

'It's coffee, Giorgio, what do you think it is?' Niamh asked, confused at why he was being so difficult. 'I bought them in the hardware store yesterday. You can get them for single cups or multiple cups. Look – you just put the ground coffee in here like this,' she said, picking up another French press to demonstrate. 'Then you add boiling water and press it down – like this. See?' She looked up at him with a wide smile.

'But why you are giving this to me? I cannot drink this.'

'Why not?'

'Nina, why are you not using the machine?' he asked, gesturing to the enormous Simonelli espresso machine behind the counter. 'Why have you not cleaned the machine to use it and make real coffee?'

'I can't work that thing.'

'What do you mean you cannot work this machine? You have never worked a machine like this?'

'No.'

'Then why are you opening a café?' he asked, confused.

195

'Well, it's mostly about the food. I'm going to focus on healthy salads and light sandwiches and things like that. You can get a coffee anywhere in this town but there is no healthy lunch place,' she said indignantly. 'I'm going to do different stuff. I love to cook and I'm pretty good at it *and* I worked in restaurants for years every summer at college. I just have to figure out some of the stuff that I don't know about yet, and that coffee machine is one of them. But in the meantime I can make French press coffee. They use them in French cafés, you know.' She placed her hands on her hips, feeling fully justified in her explanation of her coffee workaround solution.

He stared at her for several seconds, rooted to the spot. 'Nina, how much experience you have working in cafés?' He crossed the tiled floor and stared at the French press steaming on the counter. He touched the lid and shook his head.

She hesitated, wondering how honest she should be right now. 'Why? What do you mean?'

'Nina, is a simple question.' His hands were gesturing now in that typical Italian way, but she still hadn't learned how to decipher them. 'How long you have spent working in cafés in other places?'

'Well, if you want to be that scientific about it, then none,' she huffed. 'But, as I just told you, I worked in restaurants for three summers. All I have to figure out is the financial bits and the coffee. But it can't be that hard. I mean, these machines practically make the coffee themselves, don't they? It's like having a motorbike behind the counter. Look at the size of this thing!'

'*Mamma mia*, Nina. You do not understand how important coffee is to Italians! You cannot serve coffee like this, in a plastic thing like this, to an Italian. They will never come back.' He placed the French press back on the counter and ran his hand though his hair. 'I will help you before you are doomed to die for ever with no customers and lose all of your money.' He was gesturing furiously now. 'You need to learn. Come.' He sighed, shaking his head. He started dialling a number on his phone as he strode across the tiles and was gone out of the front door. She darted after him, stopping only to turn the key in the door. She heard him chattering in short, rapid sentences and ended with '*Si, adesso*'. Yes, now.

'Yes, now ... where?' she asked, but he was already too far ahead of her to hear.

She caught up with him at the end of the street. 'Where are we going?'

'To teach you to make coffee,' he said, without losing stride.

She followed obediently, trying to keep pace with him. 'Man, you walk fast!'

At the bottom of the steps he turned right and shortly afterwards he stopped in front of the Illy café.

'Oh, we're going here?'

'Yes, this is where they make real coffee. You will learn how before you make yourself crazy with this idea to open a café without real coffee and you are crying to me in two weeks because you have no customers and you are ... how do you say ... bankrupt?'

'I've been in here a few times. It's nice.'

He stopped and stared down at her in disbelief. 'Yes, it is real coffee. Here, they make real Italian coffee ... this is why it is nice.'

He walked through the door, up to the counter and shook hands with the man she recognised as the owner. They chatted in rapid Italian for a minute or two, with the owner throwing several glances in her direction. She stood sheepishly, wondering what exactly was being said, with no way of knowing what would happen next. She caught two well-dressed ladies looking her up and down and realised with no small degree of horror that she was standing at the entrance of the coffee shop covered in dust and filth.

'Ah, you are the Irish girl who will open the café on Via dei Limoni, no?' the owner asked her as he approached and extended a hand to her. 'I am Massimo. Don't worry, *signora*, Giorgio has explained everything to me. I will help you,' he said with a wide grin and a strong handshake.

'Yes, that's me. I'm Niamh,' she answered quietly, returning his handshake and just now realising that she would be in competition with this man's business.

He hesitated, looked at Giorgio and said something in Italian.

'Ah *sì*.' Giorgio nodded. 'When I tell him about you and the problem you have on Via dei Limoni, I tell him your name is Nina. Then you say your name is Nee . . . I still cannot say it. How do you say it?'

'Oh, right. No, Nina is fine,' she said to Massimo.

'Nina is OK?'

'Yes, Nina.' She smiled.

'Ah, OK, good . . . is better for me.' He grinned. He seemed a happy sort of individual.

'*Allora*,' he continued. 'And you cannot make coffee?'

'No. Well, not on one of those machines.' Niamh pointed to a similar-looking machine.

'No, she cannot make coffee,' Giorgio said firmly, glancing at her sideways.

'No problem, Signora Nina! You will do free labour for me and I will teach you to make the best coffee. At the end you will buy me free lunch in your new café! You are going to do new food, no? Is good agreement, no?'

'Yes.' Niamh smiled. 'Is good.'

'But you cannot learn to make coffee in one day. It takes time.' He hesitated and looked down at her jeans and shirt as he raised his shoulders to his ears in classic Italian style. 'And perhaps today is not the best day for you. You were busy with the cleaning, no?'

She felt her face start to flush. 'Yes, I'm sorry. I was cleaning. I didn't know I was coming here.' She glared pointedly at Giorgio. She thought she saw him attempt to hide a smile.

'*Allora*, Nina, you will come here every day for two hours. Then, in a week or two you will be able to make coffee. Anything less will be a disaster and you will have no customers and your business, it will die. *Capice?*'

'*Sì, capisco.*' Niamh nodded, indicating that she understood.

'Now I must go back to work,' Giorgio interrupted. 'Massimo, I will not come back here for coffee for two weeks, until it is safe to have coffee again. But, before I go, I will have one espresso now – that you make, please.'

'*Subito,*' Massimo replied, as he turned to face the coffee machine.

'You are with the best teacher now, Nina. Massimo has been making coffee since . . . *come si dice* . . . how do you say . . . since you are a baby.'

'*Sì, è vero.* It is true. I am more than forty,' Massimo said with an exaggerated shrug of his shoulders. He placed an espresso in front of Giorgio. '*Ecco.*'

Giorgio smiled and tipped back the espresso, turning to Nina. He nodded at her with a smile and said '*arrivederci*' as he left the café.

She watched him leave and realised that so too did every other woman in the café. He cut a fine figure as he dashed out of the door and turned to make his way back to the office. He was being so sweet to her that she couldn't help feeling drawn to him. It was the most kindness she had felt from a man in a long time. She was clearly attracted to him, but didn't want to give in to that notion. After all, she couldn't imagine any woman *not* being attracted to Giorgio. But she knew that any feelings she might have would lead nowhere, involved as he was with the 'illustrious and accomplished' Sara, and she sensed that Sara would act like a ferocious lioness in defence of her man.

You're the new girl in town, Niamh, she thought to herself. Best not go knocking off someone else's man as you try to ingratiate yourself with the locals.

She washed her hands and face in the bathroom and did her best to beat off some layers of dust from her clothes. Massimo showed her around the little café. She stood outside the counter as he made a *macchiato* for a customer and then he invited her to join him for a coffee.

They sat at a table in the back of the café and he told her about Italians and their coffee. He talked about their preferred brands and the different types of coffee. She was shocked to hear the price of the commercial coffee machines that were standard in every restaurant, café and railway station café in the country. Some of them cost several tens of thousands to buy.

'So how can a small café afford to have one?'

'Well, they don't buy it, they lease it from the coffee manufacturer,' he explained. His English was a lot better than Giorgio's, most likely because he dealt with foreigners every day of the summer season. 'The coffee makers want you to use their coffee beans, so they will offer you the machine and you can keep it for as long as you order their beans. So, they make the investment up front for the machine, but they know that you will be a customer for many years.' He leaned back against the chair. 'As long as the coffee beans are good, you will continue to order from them, so they are building many, many customers for many, many years.'

'So how come there is a machine sitting in the café on Via dei Limoni all this time if no one is buying coffee beans any more?'

'I don't know, but probably Giorgio or his brother made a deal with them when they closed the café, or probably they bought it at the beginning. The café was opened many, many years ago, Nina.'

'Yes, I heard a little about it. It's very sad.'

Massimo shook his head. 'Lena was such a beautiful woman. Marco has never been the same since that time. They were so happy together. Everybody loved her. She was a kind and beautiful woman. Everyone was so sad when she died.'

'Did Marco leave right away?'

'No, he stayed for a while and tried to . . . how do you say . . . put his life together once again, but I think that everywhere there were too many reminders of her. He and Giorgio were always the best friends, no? So it was hard for Giorgio, too, to see his brother in this much pain, you understand?'

'Yes.' Niamh nodded. 'I understand.'

'I'm sorry, my English is not so good.'

'No, it's great,' she said encouragingly.

He smiled and continued. 'So Marco applied for a transfer to a hospital in America. He could continue his medical practice there and hope to start a new life at the same time. He got a visa, and one evening he told the family at dinner that he was leaving. He left the next day. It was as if he could not wait to leave the sadness behind.'

She watched Massimo as he told the story and she could see the sadness in his face, recalling the details. 'Then, he was gone, and Giorgio was sad for this reason, too. His fiancée left him two months later.'

'That's awful. Had they been engaged long?'

'I don't know, maybe a few months. I know that he loved her, but I do not know how much she loved him. Giorgio is a kind man. He has a good career and he is a hard worker. His family has some other businesses – different real estate – that he also is involved with, as well as his own job, so he is always busy. But, I don't know how much this woman really loved him, and how much she loved the idea of him. To leave so soon after so much has happened, it says to me that she ... how do you say in English? ... She was not willing to live the hard parts of life, to have problems and stress, only easy. She wanted only the good life. That is not right.' He stood abruptly. 'I am sorry. I am keeping you from your work. I talk too much!'

'No, not at all. I enjoyed chatting with you,' Niamh said, standing too.

'Chatting? What is chatting?'

'Oh, speaking ... it's speaking, you know, casually, just like we were doing.'

'Ah, OK! So I teach you to make coffee and you teach me to speak better English!' he said with a wide grin. 'Now, I must get back to my customers. Tomorrow I will see you at ... at what time is good for you?'

'Oh, any time is fine, Massimo, honestly. You tell me what suits you and what is best for your business.'

'OK, so we see you tomorrow at nine o'clock. That way the Italians will have gone already to work and so will have had their coffee and we will not upset anyone, and the less serious

202

people, like tourists, will not be here until after ten o'clock, so we will have some time to prepare.'

'Sounds good. Thank you again, Massimo.'

'Signora Nina, you forget – you will work for free for me,' he said, grinning. 'So don't thank me yet! *Arrivederci! A domani!*'

'*A domani.*' She waved as she stepped back out into the sun.

Chapter Twenty

She quickly began to look forward to her mornings at Massimo's café. She had completely underestimated the amount of work involved in operating a small café, and she had wildly misjudged her lack of experience. Without Massimo's help, her attempts at running a little café would have been, as Giorgio had predicted, a disaster of massive proportions. The coffee machine itself and the skill required to properly make good coffee were only part of the challenge. There was so much more involved that she hadn't even begun to plan for or consider.

She was also gaining a sense of the importance of relationships within the community. Massimo knew everyone in the village, it seemed, but then he had lived here his entire life, so this was understandable. Most of them – the locals, that was – came to his café for coffee or pastries in the morning. She didn't intend to compete on the basis of coffee alone, and she explained that to Massimo, but rather she wanted to create a unique place for light, healthy lunches as opposed to the usual Italian fare of pasta and pizza. Her customers would most likely be tourists more than locals, at least initially. Tourists would be more accustomed to having salads, soups and sandwiches for lunch, as opposed to the traditional bigger

Italian midday meal, and she did have relevant restaurant experience that she could put to work.

She also learned some useful cultural information, such as the fact that Italians didn't really go in for breakfast like other cultures, but kept it simple and light, with a coffee and croissant, or *un cornetto*, as the Italians called it. Massimo explained that breakfast is such a non-issue for Italians that most of them choose to stand at the counter in the morning to have their cappuccino or espresso, rather than sit down at a table.

Massimo was a sweet man who was devoted to his family. His adorable two-year-old twins burst through the door each morning screaming, 'Papà! Papà!' and he would scoop them up into his arms. It made her smile every time she saw it. He introduced her as Nina and they each clung to one of her legs and stared up at her wide-eyed, chanting her name loudly on repeat.

Massimo's mother would take up residence at a table at the back of the café each morning a little before nine o'clock. It was a ritual that gave purpose to her day. She was a small, sweet old lady who always had a smile for anyone who came in. She would sit at the table drinking coffee, doing crossword puzzles and reading until some of the local women showed up, at which point she would hold court for very lengthy, important conversations. She was known in the café as *Nonna*, the Italian for grandmother, and it was a badge that she wore with pride.

Nonna had also started to call Niamh Nina, as she had heard the twins loudly and enthusiastically rattle off her name each morning. The old lady shook her head, and made a dramatic hand gesture that involved both shoulders, when Massimo tried to explain that Nina wasn't her actual name. It was becoming clear to Niamh that at this rate she

205

would soon be known exclusively as Nina among the Italian community, and she took pleasure from the fact as she began to feel more and more as if she were being accepted by this new tribe.

Nonna spoke no English so their conversations were limited to the little Italian that Nina had acquired, supported by a lot of hand gestures.

'Why does Nonna always dress in black?' she asked Massimo one morning.

'Ah, she is in mourning for her husband, my father,' he replied over the screech of the coffee-grinding machine.

'Oh, I'm sorry to hear that. I didn't realise that your father had passed away.'

'Nina, it was twenty years ago, but my mother has refused to wear anything but black ever since.'

'Aw, that's kind of sweet, you know, like a great romance that she doesn't want to let go of.'

'Yes, it is sad. They were best friends and had been married for almost forty years. Now she is in her early eighties, but she looks so much older because of all that black she wears,' he sighed. He shrugged his shoulders and continued. 'But, she will not listen to anyone, so what can I do?'

'Sounds like something out of an old black and white movie, you know? The widow wearing only black and mourning her husband for the rest of her life?'

'She was a very beautiful woman, but now she wears her sadness on her face in lines. I think if she did not wear all this black, it would be better. How would you say . . . it would make her feel lighter? Do you understand?'

'I do. There's a thing now called colour therapy. It's all about how different colours make you feel and when you should wear them. You know, like red is a power colour so you should wear it when you have a big meeting, or presentation, or when you want to feel in charge.'

'*Ha!* This is good information! I will wear red the next time that I go to visit my bank manager,' Massimo said, and he threw his head back and roared with laughter. 'This must be an American theory, no?'

'Probably,' Niamh agreed, giggling. 'I doubt the Irish invented it, anyway, and it does sound like something that the Americans would come up with.'

The conversation continued in easy banter for two hours each morning. Massimo would interrupt her every time she used a word that he didn't understand and he would repeat it over and over until he got used to saying it. In return he taught her some common, everyday Italian expressions, phrases that she could use right away in her new life. He taught her that it was important not to worry about grammar and structure and pronunciation, but just to start with simple words and phrases and build on them.

Giorgio had been true to his word for the first few days, but reappeared just after she arrived one morning at nine o'clock.

'*Buongiorno a tutti,*' he said, with a smile to the little crowd in the café.

'Ah, Giorgio, I was afraid that you would not come back until Nina had finished learning,' Massimo joked as he shook his friend's hand.

'I thought you were avoiding this place for the next two weeks?' Niamh asked, with her hands on her hips.

'I tried, but it is the best coffee in town. I had no choice but to return,' he sighed with mock exaggeration.

'You are late this morning, no?' Massimo asked in English with one eyebrow raised.

'Oh, ah, yes, today I start later,' he responded, sticking his hand in his pocket and plucking out his wallet. '*Un cappuccino, per favore.*'

'I think you had better make it, Massimo,' said Niamh. 'Now that he's returned you don't want to scare him off by having me make his coffee. I don't think he is ready for that just yet.'

'*Va bene*, OK, I will make,' Massimo responded, turning to face the coffee machine.

Niamh had busied herself filling the grinder with fresh coffee beans when she heard a gasp behind her.

'*Ah, Giorgio, caro,*' Nonna exclaimed as she shuffled towards him. He bent to kiss her on both cheeks. She placed her hands on the sides of his face and spoke in rapid, gentle Italian. Niamh could only guess by the expressions and the gestures that she was saying she hadn't seen him in a long time. Massimo came and stood alongside her behind the counter, placing Giorgio's cappuccino cup on a saucer.

'Yes, we don't usually see you here at this hour of the morning, Giorgio. It is unusual, no?' He turned and winked at Niamh. She saw Giorgio flash a look at Massimo that she didn't understand.

Nonna turned to him and demanded to know what he had just said to make Giorgio look flustered. When he explained in Italian, she clearly agreed with Massimo's statement. She turned back to Giorgio, putting an arm around his waist and patting his chest with her other hand.

'*Sì caro, sì,*' she said, and continued in Italian.

'She says that he always comes in too early for her so she never gets to see him. She says that it has been too long since she has last seen him and she is angry with him for this. Angry in her own kind of way, that is,' Massimo translated. 'She is telling him that she wants him to come to dinner on

208

Saturday night. Nonna is such a wonderful cook.' He gestured wildly with his hands. 'How do you say in English ... she is a magician with the food! She used to have some wonderful dinner parties in the past, but now she just cooks for family. *Mamma mia*, she can make the pasta that will make you want to cry it is so good.'

Nonna turned and pointed towards Niamh without even slowing her rapid stream of Italian. Niamh had no idea what was being said, but based on the series of hand gestures in her direction, it clearly had something to do with her and she could feel her face start to flush immediately. Why does my face do this every time, she wondered, frustrated, putting both hands to her cheeks.

'Ah, Nina, Nonna wants you to join us all on Saturday night. You will come, no?' Massimo translated again.

'Oh, really? Well, yes, of course, I would love to but ... ' she said, surprised to have been invited. 'What did she say?' she asked Massimo quietly.

'Yes. She said that Giorgio must come for dinner as he has been ... how do you say in English ... not seeing her as much recently?'

'You mean avoiding her?'

'Ah, yes!' he exclaimed loudly. 'This is the word I was look-ing for. Yes, she says that Giorgio has been avoiding her so he must come to dinner on Saturday now that she has seen him again.' He wore a wide smile, pleased with his use of his newly acquired English word.

'Yes, but what does that have to do with me?' she asked Massimo. 'Are you sure that she invited me?'

'*Sì, sì, certo*. She said that you must come to dinner also because you are the reason she has seen Giorgio again.'

'How so?' Niamh asked, now utterly confused. She wasn't

sure if it was his English or if the old lady just wasn't making any sense, but she couldn't see what she had to do with the reunion of Giorgio and Nonna.

'Yes, you see, Nina, Giorgio comes here every day for coffee at seven-thirty in the morning,' he said, leaning in and speaking quietly to her. 'Nonna is never here that early in the morning. He has come here at that time every morning on his way to work for many, many years, but today he is here at nine o'clock, because, I think, you are here, no?'

'That's daft, Massimo,' she said, feeling her face start to flush again. 'That's totally not the reason he's here later today. Maybe he is just running late. Emily said he's always late for everything!'

'What is daft?'

'Crazy, Massimo. Crazy, nuts . . . '

'Ah, I like this word. I will find many ways to use it each day in here with some of our daft customers. As for Giorgio,' he continued, 'he starts work at eight o'clock in the morning at his office. So, at seven-thirty in the morning it does not matter if he is a little late. But nine o'clock is different – this is definitely late, Nina, and there is no other explanation for it, other than you come here at nine o'clock in the morning this week and next week. This is the truth, Signora Nina!' He spoke with a flourish of his hand. 'Now, Nonna is asking if you will join us for dinner on Saturday night. What is your answer?'

'*Ah sì, Nonna, grazie*,' Niamh said, smiling at Nonna, who had still not let go of Giorgio. 'How do you say, "That's very kind" in Italian?' she asked Massimo. She didn't know what to make of Massimo's theory, but it made her feel good to think she might have had something to do with Giorgio showing up later than usual.

'*Molto gentile*.'

'*Molto gentile, Nonna*,' she repeated.

Nonna merely smiled and nodded her head. She motioned with her hand and mumbled that she would like a cappuccino. She hesitated for a moment, glanced at Niamh and then nodded towards Massimo. Even though she had just invited the new foreigner in town to join them for dinner on Saturday night, Nonna wasn't quite ready to trust her with her morning cappuccino. There was a correct order of things, and cappuccino was pretty high up on the list of the important elements of Nonna's life, along with food, wine and family. Massimo looked at Niamh and shrugged as if to say that there was no point in fighting that one.

'No problem, Massimo. There is a saying in English that goes, "All good things come to those who wait," and that definitely applies here. I'm nowhere near qualified to make Nonna's cappuccino just yet!'

Giorgio looked at her and shook his head, smiling. He peeled Nonna's arm from around his waist and turned to leave. 'My dear Nina, you still do not understand just how important coffee is to the Italians. You might have a very long wait before Nonna will order a cappuccino from an Irish girl!' He gave a wave to the small group gathered at the counter and was gone.

Niamh stood watching him leave, replaying his words *My dear Nina ... my dear Nina* over and over in her head. Don't overthink it. It's just an expression, she tried to convince herself, but she had plucked the three words from the air as soon as he had said them, just as a hummingbird might pluck sweet pollen from a bud.

Chapter Twenty-One

By the end of the week, Niamh was brave enough to start making cappuccinos for some of the regular local clients. She had perfected the art of the cappuccino foam under Massimo's stewardship and was amazed at how much skill it took to get it just right.

Saturday morning came around and she was at her post behind Massimo's counter by nine o'clock as usual. She was deep in thought as she stared into the milk pitcher, steaming the milk for the two cappuccinos that had just been ordered, when she heard her name.

'Niamh? What on earth are you doing in here?'

She turned to see Jeffrey leaning across the counter, grinning at her.

'Jeffrey!' she exclaimed, her face immediately flushing with colour.

Thankfully the pitcher of steaming milk demanded her full attention, so she turned back, grateful to have a moment to gather her thoughts. Should she be mad or pissed off at having been stood up? Or should she try to appear nonchalant and dismiss it as unimportant?

'Of all the gin joints ...' He laughed. 'What the heck are you doing here?'

'I'm making coffee. What does it look like?' she replied, her gaze focused on the jug in her hand.

'Well, I can see that, but why here? I thought you were opening your own place?'

'I am, in a couple of weeks, but I've been coming here to learn the art of the barista.' She placed the two cappuccinos on the counter. 'What are you doing here?'

'I'm in town for the weekend with Franco. So, thanks for standing me up on the pier that day. It's been a long time since that's happened, I can tell you. I had forgotten how crappy it felt! I felt like a complete jerk.'

'Nice try, Jeffrey. Are you having a coffee?' she asked, trying hard to look busy.

'A cappuccino, please, and what do you mean by that? I stood there like an idiot for a half an hour before it dawned on me that I had been stood up.'

'Jeffrey ... ' She sighed, and stopped, unsure which version of herself was going to respond. He would either get calm-and-collected Niamh, who would graciously dismiss his attempt at lying about his behaviour as meaningless and unworthy of anger, or he'd get demented Niamh, who had to admit that she felt a little humiliated at the thought of it.

'Jeffrey,' she continued. 'It's bad enough to stand a girl up, having invited her to lunch in the first place, but to lie on top of it and try to come over all smarmy and cocky like you were there the whole time is just pathetic. I was there. I was the idiot. And the fact that you stood me up and now are trying to fudge your way out of it, unable to admit that it was a shitty thing to do, makes me wonder why I even agreed to it in the first place.'

So it turned out that he got the demented version of Niamh in the end. She turned her back to him and focused her attentions instead to the milk pitcher. She was furious again and wondered if it was considered illegal to scald customers in Italy.

'I swear to God I was there. In fact, you can ask Franco. He'll be here shortly. Honest, Niamh, I was there. I was about fifteen minutes late because I had to drop Franco at the marine store to get what he needed to fix his boat's engine. It's about an hour away and on the way back there was some bad accident on the road so we were delayed. I swear that's the truth. I was there. Everyone typically runs late in Italy, so when you weren't there, I just figured you had stood me up. It never even dawned on me that you might have disappeared in less than fifteen minutes. Honest!'

She turned to look at him and he was standing with both hands held up in defence.

Bollocks, she thought, as she remembered how she had scarpered off just before quarter past the hour. He looks like he's telling the truth.

'Niamh, I'm so sorry you thought I had stood you up. I didn't have your number and neither did Franco. I went back to Genoa the next morning and I didn't know where you had moved to after you left the hotel that day, so I was kind of stuck. I honestly didn't think I'd see you again.'

She tucked her hair behind her ear and fiddled with a tub of spoons beneath the counter in an attempt to look busy. Where are all the customers now when I need them? she thought to herself.

'Well, you sure can make a decent cappuccino. Truce?' he asked with a smile.

'Truce,' she agreed.

'On one condition though – that you let me make it up to you for real. Let me take you out to dinner tonight.'

'Oh, that's nice, but I can't tonight. I have plans.'

'Of course you do. That's not surprising. OK then, how about tomorrow night? I don't have any assignments due on Monday so I'm staying in town this weekend. I can meet you any time that suits.'

'I thought you were done with school?'

'Almost. The exams are over but we had both been doing some tutoring for extra credit so we've got a bunch of reporting and paperwork due on that now and I've got one last assignment. Another week or so and we'll be free. So, what do you say?'

'Sure, why not?' Niamh said with a small smile.

'Be careful and don't be too enthusiastic about the prospect of dinner with me or I'll get a swelled head.'

'Call me cautiously optimistic. Just don't be late this time!'

'I won't now that I understand that I've got a fifteen-minute window before you go all Cinderella and her pumpkin carriage on me!'

'Well, if you're not late then you won't need to worry, will you?' she said, feeling more confident.

'Fair point,' he conceded. 'How about dinner at Da Paolo's?'

'Oh, that sounds lovely, actually. I was there once with Grace and loved it. We were told it's one of the best restaurants in town.'

'It is. I know the owner so he'll look after us. I'll see if we can get a table outside. OK, I've got to run. Thanks for the coffee,' he said with another wide grin. 'See you tomorrow night!'

The rest of the morning passed without incident, and she took off her apron and said goodbye to Massimo just after noon.

'*Brava, Nina. Oggi hai fatto bene!*' Massimo said, graciously telling her that she had done well today.

215

'*Grazie, Massimo.* I love coming here.'

'*Allora*, see you tonight, yes? Here is the address of Nonna's house.'

'OK, thanks. Is it here in town?'

'No, is up in the hills above the town. You can walk, but there are many, many steps. I forgot that you do not have a car.'

'That's fine. I can take a taxi.'

'Ah, yes, but they are not so reliable here. Sometimes they do not . . . how do you say . . . arrive? Why don't you meet me here at six o'clock and you can come with me?'

'OK, thanks. That's very kind of you. I'll see you here at six o'clock. *Ciao!*'

She made her way back to her little café on Via dei Limoni, grateful for some quiet after the busy morning at Massimo's. She surveyed the scene and took stock of what she needed to get done for the rest of the day. The place had been mostly cleared out and now looked a lot more spacious. The coffee machine had been serviced and was working perfectly, which was a relief given the inordinate price it would have cost to buy a new one. She had yet to try it for real herself and thought it might be safer to wait until she felt totally confident with Massimo's model before she started tinkering with her own.

Niamh paced up and down, counting out her steps and trying to decide how to configure the new tables and chairs for her café. For now, they were all stacked upstairs, still wrapped in their protective plastic. She had literally squealed in delight when she found them in an old furniture shop in Genoa. The place was a salvage yard of sorts, with all kinds of old doors, wrought-iron gates, fireplaces and an eclectic mix of furniture. She had wandered around the shop happily for about two hours and in the end had bargained for the little mismatched tables and chairs and an enormous chipped, art deco-style mirror. She had been quite proud of herself for pointing out all the flaws – which to her mind only added to their charm – but which had knocked several hundred euros off the price.

She had another few days of training to go at Massimo's and then she'd be ready to open up Café Limoni, as she had decided to call it. The new sign for out front was being delivered in the afternoon. It was a simple wooden sign with an etched-out coffee cup and the name of the café engraved on it. Massimo had introduced her to a local carpenter who was delighted to help her out. He gave her a reduced price for the sign as she was a friend of Massimo's, and said that he would hang it from the front of the building as soon as she was ready to announce the new café.

Now that she had the clutter cleared out it was easy to clean the small space. She spent the afternoon cleaning, scrubbing and polishing and the place practically sparkled by the time she was done. She admired the original tilework as she first dusted, then scrubbed them individually. Even the chips and dents from years of wear and tear suited them and gave them an aged patina. The back countertop had been covered in some sort of hideous plastic protective coating that was probably deemed practical twenty odd years ago. When she peeled it and the layers of glue off, she revealed a beautiful piece of solid oak wood underneath, which she polished to a high shine.

Her supplies would start arriving from Monday and she had allowed a few days to get everything sorted and organised before opening the following Saturday morning. She had found an old set of weighing scales buried under the counter, with individual steel weights that had obviously been used long ago to balance the scales, way back before the more modern versions existed. It too was chipped and rusted in places but she decided that even though she had nothing that needed weighing, it was too beautiful to discard, so she cleaned it up and it now stood proudly on a shelf inside the window.

Saturday was always a busy day in the town, even early in the season, as all the locals were out and about, so she decided that would be the best day to announce her arrival on Via dei Limoni. The thought of it alone made her anxious, and the closer the date got the more nervous she felt. She had forgotten all about tonight's dinner party as she got lost in her work, and only when the church bells struck five did she lock up and dart home to change.

Chapter Twenty-Two

Niamh had no idea how formal or fancy an Italian dinner party would be, so she opted for a simple black dress that she had bought the day she went shopping with Grace in Santa Margherita. God, that seems like months ago but it was only a couple of weeks, she thought as she got dressed. She tugged at the dress to get it up over her hips. 'Yep, you're starting to wear all that pasta you've been eating Niamh,' she said, with an exasperated sigh. 'Please, God, just let it zip up.'

The zip eventually obliged and she pulled it up the last two inches.

'God Bless Coco Chanel for inventing the little black dress – every girl's most trusted wardrobe essential. Now, earrings – I need big, fabulous, dangly earrings to distract people from the fact that after all this time I still can't speak proper Italian.'

She reached Massimo's café just as he pulled up out front. They drove for ten or twelve minutes up into the hills behind Camogli, eventually turning off the main road and down a gravelled driveway to a space that could hold about six cars. Her heels crunched on the gravel as they made their way up the narrow path towards the three-storey villa. It was painted a deep, warm red, in keeping with the collective hues of red, orange and yellow in the town and on surrounding properties in the hills.

At the front of the house a long wooden table sat underneath a pergola loaded with bright purple bougainvillea. It was set for at least a dozen people and was adorned with chunky off-white candles. The view down over the hills towards the bay was magnificent. Niamh couldn't help but stand and stare, captivated by the sight of the town sitting in a semicircle, giving way to the sparkling bay beyond it.

There were some familiar faces from the café, as well as Massimo's family. Massimo took her around to meet those that she didn't already know by name. She cursed herself for not working harder at learning more Italian, as she was limited to basic pleasantries and introductions. Nonna was nowhere to be seen. Most likely in the kitchen, Massimo explained, as she always cooked when hosting people for dinner. He gave her directions to the kitchen when she asked, and she made her way through the elegant villa to find her host.

Nonna was in the kitchen with one of Massimo's children at her feet and the other rolling out pasta shapes at the table under her guidance.

'*Buona sera, Nonna,*' Niamh said, as she handed her the bouquet of flowers she had brought for her.

'*Ah, Nina, buona sera! Grazie!*' Nonna replied with a warm smile.

'I see they are learning the art of pasta-making from a young age,' said Niamh, gesturing to the little one with the rolling pin.

Nonna hesitated and then nodded her head. '*Ah sì, la pasta, sì.*'

'Can I do anything to help you?'

Nonna understood the question and nodded, handing her

an apron. She said something in Italian that Niamh didn't understand, pointing at the child covered in flour at the table.

'I'm sorry, I don't quite understand,' Niamh replied, frustrated that she wasn't better able to communicate.

'She said that the little one rolls the dough so slow, that we will be here all night and not eat until tomorrow.' Niamh turned to find Giorgio leaning on the doorframe. 'So, you know how to make pasta?' he asked, sounding surprised.

'No, not a clue, but she can tell me what to do. I'm a good listener,' Niamh said, smiling.

Nonna handed her a rolling pin and showed her just how far to stretch the pasta before cutting it into small squares.

'You have high ambitions, Nina. First coffee and now pasta. You are brave.'

'Or delusional. I'm not sure what I'm doing here, trying to make pasta at an Italian dinner party.'

Giorgio smiled again. 'Neither do I ... but is funny to watch!'

'Thanks for the vote of confidence, Giorgio. Cheers for that.'

'So, you are ready for everything? To open the café next week?'

'Yes, I think so. I hope so!'

'I think maybe you do not understand what you are thinking?'

He ran his right hand through his hair. She realised that he did that a lot. She couldn't even guess at his age, although to be honest she was never any good at putting an age on people. But if she were forced at gunpoint, she'd probably say late thirties. He had great hair, anyway, whatever age he was. Kind of like that Irish actor who played James Bond before anyone really knew him. Wasn't he from County

Meath or somewhere? I mean, who comes from County Meath? No one! And then, all of a sudden, Ireland has its own James Bond.

'Um, is that a question or a statement, Giorgio? I'm confused. What do you mean?' she asked with a frown.

He continued, in broken English, to explain the critical nature of the short season, the importance of tourists and the tourist season, and so on, but by now she was entirely distracted. How was it, she wondered, that salt-and-pepper hair looked so great on men, whereas women went to extraordinary lengths to camouflage any signs of ageing? She could definitely see some early flecks of grey in Giorgio's hair but she had to admit that it looked good. Women, on the other hand, didn't have the same advantage. Why was that?

'Nina!' he said, with an impatient, loud sigh.

'Oh, sorry,' she said, with a jolt. She wondered how long she had been staring at him and his hair. 'Sorry, I just lost my train of thought.'

'But you weren't saying anything. I was, Nina,' he replied, with another confused frown.

'Oh yeah. That's right. Sorry, what were you saying?'

Giorgio shook his head and repeated his earlier declaration, this time with more emphasis.

'I am asking,' he said, pausing again for effect, 'if you understand what you must do and how difficult it will be with this café.'

'Oh, that!'

'Yes, that,' he replied, his gaze meeting hers.

Niamh stifled a giggle. 'Yes, Giorgio. I think I do – I'm just a bit nervous about it, TBH.'

'What is "TBH"? What does this mean?' he asked, looking perplexed.

'Don't frown, Giorgio. My mother says that you'll get wrinkles if you frown. You know the little ones between your eyebrows? Some people have them so bad that they look like actual furrows between their eyes, like in a field. You know – furrows for growing vegetables.'

She put one finger in the space between her eyebrows and frowned repeatedly to see if she could feel the onset of any furrows.

'Nina, I don't know what you are talking about. I don't know what are these furrows, or the other thing you said before that.'

'What thing?'

'I don't know. You said something about TB ... this terrible disease.'

'What? No, I didn't.'

Giorgio ran his hand through his hair again. 'Yes, yes you did. You were talking about the café. You said you were nervous about it, and then you say something about having TB.'

'What? Are we actually having the same conversation, Giorgio? What are you talking about?'

'Nina, I am not so sure any more,' he said, grinning at her.

Nonna lifted her head from her pasta-making and glanced from one to the other of them, understanding nothing of the words, but following their gestures and expressions.

Niamh's mind raced back through what she could recall of the conversation in her head.

'Oh! Wait! I said TBH!' she exclaimed, putting a hand over her mouth.

'Yes, this was it!'

'*Ha!*' She laughed out loud. 'That's not TB like the disease, Giorgio, it's T-B-H – as in "to be honest". It's short for "to be honest".'

Giorgio was now gesturing with both hands in spectacular Italian fashion. 'So if it means this, then why do you not say this? Why do you say just these letters?'

'I dunno, lots of people say it. I think it's a millennial thing. I think they made it up. It's like a pop culture thing now, you know, like LOL. None of them can type any more, either. I think that's where it comes from. You know, they shorten everything to fit into text messages and then suddenly they all wake up one day and none of them can spell! My uncle works in HR for Apple in Cork. He said it's totally a thing – that they can't spell properly.'

'No, I do not know what you are saying again, Nina,' Giorgio said, shaking his head. 'I think my English is OK, you know? And then you start talking fast like this and I have no idea what it is that you are saying. *Mamma mia.*'

His hands were enunciating every word as if the whole thing were orchestrated. Niamh bit her lower lip and turned her eyes to the ground as she watched the hand-gesture theatre unfold.

Don't laugh, don't laugh, she warned herself, as she tried to quiet the giggles rising in her throat. 'Sorry, yes,' she eventually said aloud.

'Why are you always sorry, Nina? Don't be sorry, just listen to what I say,' Giorgio said slowly, putting his phone on the table and pulling out a chair to sit on.

'You're right, sorry. I mean, yes,' she replied, her gaze still firmly directed towards the floor.

'*Allora*, Nina, is just that the season here is so short, for the tourists. All the Italian people will go back to Milano on the last weekend in August. And, in September you will find only some German tourists here. So you must make all of your money from this café in just a few months from now to the end of August, because after this, it is ... how do you say this ... there is no more.'

'It's over?'

'*Si! Esatto!* It is over!'

'I get it, Giorgio, and I appreciate the advice, but none of this made any sense from the start – not leaving my life in Ireland, not renting a café, not opening late in the season, nothing makes sense.'

'*Si, è vero!*' He agreed with a small nod of his head. 'So, you will change your mind?'

'What? No! Giorgio, nothing I've ever done in my whole life has ever felt so right or so challenging or so goddamn exciting!'

'Ah, so then you will not change your mind?' he asked with a confused look on his face.

'Hell, no!' Nina said with a wide grin.

'But, Nina, you know that you are a little bit crazy to do this, no?'

'*Si*, Giorgio,' she said with a happy laugh. '*Si!*'

He held her gaze across the table for a moment or two, until his concerned expression gave way to a genuine smile that crinkled up the corners of his eyes.

'You are funny, Nina, funny and courageous!'

She felt something contract in her belly. She watched as he gathered up his things. She watched him still as he pushed back his chair from the table. Her eyes followed him as he stood to leave and she wondered what he meant, or what he could have meant exactly. No one had ever before said that she was courageous, nor had they had any reason to, she pondered sadly. She found herself silently willing him not to leave just yet.

'Hey, so how come you know a word like courageous when

you can barely speak English at the best of times?' she said with a cheeky smile.

'Ah, I learn English from many movies!' he said, with an uproarious laugh. 'And all these movies about the war, they have the heroes who have the courage and they must go to war and be the courageous ones! And if they have the courage then they will win.' He looked quite pleased with himself.

Niamh tried to hide a smile at the idea of Giorgio watching some epic war movie and repeating the words and phrases to himself to learn more English.

'*Allora*, now I go. Nina, you have your advice about this place, so as your lawyer and your friend, I have done what is my job.' He stood, towering over her, and tucked his phone into his pocket.

'*Sei coraggiosa*,' he said with a wide smile as he tapped her nose with his finger before crossing the kitchen to say good-bye to Nonna.

She lifted her hand to her nose.

Did the fact that he had just touched her mean anything? she wondered. Did it have any significance? Was this how male and female friendships worked? Rick certainly had never been playful with her, or perhaps he had in the early days, but she couldn't remember it. Could people be playful with each other without it actually meaning anything more?

She repeated the word *coraggiosa* twice under her breath and decided that she liked both the rhythm and the round sound of it.

'*Coraggiosa*,' she repeated softly to herself. She wasn't sure that she was courageous at all, but she liked the fact that some-one else harboured the thought that, for once, she might be.

'Now I will go so that you can concentrate,' he said, return-ing to her side. 'I will go back to the others on the terrace.

Come and join us when you have finished with the pasta. Nonna always leaves this type of pasta until last so that it is made just before the cooking, so I think this will be the last job to do tonight.' He turned and spoke to Nonna in Italian and she confirmed his theory.

'She says that she will keep you only for this job and then you will both join us on the terrace.'

'Will she need help serving? I don't mind helping. In fact I quite enjoy it. Makes me feel useful.'

'No, she always has people to do this part of the evening. How do you say . . . she hires professional people for this? Is this the right way to say this?'

'Yes.'

'Good. *Allora*, she hires people to serve the meal and to clean up, but she insists on cooking and preparing everything herself.'

'Maybe she likes to feel useful, too.'

'Perhaps you are right,' he said with a shrug. 'I had not thought of it like that.'

He left the kitchen, but returned a minute later and handed her a tall glass of champagne. 'No cook should be without a drink in the kitchen. Is bad luck,' he said, and left.

She caught Nonna watching them and she heard her mumble something, but couldn't make it out.

'You won't have one, Nonna?' she asked.

'No! No!' she gestured towards the pasta, indicating that she would wait until this job at hand was complete.

They continued the pasta-making for another twenty minutes, with Nonna churning out at least three times the volume that Niamh contributed. When they had finished, Nonna patted her on the arm and thanked her, then ushered her out to join the other guests on the terrace. She made her way back out through the villa, wondering who she would have the best chance of having a decent conversation with, and hoping that some of the other guests that she didn't know so well spoke some English.

She was surprised to see Franco standing with a glass of wine on the terrace, and she scanned the small crowd to see if Jeffrey was there, too.

'Sorry, Nina, but it's just me tonight,' Franco said with a grin as he caught her glancing around the terrace.

'Hi, Franco,' she said, ignoring the quip. 'What are you doing here?'

'That's my mother over there,' he said, pointing to an older Italian lady. 'She and Massimo's wife are close friends and so we often get invited to Nonna's house.'

'Oh, right, of course. I don't know why I asked, sorry. Stupid question. I suppose everyone knows everyone else in this town.'

'Well, yes, that might be true, but it doesn't mean that everyone is friends, so it wasn't really a stupid question,' he said. 'I hear you were making some pasta in there?'

'Yes, it was great, although I hope you're lucky enough to get some of Nonna's version and not mine. Hers are perfect as you would imagine and mine look like they've had an epileptic fit and are all wobbly.'

'How's the café coming along? When are you opening?'

'Next weekend, hopefully.' Niamh sipped on her champagne.

'I'm only here in town for a couple of days so I'll miss your opening day, but good luck with it! Cheers!'

'Thanks, Franco, that's very kind of you. Oh yeah, Jeffrey said that he would be here in town this weekend. I should have guessed that you'd be with him too.'

'Yes, my partner in crime. He was very disappointed not to be invited to tonight's dinner party. He will be even more disappointed when I tell him that you were here,' he said with a mischievous grin. 'But I believe that you have plans for dinner tomorrow night, no?'

'Dinner tomorrow night? Where are we going?' Giorgio had stepped alongside them and put one arm around Franco just as he mentioned tomorrow night's dinner.

Shit, Niamh thought. Worst possible timing.

'Sorry, Giorgio, but we are not invited. Jeffrey is taking Nina out to dinner tomorrow.' He turned to Niamh and grinned. 'He already asked me what he should wear. I haven't seen him this excited about dinner in a long time.'

Giorgio looked from Franco to Niamh and then glanced down at his champagne glass. Niamh could feel her cheeks get redder by the second. She was glad it was getting dark and she hoped that neither of them would notice. She didn't know why exactly, but it felt wrong to be telling Giorgio all this, and there was no way to politely shut Franco up.

'Ah, I see. You met him at the party, no? At Sara's restaurant?'

'No!' Franco continued, laughing. 'They met one day in Portofino by chance, and then again at Sara's by chance, and then one final time by chance yesterday in Massimo's café! I think it is not just chance, but perhaps fate, no?' He was clearly enjoying this.

'Oh, I did not know,' Giorgio said quietly, glancing at Niamh.

'Franco, it was totally by chance and meeting at your sister's restaurant and Massimo's café was totally normal, as you always hang out there when you are in town.' Niamh tried desperately to tone down the implication that something greater was happening with Jeffrey. 'You're exaggerating, and it's only dinner. It's not a big deal.'

'Well, my dear, this is not how my friend Jeffrey is looking at this. He is very excited about tomorrow night's dinner date.'

Even though she was embarrassed at having this conversation in front of Giorgio, she had to admit to feeling a little bit pleased when Franco said how excited Jeffrey was about dinner. It had been a long time since she had had any excitement in her life when it came to a man. Life with Rick had become pedantic and predictable and he could never have been accused of ever getting excited about the prospect of having dinner with her. Her thoughts trailed off and she tried to remember if it had been different at the start. It must have been, there must have been a spark, but she was damned if she could recall it now.

Her attention was jolted back as they were called to the table to eat. With each glass of wine she got braver with her Italian and had several fragmented, confusing and downright funny conversations. She couldn't remember laughing this much in a long time. The group were warm and welcoming and they wished her luck with her new café, each of them promising to visit.

Two hours or so later she heard a car door close and footsteps coming up the gravel path. Sara arrived, looking as though she'd just stepped out of a couture advertisement, wearing a cream-coloured satin halter neck jumpsuit and carrying a wicker basket that contained several bottles of champagne.

'Jesus, she's like a model,' Niamh mumbled to Franco, who was sitting alongside her. She self-consciously tugged on her dress. It had gotten more and more snug with each course and at this point she was just hoping that the zipper wouldn't give way.

'Yes, I know she's my sister, but even I can see how beautiful she is,' Franco said. 'She used to be a model but got tired of it and went back to culinary school. I think half of her clients go to Sara's just to see her. The male ones, at least.' He laughed.

Giorgio got up to greet her and walked her to the table.

'They look good together, don't they?' she said to herself as much as to Franco.

'They do. A handsome couple, no?'

Niamh pretended to take a sip of wine in the hope of not having to comment further about Sara and Giorgio.

Franco raised his glass to hers. 'A toast to Café Limoni. I hope that this dream will make you happy,' he said with a kind smile.

'*Grazie*, Franco,' she replied, taking a long sip of the champagne. 'I hope so, too.'

Chapter Twenty-Three

At exactly eight o'clock the next evening she reached the narrow little alleyway entrance to Da Paolo's. Jeffrey was already there waiting for her and greeted her with a hug and a large grin. The owner came and greeted Jeffrey and ushered them to their table in the courtyard outside.

'This is adorable. We didn't get to sit here last time,' she said, admiring the small space that held only eight tables.

'I pulled a few strings to get an outside table,' he said with a wink.

He held her chair as she sat at the table, noticing with a smile that a bottle of Franciacorta had been pre-ordered and was sitting in an ice bucket adjacent to them.

'Nice touch,' she said.

'Well, I felt lucky that you agreed to have lunch with me the first time, not to mention dinner tonight, so I wanted to show my appreciation at having been given a second shot,' he replied. 'May I?' He smiled as he tipped the bottle towards her glass.

'I rarely say no,' she said, returning his smile. She realised that it felt nice to have someone pay so much attention to her and she relaxed more into her chair.

Jeffrey did most of the ordering, as he spoke decent Italian.

The menu offered an array of fresh seafood and shellfish, but as Niamh had noticed when she had had lunch there previously, most of the tables ordered the same thing. Da Paolo's was renowned for their daily specials and in this case it was oven-roasted whole fish cooked in white wine, tomatoes and capers.

They chatted easily again over dinner, Niamh telling Jeffrey about her ideas for the café and he telling her about his attempts to secure a job back home.

'I must have applied to about thirty different law firms. The competition for the top firms is really intense – a lot of smart graduates looking for a small number of top jobs,' he said as he topped up their wine glasses.

'Are they all in Canada?'

'No, I've applied to a whole bunch in the US too. New York, Boston, Chicago and DC. Franco has applied to most of the same firms, so in a way we're even competing with each other. It will be tough if one of us gets our top choice and the other doesn't.'

'Stop being such a pessimist!' she admonished. 'When do you find out? I mean, when do these firms start contacting successful candidates?'

'Well, the first round of calls could be any day now. They know that candidates apply to multiple firms, so they are equally driven to lock in their ideal choice of candidate as soon as possible. My guess is that if we're successful in the first round we'll get a call next week. If not, it will be another couple of weeks after that, once they've gone through the first round. It's just a waiting game now.'

'That must be pretty frustrating.'

'It is a bit, because I actually don't know when I'll have to leave here. However, it does mean that until then I get to hang out in Liguria for the summer and that doesn't suck. To be honest it's probably the last time I'll have any real free time for the next few years.' He laughed. 'If you're lucky enough to get into one of the top firms then it means years of long hours.'

Several bottles of local, crisp white wine had followed the initial bottle of Franciacorta when eventually the waiter placed two espressos and a plate of biscotti in front of them. Niamh looked around and realised that they were the last two sitting out there. 'We should go and let these people go home.'

'Oh, you're right. I hadn't noticed that everyone else had left. How about a drink at La Terrazza? I'm staying at the hotel this weekend.'

'OK, that sounds nice, but only if I can buy the drinks – and thank you for dinner. I had a really nice time.'

'Me too, and I think I'm man enough to let a woman buy me drinks,' he joked.

They strolled to the outdoor terrace of La Terrazza and sat with an unobstructed view of the moon, fat and high in the sky, reflecting on the bay below. The waiter brought them two glasses of limoncello, followed by another two on the house, as Jeffrey told her about the various towns and villages she needed to explore locally.

'I better head home, it's getting late. I'll get the bill,' Niamh said, as she reached for her handbag. 'Where ...' she looked left and right on both sides of her chair.

'What's up?'

'Where's my bag?' She looked under the table, stood up and took her jacket off the back of the chair, but her bag was nowhere to be found. 'Oh fuck! I must have left it at the restaurant. It was on the ground next to my chair. Shit. Do you think we can call them?'

'Um, Nina it's one o'clock in the morning and we were the last people to leave. They are long since closed. Don't worry about it. I'll get the check.'

'No, it's not just that, it's my phone and my keys, too. Fuck!'

'The keys to your apartment? Oh shit. OK, let me call the restaurant just in case there's someone there late. I doubt it, though.' He pulled out his phone and looked up the number of the restaurant. 'There's no answer. Do you have a spare stuck outside or is there anyone else in the building who can let you in?'

'No, putting a spare outside would be the kind of thing a smart person would do. I don't qualify for that description. And no, I don't know any of the neighbours in the other apartments yet because I spend all my time at the café, so I haven't met anyone else in the building. I can't exactly go buzzing their doors in the middle of the night. Not the best way to endear yourself with the neighbours, wouldn't you agree?' She wasn't sure why she was being so sarcastic with Jeffrey, as he had nothing to do with it. She put her head into her hands and let out a loud sigh. 'I'm such a fucking eejit.'

'Look, just stay with me tonight. It's not a problem and I promise I won't bite.'

She sat bolt upright. 'No, wait, I could just get another room here for the night.'

'Nina, this is Italy, not America. They don't have twenty-four-hour staff. You'd be lucky to get some night manager who might manage to find a key if you had lost your room key, but check you into a room in the middle of the night? That's not happening. Just stay with me. I'll be good. Come on, I promise.'

'Shit. OK,' she said reluctantly, as she had no other choice, and followed him back to his hotel room.

'Death by minibar?' he asked as he opened the closet door and peered inside at the contents.

'Sure, why not? Why stop now?' she asked with a shrug. She couldn't remember having this much fun in a long time.

'So . . . we have a split of champagne, some dodgy-looking whisky, vodka and a half bottle of red or white wine. What's your fancy?'

'I think I'll stick to champagne, thanks.'

'OK, here you go, you have that. There are glasses in here somewhere,' he said, rooting through the small closet under the television.

'I can't believe I left my bag in the restaurant. I hope my phone won't be robbed.'

'Nah, the staff would have had to go out to clear up after we left so they'll have found it. Don't worry, it will be there in the morning.' He walked up to her and took her in his arms. 'Here, see if a hug will help.'

She was surprised at how bulky and strong he felt compared to Rick, his arms and across his back in particular. He felt good and it felt good to be held properly, even if it felt a little strange. She couldn't remember the last time Rick had held her in his arms like that, which made her feel sad. She lay her head down on his shoulder and sighed again. 'You smell good.'

'Thanks,' he laughed, releasing her from the hug. 'Stop worrying, will you?' he said quietly. He hesitated for a second and then leaned in and kissed her. She felt her shoulders soften. He pulled away from her and looked into her eyes. 'I'll sleep on that sofa thing over there if it will make you feel better. Honestly, I don't mind.'

'No, I don't want you to,' she said, standing on her tippy toes to kiss him.

'Are you sure?'

'Yes. Stop asking me.'

She wasn't sure if the drinks had given her fake courage or if it was the headiness of being kissed by someone new again, but this time she wanted him and didn't feign any moral objections. It was probably a combination of both. She didn't feel drunk, but then again that wasn't really a true indication of her level of sobriety, as most often it was the nights she 'felt fine' that ended in the worst catastrophes. Either way, she didn't care. Here was this tall, strong, good-looking Canadian who was utterly charming and sweet, and he liked her. She hadn't had this kind of attention in a long time.

Why the hell not, Niamh? she thought to herself, wrapping her arms around his neck.

The following morning, Niamh knew immediately upon waking that she was in a strange bed. She could tell by the sheets, which were silky smooth against her skin. They felt like fancy hotel sheets. The fact that she was naked rather than wearing a T-shirt or pyjamas was the second sign that something was amiss. She turned her head and could see that Jeffrey was still sleeping. A pang of embarrassment rushed through her, as she thought back to the night before. Straggly memories like pieces of a patchwork quilt coming together started to float through her mind. Suddenly, she had a mental image of her trying to imitate a pole dancer using the four-poster bed.

Jesus, did I pole dance for him? I'm mortified! she thought with a grimace. You don't do normal dancing well, Niamh, never mind pole dancing!'

She could feel the embarrassment work its way up her neck in a hot flush again. Mortified, she closed her eyes at the memory, struggling to put the remnants of recollections back together into a cohesive picture.

She turned to look at him again. He was sound asleep. Moving slowly and quietly, she gently eased out of the bed. She shook her head again in remorse as she picked up her various items of clothing that had so clearly been discarded in haste.

'Where the fuck is my bra?' she whispered to herself.

She lifted up his trousers and shirt from the floor, hoping to find it underneath.

'Where the fuck is my fucking bra?'

She checked his side of the bed, but there was no sign of it. She knew that if she was to get out of there unnoticed, she would have to be quick. She tiptoed into the bathroom and threw on her clothes. She didn't dare run the tap to splash water on her face for fear of waking him, but instead picked up her sunglasses, her shoes and crept out. She stepped silently into the hall and turned to close the door gently behind her. Her bra was hanging on the doorknob outside the room. In a flash she remembered deciding that they should do like they did in the old movies and hang a white cloth or towel outside the door, and had the bright idea of using her bra instead.

'Oh my God. I'm mortified. How many people have seen this?' she moaned quietly, as she pulled the door shut with a click. 'God forbid you'd just use the DO NOT DISTURB sign, like a normal human. No, you had to hang your bra on the doorknob, like some pornographic lunatic.' She stuffed the bra into her pocket, slipped on her shoes and made her way to the lobby bathroom.

She had black smudges of mascara and eyeliner under her eyes. She did her best to freshen up her face with water and paper towels in the bathroom mirror. 'Looking decidedly lovely today, Niamh. Look at the state of you. If you were on the street, sitting on a piece of cardboard with a blanket wrapped around you, people might throw a coin at you this morning.'

Her hair looked like a dead, matted cat on top of her head, most likely as a result of the half a can of hairspray she had used last night. Washing it was out of the question, though – she would rather die right there than have to massage her head, followed by the pain of blow-drying afterwards, and she didn't have the luxury of the type of hair that you could let dry naturally. She would have to pull out a baseball cap when she got home and hide underneath it for the day. She caught sight of herself in the mirror and decided that she looked like a failed drag queen. 'So much for the skincare routine,' she said, as she slipped back out of the lobby bathroom unnoticed.

She had no money and no way of getting home, so she went to the only place she could think of that was open at seven o'clock in the morning.

'Of course it had to be sunny,' she moaned, as she put on her sunglasses and walked quickly to Massimo's.

Massimo greeted her with his usual sunny smile. 'Ah, *buongiorno*, Nina! You need a coffee, no?' he asked with a grin. His voice sounded louder than normal.

'Yes, Massimo, but I've no money. I left my bag at Da Paolo's last night so I have to wait until they open to get it.'

'Nina, is no problem. They will open at eight o'clock to prepare for the lunch, so you have a half an hour to enjoy your coffee. Or maybe you need two today, no?'

'Yes, maybe indeed.'

She feigned normality as she ordered two cappuccinos. She sat outside in the hope of avoiding further conversation, put her sunglasses back on again and slunk down into the hard chair. She realised that she probably looked quite strange, sitting alone at the table with two cappuccinos, but she didn't care. The coffee was helping. She was massaging her temples when she saw the other chair at her table being pulled back and someone sitting down on it. She looked up to see Emily grinning at her.

'I can spot a hangover at ten paces,' she said, pulling in her chair. 'Good grief, you look wretched. I want to know everything. What did I miss?'

Niamh looked at her and groaned. 'You don't want to know.'

'Oh, I definitely do. Whose coffee is this?'

'Mine.'

'Ah, I understand. It's a two-coffee kind of morning. For future reference, it's best to order them one at a time so the second one doesn't sit there and get stagnant and cold while you try to stomach the first.'

'Agreed, but that would have required a second conversation.'

'Ah, I see. Well, this one looks cold already, so let me buy you a fresh one, then I'm coming back and I want details.' She clapped her hands together in glee at the prospect of some juicy stories. 'You don't look so good. Can I get you anything else?'

'I feel like absolute dog shit,' Niamh said in brutal honesty.

'Charming. All right then, I'll be back with some carbs.'

Niamh leaned forward and put her head on the table. She stayed that way, relishing the cold of the steel table top against her face, until Emily returned with fresh cappuccinos and warm croissants.

'You have a lovely pattern on one side of your face now,' she pointed out.

'Marvellous. Just add it to today's list of visual horrors. What are you doing here so early? You're not an early morning person.'

'I'm going to Milan this morning. Just stopping in for a coffee before the car arrives.'

'I kissed him.'

'What? Who?' Emily asked looking genuinely surprised. 'I was expecting a good story, given the state of you, but there was kissing? What have I missed?'

'What do you mean, "who?"' Jeffrey.' Niamh groaned again and put her head in her hands.

'Good Lord, we haven't had this much excitement in town in ages. Go on!' Emily urged. 'How did this all happen and when?'

'Last night, at Da Paolo's. Well, not actually at Da Paolo's but afterwards, back at the hotel.'

'Go on! What on earth happened? This is very exciting!' Emily grinned.

'I don't know. One minute we were having a great time just chatting and laughing and the next we were kissing.'

'Were you drunk? Was he drunk?'

'I think we had three bottles of wine with dinner and I recall diving head first into his minibar, so yes, I think you can safely say we were drunk.'

'Wait ... his minibar? You were back in his hotel room? How very *Dangerous Liaisons* of you!' Emily threw back her head and gave an uproarious laugh.

'OK, fine.' Niamh placed her forehead on the table and muttered, 'That's not the whole story.'

'It rarely is, my dear. Come on, out with it.'

Niamh lifted her head off the table and looked across at her friend. 'I slept with him,' she said. She sipped her second cappuccino, shaking her head. 'I mean, what got into me? A week ago I had sworn off of men, given recent disasters, and here I am kissing a practical stranger like a dog in heat.'

Emily waved her hand in the air. 'Don't be so hard on yourself. So you slept with him. He's very charming and clearly attracted to you. What's the problem? Stop overthinking it, you were due a bit of a blow-out night.'

'It was so stupid, though. I mean, he's leaving at the end of the summer so nothing can come of it, and now I've gone and slept with someone in a small town. Stupid of me to have complicated things.' She sighed.

'Look, A, he's not from here – he's Canadian and returning home in a matter of weeks, and B, he's not weird, he likes you and you like him. Niamh, you've been pining away over that dreary excuse of a man back in Dublin, even though he's the one who left you, and for some reason you think you belong in some self-imposed purgatory. Have some fun for a while. You're young and single, and so what if he's leaving at the end of the summer? Not every relationship or fling has to be for ever, you know. There's a lot of good in the temporary versions, also.'

Niamh squinted at her through her headache. 'I never thought about it that way, but I suppose I did put myself into some sort of sad-girl, self-imposed prison, didn't I? What a loser I am. Rick is the one who left and I sat around mourning him. God, I wouldn't recognise me if I saw myself like this a few months ago.'

'You know what they say about the best way to get over a man?'

'No, I don't. Grace said something about that a couple of weeks ago too before she left. Go on, then, what's the advice?'

Emily sat back and folded her arms across her chest. 'The best way to get over a man is to get under another.'

'Emily, that's a vile way of putting it. I'm no prude, but God, that's crude.' Niamh squinted across the table.

'Like it or not, it works. If you shag someone else then suddenly you don't have only Mr Misery Guts back in Dublin in your head. Someone else is swirling around in there, naked, too. It's called the Penis Distraction Theory. It creates the little bit of distance and distraction you need to gain some perspective and move on.'

'You totally made that up. That's an Emily Drake theory, isn't it?'

'What does it matter who made it up? It works and that's all that counts!'

'Sounds like you've done a thesis on this.'

'I've done substantial groundwork, yes,' Emily said with a grin. 'Now, I must go meet my driver.' She tossed back the remainder of her cappuccino and stood up. 'I'll call you when I get back.' And with a large wave she was gone.

Chapter Twenty-Four

It felt almost ceremonial to turn the lock in the door and flip the sign around to read APERTO/OPEN to the outside world. Niamh gave a little clap with her hands and made her way back behind the counter, wondering who would be first to cross the threshold. She unwrapped the various dishes of salads that she had prepped earlier that morning and placed them in a series of large, hand-painted pottery bowls in the refrigerated display cabinet. The smell of torn fresh basil, ripe tomatoes and tangy cubes of marinated feta cheese rose up to greet her as she peeled back the layers of plastic.

Loaves of freshly baked ciabatta from the local baker stood ready to make the light, healthy sandwich options listed on her menu. She had purposely kept it short to start with, offering four types of salad and the same number of sandwiches, thinking it would be better to start slowly and get the basics right initially.

The door opened, triggering the bell that she had had affixed. An older Italian man shuffled in, stopped and looked around.

'*Buongiorno.*'

'*Buongiorno,*' she replied with the widest smile she could muster.

He fired off a stream of rapid Italian that she failed utterly to understand.

'Um ... *mi scusi, non ho capito*,' Niamh stuttered, trying to explain that she didn't understand.

'*Lei non è italiano, signora?*' he asked incredulously.

'*Io, no*,' she replied, trying to think how to say that she was Irish, not Italian. 'Um ... *io sono irlandese*,' she said, stumbling over the few words that she knew.

The little old man uttered a grunt that sounded like '*Meh!*' and with a dismissive wave of his hand he turned and shuffled back out of the door.

'Well, this is certainly a positive start,' she mumbled sarcastically as she wiped the countertop for the third time that hour. 'The first person to cross the threshold turns out to be a total racist and flees because I'm not Italian. Well, that's just rude!'

The little bell chimed again.

'*Buongiorno, signora.*'

She turned to see the postman stride across the floor.

'Oh, *buongiorno*,' she said, asking if she could get him anything.

'*No, grazie ... ecco.*' He handed her what looked like her first electricity bill.

'Charming – a rejection and an electricity bill. This has been a profitable first hour. Third time's a charm, perhaps?' she mused.

Her phone pinged with the sound of an incoming message.

Hello, love. Just checking to see how it's going there? her mother wrote. *If you're too busy to chat, I understand.*

'Chance would be a fine thing,' Niamh muttered under her breath as she replied with a whopping lie. *Yes, all good. A bit slow this morning but that's probably to be expected.*

Of course it is, love. Just wait until word gets out and you'll be run off your feet!

Niamh rolled her eyes and looked around the empty café. *Yep! Must run! Chat soon.*

She couldn't keep up a text exchange of blatant lies so she added two kisses and hit send. An hour later a text from Grace interrupted a game of solitaire on her phone.

Hi! Can you talk or are you busy?

I can talk.

Her phone rang immediately.

'Hey! I didn't want to interrupt you. How's it all going? I've been thinking of you all morning.'

'Fantastic,' Niamh replied sarcastically.

'Uh oh. What happened?'

'Nothing. Nothing is what happened. That's the problem. I've been sitting here since nine o'clock this morning and so far I've had a little old man who was lost and the postman dropping off my first bill. So far, it's a complete disaster.'

'Maybe it's just not an early town?' Grace offered.

'Grace, all the other cafés are packed every morning,' Niamh said despondently.

'Well, people probably don't know you're open yet.'

'The postman managed to find me,' she said sulkily.

'Well, he was actively looking for you. How did you announce the opening?'

'What do you mean?'

'I mean what kind of marketing did you do?'

'Well, I have the new sign outside and I put a notice up in a few places around town and I displayed a poster at Massimo's place, stuff like that.'

'But, Niamh, you're not on a main street – that location is

a bit off the beaten path! We stumbled upon it by accident, remember?'

'Are you saying this is a stupid idea?' Niamh said, her voice getting louder. 'Because it would have been great to have heard this before I ploughed so much money into this mad notion.'

'Stop being so defensive and don't get all pissy with me. I'm just saying that you might need to do some more marketing until people realise that you're there, that's all. For God's sake, don't make me regret calling you, Niamh. I'm just trying to help. Like, I don't know ... get a sandwich board and plonk it outside on the street, or put up some kind of notice or advert on the Camogli websites. They love promoting local places like that, don't they? Or, I don't know ... hire someone to walk up and down the pier with coupons or something.'

'Yeah, I suppose you're right,' Niamh agreed reluctantly. 'Maybe I could—'

Before she'd finished her sentence the bell rang and in walked two middle-aged men in shorts and bulging T-shirts.

'Gotta go!'

'OK, good luck!'

'*Buongiorno*,' she said cheerfully as they made their way to a table.

Definitely northern Europe somewhere, she mused, based on the way they were dressed and the massively overgrown moustaches. She gave them a minute to look over the menu.

'Can I get you something?'

'Ah, English?'

'Yes, well, Irish, actually, but I speak English,' she corrected in the way that Irish people the world over always felt the need to do.

One of them looked at her directly, clearly expressing that he didn't give a toss either way.

'We take a beer.'

'Ah ... well, I don't actually have any beer, I'm afraid.'

He looked at her again, this time blankly.

She sighed quietly. 'I'm afraid I don't have any beer,' she repeated slowly, enunciating her words.

He looked towards his moustached friend and back to her again. 'No beer?'

'No, sorry. I don't have a beer licence yet.'

He muttered something in German to the other moustache and they both stood abruptly, nodding to her as they left the café.

'Philistines,' she spat under her breath. 'What? You can't have a bloody sandwich without beer? I mean, I like a boozy lunch like the next girl, but it's a bloody sandwich. Have a cup of tea!'

It was almost another hour before the bell rang again. Niamh leaped up from behind the counter. 'Whatever it is you want you can have it for free, just please for the love of God don't go.' She hadn't intended to say it aloud, it just kind of came out.

She turned to see Giorgio standing just inside the door, a bemused look on his face.

'Of course, it's you,' she said, realising just how happy she was to see him at that moment, but trying desperately not to show it.

'So, this is your strategy to make money with this business? I am not so sure this will be a big success for you. But thank you, Nina, I will have an espresso, for free, no?' he said, his face breaking into a wide smile.

'You're actually going to allow me to make an espresso for you?' she asked, feigning shock.

She bent, pretending to root around for an imaginary something under the counter. Please don't notice that I'm blushing, goddamnit, she thought, as she tried to distract herself with a box of sugar sachets.

'Well, today, I am feeling brave – *coraggioso*, no? And you said it is free, no?'

'Yes. I'm just happy to have something to do, Giorgio,' she replied as she turned to face the coffee machine.

'Why? Not so many customers today?'

'Zero, actually, Giorgio. Zilch. Nada. Niente. Fuck all.'

'Ah, I understand. So you are frustrated about this, no?'

'You could say that, yes.'

'Don't worry, it will take time. You must be patient, Nina.'

'Not my greatest virtue.'

'What is this . . . virtue?'

'Um, it's a strength or positive characteristic.'

'Ah! OK, good. So what does this mean?'

'It means that I'm not the most patient person.'

'Ah, *sì*, yes, now I understand – and this does not surprise me,' he said with a grin, as he tipped back the tiny espresso cup.

He was always immaculately groomed and today was no exception. He wore a single-breasted navy suit, with another crisp white shirt unbuttoned at the neck.

I bet he's the kind of man who gets better looking with age, she thought, staring at him. He had a strong jaw and had the faintest hint of dark stubble. She only realised she was staring at him when she felt a strong urge to tuck a stray strand of hair back behind his ear.

'Exactly how many white shirts do you own, Giorgio?'

'I don't know,' he shrugged. 'I have never counted. A lot, I think!'

'You look good.'

He glanced up at her.

Fuck. Inside thoughts, Niamh, inside thoughts, she told herself in alarm.

'In white shirts I mean. It's a nice shirt . . . on you . . . '

'Ah, *grazie. È da Napoli.* I buy all of my shirts in Napoli. They are the best quality.'

'I think I'm missing the sartorial gene.'

'What does this mean? I don't understand . . . sartor . . . ? What is it?'

'Sartorial. It means good sense of style, a good inkling for fashion.'

'Inkling?'

'Oh, um . . . a good idea.'

'Ah I see. OK. *Bene.* Inkling,' he repeated.

His phone rang. This was the first time the two of them had been alone together in a while, and as she watched him pull out his phone she realised that she had missed his company.

'*Pronto.*'

She loved the way Italians answered the phone. Not by saying hello, but by saying '*pronto*' meaning 'I'm ready.' It was one of the delightful quirks of the language that she had picked up on since moving there. She had even tried saying '*pronto*' herself when her phone rang. She thought it made her sound sophisticated and helped her fit in more, but it had pissed her mother off no end and she had hung up twice, mistakenly thinking she had dialled the wrong number.

'But why do you say that when you answer the phone, Nina?'

'That's how all the Italians answer the phone, Mam.'

'But you're not Italian.'

'I know, but I'm living here now so I'm just trying to fit in as best I can. It's just a habit now.'

'But don't you see that it's me calling? Doesn't my number show up on your screen when I call you?'

Sweet Jesus, this could go on all day, Niamh thought. 'Yes, it does. You're right. Don't worry – I'll say hello in future.'

'Thank God. It's costing me a fortune with all these phone calls and having to hang up every time thinking I've dialled the wrong number.'

Niamh rolled her eyes. 'Yes, OK. I'll only answer in English from now on when you call.'

Giorgio stood and covered the phone with his hand. 'I must go back to the office. The coffee was not so bad. I think you will be OK, Nina,' he said with a wink as he left.

'What a gorgeous specimen of a man,' she said under her breath with a sigh. 'But don't wink at me if you don't mean it.'

She sat and debated whether she should just give up and close up shop for the first day, tempted just to crawl home and get under the covers. 'That's ridiculous. It's your first day, Niamh. Cop on,' she berated herself.

A hesitant knock on the door got her attention. Two short, white-haired old ladies stood outside, peering in through the glass.

'Just please don't be looking for an actual Italian person, for the love of God. Please want something ... anything ... that can be served in English. Please!' Niamh muttered as she opened the front door.

'*Buongiorno*,' she said with a smile.

The two ladies looked at each other and back to her.

'Do you speak English, dear?' one lady asked in a soft British accent.

'Yes, I do.' She held the door open for them.

'Oh, marvellous.'

They made their way to a corner table and ordered some tea.

'Are you here on holidays?' Niamh asked, as she placed two menus on their table.

'Yes, we come every year.'

'Oh, lucky you. Can I get you anything?'

'This caprese sandwich sounds lovely, but is it very big, dear? We don't eat that much for lunch at our age, you know.'

'I can divide it in half for you if you would like to share it,' she offered.

'Oh, that is so kind of you. Would you like that, Louise?'

The other lady had yet to utter a word.

'Yes, lovely,' she replied in a quiet voice.

They sat there for two hours, ordering several pots of tea and enthusiastically proclaiming her caprese sandwich to be one of the best they had ever had. Two other couples wandered in for coffee and sandwiches, an Italian lady for an espresso and a young couple asking if she had Wi-Fi. Too embarrassed to leave when she said no, they opted for a cappuccino and a slice of pie.

The two British ladies introduced themselves as Millie and Louise from London, and said that their friend had told them about the café.

'You heard about it?' Niamh asked, surprised to hear that they hadn't just stumbled upon it. 'But I only opened today.'

'We arrived yesterday from London. Our friend told us about this place last night on the terrace of the hotel. You must know her – Emily Drake?'

'I do,' Niamh replied with a smile. 'That was sweet of her.'

'She told us not to miss it and she was right. Well, good luck to you, dear,' Millie said as they shuffled out. 'See you tomorrow.'

And with that she had her first regular customers.

The next few weeks went by in a blur. Jeffrey had been

surprisingly sweet and had called a couple of times. He had even suggested another dinner date on her next free weekend. Niamh wasn't sure if it was her reluctance to get involved with anyone else again so soon, or the fact that she was totally wiped out every night and relished the thoughts of sleep over anything else these days, but either way she had put him off. She saw little of her new friends outside of the café as everything was new territory to her and when she wasn't opening, serving or closing she was getting ready to do one of those tasks. Word spread around town and some of the younger locals ventured in to try her salads and light lunch options. Unsurprisingly, she didn't do a big trade in coffee apart from the tourists, but the doorbell kept jingling as people wandered in and out. The most significant request that she was unable to fulfil was wine and it quickly became clear to Niamh that if she was to compete with the other lunch options in town she would have to figure out how to get a wine licence. Given that she herself believed that wine with lunch on holiday was more of an assumption than a luxury, she couldn't really blame those who opted to slink back out when they discovered that Café Limoni was, to all intents and purposes, a dry lunch option.

With that aside, she had built up a decent trade and, while she wasn't about to get rich based on the current numbers, she could, for the first time, see the potential of building it to a sustainable future. The older locals were curious and peered through the window, but they were never going to be her customers and after a couple of weeks she learned to make peace with that, and focus instead on those she could attract.

Chapter Twenty-Five

After a particularly long and busy week, Niamh finally turned the key in the door of Café Limoni and headed home, grateful that tomorrow was Sunday and she had the day off. It had been her busiest Saturday yet, and she walked home feeling happy about how the week had gone, and particularly proud about the day she'd had today. This was the kind of satisfaction you could never get from working for someone else and she relished the feeling after all the weeks of uncertainty. She tried to call Emily on her walk home but her phone battery was dead. She had forgotten to charge it all day due to the relentless stream of customers.

Probably for the best, she thought, as she ambled along, or Emily would be inviting me to one thing or another. Instead, I have a date with my fancy new Italian sheets and my black-out blinds.

The following morning, Niamh woke to check the time, and remembered that her phone had died the previous evening. She had obviously fallen dead asleep before she had thought to plug it in. She was standing under the steady beat of the water in the shower when she heard the noises that went on and on. Unable to make out the sound, she turned off the water to listen but it had stopped. She wrapped a towel around her and stepped into the bedroom. Her phone was lit up. There were seventeen missed calls from Grace, four from her dad and dozens of text messages. Her breath tightened and her hand started to shake instinctively from the sudden surge of adrenaline rushing through her body. She sat on the edge of the bed, with the phone cable extended to its fullest, and dialled Grace's number.

'Jesus Christ, I thought you were dead. Where the fuck were you, Niamh?'

'I'm sorry I—'

'I've been trying to reach you since ten o'clock last night.'

Niamh quickly calculated that that would have been eleven o'clock Italian time and she was already asleep.

'I'm sorry. My phone died and I forgot to charge it. What's wrong?'

'Mam is in hospital. It's bad. You have to come home.'

'What? What happened?'

'I don't know, we don't know yet. We're waiting to see the doctors this morning. She collapsed at home.'

'Jesus. Is she OK?'

'They have her wired up to all kinds of monitors at the moment. I was there last night. I haven't been in yet this morning. Robert is away so I have to drop the kids off to a friend in an hour and I'll go in then.'

'But what are they saying?'

'I don't know. I mean, they don't know. They haven't said anything yet. They're doing all kinds of tests. She was in a bad way last night, Niamh.'

'Oh shit. OK, umm, I'll check flights. I don't know when the next flight is but if you think I should go then I'll go.'

'They aren't my words, Niamh. The doctor asked about family and I said you were in Italy. He said to tell you to come home.'

255

She could hear Grace crying quietly on the other end of the phone. She felt the water drip from her hair down her back and onto her shoulders.

'Where's Dad?'

'He's with Mam. He stayed with her last night.'

'OK. I'll check flights and I'll call you back.'

Her hands shook as she pulled out her laptop. 'Come on, Wi-Fi, just fucking work today, OK?' she yelled at the screen.

There was one flight that afternoon but she had no idea what the train schedule to Milan was like on a Sunday.

'What's the goddamn train company name?' she muttered as she typed into her Google search bar. The timetable showed several trains departing Camogli, but all of them had multiple stops and none of them got to Milan in time for her to make the flight. She picked up her phone and texted Emily.

Please call me if you get this. It's urgent. I need your help.

Four minutes later her phone rang.

'What's the matter?' Emily asked.

She started to sob as she explained the situation and relayed the phone call from her sister. 'There's a flight at two o'clock but none of the trains will get me there on time.'

'Stop crying and get yourself together. You don't have all the facts so don't waste your energy on tears just now. Pack a bag and wait. I will take care of this for you. I'll call you back shortly.'

She hung up abruptly and Niamh did as directed. 'What do you pack for something like this?' she wondered as she dried her eyes and stuffed clothes into an overnight bag. Her phone rang six minutes later.

'Giorgio will be outside your door in thirty minutes. He will take you directly to the airport.'

'Giorgio?'

'Yes. I couldn't reach my driver by phone so I called Giorgio. He was at home when I called. He said he would be there in thirty minutes. Now, get your passport and put it into your bag right now. You're upset, Niamh, and likely to forget it. Then go online and buy a ticket for that flight while you wait. Don't leave it until you get to the airport, as that's a disastrous situation to deal with in Italy. And bring a pair of large sunglasses. I'm not joking about that. If you are upset then you're better off hiding behind them rather than deal with nosy individuals gaping at you. Wear them on the flight too if you need to.'

Niamh was nodding as she spoke, grateful to be told what to do. Her mind was swirling with thoughts and worries. She thought about her mother and what condition she was in, she thought about her dad, sitting by her side all night. She thought about her sister frantically dropping the boys off with a friend so she could get to the hospital quickly.

She was waiting downstairs when Giorgio pulled up.

'Nina, I'm so sorry,' Giorgio said as he got out of the car. He wrapped her in a hug.

'Thanks. I'm so sorry to ruin your Sunday,' she said, wiping her eyes dry.

'No, I am happy that I was here to help.' He took her bag and flung it on the back seat. 'Your flight is at two o'clock, yes?'

'Yes,' she said, nodding.

'OK, we will get there in plenty of time. Don't worry.'

'OK. Thank you, Giorgio. I . . . '

'There is no need to say anything. Family is everything, no?'

Her eyes welled up with tears and she clenched both fists and blinked furiously to hold them at bay. She took Emily's advice and hid behind her oversized sunglasses.

He drove like a maniac and made it to the airport in

two hours. The journey was mostly in silence, with only the Italian radio for distraction, most of which she didn't understand anyway.

He parked the car and got out, whipping her bag from the back seat.

'Thanks, Giorgio. I'll . . . '

'Come,' he said, taking her hand. 'I'm coming with you. Do you have a boarding pass yet?'

'No, I just bought the ticket online at home.'

'OK, I will take care of this for you. Don't worry.'

She felt like a little girl as he held her hand, took charge and strode ahead. She hadn't even thought about boarding passes or anything like that. The security liquids rule flashed into her head and she couldn't remember if she had even packed cosmetics or not. Giorgio presented her passport and luggage at the check-in counter. She could just about make out the conversation with him arguing with the attendant that she was not going to check her bag in. He picked it up, shook it, twirled it around, all the while gesturing with his other hand and reeling off rapid, stern Italian.

She didn't know what he said exactly, but the attendant conceded and she took her bag and boarding pass with her.

'You must be at the gate in forty minutes. The entrance to security is there,' he said pointing to a series of empty turnstiles.

'There's no one there,' she muttered confused.

Giorgio smiled at her. 'Nina, it is Sunday. Sunday is for family. No one travels on a plane in Italy on a Sunday unless it is absolutely necessary. So, this means that you will be at the gate in ten minutes from here, from this place. Do you understand?'

'Yes.'

'OK. Now, vodka or whisky?'

'Sorry?' She realised that he had escorted her from the security check point entrance to a little bar just ten yards away as they were talking.

'Vodka or whisky? It is a simple question, no? You have had a shock and a drink will help. Just one, not ten, you understand? Ten will not help, Nina.'

'Vodka, please.'

He sat her down on a chair and disappeared to the bar, coming back with a double vodka, an espresso and some sort of a baguette sandwich sticking out from a paper bag.

'I have to have an espresso too?'

'No, the espresso is for me as I will drive back to Camogli again now,' he said with a small smile and a shrug.

'Oh right, of course. Sorry, I'm not making any sense.'

He sat with her as she drank her vodka. He reached over and stuck the baguette into her bag. 'I am certain that you have not eaten today, and the food on the aeroplanes is ... how do you say ... food for dogs?'

'Dog food,' she said with a smile. She couldn't imagine Giorgio ever eating anything from a plastic airline tray.

'Ah, easy! Yes, dog food. Promise me that you will eat this before you get to Dublin.'

'I promise.' She realised for the first time today that she was hungry. It was almost one o'clock and she hadn't eaten all day.

'Do you need me to do anything for you?'

'No thank you,' she said, staring down into her drink. 'Oh, wait. Can I give you the keys of the café? I had planned to go in there today. Would you mind checking to make sure that everything is OK? There's food and stuff in there and I'm not sure when I'll be back.'

'Yes, give me the keys. I will take care of it. I will take care of everything. Don't worry . . . *va bene?*" he said, taking her hand.

She nodded her response, not trusting herself to speak, and squeezed his hand back in return.

He walked her back towards the security entrance, put her bag on the ground and held her in a strong, tight hug. She closed her eyes wanting to melt into him right there and pretend that none of this was happening. He pulled back from her slowly, put his hands on her shoulders and looked at her intently. Her heart started to pound in her chest.

'*Non preoccuparti*. Don't worry. Everything will be OK,' he said gently, as he leaned forward and kissed her on both cheeks. He put her bag on her shoulder and nudged her gently in the direction of the waiting security attendant. '*Vai*, Nina,' he said, encouraging her to go.

'Thank you,' was all she dared to say for fear that the emotions racing through her would cause her knees to give way or her eyes to flood with tears. She handed her boarding pass to the attendant, who gave it a cursory review and nodded that she could go. She turned and looked back over her shoulder. Giorgio was standing where she had left him, his hands in the pockets of his jeans, watching her. He nodded, indicating in his own way that she should continue on forward and that everything was going to be OK. The fact that he had brought her here, that he had helped her and had taken charge was utterly generous and kind. The fact that he had stayed here until she had left was enough to make her fall apart. He could easily have turned and walked away, but that one small gesture of waiting there and watching her go was the sweetest, most selfless thing anyone had done for her in a while, if ever. She gave a small wave and turned away as she wiped the tears from her face, making her way slowly and with a heavy heart to her gate.

She sat down and pulled out her phone to text her sister and saw that she had several messages. The noise of the airport must have obscured the message alerts coming in. Grace was at the hospital and their mother was stable. Emily sent her best wishes, saying to text her if she needed anything. Giorgio had sent another note simply saying not to worry and he would see her again as soon as her mother was well.

How sweet. What lovely people I've met here, Niamh thought as she stood up unsteadily, ready to board her flight home, uncertain of what awaited her when she got there.

Chapter Twenty-Six

Niamh went straight to the hospital on arrival. Her mother was weak but conscious and happy to see her. She took her hand as Niamh stood alongside the bed.

'I'm sorry to worry you, love, and have you fly all this way home.'

'Stop, Mam, it's fine. How are you feeling?'

'I don't know, to tell you the truth, with all this medicine they have me on.'

She was beyond pale. She was more a grey colour and she looked old and vulnerable lying there in the hospital bed. Grace had warned her before she entered her room, but it was still a shock to see her like that.

'You never think of your own mother as an old woman, but she looks like an old woman in there tonight. Just be prepared for that,' Grace had said as they entered the room together.

She was wired to a drip and all sorts of monitors that Niamh didn't understand. The doctors had said that they needed to run more extensive tests in the morning so that they could determine what had caused the problem. The two girls spent the evening there with Paddy, talking to doctors and nurses and sitting by their mother's bedside.

Later that night Grace said goodbye and went to collect

the boys. 'I'll be in again in the morning, Mam. Have a good rest tonight.' She bent over and kissed her on the cheek. 'Love you.'

'I love you, too. Now go get those gorgeous boys and get them to bed,' Una said with a small smile.

When Grace had closed the door behind her, Una turned to her daughter and motioned for her to sit down. 'I had a visitor earlier, when you were on your flight home. Rick came to see me.'

'Who?' Niamh asked, her mind refusing to function.

'Rick. Your Rick.'

'What? He's not my Rick. Not any more, Mam. How did he know you were in here in the first place?'

'Well, actually he called to the house looking for you and the woman next door was in her garden. She had been there when the ambulance came for me last night so she told him. It was nice of him to come and visit me, wasn't it?'

'Why was he looking for me?' Niamh asked, frowning.

'Well, he said he wants to make amends. That he made a mistake and he called to the house to see you.'

'What did you tell him?' she asked suspiciously. Niamh was afraid that her mother had always secretly harboured a hope that she'd live happily ever after with Rick. 'Boobra must have dumped him. Serves him right.'

'Who in God's name is Boobra?'

'Oh, nothing, forget it. So, what did you tell him? Did you tell him that I've moved to Italy and I'm loving my new life and I'm skinny now? Not that I am, but he doesn't know that so I hope you told him.'

'No,' her mother said slowly. 'I said you were in Italy all right, and he seemed surprised at that.'

'I bet he was. I bet he was very surprised that I was actually

263

living a life somewhere fabulous without him. You know what? I bet he expected me to be at home watching television, depressed, sobbing and eating my way through tubs of ice cream. Ha! Little does he know. Prick.'

'Nina, it's hard enough to talk. Will you stop that rambling and listen to me, for God's sake?'

'Sorry. Go on.'

'I know he hurt you but he told me that he made a mistake and he wants you back. People can change or fix their mistakes. What's the point of all those self-help books and life coaches if people aren't able to change their ways and become better versions of themselves? If you can forgive him for hurting you and if you love him entirely then you have a chance at a good future together, but there can be no room in your heart for any doubt – or anyone else.'

What exactly has Grace told her? Niamh wondered, horrified that her mother might know any details of her romantic life, scant as it was.

'Reluctance and hesitation creates space,' her mother continued, 'and space creates opportunity for problems. Why are you so adamant you don't want him back? Do you really mean it?'

'He cast me aside so easily, Mam, and I heard nothing from him for months.' She could feel herself getting frustrated already with the conversation and she was irrationally angry at the idea that Rick had seen her mother before she had.

'Well, his own family are certainly no role models for great couples. His parents hardly talk to each other and both of his brothers are divorced, but he does love you, that I'm certain of.' Una paused and took a long breath. 'But you must love him back, Nina. You have to be certain. And if you want to build a future with him then you'll have to forget about these notions of Italy. I'm just saying this because you never even spoke to the man after you broke up. You went on holiday and didn't come back. It was all very reactionary and you need to be sure that you made, and are making, the right decision. The fact is he'll never be happy anywhere else. He's too Irish. It's only a certain kind of person can uproot and start over somewhere else. It speaks to strength of character and a quiet confidence in oneself.'

Niamh sat in silence, twiddling with her fingers, unsure of what to say.

Una shifted her position in the bed. 'Will you prop up my pillow a bit for me? You know, Nina, I see how your face lights up when you talk about this village in Italy – what do you call it again?'

'Camogli, Mother.' Niamh rolled her eyes. Her mother was never going to remember how to say it, no matter how long she tried. It was English or nothing.

'Right, yes, that place. Well, I see how you are when you talk about it. You like it there.'

It was said as a statement more than a question, but Niamh answered it anyway, as if to confirm the fact. 'Yes, I do.'

There was silence for a few moments and she could see that her mother was thinking of what to say next.

'Well, that's a good thing, I'm glad you're happy there. People start new lives in new places all the time. Sometimes for no reason except they just ended up there, but other times it's a choice. When it's the right choice it can be good for your soul. Only the lucky few get to live somewhere that feels good in their soul. Most people just survive and live somewhere because that's where they live and they are too reluctant or afraid to change. Young people today have much greater opportunities to change their life and start over, but you need to decide because you can't have both, Nina. If you think there is any chance of you two getting back together then you'll have to come back home to Ireland.'

'But he threw it all away, Mam, so how can I trust him? I heard nothing from him in all this time so how can I know for sure? I mean, how do I know if he was actually the one and he just screwed up and we're really meant to be together and I should stay?'

She could hear the level of hysteria rising in her voice, try as she might to control it, but she hadn't been prepared to talk about Rick and hadn't thought about him in a while. Now, the fact that he was back and saying that he had made a mistake – it was all very confusing.

'Nina, there's no such thing as "the one", that's just a concept made up by movie companies and the people who sell books full of those romantic stories. Surely you know that much? You're a smart girl.'

'Publishers, Mam, the people who sell books are called publishers,' she sighed.

'Well, whoever they are, Nina, they just made that up to drive us all mad searching for that one true love. Then, women all over the country are depressed when they see the movie or read the book and realise that they haven't found true love but they're running out of time, so they marry the next decent fella that they meet. It's all nonsense.'

'Mam, it's not nonsense. I'm not going to just marry anyone.'

'Who said you have to get married? For God's sake, Nina, you just broke up a few months ago. Sit down and take a minute before you go rushing into marrying him, will you? All I'm saying is you should listen to him. Surely everyone deserves a second chance, or at least the chance to be heard? Isn't that what you're always saying? You ran off with this

266

hare-brained notion of living in Italy, and somehow it has worked out and you like it there, but your reaction to all this was just as bad as his. You can't just run from your problems. You have to face them. And I think you owe it to yourself to find out if there is still a chance for you two before you write him off, that's all.'

'I don't know. This is all very confusing. He left and I heard nothing this whole time. Not a word! And now suddenly he shows up and wants to talk and wants me back? Rick and I were great together at one point but even that had kind of faded into mediocrity. And everything else was kind of average, at least for me it was. I mean, he's the one who had the great job. Mine was only OK. He had a great apartment. I was still stuck living at home because I couldn't afford my own place. No offence.'

'Yes, Rick and you were good together – until you weren't, but neither of you handled the situation very well.' Her mother shifted again in the bed. 'Will you hand me that cup of water, please? My throat is getting dry from the length of this lecture.'

'Mam, I . . .'

'Will you stop it, Nina, and just listen to me for a minute. All I'm saying is that loving someone isn't enough. There has to be more than that. Look at all the relationships that the average person has before they settle down with someone – many, correct?'

'Yes,' Niamh answered reluctantly, wondering where this might be going.

'Well, don't tell me that all those people weren't in love at some level or another or at one point in time. Of course, there was love or at least real happiness, otherwise what's the point of being in a relationship? But there has to be more.'

267

'What do you mean?' Niamh asked, now more confused than ever. 'You're starting to contradict yourself, Mam.'

'Nina, you have to love yourself. That's what I'm trying to tell you. That's the most important relationship you'll ever have. You have to be happy within yourself so that you can be happy in the relationship with your partner. You have to like who you are as a person and you have to like who you are in the relationship, because people change a little bit when they are in a relationship, they have to . . . they have to compromise to make it work. And you have to like the version of you that you become with the new person.'

Una handed her back the cup to place on the bedside locker. 'Relationships burn out or end because they didn't have all the ingredients – there was love, maybe, but it's not enough. Attraction to the other person isn't enough in itself, Nina. When you meet the right partner you'll feel good about them but also about yourself and how you act or feel around them.'

'Jesus, this is like something you'd hear on *Oprah* or one of those American talk shows. Where is all this coming from?'

'Don't be ridiculous! It's nothing like those shows on tele-vision where they beat up their relatives. It's pure common sense, if you think about it.'

The nurse stuck her head around the door and nodded in Niamh's direction. 'Ms Kelly, I'll have to ask you to leave now, please. The doctor is on his way.'

'Oh, OK, no problem.'

'Don't worry too much about making the right decision,' her mother continued. 'There's no rush. When everything lines up the way it's supposed to the universe has a way of letting you know. Just give your subconscious a job to figure it out and sleep on it for a while. When you can see no clear reason not to do the thing because it all makes sense to you, then you have to just go for it. Just be true to yourself, Nina. It's OK to go after what you want, and don't settle for good enough just because you should, but weigh up all the options and have all the conversations. If you don't, you're selling yourself short and you'll always wonder what might have been.'

She patted her daughter's hand and smiled, leaning back against the pillows. 'Now, run off home with you and get some rest. I'll see you tomorrow after my tests. They are pretty straightforward so they said I should be back in the ward by about eleven o'clock.'

'OK,' Niamh replied, giving Una a kiss on the cheek.

'Oh, and bring me some black grapes and some Rich Tea biscuits. The biscuits here are terribly boring altogether.'

'Right so,' Niamh said, giving her another kiss. 'I love you.'

'I love you, too. Go home to your father and make sure he has some dinner, will you? And don't forget my biscuits tomorrow.'

Chapter Twenty-Seven

In her dream Niamh was being shoved and pushed back and forth on a boat. The boat was rocking and she with it. She didn't hear her bedroom door open. She had been home almost a week and her life had become a rotation between hospital visits twice a day and cooking dinner in the evening for her father and Grace and the boys.

The tests had shown that their mother had suffered a mild heart attack. There was a blockage in her arteries that would require surgery. It was a fairly routine procedure, but it still posed risks and would require a long rehabilitation period. Una was going to have to remain in hospital for a number of weeks, a reality she was not at all happy about.

Niamh had refused to see Rick, insisting that all her energies needed to be focused on her mother and the rest of her family right now. She knew that in truth she was partly using this as an excuse to delay having to see him, but it sounded entirely legitimate and appropriate, so he could hardly argue. She knew she'd have to see him eventually, if only to gain some closure, but for now her days were on repeat: hospital, lunch, hospital, dinner.

The surgery was finally scheduled for early the following day, which was a cause for both relief and anxiety for all of them. Niamh and Grace left the ward earlier than usual that night so that their mother could get a proper night's sleep before she was taken down to the theatre first thing in the morning. Paddy had arranged to be there early in the morning and the girls would follow a bit later. The doctor estimated that she should be out of recovery by noon.

She and Grace had stayed up late with their dad, chatting by the fire, each of them trying to defer the idea of going to bed only to lie there restless.

She was aware of being shoved, back and forth, back and forth as her brain caught up with her physical self. She heard her name called but it sounded like it came from far away. She woke slowly, opening her eyes to find Grace standing over her, her face wet with tears.

'Mam's dead,' she sobbed.

Niamh's head was fuzzy and dull from lack of sleep. Her eyes were refusing to open properly. She squinted, trying to focus on her sister. She couldn't catch the words that Grace had just spoken. She heard them, but couldn't process their meaning. She sat up with a slow fear creeping through her body.

'What?'

'Mam's dead, Niamh,' she repeated, sobbing loudly now.

The fear swelled inside her with a surge. It started in her stomach and welled up, expanding into her chest until it hurt. Her heart was pounding wildly.

'What are you talking about? I saw her last night. She was fine, Grace.' She sat up on the edge of the bed, her heart pounding loudly in her chest and her ears.

'She died, Niamh. She's dead.'

Grace sat on the bed and wailed, rocking back and forth.

'What the fuck, Grace? Tell me what's going on,' she

shouted in a panicked voice, as an unsummoned rage took hold of her. Her head was pounding.

Grace's voice had a staccato rhythm to it now as it fought with heaves and sobs for a sound. 'This ... morning ...'

'Yes, what? WHAT?' Niamh shook her shoulder frantically. 'WHAT, Grace? Tell me!'

'It was the anaesthetic,' she sobbed. 'It happened all of a sudden ... she had a reaction to it. She went into ... her blood pressure dropped, and she went into anaphylactic shock ... and they couldn't revive her.'

Niamh sat and stared at her, suddenly weakened as the surge of fear she had felt rushed down through her body to her toes. She felt silent tears roll down her face, struggling to understand what Grace had just told her.

It must be true, she thought as she watched her sister fall to pieces alongside her. 'Grace, what? What actually happened? What do you mean?'

'She had a reaction to the anaesthetic ... she was allergic to it. It's rare, but it does happen. They didn't know in advance.' Grace sobbed uncontrollably. 'They couldn't reverse it in time. Her heart just gave out.' She was wailing now, as if the words were puncturing her soul as she spoke them.

'What time is it?' Niamh asked, grabbing her phone. It was half-past eight. Her mother's surgery had been scheduled for seven o'clock. She hadn't even woken up to send her a text message before she went down.

'I wasn't even awake,' she said quietly. 'I was asleep when it happened. I was asleep when she went down to the operating theatre. I was asleep, Grace. I was asleep while she was dying.'

Grace looked at her, wiping her eyes with a soggy tissue. 'What?'

272

'I was asleep while Mam was dying. I wasn't there. I didn't even send her a note this morning.'

The adrenaline in her body was making her nauseous.

'Was she alone, Grace?' she asked, tears coursing strongly down her face now.

'No, Dad was there,' she sobbed. 'He was there early.'

'Oh my God.'

'He just called. Just now before I woke you. He said to go down there right away,' she sobbed. 'To say goodbye while she is still in the room ...' She sobbed uncontrollably again.

'But ... how is she dead, Grace? Why did she die? I mean ... she's in the hospital. It was a standard operation. You're not supposed to die in the hospital?' She sat on the bed, staring at her sister, beseeching her for answers.

'I couldn't really make out what he was saying ... just that it's a rare condition, but some people have a reaction to the anaesthetic and Mam did ... and that they couldn't bring her back.'

'Jesus.'

'I don't know anything else. He wasn't making much sense. We should get dressed,' Grace said, standing.

Niamh remained motionless on the bed. The tears that fell were silent. She hadn't started to sob yet. That would come later. Part of her felt as if she were living in someone else's bad dream. She shook her head hard and put her hands to her eyes. None of this made sense to her. It must be real, yet it couldn't be. She couldn't understand it. 'How is this happening?' she asked herself out loud.

Looking back on it, she had no recollection of getting dressed. She had no memory of her nephews' chatter when she went downstairs, or what she might have said to them. She had no memory of the car journey except for sitting stoically in the passenger seat of Grace's car, her hands clasped together in her lap, staring straight ahead into the grey, rainy day. She had no memory of dropping the boys off at crèche. She wasn't even sure if it was she or Grace who had walked them in. The only memory she had was of standing, frozen at the top of a sterile white corridor. It looked bleak, empty and soulless. The walls were hazy, blurry. It looked as if you could walk down the length of the corridor for miles and not reach the end. She remembered how her feet wouldn't move. She was rooted to the spot, her brain trying to process what was happening, what was about to happen. If she stayed there in that spot, then perhaps it might not be true. Perhaps she could stay there for ever on the precipice of both the corridor and of utter heartbreak.

Grace nudged her forward and her feet obeyed. She didn't know where they were going, only that she didn't want to go there. She wanted to slow down the walk, to not reach whatever door it was they were moving towards. Her heart was pounding again now in her chest. Grace reached the door before her.

How does she know which door it is? Niamh thought, forgetting that they had been there just the night before.

The door was numbered two hundred and twelve.

'Are there two hundred and twelve sick people in here?' she wondered. She couldn't be sure if she had said it out loud or in her head.

Grace hesitated at the door and turned to look at her sister. Niamh just turned to face her and returned the look. There was nothing to say.

Grace pushed through the heavy white door. The room was silent. Their father sat on a grey plastic chair next to the bed. He was holding his wife's hand. He looked up when the door opened and stared at them, his eyes wide with sorrow and loss. He stood and hugged them both. It was then that Niamh turned her gaze towards her mother. She lay there, silent. She looked peaceful, as if she were just sleeping, except for the colour of her face. It wasn't white. It wasn't grey. It was something in between. She didn't know if there was a colour name for it, but it wasn't a normal colour. She wondered if this was the colour that people turned when their life slipped out of their bodies and went elsewhere, or nowhere.

Grace was sobbing quietly, her head bent and her shoulders shaking as she held her mother's hand. Niamh could feel tears course down her face as she stared at her mother, but she couldn't hear any sound. She hugged her dad and felt herself sob into his chest as he did the same.

Grace stood back to allow Niamh the chance to step in beside their mother. She held her hand and leaned in to kiss her cheek.

'I'm sorry I was asleep, Mam. I'm so sorry.' The sobs were hurting her chest now as she gazed down at her mother's face.

That was all she could manage to say as her voice gave out. She surrendered to the tears and the pain that took over and bent her head down into her hands.

The door opened and a nurse bustled in. She spoke but the sound didn't seem to come from her. It seemed to come from far away and reverberate around the room. Niamh had no idea what the woman had just said. Her dad was sitting on the plastic chair, holding his wife's hand again, staring quietly at her face. Grace was sobbing inconsolably. Niamh decided then that she would have to try to be strong. Her mother would have wanted that.

The nurse was twiddling dials on the monitors alongside the bed. They were no longer connected to their patient, so

Niamh figured that she must be shutting them down, readying them to help the next patient. She wondered how much time they had, here in this little room with their mother. She stopped the nurse at the door as she went to leave the room.

'What time . . . um . . . how long . . . ?' She couldn't find the right words to ask the question.

The nurse smiled a kind smile and placed a hand on her arm. 'Take your time, love. There's no hurry.'

Those simple, kind words summoned more silent tears. Niamh nodded her gratitude. She looked back into the room and felt a searing pain in her chest as she watched her father look at her mother. She wondered if this pain was what people meant when they talked about real heartbreak. She had never really thought it was an actual thing, an actual pain, but this pain was real and she had never felt it before. Breaking up with Rick had hurt, but she hadn't felt this or anything like it. She put her hand to her chest at the point of the pain but she couldn't reach it. She couldn't touch it. It was deep inside, some sort of primal pain reserved only for the most truly devastating moments in life.

Her father sat motionless, holding her mother's hand and gazing at her face. He looked as if sadness had wrapped itself around him and he sat there smothered by it. She knew then that she could not watch him say goodbye to the woman he had loved for over forty years. Not here, not in this grim, soulless hospital room.

She had no idea how long they had been in there. The nurse came in for a second time. She never told them that they needed to leave, but Niamh sensed that their allotted time might be running out. She stepped forward and motioned to her sister. Grace nodded and leaned forward giving her mother another kiss goodbye. She was unable to speak.

Niamh leaned down and did the same, squeezing her cold hand. 'I'm sorry I wasn't here, Mam.'

She put her hand on her dad's shoulder as if to coax him from the far away, sad place he was currently languishing in. He looked up into her face and just stared at her, his eyes empty. She didn't think she had ever seen such sadness on anyone's face before. Not just sadness, but heartache. She hadn't known that a face could register heartache. She learned that it could that day. She learned that heartache was a real pain, and that your eyes would hold and show it as an emotion for as long as you felt it.

'We'll be right outside, Dad, OK?'

'OK, love,' he said as he started to get slowly, unsteadily to his feet.

She turned then and walked away. She didn't look back as she didn't want the moment that he said goodbye to his wife, to her mother, etched in her memory for ever.

The rest of the day bled into the following and into the one after that. All she recalled was the constant stream of visitors calling to the house, the low hum of quiet conversations, the steady stream of tea, vodka, sandwiches and cake as visitors both brought food to help the family and stayed to eat and drink with them in consolation.

Her mother hadn't wanted to be waked at home. She had always thought that it was a rather gruesome notion to have the coffin in the middle of the living room.

'You lying there dead and all those people just gawping at you while they have tea, and in your own living room, too. I'll be having none of that.'

Instead there was a rosary and then another prayer service the evening before the funeral. The day of the funeral was grey and wet. Niamh stood alongside her father and her sister under a black umbrella. By the time they had buried her mother and she had reached the car, she was soaking wet, but had no recollection as to why. Had she dropped the umbrella? Had she been holding it wrong? Had the rain been blowing sideways? She didn't know. All she could recall was the sight of the coffin being lowered slowly into the ground as she stood there and tried to reconcile that her mother, larger than life, was now lying lifeless inside that wooden box. She failed. Her brain failed to compute the reality of the situation as she watched it reach the bottom. She had never felt so empty in her entire life.

Chapter Twenty-Eight

For over a week after the funeral Niamh had been actively avoiding any contact with Rick. He had sent several text messages of condolence and had left two voice messages on her phone, but she was not ready to see him, not ready to talk to him. She was living in a haze of pure sorrow and lack of sleep. She hadn't had a proper night's sleep since before leaving Italy weeks before. Finally out of desperation to get out of the house as much as anything, she agreed to meet him at a wine bar in the local village.

'We were really good together. I blew it. I'm sorry,' Rick said quietly as he reached his hand out and took hers. 'I've missed you. I wasn't ready to make a commitment back then but I am now – I know what I lost, Niamh.' He squeezed her hand and looked her straight in the eye.

She sat silently staring down at her hand in his. It felt different.

'We can even talk about moving in together if that's what you want, Niamh.'

She sat opposite him at a tall round table in a quiet corner. A couple of drinks and months of ill feeling sat between them.

'This is all my fault and I take full responsibility. I was wrong. I should never have let you go. I heard that you had gone to Italy with your sister, but then I heard that you hadn't come back. I couldn't believe it. I was kind of shocked, to tell you the truth. It didn't seem like the kind of thing you would do. I felt bad about it, actually, because I had caused it or something.'

She resented the fact that he thought he had so much power over her, enough power to cause her to turn her life upside down and stay in Italy instead of coming home at the end of the week like every other normal person. She sat twirling the stem of her wine glass in her fingers, watching the legs appear on the inside of the glass.

Did he have that much power over me? she wondered. Is that really why I refused to come back home? Was I really just running away from something, from him?

She looked up at him, realising that she had stopped listening to him. 'I'm sorry, what?'

He sighed. 'I'm trying to talk to you here, Niamh, and you're making it very difficult. Can you listen to what I'm trying to say?'

'Yes. Did you know that wine has legs?'

'What?'

'Did you know that wine has legs?'

He looked at her as if she had suddenly sprouted a second head. 'Wine?'

'Yes, wine,' she repeated.

'Yes, I knew that wine has legs. I think anyone who knows anything about wine knows that wine has legs. Why?'

'No reason. I didn't know that, so I guess not everyone on the planet knows that wine has legs, but I know it now. I learned that in Italy.'

'That's great, Niamh. Can we get back to our conversation now, please? I'm really trying here.'

This was suddenly starting to feel like a lot of effort.

'Yes, you were telling me how much you missed me and how much you wanted me back.'

'What's gotten into you? Have I said something to piss you off?' He pinched the brow of his nose between his two fingers and shook his head.

'You mean tonight or back a few months? A few months ago you dumped me with some lame spiritual phrase like "we're going nowhere" or "it's not working" or something along those lines. You sounded like something out of a really bad American sitcom that got canned after the first season 'cause it was so corny. I mean, who says that to a person, Rick? Who actually says something like that?'

It was a tirade now and there was nothing she could do to stop it. It was probably a combination of exhaustion, grief and two glasses of wine. The words just came pouring out as if each of them had their own intention and determination to be heard.

'Did someone tell you to say that? I don't remember you ever being such a massive moron before that night. Did you talk to people about it? Did you get counsel on how to dump your girlfriend in such a way as to avoid mass casualties? What ... I mean, what the actual fuck was all that about?' She drew a breath, and took a large slug of wine, knowing already that she'd regret this in the morning.

'I'm sorry I didn't handle it better. I said all the wrong things, Niamh, I know. I just panicked. I thought we were going too fast and I just felt an urgent need to pull the plug. It was an asshole move, I know, and I'm sorry.'

He stared down at the table and had the decency to appear legitimately remorseful.

'What about the skinny blonde who was all but mounting you in that skanky club?'

'What club? What are you talking about?'

'Town. It's called Town, Rick. That club. I saw a photo of you with Boobra draped all over you.'

'The one at the office who works in Sales? Are you serious? She's just a player, Niamh. She'd throw herself at any man who has money and will look at her. She's desperate to land a man and it shows. She has "Rescue Me" written across her forehead. Do you have any idea how unattractive that kind of shit is to a man?'

'So why was she sitting on your lap, balancing on your balls?'

'Oh for God's sake. She sat on my lap and had someone take a photo of us. It was twenty seconds.'

'So you're telling me you didn't enjoy it?' She realised that she was at risk of sounding like a wounded victim if she kept this up, but the thought of him with the walking cleavage from Sales made her furious all over again.

'She posted that picture, not me. She took the photo and she posted the photo. It was twenty seconds and I haven't seen her since that night except in passing at work. I swear to you, there was nothing more to it than that.'

'I have to be true to myself,' she said, recalling her mother's words and sitting up taller on her bar stool.

Rick rolled his eyes. 'For fuck's sake, Niamh. What does that mean?'

'It's what Mam said to me one night before she died,' she replied quietly, blinking away the tears that threatened.

'Well, I don't go in for that kind of enlightened, self-preservation rubbish. How can you be true to yourself when you don't even know who you are or what you want?' He was frustrated now and signalled the barman for another round. 'You fucked off to Italy for a grand adventure when things weren't going your way. You started a business that you knew nothing about, blew your savings most likely and as usual you didn't know a thing about what it was you were supposed to be doing. You've never even worked in a café, Niamh, let alone run one. That's not the most responsible way to behave.' He sighed loudly, shook his head and ran his hand over the stubble on his chin. She used to like to do that. She had always liked it when he didn't shave on the weekend, and would look like a relaxed version of himself for a day and a half. 'What about your future, your career?' he continued. 'Did you ever stop for a minute to think about that? Christ, Niamh, it's not like there's a Hollywood version of your life where you get to run off to Italy and just start a new life for yourself and live happily ever after. Real life doesn't work like that and you need to think about your goals, your plans and your future. You're a dreamer, Niamh! A dreamer! Hell, I bet you haven't even closed up that café or thought about it, have you? You just left it to run home and now you're sitting here feeling sorry for yourself. You ran away from problems and made a rash decision, and now you've gone and left that one, too. Hardly big-picture thinking, wouldn't you agree?'

She could feel her posture slipping and her shoulders rounding down. Her gaze dropped to her fingers and she started to pick at the piece of loose skin by her thumbnail. Maybe he was right. Maybe it had all been a huge mistake. She did just run away from it all and never stopped to think about how anyone else felt or what it might mean for her future. The barman put two more drinks in front of them. Rick paused to take a sip of his gin and tonic.

'Look, I'm sorry that your mother died, but she'd tell you the same thing if she were here. She'd say that you're just being childish and selfish and you need to cop on and pull yourself together. Maybe you just need to hear this. You've had a mad adventure arsing around Italy for the past few weeks or however long you were there, doing whatever you felt like doing. You've had weeks and weeks out of real life, eating pasta every day and drinking barrels of wine. That's more than most normal people have their whole lives. It's time for a reality check, Niamh. It's time to quit the fantasy, grow up, come home and get back to your real life.' He paused, shook his head and stared at her.

She could feel herself getting teary and she desperately didn't want to cry in front of him. She had way too much eye makeup on, for one, and it would be sliding down her face in a slow, black rivulet if she shed a single tear. This wasn't going to plan at all. She noticed the barman frown slightly as he watched her try to hide her face in her glass, sipping slowly. She had to pull herself together.

Maybe Rick was right. Maybe it was all just a stupid fantasy, running away from her real life like that. It would certainly be easier here. Her family was here and she had friends here. She could even get her old job back if she wanted it. She didn't think she wanted it, though. It was tainted now. She used to be good at that job so there was no reason she couldn't find another one like it. It hadn't been very inspiring, but the pay was decent. Maybe she could apply for a more senior position at a different firm and make a bit more money? She could live at home until she found a place to live, or maybe there was a chance after all for her and Rick. Maybe they could start over. Maybe this time he would be really open to moving in together as he suggested because he wanted her back so much. They could get a place in town like she'd always imagined and she'd buy one of those fancy white sofas with loads of white and beige throw cushions. He'd want a massive television, of course, but they liked to watch movies together, so that would be nice. She'd get a new set of matching serving dishes and dinner set, the fancy kind that her friends would admire when they'd come over for dinner. Maybe they could get a dog? Rick loved dogs, big dogs especially. Maybe if they got a dog they'd spend more time together on the weekends. Maybe instead of going to the gym for hours at a time he'd want to take the dog on long walks in the park with her . . .

His voice cut into her reverie, scattering the mental image of her perfect new living room in their shiny new apartment along the canal, with their Labrador puppy. 'You quit in an email. After everything we've been through. Not in real life, in an email, Niamh! I'll tell you, that made me look like a right wanker at work. I got all kinds of grief over that, especially from the women, saying that I had mistreated you and you were now an emotional basket case. There's nothing wrong with you, Niamh. I hate it when women play the female card, all tragic and vulnerable. It's such bullshit. You made me look like a right prick.'

There it was. It was so obvious that it was shocking. She could feel her jaw drop slightly as her eyes settled on him. The barman raised his eyes from the other side of the bar.

'What are you looking at me like that for? What?' Rick asked, now clearly frustrated.

Another time she'd just have got mad. She'd have been furious and argued back, thrown some mean comments at him and threatened to walk out. He'd sulk, they might not talk on the way home, but eventually they'd apologise the next day and have make-up sex, and while still wrapped in each other's arms would say that they shouldn't argue with each other like that, that they were too good together, and everything would resume as normal and be fine again for a few weeks.

'I made *you* look like a prick?' she asked almost inaudibly.

'What?' he asked, exasperated.

'I said, I made *you* look like a prick? You dumped me. Dropped me without a second thought after four years. And I made *you* look like a prick?'

She started to laugh. The couple further down the bar turned to look at her. She could hear that she sounded a bit hysterical, but she couldn't help it. She wasn't being facetious or trying to annoy him – it actually sounded funny when she repeated it in her head. She slowed her laugh enough to speak.

'It's just funny that you think I'm somehow at fault here for making you look bad at work. And I just realised something. You always have to be right. You always have to be in charge, all put together and in control. You dumping me, that was OK because that was you in control and in charge, but I was supposed to just suck it up and deal with it and return to work like a good girl. Or quit! But I didn't. Instead I . . . how did you describe it? I believe you said that I had "fucked off to Italy for a grand adventure" and in your head that made *you* look bad!'

He stared at her as if she had lost her mind.

'Over the course of the last two drinks I was beginning to think that maybe you were right. It was all a big mistake. I was wrong and you were right. You knew better, as usual. And I just realised, Rick, that this is what you do – you make me feel like a smaller version of myself, like a little girl who doesn't know better. You probably don't intend to do it, and probably don't even know you're doing it, but you do. This has never been a relationship of equals but I never realised it until now 'cause I never really heard it from you so bluntly.'

'Look, Niamh, I don't know what—'

'No, let me finish,' she continued. 'You're a nice guy, Rick, and you're a decent man for the most part. You're successful and good-looking, but I just don't like who I become around you. I somehow let you take charge of everything, including me, and I become a smaller version of myself, and I don't like it. I'm loud and I'm messy and I say the wrong things and I'm not very diplomatic and I'm a little overweight and my feet smell when I wear runners and my eyebrows are too thin. I can live with all that, but I don't want to live a smaller kind of life any more.'

She scrunched her hands into tight fists on her lap and stared down at them, remembering the words her mother had said to her before she died. She looked up into his face with a sad smile, tried unsuccessfully to blink back some tears and said: 'Loving someone isn't enough. There has to be more than that.'

She slipped down off her bar stool and picked up her jacket. 'You were right to end it, Rick. We were good together for a while but we're just not the right people for each other. We're not the "happy ever after" kind.'

He shrugged his shoulders. 'How can you be so sure that there is a "happy ever after" kind?'

She wiped away what were almost certainly black tears by now. 'I can't. But I'd rather try to find it and fail than settle for good enough. Like you said, it's the dreamer in me. Goodbye, Rick.'

It was the most in charge she had ever felt around him.

Chapter Twenty-Nine

The next two weeks went by in a quiet, sad kind of ritual. There was a tangible air of true sadness in the house, dispersed temporarily only when well-meaning visitors dropped in. The number of visitors had been diminishing as people got back to the business of their real lives and left Niamh, Grace and their dad to resume theirs. The house was markedly quieter than before, the only sounds being those made by Niamh clattering about in the kitchen as she pulled together some semblance of lunch and, later, dinner.

She slept late most mornings and awoke groggy and with a headache, having had too much wine the night before, but it was the only thing that gave her solace. If she drank enough then she would fall into an unsettled sleep, but at least it was sleep and a respite from the thoughts in her head. Grace dropped in every evening with the boys and they provided a welcome distraction from those thoughts in her head and the silence that hung in the air. They also brought a smile to her dad's face, the only time she would see it all day, and when they left, it would slip away and he would settle back into a quiet sadness. He was lost without his Una, and there was nothing that Niamh could do to change that.

'That's the hardest part,' she said to Grace one evening

at the kitchen table, after their father had gone out into the garden to tend to his plants. 'Watching Dad trying to deal with being alone, without Mam. They were always together and had their little routines, you know?'

'I know,' Grace said, as she stood and looked out of the window at the back garden. She watched him lift Ben out of his carefully tended flowerbed. 'I don't know what he's going to do, but there's not much we can do to help. He'll just have to get used to it. Old age sucks. Oh God, I hope they haven't stomped on any of his flowers.'

'She wasn't even that old, Grace. She wasn't supposed to die – she was in hospital. Why couldn't they save her? I just don't understand it.'

'Yeah, I know. Poor Dad.' Grace watched him pull up some stray weeds while the boys played chasing with the dog. 'Do you want another glass of wine?'

'Yes please. I'll open a bottle. We finished that last one. Are you staying here tonight?'

'Yeah, Robert is away tomorrow at some match so I thought I'd stay over tonight and keep the boys around for Dad. I better get some kind of dinner started for the boys. What do you fancy?'

'I don't care. Whatever is in the fridge is fine.'

'Well my two terrorists aren't quite that lenient when it comes to food. How about some shepherd's pie?'

'That sounds good. Dad will eat that, too.'

Grace pulled a couple of pots from the kitchen cupboards as Niamh opened a bottle of red wine. 'What are you going to do?' she asked her pointedly.

Niamh sighed and leaned back against the sink. 'I've no idea. I've been kind of playing ostrich and not thinking about it, to be honest.'

'You mean you're in complete denial?'

'Yep.'

'Well, you can't go on like this, you know. Neither can I. Eventually we both have to return to our real lives, altered for ever as they are. I need to go back to work next week and I can't keep coming over here every evening, and you need to decide what you are going to do. As it is, you're living between two worlds. What's happening with the café while you're here?'

'That's the problem. Nothing is happening with it right now. I had no choice but to close it up and get on a plane. That was weeks ago. I put most of my savings into getting set up in Italy. I had to rent an apartment before I realised I might have been able to live upstairs. So, I had committed to it for a month initially and then I got distracted and it was easier to just extend that rather than buy furniture for the place upstairs. Then I had to buy all kinds of stuff for the café, so basically my savings are more or less obliterated. It was slow at the start, obviously, but then I started to get some regular customers, mostly tourists who wanted something other than pasta. I don't think the Italians really get it, but I had some decent tourist trade. But now it is literally just sitting there costing me money,' Niamh said with a defeated sigh.

'How come?'

'Because I still have to pay rent and bills for the place,' she sighed.

'Oh right, of course. Sorry, that was a stupid question. But look, you can go back and start it up again. You said that you had started to get good feedback from people and that the tourists liked it, so just go back and get stuck in again.'

'Well, that's the problem. Summer is almost over now and everyone has told me that once the first week of September arrives and schools reopen, all the tourists are gone. My only customers were tourists. It's all a bit of a mess and I don't actually know what to do, Grace!'

'Wait a minute. What does that actually mean – the bit about all the tourists leaving?'

'It means that there is no business, no customers from September until next April or May. Apparently it's a really short tourist season.'

'But that's ridiculous. Surely that's an exaggeration?' She rapped loudly on the window. 'Ben! Will you for Christ's sake get off that dog?' she roared through the glass. Her father turned around from his rose bushes and said something in the direction of Ben. He stood up and the dog bolted for the shed, with Ben in hot pursuit. Their father shook his head and stared after Ben, smiling for a moment before going back to his pruning.

'It's not. I asked Emily and she agreed. She said the place is pretty deserted in winter, which is charming – unless you are dependent on a stream of tourists to make some money. Why didn't I know this before I signed the bloody lease? I suppose it was a rash decision in the first place. Shit! I've gone and made things even more complicated. What a first-class gobshite I am. What am I going to do, Grace? I don't want to just give up. I don't want to be a failure and have all this hard work come to nothing. I'm demented trying to think of a solution but I can't invent tourists if they're not there.'

'Well, look,' Grace said, stirring onions in a wide pan. 'There's no point beating yourself up over this. You tried something and it didn't work the way you had thought it would. So what? It was worth a shot. It was always going to be a risk, and you knew that, but at least you tried it, at least you took a risk. I've never taken a risk like that in my life. I've always held down the safe, sensible job. This took balls, Niamh, and you should feel good about having tried it at all.'

'I suppose,' Niamh said reluctantly.

'Do we have potatoes?'

'Yeah, I'll get them,' Niamh replied, staring out of the window. 'I just don't know what to do now.'

'Well, you have to go back, don't you? I mean, you still have stuff there, you can't just disappear.'

'No, I know. I have stuff in the apartment and I have to find out what I need to do about the café lease. God, what a mess.'

'Look, it's not going to get any easier and you're wasting money paying for an apartment that you're not in, so just make the decision to go back and close it all up and come back home.'

'It feels like I'm giving up, though. I hate to think that I have to give up after I've come so far!'

'Well, what is the alternative? You said you're practically out of money and nothing happens there for the winter, so what are you going to do?'

'I don't know. It feels like total defeat if I give up and move back home. I really felt like I was starting to get somewhere, you know – starting over, building a new life, and I love it there. But I don't have any more money to throw at it and I can't afford to keep paying the rent and cover living expenses until next May. It's all very frustrating.' Niamh put her head in her hands.

'You can get a new job, Niamh. You can live here and take your time to figure things out. Anyway, it will be good for Dad to have you around.' She opened the back door and roared out. 'BEN! Get off your brother! He's not a horse. You're squashing him. Dad, can you keep an eye on them before they kill each other, please?'

'Ah, they're grand. They're only playing,' he said without even turning around.

'Look,' Grace continued, 'you had a shitty situation to deal with and you got a bit carried away and ran away from your life for a while. No one is going to blame you for that. But you can't fuck up your whole life by continuing to live in denial. It was a good run while it lasted and you got to take a few months out of real life and live some foreign fantasy for a while. That's more than most people ever get to do in their lives, me included. At some point you have to put on your big-girl pants and buckle down to some real work.'

Niamh stopped peeling potatoes and stared at her sister. 'Hang on a second, Grace. I appreciate the life advice but it's not as if I was living out some full-blown fantasy for the past couple of months. I was working my arse off. I fixed that place up and spent weeks on my hands and knees scrubbing. I was in there every morning at six o'clock to get it set up. I had to do everything myself.'

Grace rolled her eyes in frustration. 'I never said that, Niamh. Stop putting words in my mouth. All I'm saying is that you're here lolling about, unable or unwilling to make a decision and you're at risk of fucking up the rest of your life through blatant indecision. If you can figure out a way to make money in Italy for the winter and you're happy there, then by all means go back, but if you can't then you have to accept the fact that it didn't work out for whatever shitty reason, and decide what to do next. That's all I'm saying. And if you don't want to hear it then fine, I'll shut up, but someone had to say it.' She turned back to the stove, taking her frustration out on the pot in front of her.

'Oh Jesus, did I pick a bad time to come back in? Is it safe in here at all?' Paddy joked as he stepped into the kitchen. 'Just so you know, Grace, Ben ate a worm and got dirt all over him before I noticed it, so he's filthy but it's only dirt.'

'He ate a worm? Ah, for Christ's sake, Dad, why did you let him eat a worm? That's disgusting.'

'I handed it to him. I picked it up from the dirt I was digging in and handed it to him and said, "Here, Ben, eat this. It's good for you, lots of protein."'

Grace looked at her father as if he had completely lost his mind.

'For God's sake, Grace, lighten up. It was a joke. Of course I didn't give the child a worm. I turned around and he was already chewing on it with one half of the thing hanging out of his mouth. He found and ate it all by himself and swallowed it before I could stop him. Many children before him have eaten a worm and lived to tell the tale. What's for dinner?' he asked with a small chuckle as he washed his hands in the sink.

Niamh caught Grace's eye and made a 'knife across your throat' gesture indicating that they should drop the subject of Italy now that Paddy was back in the house.

'We're making shepherd's pie, Dad,' Grace replied cheerily.

'It smells good so far, fair play to you girls. You learned from the best – your mother always made a great shepherd's pie.'

The two girls stopped still and looked at him.

'For the love of God, will the two of you stop it? You can't bring her back, you know, and I'm not going to stop talking about her. If she were here now she'd give out yards to the both of you for being so soft. Your mother made a great shepherd's pie and that's all there is to it. We can't pretend that the woman never existed.'

'No, I know, Dad, it's just that, well . . . we thought it might be upsetting to talk about her, that's all,' Grace said slowly.

'Well, that's just daft, Grace. What are we going to do? Never talk about your mother again? That makes no sense at all. We all miss her and we wish she was still here, but she's gone and you can't pretend otherwise.'

It was the most direct and no-nonsense speech the girls had heard him give in weeks and it gave them both pause to take a sigh of relief. Maybe they didn't have to walk around on eggshells after all. Maybe their father was actually coping better with their mother's untimely death than they were.

'Now, just make sure you do a decent job with that shepherd's pie and don't cock up her recipe,' he said, eyeing the two of them over his glasses. He picked up his newspaper and headed for his armchair. 'Oh, and you better bring those two in out of the rain or they'll be like little mud babies out there.'

'Christ!' Grace said, bolting for the back door. 'I didn't know it was raining.'

The two were covered in earth and mud and would need to be deposited directly into the bathtub. 'Can you do dinner, Niamh? I have to power hose the garden off of these two.'

'Yep,' Niamh said, grateful for the change in conversation and the distraction. She turned down the heat under the pot of boiling potatoes and pulled open a drawer. She took out an old black apron and shook it out of its wrinkled coil. She made as if to place the strap around her neck but hesitated. She could see her mother standing there in the kitchen. She held the apron to her face and could smell her mother's perfume from the last time she'd worn it. She closed her eyes and inhaled deeply. She could feel tears sting the backs of her eyes and blinked them away furiously. For all the casual comments her dad had made, she knew instinctively that seeing her get upset was more than he'd be able to handle right now. She folded it and placed it gently back into the drawer. It was just too soon, she decided, as she closed the drawer and turned her attention back to dinner without the apron. 'Some things just take more time than others.'

Chapter Thirty

Niamh loved it when Grace stayed over with the boys as it gave her a purpose and provided a genuine distraction from her thoughts. She could tell, though, that Grace was anxious to get back to her regular life and routine, but that she was making herself available to give Paddy time to readjust to the new order of things.

Both of them were surprised at how well he seemed to be coping. They had expected a lot of sadness, which there was, of course, but they had also expected him to be listless and helpless, and neither condition was apparent in any shape or form. He got up each day and busied himself with his little jobs around the house, he took a stroll into town each day to get the paper, do a bit of grocery shopping or just drop into the local café, and he tended to his plants and garden religiously each afternoon. He was doing a decent job of keeping himself occupied.

Niamh was beginning to think that of the three of them, she was the one having the hardest time moving on and accepting things as they now were. She suspected that being in limbo between her old world here in Dublin and her new world in Italy wasn't helping and that the sooner she made a decision either way, the better off she would be. Although she was reluctant to admit defeat and relinquish her new life in Italy, she was beginning to see how easy it would be to slip back into a regular life again in Dublin.

She had no intention of going back to her old job – that was one thing she knew for sure – but she had to admit that it would be so much easier to find something else here in Dublin, rather than try to reinvent herself in Italy. While she hadn't been in love with her previous job, she had been good at it and she knew now, with the benefit of hindsight and the perspective that her escape to Italy had given her, that she could apply those skills again in another company. She had good experience at a growing startup, and that whole industry in Ireland was booming. From her experience at PlatesPlease she knew that there was a ton of funding being invested in new and exciting companies, and most of them were going through major hiring spurts. She knew a little about raising money, recruiting employees and running the administrative side of things, so that experience was bound to have some value.

Niamh also had no intention of going back to Rick. That notion had now been firmly ruled out in her mind, and if she were to remain in Dublin she would rather do so on her own terms and start over. In fact, being more independent for a while might not be the worst thing she could do. She would dust off whatever friendships she could still claim post-breakup, and get out there and make new ones to replace those that she lost to Rick.

She had a place to live here at home until she decided what she wanted to do in the future. Her dad was easy to live with and wouldn't bother her, and he made for pleasant, easy company in the evenings. She suspected that it would be good for him to have her around, too, rather than being left all alone in the house. All in all, the signs seemed to be pointing towards returning home and starting over, but to do so meant that she had to deal with all of her responsibilities in Italy and close everything down. There was no way to avoid it. She would have to go back and deal with it all in person.

Now that the peak summer period was over there were plenty of cheap flights to Milan. She could just take the train from there to Camogli, spend a few days packing stuff up, deal with any necessary paperwork and finances, ship a few things back to Ireland and fly back. She figured that she could get everything done in a week. She could ask Grace to stay over for a few nights while she was away so that Dad wouldn't be on his own. I'll ask her the next time I see her, she thought.

She opened a bottle of wine and poured herself a glass as she started to get dinner ready for the two of them.

'Is it just the two of us tonight?' Paddy asked, as he walked into the kitchen.

'Yep. Just us.'

The house was decidedly quieter without Grace and the boys. Niamh put on one of her mother's aprons, one that hadn't been worn since it had last been laundered and so it wouldn't torture her with the scent of her mother's perfume. Before sitting at the table her father poured himself a glass of milk.

'Have you thought about when you'll go back to Italy? I was only thinking today that you must be home about a month at this stage. Am I right?'

'Yes, just a couple of days short of a month, actually,' she said as she placed their plates on the table. 'I don't know. To be honest I was beginning to think that maybe it was all just a mad idea in the first place and that I'd be better off here at home, especially with everything that's happened.'

'What do you mean "with everything that's happened"? Surely everything that's happened is even more reason to get back to your new life out there? I thought you were loving it?'

'Well, I was, but then when I had to come home I had to close the café and now it's heading into winter and it's a bit of a ghost town from what I hear.' She hesitated, wondering how much she should tell him.

'Go on . . .'

'Well, I've used up most of my savings in getting the place ready, and paying rent and all that, and I had only just opened the café when I had to come back, so it's all kind of screwed up now, and I don't really have the means to survive through the winter, 'cause I can't get any other job.'

'So you're just going to give up?'

'No, it's not that I'm giving up. It just didn't work out in my favour. The timing was wrong. It took me too long to get the place open so I missed most of the summer, and everyone tells me that there's no one around for the winter. Some things are just not meant to be, Dad. I tried and it just didn't work out. Anyway, it will be easier to get a job here.'

'So you *are* just going to give up, then. I'm surprised at you, Niamh. You were never a quitter.'

'That's a bit unfair, Dad.' Niamh waggled her fork in the air. She took a sip of wine and stared down into her plate.

'Niamh, life is unfair. Shitty things happen to good people every day. No one said that any of it was going to be easy or fair, but you haven't given this thing in Italy a fair shot.'

She looked up at him, wondering where this was going.

'It was unfortunate that you had to come home, but that's just how it played out. Your mother was sick, you came home and then she died, and you've been moping around here ever since. Do you think that's what she'd want for you? Do you think she'd want to see you around the house like a lunatic with the hoover, cleaning the place as if your life depended on it, instead of going out and making your mark on the world?'

'Well . . .'

'Of course she wouldn't,' he continued. 'She'd want you to go back there if it would make you happy, and that is what I want too. You've no business living at home with your father at this hour of your life, looking for another job that will just pay the bills.' His voice trailed off and he sat quietly for a moment, staring into the distance. 'You only get a few chances in life, Niamh, and I think that this move to Italy, mad as it was, might be one of them. It made no sense whatsoever when you announced that you weren't coming home, but that meant that you were following some kind of dream or something in your heart.'

Her mother had always been the one to give them lectures on life and share her many nuggets of wisdom, but her father rarely did so. Her mother's ramblings must have rubbed off on him.

'Most people don't get to live like that, Niamh. They grow up, get a job, get married and have children or not, and that's them for the rest of their lives. Most people don't get to just up sticks and start over somewhere else, because they have too much tying them down at home. You don't, so for the love of God will you do something with that privilege?'

'But won't you be lonely here at home in this house, all by yourself?'

'I'm actually thinking of going over to my brother in London for a while.'

'Oh,' she said, unable to mask the surprise in her voice. Her father hadn't been out of the country in years.

'Sometimes life is unkind to us Niamh. Your mother is

gone too soon and there's nothing we can do about that. But if this teaches us anything it's that life is too short, and that we should take advantage of every day we've got. So, I'm going to see my brother for a while and you should get your head out of the clouds and think about what you actually want to do, not what you think you should do. And, for God's sake, don't go choosing the easy way out, it rarely ends in happiness.'

She couldn't think of a single thing to say, so she just nodded.

'They were grand lamb chops, weren't they? You did a fine job of those, I must say.' He put his knife and fork on the plate. 'My show is about to start now. I'll put on the kettle. Will you have a cup of tea?'

'I will, thanks,' she said slowly.

She sat at the kitchen table as her dad made two cups of tea and slowly realised that she had just been given the permission she hadn't known she needed to follow her heart and choose the unknown over the practical, to leave her life in Dublin, to do it properly this time, and try again. She knew then, sitting at the kitchen table in her mother's second apron, that she had to go.

Chapter Thirty-One

While it had been hard saying goodbye to Dad and Grace, Niamh felt a sense of relief that she had made the decision to return to Camogli. She had booked a one-way ticket to Milan, but the flight landed too late to connect with the last train to Camogli, so she would have to spend the night in the city. She had texted Emily for a recommendation as she herself knew nothing about the city and had spent no time there. The last time she had arrived in Milan had been with Grace, whose company had paid for a car service to meet them at the airport and take them to Liguria.

'Not so this time, Niamh,' she said to herself as she sat down to text Emily. 'This time you're on your own. No fancy car service for you. You'll be putting your broke arse on the train or the bus!'

To her surprise, Emily came right back to her. She was not normally one to live on her phone. In fact its usual state was to be on silent, stuck in the bottom of a handbag or in a drawer.

Oh, perfect! I'm going to be in Milan then, too. I am badly overdue for a haircut, and I'm staying for the weekend. Oh, this will be fun! I know exactly where you must stay. Let me check to see if they have availability. I'll be right back!

You travel to Milan to get your hair done? It's a two-and-a-half-hour drive each way, Niamh texted back, unsurprised at the fact, but still amused by it.

As soon as she sent the message, her phone rang. It was Emily.

'Good Lord, it takes far too much energy to type like that. When did people stop actually talking on the phone?'

'Well, you're just slower than most because you insist on using proper English and correctly spelled words all the time. Most normal people use abbreviations, so it's faster.'

'You know, if we're not careful we'll all become a nation of savages, unable to form complete sentences any more. As for my hair appointment – we live in a fishing village. A fishing village, where real people actually fish and then others actually cook that fish for a living. Not a whole lot of experienced hairstylists milling about the place.' Niamh could just imagine Emily shaking her head at the other end of the phone at the thought of even contemplating a hair appointment anywhere but at a top salon. 'Now, I just spoke with a good friend of mine who happens to be the hotel manager at the most divine property and I reserved a room for you for Saturday night. It's my treat. I'll just be so relieved to get you back to Italy that it can be cause for a little celebration. What time does your flight land and where?'

'I land just after six o'clock at Linate airport, and you don't have to pay for my hotel room. Thank you but—'

'Perfect, you'll be at the hotel within twenty minutes, darling, and the hotel room is already taken care of. You can change and we'll meet for drinks. I'll book dinner for about eight-thirty. Oh, how fun! This will be fabulous. I thought I'd be wandering the halls of the hotel all by myself. This is so much better!'

Niamh doubted that Emily would have been wandering the halls of any hotel on her own as she always seemed to be surrounded by keen suitors or elegant friends. 'Is the hotel really fancy?' Her question was met with silence. 'OK, sorry,' she continued. 'Stupid question! Don't worry, I'll pack accordingly. Do I need a cocktail dress, or exactly how fancy are we talking here?'

'You won't need a cocktail dress, no, but the hotel is very elegant and the restaurant we'll go to is exquisite.'

'Got it,' Niamh said, rolling her eyes. She shook her head, realising that the majority of her new cute outfits were still in Camogli. It wasn't as if she had needed to pack any for the trip back to Ireland. 'I'll have time to shop for something tomorrow before I leave Dublin.'

'Marvellous. I'll send you the hotel details. Send me your flight information so that I can track your flight. See you tomorrow night, darling!'

Niamh smiled as she ended the call. She wouldn't have considered Emily the type to track a flight. In fact she would have gone so far as to suggest that she wouldn't know how. She certainly wasn't the most technically adept individual, but in a short period of time Emily had become a good friend. She was the one person who had checked in with her regularly over the past month in Dublin. She had even offered to come to the funeral, but Niamh had dissuaded her.

Her plane landed a few minutes early. She stepped off the plane and onto the steps leading down to the tarmac. They had been directed to a gate in the older section of the airport, as yet unrenovated, and so most of the flights disgorged their passengers onto the tarmac. She stood at the top of the steps and took a deep breath of air. It smelled foreign yet familiar. She made her way through to baggage reclaim, grabbed her overweight suitcase from the luggage carousel, heaved it up onto a luggage trolley and proceeded to customs.

Before leaving Dublin she had made several trips to Penney's – Ireland's preferred, inexpensive shopping solution to any impending night out or holiday. The average piece of clothing ranged from eight euros to thirty euros, yet she had somehow managed to spend almost three hundred euros in each of two Penney's locations. All the new autumn and winter lines were in and she figured that though they were radically inexpensive, no one in Italy would have them, or know just how inexpensive they were in reality.

As she exited through customs, she was greeted by a man wearing the typical uniform of black suit and tie, with a black cap. He was holding a sign with her name on it. She giggled to herself as she said hello. So that's why she wanted my flight information, she thought. The driver took her luggage trolley and she stood a little taller, swinging her handbag over her shoulder. She just wished it were summertime right now so she could fish out an enormous pair of sunglasses and act like she was fabulous or wealthy.

Chauffeur-driven cars had priority parking so they were in the car within minutes, and before she knew it she was whizzing through the city. She stared out of the window as the city morphed from functional business districts to increasingly elegant streets and buildings. The car slowed to a crawl in less than twenty minutes, and the driver turned onto Via Manzoni and pulled up in front of an imposing limestone building.

The five-storey hotel stood proudly on a corner, with double doors leading to a plush, elegant lobby. A highly polished brass plaque on the wall read LEADING HOTELS OF THE WORLD. She knew she had seen that plaque somewhere before and she gasped as she realised that this was the same group that the hotel in Santa Margherita had been a part of. If that experience was anything to go by, then she was in for a treat.

She checked in and was graciously welcomed as a friend of Signora Emilia, and escorted to her room on the fourth floor. A note from Emily and a bottle of Franciacorta was on ice awaiting her arrival.

'Welcome back! Open this and imbibe as you get changed. I'll meet you in the lobby bar on the ground floor at seven o'clock!'

'Don't mind if I do,' Niamh said with a grin, as she popped the cork on the champagne.

Unsurprisingly, Emily was holding court at the bar when Niamh arrived downstairs. As she made her way through the lounge she was relieved to see that she hadn't overdressed, but in fact could maybe, at a stretch of the imagination, pass for being as glamorous as the other ladies in the room tonight. She had picked up a capped-sleeved black sequinned dress that fell to just above her knees. It shimmied as she walked and, given its shift pattern, it was very forgiving. She wore a pair of new nude heels and walked slowly towards the bar to ensure her feet wouldn't slip out of them. Maybe that's why celebrities always walk slowly and purposefully, she thought. Maybe they're just trying not to fall out of their shoes.

Emily turned and saw her. She jumped down from her bar stool and hugged her tightly. 'Welcome back, darling! So good to see you!'

'You too! This was a great idea!' Niamh turned to greet the two men in suits and stopped short. 'Giorgio!' she said in utter surprise, and with just a little too much enthusiasm. Her breath caught in her throat. God, he looks good, she thought to herself, hoping she wouldn't blush.

He looked equally as surprised to see her. 'Nina! *Buona*

sera. What are you doing here?' He stood up and kissed her on both cheeks.

'I'm on my way back to Camogli. What are you doing here?' She glanced at Emily, who shrugged and raised her eyebrows as if to say this was all perfectly normal.

'I am also on my way back to Camogli. I arrived from America this morning. I have been to visit my brother in Chicago.' He hesitated for a second, glanced at the other gentleman and then said quietly, 'Nina, I am so sorry for your loss.'

'Thank you,' she said with a small smile, as she looked down at the floor. 'If it's OK, I'd rather not talk about it. I can't yet. I don't mean to be rude.'

'No, no, of course not. I am sorry. I understand.'

She saw him glance at Emily awkwardly. Emily knew better than to bring up the subject of her mother at this time, so instead she introduced her to the other gentleman at the bar. 'Niamh, this is my dear friend Antonio. He is the general manager of this wonderful property, a firm favourite of mine.'

'It is my pleasure,' Antonio said, taking her hand. 'Emilia is too kind, but she has been a very good friend for many, many years now and one of our best clients.'

'Less of all that talk of many, many years, darling, if you please? It never does a lady good to highlight the years.' Emily smiled as she sipped a Martini. 'Niamh, darling, what will you have to drink?'

'Oh, umm, a Martini sounds great, actually.'

'My pleasure, *signora*,' Antonio said as he motioned for the barman. 'We are delighted to have you stay here with us. If you need anything at all during your stay, please do not hesitate to contact me.' He handed her his card. 'Emilia's friends are always welcome here, and now you are a friend too.' His

English was flawless and he was impeccably dressed. 'Now, I will leave you all to catch up. I will see you later this evening, no?' he asked with a nod and a smile towards Emily. She tipped her glass in his direction and smiled back at him.

'Cheers, darlings!' she said raising her glass to Niamh and Giorgio.

'Cheers,' they replied in unison.

'You look wonderful, my dear,' Emily said as she leaned over and patted her friend on the knee.

'Yep, amazing what dropping five pounds will do for those second and third chins,' Niamh said with a grin. 'Can't say I'd recommend it, though, the grief diet that is, pretty miserable actually.' She bit her lip and stared down at the floor, regretting the fact that she had brought it up at all.

'Well, you look marvellous, that's all, and it's great to have you back. Isn't it, Giorgio?'

'Yes, she does. You do,' he said, staring at her. 'I almost did not recognise you when you walked in.'

'That's just because you've never seen me in sequins and mascara,' Niamh joked, grateful for the abrupt change in conversation. 'You usually see me buried under layers of dirt and dust.' She had meant it flippantly, but the word 'buried' slipped out before she knew it. Fuck, this is hard, she thought. How do you carry on as if everything is normal and behave appropriately when every other thought drifts back to your mother's funeral just weeks ago? She could feel tears threaten, but she refused to let them win right now. That could wait until later when she was back in the privacy of her own room. She pretended to drop her handbag and moved to get it, only to bump into Giorgio's head, who appeared equally keen to jump to attention in order to change the direction of the conversation.

'Ouch, shit,' she mumbled, rubbing her forehead.

'*Dio, io,*' he uttered, doing the same.

'Are you all right?' Emily asked, feigning concern. It was clear that she was trying not to laugh outright. 'Not to worry, drink up, it will numb the pain.'

Niamh sat back on her stool, rubbing her forehead.

'I'm so sorry, are you OK?' Giorgio asked, touching her forehead.

'Yes, I'm fine,' she said with a smile. It felt good to be out in a nice social setting with these good people. She hadn't realised how much she had missed it. 'This hotel is stunning, Emily.'

'Yes, I stay here all the time. When I heard that Giorgio was arriving back this morning I insisted that he join us. I just hope you aren't too jet-lagged, darling?'

'No,' he said firmly. 'I don't believe in jet lag. I don't accept it.'

'Spoken like a true lawyer,' she joked. 'So, how was your trip?' She turned to Niamh and placed a hand on her knee. 'Giorgio just walked in about four minutes before you did, so I've heard nothing of his trip yet. Speak, darling, speak!' She raised her Martini glass to her lips.

His face broke into a wide grin. 'I am going to be an uncle!' he said, with an effusive hand gesture.

'What? Really, but, how?' Emily asked, her tone of voice causing Niamh to cast her a second glance.

'My brother, he has met someone in Chicago. They have been together for almost a year and now she is pregnant.'

'That's terrific. I didn't even know he had a girlfriend out there. Did you know?'

'No, I knew nothing. He didn't want to say anything until he was certain that this was, you know, real, that it would work – especially after Lena.' A look of sadness crossed his

309

face momentarily. His brother's loss probably reminded him of his own subsequent loss too, Niamh thought.

'Yes, of course, that's understandable, darling. How wonderful.'

Giorgio's grin reappeared almost immediately. 'And now she is to have a baby, and I am to be an uncle! It makes me so happy!' He raised his glass to no one in particular.

'I didn't know you liked children so much,' Emily commented, narrowing her eyes slightly. 'Is this new?'

'No, I always wanted children, and if I can't have them of my own then this will have to be good enough.'

'If you're not careful, darling, that grin might become permanent and people might accuse you of actually being happy.'

'It is wonderful news, no?'

'Indeed.' Emily seemed genuinely surprised at his reaction to this news.

'That's fabulous, Giorgio. When is she due?' Niamh asked.

'Ah . . . in the spring. She is two months pregnant. I will be a spring uncle!'

'I know what it's like to have little nephews. You're going to be a great uncle.'

'*Salute!*' he said, raising his glass again. His happiness was almost infectious.

'All right my loves, we should make a move soon,' Emily said, changing the subject. 'We can talk more about this over dinner. Our car should be out front by now. Finish up your drinks and I'll meet you both out front in five minutes. I need to grab my wrap from my room.'

She moved through the elegant crowd with ease.

'She has a way of walking that makes it look like she's gliding or something, doesn't she?' Niamh said quietly as she watched her leave the room.

'Yes, she is a very elegant woman.'

They were both staring after her now.

'I was surprised to see you here,' Giorgio said, turning back to face her. 'I was not sure that you would return to Italy.'

'I wasn't either, to be honest. I only decided for real a couple of days ago. It was hard, you know? Part of me wanted to stay at home for my dad's sake, and the other part of me wanted to come back here, so it was hard to decide in the end.'

'So what made you decide to return?'

She realised that she had probably never had as long or as real a conversation with him before this. She certainly hadn't had his attention for this long before, and she found his presence intoxicating. She wanted to admit right then that he was part of the reason she had wanted to return. She had tried to deny her feelings for a long time, but realised on her return to Ireland that it wasn't only the country of Italy she had missed. She had missed Giorgio, too. She wanted to say that she hadn't expected to fall for someone else so soon, but she had. She wanted to tell him that, foolishly or not, when she visualised herself in Italy, he was always part of that picture. But she knew that she couldn't or, at least, shouldn't. He was with Sara and she had to accept that, reluctant as she was to do so.

'Well, it was something my dad said. He said, "Your mother would want you to go out and live your life, not sit around here moping", or something like that.' She looked down at her hands and fiddled with her fingers, willing herself not to get teary.

'Your father sounds like a kind and sensible man,' Giorgio said kindly. He reached over and placed his hand over hers. 'You are lucky for this reason, no?'

Her eyes welled up with tears despite her best effort. 'Sorry,

311

I thought I'd do a better job of holding it together. I didn't mean to get all teary and emotional,' she said, wiping a tear from the corner of one eye. 'I'll pull myself together, I promise.' She took a deep breath and sat up straight.

'Don't apologise for being sad. You have every right to sadness, just as you do happiness. Now is a time for some sadness. The time for happiness will return again soon.'

Sensing that she needed a shift in tone, he stood up from his bar stool. 'In the meantime, how about we choose happiness, just for now, over dinner? I will tell you about my plans for being an uncle. It would be a shame to cry onto our plates, no?'

She laughed despite herself, and got up from her stool. 'Yes, that would be a shame. Your English is getting better, Giorgio!'

'I have been learning a little,' he replied, and held out his left elbow for her to take.

She glanced up at him and all she could see was a kind smile on a handsome face. She hesitated for just a second, and then she accepted the genuine gesture and linked her arm through his. Emily was waiting for them at the door. Niamh saw her eyes drop for a split second down to her arm linking through Giorgio's and could have sworn she saw the faintest hint of a smile. She couldn't be certain, though, because a second later Emily waved at them wildly and swept out through the door into the waiting car.

Chapter Thirty-Two

Niamh had forgotten to close the blackout blinds fully before collapsing into bed at one o'clock in the morning. Slatted bands of light crept slowly across her bed, inching their way towards her pillow. She had fallen into a deep sleep as soon as her head hit the pillow, and had barely moved in the night. The hotel room was cast in the soft white glow of early morning light and she lay there quietly admiring her elegant, monochrome surroundings. Even though she was exhausted, she felt relieved to be back in Italy.

She sat on the edge of the bed, willing herself to stand up. The past few weeks had been an emotional minefield and today somehow felt like a new beginning, a fresh start. She was back and, although she felt a pang of nervousness about what lay ahead, she was cautiously optimistic. She had to figure this out. Shaking her head to dislodge the last of her sleepiness, she felt as if today were symbolic in a way. She padded barefoot to the bathroom.

'I've got to figure out how to work these bloody Italian radiators,' she muttered as she put a hand on the ice-cold old cast-iron radiator. It had an old dial that only went on or off, meaning that you either remained cold or you had screaming hot steam hissing and screeching from the pipes. The noise had been too much for her as she'd got into bed in the wee hours earlier this morning, so she had twisted it to off.

The hot water rattled in the pipes now as she ran the shower. It coughed, spat and splattered its way out, as if resenting the fact that it had to do anything at all. At first it was too hot to step into and then gradually it got cooler until it turned cold. She had read somewhere once that Jennifer Aniston only took three-minute showers, so she felt that three minutes should be enough for her, too.

'You look like you slept in a ditch, Niamh,' she said to her reflection in the bathroom mirror. 'If today is symbolic of a fresh start back in Italy then you need to look the part,' she mumbled quietly as she stood under the pulsating showerhead.

Thirty minutes later she spotted Emily at a window table in the ground-floor restaurant, sipping on a cup of steaming hot tea – a British tradition that she had refused to relinquish on moving to Italy.

'Did we order more champagne when we got back here last night, darling?' Emily asked with a smile.

'Yes, we did,' Niamh said. 'It was a great idea at the time! I'm exhausted.'

'Good Lord, where is your spirit this morning? You're in Milan, darling! So much opulence, so much elegance, so much fun!'

'Where's Giorgio?' Niamh asked, sipping on a freshly squeezed orange juice.

'He was up and out early. He was meeting some friends for breakfast. Now, the plan for the day is as follows. The car is picking us up here at four o'clock. I have my hair appointment this morning followed by a spot of shopping. Let's meet for lunch, shall we?'

'OK, that sounds good.'

'Just get out and take a walk. There is shopping to be done and you're in the right neighbourhood! Every shop you could wish for is right here.'

Niamh had a feeling that Emily's idea of shopping and hers were two very different creatures. She decided she had been right later that morning as she strolled past the high-end labels and couture shops. Not an H&M in sight. Even Zara wouldn't get a look-in here, she thought, as she wandered the narrow, elegant streets of the Montenapoleone neighbourhood. She happily passed the time wandering the neighbourhood until lunch, when she followed the directions from the concierge to reach the restaurant that Emily had reserved for them.

Niamh smiled as she reached the entrance. It was inordinately elegant – not that she had expected anything less. A narrow, wrought-iron door led from the street down an arched alleyway that opened up into a small wine bar. The wall opposite had two sets of double French windows that opened out onto a charming courtyard. Ivy and wild roses grew up white trellises and three-foot urns held ancient olive trees. It was the epitome of understated Italian elegance.

Emily had already been seated at a corner table in the courtyard, her back to the fragrant roses on the wall behind her, facing the elegant crowd of diners. She wore a beige cashmere coat and oversized sunglasses, her hair piled atop her head in an elegant chignon.

'I had to start with a glass of something chilled. Won't you join me?' Emily said as Niamh took a seat across from her.

'Yes, that sounds lovely. This place is beautiful, Emily,' Niamh said, taking in the scene around her in the courtyard.

'Yes, it's one of my favourites here in the city. The menu is short and simple, the food is all local and they only serve what is in season.' She turned to the waiter, who was seating

315

Niamh at the table. 'Can you please bring another glass of this?' she asked, raising her glass and drumming her perfectly manicured fingernails on it.

'*Certo, Signora Emilia, subito.*'

'I wasn't sure what your preference might be, so I hadn't ordered a bottle yet. Now, take a look at the menu and let's order. I'm famished.'

All the items on the menu were small plates. The menu was designed with tasting and sharing in mind, with dishes that could be sampled and shared amongst friends.

'For such a fancy place, this menu is surprisingly simple,' Niamh commented.

'It is. The chef is very talented and the focus is on the produce as opposed to overtly fancy dishes. I think it's only a matter of time before she gets a Michelin star for this place. I love their wine list, too. They have the most amazing selection of wines by the glass here, which is quite a treat.'

They ordered a selection of dishes, including late summer tomatoes and burrata, fusilli pasta with wild mushrooms, garlic and thyme, and grilled baby quail. Each item listed on the menu came with a suggested wine pairing, which they elected to have.

'So I'm guessing that we're not in any hurry and that this is going to be a long lunch, then?'

'Yes, darling, the best always are. Cheers!' Emily said with a smile as they clinked glasses.

Overhead outdoor heaters kept the chill from the September air. The high surrounding walls fashioned a kind of natural amphitheatre, cocooning the sounds of chatter, laughing and the clinking of glasses and crockery, creating a warm, buzzy atmosphere. Emily was always easy company and Niamh could feel herself relax more with every sip of wine. Knowing that she didn't have to worry about making her way around a still as yet strange city, or deal with public transportation to get back to Camogli made it all the easier to sink into a sense of relaxed comfort and enjoy every moment of the lunch. The idea of slipping into the back of a chauffeur-driven car and having someone else take care of everything was very appealing right now.

Each of the courses were delectable, but even more interesting were the wines they were paired with, some of which Niamh had never heard of before.

'I love this wine list, so many local choices ... I've always been into wine – I think I told you that – but most of these bottles you just can't get outside of the country. Some of them I've never even heard of and I thought I knew a lot about wine.'

'Very perceptive of you, Niamh. This place is actually renowned for its wine list. A lot of these wines come from small producers and are never mass marketed or exported, so the only way you'll find them is to drink them at the source. That's rather the beauty of it.'

'I'm really impressed. I know the usual suspects like the big-name, famous wines from Tuscany and Piemonte, but I didn't realise there were so many little local producers and local wines.'

'Most people don't until they come to Italy. The big winemakers are like merchants in any business. They've got marketing dollars and savvy and they take a few good bottles and mass-promote them to large markets. It's merely "Marketing 101" in its simplest form. So what you see outside of the country are wines from big producers with big influence. The small, local producers just don't have the marketing dollars to compete but they are still excellent wines.'

'It's a pity there's nothing like this in Camogli, isn't it?

Although I suppose places like this are usually only in big cities.'

'Well, I suppose that's part of the attraction of the best cities – a wide variety of great restaurants, cafés, wine bars. I mean, shopping you can get anywhere, but some cities do food and wine better than others. It's why I come to Milan as often as I do. It's elegant, refined, cultured but yet it's relaxed, and it's nothing like as frenetic as other major metropolitan cities. I like the pace of life here.'

'I can understand why,' Niamh said, sitting back in her chair and looking around at the contented faces of the other diners. 'It's just lovely here. I mean, I love Italy in general, and have definitely fallen in love with Camogli, but I had no idea that Milan was such an elegant city. Everyone talks about Rome being so beautiful, but you don't hear as much about Milan.'

'No, it's rather misunderstood, actually, but that's part of its charm because as a result it's not as overrun with tourists. It's much more of a local city and feels very Italian. Once you get under the skin of Milan it's actually rather like an onion that keeps revealing layers and layers. It's most definitely my favourite Italian city and you're beginning to see why.' Emily smiled as she turned her attention back to the menu.

Niamh sipped on her wine and let her mind wander. They sat in silence for a few minutes, each of them lost in their own thoughts.

The quail course arrived and, just like the other dishes before it, was beautifully presented. Another waiter arrived at the table and poured each of them a glass of Barbaresco. Niamh swirled her bulbous glass around and around on the white tablecloth and inhaled deeply. She watched the orange-brown hues of the wine circle the glass and, holding the glass to her nose, closed her eyes and inhaled the earthy scent. Taking a sip, she looked across the table towards Emily.

'Delish,' she said, precisely. 'I've never met a bottle of Barbaresco that I didn't love, but to be honest it's not that easy to get in Dublin – only in the fancier restaurants. I went a few times with Rick for special occasions, but he wasn't that into wine so I never really got to experiment as much as I'd have liked,' she said, thinking how long ago that all seemed now.

'My sentiments exactly, my dear. Barbaresco doesn't get enough credit in my mind. It's always overshadowed by its more popular neighbour Barolo, but there is an earthiness to Barbaresco that I just adore.'

'That's exactly the word I was thinking when I tasted it. It's like you can actually taste the earth, or maybe you can smell it, I'm not sure, but either way it's there. Do you know what I mean?'

'I do, and I agree. Divine,' Emily said, taking a long sip of the luscious red wine.

'Camogli needs a place like this. I know it's only a little village, but wouldn't it be lovely to have a place like this to hang out in, with great wines? You know, a local spot that wasn't a restaurant, just a wine bar – and Liguria has such great local wines. I'd never heard of most of them either until I got there.'

'That's true,' Emily replied, swirling her glass on the table. 'To get a glass of wine anywhere you have to beat off the tourists at the restaurants. And even the restaurants with tables outside on terraces are more likely to seat people who want to have dinner, not just drink wine.'

'Unless it's you, of course,' Niamh laughed. 'I can't imagine anyone refusing to seat you ever – Camogli or elsewhere!'

Emily laughed. 'I should hope not! Thank God for La Terrazza where we go for Aperol spritz at sunset. That's about

319

the easiest place in town just to get a drink.' She picked up her wine glass and looked across at Niamh. 'What?' she asked. Niamh was staring at her in the oddest way. 'You have a very peculiar look on your face, darling. What is it?'

'No,' Niamh began slowly. 'It's just that I think you're right. There is nothing even close to this in Camogli apart from La Terrazza and that's part of the hotel. Other than that the only place you can go to have a glass of wine is a restaurant. In fact, I think that the best selection of wines by the glass is at your apartment, Emily.'

Emily laughed. 'You're probably right.'

'But seriously,' Niamh continued, leaning in across the table. 'What if the café wasn't a café? What if it was a wine bar instead? I mean, change it up and set it up as a proper wine bar?'

'Do you know?' Emily leaned back into her chair. 'I think you might be on to something. This wine bar idea has appeal for both locals and tourists alike, so you wouldn't have the same problem of relying merely on summer traffic. And Lord knows, as you correctly stated, there isn't a decent place to go and get a drink without them wanting to force-feed you pasta or fish. And that, my dear, is an opportunity. Plus I love the idea of being able to go somewhere fabulous, that's not my apartment, and drink great wines!'

'Why didn't I think of this the first day?'

Emily shrugged. 'Sometimes the best ideas take time.'

'Do you really think I could pull this off?'

'Niamh Kelly, where is the enthusiasm and excitement of mere minutes ago? Don't let the old, hesitant you creep back in!' Emily admonished. 'Of course you can pull this off!'

'You're right, you're right. Sorry,' Niamh said in agreement. She sat up straight and folded her arms in front of her on the table. 'OK, where do we start? I have to change the place enough that it doesn't look like a wannabe wine bar. It has to look legit, and I'm on a budget, so I have to do it all on a shoestring. Last time around I went all in but now I'll have to prioritise, so I'll have to be really smart this time. What do you think?'

'I think it's probably quite simple, actually. You just need to reconfigure the inside so that it looks less like a cheerful café and more like a soulful wine bar, you know, colour scheme and soft furnishings, things like that. Then, get rid of the existing menu and food displays and offer something simple, something more suitable to a wine bar, like this.' She pointed to the small snack menu that stood on the table. 'And stock up on great wines!'

'And if I offer a fabulous selection of wines by the glass that locals can't get anywhere else in town, then I have something new and shiny to offer.'

'Exactly! Ooh, how very exciting!'

'But isn't it impossible to get a licence to sell wine? I tried when I opened the café but I couldn't get one.'

'Nothing is impossible, darling. It will just take a bit of time and will require that we approach the right people.'

'What do you mean?'

'Italy is about as corrupt a first-world country as any and there are still officials not opposed to greasing the tracks a little for you, in return for an incentive. Also, there are the normal channels to go through for all the oceans of paperwork, and then there are other channels that one can use, to ensure a faster, smoother result. It's simple. You just didn't know the right channels to go through. You were an outsider who filled out an application form. Nobody cared. It was a standard rejection and that was that.'

'I have no idea what you are talking about, but it sounds like you know how to make this actually happen?'

'Everyone does. You just have to ask the right people the right questions. Most European countries are bureaucratic to the point of exhaustion. You just have to know the right people and the right channels.'

'So you're fairly sure I could get a wine licence?'

'I know you can,' Emily said with a wink. 'This isn't my first time dealing with Italian bureaucracy so I've already learned what not to do, and who to recruit to help smooth the way.'

'Unreal. I never really stood a chance with the café, did I? I had no idea about anything, least of all how local politics worked.'

'Don't beat yourself up. It's the same the world over. There are easy ways to do things and hard ways to do things. You just chose the latter because you didn't know any better, that's all.'

Emily had a knack of making everything sound less complicated that it was. She seemed to go through life effortlessly, but whenever they talked about anything tough or challenging, Emily would always refer to 'hard lessons learned', as if she had personal experience of them. Niamh didn't know if she was just a great orator of other people's struggles and victories or if in fact she had lived through so many challenges, and learned so many lessons, that everything now was truly effortless.

'Now, the first thing you are going to need is advice on how to approach the legal application with the local council. Know of any good lawyer that we could seek advice from?' she said, a slow smile spreading across her face.

'Giorgio?' Niamh asked, wide-eyed.

'Precisely. He's not corrupt but he knows his way around

the system, he knows everyone in the council and he has some friends in high places. That should be our first conversation.'

'You're actually serious, aren't you? You really do think that I can turn the café into a wine bar and pull this off,' Niamh said, a wave of emotion rising inside of her.

'It was your idea, darling. I believe in jumping all over an opportunity when it presents itself and this sounds like a great opportunity to me. Plus, I don't really see any other options if you want to remain in this country, and I'm quite certain that you do – am I right?'

'Yes,' Niamh replied emphatically. 'More than anything.'

'Well then, that's settled. We have some work to do, don't we?' With that Emily waved for the bill and fished her sunglasses out of her bag. She picked up her phone and tapped at it for a few seconds. 'The driver is waiting outside.'

'Was he just sitting waiting for you the whole time?' Niamh asked, amazed that Emily had so many people at her beck and call.

'I pay him to do that. You can solve many problems by throwing money at them, darling. It makes life so much easier,' Emily replied, grinning as she stood up from the table. 'Excellent lunch, and we're leaving here with a Plan B for Niamh Kelly. Not bad for an afternoon's work, wouldn't you say?' She picked up multiple shopping bags and swept through the restaurant gracefully, leaving a trail of turned heads in her wake.

Niamh walked quickly to catch up with her, wondering if she would ever possess the grace and charm that Emily had in spades. As she tripped over the handle of a woman's handbag on the ground and bumped into an adjacent chair, she rolled her eyes and thought, most likely not.

Chapter Thirty-Three

Niamh turned the key in the door of Café Limoni as the sun started to come up. The little streetlamps cast orange shadows in random patches across the cobbled street. The door creaked open, the sound reverberating in the early-morning silence. She stood, taking in the scene around her. It was exactly as she had left it. Thoughts of the last time she'd stood here in the café came flooding back. The rush the next day, the desperation to get out of there and get to the airport, the crush of worry she had felt in her chest. They were now replaced by thoughts of the hospital visit, the funeral and the weeks that followed. Everything flashed through her mind like a movie projector at high speed. She didn't even realise that she was crying.

She switched on the overhead light, the sharp jolt of the bulb stinging her eyes. There was a fine layer of dust on each of the tables. She ran one finger across the table closest to her as she walked by it, watching her finger leave its trace as she went. She stood behind the counter, running her hand across the tiles. The place had the musty smell of an old property that had been closed up for too long. She knew she should fling open the windows and let in the autumn breeze, but instead she sat on the stool behind the counter and put her head into her hand, suddenly feeling overwhelmed. She pressed the backs of her wrists hard into her eyes until she saw circular rings pulsating in the darkness behind her eyelids. The last conversation she'd had with her mother ran over and over in her head and she wished she could just pick up the phone and call her. But she couldn't, and with the pang of loss she felt the physical ache again in her heart.

'Cop on to yourself now, Niamh,' her mother would have said to her in her no-nonsense voice. 'You have work to do and it won't get done with you sitting there feeling sorry for yourself.'

She smiled, despite herself, at the memory of her mother's way of wrapping up words of encouragement in words of minor admonishment, wiped her eyes with the backs of her hands and started cleaning. Small clouds of dust rose from each table as she made her way around the little café.

The door burst open. 'I brought baguettes and coffee from Massimo's!'

Niamh jumped up with a start to see Emily standing just inside the doorway, her nose scrunched up in disgust.

'Good Lord, Niamh, open some windows. It smells like old men's shoes in here!'

'What are you doing here? It's eight o'clock in the morning.'

'I couldn't sleep.'

If Emily noticed Niamh's tear-stained face, she didn't show it. She placed the paper-wrapped warm baguettes on the countertop.

'Seriously, Emily, what are you doing here? You're not a morning person. You don't do early mornings.'

'Well, it's quite simple, darling. The sooner you transform this place into a wine bar, the sooner I'll have somewhere

325

lovely to drink great wines that is not my own apartment. I was too excited about this whole wine bar notion to stay in bed, and I figured you might need coffee.'

'Fair enough.'

Emily stood, hands on her hips, and took in her surroundings, as if looking at it with fresh eyes for the first time.

'It won't take much at all to convert this place into a wine bar. To be honest I think all it really needs is a drastic shift in ambience. Kill the overhead lights, bring in an overabundance of lamps and candles, paint the walls a moody colour and get some top-quality wine glasses.'

'What's wrong with the colour of the walls?' Niamh asked, aghast at the thought of having to paint them. 'I thought accent pieces might be enough to change the look of the place, no?'

'Well, darling, first of all, white is too clinical for a wine bar. It is perfectly fine for a café, early morning, lunch, bright, sunny and shiny and all that, but people won't frequent a wine bar until evening, and you need to create the right mood. I think a nice cool grey colour would work very well in here, and it's trending in all the great interiors magazines. Cool grey, that is. And secondly, you didn't have to paint the place last time around. You just dusted it off and touched it up. So, I'm sure it's desperately needed at this point. This is not the time to be cheap, darling. It will show.'

By now Emily was pacing the room downstairs, pointing out things that had to go and things that had to change. Apart from the idea of having to repaint the walls, Niamh was actually relieved to have someone with strong opinions to suggest what she needed to do.

'We'll have to have some kind of spectacular, over-the-top wine display for dozens and dozens of bottles. We don't want to have confusion or uncertainty about what this place is. I think the only answer is to get one custom made.'

'What?' Niamh cried. 'We need a custom-made wine cabinet? Are you mad? That would cost a fortune.'

'Not at all, my dear. I know someone locally who can make it out of regular wood and we'll have it painted and scuffed – kind of shabby chic. What do you think?'

'As long as you know what you're doing, that's fine by me. I wouldn't know where to start.'

'Now, one other thing. Why don't you move in upstairs until you get back on your feet financially? Get rid of the Airbnb and stick in a bed upstairs. I think it's ideal given that there is already a bathroom and it would save you a small fortune. What do you think?'

'No, you're right. I had thought about doing that and getting the place all cleared out and then, well, you know ...' Her voice trailed off.

'Yes. Quite. You got distracted.' Emily stood up and closed her laptop. 'Well, Niamh, you're just going to have to grab hold of this one by the arse. Own it! Things were different before and you didn't have to try to think at this level, but now you do. You need to conserve what finances you have left to get this place up and running. Just terminate your Airbnb rental, which you are fully entitled to do with sufficient notice, and move in upstairs. I really don't see any other way around it. I can talk to them if you like.'

'You can?' Niamh asked, her mouth agape. 'Would you? I don't even really know them. I'd be so grateful.'

'Yes, of course. They are good people. I'll have a chat with them and explain the situation. It won't be a problem.'

'If you can that would be marvellous. It would be great to be able to live upstairs. Thanks, Emily, I really appreciate it.'

'Not at all.' Emily gave a casual wave of her hand. 'Now, what are we going to call the place?'

'What about just calling it "The Wine Bar"? You know, so when people ask, "Where are you going?" the answer would be "to The Wine Bar".'

'I love that idea! We'll need to get a sign made for outside, and a logo. We need to decide on an opening night and then promote the hell of it around town. Anything else that I'm not thinking of?' Emily asked, tapping her fingers against her bottom lip.

'I don't think so, except for the obvious.'

'What's that?'

'The wine?'

'Oh right, yes, of course. I'll come up with a plan for the wine to get us through opening night, at least, and I'll see if we can get some time with Giorgio today or tomorrow. We'll need his help with the licence and probably getting a sign made and hung if we're to open in a couple of weeks. Remember, it doesn't have to be perfect for the launch, just fabulous. There is a difference, you understand!'

'Yes, I'm learning that.' Niamh smiled, pulling on a pair of rubber gloves.

'Now, I'm in desperate need of another coffee, so I'll dash. Come to my place for lunch. I'll have lunch ordered in for us and we can get online and order all your lamps and candles and other supplies. I think the place needs some cool art-work, too. We can do all that over lunch. Say one o'clock at my place? I'll have a plan figured out for the wine by then. In the meantime, you get stuck in here and get rid of any glaring signs that this was ever a café. Stick everything in a corner for now in case Giorgio wants to keep some of the marginally valuable stuff that was here before you, but otherwise, it all goes. *Va bene?*' Emily had a wide grin on her face. It was clear that she was enjoying this.

'*Va bene*, OK,' Niamh agreed with a nod.

'God, I hadn't realised how bored I was until I started thinking about this project. This will be fun, darling! See you at noon.'

Apart from ducking out for a cappuccino around ten o'clock, Niamh got stuck in and didn't stop dumping, moving and cleaning until almost one o'clock. It felt good to be busy again, and she had to admit that she was excited about the wine bar idea, especially as she had support from Emily. She wasn't sure she'd have managed to pull it off on her own. She freshened up in the little bathroom downstairs and dashed to Emily's place with a few minutes to spare.

The two of them spent the afternoon mapping out plans for the wine bar. They decided that Niamh could start with the painting and they could recruit help as needed for the parts she couldn't reach. They decided on a soft, pale grey colour from magazine images and Emily told her where to go and buy paint in town. They'd deliver it by the next day so she could get started right away. They scrolled through websites that offered Italian-designed products and delivered locally, both of them agreeing that the place should have an Italian feel to it if they were to attract the locals. By comparison, more modern designs in restaurants and bars both in Camogli and other towns locally had never been popular with the locals and had therefore proven unsustainable.

They found a company just outside Milan that created spectacular old-school candelabras and scrolled through pages of designs. They ordered several tall floor-standing versions as well as elaborate twelve-candle countertop designs.

Miniature single candleholders in the same design would be perfect for each individual table.

'Lamps would definitely be easier and less messy, but this is going to be stunning and more unique,' Emily announced with a proud smile as they hit the order button on the website.

'I think the servers, myself included, should wear all black, but it should be stylish, not some lame shirt and pants,' Niamh suggested

'Excellent idea! Why don't we pick something from a high street store that carries that kind of thing all year round so, as your people change, you can just order more. I don't like those restaurant-industry options, they're too stiff for what we're trying to create here and they're terribly expensive. They don't all have to be identical but they do need to be functional and elegant. You need to get this up and running on a shoestring.'

'And the wine glasses should be those really fancy thin-stemmed ones that they have in the good places in Milan and Portofino. I know they're more expensive and they break easily, but they kind of say something about the place, don't you think?'

'Agreed, and I know the brand you are referring to. I'll pull up their website.' Emily leaned back in over the laptop again.

'I wonder if Massimo might be able to get me a trade discount on the glasses, you know, because he has a café?' Niamh wondered aloud.

'It's worth asking, darling. Every euro counts now, and the further you can spread it, the better the place will look and feel. OK, so it looks like everything will be delivered within the next seven days,' Emily continued, scrolling down her laptop screen. 'So I think it's safe to say you'll be ready to open in . . . what? Two weeks?'

'That sounds doable. All of the really hard work is done from the first renovation of the café, apart from repainting the place. The only question is how long it will take to make the wine-display cabinet. How long do you think?' Niamh asked, slashing items off their to-do list.

'Let me worry about the wine-display unit. We can always throw money at the problem to get it done in time.'

The one thing they compromised on was artwork. They didn't have a budget for original art and they didn't have the time to scour local artists, so they ordered a number of oversized prints from an online outlet, including artists like Rothko and Picasso.

'We don't want a sunflower or French lily pond vibe, we want something more striking and less . . . I don't know . . . melancholy or moody.'

'Right, not a Monet in sight. Got it!' Niamh said, giving Emily a mock military-style salute.

By the end of the day they had everything ordered, planned and plotted out on paper. They settled on an opening date in a little under three weeks' time. It had to be a Saturday night to try to maximise the local crowd. Niamh gathered her things and stuffed the lengthy to-do list and a whole lot of notepad pages into her bag.

Emily's phone buzzed. 'Oh good, it's Giorgio. He says he's on his way. I asked him to drop by after work.'

'Does he know what for?'

'No, he has no idea, but I didn't want to get into it over the phone, best to ask these delicate questions in person, I find. Do me a favour and pull a bottle of white wine from the wine fridge and fill the ice bucket.'

'Sure. Does Giorgio even drink white wine? I don't think I've ever seen him drink anything but Italian reds.'

'Of course he does, especially the good stuff. But, more importantly, I do, and we're in my apartment,' Emily said with a grin.

Niamh went to the small room just off the kitchen and pulled a chilled bottle from the impressive collection. It had originally been intended to be a larder or storage room of some sort but Emily had had it converted into a wine cellar that now held several hundred bottles. As she put the bottle in an ice bucket, the door buzzed.

'Niamh, can you get that?' Emily shouted from the living room. 'I'm on the phone with one of the vineyards.'

Niamh opened the door to Giorgio.

'Oh, *ciao*, Nina,' he said, smiling. 'I didn't expect to see you just now. I thought it was just Emilia.'

'We've been here all afternoon working on stuff. Come on in.' She tried to sound casual but there was something about his presence that always made her feel . . . she couldn't even describe it . . . unsettled. She didn't know what it was, exactly, but she had never felt it before with any other man. He was handsome, certainly, and impeccably dressed always, but there was something about his demeanour, the way he held himself, his confidence and his quietness that she felt drawn to. He had a warm side that wasn't immediately apparent. Niamh felt that it was most likely due to the nature of his work and the need to maintain a professional persona with clients. 'I'm opening a bottle of wine in the kitchen. Emily is on the phone. Would you like a glass?'

'Yes, thank you.'

He followed her to the kitchen. She pulled the bottle from the ice bucket.

'Carricante. Nice choice,' he said appreciatively.

'It's a nice collection!' she said with a big smile. 'I'm trying to beef up my knowledge of local wine and taste some of the ones that I wouldn't have had access to in Ireland. So this Sicilian Carricante white wine is today's market research.'

'Beef? Why do you say beef?' he asked, tilting his head as he did when asking a question.

'Beef? What?' Niamh responded, confused.

'Just now ... you said you beef ...'

'*Oh!* Beef up!' she replied, laughing. 'I said I was trying to beef up my wine knowledge. It means improve, like ... improve my wine knowledge.'

'Ah, another new expression! See? The more time I spend with you, the more English I learn. This means you are good for me, Nina, no?' he said with a grin.

She felt her stomach flip upside down.

Jesus, Giorgio, you really can't say things like that to a girl. Not when you're that hot. She could feel her cheeks start to flush as she fumbled with the corkscrew.

'You look happy today, Nina. It is nice to see,' he said, stepping towards her. 'Please ...' He took the corkscrew from her hand. Subconsciously, she touched the place where his hand had touched hers.

She leaned against the kitchen island and watched as Giorgio proceeded to open the bottle with a couple of deft movements. She couldn't help but think that if that had happened with Rick she'd have gone all bat-shit crazy feminist, ranting about how she was perfectly able to open a bottle of wine and how presumptuous and controlling he was. But with Giorgio it always felt like more of an invitation than an order. She always felt like part of the conversation or the event with Giorgio, as opposed to having to argue for her place in it.

They sat on high stools waiting for Emily to get off the phone, and Niamh rattled on, telling Giorgio about the plans for the wine bar. She avoided the subject of the licence as she thought Emily would be better equipped to handle that conversation. And, anyway, she herself didn't know exactly what was involved, only that they needed it fast.

'When you get everything ready and you are finished with all of this extra work, on your first Sunday off I will take you sailing,' he announced with a smile.

Her heart gave a little skip. He had never invited her anywhere before.

'Most Sundays I take the boat out with Sara, Massimo and some friends. You must come with us!'

Niamh cringed inwardly on hearing him say Sara's name. She couldn't understand their relationship. Yes, Sara was easily one of the most beautiful women that Niamh had ever met, but she had been cold to her from the very first time they had met, and no matter how pleasant or polite Niamh had been towards her, nothing had changed. Giorgio wasn't the type to be struck by looks alone, surely, so what was she missing? She realised that she envied Sara her relationship with Giorgio, which was irrational and futile, but she couldn't help it. She had to try hard to make an effort to be nice to her around Giorgio, as her instinct was to be jealous, which her mother would have pointed out was a nasty character trait that should be stomped on.

'That sounds great, thanks,' she said. She was saved from having to feign delight at the invitation to join him and Sara on his boat by Emily's arrival in the kitchen.

She wasted no time in explaining what they needed and

she asked him directly if he could help them. In true Italian fashion, he shrugged his shoulders in response and picked up a grape from the bowl.

'*Sì, certo,*' he said in response. Yes, of course.

Niamh marvelled at how it all worked here, but didn't dare to interrupt. They were making real progress and she had just got one giant step closer to opening The Wine Bar and to her rescuing her dream of a fresh start and a new life in Italy.

Chapter Thirty-Four

The following weeks went by in a rush and Niamh's days were full of tasks like painting, fixing, ordering, stocking and planning. They had multiple wine deliveries from small producers several times a day, so Niamh based herself in the little café, leaving only to run a necessary errand or grab a coffee at Massimo's. The painting of the walls took her four days and she was particularly proud that she had managed to do it entirely on her own. The place changed every day and she was beside herself with excitement as she watched its progress.

She had erected the candelabras and placed a miniature version on each table. She had been lighting the ivory-coloured candles for a few hours every day, just as Emily had advised, to avoid having the place look shiny new. Instead it would have a patina of age on it with the candle wax dripping and frozen in time. Niamh smiled as she examined them every morning and saw how they were already creating wax shapes like those ice structures you see in caves – either stalagmites or stalactites, depending on whether the ice rose upwards from the ground or hung down from above, but she was damned if she could remember which was which. 'Either way you already look very pretty,' she said to the candelabras as she walked by them, touching their new wax sculptures gently.

With only a few days to go before opening night, she really didn't have any spare time, but when Giorgio had called on Saturday evening, he had been insistent that she meet him at Massimo's early the next morning.

She dressed in jeans, boots and a sweater, grabbed her coat and an oversized scarf and picked up her bag. She opened the door onto the narrow, cobbled street and stepped out into the cool air. Late October had brought with it a distinctive chill both early morning and late at night.

She walked the ten-minute walk to Massimo's café, the chilly sea breeze helping to wake her up.

'And on a Sunday, too,' she mumbled into her scarf.

She walked along the series of narrow streets, her head down against the wind, mentally running through her check-list for the day.

She stepped into the warmth of Massimo's café and peeled off her scarf.

'Ah, Signora Nina! *Buongiorno!*' Massimo said warmly. 'You are ready for the big party, no? Everything is prepared? I know that you are very busy with all this work. You need a coffee, no?'

'*Sì, Massimo, certo oggi,*' she replied with a smile. Yes, definitely today.

Giorgio sat at a table at the back of the café. That's unusual, Niamh thought. He usually stood at the counter for an espresso or cappuccino, or on occasion he would sit at a table right in front, and she had never seen him sit at the back of the café. Maybe he doesn't want to be spotted by clients on a Sunday morning and he's hiding out, she thought, as she made her way towards him.

'*Ciao, buongiorno,*' she said with a smile.

'*Buongiorno,* Nina. How are you today?' he replied, but he didn't smile.

'Umm … tired, busy, stressed. I think that about sums it up,' she joked.

Massimo arrived with two cappuccinos and a plate of biscotti. '*Ecco signori!*' he said, placing the cups on the table.

'*Grazie, Massimo,*' Giorgio replied, looking up at him. He turned his attention back to his cup as he stirred a sachet of sugar into his cappuccino.

Niamh realised that she hadn't seen him smile yet this morning.

'So what's up?' she asked with a small frown. Although she loved nothing more than to be in his company, she was woefully behind schedule and Giorgio didn't seem to be in the best of moods.

'I'm afraid that I have some bad news, Nina,' he responded, not lifting his eyes from his cup.

Her heart sank in one plunging dive to the pit of her stomach.

'What do you mean? What kind of bad news?' She sipped her coffee nervously. 'Oh my God. Have they denied my application?'

'What application, Nina?' Giorgio asked, looking confused.

'My wine licence? Have they denied it?'

'No,' Giorgio replied, his eyes cast down towards his feet. 'I'm afraid there is an offer on the building.'

'What do you mean, an offer?'

'There is an offer for the building … to buy the building. I didn't know how to tell you this news. I just found out last night,' he said without looking at her. 'But I think that there is no good time to tell you this.'

'My building?' she asked incredulously.

'Yes. Well, it is not your building, it is my brother's building, but yes, that building.'

'But I don't understand. How could there be an offer on it. Is it sold?'

'No, the offer was just made yesterday, but my brother says that he is happy with the offer and that it is perhaps a good thing for him, so I must tell you that he will accept it.'

'What?' she asked, incredulous.

'I know. I am sorry, Nina.' He shook his head slowly, staring at his untouched cappuccino.

'But how, Giorgio? I mean, how could this happen? The building was empty for two years ... two whole, entire fucking years. Nothing. Then I fixed it up, opened the café, am getting ready to reopen it as a wine bar and now it's being sold?' Her voice was rising with every word. 'And my lease expires after the initial six months. Oh my God. What a rookie mistake that was. I didn't think I needed to lawyer-up for my little café in Camogli. I feel pretty fucking naïve right now. No one even rented the godforsaken hole until I fixed it up, and now some fucker buys it from under me? How is this happening?'

'Yes, I am sorry, Nina. I think my brother is a fool to sell the building. It is only going to increase in value with all the investment that is being made in Camogli. I told him this, but he did not listen to me.'

'I couldn't give a shit about your brother's investment, Giorgio. What about my investment? What about me?' Her voice was rising and she could see the couple at another table look in her direction.

'*Lo so, lo so. Mi dispiace, mi dispiace* ... I am sorry,' he said, running a hand through his hair.

He looked remorseful, but Niamh didn't care. She had bet

everything on coming back and starting over again, and now she was in danger of losing it all. She wasn't sure which of them she was more furious with right now. Giorgio's brother, certainly, even though she had never met him, and whoever put an offer on the building, and even Giorgio himself just for being the messenger.

She felt an irrational sense of rage but was simultaneously welling up with tears.

'Sorry? Fuck, sorry, Giorgio. I put everything into that place. All my savings – you know that! How could you do this?'

'Nina, calm down. I—'

'Calm down? Calm down? I just got back from burying my mother and thought I was coming back to pick up my life again and get back to work. But no, I can't do that 'cause the building is about to be sold. How the fuck was the building sold? I didn't even know it was for sale.'

'I know. I am sorry. It is complicated because I don't have all the information. And no, it was not for sale.'

'OK, you are making zero sense now. Zero! How could the building be sold if it wasn't for sale? Is the goddamn building sold or not?'

'Please don't get so mad, Nina. Yes, yes, the building is being sold, but it was not for sale. I mean that my brother had not put it ... how do you say ... for the market?'

'Don't get mad? It's too late for that. I've just been royally screwed! And it's *on* the market, Giorgio. *ON*.'

'OK, on the market. So, it was not on the market. But yesterday my brother called me from Chicago to tell me that he had agreed to sell the building to someone.'

'Agreed to sell it? To who?'

'I don't know. He just told me that he had an offer on the building and that he will sell it.'

'So, it's not sold yet?'

'Yes, he has agreed that he will sell it.'

'But have they signed anything? I mean is it actually sold?'

'I don't know. I don't think so but I only know what he told me when he telephoned me yesterday.'

'I don't believe this! You have find out, Giorgio! I need to know if it's too late or if I can do anything about it.'

'I can call him first thing in the morning, in his morning time, I mean. Now, it is still night-time in Chicago.'

'OK, OK.' Niamh sighed as she put her head down onto her folded arms. 'I really don't believe this is happening now, after everything I've been through. Who put an offer on the goddamn building?' She wiped one silent tear from her eye and turned her face away from him.

'I am sorry, Nina. It is not mine. The building is not mine. There is nothing I could do. He just called and told me that this had happened and I was the one who had to tell you.' He reached out and put a hand on her arm. She sat back, pulling her arm away and stared out towards the front of the café.

'Can you please call him later today and let me know what he says?' she asked, standing up and pushing her chair from the little table. It made a scraping sound on the tiles.

'Yes, of course. I will call you as soon as I speak with him. Nina . . . ' He stood up and stepped towards her, but she swept up her bag and strode towards the door.

She left the café and made a left turn, walking back along the promenade. It was quieter now that the tourists had left. Some locals walked along the seafront, older couples wrapped in coats and scarves against the cold sea breeze. She folded her arms and hid behind her sunglasses, head down as she walked into the breeze, back in the direction she had come only twenty minutes earlier. Tears fell silently down her cheeks. She didn't even attempt to wipe them away. It didn't matter. She didn't care.

She had thought that this time it would be different. She had really believed that she'd get her second chance and things would turn out better. She had put so much into turning the café around, trying to prove as much to herself as to anyone else that she could do it. All the feedback she had received over the past few weeks was hugely positive. Even the locals seemed curious about the idea of having a wine bar in Camogli. But everything was now in question, and once again she didn't know where she stood. She didn't know if she would even have the place by the weekend, or if she was basically running it for someone else now that it had been sold. It was all a disaster – again.

She turned to go up the steps to the upper level, making her way back to the apartment. She locked the front door behind her and did the same with the door that led to the upstairs. She twisted the dial on the heater until it hissed out steam, took off her jeans and curled into bed. She leaned one elbow against the pillow and switched her phone to silent, realising as she did so that the building was also the place that she now lived. 'Homeless too. That's a thrilling prospect,' she muttered into her pillow, before falling into a restless sleep.

Chapter Thirty-Five

She awoke just after four o'clock in the afternoon and turned to sit up, feeling normal for just a moment. Then the conversation with Giorgio came racing back into her mind and she sank back into the pillows. She pulled out her phone and texted Emily.

Can you meet me for a drink? I need to talk to you.

Her phone lit up almost immediately with a response.

Of course. Where and when?

Now and I don't give two fucks.

Ah. OK. How about the little place at the end of the pier?

OK. Heading there now.

OK. See you in 20 mins.

Niamh was already sitting on the terrace of the restaurant all the way at the end of the pier when Emily arrived. She was facing the sea but wrapped up in a jacket and scarf as it had started to get colder in the evenings now. It looked very different to how it was in the summer. The light was thinner, not as big and golden, but it was still beautiful.

She had replayed the earlier conversation with Giorgio over and over in her mind, trying to find a solution, but it was hopeless. She knew that if she lost the building and the wine bar failed then she didn't have an alternative, as this was all she could do here without any proper Italian skills. She didn't speak enough Italian to get a regular job, there were no English schools in the area so teaching English wasn't an option and the tourist season was already over for the year. She had put everything into the café and, with Emily's help, had mustered the energy and resources to do it all again with the wine bar idea, but she was at the end of the road and she knew it. The wine bar had been Plan B and she didn't have a Plan C.

Emily pulled out a seat at the table and motioned for the barman. She was wrapped in an oversized camel-coloured cashmere wrap and wore her signature Chanel sunglasses. Her nails were perfectly manicured, as always, Niamh noticed.

'Thanks for coming,' she said quietly.

'Of course, darling. It sounded rather urgent but in truth you know I rarely turn down the opportunity to drink outdoors.'

She ordered a bottle of local red wine.

'Now, what seems to be the problem?'

'Giorgio asked me to meet him this morning at Massimo's café. The building is being sold.'

'I know.'

'What do you mean, "you know"?'

'I know. He told me yesterday. He called me to ask me how he should tell you. I must say he was distraught at the idea of being the one to tell you the bad news.'

'Why didn't you tell me?'

'Because Giorgio was adamant that he should be the one to do it as you had agreed the whole deal, contract and all, with him.'

'And now it's all shot to shit.' Niamh sat forward and put her head in her hands. 'I can't believe this is happening. Can't the universe just give me a break and throw me a goddamn bone?' She sighed dramatically.

'Look, all is not lost,' Emily replied, pulling her wrap tighter around her shoulders against the chill of the sea breeze. 'You know the little man who sells pizza by the slice?'

'The one at the other end of the pier?'

'Is there another one?' Emily asked, raising one eyebrow.

Niamh wasn't in the mood for jokes. 'I don't know, Emily. Yes, I know that guy. What about him?'

'Well, he had an internet café here in town some years ago. He spent an absolute fortune kitting the place out with computers, modems and cables – whatever one needs for an internet café . . . I don't know. Anyway, my point is that he ran an internet café, which made perfect sense when he opened it, but then a year into it laptops and smartphones became mainstream and suddenly he had no business.'

'*Ecco, signore*,' the waiter said, smiling as he deposited two glasses and a bottle of wine in front of them.

'Anyway, as I was saying, the man suddenly had zero business and so he totally reinvented himself. He borrowed money from somewhere, recruited some locals to help and turned the place into a very basic pizzeria offering pizza by the slice. Of course, the town was appalled at first, as they'd never even considered pizza by the slice, but the tourists loved it and so grew his business. He had the courage to stay in it and figure it out. He found a solution to his problem and moved forward.'

She sat back with a wide smile, looking very pleased with herself. Niamh was certain that there was a lesson in this somewhere – something about the need to reinvent herself, but she couldn't determine what exactly it was.

'Great story, Emily, but there's one minute detail that differs from his story and my Greek tragedy of a life.'

'What's that?' Emily asked, still beaming.

'That guy had a building. He just traded a bunch of computers for a pizza oven and some dough and off he went with his new business. Small problem – I don't have a building. I *used* to have access to a building until some wanker went and put an offer on the building and my greedy landlord jumped at it.'

'Well, if that's how you feel about me?'

'What?' Niamh squinted up at her with a pained expression on her face. She was tired, emotional, and stressed and this conversation wasn't making much sense. This was clearly one of Emily's 'Let's have a deep and confusing conversation about nothing' kind of days, but Niamh just couldn't cope with it right now.

'I'm your wanker.'

Niamh looked up from her wine glass and stared her right in the eyes. 'What?' she asked again, shaking her head. This was becoming maddening.

'You said, "some wanker went and put an offer on the building" – you said that just now.'

'Yes. So?'

'So, I'm your wanker, darling. Although I'm not terribly fond of the term. In general it's perfectly fine, and in fact I know many wankers personally, but not to describe me. I understand where it was coming from, of course. Perhaps we could find another word for me, though. Something a little more flattering?'

She sat back against her chair, took a sip of wine and watched the realisation work its way across Niamh's face.

'You?'

'Me.' Emily nodded.

'You bought the building?'

'No, I put an offer on the building.'

'But . . .'

'But what?'

Niamh could see that Emily was enjoying this now. She sat up straighter. 'But, I mean, why did you . . . do you want to buy the building? Why would you do that to me?'

'Not *to* you, darling, *for* you. I want to do this with you. Don't you understand?'

'No actually, I don't.'

'Look, Niamh, it's really quite simple,' Emily said, leaning into the table to face her. 'You were gone for almost a month and I realised that you are the only non-Italian person here that I really like. The rest of the expats are either pretentious snobs or entitled pricks and they think that the fact that we all speak the same language somehow binds us together in unity or solidarity as expats and they've forgotten the fundamental principle of forging friendships – that you have to actually like someone before you allow them into your life. And I don't, for the most part, *like* most of the expats here. Anyway, then along comes you, not really giving a toss what anyone thinks of you and just getting on with it, and you open this café that sells lovely salads that no one except tourists wants to eat because the Italians haven't quite grasped the Californian ideals of "clean food" and heart-healthy alternatives. To top that off, you offered average coffee that no Italian will ever spend money on, and you opened smack in the middle of summer. The odds were stacked against you from the start, my dear.'

'But you're buying the building . . .' Niamh said slowly.

'Precisely,' Emily said firmly, with a nod. 'This really is awfully good wine. It has great body for a four-year-old wine, don't you think?' She swirled her glass and took a long sip.

'Yes, I suppose. Anyway, you were saying . . .' Niamh

offered, trying to rein in the conversation and nudge Emily back in the direction it had been going.

'Look, darling, it's all quite simple really. While you were gone the town council finally granted permission to build that new luxury hotel on the periphery of the town. That's going to increase the spotlight on Camogli and the town is only going to get busier. More hotel inventory means more tourists, which is a good thing for locals who will benefit from increased tourist traffic. However, it will also have implications for real estate and so people are already speculating that property prices – especially those in the centre of town – are going to rise. So, you come along, dust off the grime from the old café and then announce that you're turning it into a wine bar. Lo and behold, some simpleton with absolutely no imagination of their own decides they should buy it now that it's all shiny and new again. They couldn't see the value of it when it was ramshackle, but the moment it shows promise as an investable entity, they dig into their grotty little pockets, call Marco in Chicago and make him an offer.'

Niamh couldn't believe what she was hearing. She just sat and stared at Emily, trying to process what she was saying.

'But how did you know that someone had made an offer?'

'Giorgio called me yesterday and asked my advice on how to tell you. He was devastated at the thought of disappointing you.'

'But if someone else made the offer, how are you going to buy the building?'

'Well, I merely intervened. There is one caveat, though.' Emily sipped her wine and turned the bottle towards her so she could read the label. 'Hmm, this is surprisingly good. I haven't seen it on the menu before. It must be new. You see – this is why we need the wine bar, so we don't have to sit outdoors on freezing cold terraces in autumn!'

Niamh thought she might lose her mind soon. 'Go on,' she urged.

'Oh yes, so I called Marco earlier today and said I would pay one euro more than the offer he had currently on it and that I was his dear friend and I reminded him that he owes me a favour. So he laughed and said OK. He doesn't care about the ins and outs of the deal, he just wants to take some money out now that he's going to start a family.'

Niamh's head was beginning to spin. Her mind was racing. 'He just laughed?'

'Yes, like I told you, he really wants nothing to do with all this negotiation and paperwork, he just wants to take the cash and get back to his life in America.'

'So, what's the caveat?' Niamh asked, nervous at what she might say next.

'Well, a lot of my capital is tied up in other investments and it will obviously take me some time to access it ...' Emily's voice drifted off as she did some mental calculations.

'Obviously,' Niamh repeated, having zero concept of how long it might take.

'I'm probably going to need sixty to ninety days, and the issue is that the other buyer is a cash buyer.'

'So what does that mean?'

'It means that we need Marco to be agreeable to the idea of turning down the initial offer and having to wait a few months for my money to come through.'

'OK, but even if he did agree to those terms, how would it work? The financial part, I mean?'

'Simple. I'll front the capital required to buy it initially and we'll work out a revenue-share arrangement so that you can contribute to the payments of the building and ultimately be co-owner. Are you following?'

'Yes, I think so,' Niamh replied slowly, finally taking a breath and reaching for her glass of wine. 'So you'd buy it and I'd buy my share of it over time?'

'Exactly. I'm not loaning you the money, Niamh. I want to be your business partner. I'll buy the building, you'll run the business and commit to a payment plan over time.'

'But why? I mean, you could have bought a building any time before this but you didn't, so it can't just be for the real estate opportunity.'

'Well, primarily, darling, because I'm bored, and second-arily, I like the idea of having a place I can go to drink great wine and feel like I own the place. Can't get barred from your own wine bar, after all!'

'So what do we do now?' Niamh asked, determined to keep the conversation moving forward.

'Well, I don't want to get into a bidding war, so we need Giorgio to keep the other buyer at bay temporarily until we sign the deal with Marco. If the other buyer gets wind of a counter offer then he/she might well counter again, and I can't afford to let this escalate in price.'

'Does Giorgio know about all this?'

'I don't think Giorgio even knows that I've made a coun-ter offer yet. But Niamh, you have to act as if nothing has changed and open the wine bar on schedule as planned. Understand? We need to act as if we know nothing about this offer, and continue with life as normal, because whoever made that offer is most likely here.'

'*Here?*' Niamh said loudly. 'Do you think it's someone we know? Like, someone who knows us? Oh my God! Traitors!'

'Yes, treacherous, darling, but such is life. That is precisely why you have to proceed with opening night without as much as a hint of anything being awry. If they made an offer once, they could well do it again,' Emily replied matter-of-factly as she pulled out her phone and dialled Giorgio's number. 'Might as well bring him into the plan if he hasn't already heard.'

The conversation with Giorgio was short, with Emily saying a lot of 'yes' and 'that's correct' before hanging up less than two minutes later. 'Turns out he had heard. Marco called him as soon as he hung up from me to tell him to stall the deal with the first offer. Giorgio just needed to verify what was discussed.'

'So he understands what's happening? I mean, about us needing time to get all this straight?'

'He does. He said to leave it with him, that he was well used to having to play politics with property deals and that he would delay getting back to the original bidder as much as possible.'

'Do you have any idea who it might be?'

'The original bidder? No, and I hope that I don't find out because if it's anyone I know and I find out that they have undermined me and tried to buy the building that houses my new business – sorry, our new business – out from under me ... well, you know what they say. Hell hath no fury like a woman scorned.'

For the next four days, Niamh continued with life as normal to all intents and purposes. The reality was that on the inside she was a mess. She felt completely powerless, as she herself could do nothing to resolve the situation. She continued to run about town, preparing for opening night on Saturday, but the precariousness of her situation was never far from her thoughts. The uncertainty was overwhelming.

Emily had tried to lift her spirits by saying that there was a chance that the other buyer, if successful in his or her bid, might want to keep the wine bar open, in which case Niamh could most likely remain on. But in Niamh's mind, the fact that she would then be working the bar for someone else, made her just a barmaid, an entirely different situation. It was untenable and she knew it.

'How much is the building?' Grace asked, when she called Niamh that afternoon.

'The offer was eight hundred thousand euros, so Emily offered eight hundred and one thousand euros to counter.'

'She's nuts! Imagine having that kind of money.'

'Well, that's the problem, she doesn't have all that, at least not liquid, anyway, that's what she said,' Niamh explained as she sat at one of the small tables in the wine bar. 'So she needs to liquidate some other investments in order to buy the place before the other buyer can make a counter offer.'

'Right, so she'll just liquidate a few investments and hope that the other buyer doesn't get wind of it. Well, that should be easy enough,' her sister said sarcastically. 'And in the meantime, are you losing your mind?'

'Yes. Totally. I can't do anything. It's all down to Emily, and I just have to carry on as if nothing is happening. She's talking to some people back in London and Giorgio is trying to keep the other buyer at bay until she has some idea of how quickly she can access the cash.'

'But what's the hurry? Why the urgency, all of a sudden?'

'Well, now that the brother has had an offer on it, he's decided to go ahead and sell it. They're having a baby in the spring, and apparently he's applying for his green card, so it's not like he's coming back here any time soon, so I guess the money sounds attractive. Can't say I blame him. I'd cash out too if I suddenly found out that some random building I owned was worth almost a million euros and someone wanted to buy it in an all-cash deal.'

'That's true. What are you going to do? If it doesn't work out, I mean. Sorry to be Negative Nelly, but I don't want you to be blindsided if it all goes pear shaped. Have you thought about it?'

'Thought about it? That's all I do! I haven't slept properly since this all started. My head is melted from it all,' Niamh said, exasperated.

'I can imagine – but do you have a Plan B? What if it all goes pear shaped?'

'No, Grace, *this* was Plan B. I had this mad idea and forged ahead with it, never in my dreams or nightmares thinking that some fucker would turn the whole thing upside down behind my back.'

'And you've no idea who it is?'

'None. The brother hasn't said, which makes me think that I know the person.'

'Well, not necessarily, maybe that's just a professional courtesy or something. You know, don't name the bidder until the deal is done or something?'

'I don't know, but it's a weird feeling thinking that someone around here just did that to me and I don't know who.'

'Well, you don't know that it was someone who's actually there. They could have been passing through and spotted it. Don't go getting all Sherlock Holmes, thinking your neighbours are out to get you. That will just drive you mad.'

'Yes, you're right. OK, I better get back to work. I've some wine deliveries arriving this afternoon. I'll see you Friday!'

'OK, I'll text you from the airport before I fly. Good luck with the last-minute stuff.'

'OK, thanks. Bye!'

Chapter Thirty-Six

'I still can't believe that you flew over here for this,' Niamh shouted to Grace through the bathroom door a few days later.

'Well, I've never been one to miss a good launch party!'

Grace had arrived earlier that afternoon and the two sisters had caught up over a quick lunch along the promenade before returning to Niamh's apartment.

'Anyway, it's not every day your little sister has the balls to do something like open a wine bar! The fact that it's in a gorgeous part of Italy is just icing on the cake,' she shouted back.

Grace came out of the bathroom in a mist of perfume.

'You look amazing, Grace. Did you lose weight?'

'Maybe,' Grace said with a shrug.

She wore a simple, Bardot-style black dress with off-the-shoulder detail.

'So did Robert lose his mind at the thought of having the boys for the weekend?'

'They're his kids too, Niamh,' Grace snapped.

'Jesus, sorry. Sensitive much? Who peed in your Cheerios?'

'No, it's just that it's frustrating that's all. Why is it that I'm expected to look after them twenty-four-seven, but if Robert has them for one weekend then it's "How is poor Robert going to cope?"'

'Didn't mean to trample on a nerve there, Grace,' Niamh retorted, rolling her eyes.

How was it that after only a couple of hours together they always ended up sniping at each other over something stupid? Niamh wondered.

'Honestly, you'd swear a man wasn't to be trusted to keep his own kids alive for one lousy weekend,' Grace continued, undeterred. She rummaged about in her suitcase, pulled a necklace from a small suede pouch and clasped it around her neck.

'That's fab!' Niamh exclaimed, happy to have found an opportunity to change the subject. 'Is it new?'

'Yep.'

'Nice gift!'

'As a matter of fact, it was a gift to myself.'

Niamh raised her eyebrows. 'Oh?' She fingered the amber pendant at the end of the gold chain.

'Well, when your husband is away on business for your birthday and comes home only to have forgotten all about it entirely, what do you do but go shopping for a consolation prize on his credit card?'

'You did not!' Niamh laughed.

Grace looked at her without so much as a smile. 'Give them an inch and they'll take a mile, Niamh. Perhaps the shock of seeing the line item for twelve hundred euros on his credit card bill will be enough to ensure he doesn't forget as easily in the future.'

'You spent twelve hundred euros on a necklace?' Niamh shouted incredulously.

'Yes, I did. Isn't it divine?' Grace said coolly as she eyed her reflection.

'That's nuts, Grace. That's rent money! Who spends that kind of money on jewellery?'

'Well, not sane people, I'll give you that, and normally I wouldn't either, but I just got pissed off and that was the one piece that caught my eye. Trust me, this was on the lower end of the scale based on what I saw on display in Brown Thomas. Normally I'd be lucky to get something from Zara from him, but he completely forgot and it pissed me off so I thought "fuck it" and went shopping.'

'Did he freak out?'

'He lost the plot initially, but when I suggested that he just not forget about his wife's birthday in future he shut up. He was fuming, but how could he object when he had been such a knob? I mean, who forgets their wife's birthday? Now, come on,' she said, swiftly changing the subject. 'What are you wearing to the grand opening? And what time do you need to be downstairs and ready? Didn't the invitation say six o'clock?'

'Yes, but I need to be ready before that. I need to start opening the place up in about half an hour,' she said, pulling a hanger from her wardrobe.

Grace looked from the green midi dress to Niamh and back to the dress. 'That?'

'There's no need for that tone of voice, Grace,' Niamh said defensively. 'What's wrong with it? It's *new!*'

Grace sighed. 'It's fine, but it's just not . . . I don't know. It's fine for a regular summer's day. It's cute, but I don't know – it's fine if you want to blend in and don't want to make a statement.'

'If I just want to blend in?' Niamh repeated, as she stood defiantly with her hands on her hips. 'Yeah, I go out all the time with the intention of wanting to blend in and be wall-paper, Grace.'

She turned around and rammed the hanger back into

the closet. 'One day I put on a really cute dress by mistake but I saw myself in the mirror and immediately said, "Take that off right now, Niamh! That one looks cute – you don't want to impress anyone, remember? Your goal is to be wallpaper!"'

'Oh, for crying out loud, calm down. The dress is fine ordinarily, but tonight is a big deal – you're opening your own wine bar, Niamh! Who gets to do that? Tonight you need to look like a million dollars! You need to be your A-game, most glamorous, sophisticated version of yourself. Now stop arguing with me, take that pissed-off expression off your face and pull out your sassiest numbers.'

'Sassy?' Niamh said reluctantly, staring at the options in front of her. 'You forget that I shop in H&M and Zara, Grace. I don't think I can afford sassy. I can afford cute, like normal people.'

'OK, stop with the defensive attitude. Let me in there. You're bound to have something suitable,' Grace said confidently, as she flicked through hangers. 'It's not about how much you spend. It's about fabric, the cut – you just need to have an eye for detail and know what looks good on you, that's all.' She pulled a black chiffon dress from Niamh's wardrobe. 'What about this? It still has a tag on it.'

'Yeah, it's new. I just wasn't sure it would work for tonight. Is it too formal?'

'Nonsense. This is perfect,' Grace replied, as she snapped off the price tag.

Within twenty minutes, Niamh was dressed in the new dress that fell just below her knee and had accessorised it with oversized gold hoop earrings and black wedge sandals. She twisted her chestnut brown hair into a messy bun and secured it with a couple of hair clips.

'There!' Grace said with a satisfied smile. 'Now you look like someone to be reckoned with.'

'Hmm, OK, thanks.' Niamh nodded with a small smile as she checked her reflection in the mirror. She looked at her watch and her stomach gave an anxious flip.

'Go! Don't even think about getting nervous. I'll see you in a half hour,' Grace said, as she shoved her sister towards the door.

Opening night had been planned meticulously. Niamh had sent a formal written invitation to everyone she knew locally and Emily had done the same in both Camogli and across the neighbouring towns. Giorgio had invited all his clients and Massimo had put up a promotional poster and had told anyone who would listen at the café. Franco had promised to show up with a bunch of his local friends and even some from as far away as Genoa. Niamh and Emily had decided to offer a red wine, a white wine and Franciacorta on the house, but the other, more expensive bottles would have to be charged for if requested. It was a business, after all.

Niamh had been counselled by Emily in earnest the week prior. She advised her not to make the mistake of being too busy serving that she couldn't meet and talk to her guests. Emily explained that in any business it was critical to have a relationship with your best clients, and that these Camogli locals would ultimately be her best clients, so it was a big opportunity to meet them and have them get to know her.

'You need to put your personality on this place. You need to become known as the owner. People like to be recognised and welcomed when they return somewhere, so it's important that you get to know your customers. Wear something fabulous on opening night and put an apron over it, that way, you can show that you're serious about it and not afraid to work, but when you remove your apron you will appear as the owner, not the server. I've watched Sara work this strategy to her advantage for years, so you'd be wise to do the same. At the end of the day, people do business with people they like, it's as simple as that.'

Niamh grimaced at the mention of Sara's name and she wasn't sure she liked being compared to her in any manner. Still, though, she couldn't help but admit that Sara's business was a raging success, so she let the comparison slide and took the advice as being well intentioned.

She stood alone now in the centre of the wine bar, turning full circle to look around.

What have I forgotten? I'm bound to have forgotten something, she mused, drumming her fingertips to her lips. She whipped out her phone and checked her To-Do app again.

Nope, this is weird. This feels weird. Actually having everything ready is a bit weird, she thought, still in the centre of the room. She walked behind the counter and checked all the wine coolers. Everything was fully stocked. She pulled open the door of the fridge to make sure all the hors d'oeuvres were ready. Platters of food were filled with bite-sized pieces of food, specially prepared to ensure they would be easy to eat with one hand while the other was holding a wine glass.

Rows of long-stemmed wine glasses stood ready for deployment, alongside still more rows of old-fashioned champagne coupes. Niamh had decided to inject a little old-world opulence into the interiors and opted for the coupe over the regular champagne flutes. She had mirrored those choices in the mismatched porcelain plates she had bought for the small plates on the menu.

She tested the surround sound system one last time and then checked her watch. It was ten minutes to six. Her stomach gave a nervous flip as she selected 'Fly Me to the Moon' on the stereo. It had been her mother's favourite song. She thought of her then, for a moment, as she adjusted the volume and decided that Una Kelly would have been proud of her in that moment. She crossed her fingers and said a silent prayer that it would all work out. She was afraid to hope, but couldn't allow herself to dwell on that now. She had guests to greet and a role to play, and she intended to do it justice.

'Oh my God, the place looks amazing!' Grace gushed as she burst through the door from upstairs. 'I'm so bloody proud of you, Niamh!'

'Thanks. Yeah, it does look nice.'

'Nice? Are you mad? It's fabulous!'

'Sorry, you're right. It is.'

'Don't you go apologising for nothing again now, Niamh Kelly. I haven't seen sight of that old version of you for some time now and I'm not allowing her back! Look at what you've accomplished! This is amazing!' her sister said, engulfing her in a hug.

Moments later, the first of the guests started to file through the door. Niamh had hired two local guys to help serve drinks so that she could divide her time between serving drinks and playing hostess. There had been a steady stream of guests for the first hour and the room was filled with the buzz of happy chatter.

As the crowd started to build in the cosy front room of the wine bar, Niamh was becoming increasingly frustrated as she struggled with bottles of wine in the little galley kitchen.

'What's up with these bottles of red wine?' she said with a loud frustrated sigh.

'*Che c'è?* What is wrong?' Giorgio asked, sticking his head inside the door.

360

'These bloody corks keep breaking. It's not like I haven't opened a million of them in my life, but these are getting the better of me.' She tucked another bottle between her knees and tugged on the corkscrew.

'And this is how you do it?' he asked, nodding towards the bottle jammed between her knees.

'I'm doing it the same way I've always done it, but they keep breaking, dammit!' she said as the corkscrew flew up with half the cork attached.

'*Dammelo*,' he instructed, reaching out his hand for the corkscrew. 'Give it to me.'

She sat down on a tall bar stool with a huff.

'I think we have had this conversation, Nina, no? You have to be more patient. *Pazienza, Nina*.'

She watched him deftly manoeuvre the corkscrew into the mangled cork and gently coax it out.

'*Allora*,' he said as the cork gave way. 'You just need to do it slowly. Some of these older bottles of red wine, the corks they are tighter, so you must be gentle. *Pazienza, Nina*. If you rush, then you will have this problem.' He nodded his head towards the three aborted wine bottles on the counter.

'Thanks. I'll just add this to the list of things Italians do better than me,' said Niamh with a sigh.

'Maybe, yes,' Giorgio said, turning back to face the counter. '*Allora*, you go and pour some drinks for your guests and I will rescue these other bottles for you.'

He had seemed tense when he arrived and still wasn't his usual calm, easy-going self, but she was grateful to him for rescuing the bottle situation.

'You're very quiet tonight.'

'Ah, just many things on my mind today.'

'Well, come and have a drink when you've rescued those

other bottles and forget about it. Pull your happy face out of your pocket, will you? This is supposed to be a party, after all!' She gave him a playful shove.

He responded with what was definitely a forced smile. 'Yes, yes, I will come.'

She looked at him for a moment but, he wasn't giving anything away.

She stepped back into the main room, which by now was packed and she couldn't stop a grin from spreading across her face. Grace was holding court with two Italian men in suits and caught her eye across the room. As far away as she was, Niamh could tell that she was in good spirits and loving the attention. She looked like a peacock with her feathers out on display, she decided. Squinting over at the two men in Grace's clutches, Niamh realised she didn't even know who they were, which she took to be a good sign, and her frustration from the kitchen started to dissipate.

Real strangers means that word has spread! How cool is that! she thought with a chill of excitement.

Niamh felt a tap on her shoulder and turned to see Sara standing in front of her. 'Congratulations, Niamh, this place looks wonderful,' she said with a smile.

Niamh wasn't sure if she was more surprised to see her standing there or to see her smile. She was quite sure that Sara had ever smiled at her directly before and she couldn't mask her surprise.

'Oh, umm, thanks. I didn't think you would come.' Niamh had uttered the words before she could stop them. 'I mean, I didn't think you'd be able to make it, you know . . . with the restaurant and all that.' She wondered what the hell Sara was even doing there.

'No, I understand, but I wanted to come,' Sara said quietly, casting her eyes to the ground. 'I owe you an apology.'

'Me? What for?' Niamh asked, genuinely confused.

'It's kind of you to act as though you don't know what for, but I know that I have not been very kind to you since you arrived.'

'Oh, that.'

'Yes, that. I know that tonight is not the right time, as you are so very busy, but I wanted to come and say congratulations and to offer my support – and to apologise.'

'But I don't understand. I mean, did I do something to upset you? Because if I did then you should have just told me. All I heard from everyone the whole time was how wonderful you were and how friendly and how sweet and blah, blah, blah. But you were kind of a bitch towards me so I just never saw it.'

'I know. I'm so sorry, I ...'

The fact that Sara had chosen this night and this moment to have a meaningful conversation about their lack of relationship irked Niamh. She had enough to deal with on opening night, not to mention the issue of the building being under offer. She didn't have time for this right now, but neither could she afford to be seen as the witch in this scenario. Sara was extending an olive branch, so Niamh could hardly beat her over the head with it.

'Look, Sara, I'm sorry, but I really don't have time right now. I don't want to be rude but I have a room full of guests to attend to so maybe we could ...'

'I understand, of course. There is no excuse for my behaviour and I know that it was wrong of me. It's just that I was jealous of you, that's all. It has always been a terrible character trait of mine, that I try to keep in check, but this time it got the better of me.'

Niamh stood rooted to the spot. 'Jealous? *You* are jealous of *me*?' she asked incredulously.

'Was. I *was* jealous of you. I'm not any longer. You did nothing wrong and I know that now and I'm sorry that I misjudged you.'

'But . . . how? I mean, what possible reason could you have for being jealous of me?' Niamh asked, unaware that her jaw had dropped in absolute incomprehension.

'But you must know, surely? Niamh, from the very first night I met you at the cocktail reception in Santa Margherita I have spent so much time wishing you had never dropped into my life. I realise now what a mistake that was, and that I should have been grateful to have you here, but I was wrong.'

'Santa Margherita?' Niamh squealed, now utterly confused. 'What?'

Sara gave a little laugh. 'You really don't know, do you?'

'Know what?' Niamh asked suspiciously.

'That since the very first night that I saw you with Giorgio, I knew we wouldn't last much longer and I blamed you for that. You see, Giorgio and I had been friends for a very long time, and soon after his fiancée left him we became a couple. I was the one who initiated it. I had been in love with him for a long time and I knew he didn't feel the same way about me, but when she left he was heartbroken and so we sort of fell together.' Sara clasped her hands together, avoiding eye contact with Niamh. 'I think I hoped that his feelings would change over time and that he might love me the same way I loved him. I was just grateful for what I had . . . for what it was, and it was wonderful for a long time. But when I met you that night and saw you with him I knew without any doubt that he would never look at me the way I saw him look at you. It was as if perhaps he realised that then, too, and so everything between us changed.' Sara glanced up at Niamh's face. 'I thought it was your fault. I blamed you.'

Niamh stood silent as the small crowd of people swirled around her.

'When there is an attraction, a chemistry between two people, it cannot be denied and it was obvious to me from the very beginning, even if it was not so obvious to you,' Sara continued. 'It took me some time to realise that, of course, it was not your fault. I behaved badly towards you and for that I am truly sorry,' Sara said, this time meeting Niamh's gaze properly.

Was this actually happening for real? Could Sara actually have been jealous of her? wondered Niamh. Where was Giorgio, anyway? She hadn't seen him since the wine bottle incident in the kitchen. She searched the crowd but couldn't see him.

Then Grace was at her side, having seen the conversation between Sara and her sister from across the room and coming in case Niamh needed to be rescued.

'Niamh, I think it's hard for people to reach the bar, there are so many people here,' Grace said, pointing in the direction of the narrow bar counter.

'Oh, right, I hadn't noticed,' Niamh admitted, grateful for the distraction. 'Are the two guys not passing enough drinks around?'

'No, no, that's not the problem. All the food is on the bar counter and people can't get to it. I think you should pass it around the room.'

'You're right,' Niamh replied. She turned to speak to Sara, but Sara shook her head. She put a hand on Niamh's shoulder. 'Please. I have distracted you enough. We can talk later. Tonight you have important work to do. I brought two of my new staff members here tonight to see your wine bar. Don't worry, I will ask them to help. If you want my help, that is?'

Niamh hesitated for a moment, still reeling from Sara's confession. She didn't quite know what to say, but she had to agree that she had other priorities right now and that she could use a little extra help.

'That would be great, Sara,' she said appreciatively. 'I thought two people would be plenty but they are stuck serving drinks. I didn't think we'd get this big a crowd, to be honest.'

Sara smiled at her as she gestured to the two girls. 'Niamh, this is a good problem to have. It means that you have under-estimated the crowd and tonight will be a big success. Don't worry, the girls will be happy to help.'

The two girls, figuring they had the night off, had already had a couple of drinks, but they donned black aprons in the kitchen and loaded mini bites of food onto round trays. As they headed towards the door, Niamh thought she saw one of the girls stumble in her heels.

'Are you OK?'

'Ah, *sì*! New shoes,' the girl replied, kicking up her heel to explain the stumble.

Niamh decided that she really needed the help, so she probably didn't have a choice and, anyway, the girl worked for Sara so she was definitely properly trained.

It didn't take more than a couple of seconds for her to hear the commotion on the other side of the packed bar. Emily, stationed on a high stool at the counter, had seen the initial pieces of prosciutto-laden crostini become airborne as the girl, deep in conversation with two Italian guys her own age, took another wobble. The girl hadn't even noticed a couple of appetisers roll off the side of her tray and down the sleeve of an expensive Italian suit. Emily scanned the crowd and caught Niamh's eye across the room, drawing one hand across her throat in a 'cut her off' motion. Before anyone could intervene, a fit of giggles caused the offending tray to wobble again, and this time several pieces of tomato bruschetta landed on the lap of a very elegantly dressed woman. Niamh watched in horror, making her way through the crowd. She had been introduced to the same woman earlier that evening and knew that she was a highly respected writer from *Food & Wine* magazine in Milan.

'No! Not her!'

Before Niamh could even reach the scene, Sara had stepped in and plucked the tray from the unwitting girl who was still, at this point, deep in conversation. With an ice-cold look that could freeze molten tar, Sara snapped her fingers loudly. '*Vai!*' she said in a voice that indicated she was not to be argued with, and motioned towards the door.

Niamh stood mortified as Sara spoke in a rapid stream of Italian, apologising to the lady and assuring her that she would take care of it. The lady stood and turned to Niamh, whose face was now bright red.

'Don't worry about it. It's my own fault,' she said graciously in flawless English. 'Who wears white to the opening of a wine bar? Please don't even give it a second thought. The dress will be fine.' She gestured towards the pale red stain. 'And I'm here as a friend of Massimo's so, officially, I'm not on duty.'

It was such a kind gesture and Niamh, already on edge and anxious, was almost brought to tears.

'I am so embarrassed,' Sara whispered in her ear, clearly fuming over the incident. 'I didn't know she had been drinking. I am so sorry. I need another apron.'

She turned to the second girl and fired off a couple of sentences in stern Italian. Niamh didn't catch what was said but the threatening tone was clear.

'No, no,' the second girl insisted, seeming to reassure Sara somewhat as she continued about the room with her tray.

She turned back to Niamh. 'You have another apron?'

'Yes, in the kitchen, on the back of the door. But who . . . ?'

'Tonight, I work for you,' Sara said with a nod as she disappeared in the direction of the kitchen.

Stunned, Niamh turned to watch her go.

'What excitement!' Emily declared with a sparkling laugh, as she came to stand alongside Niamh and Grace. 'Sara had been speaking to some people in that corner and she saw the whole thing happen. I watched her lurch across the room like an animal stalking its prey,' she continued with an amused smile. 'I'd hate to be that poor girl tomorrow!'

'Well, it's not her fault, poor thing. She didn't know she'd end up working tonight,' Niamh offered in the girl's defence.

'Niamh, darling, you don't go out with your boss and get hammered. My word though, did you witness the snap of her fingers?'

'Yes, impressive!' Grace said in reluctant admiration.

'I kind of want to learn to do that, and to be more like her actually. She was fierce!' Niamh said, her head reeling. 'Although if I acted like that I'd probably be sued for harassment.'

'Now,' Emily said, leaning in conspiratorially towards Niamh. 'Not meaning to change the subject or anything – but I'm going to. There's a man in that corner I simply have to meet. Do you know him?'

'Who?' Niamh asked, craning her neck in the direction Emily was pointing.

'That gorgeous creature in the pale blue shirt. Just look at those arms. He's positively bursting at the seams, and so am I. I think I feel flush!' Emily said with a salacious grin.

'No, I've no idea who he is. How did these people find out about this? And how are there so many hot men here? Is this actually happening?'

'Word of a party travels fast in a small town. Now, hand me two glasses of your finest champagne, please, dear girl!'

'You're just going to rock up there and talk to him?'

'Good grief, no. With a bit of luck I'll rock up there and seduce him!' Emily grinned before making a beeline for the corner.

The crowd had started to whittle down after eleven o'clock, with only a couple of stragglers left in the bar.

'God, this certainly isn't an Irish party,' Grace said, gripping her champagne glass tightly. 'I don't think an Irish party can officially end until all the alcohol has been consumed. Emily! Are you leaving? You can't leave!'

Emily was making her way to the door on the arm of her prey.

'We're going to La Terrazza to meet some of ... what's your name again, darling?' she asked the man, who was easily fifteen years her junior.

'Alessandro,' he said, leaving her side to introduce himself to Niamh and Grace. '*Piacere*,' he said politely. 'We are going to meet some work colleagues of mine. You are welcome to join us.'

'Ooh, sounds like fun,' Grace said, with champagne-fuelled enthusiasm. 'Niamh?'

'Sure, why not? I think I've earned a drink tonight,' Niamh said. 'Go ahead. I'll follow you in a few minutes. I just have to lock up here and grab my coat from upstairs. I'll leave this mess until tomorrow.'

Chapter Thirty-Seven

Niamh flipped the little sign on the door to read CLOSED. Giorgio was outside, pacing up and down, talking on his phone. Niamh's stomach flipped as she stood watching him through the blinds. She wondered if he was coming back to join the party or if he was coming with an update on the deal. She could feel her heart pound harder in her chest and felt irrationally nervous. He was coming in with some sort of news. That much was obvious. What she didn't know was whether it was good or bad.

He kept pacing, and had all the shoulder shrugging and gesticulating of an Italian in intense conversation.

Niamh texted Emily:

Have you heard anything from Giorgio about the deal?

Moments later a response flashed up on her screen. *No, nothing. Why?*

Because he's pacing up and down outside the wine bar like a deranged caged animal.

There was silence for a moment and the three dots to indicate that someone was actively typing had disappeared.

Why have you gone silent? What are you not saying? Niamh asked.

He does that when he's stressed or angry. I've seen it before.

Shit. Do you think it's bad news?

I don't know.

Giorgio pushed open the door. The little bell tinkled overhead.

'*Buona sera,*' he said, as he dropped his briefcase on the banquette along the left wall. 'Are you busy? Can I speak with you?'

'For the love of God, Giorgio, yes, spit it out. I've been watching you pace for the last ten minutes,' Niamh said, her arms flung out at her sides.

He frowned and looked confused. 'I don't understand, but I have some news about the deal.'

He sat on the banquette and she took a seat alongside him.

She groaned and bent over at the waist, putting her head in her hands. 'It's not going to work out, is it? I can tell by your face. You're all serious. I knew it was impossible. Goddamnit it, anyway.' She lifted her face and shook her head with a wry smile. 'I was so close.'

'Nina, will you listen to me?'

'Sorry, go on,' she said in a quiet voice. Her mind had already left the conversation as he talked about different numbers, percentages and valuations. She wondered how long she had before she would have to return home. She wondered exactly how much money she had left in her bank account. She thought about the invoices to suppliers that had yet to be paid. She would have to cover those, for sure. She couldn't just walk away from those and not pay them just because she'd screwed up her own finances.

'Nina, are you listening to me? I don't think you are listening to me,' he said, sounding exasperated.

Niamh turned to see Giorgio gesturing with both hands.

'Sorry, no, I wasn't. I am now. Sorry.'

'So my brother will own half.'

'Sorry, what? I wasn't listening. Sorry.'

Giorgio sighed and shook his head and spoke slowly. 'I explain to you, Nina, that Signora Emilia will own fifty per cent of the building and my brother Marco will own the other fifty per cent.'

'But how come? I don't follow.'

'*Dio io*. You were not listening to one word I have said.' Giorgio got up and stood in front of her. 'I tell you now again. OK. I have spoken with my brother on the phone in Chicago three times yesterday and two times again today. I have told him that he is crazy to sell the building. The building will only increase in value. Each time I tell him this he tells me that he will soon have a baby and a wife to think about and so he now wants to sell the building. So I ask him how many dollars exactly do you think you need to buy ... *Dio io*, what do you call these things? Nappies! Yes, and milk for the baby? Do you think you need eight hundred thousand dollars' worth of these things?' Giorgio was gesticulating wildly again and running his hands through his hair. 'So finally today he hears me for the first time. I say is it not better to have an investment for the future if he is to have a child? I say is it not better to save for university in America as this costs so much money? I tell him that right now he does not need the money, he just wants the money – there is a difference, no?' He continued uninterrupted while Niamh stayed rooted to the seat, clinging to his every word.

'So finally I suggest that if he wants money now that he sell half of the building to Emilia and retain the other half ownership. That way he gets money for baby milk and he keeps a share of the building for the future. And Emilia does not need to worry about liquidating her other investments. After two days of these conversations he tells me that this is a very good idea.'

He looked exhausted.

'So, you mean he's going to sell half of the building to Emily? Like fifty per cent? And he's happy to hold on to the other fifty per cent?' She realised that she was speaking as a nine-year-old might, in trying to understand the situation, but she was terrified that she had somehow misunderstood.

'*Sì.*'

'And is Emily OK with this?'

'I have not spoken with her yet. That was my brother just now on the phone. But I think she will agree that it is a better deal for her as she can retain her other investments. She would have had many, many tax implications if she had had to liquidate her investments before they had matured.'

It still amazed Niamh how articulate Giorgio could be when he talked about business or finance, and yet at times couldn't utter a simple sentence in English, but she decided that this was not the time to mention it.

'And, he's not selling to the other bidder?'

'No.'

'So, we keep the wine bar?'

'*Sì,* you keep the wine bar,' he said, looking at her with a smile.

'*Oh my God!*' was all she could say. She put both her hands to her mouth. They were shaking.

'Nina, why are you so surprised? I know a good deal when I see it. I just had to explain it to my brother that he is being a fool to sell. So now, this way, everyone wins.'

'Thank you, Giorgio! Thank you! Thank you!' She leaped up, threw herself against his chest and kissed him. She hadn't meant to. At least, she didn't think so. She certainly hadn't thought about doing it – it just happened. She was over-whelmed with relief and excitement that all this was finally

373

over and she could get on with her new life here. She pulled back, put her hand to her mouth and looked at him. 'I'm sorry. I didn't mean to. I was just ... I don't know ... sorry,' she mumbled from behind her hand, her head reeling once again. She sat back down on the banquette and could feel the tears welling up behind her eyes.

'Are you? Sorry?' he asked, looking down at her.

'No, that was a lie,' she said with a small laugh, wiping away one errant tear.

He took her hand and slowly pulled her up from her seat.

'Why are you crying?' he asked softly, tilting his head to one side again, a gesture she had come to love.

She didn't trust herself to speak for fear she might give in to all the emotions welling up inside her. Relief that the building would not be sold from under her, excitement that opening night had gone so well, pride that she had pulled it all off and was on the way to rebuilding her life, this time the way she wanted, and emotion that she was afraid to name or afraid to hope for, given the conversation with Sara. Instead, she just shook her head and blinked away the next round of threatening tears.

She took a deep breath. 'Sorry,' she shrugged. 'It's just a lot right now, that's all.'

'There you go apologising again,' he said, putting his hand under her chin. 'But this is OK. It is a lot and you have done so much. I hope you are proud of yourself tonight, Nina. I know that I am.'

He put his hands on her shoulders and looked at her for just a moment before pulling her back into his arms and enveloping her in a hug. He tilted her chin up towards him and this time the kiss had intention. She could feel her body soften and relax against him as her heart beat faster in her chest. He put one hand behind her head and, with the other on the small of her back, he pulled her gently in towards him. She wrapped both her arms around his back, her hands on the curve of his shoulders and breathed into him. She wanted to stay there for ever, not moving, not changing anything.

He pulled back from her and smiled, his eyes crinkling at the sides. He slowly brushed her hair back and put both his hands on the sides of her face. 'I have wanted to do that for a very long time. In fact since the first day that I met you, the crazy Irish girl with the funny name and the big laugh, I have wanted to do that. Most of the women I have known in my life are the same. They want the same things, they do the same things, and they behave the same way. You are different.'

'But what about Sara? I spoke to her earlier, but ...'

Giorgio shook his head. 'Sara is a dear friend, we were together for a while but it was never ... *come si dice*, how do you say ... a forever kind of love. I helped her with some problems in the past, and she was there for me over the past year. I think we both knew it was not this forever love, but ... but then I met you.' He brushed her hair back again and smiled at her as though allowed to for the first time. 'I love that you are different. You do things your way and you are not afraid of anyone or anything.'

'That's funny, because I think I'm terrified of most things actually, but I like the version of me that you see.' She stopped dead in her tracks and put her hand to her mouth with a gasp.

'What's wrong?' he asked, seeing the change in her expression.

She felt tears well up and threaten behind her eyes and she blinked them away furiously. 'Sorry, it's just something that my mam said to me before she died. She said that you have to like the version of you that you become with someone new, you know, like in a new relationship, and that's kind of what you said just now. It made me think of her.'

'That is a good thing, no? Your mother was right. I wish I could have met her.' He smiled and bent down to kiss her softly again. 'I was afraid to hope for this for a long time, Nina.' He put one arm around her shoulder and pulled her into his chest.

The bell jingled over the door. A young couple holding hands stepped just inside the doorway, but hesitated on seeing the CLOSED sign on the front door.

'Excuse me ... oh, I'm sorry,' the young man said, seeing that he was interrupting something. He looked back at the sign and back again towards Niamh and Giorgio.

'Umm, the sign says this place is open until midnight and it's not midnight yet,' he said, checking his watch. 'Umm, we were just wondering ... '

'Are you open?' the young woman asked with a hopeful grin as she stuck her head around the door.

Niamh looked up at Giorgio, raised her eyebrows and gave a little shrug of both her shoulders as she had seen him do so many times. She looked back to the couple at the door. 'Yes,' she replied with a wide grin as she squeezed his hand. 'Yes, we are!'

Is It Really Too Much to Ask?

Jeremy Clarkson began his writing career on the *Rotherham Advertiser*. Since then he has written for the *Sun*, the *Sunday Times*, the *Rochdale Observer*, the *Wolverhampton Express & Star*, all of the Associated Kent Newspapers and *Lincolnshire Life*. Today he is the tallest person working in British television.

By the same author

Motorworld
Jeremy Clarkson's Hot 100
Jeremy Clarkson's Planet Dagenham
Born to be Riled
Clarkson on Cars
The World According to Clarkson
I Know You Got Soul
And Another Thing
Don't Stop Me Now
For Crying Out Loud!
Driven to Distraction
How Hard Can It Be?
Round the Bend
The Top Gear Years

Is It Really Too Much To Ask?

The World According to Clarkson
Volume Five

JEREMY CLARKSON

MICHAEL JOSEPH
an imprint of
PENGUIN BOOKS

MICHAEL JOSEPH

Published by the Penguin Group
Penguin Books Ltd, 80 Strand, London WC2R 0RL, England
Penguin Group (USA) Inc., 375 Hudson Street, New York, New York 10014, USA
Penguin Group (Canada), 90 Eglinton Avenue East, Suite 700, Toronto, Ontario, Canada M4P 2Y3
(a division of Pearson Penguin Canada Inc.)
Penguin Ireland, 25 St Stephen's Green, Dublin 2, Ireland (a division of Penguin Books Ltd)
Penguin Group (Australia), 707 Collins Street, Melbourne, Victoria 3008, Australia
(a division of Pearson Australia Group Pty Ltd)
Penguin Books India Pvt Ltd, 11 Community Centre, Panchsheel Park, New Delhi – 110 017, India
Penguin Group (NZ), 67 Apollo Drive, Rosedale, Auckland 0632, New Zealand
(a division of Pearson New Zealand Ltd)
Penguin Books (South Africa) (Pty) Ltd, Block D, Rosebank Office Park,
181 Jan Smuts Avenue, Parktown North, Gauteng 2193, South Africa

Penguin Books Ltd, Registered Offices: 80 Strand, London WC2R 0RL, England

www.penguin.com

First published 2013
001

Copyright © Jeremy Clarkson 2013

The moral right of the author has been asserted

Set in 13.5/16pt Garamond MT Std
Typeset by Jouve (UK), Milton Keynes
Printed in Great Britain by Clays Ltd, St Ives plc

A CIP catalogue record for this book is available from the British Library

HARDBACK ISBN: 978–0–718–17867–3
PAPERBACK ISBN: 978–0–718–17868–0

www.greenpenguin.co.uk

Penguin Books is committed to a sustainable
future for our business, our readers and our planet.
This book is made from Forest Stewardship
Council™ certified paper.

In loving memory of Caro

The contents of this book first appeared in Jeremy Clarkson's *Sunday Times* column. Read more about the world according to Clarkson every week in the *Sunday Times*.

Contents

Hounded by the ash cloud on my escape   1

Help, Mr Spock, I need you to pilot
     my hi-tech new flat   5

Traffic storm troopers won't let me buy a bra   9

Roll up to look at my pebbles – just £5 a ticket   13

Madam Minister, your briefs are full of
     flirty, dirty talk   17

Sheep are the robbers' new bullion   21

Please, carry on filming, I'm only
     burning to death   25

Surgery to solve the deficit – cut off Scotland   29

Give to my new charity – Britain's Got Trouble   33

No prison for you – just lick my cesspit clean   37

Move along, officer, it's just a spot of dogging   41

Burial? Cremation? Boil-in-the-bag?   45

Don't misread the whiff of Cameron's armpits   49

A few song lyrics could have done for Piers   53

England's fate is in your hands, Ambassador   57

Concussion is what holidays are all about   61

I've sprayed wasps with glue, now what?   65

Naughty bits & melons – I learnt it all in Albania   69

Beware – Arabella won't stop at hay rustling   73

One dose of this and you could turn into
a werewolf   77

But I've killed Baz already, Mr Safety
Instructor   81

This tired old bird deserves another
chance   85

Just speak English, Johnny Europe   89

Turkey joining the EU? Over my
dead dog's body   93

No one needs to know their adze
from their elbow   97

Use Jordan and Jemima to sell Britain   101

Foraging – an old country word
for violent death   105

WikiLeaks – I dare you to face
Roger Sensible   109

Stop all the clocks for British No Time   113

The small society built on jam and dung   117

Proud to sponsor this police shootout   121

Hello, reception. I've actually used
my bed, please don't be angry   125

This kingdom needs a dose of Norse sense   129

Big smile – and check me down below
for ticks   133

Cancel the breast op and buy an iron lung   137

A man's ego hangs in his downstairs loo   141

We didn't have an affair – and that's
all you need to be told   145

Garçon! A hike in my flat's value, please 149

A quake's nothing until it becomes a wobbly
iDisaster 153

I'm going to cure dumb Britain 157

Advice for men – don't try to keep your
hair on 161

We demand our weekends back,
Adolf Handlebar 165

Houston, our spaceships are ugly 169

Look what that little DVD pirate is really
doing 173

Dear BBC, why d'ya think Dick Whittington
gave Salford a miss? 177

Okay, I'll come clean on Rebekah and
the Chipping Norton plot 181

Okay, tontine tango birdie, let's baffle 'em
with insider talk 185

Get on your roof, everyone, and give
Biggles an eyeful 189

That's it – one fluffed backhand and I'm
broken as a father 193

French porn and a little software can save
our schools 197

Oh, Berbatovs – I've got to learn
footballspeak 201

My daughter and I stepped over the body
and into a brothel 205

Own up, we all had a vile streak long
before going online 209

Down, boy! Fido's fallen in love with the
vacuum cleaner   213

Street lights and binmen? Luxuries we just
can't afford   217

Ker-ching! I've got a plan to turn India's
pollution into pounds   221

Look out, dear, a carbuncle is heading
your way   225

Oh, the vita is dolce. But the music?
Shaddap you face   229

Down periscope! I've found an airtight
way to quit smoking   233

No more benefits: I'm putting the idle on
the bread and sherry line   237

I walked tall into Savile Row – and left a
broken man   241

Harry's chopper makes mincemeat of
Will's whirlybird   245

A *Daily Mail* scoop: I'm a nurse-killing
Hitler in blue jeans   249

My RAF training was dull – until I got to
bomb Piers Morgan   253

A Commons or garden blunder by the
duke of digging   257

No, Fido, the law says you can eat Raffles – not
Postman Pat   261

Skis on, break a leg . . . and take Sarko to
the cleaners   265

We've got a million words for sex but not
    one for best friend   269

Carry on sniping at the rich, Ed, and I just
    might steal your seat   273

Having to sell the family silver – it's
    comedy gold   277

Listen, officer, that gravy boat is the key to
    Whitney's death   281

Lord Lucan must be dead – no one can
    escape YouTube   285

Those pesky stars just won't expose
    themselves any more   289

Three men go into a bar . . . and I couldn't
    hear the punchline   293

Even James 'Thunder' May couldn't make
    wind farms work   297

Smell my cologne: it's called Girlie Tosh
    pour Homme   301

A cheap booze ban will just drive your
    pooch to hooch   305

Exploding Art Snob – it's the best Hirst
    masterpiece yet   309

Where's the Dunkirk spirit? Doing a
    runner to Australia   313

Welcome to the fifty-fourth series of
    Top Gear. I'm seventy-seven, you know   317

Heston's grub is great – but so what if your
    date is ugly?   321

One hundred lines, Miliband Minor: 'I must
    not show off in class'   325

Girls, gongs and JR – if only I'd worn a
    jockstrap   329

I'm desperate to be a German – call me
    Gunther Good-Loser   333

Go on, troll me – but leave your name and
    address   337

Kaboom! It's my turn to play fantasy
    climate change   341

They've read Milton, Mr Gove, now
    get 'em to rewire a plug   345

Blow me up, Scotty, before I land on your
    Manx home   349

And your premium bond prize is . . . a seat
    in the Lords   353

Cheer up, Mewling Murray, you've made
    it into *Boohoo's Who*   357

We're all running as Team GB, the grim
    bellyachers   361

Stop, or I'll shoot . . . about 100 yards off to
    your right   365

Listen, Fritz, we'll do the efficiency
    now – you write the gags   369

Arise, Sir Jeremy – defier of busybody
    croupiers and barmen   373

P-p-please open up, Arkwright, I need
    some t-t-t-trousers   377

Oh, my head hurts – I've a bad case of
    hangover envy   381

If breasts are no big deal, girls, don't get
    them reupholstered   385

Call me Comrade Clarkson, liberator of the
    jobsworths   389

If foreigners weren't watching, we'd be
    lynching bell-ringers   393

Take another step, Simba, and you'll feel
    my foldaway spoon   397

So, the Scouts came to earth in a reptilian
    space plane, right?   401

This lanky git will call you what he wants,
    ref – you blind idiot   405

Chew on a Big Mac with fibs before you
    answer a survey   409

Yes, siree – count me in for genocide and
    conservatory-building   413

Coming soon, *I'm a Terrorist . . . Make Me
Lick Nadine's Toes*   417

Write in now, eel fanciers, and claim your
    million quid   421

Of all the towns in all the world, Cold,
    Wet and Closed is best   425

Help, I've lost track of world affairs in
    Bradley's barnet   429

Stand by, Earth, to boldly look where
    there's no point looking   433

Dim staff and no stock: the key to hanging
on in the high street   437

Forget the cat and the pension, wrinklies,
a gap year beckons   441

Your next HS2 service is the 3.15 to
Victorian England   445

Oh, waiter, can I pay with this microchipped
finger?   449

Hello, sailor. Show me what Britain is
really made of   453

Work on the accent, Brum, and Tom
Cruise will be in for a balti   457

As Russians say, manners maketh
the British late   461

Hounded by the ash cloud on my escape

On Thursday morning I woke up in Colditz Castle, drove to Poland and found that I couldn't fly back to England as planned because all of northern Europe was shrouded in a cloud of ash that was thick enough to bring down a jetliner. But, mysteriously, not so thick that it was actually visible.

Brussels, then. That would be the answer. We'd drive at 180mph on the limit-free autobahns to Berlin, fly to Belgium and catch the Eurostar to London.

This, however, turned out to be ambitious, because the only vehicle we could lay our hands on was a knackered Volkswagen van that had a top speed of four. So Prague, then. That was nearer. Yes. We'd start from there instead.

Unfortunately, the index of our map was broken down into countries. And we didn't actually know which country we were in. We'd see a sign for Lückendorf, so I'd look it up in the index. But would it be filed under Germany, Poland or the Czech Republic? And how would it be spelt? The Germans may call it Lückendorf but the Poles might call it something entirely different. In much the same way that people in India call Bombay 'Bombay'. But the BBC insists on calling it 'Mumbai'.

By the time I'd decided Lückendorf doesn't really exist, we'd found a sign for Bogatynia and that doesn't seem to exist, either. The confusion meant that pretty soon we were on a farm track, our path blocked by a tractor that seemed to be scooping mud from a field and putting it on to the road. This encouraged us, since it seemed like a very un-German thing to do and all the Poles are in my bathroom at the moment. We had, therefore, to be near Praha, as the BBC doesn't call it. But should.

We were, and our worries seemed to be over. But they weren't. By this stage the invisible cloud of ash had settled on Belgium and Brussels airport was closed. No matter, we decided. We shall go to Paris and catch the train from there.

Oh, no, we wouldn't. We learnt that all the Eurostar trains were chock-full but we figured that would be okay. We'd fly to Paris, rent a car and we'd drive home in that. Job done.

To celebrate, we went for a beer. I had a lot, if I'm honest, because I wanted to be too drunk to drive this last leg. I had so many that after a while Barclaycard decided it'd be fun to cancel my credit card. And I couldn't phone to explain that if it didn't turn the credit back on again, I'd come round to its offices with an axe. Because by this stage my phone was out of bullets. And then we found that our plane was due to land at Charles de Gaulle just five minutes before that shut down, too. Any delay would be catastrophic.

Normally, people getting on to a plane are fairly polite. We're happy to stand in the aisle for hours while people try to fit the dishwasher they've bought into the overhead locker. I chose not to be so patient on this occasion, though, and as a result there were many injuries. But because of the violence, the plane took off on time and landed just before the Paris shutdown was due to begin.

By now I was Cardiff-on-a-Saturday-night drunk. And fairly desperate for a pee. But not so desperate that I failed to realize the gravity of the situation at Charles de Gaulle. You know those last moments in *Titanic* when the ship is finally going down? Well, it was nothing like that. It was worse.

In the baggage claim was a pretty girl asking if anyone could give her a lift to North Jutland. In the main concourse

were businessmen begging rides to Amsterdam. And everyone was being approached by dodgy-looking North Africans
with gold teeth and promises of taxis to anywhere. For you,
my friend, special price.

Of particular note were the queues of people pointing
and shouting at airline staff as though they were responsible
somehow for the eruption. This seemed like an odd thing to
do. I very much encourage assault, verbal or otherwise, on
useless members of staff who won't help. But yelling will not
bring order to the planet's mantle.

It's funny, isn't it? The airports had only been closed for six
hours and society was cracking up. Not that I cared much
about this because we had secured the last rental car in the
whole airport and were in a rush to catch the midnight train
from Calais. This meant there was no time for a pee.

By Senlis, my bladder was very full. By Lille, the pressure
had become so great the contents had turned to amber. Ever
peed from the window of a moving car? I have. It came out
as pebbles. But it was worth it because at three in the morning I climbed into my own bed at home. Five countries.
Planes. Trains and automobiles. And all because Mother
Nature burped.

There is a warning here, because on the volcanic explosiv-
ity index (VEI) – which goes from one to eight – the eruption
at Eyjafjallajokull will probably be classified as a two. And yet
it shut down every airport in northern Europe. There are
much bigger volcanoes in Iceland. They could, in theory,
shut the whole world down for years.

Let's not forget that back in 1980 Mount St Helens in
Washington state blew with a VEI rating of five. It was a
huge blast but only local air traffic was affected.

What's changed, of course, is our attitude to safety, brought
about in the main by our fear of being sued. Could volcanic

ash bring down a jetliner? Fifteen-hundred miles from the scene of the volcano itself, it is extremely unlikely, but so long as there are lawyers, licking their lips at the prospect of proving the crash could have been avoided, air traffic controllers are bound to push the big button labelled 'Stop'.

It won't be a volcano that ends man's existence on this planet. It'll be the no-win no-fee lawyers. They are the ones who brought Europe to a halt last week. They are the ones who made a simple trip from Berlin to London into a five-country, all-day hammer blow on your licence fee. They are the ones who must be stopped.

18 April 2010

Help, Mr Spock, I need you to pilot my hi-tech new flat

In the olden days it was easy to make a television work. You plugged an aerial cable into the back, then bashed the top with your fist until, eventually, Hughie Green stopped jumping up and down. Things have changed. Have you tried to make a modern TV work? It cannot be done. No, don't argue: it can't. You have to get a man round and then it still won't work because you have absolutely no idea what to press on the remote-control device. I am looking now at the plipper thing for the TV in my office. It has thirty-two buttons on it, including one marked 'COMPO/(rgb 8)'.

Any idea what that does? I haven't. I do understand the one marked 'Power', but this does not actually turn the television on. So far as I can tell, nothing does, which is why, for three years, it has been off. Frankly, for getting the news I'd have been better off building a chain of beacons.

Then there is the world of the mobile phone. Sometimes my wife asks me to answer her Raspberry and not once in a year have I been able to do so before the caller rings off. To my way of thinking, it's not a communication device. It's a sex toy for geeks. A laptop enthusiast's Rabbit.

However, my life took a dramatic turn for the worse last week because I took delivery of a new flat in London. It's been done up by a developer and fitted with every single item from every single gadget magazine in the universe. This means I cannot operate a single thing. Nothing, d'you hear? Nothing at all.

Let us take, for example, the old-fashioned pleasure of

making a cup of coffee. For many years this involved putting some water in a kettle and boiling it. But now kettles are seen as messy, which is why my new flat has a multi-buttoned aluminium panel set into the wall. The idea is that you fill it with beans and the boiling water is instant. Sounds great, but the instruction book is 400 pages long and I'm sorry, but if I waded through that, my longing for a cup of coffee would be replaced by a fervent need for a quart of Armagnac.

The coffee machine, though, is the tip of the iceberg. There's a music system that can beam any radio station in the world into any room. Last night I selected a classic rock station from San Francisco and was enjoying very much the non-stop stream of Supertramp, until I wanted to go to bed. This meant turning the system off and, for me at least, that is impossible.

Normally, of course, you just hit the offending electronic good with a hammer or throw it on the floor – this works well for alarm clocks in hotel rooms – but I was holding a remote-control device. Smashing that into a million pieces, I realized, would not stop the noise. I needed to find the actual box and I couldn't. So the only solution was to fly to California . . . and burn the radio station down.

I considered it but in the end went to bed to 'The Logical Song'. The irony was not lost on me. This morning the station was playing 'Dreamer'. The irony was lost on me there, though. In a boiling torrent of rage. It's not just the music system and the kettle, either.

The extractor fan above the hob has seven settings. Why? What's wrong with off and on? I can't think of anything that's less in need of seven settings . . . apart from maybe a pacemaker.

Other things? Well, I can't open the garage door – it's remote control, obviously – and the entry phone doesn't appear to be connected to the front door. That means there's an increased chance it's connected to air traffic control at Heathrow and, as a result, I daren't go near it.

Burglar alarm? Nope. Television? Nope. Broadband? Not a chance. And the cooker? Hmm, you could use its controls to remotely pilot a US Air Force spy drone. But to make a shepherd's pie? Not in a million years. And, of course, I can't contact the man who installed any of this stuff because he's in Aspen. People who install high-tech equipment are always in bloody Aspen. This is because they're always American.

They go to gadget shows in Las Vegas, get completely carried away and then come to Europe to install systems that no one over here can understand. We've only just got over drawbridges, for Christ's sake. Then they disappear and the people who made the various bits and pieces go bust. Which means you're left in a house that has everything – and nothing at all.

In a desperate attempt to turn everything off, I thought I'd find the fuse box. Fuse box? To an American gadgeteer, a fuse box is as Victorian as a horse and carriage. So, in my new flat, the fuse box is a fuse room. And it's not hard to find, because you can hear the circuitry humming from a hundred yards away. Or you could if you weren't being deafened by 'Even in the Quietest Moments'.

Then you open the door and, Holy Mother of God, it's like stepping on to the bridge of the *Starship Enterprise*. I am not joking. There are rows and rows of switches and thousands of tiny blinking green lights. Thousands? Yes. Thousands.

I have been on the flight deck of a modern Airbus jetliner and I assure you there are fewer switches and lights up there than there are in the bowels of my three-bedroom flat. It's so scary that you don't dare touch anything in case, when you come out again, you are in Chicago.

Apparently this is not unusual. Many modern properties have rooms such as this, full of warp cores and modems and circuit breakers. The fans needed to keep it all cool would propel a military hovercraft; the power needed just to power itself would light Leeds; and it's all for no purpose whatsoever because no one in the real world understands any of it.

As I sat on the floor, then, with no heating, no kettle, no freezer, no television, no broadband, no light and no hope any time soon of turning the situation around, a profound thought wafted into my head. Our endless pursuit of a high-tech future seems to have taken us back to the Stone Age.

2 May 2010

Traffic storm troopers won't let me buy a bra

Now that the general election is over, we can turn our attention to one of the most important issues in our lives today: my local cobbler has closed down. I can't say that I ever used it because that would be a lie; I didn't, but I liked having it there. A genial old man in a brown coat, stitching up battered clogs, reminded me of a time when we didn't simply throw our training shoes away because they went out of fashion or because our football team signed a sponsorship deal with Puma. Waste Not. Want Not. It wasn't called that, but it should have been.

The florist has gone, too. I can't say I ever used that, either, mainly because the girl who runs the rival business on the high street is much prettier. But, again, I liked having it there. I liked living in a town that had two florists and now I don't any more.

Other shops that have closed down in the past couple of years include the hi-fi shop, the bra shop, the children's clothing shop, both off-licences and the delicatessen. Now, I should explain at this point that I did use the deli. Once. I bought some cheese there and it was very nice. Not so nice, sadly, that I actually bought more, but I liked the idea, should I be in town buying some stamps or getting my shoes mended, that if I were overcome by a need for a spot of Wensleydale, I could sally forth etc. and get some. And now, I can't.

Obviously, I am writing about Chipping Norton, and this news, you may think, would be of some interest in the

Chipping Norton Gazette. But we have no such thing. And, anyway, I bet exactly the same thing is going on in your town; that it's now just a bland, featureless desert of estate agents, fast-food joints and charity shops.

I know that charity shops perform a vital service. I am aware of this and I wish them all the very best as they leach into the premises once occupied by butchers, bakers and candlestick makers. The trouble is, I hate them.

I never want to buy a Victorian teapot. And I don't like to be reminded when I go into town that it's still possible. A Victorian teapot is no good when you want cheese or a romper suit. A Victorian teapot is no good even if you want a cup of tea. So I don't want one, even if it's only 3d – as it usually says on the label in these places.

I suppose, if push came to shove, I'd rather have a charity shop than a set of whitewashed windows that sit like broken teeth in the gums of the high street, reminding their former owners of their failure. However, what I really want is the cobbler back. And the bra shop and the florist and at least one of the offies.

They won't be back, though. They're gone for good. And it's a worry because when you take away a town centre's independent retailers, you take away its soul. You also take away the reason for going there. And then what? Why live cheek by jowl in the flabby doughnut when there's no jam in the centre?

I do not intend to dwell on the consequences here because I'm more interested in stopping the rot. And to do that, we need to work out why, all of a sudden, so many small shops are shutting up for good.

Some, of course, blame the recession. But many of these places had signs above the door saying they were established in 1890. That means they'd survived recessions in the past, and wars and diphtheria.

The most common scapegoat is the supermarket or the out-of-town retail park. People say that it is much cheaper to buy cheese from Asda than it is to buy it from a chap in an apron in your local deli. This is true. But if it's cheapness you want, then surely it'd be best to make the cheese yourself. All you need is some milk, some rennet and the bassist from Blur.

No. I suspect the reason we choose to visit a supermarket rather than flog around a town that was designed by King Alfred is that it's so much more convenient.

And that, I think, is where a solution to the problem of urban decay can be found. Realistically, we can never do anything to reverse the spread of supermarkets, but we can level the playing field. We just have to make town-centre shopping easier. And that can be achieved by getting rid of traffic wardens. Or civil enforcement officers, as they are now called. And how Russian is that?

Whatever they're called, I'm not suggesting they should be put in a vat and melted down, but if this were necessary, then so be it. The fact is, they have to go. All of them.

Every single time I go into my local town, I get a parking ticket. I'm driving along, I am suddenly consumed by a need for a bra, I park in a perfectly sensible place that causes no inconvenience to anyone, pop into the shop, find it's selling only Victorian teapots, come out again . . . and blam. I've been done. If they put that much effort into catching terrorists, nothing would ever explode ever again.

In Oxford I work on the basis that I'm going to be done anyway, so I just park right outside where I want to be. The last time I went there, I parked in a bus lane and went to watch a film. The fine was the same as if I'd made an effort.

It's as though towns don't want people to stop and shop. And, of course, many don't – those run by people who still cling to the outdated and now completely discredited theory that man causes global warming, for example. They would rather the locals stayed at home and beat themselves with twigs. But even enlightened boroughs continue to employ civil storm troopers. Which means they are employing a body of people whose sole job is to kill the town.

Do they think that, if left to our own devices, we'd all park on zebra crossings for a year? If they do, it means they don't trust us. And if they don't trust us, then the relationship has broken down and it's time for some civil unrest.

9 May 2010

Roll up to look at my pebbles – just £5 a ticket

As we know, European flights have been a bit tricky these past few weeks. Couple that to the dreary industrial action at British Airways, the lousy exchange rate and the complete shambles that is our economy, and it's certain that many people will be thinking about taking their holidays in Britain this year.

Indeed, I was in Cornwall last week and, even though it's only the middle of May, the beaches were already peppered with families, huddling behind windbreaks and peering at the horizon through their anorak hoods, fervently hoping for a triumph of optimism over meteorological fact.

This is the problem with holidaying in the British Isles. We have good weather, of course, but it's like an unreliable old friend. You never know when it will drop by to brighten your day. And it never stays long. It has other places to go. France, usually, or the Caribbean.

So let's think about that for a moment. This year there will be more holidaymakers at large in Britain than ever before. They will not be able to lie on a beach reading a book because the same northerly winds that brought the ash cloud are keeping temperatures down to the point where nitrogen freezes. So we have thousands and thousands of people, on holiday, bored and with all the money they didn't spend on flights burning a dirty great hole in their pockets. I sense a great business opportunity here.

While in Cornwall, I couldn't help noticing that there was a bee museum. Yes, that's right. A bee museum. The bees do not balance balls on their noses or juggle miniature chain-saws. You just pay cash money to watch some bees fly about, being bees. It was just down the road from a gnome reserve, where you can go and trundle around the garden of someone who has very poor taste.

So, there is money to be made from insects and plastic garden ornaments. But for some reason what the bored British holidaymaker likes best of all is stones. If the stones are fastened together in the shape of a church, or an old house where someone's wife used to live, then you are quids in. But don't worry if this isn't the case.

Fallen-over stones are still massively popular with the army of moochers. They will spend hours, and pay out God knows how much on booklets and postcards and ice creams, and all you have to offer them in return is some rubble that you can claim once used to be an abbey.

Amazingly, though, you can even make money if the stones are just stones.

Round where I live there are some stones in a field. If you pay a pound, or 50p for children, then you are allowed to go and look at them. How brilliant is that? You almost certainly couldn't design a new type of Apple iPod or an Aston Martin DB9. But don't worry. You don't have to.

To make a living you just have to charge people to look at some stones that someone, a long time ago and for unclear reasons, up-ended in your top paddock.

There are some enormous stones in a field in Wiltshire that are free if you look at them from the nearby road. But the druids, or whoever manages the site, will charge you a whopping £6.90 if you want to see them close up. That's a fantastic business. Especially when you throw in the sale of the guidebooks, all of which say the same thing: 'We don't have a clue why these stones are here.'

Mind you, the guardians of a stone I saw in Cornwall go one better. They have got hordes of people paying £3 to see a stone that may or may not mark the burial place of King Arthur. A king who didn't actually exist. How mental is that?

There are some stones by the stream on the farm I've just bought. I'm going to claim they mark the birthplace of James Bond, open a gift shop and charge people a fiver to come and stand near them for a few minutes. You should be thinking along the same lines. If you have any sort of geology in your garden, put up a leaflet in the local post office and Wallace Arnold will be bringing them round in droves for a gawp.

The capacity British holidaymakers have for finding uninteresting things so interesting that they will pay money to look at them beggars belief. They will pay to watch cows being born. They will pay to see needlework. They will pay to look at your flower beds. If you have a hobby, no matter how nerdy it may be, you can make money out of it from June to the end of September.

Unless your hobby is looking at pornography on the internet. You probably won't be able to make anything out of that. But don't despair.

Industry is an excellent draw, especially if it's closed down. There's a disused tin mine in Cornwall that charges adults eight quid and children a fiver. And what do they see? A hole in the ground that is no longer producing one of the most dreary commodities in the already not very exciting world of metallurgy.

Imagine the possibilities. You could charge people money to go and look round your branch of what used to be Woolworths. 'This is where people used to choose their sweets, and if you follow me we'll have a look at where the racks of DVDs used to be.'

What else are tourists going to do? They've seen some stones. They've looked round the gnome reserve and they've watched bees. It's still raining, the children are still bored, you have their attention and that means you have a direct line to their credit card.

I met a man last week who rents wetsuits to people who want to go swimming but can't in the costumes they've brought because it's always too cold. He will also rent you a slab of polystyrene on which you can play in the waves. He has a £100,000 supercar, and I'm guessing now but I'd like to bet that by milking the misery of the trapped British holiday-maker, he's able to take his holidays abroad.

16 May 2010

Madam Minister, your briefs are full of flirty, dirty talk

There seems to have been some sort of brouhaha about a shortage of women in the new Camerclegg cabinet, and I must say, it does seem to be a bit unbalanced. This, I fear, is very unhealthy. There is nothing that fills my heart with such dread as an all-male gathering. This is why I avoid stag nights and 'lads' nights out' with the same fervent determination as I avoid close encounters with nettles and rabid dogs. I do not understand business, cigars bore me, I have no interest in cricket and if anyone slaps me on the back, I am filled with a sometimes overwhelming need to respond with a punch to the face.

When men are not talking about business and cricket and slapping one another's backs, they talk nonsense, wondering, for instance, if it is possible to live upside down, or cross the Atlantic on a vacuum cleaner. This sort of thing is useless when you have been charged with running the country. You may start out with every intention of working out how the Department for Business, Innovation and Skills could be abolished. But pretty soon, after you've checked on the cricket scores, you're going to be wondering if it's possible to ingest ice cream through your nose.

Men need women in order to function properly, and the reason for this is simple: a conversation with an interesting man is just a conversation with an interesting man. Ultimately, it's going nowhere.

Whereas a conversation with an interesting woman, provided she isn't completely enormous, could go out of the door, up the stairs and into the bedroom. Or into the garden. Or to the back seat of the car. It could go anywhere.

This is why men are much funnier and cleverer when women are around. Because we flirt and women flirt back. And flirting is the oil that lubricates the engine of ingenuity and wit.

I cannot be arsed to think a single original thought when I'm surrounded by men. But throw a woman into the mix and usually I have developed a new world order by teatime. Unfortunately, I'm not sure the cabinet is the right place for such behaviour. Trying to make Theresa May understand the need for national service is one thing. Trying to make her understand while imagining what she would look like naked adds all sorts of complications that the country can well do without at the moment.

What's more, we are talking about people here who are separated by many miles from their families. They are cooped up in a room together and it is at times like this when flirting can lead to all sorts of other problems. If you are not careful, you could end up in the bath with Edwina Currie.

Right now, the government has no money at all to pay for the war in which we are engaged or even the medicines needed to put the soldiers back together again. And it's hard to think how this can be sorted out if Liam Fox is playing a secretive game of mental footsie with Caroline Spelman.

You may argue, if you wish, that grown men and women with big jobs do not flirt, but I disagree. Only the very dull and the very dead do not. When a person is tired of flirting, they are tired of life. And we don't want people like that in charge of anything.

So, you might imagine that the best solution is to be governed entirely by women. Thanks to her multitasking skills, a woman in government could look after defence in the morning, work and pensions in the afternoon and health while doing the ironing. You therefore wouldn't need twenty-eight seats round the table. Just four.

However, I'm not sure an all-woman government would work at all because have you ever heard women talking when they think no men can hear?

We imagine it's all schools and shopping and needlework. But it isn't. I've been in the position these past few days to eavesdrop on a group of girls. Bright girls with important jobs. And what they've talked about – non-stop – is sex.

Not romantic, swoony, Mr Darcy-in-a-lake sex, either. Real, hardcore, back-end-of-the-internet sex. Who's been sodomized by whom and where. Who's had surgery on their inner labia. What lesbianism would be like. At one point I thought they'd moved on to gardening because I thought they were talking about a nearby clematis. But I'd misheard. It was clitoris. And it seemed to occupy them for hours.

One girl explained last night, when she thought I was asleep, that she got her builders to do as she wished by stopping on the way home, taking off her bra and standing in the cold for a few minutes. But they were quickly back on labial surgery.

£222,281

Often, invitations were extended for the others to have a look at an interesting piece of pubic topiary. I found this amazing. I have been a man for fifty years and I have never been invited by another man to look at his penis. Nor have I felt the need to ask a mate to check out my testicles to see if they are 'normal'. And certainly, I've never got my builder to do as he's told by coming home with my old chap hanging out.

The women I've been with aren't unusual, either. A few weeks ago I overheard two girlfriends chatting, and the subject – for several hours – was masturbation. Was the Bullet better than the Rabbit? What positions worked best? And what fantasies? It was extraordinary because, again, I cannot imagine men discussing onanism in the same terms. In fact, I cannot recall it being discussed at all.

When we understand all this, we can see perfectly well why committees don't work. There are too many distractions.

This is why companies and countries run by one person are so productive. Because they don't spend all day flirting or talking about sex or seeing how far they can lean back in their chair without falling over, they get things done. I therefore have a suggestion. Soon, we will be asked if we wish to change the voting system. I think we should seriously consider introducing a dictatorship.

23 May 2010

Sheep are the robbers' new bullion

Alarming news from the north. Last week someone broke into a field on the outskirts of Knutsford in Cheshire and stole a hundred mummy and baby sheeps. The farmer's wife is distraught as one of the stolen animals was a pet. And they took its new lamb as well. It's all just too heartbreaking for words. And it's by no means an isolated incident.

Just a few days earlier in Lancashire, a farmer in Ramsbottom – I'm afraid I'm not making that up – woke up one morning to find that someone had half-inched 271 of his flock.

Meanwhile, in Wales, 200 were nicked, a similar number went missing in the Borders, and in Cumbria alone fifteen farmers have been targeted. It seems, then, that up north, sheep are the new bullion.

It's not just sheep, though. In Tamworth, Staffordshire, someone has been nicking piglets; in Norfolk, Mrs Queen lost £15,000-worth of cows; and in Shropshire some chap rang the police the other day to say someone had stolen 800,000 of his bees. That's on top of the 500,000 bees that were stolen from Lothian last June. At this rate I may have to think about fitting a burglar alarm to my tortoise.

So what's going on here and, more importantly, why has no one yet been caught? I mean, how hard can it be to find someone who has stolen a million bees? Surely he'll be in a hospital, swollen beyond all recognition and moaning the low moan of deep, relentless agony.

I want to catch him, frankly, because stealing someone's

bees is a bit like stealing someone's eczema flakes. What exactly are you going to do with them?

Then there is this sheep-rustling business. To steal 271 sheep with no one hearing, you need to have several things: some experience of how sheep behave, a knowledge of the countryside, a fleet of dogs and a big lorry. Now I'm no detective but I reckon that if we examine this evidence, the culprit is almost certainly going to be a shepherd. Interestingly, however, police investigating the crimes are not looking for someone sitting on a fence, in a brand new smock. Instead, they seem to have decided that crime syndicates are at work here. Wow! The Wurzels with sawn-offs.

Actually, it's a bit more complicated than that. Apparently, stolen sheep and underground, unlicensed slaughterhouses aren't troubled with European Union hygiene regulations. Which means the market could soon be flooded with a surplus of dodgy joints. It sounds to me as though there could be a Mr Big at large in the hills. Pablo Esco-baa, perhaps.

Frankly, though, I can't imagine the profits are that large. Which is why I find myself wondering why we now have Ronnie and Reggie Gummidge from the Cosy Nostra rushing about in the uplands stealing sheep when they could be doing the traditional gangster thing: robbing banks.

I always wanted to be a bank robber when I grew up. As a career, it seemed ideal: short periods of glamorous and interesting work followed by lengthy spells of relaxation in Spain. All my heroes were bank robbers: Butch and Sundance; Jack Hawkins's League of Gentlemen; Bonnie and Clyde. Bank robbers were cool.

There was a time when a bank was robbed every other night. We became used to waking up in the morning to the sound of Dixon tearing past our house in his Austin Westminster, on the trail of some blagger in a stripy jersey and a Jag.

You'd imagine that today bank robbery would be even more popular.

We all know the police are mostly engaged in the lucrative business of apprehending motorists. And the few who are allowed to concentrate on proper crime are either back at the station, filling in forms, or on courses, learning how to climb over a garden wall. The chances of being caught, then, are almost zero.

Obviously, if you wander into your local branch of Barclays and, halfway through the robbery, you succumb to the drugs you've taken and fall asleep, then, yes, you're going to get nicked. But if you really concentrate on planning and get all the details just so, you'll be fine. The only problem would be the crowds of well-wishers showering you with rose petals as you ran for the getaway car.

And yet despite all this, the last really big bank job on UK soil was in 1994, when raiders made off with £26.5 million from the Northern Bank in Belfast. That's an astonishing sixteen years ago. So what's happened? Why have people stopped stealing wedge, which makes you popular and cool and rich, and started stealing honey bees, which makes you go to hospital?

I wouldn't mind, but the people behind the Belfast heist have never been caught. And most of the money has never been recovered. One night's work: £26.5 million. And no time in the slammer. That's got to beat traipsing around the freezing moors at night, whispering orders at Shep in the hope that you can flog a dodgy chop to Mrs Miggins at No. 22 for a couple of quid.

It's odd, but I think I have the answer. If you go to a hilltop farm, you will find a sheep. But if you go to a bank, you can be pretty certain you will not find any cash. Obviously, they've given most of it to the Greeks, but what about the rest? I think it's melted because I haven't seen or used any for years. So to be a bank robber in the twenty-first century you don't need to be able to crack safes – just computer codes. And I'm sorry, but fiddling about on HSBC's hard drive is a miserable pursuit. Certainly, it's way less cool than nicking the Queen's cows.

It gets worse. Modern cars are almost impregnable, modern art is worthless, half the world lives with a panic button and a can of Mace under its pillow, CCTV has made all city centres no-go areas and most of the police are tooled up with shooters.

This, then, is why there has been such a spate of animal thefts. Because these days, what else is there to nick?

30 May 2010

Please, carry on filming, I'm only burning to death

With the next series of *Top Gear* just weeks away, we are in a frantic race against time to finish off all the films. I won't say what they're about here, though, because obviously you already know. This is because every single thing we do is photographed and videoed by passers-by. And then either posted on the internet or sold to the newspapers. Now that everyone has a camera in their pocket all the time, everyone is a paparazzo, and that has changed my life completely. I'm not complaining because, obviously, life will be a lot more worrying when the attention stops. But, that said, could I please make a small request.

When you stop me in the street to ask for a photograph, have some clue about how your phone camera works. That way, when you ask a witless passer-by to take a photograph of us, he won't spend twenty minutes holding it the wrong way round and taking endless shots of his own nose.

There's another annoyance, too. Yesterday I was snapped walking up Holland Park Avenue, going into Tesco, buying eggs, driving up the M40 and relieving myself in Oxford services. I'm not joking. I turned round while I was having a pee to find a lorry driver filming me. Doubtless, this riveting scene is already on YouTube. Unless, of course, the chap wants it for some kind of bizarre private collection.

I feel fairly sure that if I were to catch fire, no one would try to beat out the flames or find an extinguisher. They'd simply record the event on their phones.

You think I'm being silly? Well, you may recall that in the

run-up to the election, the former UKIP leader Nigel Farage decided to tow a banner behind a plane, urging people to, I don't know, stamp on a bratwurst. Unfortunately, the banner got entangled in the plane's tail fin and it crashed.

I'm certain you recall the photographs of him in the wreckage, with blood pouring down his face, and of the pilot, seriously injured in the seat next to him.

Now here's the strange thing. Someone took those photographs. Someone raced to the scene, saw two injured men hanging upside down and thought: 'I know. I'll get my camera out and take a picture of this.'

Of course, it's possible that the person responsible was a professional photographer, in which case the boundaries are blurred. It is a professional photographer's job to record events, not shape them. But I think this mainly applies during periods of civil unrest and war.

However, it is also possible the person responsible was a bank manager or an accountant. And I don't know about you but I think if I were presented with a badly injured man in the wreckage of a plane – no matter how much I disagreed with his opinions – I'd think about neck braces and mouth-to-mouth and fuel leaks rather than exposures and angles and what some pictures might be worth.

We saw a similar problem recently with the sun-dried baby on the beach. Someone decided that the best way of helping the poor infant, who suffered 40 per cent burns, was to take some pictures of him.

And then you have those people – and for some reason they're almost always German – who think it's a good idea to climb over the security fences at zoos.

Maybe they think the leopard or the tiger looks cute but, of course, as soon as they're actually in there, they quickly realize that it wasn't such a good idea after all. Usually as the creature is eating their leg. What would you do if you saw someone being eaten in a zoo? Throw things at the animal? Try to find a rope so what's left of the person can climb out?

Yes. I'd do something like that, too. But most people, if the internet is anything to go by, whip out their cameras and make a grisly little film.

It's almost certain these days that if you got into trouble at sea, you would not be rescued.

The police, as we know, are not allowed to help. David Hasselhoff is gone. And onlookers would simply take out their phones. You'll get your fifteen minutes of fame, all right. But it will be the last fifteen minutes you ever have.

What the camera does, of course, is detach the onlooker from the events unfurling in front of them. There's a sense as you operate it that you are watching the scene unravel on television and that, as a result, you are unable to help. In short, cameras dehumanize humanity.

But there is an upside. Because in recent years I've noticed that 'news' is not what's happened. It's what's happened on camera.

If a herd of tigers runs amok in a remote Indian village, it's not news. If a gang of wide-eyed rebels slaughters the inhabitants of a faraway African village, it's not news. But if it's a bit windy in America, it is news. Because in America everything that happens is recorded.

I find myself wondering if last week's Israeli raid on a Turkish ship in a flotilla carrying aid to Gaza would have had the coverage it did if the battle hadn't been captured on film. And likewise the racing driver who broke a leg after crashing in the Indy 500. It only became a big deal because we could watch the accident from several angles in slow motion.

In recent months this phenomenon has even spread to the natural world. I mean it. When an animal does something normal, it's not news. But when it is 'caught on camera' doing something normal, then it's in the *Daily Mail*. These days, if you snap an owl catching a mouse, you are Robert Capa.

In the end, this can only be good for all of us. Figures out recently show that more people in India have access to a mobile phone than a lavatory. Soon, it will be the same story in China and Africa. And then, when all the world's being filmed, all of the time, we can go back to a time when news was something interesting rather than something we can simply see.

That way, I wouldn't have to spend half my morning looking at pictures of Twiggy going shopping. And an eagle eating a fish.

6 June 2010

Surgery to solve the deficit – cut off Scotland

As we know, the country is in a terrible mess, and as a result, the head of every government department has been told to go away and implement cuts.

This all sounds very sensible but because I'm a television presenter, I know it won't work.

Here's why. Every Thursday night, the producers of *Top Gear* stitch together the various elements of the show to create a finished product that is around seventy minutes long. Because this is eleven more than the time slot, we have to make cuts.

Or as Clive James used to say when he was making TV shows, we have to throw away our babies.

It's extremely annoying. You've edited a segment to be as good as possible, and now you have to start with the scissors, losing the odd fact here and the odd joke there. It takes an age, it hurts and the same thing always happens when you've finished. The programme is better, tighter and sharper. But it's still six minutes too long.

So it's back to the drawing board. And this time, you must lose links and explanations. You are no longer performing liposuction on fat. You're cutting away at bone and muscle. Important stuff. You are bringing it in on budget but the finished product won't stand up. Think of it, if you like, as a hospital with no electricity. It's still a hospital but it's not much use if the iron lungs don't work.

To prevent this happening on *Top Gear*, we try not to trim

muscle and bone. When we're desperate to cut time, we lose limbs.

You may have seen the Vietnam special we produced a couple of years ago. What you didn't see in that show, however, was a sequence involving the Stig's Vietnamese cousin. This had been tough to make. We'd located a local motorcycle stunt rider, we'd shipped a bike over from Japan, we'd done two recces and written several treatments, and twenty-five people had spent a whole day filming the scene under a sticky sky and watchful gaze of government officials who kept wanting to see the rushes.

The reason you didn't see it is because so many unforeseen things had happened on the trip, the finished programme was miles too long. And when we'd slashed and burned the fat, there was still twelve minutes to go. So instead of slashing and burning at the muscle and bone, we threw away a whole sequence. Better, we thought, to lose an arm than ruin every organ in the body.

And that brings me back to Britain's economy. Yes, the NHS can sack a few managers and the Department for Transport can shelve plans to widen the B3018. Little things such as this will save millions but there will still be millions to go, which is why David Cameron and Cleggy, the tea boy, must think long and hard about losing the Vietnamese Stig. They must think about chopping a whole department. Obviously, I would suggest the Department of Energy and Climate Change because it's silly, when times are tight, to have a whole ministry attempting to manage something over which humankind has no control. It'd be like having a Department of Jupiter.

But the climate change department is relatively small, and cutting that when you are a trillion in debt would be like trying to solve a £50,000 overdraft by not having your hair cut any more. No, Cameron and the shoeshine boy need to lose something big and I believe I have the answer: Scotland.

Let us examine the benefits of this. In the last election the Scottish National Party, which wants independence from England, took nearly 20 per cent of the vote in Scotland. Add this lot to the non-voters who also want to go their own way and you realize there is significant support north of the border for Hadrian's Wall to be rebuilt.

Economically, the SNP thinks Scotland would be fine. I don't know why, since Scottish public spending is 33 per cent higher per head than it is in the south-east of England.

But on its website, the party says that Ireland is independent and is the 'fourth most prosperous country in the world' (really?) and that Iceland, another small independent state, is the 'sixth most prosperous country in the world'. (Apart from being totally bankrupt, obviously.)

Let's not get bogged down, though. The upsides go on and on. Without Scotland on the electoral map, Cameron would have a majority in the House of Commons, so he could lose the Cleggawallah, we'd never again have a Scottish prime minister and Scotland would become abroad – which would make it an exotic holiday location.

I think we could take this further. Why not draw the boundary between England and Scotland at York? This way, the SNP would feel that William Wallace's sacrifice hadn't been in vain and, better still, all the northern English constituencies could be governed by the sort of left-wing, wetland-habitat, save-the-bat and build-a-wind-farm government they seem to like so much.

So what, you might be thinking, is in it for those who remain – the Welsh and those in the south of England? Well, there's no doubt that letting Scotland go would be very painful, especially after 300 years of friendship. But what are the alternatives? The NHS? The Ministry of Defence?

No. I'm afraid it has to be Scotland. It costs the UK £5 billion a year and saving that, on top of the £6 billion in cuts from the fat elsewhere, would go a long way towards solving our debt crisis.

Oil? Well, obviously the Scottish oil companies such as, er, whatever they're called, will continue to pump the black gold into Aberdeen while the others, such as BP and Shell, could simply divert their pipelines to Kent. That's fair. Oh, and we'd have to move the Trident submarine fleet as well.

I want to make it plain to my Scottish readers that I do not want to throw you on to the cutting-room floor. I shall miss you with your funny skirts and your ginger hair. The SAS will miss you, too, since over the years 75 per cent of its soldiers are said to have been from north of the border. But we simply cannot afford to stay together any more. Goodbye, then, and good luck.

13 June 2010

Give to my new charity – Britain's Got Trouble

Oh, dear. I think I've been a bit naive again. Because I sort of assumed that in the run-up to the general election, all three political leaders had made it pretty clear that cuts would be necessary, and that as a result, all of us had reconciled ourselves to a few years of eating less and buying fewer electrical gadgets.

I figured also that after we'd finished laughing uproariously at the plight of the Greeks, we'd realized that we, too, would be in for a similar period of austerity. But I was wrong, because so far as I can see, no one is prepared to change their lifestyle one iota.

Let us examine the case of Nottinghamshire. The Tory-controlled county council and the Labour-run Nottingham council propose to shave a total of about £100 million from their spending and lose 2,000 jobs in the process. Have those affected reacted with a shrug of inevitability? Not a bit of it. They're all working to rule, and their union is making Churchillian noises about going to war.

It's not just council staff, either. You've also got a lot of middle-aged ladies jumping up and down on village greens protesting about plans to close their local library and not listening when anyone tries to explain it's all on the internet anyway.

Elsewhere, tax workers were outside the Treasury because their office-opening hours have been cut and students in Glasgow were to be found waving banners over plans to lose eighteen staff from the university's biomedical and life sciences department.

Doubtless, the druids will be similarly angry after Danny Alexander told the Commons that a £25-million visitor centre at Stonehenge will not now be built. I don't know how druids express anger but if Alexander turns up for work with a lot of warts on his face, I guess we'll know.

Whatever, the point is that no one seems to recognize the need for cuts in spending, and if they do, they don't think they should be involved. So what's to be done?

One chap called the *Jeremy Vine* radio show last week to discuss the problem with David Cameron. In a thick Birmingham accent, he pointed out that if you took all the money from the richest 100 people in Britain, all of our problems would be addressed and the other sixty million people could carry on as before.

Amazingly, Cameron didn't think this was a very good idea, so the man from Birmingham came up with another one. The prime minister should work for nothing. And therein lies the problem. It's impossible, really, to get people to accept the cuts when so many of them are bonkers.

And because they're bonkers, there can be no doubt that when the cuts do start to bite, there will be much wailing and gnashing of teeth, along with a selection of petrol bombs and much police brutality. We are, it seems, on our way back to 1979.

Last week I suggested a way of averting this would be to cut off Scotland. But no one in power seems to be taking that idea seriously. So I have come up with another rather brilliant wheeze: register Britain as a charity.

The last time I looked, British people were giving more than £10 billion every year to help those less fortunate than themselves. That works out at more than £200 for everyone over the age of sixteen.

We put money in the slot to cure cancer, buy swimming

pools for wounded soldiers, build orphanages in Romania, help keep drug addicts off smack, improve living conditions in Gaza: the list is endless. We give so much to charities for the blind that there are now more guide dogs than there are people for them to guide.

In recent months, I've bought pictures to provide music lessons for kids with learning difficulties, signed several rugby balls, supplied a boot full of dung to help keep my local town's lido open and then I spent a night with Louis Walsh to raise cash for Palestine. I even bought the chef Richard Corrigan at one party and I'm damned if I can remember why.

Then there's *The Big Issue*. I don't like it. I think it's boring. But it is the only magazine that I get every week. Sometimes I buy the same issue three times. Why? When I read *Private Eye*, which I enjoy hugely, I don't think, 'Ooh. That was brilliant. I'm going to buy it again.'

The reason is simple. We enjoy giving our money away. It makes us feel all warm and gooey. Which is why we almost always give whenever we are asked. No, really. I reckon that if I knocked on your door this afternoon, explaining that I was doing a sponsored drive to London, in a comfortable car, to raise money for the Amazonian tree warbler, you'd give me a tenner.

And think about what you're doing when you roll a 10p-piece into the lifeboat on the bar of your local pub. You are paying to rescue some drunken idiot from Surrey who's had too many gin and tonics and fallen off his yacht in the Solent, that's what. But it doesn't stop you giving, does it?

Of course, when you are really passionate about a charity's aims, we are no longer talking about the odd 10p. People are prepared to move mountains, or at the very least climb them, to raise thousands. Tens of thousands, even. And that's where my scheme comes in, because we are all passionate about the state of our nation.

I'm proposing, then, that your local MP comes round to your house every week with a collecting tin and that instead of organizing strikes and what have you, unions organize sponsored bike rides to Germany. We can all get behind this, eating as many pork pies in a minute and jumping out of aeroplanes, and then we can appear in our local newspapers, in fancy dress, handing over massively outsized cheques for huge amounts to the exchequer.

Other charities may react in horror to this but they shouldn't, because when the cuts come, they will suffer just like everyone else. If we adopt my scheme, the cuts won't come at all.

20 June 2010

No prison for you – just lick my cesspit clean

For reasons that are not entirely clear, the question of prison reform seems to have cropped up again. Good. It's very important we reform the system so that prisons become disgusting and unhinged. No electricity. No light. No heat. And full to overflowing with inmates who are allowed to eat only what they can catch, or grow in window boxes. Window boxes that they must make from their own fingernail clippings.

Unfortunately, other people think that prisons should be about rehabilitation rather than punishment. That they should be places for quiet reflection, whale song and afternoon poetry by interesting lesbians. Dostoevsky thought this. And so, to a certain extent, did Winston Churchill.

There is even a charity that exists to campaign for the rights of inmates and their families. And I'm sorry, but isn't that a bit weird? Because when you decide to help those less fortunate than yourself, there are so many worthy candidates. People with no homes, no arms and no chance. People with hideous diseases. People with their heads on back to front. And that's before we get to the heart-melting question of children and animals. So why, I wonder, did someone wake up one day and think, 'I know who I'll help. The man who stole my bicycle'?

It actually happened, though, and as a result we now have the Prison Reform Trust, which apparently believes that a prison sentence should be used only for the likes of Peter Sutcliffe. And, even then, that he should be treated with tenderness and a lot of crisp Egyptian cotton.

Well, let me make something quite plain to the lily-livered eco-hippie vicars who think this way. If you come round to my house this evening, asking if I'd like to buy the man who stole my television a gift, I shall say, 'Yes. But only if I can shove it up his bottom.'

It gets worse. Only last week one of the peace 'n' love brigade tried to claim that Britain's judiciary was in love with custodial sentences. Really? Because recently a furore erupted over a case in which Cherie Booth QC told a man found guilty of breaking another man's jaw that he would not go to prison because he was a religious person.

On that basis, the devout Osama bin Laden can hand himself in, knowing Cherie will simply fine him fifty quid. And the Archbishop of Canterbury now has carte blanche to kill as many badgers, and children, as he likes.

Strangely, however, the Haight-Ashbury views of the trust are shared by the outgoing head of the prison service. Yup. Mr Mackay wants fewer people sent to jail as well. And so, too, do the Prison Governors Association and Napo, the probation officers' union.

Such is the weight of opinion behind the call for more community-based punishments, I decided to do a spot of research. And I uncovered some interesting statistics. Last year 55,333 people were jailed for six months or less, at a cost of £350 million. And, apparently, as much as £300 million could be saved if they were given community jobs to do instead. That's a powerful argument, now that an ice cream costs £700.

And consider this. It seems that only 34 per cent of criminals given community punishments reoffend, compared with 74 per cent of those sent to a nice warm prison.

It's easy to see why this might be so. At present, criminals tend to mix with other criminals. I, for instance, do not know any smugglers or murderers, and in all probability you don't either. That's because these people live in a society where their crimes are considered the norm. At my old school, the worse the misdemeanour, the greater the so-called 'lad values' that encouraged us all to be more and more badly behaved. And I dare say it's much the same story in Wandsworth nick.

Before you think I've gone all soft, consider this. If we take them out of their cells, dress them in orange jumpsuits, shackle their legs together and get them to hoe the municipal roundabouts in our local towns and villages, then they will no longer be among their own. They will be among us.

As a result, we will be able to tell them things. And after they've spent six months on a roundabout, being told things, quite loudly, they may start to understand that their life is not normal and there is nothing particularly brilliant about shoving a pint pot into another man's face.

How brilliant is that? The hippie vicars are happy because the crims are out in the open air, getting fit and doing something useful. And we're happy, too – especially if we are allowed to throw things at them as we drive by. Tomatoes. Eggs. Bricks. And so on.

I'm starting to like this community punishment idea very much. And already I'm thinking of jobs around my house that need doing. Painting. Decorating. Licking the cesspit clean. Think. The offender would be able to see how a normal family lives and I would be allowed to call him names and hit him over the head with a stick.

Criminals could be made to retrieve shopping trolleys from Britain's most disgusting canals. They could be made to perform dangerous stunts at theme parks with killer whales and lions. And put the cones out on motorways. Imagine Boy George being made to put his head up a cow's bottom to see if its calf is the right way round while you call him names and pelt his backside with veg.

It gets better. Because if lags are made to pick up litter and weed central reservations, we'll need fewer expensive prisons, it will save local authorities a fortune and, what's more, the decent people currently employed by councils to do menial jobs would become free to earn a proper living in the private sector – inventing wireless routers that work, for example.

I can see now that my views on prison have always been naive. And I can see why prison officers are so in favour of community punishment instead. Because, to put it simply, everyone wins.

27 June 2010

Move along, officer, it's just a spot of dogging

The last government was so enthusiastically bossy that in thirteen years it introduced 4,300 exciting ways for us to break the law. It even made it illegal to detonate a nuclear device. But there's nothing new in this, really. All governments like to think up new rules. It's natural.

That's why I smelt a rat the moment Nick Clegg emerged from behind his urn and asked 'the people' to say which laws they wanted repealing. The deputy prime minister? Of Britain? Asking us if we want fewer laws? Nah. Plainly there was dirty work afoot.

And so it turned out, because on the very same day, a senior police officer was explaining that proposed government cuts meant there would be an inevitable drop in the number of officers. 'Aha. So that's it,' I thought. 'They have to cut the number of rules because they simply don't have the money to police them.'

This all sounds very brilliant, and you may be thinking that soon it will be all right to smoke in the pub and drive in the outside lane of the M4 and even, perhaps, use your dogs to scare off the fox that's eating your children. But don't get your hopes up because I'm willing to bet that in the next five years the number of laws that do actually get repealed is roughly none.

So therefore we must turn our attention to the police force and wonder what might be done to save money there. Many may suggest that, instead of cutting officers, those in charge might like instead to cut the number of courses constables are obliged to attend before being allowed to climb a ladder, or ride a bicycle, or dive into a lake to save a drowning child.

This, however, is probably fatuous, so I propose that we turn for inspiration to the Dutch. I realize, of course, that the Dutch police do not have the best reputation. Harry Enfield and Paul Whitehouse once did a marvellous sketch – 'I'm sitting here with my partner and, I'm alsho happy to shay, my lover, Ronald' – that reinforced a commonly held view that Dutch policing is one part crime-fighting to ninety-nine parts homosexuality.

More recently, we were told that in an effort to combat anti-Semitic crime in Amsterdam, Dutch policemanists were using 'decoy Jews'. The whole idea was ludicrous, even before we get to the question of: why not use real ones? Because, let's be honest, Rutger Hauer in a skullcap isn't going to fool anyone.

I first experienced the Dutch police back in 1975 when a group of Indonesian Christians from the South Moluccas hijacked a train outside the Hollish town of Assen to complain about . . . actually, I can't quite remember.

Anyway, this was on the news a lot at the time and what I do remember is being staggered by the Netherlandic forces of law and order that turned up at the scene. In Britain at this time policemen were all Dixon of Dock Green, but over there they all looked like a cross between Jesus and Jerry Garcia. The main spokesman was wearing loon pants and a bandanna and had hair so long, I felt sure he would trip over it should an attack on the train be deemed necessary.

But here's the thing. I bet you can't remember what the Moluccans wanted, either. Nor, I'm sure, can you remember how the stand-off ended. All we know is that a terrorist organization was formed, it struck . . . and then it simply vanished.

In Britain, it took our smart, clean-cut, well-turned-out officers thirty years to deal with the IRA. And the way things are going, it'll be even longer before they get to grips with Johnny Taliban.

So you have to wonder. What do the Dutch have that we don't? And if they do have something, could it work over here, now our police force is made up of two constables, one stapling machine and an elderly dog called Sam?

I posed this question to a Dutch friend recently, and while I may have been drunk – or he may have been stoned – he said, 'Yes. We are different from you. We can play football, for a kick-off.' He went on to explain about how law enforcement works. Here, if you put one wheel into a bus lane, you can expect to go to prison for several thousand years. But there, if there is a sensible reason and no bus was present at the time, the police will get back to their tender lovemaking and leave you alone.

Fancy some sex in the park? Try it here and you'll still be struggling out of your underpants when Plod turns up. In a main park in Amsterdam, officers are advised to turn a blind eye, provided the coupling is fairly discreet. Want a joint while walking through Amsterdam? Well, you can't. It's illegal. But provided you don't bother anyone else, the police won't bother you.

We have a word for that here, too. Well, two, if we're honest. Common sense. And I wonder what would happen if it were applied; if you could make a phone call in a car if you were in a traffic jam at the time, or you could smoke indoors if everyone else wanted to smoke as well, or if you could read poetry at a summer festival without having to buy a licence.

Imagine it. The police could worry about crime that does matter and ignore crime that doesn't. The savings would be huge and the increase in efficiency dramatic.

Of course, this would require some discretion from the policeman at the scene. And that could be a problem. I know plenty of Plod I'd trust with the job but, equally, my life in Fulham in the 1980s was ruined by an overzealous constable who really would have done me for 'walking on the cracks in the pavement' if he'd thought he could get away with it.

So here's what I propose. We adopt the Dutch system – if such a system exists outside the football-addled mind of my friend – only we give it a little tweak. If the case is brought to court and the magistrate deems it to be a waste of his or her time, then the arresting officer is made to pay – out of his children's piggy bank if necessary – the cost of getting it there.

4 July 2010

Burial? Cremation? Boil-in-the-bag?

As we know, death is a great leveller; communism in its purest form.

Your family may choose to remember you with a giant pyramid on the outskirts of Cairo, or they may choose to mark your passing with a bunch of petrol-station chrysanthemums, crudely tied to the railings on a suburban dual carriageway. But you're still dead.

It's much the same story with the bodies of those brave First World War soldiers that were recently exhumed from their mass grave in France and buried with more dignity elsewhere.

Now, their families can pay their respects in quiet reverence, which is very nice. But the soldiers themselves? Still dead, I'm afraid. I write about death a lot. It bothers me. I don't like the uncertainty of not knowing how or when it will come. Will it be tomorrow and spectacular or will it be many years from now with a tube up my nose? And what happens afterwards? That bothers me, too.

In my heart of hearts, I know that nothing happens. But of course I could be wrong. We may come back as mosquitoes – in which case I will find Piers Morgan's house and bite him on the nose just before he becomes Larry King. Or we may come back as lions. In which case . . . I'll do pretty much the same sort of thing.

Or there may be a heaven. If there is, I shall remind St Peter that Christianity is based on forgiveness, say sorry for not going to church, ever, and demand that I'm allowed in. And that – that is really what bothers me most of all about dying.

They say that we leave our body behind when we're dead, but what if we don't? What if there is a next life and we go into it in the same carcass that's transported us through this one? It's why I don't carry a donor card. Because I shall be awfully hacked off if I am gifted an eternity of milk and honey but I keep bumping into things because some bastard back on earth has my eyes.

It is for this reason that I have made it plain that, when I go, I wish to be buried and not cremated. Because you're not going to have any fun at all with the angels if you arrive at the Pearly Gates looking like the contents of a Hoover bag.

I'm bringing all this up because last week some Belgian undertakers announced that they will soon be offering the dead a 'third way'. A burial? A cremation? Or would sir like to be dissolved in caustic potash and then flushed away down the sewers? No, sir bloody wouldn't.

The process is called resomation and it works like this: you are placed in a silk bag with some water and some potassium hydroxide and then you are boiled until you become a greeny-brown paste.

Hmmm. Even if we leave aside the question of how you might manage in the afterlife as a paste, we must also address the question of reverence for the deceased. Many people may wish to urinate on John Prescott's grave, but chances are, when there is such a thing, no one actually will.

Think about it. Churchyards are rarely vandalized and no one plays ball games in them. Ships that go down with hands still on board are designated as graves and may not be investigated by diving teams. The ashes of those who've been cremated are scattered in places of great beauty. Not chucked in a dustbin lorry. This is because we have a respect for the dead.

And I'm sorry, but where's the respect in turning grandad into a paste and flushing him down the lavatory?

Yes. You are given some powdered bones after the reso-mation is complete, but every day you know that the paste is out there, too. It'll haunt you. Wondering if you've just caught a fish that ate it. Or whether you stepped in it on the way to work.

Needless to say, the engine behind the concept comes from the murky and dirty world of environmentalism. The Scottish company responsible says that cremating a body creates 573lb of carbon dioxide and that with its new system this is cut to virtually zero. What's more, the company says that if we dissolve the dead, there will be less pressure on space in graveyards.

This is like arguing that Prozac upsets the ecosystem and, once in the water, causes all fish to turn right. It may well be true but it's better than having the streets full of middle-aged women sobbing because they've got a parking ticket. And shampoo. Washing your hair in 'peace soap' made from mung beans may well ensure Johnny Polar Bear has a home for many years to come but you will have a dirty beard.

It's the same story with this caustic potash business. Melt-ing the dead may be practical but it is also absolutely horrific. Because let's be honest here; let's cut to the chase. We are talking here about boil-in-the-bag, aren't we? And that's just not on.

Boil-in-the-bag works – just about – for parsley sauce. But not for your mum. She breastfed you. She raised you. She was only ever as happy as you were. And you are going to boil her in a bag and make her into paste. To save a polar bear. It's the worst thing I've ever heard of.

If all we're bothered about is the environment and to hell with the dignity, why do we not throw our dead into the sea or into landfill? Or why do we not simply feed them to our dogs? This makes perfect sense, if you think about it. There are no eco-implications at all. No grave is required. The dog gets a tasty midday snack. Everybody's happy.

Except, of course, we're not happy, are we? Because you cannot feed your nearest and dearest to Fido. It's bad enough clearing up the dog eggs on a normal day. But clearing them up when you know they are Uncle Ernie? It's just a no, isn't it?

So's resomation, and I can't believe the Belgians will actually go for it. Because if they do, and my fears about death are correct, all they'll have to look forward to after a life in Belgium is being used by God for all of eternity to stick his wallpaper to the wall.

11 July 2010

Don't misread the whiff of Cameron's armpits

Have you ever watched a vast swarm of starlings reel around the sky in Africa? Or a million-strong herd of wildebeest? If so, I'm sure you've marvelled at their ability to communicate without actually appearing to do so. But you know what? I think humans can do exactly the same thing. Back in the 1980s the Comedy Store in London would allow a queue of wannabe comedians each to have ten minutes on the stage after the main performers had finished. By this time of night, most of the audience was either hopelessly drunk, extremely chatty or at home in bed.

So it was a tough crowd, even for a seasoned campaigner. For a bag-of-nerves newbie, hoping to get noticed, it must have been a nightmare.

And for one particular girl, on a night when I was there, it must have been even worse. She came on to the stage, picked up the microphone and delivered what we had to assume was her best line. You always deliver your best line first. That way, you have the audience on your side from the get-go. So she delivered her best line and she was greeted with absolute silence.

It was a fairly funny line but – as one – a couple of hundred people in varying degrees of inebriation decided not to make a sound. If someone had heckled, then she'd at least have had a well-rehearsed put-down to fire off. A heckle could have saved her. But none came. You could have heard a pin drop; well, you could have done were it not for the deafening sound of a poor girl dying from the inside out.

I've always been fascinated by that moment. Because how did all those people suddenly decide, without communicating, to behave in exactly the same way?

Clive James, the veteran broadcaster, wit and raconteur, always maintained that you will get a bad audience if you have a bad script. And that, conversely, if you are good, the crowd will be good, too. But I've now proved this to be incorrect. Two weeks ago, while recording the *Top Gear* show, James May, Richard Hammond and I talked for a few minutes about the new Nissan Micra, and there was the sort of quietness normally associated with church services. As a result, the whole scene was edited out of the programme.

However, as a test, we did exactly the same story again last week. The same people saying the same words on the same day of the week in the same place. And the audience laughed until their buttocks fell off. I found that very, very strange, so I did some research.

Back in the early 1970s, an American woman called Martha McClintock, from Wellesley College, Massachusetts, asked 135 college girls living in dorms to record their period start dates. To her amazement she found that, as the academic year wore on, the dates became closer and closer together. The girls were getting in sync.

How was this possible? Well, it seems that plants and insects – even cows – communicate with one another using pheromones. And some scientists believe that humans emit pheromones, too, through their armpits. Could it be that back at the Comedy Store in the 1980s we could smell the comedian's fear radiating out from her pits, and responded to it?

Is that possible? Could it be that the stock market goes haywire from time to time, not because there is anything fundamentally wrong with the system but because of hidden

messages in someone's body odour? If so, we should all be a
little bit terrified. Because what if reason tells us to do one
thing but we are then compelled by our noses to do something else?

I do not want to buy Peter Mandelson's new book. I don't
see why he should have any more of my money. But I'm
frightened to death that I may soon be standing next to
someone in a bookshop and, as a result of their whiffy pits,
feel compelled to buy it. Likewise, reason dictates that if I
see Mandelson crossing the road in front of me, I should
press the accelerator as hard as I can and try to run him
down. But what if, at the last moment, I get a hint of Mando
juice and decide to hit the brake pedal instead?

It gets worse. Right now, all of us are in agreement that the
country is broke. The human part of our brains is telling us
we have more debt in relation to gross domestic product
than almost any other country in the world and that savage
cuts, along with tax rises, are the only answer. Of course,
there are murmurings about the abandonment of free swimming lessons for the elderly, and arty people were running
around last week moaning about a proposed Arts Council
budget cut. But as a collective whole we are all agreed that
something has to be done.

Unfortunately there is no doubt that, at some point in the
not-too-distant-future, we will all decide – as one – that the cuts
are not necessary and that the price we're paying is far too high.
We shall simply wake up one morning and decide that David
Cameron is a stupid idiot and that we must have a Labour government back in power as soon as possible. It is inevitable.

We see this all the time. Everyone has a Nokia phone.
Then everyone has a BlackBerry. Everyone believes in global
warming. Then everyone thinks it's rubbish. Everyone loves
Jonathan Ross. Then everyone doesn't any more.

I've never understood what causes this to happen. But now it's clear: the cow/starling part of our brain is responding to messages in the ether. Like bulls, we are being led around by our noses. Someone, somewhere in the world turns left, so we must all turn left. This is not a sound platform on which to build an economy. Let alone a species.

I can only suggest that, in the coming months, Cameron focuses very carefully on personal hygiene. He can make the speech of his life, but unless he delivers it from behind an impenetrable wall of Right Guard, it won't make the slightest bit of difference. Deodorant. It's the only way we can survive.

18 July 2010

A few song lyrics could have done for Piers

For the past few years, many millions of people in this country have been scared to pop to their local shop or petrol station in case they bump into Piers Morgan. Well, I have good news. He's been given a new job hosting a television show in America, which means you can go to the bakery for bread knowing he can't possibly be in there.

Doubtless he will have received a Google alert about this mention and even as we speak will be scribbling furiously in his little diary about how I haven't been offered a job on television in the States because my teeth are too beige and I have a fat stomach.

Well, sorry, Piers, but I was in fact asked to meet with all the main American networks a few years ago. I even went over there for some meetings and it was all very grown-up. But in the hotel bar one night I did some maths and uncovered a problem.

They sign you up to do a pilot – quite why I had to make a pilot of a car show I have no idea – and if they like it, you are required to make six shows. If they go well, the run extends to twenty-five shows, and if those get high ratings, they demand a hundred more.

So you go over there to make one pilot and, whether you like it or not, you could still be there five years later. Now, of course, I realize this isn't an issue for Morgan but I have friends in Britain and after five years I'd be missing them terribly. I'd almost certainly become a mental, launching into anti-Semitic tirades at policemen and hurling telephones at hotel receptionists.

Aha, you may think, but what about the money? Well, for sure, if your television programme is a big hit on an American network, then yes, you will be very rich. So you'd be there in your Jacuzzi, with two Las Vegas showgirls, eating some swan, and your children would be 5,000 miles away thinking that, perhaps, you loved cash more than you loved them. I don't think that would be very healthy.

Besides, lots of people move to a new job for money and it rarely works out. Morecambe and Wise. Trinny and Susannah. Barry and Norman. You take the corporate shilling and your career will be over in a jiffy. I don't, by the way, include poor old Jonathan Ross in this. He is an extremely nice and kind man whose move to ITV was thrust upon him by people with an agenda. I'm sorry to say this here, but I think the whole episode was disgraceful.

Anyway, I had a problem. I was in America and due to meet all the big networks for a job I really didn't want. I therefore made a plan with my producers. Upon entering each meeting, we would take it in turns to name a band. And then each of us would have to get as many of their lyrics as possible into the conversation.

This is why, at one network, we were asked what made *Top Gear* so appealing, and my producer, Andy Wilman, answered: 'It's the karma karma karma karma karma chameleon.' It's also why, at the next meeting, I said it was 'art for art's sake' and that 'life is a minestrone'. I was so pleased with that one, I then said, 'served up with parmesan cheese'. Which may have been a mistake. Certainly no job offers were forthcoming afterwards.

I cannot tell you how much fun this is. You're being asked about back ends and put options by some of the brightest, sharpest people in television, and you're sitting there wondering how 'The Logical Song' went and if any of its lyrics have anything at all to do with anything anyone is saying.

Of course, you will argue that this is all fair enough if you don't really care about the outcome of a meeting. But sitting there running through Don Henley's back catalogue in your head would be stupid if you did. Really? Because I put it to you that all meetings are a waste of time and that you would achieve more if you simply sat on your hands and whistled Dixie. So you may as well play song-lyric bingo.

Think about it. If you have a meeting to agree a deal, then both sides will have to compromise, and that means every-one leaves feeling a bit disappointed. If you decide not to compromise, then what's the point of going? So, there can be no such thing as a 'good' meeting. It's either disappointing or useless. There is no other way.

As evidence, I give you the Copenhagen summit. Last year 115 world leaders flew to Denmark to discuss what might be done should global temperatures rise. After eight draft texts and an all-day get-together, involving thousands of people, everyone agreed they couldn't agree on anything.

It was always thus. As a cub reporter on a local newspaper I sat through thousands of council meetings that achieved absolutely nothing. I remember one in which the members spent an hour discussing whether they should have a glass or a plastic water jug at future meetings. And they ended by suggesting they discuss the issue in more detail next time they met.

G7? You may remember that after much pressure from Bonio and St Bob, Gordon Brown and co decided to discuss the possibility of cutting Third World debt to zero. So they talked for ages and discovered they all disagreed with one another.

Now stop and wonder how many meetings have been held between Israel and various other Middle Eastern states over the past fifty years. Anything achieved there? Well, a bloody great wall, but that's about it. They'd have achieved more if Binyamin Netanyahu had greeted President Bashar al-Assad last time they met by saying, 'Rudy's on a train to nowhere.' Why not? Nothing else has ever worked. And who knows, maybe Syria's president is a Supertramp fan. Maybe that's the key that would sort out the West Bank.

Let me finish on one final piece of evidence that all meetings are a waste of time. Someone in America recently called one to discuss who should replace the CNN chat-show host Larry King. And they decided that, of the six billion or so people on earth, the answer was Piers Morgan. My case rests.

25 July 2010

England's fate is in your hands, Ambassador

Britain has just sent a new ambassador to Finland. He is called Matthew Lodge and he will be living in a historically important house that was thoroughly modernized back in the 1980s using Finnish stone. I'm sure he will be very happy there. But how, exactly, will he fill his days? If you are the British ambassador in Washington, or Berlin, then obviously there is much to be done. There will be cocktail parties to attend, and UK citizens will lose their passports and need new ones. But Helsinki? The Foreign and Commonwealth Office says that Lodge will be responsible for relations between Britain and Finland.

What relations? We get on with the Finns in the same way that I get on with my neighbours. I know they exist. The end.

I realize, of course, that Britain and Finland are the only two democracies in human history ever to declare war on one another but it seems highly unlikely that this will ever happen again. So what are the ambassador's weekly reports going to say? How many different ways can he find to say, 'Relations between Finland and Britain remain cordial'? They've been that way since 1945.

We're told that Lodge will also be responsible for the well-being of British nationals living in Finland. Right. I see. And how many of those are there? Two? Seven? Nobody lives in Finland. Not even Finns. It's almost completely empty. You may as well be the British ambassador to Mars.

And I'd like at this point to apologize to Lodge for singling

him out because, of course, it's pretty much the same story
for our man in Denmark, Norway and indeed right across
Scandinavia. The globe, too. I mean, what does the British
ambassador to Slovakia do? No, really. What?

I should imagine he spends the first half of his year planning the annual cocktail party and the second half clearing
up the Ferrero Rocher wrappers.

All of this conjecture brings me on to a breakfast invitation
I once received from the German ambassador in London.
There were just the two of us, in a huge room, and we had cold
meats until, after an hour or so, a butlery sort of chap came in
and coughed discreetly, signalling that my time was up. So I left,
and as I did so I wondered: what on earth was that all about?

The only possible reason for the invitation was that, having
had some cold meats in a very agreeable room overlooking
Belgrave Square with an absolutely charming man, I would
feel better disposed towards the Hun. And you know what?
It worked. He gave me some ham. I bought a Mercedes-Benz.

This is why I am delighted to hear David Cameron telling
British embassy staff all over the world that the days of croquet and gin slings are over; that they must now push hard to
support British business. And it's also why I'm thrilled to see
he's gone to India.

For too long Britain has concentrated its efforts on America in the vague hope of keeping the special relationship
alive. But, truth be told, there is no special relationship. The
idiots in the middle bit have never heard of us and the rest
still hate us for shooting up the White House or pulling their
forefathers' toenails out.

We helped them become part of an 'international' force in
Iraq and Afghanistan. We helped them secure their need for
oil. And what did British business get in return? A bollocking
for spilling a bit of it on one of their beaches. How many US

construction companies buy JCB diggers? How many Eurofighters are there in the US Air Force? Quite.

But if our giddiness with America was bad, then our attitude to the rest of the world was even worse. We either ignored it or dispatched John Prescott to tell them that they couldn't have cars and power stations because of the environment.

Tony Blair and Gordon Brown, meanwhile, maintained an ethical foreign policy that meant we just told foreigners in dresses and hats they had to stop whatever it was they were doing and behave like us.

All that has to change. We have to stop lecturing the men in dresses and beg them to think British. And the best person to do that is not Prince Andrew. No, it's the people who live there. And the people who live there are our ambassadors.

We must therefore pull them from whatever secretary happens to be filling their afternoons these days and set them to work, as salesmen. Our man in Delhi gives a local dignitary a cup of tea and a cucumber sandwich and, in return, he buys a Eurofighter. Well, it worked for me.

The big problem is, of course, what else will they sell? Tesco's home delivery service? A mobile dog-grooming service? Britain is a nation now of people who go to work, send emails and come home again. If you look at the business leaders who accompanied Cameron on his trip to India, few of them run companies that make anything.

And that – that – has to be the starting point. Because it's no good forging a special relationship with India or Finland or anywhere else if we have nothing to offer. It's no good giving our ambassador to Slovakia a Ford Mondeo to travel the country as a salesman if he has no samples to put in the boot.

Now is the time to turn this around. People will lose their

jobs over the coming months and years. They should be encouraged to go into their sheds and make something. Because now you won't need to worry about marketing. You have the ambassadors to do that for you. And you don't need to worry about a shop front, either. Because it's the British embassy in just about every capital city in the world.

The days of Brown and Blair are over. The days of patronizing, hectoring, ethical nonsense are gone. Britain is now back in business. We just have to work out what that business is going to be.

1 August 2010

Concussion is what holidays are all about

It's funny, isn't it? At home, you make sure your children wear cycling helmets when they go for a bike ride, you wear a high-visibility jacket when you are on a building site and you treat your fuse box like it may explode at any moment.

However, as soon as you go on holiday, you are quite happy to jump off a cliff and eat stuff that you know full well has spent its entire miserable life living on a diet of nothing but sewage.

We heard recently about a man who fell 150ft to his death while parasailing on the Turkish coast.

He looked like a normal sort of bloke who would take care when crossing the road and so on, so why did he suddenly think it was a good idea to be tied to the back of a speedboat, by a young chap, using a sun-ravaged harness, and then hoisted into the heavens?

You may think it was a freak occurrence. But if you type 'parasailing accident' into Google, you will quickly get the impression that no one has ever returned to earth at anything less than 180mph. Parasailing, it seems, is more dangerous than smearing yourself in Chum and swimming with some crocodiles. But will that knowledge keep me from the big blue yonder when I go on holiday later this month? No.

It gets worse. At home, I make sure my children are kept out of harm's way as much as possible, but on holiday I once watched them being attached to some parasailing equipment by a man who actually had to put down his spliff so he could tie the knots. Well, when I say knots . . . Then, later, I put my boy in an inner tube and towed him around the Caribbean at such enormous speeds that he fell out and was knocked unconscious. What was I thinking of? He is my son. He means everything to me. So why did I think it would be 'fun' to tow him across the sea, at 40mph, on his face?

Then we get to the question of vehicular transport when you're on holiday. At home, you have your car serviced regularly and put through an MOT without complaint. You like to know it's safe and that the brakes work.

But on holiday you are quite happy to rent something from a man called Stavros who makes you sign all sorts of forms you can neither read nor understand before you belch away in a cloud of burning fluids. Or you rent an amusing scooter that you ride much too quickly in shorts and a pair of flip-flops.

Would you let your eleven-year-old daughter ride about at high speed on such a thing? Of course not. It would be foolish, because if she fell off, she'd be peeled. Right, so why do you let her go on a jet ski? I do.

My youngest daughter and I have spent hours seeing how high we can jump over the waves and who can go the fastest while chasing the flying fish. And get this. When we've finished, I let her go snorkelling, knowing full well that the jet skis we've just climbed off are now in the hands of other father-and-daughter speed combos who really won't notice a little girl's head bobbing about in the waves.

The sea is an almost endless source of death and despair. Earlier this year, I plunged into it with a mate and spent several carefree minutes being bashed about by waves that were even taller than me. Then my friend was knocked over with such force that his arm was wrenched completely out of its socket. But did I get out of the water? Again, no. I'd seen what the water could do to a man . . . and I liked it.

Then we have the banana boat. You let your eldest daughter go in the speedboat while you climb on to the big inflatable penis with the rest of the family and then you sit there, trying to pretend it's exciting while simultaneously pretending not to notice that the rapist who's driving the towboat is playing tonsil hockey with your daughter.

And you think: 'This is harmless. Boring even.' And it is, but have you ever fallen off a banana? That's not boring at all, because usually, just before you hit the water, you get your wife's knee in your face; so now you're drowning in a sea of stars and bewilderment, wondering if she did it on purpose.

Eating? At home, you wash your vegetables and cook your chicken until it's technically coal. But on holiday? Well, after the swarthy waiter has stopped staring at your daughter's breasts and explained that tonight's special is a 'local delicacy', you're perfectly happy to put it in your mouth. Despite the fact that it's obviously a wasp that's plainly been cooked in a bucket of blubber, in a bag bearing the label 'Best before the Boer War'.

Then there's the wine. You like it not because it's cheap or tasty but because the hideous little oik in the apron has told you it's made by his brother. You know he means his brother works at the chemical plant that produces a wine-based substitute as a sideline but you feel that because there's a family connection, it's authentic and earthy, and so you drink lots of it, and then you climb into the deathtrap that has three brakes and wobble home in a blurred tunnel of double vision and stomach cramps.

Of course, you know drink-driving is stupid. Except when you have a sunburnt nose and you've spent the day on the beach. Then it's okay.

What is it then, I wonder, that makes us become so very different as soon as the Ryanair jet touches down in some dusty sun-baked tourist trap? Why do we suddenly think that it's a good idea to jump off a 100ft cliff into a puddle and let our children climb around on outboard motors that are still running? Why do we take leave of our senses?

Strangely, I think we don't. I think that on holiday we become what we're designed to be: thrill-seeking, fun-filled, risk-taking, happy-go-lucky wonder beings. And that when we go home, to the drudgery of everyday life, we are obliged to become something we're not: frightened and ever so slightly dull.

8 August 2010

I've sprayed wasps with glue, now what?

There seems to be some talk that the retirement age will soon have to rise to ninety-eight for men and one hundred and fourteen for women. And that since the country can no longer afford to pay a state pension, everyone will be expected to finish their last shift by getting a carriage clock and then jumping into one of the machines at the factory. This is excellent news. And I'm speaking from some experience because on Monday I jacked everything in. I retired.

Top Gear is a monster and feeding it takes up all the conventional hours – and a few that haven't been invented yet.

And to make matters worse, we decided that while we were filming the last series, it would be a good plan to make a few items for the next one as well.

I'd film all day, then write until the wee small hours, waking up in hotels and spending the first fifteen minutes of the day wondering where the hell I was. Occasionally, I'd get calls from the family saying they were in Mallorca, or Devon, or Cornwall, and having a lovely time, and I was consumed with a jealous rage. Why wasn't I there, too? Kids, you know; they don't grow up twice.

By June I was absolutely knackered. By July I think I was starting to go a bit doolally, and by last week, after three months without a break, I'd had enough. So I made my mind up. I would go home from the last shoot on Sunday and I would retire.

I began to long for it; dream about what I'd do. And what I would do, mostly, is absolutely nothing at all. It became all-consuming, to the point that I was counting the hours until it was all over – something I hadn't done since double physics with Dr Jones back in 1975.

And then the day came. I woke at seven and went down-stairs, without shaving, and I read the papers until about eight, when I had a good stretch and made another cup of coffee. Then I was bored.

I decided to look in the fridge but it was empty, so with absolutely nothing to do, I read the business section of the papers, even though I had no idea what any of it meant. By ten, I was so desperate that I was reading the *Daily Mail* and trying to understand why it had published a picture of Kelly Brook. I failed, so I went to look in the fridge again. Then I looked out of the window.

As the clock ticked round to midday, I thought it would be nice to meet friends for lunch. But they were either away on business or on holiday. My children? That was a no, too. They were all too busy with 600 of their closest personal friends.

I thought then that I'd have a wander round the garden to see if anything needed doing. And I found a tree that needed planting. 'Excellent,' I thought. 'That will keep me busy for ages.' And I was right.

It took me a full fifteen minutes to find the gardener and another six to explain what I wanted. Then I had another look in the fridge to see if perhaps there was a cold sausage that I'd missed earlier.

There wasn't, so I went for a walk to see how things were getting along on my farm. I noticed immediately that the bar-ley was ripe, or medium rare, or whatever it is when barley's ready for harvesting. So I rang the farmer and asked him to fire up the combine. Then I went home again and, because no cold chicken had hatched in my fridge, I tuned in to a pro-gramme hosted by a man with a bright orange face in which people tried to sell stuff they'd found in their attic. Apparently, many retired people watch this, and after half an hour most determine that it's better to be dead, so they have a stroke. I didn't want a stroke, so I decided immediately to start a hobby.

But what? I dislike golfers, I am to DIY what Nicholas Witchell is to cage fighting, and I happen to know you can't put a ship in a bottle using the only tool that I can wield with any confidence – a hammer.

Undaunted, though, I came up with the best pastime in the history of man. What you do is find an aerosol tin of spray adhesive, such as you would use to stick posters to a wall. You then lie in wait and when a wasp flies by, you leap out and give it a squirt. Bingo. One minute it's flying; the next it's tumbling silently out of the sky with a confused look on its stupid little face.

I realize that these days you get into terrible trouble if you say you've shot a baboon in the lung but this is different. Because there are not millions of baboons flying around in your garden, ruining any attempt to sit outside and have lunch. Baboons don't sting you for fun, either. And anyway, gluing a wasp together in mid-air requires patience and skill and gives the creature a sporting chance.

Plus, putting a paralysed wasp in the bin while shouting, 'Ha. Now what are you going to do, you little bastard?' is much less cruel than enticing it into a jam jar and letting it suffocate in a pile of its mates' corpses.

In fact, I shouldn't be surprised if the RSPCA doesn't give me a medal or a certificate of some kind.

The only downside to my new game is that you will miss more often than you hit. And this means a great deal of glue ends up on your furniture and your computer. But trust me. The satisfaction of seeing a wasp suddenly stop flying? It's worth ruining your house for that.

Unfortunately, this is a seasonal pastime and soon the wasps will be gone. Then what? No, really. What do you do to fill your days when you are old and there are no insects and no work? You die, really, because having tried it for a whole day, I've decided that thinking of things to do is far more exhausting than getting up and doing them.

15 August 2010

Naughty bits & melons – I learnt it all in Albania

Every year, I tell my children, with a serious, Dickensian face, that they may have a fun holiday at Easter but in the summer we must go somewhere that will expand their minds. Cambodia. Alaska. Bolivia. These are the places I always have in mind. Unfortunately, I'm always too busy to enforce these rules, which is why, this year, we ended up in Kassiopi in Corfu. And all you can learn there is how not to catch chlamydia.

And so it was on the third day I decided that the kids must put down their vodka shots and their new Italian scooter friends and come with me on an expedition to Albania. We would go to the ruins at Butrint. And we would learn about how the Romans invented mortar.

Sadly, though, the ferry to Albania is almost certainly the slowest moving vessel in history. It does half a mile an hour and I couldn't help noticing it had a funnel made from cardboard and gaffer tape. It was the *Herald of Not So Free Enterprise*.

I therefore decided, in a strident way, that we would charter a boat, and so it was, after a complicated exchange with Greek customs, during which there was much blowing of whistles, we pulled into the Albanian port of Saranda in a 68ft Ferretti motor yacht. There was nowhere to park it, so we tied it to the coastguard's boat, which had sunk – in about 1956 – and went to have our passports checked in what appeared to be a Russian public swimming baths, only with more smoking.

We then hired a guide called Fatso and he was delighted. 'British. Very good comedy,' he said. 'Norman Wisdom. Mr Bean. And number one funny show: *Top Gear*. In Albanian, word for man organ is pronounced "car". You make show about cocks,' he said, poking me in the chest and roaring with laughter.

It wasn't quite the education I'd had in mind, but no matter. Off we set through what looked like a cross between Odessa, Miami South Beach and Benidorm in 1969. If you can imagine such a place.

All guides who grew up with communism like to give you facts and figures that prove their country is better than yours. This was a point picked up deliciously by Sacha Baron Cohen, who famously pointed out that Kazakhstan is the 'world's number one exporter of potassium'.

Fatso, however, made Borat look like an amateur. After explaining that there were now two roads to the ruins – two! – and how much each of them had cost, and how Saranda is the sunniest place in all of Europe, he suggested we stop off at a nearby spring. 'Albania has more water than any other country after Norway,' he explained, before revealing how much water, exactly, is produced by the spring in question. 'It's 375 cubic metres every second,' he said, thumping the steering wheel of his van with joy. 'That is 1.35 million cubic metres every hour. And that is 32.4 million cubic metres a day. Albanian water, too. Best water in world.' He was nowhere near finished. 'In this region we produce 45,000 tons of watermelons every year. Second best region for watermelons in all of Albania,' he added, grabbing his heart and blinking to stop himself crying with pride.

My son, annoyingly, wasn't interested in these remarkable statistics and asked if there was a shop where he could buy an Albanian football shirt. Fatso was overcome with rage:

'Albania football team number one in world, but every match, referee is biased,' he thundered. 'One time, John Terry cut off Albania striker's head and Albania striker was sent off. In a match against Dutch peoples, we scored nine goals, all disallowed by referee.'

By this stage, I was eating the inside of my face in an effort to stop myself laughing. And that was before we got to Albania's crime rate. 'None,' he said, bouncing up and down in his seat. 'There is no crime of any sort. And Christians live side by side with Muslims in perfect harmony.'

We turned to Albania's recent past. 'In communists' time, there were some things good. Some things bad. Bad things? One man say to government spy that he had no spoon for his sugar and got seventeen years in jail. Another man ask why Corfu harbour have a light when we have no light. He got twenty-five years.' So what were the good things? 'Everyone have job and supply of water under control.'

At this point, we arrived at Butrint. This, it's said, is where Hector's missus and a few mates set up shop after the fall of Troy. It was very hot, and the guide there was keen to show us every building and how we could tell which bits had been built by the Greeks, which bits by the Romans and which by the Venetians. It's exactly what children should do on a summer holiday, this. Learn stuff. Not just drink vodka and snog.

But I wanted to get back in the van with Fatso and learn more about the glorious nation of Albania. He was waiting in the car park with an Albanian beer. 'Best in world,' he said. And it was. But then beer always is when you're hot and it's not.

On the way back to Saranda, I noticed that a sizeable percentage of all the cars had British plates. 'How come?' I asked. 'Ah,' said Fatso, 'many Albanians go to England, get job, buy car and come here with it on holiday.' I see. Another thing I noticed is that most of the houses had been knocked over. 'Why's that?' I asked. 'Earthquake,' he said with an impish smile. 'Government earthquake. You build house with no permission, special forces come with bulldozers and knock it down.'

And so there you are. We'd gone to Albania to learn about cement but we'd come away with minds enriched by so much more. We knew how much water is produced every hour by the spring. We knew how many watermelons are produced each year. We knew about planning regulations in Saranda and the Albanian word for 'cock'.

That's the thing about going on holiday with me. It's so much more fun. I should be a tour operator.

5 September 2010

Beware – Arabella won't stop at hay rustling

Sinister news from the shires.

After a summer that was too dry and then too wet, the hay harvest has been hopeless, and as a result, the price has reached £6 a bale. That's more than double the price last year and so it's now more expensive than marijuana. Yup. Grass will now cost you more than, er, grass. And that's if you can get hold of it at all.

One poor girl with a hungry horse rang me a while back to ask whether I was in a position to help since I'm now a farmer.

So I went to see the man I'd employed to cut my hay and he was perplexed. 'Let me just get this straight. You want a few bales for your friend?' he asked incredulously. It was as though I'd asked him if I could watch his wife take a shower. The answer was a big fat no.

As a result of all this, the nation's horse enthusiasts are in a state of blind panic. In the coming winter their precious animals may die of starvation, and consequently many have turned to crime. At night there are thousands of middle-aged ladies sneaking around the countryside, stealing bales of hay that have been left in the fields. Farmers all over the country have been targeted and are at a loss.

Hay can't be stored indoors, under lock and key, because it has a nasty habit of catching fire, and it's not possible to shoot the thieves because of various laws. One solution is to package the hay in bales so large they won't fit in the back of a Volvo but there's a danger, if you do this, that the enormous barrel could roll down a hill and kill one of the early members of the Electric Light Orchestra.

And so here we are. It's 2010. And such is the pressure on space that perfectly decent women called Arabella are stealing grass from farmers to feed their pets. What's it going to be like when it's not food for horses that becomes scarce but food for people?

As you may have heard, the harvests in Russia and Ukraine failed this year and now, with the biggest grain shortage for twenty-six years, the price of a ton of wheat has doubled to about £200. A bit of wonky weather in a couple of countries and suddenly a loaf of bread costs about the same as a pound of myrrh.

Without wishing to sound like an A-level politics student, it's easy to see what's gone wrong. There is simply not enough space on earth to grow food for the planet's ever-increasing population. And the consequences of this will be dire. Because if a woman with clipped vowels and a hairdo is prepared to become a thief to feed her horse, how low will she stoop when she needs to feed her child? For sure, there will be hair-pulling at the bakery. Maybe even some biting.

It's hard to know what to do. Even if we manage to inject some family-planning sense into the Roman Catholic Church, the population will continue to grow and this means that, one day, people are going to start to get hungry. And then they are going to start to starve. And then many will die. It's a fact. Genetically modified crops may delay the moment but it's coming. It's a mathematical certainty.

Unless, of course, we can find more land on which to grow stuff. You may think this is unlikely. We've been to the moon and it seems entirely unsuitable. Mars appears to be a dead loss as well, which means we have to look closer to home. And guess what. I've found some. Lots of it.

Mile upon mile of juicy soil, ready and able to produce millions of tons of delicious food for all the world. It's called the English countryside.

Last year I bought a farm in Oxfordshire and was delighted to discover that the government would pay me to grow nothing at all on about 400 acres. I can also get money to keep stubble in the ground for a bit longer than is sensible and for planting hedgerows. That's right. You work all day. Pay your tax. And the government then gives it to me so I can plant a nice hedge.

This is because of the skylark. Or the lapwing. Or some other whistling, chirruping airborne rat that doesn't matter. I like a bird. I'm even a member of the RSPB. But the notion that more than half my farm is a government-subsidized sanctuary for linnets while the world goes hungry is just stupid.

Especially as there's plenty of evidence to suggest it doesn't work. Examination of the latest environmental stewardship programme suggests that the only birds to benefit are the starling and lapwing. Which means the government is proposing to spend £2.9 billion on a programme, at a time of hardship and hunger, even though it knows one of the few beneficiaries is the starling – a bird that can knock down buildings with its urine and eat a whole tree in one go.

Now it may well be that this bird business is just a cover story to mask an undeniable truth – that, left to its own devices, farming would cease to be a viable industry. I must say I'm staggered by the smallness of the returns you get. You'd be better off spending your money on a powerboat.

However, I find it morally reprehensible that the previous government stated that it wanted 70 per cent of Britain's utilizable agricultural land to be in an environmental stewardship scheme by 2011. Did it not have calculators? Could it not see there's going to be a global food shortage soon and that setting aside nearly three-quarters of Britain for the benefit of a sparrow is moronic?

Of course, I'm not a farmer. I don't understand the complexities of the industry. But I am a human being and, while it's nice to walk through my fields, listening to the starlings eating my trees, I do think that giving me money to leave land for the birds is madness.

I therefore have an idea. Instead of giving farmers vital subsidies not to grow food, how about this? Give them subsidies to grow some.

14 September 2010

One dose of this and you could turn into a werewolf

This morning, all being well, my wife should be on her way back home from a charity bike ride to Arnhem in Holland. This involved cycling eighty miles a day, every day, for a week, and of course a great deal of effort and sweat was needed to get ready.

As a result, she spent much of the year in a gym, picking things up and putting them down again, very quickly, while listening to music such as Basement Jaxx and N-Dubz. Until – disaster. Just two weeks before the start date, *ping* – something important snapped in her neck.

I tried explaining that my neck was fine because I spent the year sitting in a chair watching television but this went down badly, so she went to the doctor, who suggested a muscle relaxant and painkiller called Voltarol. A packet of pills that, I kid you not, comes with an instruction manual.

Now, as we know, any man who consults an instruction manual must consider himself a failure. Instruction manuals are for the weak and the indecisive. They are for people who happily accept that someone, somewhere, knows better than they do. 'Grunts': that's what they're called in the American infantry. However, I couldn't work out why a packet of non-prescription pills should require instructions, so I had a read. And it was amazing.

First of all, you are told how to take the pills. You swallow them with a glass of water. Unless, I presume, you are French, in which case you push them up your bottom. The French ingest everything up their back passages. I'm surprised they don't eat this way as well. I'm also surprised they manage to have children.

Anyway. Back to the Voltarol and, specifically, the section on 'common' side effects. These include diarrhoea, nausea, vomiting, headaches, dizziness, vertigo, a rash and a change in liver function.

Now, call me a party pooper if you like, but on balance I think I'd rather have a sore neck than run the risk of cycling to Holland with diarrhoea running down my legs, vomit exploding over the handlebars and a liver that thinks it's a piece of Lego.

It gets worse. Less common side effects include chest pains, yellowing of the eyes, collapse, swelling of the tongue and a propensity to vomit blood. In other words, if you take one of these pills to make your neck feel a bit better, there's a 1 in 1,000 chance you'll become a werewolf.

Sadly, though, it could be even worse. Because there's almost a 1 in 10,000 chance you could suffer blistering eyes, bleeding, blurred vision and confusion. In other words, you become a zombie.

So far, I have singled out Voltarol, but a trawl through the big wide world of medicine reveals that nearly all household pills 'n' potions can have dramatic side effects. Nurofen, for instance, can increase the risk of old people becoming deathly white and having a heart attack. Imodium can make your intestine paralytic, while a pill I was once prescribed for a slipped disc could, it seems, cause my gums to disintegrate and my teeth to fall out.

Boots, meanwhile, will happily sell you a hay fever relief that could cause your face to swell up, while it seems Sudafed is basically a magic mushroom. It can cause you to have nightmares and run about the garden imagining you are being chased by Jesus.

Then, of course, there's the big daddy. Viagra. This will cause your penis to stiffen, enabling you to have penetrative sexual intercourse – but with whom? That's the question. Because, according to the instruction manual, it will need to be someone who's turned on by a man who might be bleeding from his eyes and his nose. Still interested? Well, beware, because other potential side effects include nausea and 'sudden death'.

So, there you are. You start out with a bit of rumpy-pumpy and wind up covered in sick and blood, with a dead man on top of you.

Of course, this is all nonsense. We are all well aware that all drugs are subjected to rigorous tests before they are allowed on to the market and that if Voltarol really did turn patients into flesh-eating zombies with altered livers and blistered eyes, someone would have noticed during clinical trials.

You may recall, several years ago, six healthy men were given a new anti-leukaemia drug called TGN1412 to see if there were any unpleasant side effects. After a short while, apparently, they began to run about the surgery, tearing off their shirts and complaining they were going to explode; heads swelled up to three times the normal size, toes and fingers began to fall off and immune systems collapsed. As a result, TGN1412 is now not on the market.

Its maker didn't say: 'Well, there you are. A complete success. It cures leukaemia and all we need do is pop a little instruction manual in the box saying that there's a chance the patient might turn into the Elephant Man and explode.'

That's the point of clinical trials. You test the drug on animals. Then you test it on people. And if it all goes horribly wrong, you can't put it on the shelves. We know this. We know the drugs we can buy are safe. Why, then, do we have these stupid leaflets saying we may suffer from sudden death?

Well, it's the same reason my quad bike is festooned with stickers telling me that if I get on and ride it for even a short while, my head will be severed and I will catch fire. It's why the sun visor in my car is smothered in ugly notices telling me that a possible side effect of the airbag is that it will kill me. It's why police community support officers aren't allowed to help children cross the road.

It's because when there's a chance of something bad happening, there's always a lawyer in the background who can argue that the person concerned should have been warned. And that brings me back to a small point I made earlier.

I suggested the French habit of putting everything up their bottoms dramatically reduced their chances of having children. But I was forgetting something. Sex this way is how you end up with a lawyer.

19 September 2010

But I've killed Baz already, Mr Safety Instructor

Like all right-minded people, I rejoiced when David Cameron announced last week that he would drive a bulldozer through the health and safety rules that have paralysed industry, killed millions and removed all sense of personal responsibility from absolutely everyone in the land.

Sadly, however, his announcement came too late for me because just a day later I was due to attend my first health and safety course. It's now compulsory for any BBC employee who travels to parts of the world that aren't Stow-on-the-Wold or Fulham.

I was seething with rage because it would be unpaid and it would last from eight in the morning until seven in the evening for an entire working week. So when was I going to write my newspaper columns? Or prepare scripts? Or do any actual work? This is the problem with health and safety people. They simply don't understand that we have work to do and that there's just no time for their high-visibility, no-job's-worth-dying-for nonsense.

Because you know what? As a journalist, I reckon some jobs are worth dying for. If a journalist had got advance word of the massacre in Rwanda, then maybe it could have been stopped. Would that have been worth a life? Damn right it would. And the life I'd have taken is that of the stupid health and safety officer who thinks you should be on a how-to-use-a-ladder course rather than the front line.

And anyway, how, in six days, could they possibly hope to cover all of the hazards a programme such as *Top Gear* might face on its travels? Altitude sickness, what to do if you get a fish in your penis, extreme cold, road accidents, how to be beheaded with dignity and what to do while being shelled in Mogadishu. The suggestion was that we'd emerge after a week as a cross between Dr Christiaan Barnard and James Bond.

The first morning suggested this wouldn't be so. We were taken into the gardens of the conference centre in Bracknell in Berkshire, where, among the rhododendrons, two firemen called Baz and Tel were staging a mock battle using a mock gun. Then Baz fell to the ground with mock blood spurting from a mock prosthetic wound in his arm. Apparently, we were supposed to have heard a shot but, sadly, Tel's mock gun had jammed.

It was like watching the Wokingham Amateur Dramatic Society stage a version of *Apocalypse Now*, and I thought: 'Holy shit. I've got six days of this.'

Afterwards, we were taken to a classroom for a lecture on how to deal with the sort of bullet wound we'd seen but I couldn't really concentrate because I was dying for a cigarette and it was two hours until break. The morning passed in a blur of acronyms, none of which I can even remember now. DRAB. Or is it BARD? And what do the letters stand for? All I do remember is that, thanks to the Labour government, we must now refer to an RTA (road traffic accident) as an RTC (road traffic collision) because accidents imply no one was to blame whereas collisions don't.

And blame? That's another whole industry filling a million more crap hotels in Berkshire with their courses and their fat women in trouser suits.

Then, the lecturer's radio crackled. There'd been an accident in the grounds: Baz had fallen out of a tree. So off we rushed to see what could be done. And there was more fake blood pumping out of yet another fake wound. This is how it went on. Lecture. Baz had a horrible accident. Lecture. Baz had a horrible accident. Lecture. Baz fell out of trees, trod on landmines, crashed his car, got shot, got blown up. Baz was the unluckiest fireman in history.

And, to make everything a bit more weird, a funeral was held at our hotel on Thursday. Now, I hope and pray that the deceased did not die in a hail of gunfire because during the post-crematorium 'do', we were running around outside, learning how to take cover in a gunfight.

And, to make everything worse, when one of the mourners approached to ask for our autographs, James May shot her in the face with a water pistol.

I was learning very many things and what I was learning is this: it is impossible to see a tripwire in a wood, it is disgusting to stick your fingers in an open wound, Serbian checkpoint guards cannot be reasoned with and unexploded ordnance has an acronym but I'm damned if I can remember what it is. Oh, and if you have a beard and you have a heart attack on the street, you are 40 per cent less likely to survive . . . because passers-by are unwilling to give the kiss of life to someone with facial hair.

Later, I learnt that men with spinal injuries get a hard-on and that it's impossible to work out where gunfire is coming from. Which is why, when the shooting started, Richard Hammond hid in front of a bush. And was killed.

On Thursday afternoon Baz fell out of another tree and needed to be moved because the Wokingham Amateur Dramatic Society was threatening to cut our heads off. We rolled him on to a blanket in the correct fashion but we couldn't move him because none of us had been on the BBC's manual labour course. I wish I was joking about that but I'm not. Baz died, I'm afraid. Again.

At this stage you probably imagine I'm going to sign off by saying it was all a complete waste of time and that in six weeks' time almost all of what I learnt will have been forgotten. But here's the thing. On day one, Tel told us about a twelve-year-old girl who had been hit by a car.

She rolled on to the bonnet, with a broken leg, and then slid down on to the road, where she banged her head and fell unconscious. A crowd gathered and everyone agreed that she should not be moved because she might have a spinal injury. She died. And she died because her tongue was blocking her airway.

I now know what to do in that situation. And was that one single retainable fact worth a week of my time? Honestly? Yes.

26 September 2010

This tired old bird deserves another chance

Last week we were told, for the umpteenth time, that unless eleventy million pounds is raised by next Tuesday, the last airworthy Vulcan bomber will be mothballed in a shed, where it will be eaten by rats and used by birds as a lavatory.

You're probably fed up with these stories. We're always being told by those who rescued this plane from oblivion that they've spent the £100 you gave them last year and that now they will dangle from your heartstrings until you give them some more.

There are many worthy organizations that want your money.

Sick kiddies. Landmine amputees. Our Brave Boys. So why give it to a lot of people with adenoidal problems and cheap shoes just so they can indulge their passion for a plane that was used only once in anger in its entire twenty-four-year service life? You may remember. It flew all the way to the Falkland Islands to bomb the runway at Port Stanley. And mostly missed.

I understand your cynicism but if we take this argument to its logical conclusion, then there is no point in paying millions of pounds every year to keep the Tower of London upright. It, too, served no useful purpose when it was new and is now nothing more than a glorified safe, guarded by thirty-seven pensioners in silly dresses. Let's pull it down and sell the land to Wimpey.

Stonehenge is also a waste of time and money since nobody knows what it was for then, and now it's just a magnet for lunatics. And why should I give Bill Oddie any of my hard-earned cash just so he can sit in a box, counting ospreys? Screw 'em. What have they ever done for me?

Happily, in this country, we are extremely good at preserving things that we think matter. Many of our magnificent old houses are kept in tip-top order and those who sit on the summit of the *Sunday Times*'s Rich List donate millions each year to keep a few dabs of Constable's oil in air-conditioned comfort.

Recently, Rowan Atkinson announced that he wished to build a splendid modern house, designed by an esteemed architect, in the Oxfordshire village where he lives. But the neighbours went nuts, suggesting that it would look like a petrol station and would consequently ruin the olde worlde charm of their surroundings. Yup. They were prepared to stone a national treasure to death to keep things as they had been for 200 years.

I experienced similar problems with my house, albeit on a smaller scale. Planners allowed me to make many modifications using modern materials such as glass and steel. But they were absolutely insistent that the door between the hall and the kitchen must remain. 'It is a very important door,' said one expert.

It's not just doors, either. Beavers, stamps, hedgerows, bats, books, woodland, monuments, boats, pottery, sporting equipment, poetry, record players. Find something old and I'll find you a group of enthusiasts who are working round the clock to preserve it for future generations. I even know of one man who collects and restores vacuum cleaners.

However, we seem to have a very different attitude to machinery. After the war, for instance, most of the aircraft that had helped to keep Johnny Hun at bay were taken to fields in Wiltshire and Blackpool and chopped into tiny pieces. We didn't need them any more in the jet age so Wellingtons, Lancasters, Blenheims and Sunderlands were simply scrapped. That's why, today, there are only around fifty working Spitfires in the whole world.

It was much the same story with Brunel's steamship, the SS *Great Britain*, which now resides at the docks in Bristol. This was a massively important piece of engineering, the first ocean-going steel ship to have a propeller, and it was big, too. A hundred feet longer than anything that had gone before.

I'm delighted to say the lottery fund stumped up much of the cost of renovating Brunel's masterpiece. But it drew the line at the 1,000-horsepower engines. Even though these were really what set the ship apart and made it interesting, it would not cough up and, as a result, the motors that visitors see today are electrically powered fakes.

Then you have the Science Museum. Only a tiny fraction of its exhibits are on show in London. The rest – some 200,000 – are housed in a collection of dingy hangars near Swindon. And, of course, a recent application to the lottery to turn this site into a full-on museum where visitors could see the cars and the missiles and the planes that made Britain an economic powerhouse was rejected in favour of a cycleway or some such nonsense. 'Preserve a car?' To the Miliband boy and his mates, that would be like paying to preserve the bubonic plague.

Generally speaking, the job of maintaining Britain's mechanized past is the responsibility of wealthy individuals. Nearly all the working Spitfires, for example, are in the hands of rock stars and blue-bloods. It's the same story with most of our country's automotive history, and that's before we get to the traction engines that are maintained by a group of people who think Fred Dibnah was a god.

The idea of getting a grant or sponsorship to preserve a Type 42 destroyer or a Tornado is simply laughable. And that's why it is important we do whatever is possible to help the men in plastic shoes keep that Vulcan airworthy. Sure, it's not as glamorous as a Spitfire, which is why, when it flew low and slow over my house the other day, my children couldn't have been less interested. My dog thought it was noisy and wet itself. Nobody could really understand, therefore, why I was running about in the garden, pointing and grabbing my private parts.

It's true, of course, that this big, loud, delta-winged, retaliatory fist never did anything noteworthy. But since it was built, purely, to drop nuclear bombs on Russia, we should all thank God for that. And be grateful, when we hand over a hundred quid to keep it up there, that we still can.

3 October 2010

Just speak English, Johnny Europe

So far, David Cameron's cuts aren't too bad. A few middle-class babies will have to suckle on their mother's breast milk until they are fourteen, George Osborne has decided to use his own money to buy a Christmas tree for No. 11 and various workers on the tubular railway have been told to get out of their cosy ticket offices – that no one uses any more – and do a spot of work.

However, we all know worse is to come. Free swimming lessons for the elderly will end, greasy women in the north will have their flatscreen televisions confiscated and the navy could lose an aircraft carrier.

That's why I've spent the week racking my brains for a big cut that won't affect anyone. And I think I have an idea.

We must tell people who work for the European Union to stop pretending they can't speak English.

Let me explain. There are twenty-three recognized languages in the EU, which means there are 506 possible bilateral combinations. And because of the impossibility of finding someone who can translate Danish into Estonian, the EU now has to use a chain of translators, which, I'd imagine, massively adds to the chance of a misunderstanding.

Certainly, I know if I was sitting in one of those booths, translating a dreary treatise on fiscal stability from Welsh into Hungarian, I'd never be able to resist changing what had actually been said just a little bit. Maybe dropping in the word 'nipples' occasionally. Or 'testes'.

But worse than the complexity and opportunity for

tomfoolery is the astronomical cost. It's around €1 billion (£875 million) a year and, thanks to various lunatic Basques, things could get worse. The cost isn't just borne by taxpayers, either. If you invent a new type of nasal hair-remover and wish to patent it in all fifty American states, the cost will be £1,600. If you want to patent it across half of the EU, the cost will be £17,500 – thanks to a £12,250 bill for translation services.

For all we know, a Greek bloke invented the Apple iPad back in 1958 but he's still waiting for someone to translate his idea from Hungarian into Portuguese.

Plainly, something must be done, not only to save all the member states money, but also to make our industry more competitive. And it's obvious, isn't it? Those translators have got to go.

The raw data suggest this will not be too much of a hardship, even in Britain, a country famed for its blinkered attitudes to the noises other people use to communicate. According to official figures, 23 per cent of the population here can speak, read and understand French.

Unfortunately, these figures are nonsense. You may claim that you can speak French, by which you mean you can order a loaf of bread and ask for the pen of your aunt. But do you know the French for jump leads? Or Scart lead? Or collywobbles?

The acid test is to imagine yourself in bed with a French girl who can speak no English. Do you have enough to get by? Really? Because, trust me on this, if you say, 'Et maintenant, comme le chien,' she is going to be very angry. And point out that it is, of course, 'la chienne'.

That's the trouble with French. You may know the word for railway station but do you know if it's male or female? Of course you don't, which is why you would come a cropper if you were asked to speak to Monsieur Nicolas Sarkozy about the possibility of sharing nuclear submarines. You'd probably end up giving him your mother's recipe for toad-in-the-hole.

No, when they tell us that 9 per cent of people in Britain can speak German, what they mean is that 9 per cent of people in Britain either have an O level in the subject or once went to Cologne on a business trip. They do not mean that 9 per cent of the British population could hold important talks with Angela Merkel on Chinese trade tariffs.

The fact of the matter is this: thanks to our absurd school league tables, only 5 per cent of A-level students sat an exam in a modern language last year. And even those that passed can hardly claim they were fluent.

So, without translators, almost everyone in Britain is sunk. But that is emphatically not the case with Johnny Foreigner, because contrary to what he may claim when you ask for directions, he does speak English.

English is the mandatory first foreign language for school children in thirteen EU member states. Couple that to the fact that most kids in Europe would rather watch Bruce Willis than some French idiot in black and white smoking a cigarette while pondering the meaning of his ham sandwich, and would rather listen to Lady Gaga than whatever it is the Italians call pop music, and you end up with a government statistic that does appear to be true. Around 90 per cent of European kids can speak English better than many people in Newcastle.

Things are less clear-cut with the older generation, but I'm sorry: if you can't speak English, then you are simply not intelligent enough to represent your region in the European parliament. Your neighbours may as well elect a table or a horse.

The time has come, therefore, for the whole continent to stop communicating with its silly grunts and noises, and take up English. We can explain to the French and the Germans that they may speak in their oh-la-la Gott-im-Himmel language when they go home at night but, to save money, it has to be English at work.

Who knows, we could roll this out all over the world, which would save the United Nations and the G20 a fortune as well. And we should, because it's ridiculous that taxpayers have to cough up simply because some halfwit from Zimbabwe thinks he's making a statement by speaking in ticks and clicks at important meetings.

Nobody really understands how language has evolved but we must understand that today, in a world of fast communications and global consequences for the smallest of things, it's time we waved it goodbye.

10 October 2010

Turkey joining the EU? Over my dead dog's body

Back in the summer, Mr Cameron made an impassioned plea for Turkey to be allowed to join the European Union.

He pointed out that for many years this great bridge between the world of Christianistas and Muslimism has been a NATO missile launch pad and that you can't expect someone to guard the camp and not be allowed inside the tent.

I'm sure that up and down Britain people called Nigel and Annabel nodded sagely at these kind words.

Many middle-class couples take boating holidays off Turkey's idyllic coast and come home with ornate birdcages and lovely rugs. Apart from the boatman who slept with their daughter, they like Johnny Turk very much.

How, they wonder, can the EU possibly turn its back on Turkey, with its lovely 'for you my friend special price' traders and excellent restaurants, while granting membership to the revolting Bulgarians? And the Romanians, with their silly pork-pie hats and donkeys? It's ridiculous.

In the past, Turkey's applications were denied because they liked to cut off people's heads, and such a move would have infuriated the Greeks. Today those excuses no longer hold water. Turkey has abolished capital punishment, and infuriating the Greeks is now seen, especially by the Germans, as a good thing.

Turkey has even managed to sort out its prison system. In the past, you were beaten on the soles of your feet for no particular reason and male rape was encouraged. We know this because we've seen *Midnight Express*. Now, torture is discouraged and the homosexuality is apparently quite tender.

It all sounds fine, then. But I've just spent a bit of time in Turkey and I don't think it's fine at all. And not just because the barmaid at my hotel had only one word of English, which was 'no'. This made ordering a beer extremely complicated.

First of all, I didn't go to Istanbul or one of those turquoise coves you see in the brochures, because that would be like judging Britain on a brief trip to London and Padstow in Cornwall. No, I went to the eastern part. The region the Foreign Office advises us to avoid. Turkey's Lancashire. And I'm sorry, but the only thing I want less in the EU is rabies. It was absolutely awful.

In my view, a country must have certain standards before it can become a member of the EU, and my No. 1 line in the sand is: dead dogs at the side of the road. Of course, you occasionally see a rotting mongrel in Portugal and it's very sad. But in Turkey they lie there like the forest of single shoes we see by the A1. Thousands of them. Maybe they are used as handy direction pointers when one is having friends over for dinner: 'Left at the Labrador. Right by the Dalmatian's head, and if you see the sausage dog, you've gone too far.'

The EU is supposed to be a group of civilized countries working as one. And I'm sorry again, but accepting a country that can't be bothered to clear up its dead dogs would be like Boodle's private members' club accepting a man who thinks it acceptable to masturbate in public.

Sadly, though, there are other issues that must be addressed. Petrol, for example. I realize, of course, that if you water it down a bit, you can increase profits dramatically. Furthermore, when your customer breaks down with a ruined engine, he will be many miles away, with no means of coming back to your place of business with a pickaxe handle. But it's not on. Even the Spanish have cottoned on to this.

It's the same story with plumbing. The idea is that when you pull the chain on a lavatory, the contents of the bowl are taken far away from your nose; not fanned directly into the air-conditioning system, which itself is made from decaying dogs. This sort of thing may be acceptable in Mexico, but not in what should be seen as the world's boutique.

We must also address the violence. Yes, we have road rage in Britain and it's not particularly edifying, but in Turkey it seems that if someone carves you up in traffic, you are legally entitled to leap from your car and beat him to death.

And then there is the transport infrastructure. A road is a complicated piece of engineering. Foundations must be dug. Many different types of stone and gravel must be laid and compressed and hardened before a top coat of asphalt is laid. Filling a crop-dusting aircraft with grey paint and flying over the desert may be cheap, but you end up with something so bumpy that your eyes stop working properly and you fail to see the next military checkpoint.

Of course, we cannot deny Turkey's membership of the EU because it has military checkpoints. We have such things at Heathrow from time to time. And Northern Ireland. But when the soldiers point their automatic weapons directly at your head through slits in sandbag walls and there are tanks, it all feels very far removed from, say, the Dordogne.

I like the diversity of Europe. I like that the Spanish kill cows as sport and northern Englanders race pigeons, a bird the French call 'lunch'. It's a wonderful melting pot, but some things would sit in the stew like a – well, like a dead dog, actually. And being asked for your papers by a man in a tank? That's one of them.

The problem is that Turkey simply doesn't feel European.

Poland does. Ireland does. Even Bradford does. But Turkey feels odd. It feels like part of the East. It's an interesting place and a nice spot for a holiday, I'm sure. There is economic growth, too, but having it in the EU would be as weird as having Israel in the Eurovision song contest. Oh, hang on a minute . . . No. It would be like having a branch of Primark on Sloane Street.

And there's the thing. Mr Cameron says it's not reasonable to expect someone to guard the camp and then not be allowed inside the tent. But that's not true, is it? My local policeman guards my house from vagabonds and thieves but that doesn't mean I want him to come and sit by the fire every night.

31 October 2010

No one needs to know their adze from their elbow

Last week a colleague of mine called James May claimed that any man who could not land an aeroplane and put up a shelf and defuse a bomb was nothing more than an organic bag for keeping sperm at the right temperature until it's needed by a lady.

Speaking to us from the pages of the *Radio Times*, he says traditional skills are disappearing from the curriculum and that there are now many men who think it's endearing and cute to be useless. It isn't, he says. 'It's boring and everyone's getting sick of it.'

I should explain at this point that Mr May is fanatical about the workings of things. For fun, he will take a motorcycle engine to pieces, and for relaxation, he will countersink a screw. At night, he takes penknives or model trains to bed so he can, as he puts it, 'look at them'.

Unfortunately, like all fanatics, he cannot understand the mindset of those who do not share his opinion or abilities. Me, for example. He is right because he draws outlines of all his tools on the wall so he can see at a glance when one is missing. I am wrong because I am confused by zips. He is right because he is organized and methodical and interested in the teachings of Michael Faraday and James Watt. I am wrong because I've got better things to do than read the instruction manual for a vacuum cleaner.

I drive him mad because I cannot see how things go together. Once, he spent fifteen minutes, in a state of increasing exasperation, watching me struggling to attach a strap to a pair of binoculars I'd bought. Eventually he could take no more, snatched the rat's nest that I'd made away and did the job for me. And that is the point. If you cannot do something, then get someone who can to do it for you.

Mr May says children should be taught basic woodworking and needlework skills at school. I disagree. I was taught for many years how to do long division. I even had extra lessons in the hope that the secret of this arithmetic witchcraft could be unlocked. But it was all to no avail. I am now fifty and I still don't understand it. So when I need to divide one number by another, I fire up Mr Samsung and get him to do it on my behalf.

It was the same story in the school woodwork centre. So far as I could tell, every single tool in there seemed to have been designed specifically to puncture my lungs. Telling me that I had to learn how to use a lathe was like telling me I had to learn how to use a tampon. It was pointless. And painful.

And again, that still holds true today. Whenever I attempt even the simplest job around the house, we need scaffolding for eight weeks to put the place in order again.

Every day, at least three white vans with ladders on the roof will come to my house and disgorge men in bobble hats who chew pencils, listen to Radio 1 and mend stuff that's gone wrong. Stuff, Mr May says, I should have been able to mend myself.

But I really and genuinely can't. I can't ever find the end on a roll of Sellotape. I don't understand clasps. Plumbing is a dark art. My lawnmower is a vindictive swine that wants to kill me. The only good news is that you have to pull on a rope to make it begin. And this has never once, ever, worked.

I am not unusual. History is littered with the corpses of people who thought they could save a few bob by doing a job themselves. Lord Finchley, for example, who attempted to mend an electric light – an endeavour that prompted the writer Hilaire Belloc to say: 'It is the business of a wealthy man/To give employment to the artisan.'

Like Finchley, I am not wired up to understand engineering, which is why my respect for those who are is boundless. I can cook an egg, so I don't really have much admiration for Gordon Ramsay. I can write a sentence, so I don't fawn over Sebastian Faulks. But I cannot drill a hole in a wall without knocking it down. Which is why I go all weak-kneed over Isambard Kingdom Brunel.

And, to a certain extent, James May.

He's boring and pedantic and methodical to the point where you want to cut his head off. But we need people like him who can weld, in the same way as he needs people like me who can . . . er . . . . I'll get back to you on that.

When he buys a gun, for example, he takes it into his workshop and inspects every detail of its design and construction. When I buy a gun, I take it outside and shoot the sky near where a pheasant had been moments earlier. And when the gun goes wrong, usually because I haven't cleaned it, I take it to the gun shop, where a man – who Mr May would put out of work – charges me a small amount to put it right again.

But back to Mr May's claim that basic woodwork and needlecraft skills should be taught in school. There are two problems with this. First, there's no point trying to teach someone like me how to make a bookcase. I can't. And second, we are no longer living in 1953.

Teaching someone how to rivet is like teaching someone how to do cave paintings – it's simply not relevant today. Woodworking is fine only as a hobby, and you should never trust a man who has a hobby. Hobbies are for people who were caught masturbating by their mums.

'Stop that and go and do something useful.'

Today the only engineering a child needs to understand is electrical. How to mend a wireless broadband router. How to align a satellite dish. How to transfer iTunes from one computer to another.

And permit me at this point to let a little secret out of the bag. James May can do none of those things. He doesn't like electricity. He doesn't trust it. He even told me once that he doesn't believe it exists. So, when his router goes wrong, like you and me, he spends all day on the phone to a man in India.

7 November 2010

Use Jordan and Jemima to sell Britain

Last week Mr David Cameron breezed into China – where hardly anyone has heard of either him or the country he represents – and explained that it really is no good having a one-party state with censorship of the internet. I don't think this was a very good idea.

I realize, of course, that he has to make some noises about human rights, or the bleeding-heart liberals back at home get all angsty. But really. How would you like it if a complete stranger barged into your kitchen one day and explained that you are not bringing up your children properly?

Quite. Well, that's undoubtedly what the Chinese thought of Mr Cameron's lecture. Who are you? Shut up. And would you like to buy some training shoes?

The purpose of Mr Cameron's visit is to make the Chinese aware of British business in the hope that after we've bought 25 billion pairs of their nasty shoes, they would perhaps like to buy a packet of Prince Charles's Duchy of Cornwall biscuits.

So why begin with a spot of light criticism? When you walk into a boardroom, hoping to sell the assembled buyers your wares, your opening gambit should not be 'I don't like your carpet very much'. It's for this reason my local green-grocer does not collar me as I walk past his shop with the words, 'Oi, fatso, do you want to buy some potatoes?'

Let's gloss over this mistake, though, and move on. By 2015 Mr Cameron hopes to have almost tripled Britain's exports to China from £7.7 billion a year to a whopping

£18.5 billion. God knows how. The Chinese have already said they are not interested in our telecom, insurance, banking or media. So, what's left? I assume that's why George Weston, boss of British Associated Foods, was there, too. Because if Mr Cameron wants to do that much trade, the prince's biscuits on their own will not cut it. He must be planning to sell some Ovaltine as well.

I like this about Mr Cameron. He seems to understand that doing business around the world will make everything a bit better at home. But, again, I sense a mistake. He was accompanied by three big-hitters from the cabinet and a selection of business leaders. There was the aforementioned Mr Weston, with his malty mug, and more than forty others.

But, foolishly, he did not take the pin-ups from his newly created pool of commercial ambassadors – Anya Hindmarch, who makes a living selling handbags to my daughter, and Tamara Mellon.

The *Daily Mail* printed a picture of the latter naked last week, and pointed out her dad was once linked to Diana Dors and she used to dabble with drugs. This may or may not be true but, either way, it's irrelevant. What is relevant is that she started the successful Jimmy Choo shoe business and is, how can I put this, easy on the eye.

Johnny Chinaman may not care much for Mr Cameron – especially when he was probably expecting Winston Churchill – but I can assure you he would have listened to what Ms Mellon had to say. And Ms Hindmarch, who has beautiful eyes.

There was some debate last week about the television programme *Countryfile*. It seems that when the show moved to a primetime slot, four presenters were relieved of their duties because, it is claimed, they weren't pretty enough.

This, from their point of view, is very sad and I hope they

do well in their new careers. On the radio. But the fact is this: most people prefer to be spoken to by someone who is attractive, and so, given the choice of two equally qualified TV presenters, it makes sense to employ Julia Bradbury. Especially on a chilly day.

And so it goes in the world of business. If an ugly man comes to my office trying to sell stapling machines, I will probably not listen to a word he says. But if the same company sends a pretty girl, I will probably buy half a million. Please, do not hold that against me. I can't help it. I was born with a scrotum and it messes with your head.

Of course, I'm not suggesting Mr Cameron should have gone to China with a selection of girls from the pages of *Razzle*, but I do think that when British business is being sold on the world stage, it is important we hold our hosts' attention.

President Nicolas Sarkozy can rock up with his lovely and clever wife, Carla Bruni, who can help keep everyone awake when the speeches have gone on a bit, and Silvio Berlusconi usually has a tribe of weathergirls in tow. This has been a problem for British prime ministers in the past. Without wishing to be mean, Audrey Callaghan was not exactly Michelle Obama. And Cherie Blair, by all accounts, could be awfully bossy. Samantha Cameron would appear to be the perfect combination, except that she's not really interested in going to China and selling Prince Charles's biscuits. Which is where Jordan comes in.

Jordan, or Katie Price, is best known for having massive breasts and too much make-up. But peel all that away and you are left with a surprisingly pretty girl who is extremely clever. She must be. She has amassed a small fortune by simply not getting into cars very carefully.

Then you have Victoria Beckham, who's bright enough to

have stayed famous by simply not eating very much. She'd be a tremendous trade envoy because she's sharp and pretty and can talk about football.

Britain, in fact, is awash with women who could sell the nation's biscuits. There's Alice Temperley, who is a dress designer; Helena Bonham Carter, who is an actress; and Jemima Khan, whom the papers call a 'socialite'. Sprinkle a bit of Helen Mirren into the mix, garnish with a generous portion of Konnie Huq, and you have a world-class sales team. Send that lot in to bat and the people of Poundbury would be in employment for a thousand years. I bet they could even flog Rolls-Royce jet engines to the Australians.

14 November 2010

Foraging – an old country word for violent death

Like many people, I enjoy settling down on a Sunday evening to watch *Countryfile*. It's so peaceful and right. No badger ever has tuberculosis. No one ever rips their face off on barbed wire. And all the presenters are so attractive. There are no old boilers messing up the lovely pastoral views, apart from John Craven, obviously. But mostly he's marooned back at base these days, flogging calendars with deer on them to old ladies. In last week's show, after they'd introduced us to the man who invented walking in Ireland and shown us a boat that went on a river, they presented an item on foraging.

It was great. Lots of extremely attractive middle-aged women went into the countryside with wicker baskets where they picked leaves and weeds and kelp. And then they all gathered in an agreeable barn to cook and eat what they'd found.

It looked fantastic. And it sounds idyllic, doesn't it, taking your family out on a crisp, frosty morning to forage for breakfast? Indeed, a few days earlier a group of Londoners had decided to descend on Hampstead Heath to pick wild mushrooms. Unfortunately, that expedition made it into the news because it infuriated local environmentalists.

Jeremy Wright, who does something green and worthy at a college in London, was quoted as saying he'd seen one person stuffing a hessian sack with fungi. And then said that if everyone picked wild mushrooms on the heath, there would be none left. Plainly, he would rather our mushrooms were flown into Tesco every morning from Israel.

I had a similar problem recently while out picking samphire at my holiday cottage. Even though it was in my garden, a local eco-ist informed me sternly that I was killing tigers or bears or some such nonsense and that I must stop immediately. Which I did . . . n't.

Now, obviously, anything that enrages the green movement is a good and worthwhile thing, but before we all sally forth, it is important to make a couple of points on the mushroom front. Because we live in a police state, it is illegal under the Theft Act of 1968 to pick fungi for commercial gain. And later in the day you will almost certainly suffer an agonizing death. Either that, or you will suddenly find your toaster hysterically funny.

The problem is that there are thousands of varieties of mushroom – there are 340 on Hampstead Heath alone – and many are either hallucinogenic or fatal. The parents of Daniel Gabriel Fahrenheit went west after eating mushrooms they'd foraged. And he must have been mentally affected, too, otherwise why would he decide that the freezing point of water is 32 degrees? And the boiling point 212?

It is impossible here to tell you what danger signs to look out for. There are simply too many. But I can tell you when you'll be safe.

If the mushrooms are a pale, er, mushroom colour and come ready-cleaned in cellophane in a big shop with fluorescent lighting, all will be well.

On a foraging expedition, however, the message is simple: beware. So what else is there?

Well, on *Countryfile*, they were uprooting just about everything, as though the whole of England is one giant snack. But trust me on this – it really isn't.

According to the Safe Gardening website, you will die badly and in great pain if you eat the berries from Boston ivy,

English ivy, lantana, Virginia creeper, yew, privet, the castor oil plant, mistletoe, holly and – weird one this – potatoes.

Now, I know what a potato looks like, but all the others? Haven't a clue. Only today, I was out walking with my dogs when I encountered a bush laden down with what I thought were sloes. And since I'm partial to a pint or two of fruit-infused gin before bed, I thought I'd pick some. But were they sloes? Or were they berries from deadly night-shade, which, apparently, are the same colour? I shan't know until I'm hunched over the lavatory one night, vomiting my own spleen out of my nose.

What about apples, then? Well, in the olden days, foraging for these used to be called 'scrumping' and would earn you, at worst, a clip round the ear from the local bobby. In my garden, though, it's called 'theft' and the lead poisoning you will receive from my Beretta will do you no good at all. The same goes for my crab apples and raspberries.

So. Not mushrooms, then, and not fruit. Which leaves us with what? Well, according to our man on *Countryfile*, you can pick pennywort, which he says is great in salad. Do you know what pennywort looks like? Nope? Me neither. And the same goes for sorrel and all the other things he plunged into his basket. So far as I'm concerned, it's all just wide grass.

There's another problem with foraging.

A problem that became blindingly obvious on *Countryfile* when the yummy mummies served up all the food they'd picked and cooked. The assembled throng did their best to look like they were dining on peach and peacock but it is impossible, even if you are Robert De Niro, to pretend that something tastes delicious when, in fact, it's a nettle gar-nished with seaweed.

Oh, they made all the right noises about nature's larder and the bountiful green and pleasant land but each time they spooned what they'd found into their mouth, they really did look like a bunch of bulldogs chewing on wasps.

So, there we are. While foraging may appeal to the thrifty, nature lovers and people who just want to enjoy the simple things in life, you must know before you set off with your trug and your rosy-faced children that, at worst, you will not survive the day and, at best, what you come home with will taste absolutely disgusting.

Happily, though, there is a way round this. It's called Waitrose.

28 November 2010

WikiLeaks – I dare you to face Roger Sensible

Guests who stay in our spare room imagine that having climbed a rickety back staircase in an adjoining barn, they are far away from the main bedrooms. But they are not. They are right next to where I sleep and I can hear every word they say.

This often makes for a frosty mood around the breakfast table the next morning. They sit there, not understanding why I am slamming their coffee cups down and telling them that if they think my culinary endeavours are so terrible, they can bloody well cook their own bacon and eggs.

Over the years, I've heard every conceivable complaint. My fireplace is hideous. My dog has a crotch fixation. And how I must surely be making enough money to provide a bit of central heating. It's jolly hurtful. But I can usually fight back by advising them that they'll never have children if they continue to make love like they did the night before.

Can you even begin to imagine how many friends you'd have left if they had been able to eavesdrop on your post-mortem analysis of their parties? Precisely. The world cannot function without secrets. And that's why I'm so disappointed by this WikiLeaks nonsense.

It is important that America's embassies around the world can provide candid reports to the power brokers back home about the sex life of French ministers, the temper of Gordon Brown and exactly what sort of parties Silvio Berlusconi is hosting. But if the sender knows his reports will be read by the person he is writing about, his observations will be next to useless. Obama Barack would be sailing along, imagining

Vladimir Putin is kind to animals and that George Osborne has a deep and booming voice with much gravitas and depth.

It goes deeper, too, because if everyone thought everything they said would be broadcast to the entire world, no one would say anything at all. It's hard to be a trade envoy to the Middle East if all you can do is smile and nod.

Silence can work in certain diplomatic situations – when a couple split up, for instance, it's always tempting to say, 'I never liked her anyway. She was a witch and her bottom was massive,' but prudence requires that you pull benign faces and mumble platitudes because you know there's always a chance that two weeks later they'll be back together again.

However, when you are the British prime minister and you are asked by the American ambassador for your government's stance on Pakistan, mumbling just won't work. He needs to know the truth. And you need to tell him. And you need to be able to do so, safe in the knowledge that the Pakistanis will not find out what you said.

Those who believe that everyone has a right to know everything say that cables from US embassies around the world should be reproduced on the internet. Well, if that's true, why does the founder of WikiLeaks not simply post his location on Google Earth? If he thinks we should know everything about everybody, why – at the time of writing – is he in hiding?

Apparently, it's hard to see what law has been broken. The Americans are saying that if there is a loophole, then they must work fast to close it. But this is fraught with difficulty because you are rummaging around in the foundations of a democracy. Pretty soon, newspapers would be unable to run stories about footballers who've been sending inappropriate pictures of themselves to two-year-olds.

You need to be careful that by shutting the door on disgruntled government employees whose stupidity could cause all sorts of international incidents, you are not also shutting the door on a journalist's remit to get to the truth. Which is why, once again, we must visit my idea for an all-powerful Ministry of Common Sense.

It was first mooted many years ago when a chap called Peter Wright planned to write a book about his time in MI5. There was much debate at the time about whether this should be allowed and, legally, both sides seemed to have a point. So, I decided what we needed was not an expensive recourse to law but to a government-appointed bloke in a jumper who would realize that, morally, it made no sense to publish the book and put a stop to it.

Since then, there have been many occasions when councils and health and safety zealots have acted within the framework of the law but outside the parameters of common sense. Again, victims should have been able to appeal to the minister. I like to think he'd be called Roger. In my experience, people called Roger are usually quite level-headed.

Roger's job, then, would be to sit in an office, listening to both sides of an argument before deciding what would be best. This week, for instance, he'd be asked whether Ann Widdecombe should be allowed to stay in the dancing programme. Some would say it's her right and that, obviously, the sort of people who can be arsed to vote wish her to remain in place. Others would say she's ruining the competition for people who can do hopping with one leg over their shoulder. And he'd decide that she should go.

Then he'd have to deal with Ray Wilkins, the Chelsea assistant manager sacked by Roman Abramovich last month. 'Yes, of course you should have your job back.' And then he could turn his attention to the students who are keeping warm on these chilly days by kicking police cars. And then you'd pop in to say you'd been caught doing 33mph, in the middle of the night, when no one was around, and he'd let you off.

In my life, I've been to court twice, and on both occasions I've been on the moral high ground. But, technically, I've been wrong and have lost as a result. This is why we need a minister of common sense. Because immediately he'd get to the bottom of this WikiWee business. What it is doing is in the public interest and probably legal. But what it is doing is also wrong.

5 December 2010

Stop all the clocks for British No Time

Earlier this year, various people – including David Cameron – started to wonder out loud if it would be a good idea to stick with British Summer Time all year round. It seems a fairly harmless suggestion but it met with considerable hostility.

Those who rise early say that, in fact, we would be much better off sticking with Greenwich Mean Time all year round.

And then you have those who say that we should have British Summer Time in the winter and then double British Summer Time in the summer. This is what happened during the war.

But this argument seems to find little favour with Europhobes. 'No. We can't have the clocks going even further forward than they do now because then we'd be in the same time zone as the Hun and the bally Frogs.'

You even have Cornish people saying that, under the present system, they have midday when it's still only 10.30 in the morning. And that any change would cause noon to fall between their bacon and their eggs. And in Scotland, of course, where it's permanent daylight in the summer and constantly dark in the winter, it makes more sense to dispense with time altogether and become a hedgehog.

Naturally, road-safety organizations are particularly vocal on the issue. They say that year-round lighter evenings would make it safer for 'kiddies' coming home from school – and this is probably true. But on the downside, it would surely increase the number killed while fumbling their way to lessons in the pitch-black mornings.

I know this probably hasn't occurred to the Royal Society for the Prevention of Accidents – an organization that endeavours to prevent an incident that, by its very nature, cannot be foreseen – but if I've got to be hit by a bus, I don't really care whether it's in the morning or the afternoon. I do, however, care about the question of time. My life has become so hectic in recent years that I did not even have time yesterday to go to the lavatory. And the day before, I was so busy I missed the office party.

I'm sitting here now with a dull ache in my groin. This has nothing to do with the picture I've just seen of Gwyneth Paltrow in her amazing new dress. It's been throbbing for weeks. I suspect it's a hernia. But I do not know for sure because I have not had a moment even to telephone the doctor for an appointment.

I suspect I'm not alone, either. I bet thousands of people die every year because they simply didn't have the time to get better.

We're all in the same boat. It used to be easy to meet friends for a drink or dinner. Not any more. Now, they are always chained to their laptops or stuck in a meeting. And woe betide the man who suggests 'one for the road' at the end of the evening. Because everyone has to be up at five to fly to New York.

Never mind British Summer Time. Hosts now need flexible British Party Time to accommodate those who are popping in after work because they need to be up early and those who have been in the office till gone midnight. You are just finishing serving one lot with coffee and mints when the next batch arrive and want a prawn cocktail. This means you can go next door and get jet lag.

I don't understand why this is happening. I have exactly the same job now that I had five years ago. All my friends have exactly the same jobs, too. And, thanks to electronic communication, those jobs should be easier. Even allowing for the fact that we must set aside two hours of the day to root about in a cupboard, trying to read the serial number of the Wi-Fi router so it can be fixed by a man in Mumbai, we can still deal with stuff far faster than we could in the days of ink and stamps.

There's more. In the past, we needed to go into a town and park if we wanted to do some Christmas shopping. Now, we can do it all online. Cooking? No need. I just move the mouse around a bit and in a matter of moments a motorcycling Pole is at my door with a steaming pile of pad thai.

In my kitchen there is a tap that delivers boiling water from what feels like the centre of the earth, so that I don't have to stand around waiting for a kettle to boil. Coffee comes instantly from the wall. The air is conditioned so I don't need to step outside for a breather.

All of these things should mean I now have several free hours in the day to ruminate on John Prescott and write thank-you letters and do stuff with the kids. And yet. My son broke up from school six days ago and I have not seen him once. Not even fleetingly. Because I'm so busy, I'm getting up just as he's thinking about maybe going to bed.

My mother says often that I should slow down. I bet yours does, too. But this is not possible. If I had chosen to spend the past few hours making daisy chains, this column would not have been written. Which would have made me very sacked. This, therefore, is the problem we need to be addressing. Instead of listening to a few racist Corns and Jock McSheep-Fan, we need a whole new strategy.

At present, it's a nuisance changing all the clocks in your house twice a year, so here's what I propose. For eleven months of the year, we have British Work Time, when we do our jobs and mend our routers and have heart attacks.

And then, every August, we have British No Time, when the speaking clock is turned off and Big Ben is covered with a tarpaulin. You get up when you feel like it, sit in the garden until it's too chilly and go to bed when you are tired. They have a similar system in France. It's one of the reasons they all live to be 147.

There's another, too. They understand that time is useful only if you're doing something useful with it.

19 December 2010

The small society built on jam and dung

Poor old David Cameron seems to be struggling to explain what he means by the 'big society'.

And I'm not surprised because, in the five seconds allocated to politicians on the evening news, it's difficult to outline a seismic shift in the way we all think and behave and live.

To most people, the big society means that if you cut your leg off in some farm machinery, instead of expecting to be saved by a government-funded ambulance driver, you should sew it back on yourself. Many find this idea unappealing.

What's more, Margaret Thatcher once said there was no such thing as society. So now the Conservative party is telling us it wants a big version of something it used not to believe existed at all. Which means that, all of a sudden, the atheist wants to build a cathedral.

To try to get a handle on the subject, I took the trouble of reading a big society speech Mr Cameron made last week and I'm afraid I'm none the wiser. He seems to be saying that we have to expect less from the government – which is what Mrs Thatcher said – and that if we are not happy with our local school we should simply get together with our neighbours and build a new one. Which is broadly what everyone on the corner of Haight and Ashbury was saying in 1967.

I'm not sure I'd know how to go about building a school. And I'm not sure my neighbours would be much help, either, because last week one of them died. And the other one's a bit busy because he's the prime minister. So, all on my own, I'd need to find some teachers and make sure they weren't kiddie fiddlers, which is likely to be more complicated in future. And then I'd need loads of bricks and cement. I think it would be easier – and cheaper, frankly – to hoick my kids out of the school I didn't like and send them to Eton.

The trouble is, however, I like the smell of Mr Cameron's idea. I don't understand the details and I don't like anything with the word 'big' in it – it sounds like a promotion at a sofa shop. But I can catch a whiff of what he's on about and, in short, it's this: 'Ask not what your country can do for you but what you can do for yourselves.' And that brings me on to the Oxfordshire town where both Mr Cameron and I live, Chipping Norton.

In 1932 the people of this hilly outpost got together and bought themselves a fire engine. And then, after the war, they sold it to the newly established, government-run fire brigade. The money raised from the sale was used to pay for a football pitch, a cricket field and some tennis courts.

Plainly, this sense of independence was still going strong in 1963 when the townspeople came together once more to raise money for a swimming pool. This lido was subsequently built, and eventually the cost of running it was taken over by the West Oxfordshire district council.

However, in 2002, the council announced that it could no longer afford to run a heated outdoor pool, especially as it had just opened a new leisure centre, and that, as a result, it would be closed down. Nothing unusual in that. The *Jeremy Vine Show* is rammed with people saying they now have to swim in puddles and skips. Swimming pools are closing faster than pubs.

However, in the fine town of Chipping Norton a handful of locals decided that instead of ringing the *Jeremy Vine Show* and moaning, they'd form an action committee to keep the pool open.

And pretty soon this committee decided to hold a fund-raising auction.

I remember it well. The old town hall was stuffed to the gunwales with people who'd donated prizes. There were hundreds of them. I know because I was the auctioneer and it went on for hours. 'A jar of home-made jam, sold to you, sir, at the back. Two bags of dung. Who'll give me a tenner?'

It was a fantastic evening.

There was lots of hub and tons of bub, and at the back there were shifty-looking people from the council thinking, 'Oh no, we're going to lose our seats,' and that spurred us on.

It was like a scene from an Enid Blyton book. The butcher bid. The baker bid. The candlestick maker bid.

My daughter, who was only seven at the time, couldn't quite understand why we were there. 'Why do we need to save the town's pool?' she said. 'We have our own.' But even this budding Thatcher soon got into the swing of things and helped her dad by bidding for things that wouldn't sell. We went home with a puncture repair kit and six signed copies of my own book.

From memory, the evening raised £12,000, which was – with a bit of help from the town council – enough to keep the pool open for a year. So, twelve months later, we were back to do it again. And we've been back every year since.

The result? Well, the pool is still open, providing local people with a nice place to go on a summer's day. But, more than that, the fundraising evening means the man from the pub who donates a free dinner with wine gets to meet the man from the bookshop, and the woman from the florist gets to meet the kids from the local school band. When I pop into the town now to buy a packet of fags, the people I see are no longer strangers, and that makes it a happier place to live.

I intensely dislike the word 'community' because it is constantly misused in news reporting. What is the Muslim community? The very idea that every single Muslim in the country has exactly the same opinion about everything makes me feel queasy.

There's no such thing as the Chipping Norton community, either. It's a town full of different people who think differently about many things. But now, thanks to the swimming pool and the fundraising efforts needed to keep it open, there is a community spirit.

It's not a big society. It's better than that. It's a small society, and I urge you all to give it a bash where you live.

20 February 2011

Proud to sponsor this police shootout

While appearing on television recently, I questioned the wisdom of car companies sponsoring football teams. Because while those hideous Audi-branded seats at Old Trafford do much to endear the German motor manufacturer to Manchester United's million-strong army of fans, they have the reverse effect on the billion or so people who support a different team.

Audi is therefore paying hard-earned cash to ensure that my son will never ever buy one of its products. He couldn't bear the thought that some of his money would be going to Sir Alex Ferguson, who he thinks might actually be the devil.

Sponsoring a football team is a bit like sponsoring a religion: 'Tesco. Proud to be the official supplier of fine foods to Britain's synagogues.' You can see that there would be problems with this. It'd be like Apple sponsoring abortion clinics in the Bible Belt. Or a man I know who once tried to get his company, a well-known cigarette brand, to sponsor public executions in West Africa.

If I were running a large company and I wanted to put its name in front of millions of people, I'd sponsor a hospital. Because there are only two possible outcomes for those who pass through the portals. They either die, in which case nothing is lost, or they are repaired, in which case they will be forever in your debt.

On the face of it, sponsored vets look like a good idea, too. If they perform a successful operation on your dog, they could shave Audi's logo into its fur and few would complain.

Especially as the sponsorship deal would make the operation less expensive.

But I see a downside to this. If the vet who fired a bolt gun into the back of my donkey's head had been wearing a Sony jacket, I'd have emerged from the experience feeling less well disposed to the idea of buying a Vaio laptop any time soon.

You might imagine that it's a good idea to sponsor a television programme since it's safe to assume that everyone watching is doing so on purpose and will like what they see. But today, with Sky+ and online availability, most people will zoom through your carefully constructed messages. Or if they are watching live, they will dislike you for wasting their time. Certainly, I made a solemn vow in series three of 24 never to buy a Nissan. I had tuned in to see Jack Bauer shooting swarthy-looking men in the knee, not some dizzy bint driving about the place in an off-road car.

Sponsorship, then, is a tricky business. You need to ensure that many people will see your company's name, that all of them are happy with the positioning you've chosen and that no one's donkey is killed. Which brings me on to proposals to sponsor the police.

This isn't a joke. The Hertfordshire force now has so many faith advisers on its chaplaincy team – including humanists – that it is extremely short of money. And, as a result, a senior officer has written to local businesses asking them to sponsor ten vehicles used by special constables.

In return for cash, the businesses would get their name on the cars, which, says the letter, will provide the 'benefit of being associated with the constabulary brand'. Did you know the constabulary was a 'brand'? Me neither. I thought it was just a lot of people in plastic shoes pretending to be Nigel Mansell. However, despite the upbeat nature of the letter, I'm not sure it's a good idea to let Currys or DFS or Asda sponsor the police force. Or service. Or whatever silly name the government halfwits have dreamt up now.

First, and this is a serious point, if a policeman in, say, a PC World jacket turned up in a car with PC World written down the side to investigate some wrongdoings at the company's headquarters, many people, myself included, would assume he would emerge after a short while to say that everything was in order. In other words, there'd be a perception that fat cat bosses, as we must call them these days, are simply buying immunity from prosecution.

There are other problems, though. A lot of people do not much care for the police. Some of these people are burglars and robbers, and a company might decide it's not too bothered about alienating them by visibly supporting the force. But what about when the police run radar traps and fine you for driving a bit too fast? Certainly, if I were to be apprehended by a sergeant in a Burger King hat, I'd ensure that from that moment on I never ate another Whopper.

My biggest problem with this sponsorship idea, though, is dignity. There was a time when British policemen looked good with their tall hats and shiny buttons. Today, they either look like everyone else with their silly high-visibility jackets or they look like cartoon characters from shoot-'em-up video games with their black overalls and their sub-machine guns.

Neither outfit lends itself to sponsorship logos. I mean, seriously, can you imagine how the world would react should there be a televised gunfight in the middle of Hitchin and all the goodies were running about in jackets promoting a local garden centre? We'd be a laughing stock and rightly so.

Plus, one of the less savoury jobs performed by officers is informing families that someone dear to them has been killed in some awful way. I don't think they'd be able to achieve the right level of gravitas if they were dressed up as the Michelin man.

We know that, as a rule, the government is completely useless at running anything and that Richard Branson and Sir Sugar will always do a better job. If I were in No. 10, I'd hand over pretty much everything to the private sector – starting with the forests – but even I would be forced to conclude that some aspects of government work must be run by public servants using public money. The armed forces are one of these things. GCHQ is another. And so are police.

Besides. I pay half what I earn in tax.

And it's nice to think I'm getting at least something in return.

27 February 2011

Hello, reception. I've actually used my bed, please don't be angry

For the past few weeks I've been travelling the world, and once again I'm filled with a sense that no one knows how to run a hotel properly. For example, when you are staying at the top of a thirty-storey skyscraper, four lifts are not enough. Because at eight in the morning, when everyone is going downstairs for breakfast, you can be waiting until lunchtime for a car to arrive.

And it's even worse when you get back at night and you are busting for a pee and one of your colleagues, who's staying on the fourth floor, decides it would be amusing to press all the buttons as he gets out.

Mind you, the vertical nature of a hotel is nothing compared with those that are laid out horizontally. Because it can often take several days to get from the reception area to your room, where inevitably your electronic key card does not work so you must go back to the front desk and start all over again.

At some hotels these days it's best to book another room on the way to the actual suite you've been given so that you can store basic emergency supplies: pants, soap and some high-energy chocolate bars.

Then we have the problems of learning how your room works. I realize, of course, that many hotels send a porter to explain everything when you arrive but you never listen because you are too busy rummaging surreptitiously through your wallet to find a suitable tip, and then doing mental exchange-rate maths to work out whether you are about to give him £2,000. Or, worse, 2p.

The upshot is that, later on, when you want to turn out the lights, you have absolutely no clue how this might be achieved. And when you finally manage it, by hitting the light fittings with your shoe, you realize the air-con is still on and you must find the control panel in the dark.

Then you wake up at two a.m. with jet lag and decide to watch television. Well, in every single modern hotel this is not possible because the remote-control device has 112 buttons, all of which are the size of a match head, and you can't locate the switch to turn the light back on to find your glasses.

So you stab away at what looks promising and all you get are messages from the Japanese engineer who designed the set to the man whose job it is to install it. Why can't hotel managers understand that almost all of their guests need just three things: a button for volume, a button for news and a button for porn? I don't want to adjust the contrast or the aspect ratio. I just want to find out what's going on in Japan and see some ladies.

Oh, and when I'm taking a shower, I am not wearing my spectacles, which means I cannot read the labels on all the little bottles in there. I'm therefore fed up with washing my hair with body lotion.

The worst aspect of staying in a hotel, though, is trying to do your laundry. It shouldn't be that difficult. You just bung it all in a bag and give it to someone at the reception desk.

But no. There's always a form on which you must say precisely what you are handing over. The form lists every possible item of clothing that anyone anywhere might want cleaning. Ball gowns. Scuba suits. Fencing masks. Ruffs. Doublet and hose. Army uniforms. G-trousers. All of this is intended to demonstrate what a wide and interesting clientele comes to the hotel but it's a bit annoying when all you want is some clean underwear.

You search and you scan for the right box to tick but it's never there because, in hotel management-speak, 'knickers' is a rude word. Eventually, between ostrich feather hat and quilted smoking jacket, you find the word 'pants'. But this, you then realize, means 'trousers'.

So the search begins again until eventually you work out that, in business land, shreddies are known as undershorts. With a sense of triumph you fill in the box called 'guest count', saying you have eight pairs you'd like to be cleaned – but wait, what's this? It's another column called 'hotel count'. In other words, it's a form in which you give the hotel your opinion on how many pairs of dirty pants you have and then it is given the opportunity to disagree.

This says it all. In essence, the hotel guest these days is nothing more than a robber and a cheat. A person who has checked in to drink the gin and fill the empties with water, claim for underwear they don't own and check out without paying. At best, we are a nuisance.

Certainly, I felt that way while staying at the Palazzo Versace hotel on Australia's Gold Coast. This is the place where contestants from ITV's *I'm Not a Celebrity* come to vomit up the bugs they've eaten while living in 'the jungle'. And I can see why. It is very Peter Andre. Here, I was not made to feel like a thief but I was made to feel very ugly. The corridors were full of pictures of beautiful, famous people in varying degrees of undress. None had a pot belly and a suitcase full of dirty shreddies. Downstairs there was a salon offering 'eye couture', and in the room a booklet 'suggests' what guests might like to wear at any given time of day. Jeans and a T-shirt didn't get a mention.

It's also very clean. And to keep it that way, guests are constantly made to lift up their feet so that a tribe of former boat people can mop up bits of imaginary food that have been dropped on the floor. Then, at night, an army of yet more cleaners patrol the open spaces with factories on their backs, fumigating and vacuuming and desperately trying to rid the building of any evidence that it might have people in it.

But the best bit came one morning when the manageress came over to our table to announce that she'd reviewed the film from the previous day's CCTV cameras and had noticed two of our party playing the piano in the reception area. It's hard to think what else one might do with a piano but she was most insistent. It mustn't happen again. Behind her, I couldn't help noticing, there were two fully-grown men snogging.

27 March 2011

This kingdom needs a dose of Norse sense

Every so often an organization with a bit too much time on its hands does a survey and concludes that Norway is the best country in the world. We're told that no one has ever been murdered, the cod is superb and there are many dew-fresh meadows full of extremely tall blonde girls who have nothing to do all day except knit exciting underwear.

Economically, we're told, they are also better off. Thanks to all the oil, Norway is the second-wealthiest and most stable country in the world and has the second-highest GDP per capita, after the statistical anomaly that is Luxembourg.

And, of course, we mock. We explain that it's all very well living in a crime-free gated community where everyone seems to be out of a commercial for Ski yoghurt, but unless you occasionally step on a discarded hypodermic needle and catch AIDS, you aren't really living life to the full.

If none of your buses is full of sick, you become one-dimensional and boring. This is why so many Norwegians commit suicide. It's also why, in all of human history, Norway has produced only a handful of people who've made it big on the international stage. One painted a figure screaming. One walked to the South Pole. And the other made a name for himself by suggesting that the sun only shines on TV. Which suggests that he only ever watches *Teletubbies*.

And that, it seems, is what Norway's all about. Designed by Playmobil and run along the lines of Camberwick Green, it's the set for a children's television show, with lots of rosy cheeks and a *Midsomer Murders* attitude to immigration.

Lovely, but so far as the rest of the world's concerned, there's not much of a there, there.

Well, for reasons that are not entirely clear, I've been to Norway quite a lot just recently and I'm sorry, but I can't quite see what's wrong with it. I suppose the speed limits are a bit low, and the only way you can enjoy a cigarette and a glass of wine at the same time is to buy a house. Also, it's a bit chilly, but that just gives you an excuse to put on an excellent Kirk Douglas *Heroes of Telemark* jumper and some splendid woolly mittens.

Let me give you one small example of why I like it there. When a British person asks for my autograph, the request always comes with a back-handed compliment: 'I dislike your programme very much and I hate you on a cellular level but my son is a fan, so sign this or I'll ring the *Daily Mail* and explain that you ruined a small boy's life.'

Russians explain that if you don't stand still until they've gone back to their hotel room for a camera, they will kill you. Aussies slap you on the back a bit too hard and Americans get massively carried away. But in Norway, you get a 'please' and an 'if it's not too much trouble' and a 'thank you'. One man became so excited that I'd posed for his picture, he took out his penis and began to masturbate. I've never experienced gratitude like that anywhere.

Then there's the spirit of *janteloven*. It's a tall-poppy thing that dictates you really mustn't be a show-off, no matter how much money you have. Delightfully, there's no such thing as Cheshire in Norway. It's why 19 per cent of Norwegians who win the country's lottery buy a Toyota. Only one has ever bought a Porsche.

Politically, Norway is sort of communism-lite. Thirty per cent of the population are employed by the state, 22 per cent are on welfare, 13 per cent are too disabled to work and, as parents are given twelve months' combined paid leave when they have a baby, the rest of the population is at home changing nappies. This is probably why there is absolutely nothing in your house bearing the mark 'Made in Norway'.

Interestingly, and contrary to what you'd expect, there is crime. An American was pickpocketed in 2008. And there are beggars. Mostly, though, they are from Romania and that does raise a question: why Norway? Why leave the warmth of your homeland and settle in a country where a glass of beer is £40 and if you sleep on the streets, you wake up with your face stuck to the pavement?

Well, I asked, and the answer was surprising: 'Because in Norway when you ask someone for money, they give it to you.'

Can you see anything wrong with any of this? Kind-hearted souls in excellent jumpers giving away their money to those less fortunate than themselves. No Premier League footballers bombing about in Ferraris. No bankers smoking cigars the size of giant redwoods. No grime. No graffiti. And a range of first-class shops that aren't full of anarchists weeing on the Axminster.

And now we must ask ourselves: how could we achieve such a level of harmony here? We are northern European, just like the Nors. We like a drink, just like they do, and we like to have a fight afterwards. Which they do as well. I'm tall and have blue eyes so, probably, my great-great-grandad was a Viking. Just like yours. So why is Britain such a mess when Norway is the living embodiment of civilization?

Some might say that Norway excels because almost no one there goes to church. They are the least religious people on earth. But we aren't a nation of Bible-bashers, either. So it must be something else. Others say it's the oil. But Norway has had one of the highest standards of living since the seventeenth century. So that's not it either.

No, I reckon the reason Norway is so nice is that the population is tiny. And countries with a small number of people in them – Iceland, Estonia and, er, the Vatican – work better than those that are filled to the gunwales.

I'm afraid, then, the only way of getting the UK to match the Scandinavian model is to abolish the UK. Norway separated from Sweden in 1905, and we should follow suit by severing the knots that bind together the wildly disparate bits of Britain. In short, I think the sovereign state of Chipping Norton would work rather well.

3 April 2011

Big smile – and check me down below for ticks

I wonder. Have we lost the ability in this country to rejoice in the good fortune of others? To be happy for someone else? Buy a big house and 'it's all right for some'. Have the big house taken away and 'it serves you right'.

Let us take the case of Kate Middleton's mum. Her daughter is marrying a prince and so we should be happy for her. But we keep being told that she's a social mountaineer who has been engineering this marriage since the days when Kate was a foetus. And that she used to be an air hostess. A bloody trolley dolly. Pushy cow.

We saw the same sort of thing when Judith Keppel became the first person to scoop the big prize on *Who Wants to Be a Millionaire?* Because she lived in Fulham and said 'bath' properly, we were invited to despise her on a cellular level. Lucky cow.

And woe betide the celebrity who dares to take a stroll on the beach while on holiday. Look at her! She may have fame, success, money and a pretty face but her swimsuit is disgusting and she has cellulite and we hope that very soon she catches cancer and dies a screaming, agonizing death.

Have you ever looked at the comments left by readers on a newspaper's website? They're just a torrent of bile and vitriol. Protected by the anonymity of the internet and freed from the social niceties of physical contact, people go berserk. Lottery winners are particularly vulnerable, it seems. And Nigella Lawson? Fat cow.

No one can earn more than the prime minister, no one can

be better looking than Ena Sharples, and good luck to anyone who dares to appear on the television talking like Brian Sewell. Did your parents go to university? Well, you've had all the chances that life can afford, so you can clear off.

This unwillingness to be happy for others is now so acute that we don't even seem to be able to be happy for ourselves. I realize, of course, that people in Birmingham have suffered from this for centuries. Joy is not a Brummie thing. Everything, even if you've made it yourself, is rubbish. There is no word in the West Midlands for 'wow'.

Now we're all in the same boat, a point that was proved exquisitely on the BBC local news programme that was transmitted in my area on Tuesday evening. It had been an absolutely beautiful day: cloudless, warm and awash with the scent of blossom. The sort of day that made you glad to be alive.

In the olden days, a local news programme would have shown us spring lambs frolicking about on their rickety legs and small children dribbling ice cream in the park. Not any more. Now you could see the news team desperately trying to persuade the water company that the good weather would mean a hosepipe ban very soon. And then when that failed, calling the local hospital to see if anyone had been admitted suffering from sunstroke. 'Well, what about a malignant melanoma, then?'

Doubtless they will have scanned the *Daily Mail* to see if there is a link between warm spring sunshine and the arrival of more immigrants, or a catastrophic fall in house prices. And then the *Guardian* to see if it was yet more conclusive proof of global warming and that soon we would all perish in terrible heathland fires.

The news editor must have been tearing his hair out: 'We can't tell people that it's been a lovely warm spring day. There must be some danger. Some terror. Some death. Get me some misery.' And boy, oh boy, did one of the reporters come up trumps.

We were told that the warm weather may appear to be lovely but that there is a hidden menace out there: the tick. A perfectly healthy-looking woman was brought in front of the cameras to explain that she had been bitten by a tick two years ago and her life had been ruined as a result. Then a professor was wheeled out to say that the long warm spell followed by a late Easter would cause many more people to be out and about in the countryside and that we were facing a . . . please say 'perfect storm'. She didn't. She said it was a 'high-risk situation'.

It turns out that we've just had a Tick Bite Prevention Week – I'm surprised you missed it – during which people were advised what to do if they discover they are being bitten by a tick. First, you must not under any circumstances try to remove it, as this may cause part of the mouth to remain in your skin, spreading Lyme disease. Nor must you swat it with a rolled-up newspaper, as this may cause the arachnid to vomit into the bite wound.

There is, it seems, only one safe way to remove a tick that's in the process of gorging on your blood, and that's with a specialized tick removal tool. If you are one of the few people not to have such a thing handy when disaster strikes, a small pair of tweezers can be employed, if you know what you're doing. Which, let's be honest, you don't.

The best solution, however, is not to get bitten in the first place. Experts suggest wearing light-coloured clothing and recommend that, after you've showered in insect repellent, you tuck your trousers into your socks.

And here's the best bit. After you've been for a walk, you should thoroughly examine your entire body and get someone else to 'inspect the areas that are hard to see'. I am not making this up. These mongers of doom are suggesting that after you've been for a stroll in the wood, you should get naked and insist that your wife has a good ferret around in your undercarriage for evidence of tick infestation.

See what I mean? It's a lovely day. You fancy a nice walk. But there's misery out there not just for you but also for your nearest and dearest, who must spend the rest of the day snouting around in your dingleberries.

Still, in the spirit of what Britain has become, I'd like to finish off by saying this: last year, about 60 million people did not contract Lyme disease from a tick bite, whereas 3,000 came a cropper. And that, of course, serves them right for being ramblers.

24 April 2011

Cancel the breast op and buy an iron lung

The National Trust announced last week that the public will soon be allowed to look round the Oxfordshire house of William Morris. It will, says the Trust, be a marvellous trip down Memory Lane, since none of the contents has been touched since the motor industry magnate's death in 1963.

It will also be a trip into the soul of a truly great man. Because although Morris was Britain's richest self-made man, visitors will note that the carpets in his bedroom were offcuts from his factory in Cowley.

Closer examination of the wardrobe will reveal a collection of Phillips Stick-a-Soles, suggesting he liked to repair his shoes rather than buy a new pair.

Morris, then, did not spend much money on himself. But, my God, he lavished a fortune on others. He gave away more than £30 million of his fortune to worthy causes – that's equivalent to about £700 million today. He funded Nuffield College, Oxford, and during the polio epidemic of the 1940s and 1950s he paid for 5,000 iron lungs to be distributed around the Commonwealth.

My great-grandfather was similarly generous. While researching my family tree for the BBC's *Who Do You Think You Are?* TV programme I was amazed – and a bit distressed – to discover that he gave millions of pounds to the Methodist church. If you worship today in a chapel up north, be aware that the windows, pews and roof . . . well, to be blunt, they're mine.

Of course, a lot of people today ask what happened to the

spirit of philanthropy. There was even an editorial in Her Majesty's *Daily Telegraph* lamenting the fact that the attractive combination of personal prudence and public generosity seems to have gone out of fashion.

There's a very good reason for this, I think. It's because in the days of Morris and my great-grandad there really wasn't much you could actually buy. In the 1930s there were no Sunseeker yachts or Ferraris or time-share opportunities in Portugal.

We were told last week that Kate Middleton's brother is on course to make 'serious money' from his upmarket cake business. Upmarket cakes? There's another drain on the resources of today's rich. Another temptation that was not placed in the path of Morris.

He was able to buy all those iron lungs because his wife was not sitting at home thumbing through OK! magazine and wondering if she should have a new pair of Christian Louboutins because Amanda Holden's got some. Nor would he have been invited to spend £750 on a haircut.

When you make a few quid today you are inundated by a horde of oily Uriah Heeps who arrive in your inbox, genuflecting like seaweed and offering you a service that can provide a dozen black orchids at three in the morning anywhere in the world. Would my great-grandad have been so generous if he'd been tempted by the private-aircraft salesman from NetJets? And if Morris had been shown a watch with a button that summons International Rescue should he be in distress, would he, perhaps, have provided only 4,999 iron lungs?

The other day, at a swanky London restaurant, I ordered a pot of tea for four and the bill was £78. I have framed the receipt and it sits on my office desk as a constant reminder that the world has definitely gone mad.

Then there was a friend who said to me: 'I tried to buy

some cheese at Daylesford this morning. But I only had £162 on me.' Ridiculous? Perhaps. But at the Gloucestershire greengrocer it seems £162 barely gets you a beetroot.

Last week I needed a coffee table, so I went to a coffee table shop and discovered that prices started at £600. Of course, it's always been possible to spend a vast fortune on furniture but very few people actually did. Now, though, the coffee table shop is rammed full of women with £500 Nicky Clarke hair and £200 sunglasses spending four grand on a chair. To go in a room they don't use, in a house where they don't live.

There's no space for philanthropy in a world where the path of the righteous man is beset on all sides by the iniquities of the selfish and the tyranny of greedy men. Men who think: 'Yes, I could let that silly woman spend her money wisely but instead I'll get her to think that she ought to buy a coffee table for £600.'

In many ways I am one of those silly women. I recently bought a farm. I didn't need a farm and I don't know anything about farming, a point made very clear by the vast swathes of red ink in the accounts book. The only pleasure I get from it is walking through the big wood, thinking: 'This is my tree.' I really am a tragic, pitiable waste of blood and organs. And so are you if you've got an iPad. Or a whirlpool bath. Or anything you don't really need. Which is pretty much everything you own.

The problem is, of course, that we think everything is necessary. We've got it into our heads that the eggs from a chicken won't do and that they must come from a gull or a quail. We think people will laugh if our phone is a year old. We know that we need a holiday cottage. And we think the wanton excess is okay if we turn up at a charity fundraiser once a year and buy a signed rugby ball in the auction.

Look around your house this morning. Look at your coffee machine and your fridge with the ice-making machine in the door. How much pleasure do you get from these things, compared with the pleasure you would have got if you'd spent the money instead on an iron lung for someone else?

I know a man of fairly modest means who funds two schools in Africa and the Philippines. Then there's the footballer Didier Drogba, who, it seems, runs what's left of Ivory Coast's education department single-handedly. They are philanthropists, and I would suggest that ultimately their investment is going to make them a damn sight happier than the man who spent his cash on a new pair of breasts for his wife.

1 May 2011

A man's ego hangs in his downstairs loo

If you were to be awarded the Nobel prize in literature, you'd be very proud and, consequently, you'd want to hang the certificate somewhere prominent. But not so prominent that it looks like you're showing off. Not on the outside of your front door, for instance: that would be poor form.

People face a similar problem when they are photographed meeting Mrs Queen. They want everyone to know that this has happened, but hanging the picture in the hall? No. That's too soon. It's the same as saying: 'Do come in. Would you like a drink? Oh and did you know I once met Her Maj?'

There is only one room, in fact, where it is possible to place evidence of your accolades and achievements. And that's the downstairs lavatory. I was at a friend's house last weekend and you simply wouldn't know from anything about him, his family or the main rooms in his house, that he used to be pretty famous. But pay a visit to the bog and, holy cow: every word that's ever been written about him, every glowing review, every gong. They're all there, strutting their stuff in front of what, let's face it, is a captive audience.

He's not alone, either. There's a well-known British comedian – you know who you are – whose whole demeanour says, 'I'm just an ordinary bloke doing an ordinary job. Nothing to see here.' But go for a pee in his house and all of a sudden it's, 'I'm GQ's Man of the Year!'

Check this out. Next time you are at someone's house, excuse yourself from the dinner table, go into the hall, past the black-and-white pictures of the kids when they were blonde and lovely, turn left at the skiing montage and have a look in the bog. It'll be crammed with letters from Henry Kissinger and faded reviews from the *New Musical Express*. It's entirely possible you may even have to move a Bafta to close the door.

People may argue that they put all this stuff in the bog precisely because they don't want it to be seen by visitors. But if that's the case, why not put it in the attic, or the laundry cupboard? Or even your own bathroom? You know full well that at some point everyone who comes to your house will go for a pee. Which means you know full well they are going to learn that back in the Seventies, before you became an accountant, you were in a band that Julie Burchill quite liked.

I bet that this weekend hundreds of couples are sitting around their breakfast tables thinking: 'Where on earth do we put this picture of us going into Westminster Abbey for the royal wedding?' And all of them will come to the same conclusion: 'Let's take down the unfunny Victorian shooting cartoon from above the cistern and put this up instead.' They can convince themselves that no one will see it there while basking in the warm glow of satisfaction that, in fact, everyone will.

However, there's another issue here. I have a photograph of me being hugged by Cameron Diaz and, obviously, that goes behind the bog itself, because it's a picture I want men to see while standing there, with their old chap in their hand.

But if I'd been at the royal wedding? That's different. That would need to go on the wall facing the bog so it could be seen by girls while they were sitting down.

You in earnest conversation with Lord Carrington? Behind the bog. You sharing a joke with George Clooney? Facing wall. You out for dinner with Kate Moss? Hmmm. Top of the loo seat, probably.

Downstairs bogs are a portal to a man's ego. I know a man

whose khazi walls played host to a £5-million Degas. Where's he going with that? What's he saying? Frankly, you don't need to be a head doctor to work it out. He's saying: 'Oh, that old thing.' Which is what people say when they turn up at your house in a Rolls-Royce Silver Ghost.

People were speculating all last week about whether or not Obama Barack should release the pictures of Osama bin Laden's body, to prove to a sceptical world that he really is dead.

I still can't quite believe we've arrived at a time when the president of the United States goes on television to say the world's biggest terrorist has been killed and we all think: 'Yeah, right.' But that's by the by.

It was eventually decided that the pictures could not be released for fear they would be used as a rallying point for the disaffected and the daft. So what will become of them? Obviously Obama cannot place them on top of his piano or on a worktop in the kitchen. Putting framed pictures of a Muslim who's been shot in the face among the holiday snaps would look a bit weird. But neither can he simply put them in a drawer in his office. When he's old, he wants people to say: 'Oh my God, were you in charge when they shot bin Laden? Tell me more about how you succeeded where Bush and Clinton failed, oh mighty one.' He wants them to be seen by people, but only if the people in question think they were not meant to be seen. It's definitely the bog, then.

Or is it? Because Obama – as we now know for sure – is an American. And I'm not sure Americans are very concerned with the bothersome business of modesty. You can rest assured that Margaret Thatcher has the *Sun*'s 'Gotcha!' headline from the Falklands war hidden away in the smallest room, whereas if she were an American it would be projected each night on to the front of her house.

You walk into a British doctor's surgery and you may well spot a small certificate on the far wall, behind some cupboards, saying that he's qualified. In America it'll be in a huge gilt frame on his desk.

I bet you any money, too, that nearly every Oscar ever awarded to an American lives in their sitting room, with its own spotlight. But where do you suppose Colin Firth put his? Next to the bog brush, I should imagine. Whereas the picture of him coming out of the lake? Facing wall. Definitely.

8 May 2011

We didn't have an affair – and that's all you need to be told

The press should not be free to screw up the lives of my children. That's why I'm pro-injunction.

It had been a fairly normal day. Woke up, rowed with the kids, spoke to my mother about yet another operation she needs, made breakfast for a ten-year-old Japanese girl who's come to stay. In the afternoon I faced up to the fact that *Top Gear* is being sued for libel and malicious falsehood, dealt with the fallout from recent tabloid allegations that I'd fed a pretty blonde some lettuce and at around midnight settled down to write some newspaper columns. Then my phone exploded.

Someone on Twitter had claimed that Jemima Khan had taken out a super-injunction to prevent intimate photographs of us being published. Jeremy and Jemima? Presumably the claimant has some kind of *Chitty Chitty Bang Bang* fixation.

Now if you are going to be romantically linked with anyone, then I'd rather it was Jemima Khan than, say, Huw Edwards. But, even though I hate doing this, I'm duty-bound to say that the claim is incorrect. Although I know Jemima quite well – my wife and I had been round for dinner with her the night before – we have never been alone together. There are no intimate photographs. The end.

Naturally, Jemima was very upset. Rather too upset, I thought. She tweeted to say she was 'in a bloody nightmare'. She found the very notion of being intimate with me 'upsetting'. After a while I began to think, 'All right, love. Steady on.' I know I'm a bit fat and my hair's pubic and I have teeth the colour of plywood. But there's no need to tell the world you're feeling sick at the mere thought of being intimate with me.

At work, it got worse. My producer said the idea was comical. At this stage I began to get quite upset. If we look at Jemima's previous loves – Imran Khan and Hugh Grant – I fit right in there.

Slap bang between the two. In my mind.

And in the mind of the *Daily Telegraph*, too, because the next day it ran big pictures of us on its front page, saying that we hadn't had a fling. Which is the same as saying, 'They bloody have, you know.'

The *Daily Star* went further. '*Top Gear* Jezza in sex pics fury' screamed the front-page headline. It then said in tiny letters that the allegations were 'false' and, in an editorial on page six, that 'it's all rubbish'.

You don't see an editorial, though, when you're walking past a newsagent. My kids simply saw a story saying that I was caught up in a sex-picture tangle. As their friends saw it too, they had a bad day.

So. Had I known about this story before midnight, would I have taken out an injunction to stop it appearing? To protect my children? Yes. In a heartbeat.

And that's a point everyone seems to be missing in the big debate about press freedom. Yes, we want a free press but we don't want a press that's free to wantonly screw up the lives of my children, or Jemima's, or yours.

I realize, of course, that injunctions, allied to Max Mosley's drive to make the papers reveal stories to victims in advance, will pretty much put the tabloid press out of business. They'd be reduced to printing pictures of a shark leaping out of the sea. Which is what the *Mirror* did on Tuesday.

Deciding which of these injunctions should be granted is

tricky. What's personal and what's not? When does a private life stop and a public image begin?

According to Charlotte Harris, a media lawyer: 'There has been a terrible mis-characterization of the people involved.' Apparently, 80 per cent of injunctions go to the victims of blackmail, harassment and stalkers and those who suffer threats to their families. Only a tiny minority are given to footballers who have been in bed with a teenager.

So it's all very well saying that all injunctions should be overturned now, but if they were, it would be a charter for lunatics and blackmailers to do and say pretty well whatever took their fancy. Moira Stuart likes to smash up wheelchairs. The editor of the *Daily Telegraph* is at the centre of a paedophile ring. Just so long as the newspaper says the victim denies the allegations, it's all legal.

If newspapers were a bit more fair-minded, if people thought their side of the argument would be heard, instead of relegated to page ninety-four, there would be no need for so many injunctions.

I am not a saint. And as I'm in the pay of the BBC – a publicly funded body – it might seem reasonable for newspapers to question some of my lifestyle choices. But they wouldn't question them. They'd demand that I be sacked. They'd say I'd sparked fury and work themselves into a frothing rage. That would alarm my family and that's why I try to keep my private life private. It's why I'm pro-injunction.

It is said only the rich and famous can afford a gagging order. But only the rich and famous ever need one. Others say that everything anyone at the BBC does should be published. What? Sophie Raworth's sexual fantasies? Pictures of Jeremy Paxman on the lavatory? Where do you draw the line?

I suppose we could start by drawing it just above the point where someone says on Twitter that Jeremy Clarkson and Jemima Khan have had an affair. And even though everyone knows it to be rubbish, it somehow becomes front-page news for two days.

15 May 2011

Garçon! A hike in my flat's value, please

I've never quite understood this country's obsession with property prices. Because if the house you're trying to sell has fallen in value, it stands to reason the house you're trying to buy has fallen in value as well. So what does it matter?

However, it is possible to make your house shoot up in value while everyone else plummets into a world of negative equity, unpleasant letters from the bank, despondency, despair and, eventually, death. Simply open a really good restaurant at the end of the road.

Checklist: balsamic vinegar and olive oil on the tables; lots of weird bread items in a nice basket; some silly cheeses; and pretty waitresses in jeans. That's about it, really.

Let us examine the case of Padstow, a fishing village on the north coast of Cornwall. It's always been a popular holiday destination and, as a result, property prices in the area were always 20 per cent higher than anywhere else in the county. But then along came Rick Stein, who opened a jolly good restaurant, and now, as a direct result, Padstow property is 44 per cent more expensive than the Cornish average.

Then you have Bray, in Berkshire. For centuries you would want to live there only if you were keen on brass rubbing. But then up popped the Fat Duck and the Waterside Inn and now you can't even buy a can of pop in the village shop for less than £1 million.

I am similarly fortunate. Not that long ago a superexpensive farm shop and restaurant opened just a few miles from my house and, as a result, every metrosexual in London now wants a country retreat in the area. The result? Well, last weekend some *Daily Mail* reporters stood at the end of my drive for a while and decided my sorry little collection of ramshackle outbuildings was worth a whopping £2 million*.

I don't really understand why restaurants have this effect. But nothing else will transform an area quite so drastically. Last week, for instance, a £35-million modern art gallery opened in Wakefield. It looks a bit like the Guggenheim – if you stand very far away and squint – and it houses forty-four sculptures by Barbara Hepworth, who everyone has heard of. I imagine.

Feeling a need to move to Wakefield as a result? Of course not, because an art gallery, as we know, is just a building behind which children on school trips can go for a smoke.

Then, of course, just up the road in Doncaster there was the ill-fated Earth Centre. Built with millions of our money, it was a place where visitors could look at a yurt and watch their own excrement being disposed of in an eco-friendly way.

Doubtless the locals felt that such an attraction would cause the value of their houses to soar. They were to be disappointed.

As soon as it opened, property prices in the nearest village fell and didn't start to rise again properly until after someone realized that nobody wanted to look at their stools being mashed and the Earth Centre was closed.

Shopping centres don't work, either. They just mean more traffic in the area. And while public transport links are good, you can't exactly buy a house in the hope that someone will

---

* This number should be taken with a pinch of salt because they also valued my car at £70,000 – almost exactly twice what I paid for it two years ago.

come along soon and build a railway station in the back garden.

It's the same story with Richard Curtis. I could have bought a house in Notting Hill for about £2.50 before the film came along. Afterwards, the same house would have been worth £2.5 billion. Had we known in advance about that movie, we all could have made a fortune. But we didn't, and that's the problem: guessing which area is about to become hot. And that brings me back to the question of restaurants.

Next week a friend of mine who has had much success with clubs and bars all over the world is opening a pizza joint on Portobello Road in west London. You may scoff at this and claim the area is already so expensive that one new cafe can't possibly make a difference. However, what you don't know – I didn't – is that Portobello Road is the longest road in the world.

It starts in Notting Hill, and this is the bit we all know. Pretty art students selling fascinators from trestle tables and Paddington Bear wandering about looking for Mr Gruber. Then it goes all trendy and there are many people in bars, wearing extremely thin spectacles. And then it reaches the A40 flyover and you assume it stops. But it doesn't. It keeps right on going, plunging north through parts of London that have no name until, eventually, it gets to what looks like West Beirut. In one of the windows I could make out the bulky form of Terry Waite, chained to a radiator.

And as I sat there at a pre-opening dinner, drinking rosé with the trendiest people in all of London, local hoodie types emerged from nearby houses on those stupid small bicycles all people on council estates seem to have. They couldn't believe what they were seeing. They didn't realize that spectacles could be so thin. And many had very obviously never seen a real live homosexual before. There was much pointing.

Here's the thing. Soon, and I can guarantee this, they will all be gone. This one restaurant, all on its own, will cause the small bicycles to be replaced with Vespas. The shops currently selling taps and hens will be sold to bijou furniture designers who will fill the windows with driftwood coffee tables at £4,000 a pop.

And the flats in the area? You could probably part-exchange one today for a tin of boot polish. Whereas next year, when Jude Law is living there, and Sienna Miller's popping past your window to buy a granary loaf, a one-bedroom basement flat will fetch half a billion. You mark my words.

Oh, and before I go, here's another tip. I gather Curtis's next film is to be set in Hitchin. Or I might be making that up.

22 May 2011

A quake's nothing until it becomes a wobbly iDisaster

Last week Iceland exploded again. Against a backdrop of images that looked like an atomic bomb had gone off, weathermen were saying the resultant ash cloud was heading our way and that soon all Britain's airports would have to be closed.

This would have caused inconvenience to thousands of us, as we'd have been forced to spend the next few months listening to friends telling very improbable stories about how they got back from Prague. 'I had to crawl to Madrid and then I got someone in a rickshaw to take me to Toulon, where George Clooney offered me a piggyback.'

Weirdly, it seems only yesterday that Europe was shut down by the first cloud of Icelandic high-altitude dust and I was boring anyone who'd listen with the astonishing tale of how I got home from Warsaw. To précis: I drove.

And it's not just Iceland that has gone wonky recently. Who could have guessed after the 2004 Boxing Day earthquake and tsunami that, just over six years later, there'd be another double whammy off the coast of Japan? An event so massive we all forgot instantly that only days earlier a tectonic shiver had reduced the wonderful New Zealand city of Christchurch to a crumpled pile of broken sewage pipes, decapitated churches and shattered dreams.

In the twenty-first century alone, we've had Haiti. And Pakistan. And the floods in Queensland. And Hurricane Katrina. And a seemingly never-ending stream of tornados reducing America's Bible Belt to matchwood. And the French heatwave that killed almost 15,000. And swine flu.

When I was growing up in the 1960s the natural world seemed so stable and safe. I don't remember my parents ever feeling the need to hoard soup and paraffin. Sure, they'd occasionally make me send food I hadn't eaten to a place called Biafra, and while Aberfan was grisly, it was a) man-made and b) not really in the same league as the Asian tsunami.

In short, we used to be surprised when we woke in a morning to find that Mother Nature had girded her loins while we were asleep. Now it's the other way round. We're amazed when we wake to find the world is pretty much as we left it when we went to bed.

So what's going on? While eco-mentalists are examining the sky for telltale signs of impending doom, and NASA is scanning the heavens for the pinprick of light that will herald the dawn of our extinction, is some major Hollywood-style catastrophe unravelling in the upper mantle? Is the crust cracking up? Is the world falling to pieces? Or is it all down to the iPhone?

Iceland is always exploding; has been since a volcanic burp brought it into existence in the first place. As recently as 1963 there were no islands of any note off the south coast but then the planet decided to be sick and by 1967 the region's guillemot community had a whole playground. It's called Surtsey and it's a mile across.

Today the arrival of a new landmass would keep the rolling news channels going for years, but back then no one had a smartphone, which meant that, to all intents and purposes, the event never happened. If the recent Japanese earthquake had happened in 1970 it would have made a few paragraphs on page twenty-nine of *The Times* and that would have been that. Now, though, CNN needs to be fed, twenty-four hours a day. And it's not picky about what it eats. If it's on film, it's news. If it isn't, it isn't.

In many ways this is a good thing. In the past a tsunami was something that really only existed in schoolbooks and we in Britain had absolutely no idea what it might be like to be stuck in an earthquake.

Now, though, thanks to a Japanese office worker who filmed the shaking filing cabinets in his office, we do. And in case we forget, YouTube is on hand to remind us.

Floods? Well, in Britain they used to come up to the news reporter's ankles, and only then because he'd spent an hour before the broadcast looking for the deepest puddle in which to stand while delivering his report. Now, thanks to Apple and Nokia, we know what it's like when a flood picks up an articulated lorry and smashes it into a petrochemical refinery. We know that floods don't lap. They rage and boil and ruin rather more than your new button-back settee.

There's more. Without mobile phones, few of the uprisings in the Arab world this year would have had much traction. A few youths would have gone on the streets, thrown some stones and been shot. It wouldn't have been news here because we wouldn't have been able to watch it.

Remember Rodney King? He was a black man in America who was ordered out of his car after a police chase and beaten up. News? Not really. I imagine that sort of thing happens a lot. But because the beating was videoed, it was on the front pages.

So, yes, now that we all have them, the camera phone is a tool for justice, and for putting us closer to the action when the world springs a leak. However, there is a problem.

In April 1994 there were many pictures on the news of Kurt Cobain, a rock star who had apparently killed himself.

And then there was the televised death of the Formula One driver Roland Ratzenberger at an event in Italy. There was, however, little coverage of the unfilmed Rwandan genocide that saw about 800,000 people hacked to death in 100 days. Only when pictures of the aftermath started to roll in did it get noticed.

This is still going on today. Whenever Bangladesh is over-run by some terrible natural disaster, we never really know. This is because the only means most people over there have of recording it is with an easel and some oil paint. Whereas whenever it rains in America, we are treated to some grainy, wobble-vision mobile footage of a fat man sobbing and pointing at his upside-down Buick.

It used to be said that if it bleeds, it leads. Now, though, if you want it to stick, you need a pic.

29 May 2011

I'm going to cure dumb Britain

Normally, when a couple decide they need a nanny to look after their child, the list of requirements is quite small. Can you cook a sausage without blowing the house to smithereens? Do you have a rudimentary grasp of English? And are you able to walk past our fridge without eating every single thing inside it?

Actually, I'm being a silly. A mother is bothered about these things. A father tends to worry mostly about aesthetics. Well, I did. I wouldn't deliberately choose an ugly sofa or a hideous coffee table, so why would I want to clutter up the house with a nanny who looks like Robbie Coltrane?

Anyway, according to various reports last week, the actress Gwyneth Paltrow and her crooning husband, whose name has temporarily gone from my mind, have advertised for someone to look after their children, aged five and seven. And their list of requirements is enormous.

The successful applicant must be able to teach ancient Greek, Latin, French and either Japanese or Mandarin. He or she will also be proficient in painting, sailing, a martial art, chess and drama. So what they seem to want is a blend of Julie Andrews, Robin Knox-Johnston and Boris Spassky. Maybe Stephen Fry would do – except, perhaps, for the martial art – but I fear the salary of £62,100 plus expenses, and a free flat, might not be quite enough.

The story attracted much tut-tutting on the radio and in the newspapers. But there will be no scoffing from me because, if the story is true, I think the couple should be applauded for setting such high standards.

In the olden days, cleverness was celebrated. People would flock to exhibitions to see new machines and meet the men who'd invented them. Talks were popular. Authors were the rock 'n' rollers, and poets deities. Not that long ago, you could be an engineer and rich . . . at the same time. But then along came *Blind Date* and that changed everything. Because here was a show specifically designed for morons. Occasionally, for comedic effect, a clever person who could speak properly was invited into the pink and purple idiot chamber so that the host, Cilla Black, could make mocking 'oooh' noises on discovering that they had been to university.

Suddenly, it was uncool to be intelligent and well read. Cilla told us every single Saturday night that it was much better to be a hairdresser. And, as a result, the future wasn't bright. It was orange.

Blind Date was the master and originator of the 'all right for some' mentality that now pervades every part of our lives. Anyone good-looking, or rich, or lucky is perceived to have committed some kind of crime against the chip-eating masses. Today, this has reached such an absurd level that we are expected to weep at the loss of Jade Goody and are bombarded by the antics of minor-league non-celebrities who have pretty much the same genetic coding as a cauliflower and a bit less intelligence than a dishwasher.

I was told last week by someone who worked on *The Only Way Is Essex* – it's a TV show, apparently – that, when asked to name the prime minister, one of the stars said: 'What? The prime minister of Essex?' Upon being told that there is no such post, he thought for a while and then said: 'Gordon Ramsay.' Meanwhile, on the other channel, Andrew Marr was talking about the origins of cities. And no one was watching.

Clever people, today, are scary. Stephen Fry is bright enough to know this. It's why he does knob gags. Stupid people only really like to see other stupid people on the television because it makes them feel good about themselves.

They reckon that if someone with the IQ of a cylinder head gasket can get on the box, there is hope that they can too.

Obviously, if this continues, Britain will be sunk. If our children feel they must be gormless to fit in, we shall soon be a big, dark backwater full of fat people celebrating their idiocy with another bag of oven-ready E numbers. And so, obviously, it's important to turn things round. But how?

Earlier this year, a man with an IQ of 48 was barred by the High Court from having sex. It said that he was too stupid to understand the consequences and health risks. Yes. But what it also seemed to be saying is that he might produce a child that's just as daft as him.

There are those, I know, who think that the judge was correct and that all stupid people should be neutered. But I reckon it's better to undo the teachings of *Blind Date* and humiliate the nation's morons into changing their ways. I believe this is possible. When I worked in Rotherham, I met many people who could barely speak. If you'd asked them to write down every single fact they knew on a piece of paper, they'd have needed only a stamp. And yet, despite having less knowledge about the world than a tree, they could add up a darts score faster than a Cray supercomputer. This means people have the capacity to be bright and useful but that no one has worked out a way to make them realize it. Until now . . .

Tomorrow morning, I have a meeting scheduled with the controller of BBC1 and I'm going to suggest we make a new TV game show in which contestants are picked at random from the streets and told that, if they answer a selection of fairly simple questions correctly, they will be given sex with a supermodel, much money and a speedboat. However, if they get one of the questions wrong, the studio audience will be encouraged to howl with laughter at their stupidity. Maybe we could go further and put up signs outside their house saying: 'The person who lives here thought the capital of France was Southend.'

I think it would be a long-running smash. And I very much look forward to the day when the children of Gwyneth Paltrow appear and sail off into the sunset in a shiny new speedboat with a bag of cash.

5 June 2011

Advice for men – don't try to keep your hair on

I don't want to be unduly rude about Wayne Rooney, but it seems the irritating little brat, who plays annoyingly well for Manchester United and annoyingly badly for England, has had a hair transplant. And I'm sorry, but what on earth is the point of that?

He was a very ugly little troll with sticky-out ears and a bald head, and now he is a very ugly little troll with sticky-out ears. It's an improvement but only in the same way that Dawn French's recent diet is an improvement. The fact is, you'd still want her on your team in a sumo wrestling match.

I wonder about this hair transplant business. Did Silvio Berlusconi, for instance, think that if he emptied the sweep-up bag from the local Hair Port beauty salon on to his bonce, he could burst back on to the world stage looking like George Clooney? He doesn't. He just looks like an oily, perma-tanned buffoon with a hair transplant.

I have a hair-loss problem. It's all fallen out at the back. And I know that for several thousand pounds I could have it fixed. But what would be the point? I'd still look like a telegraph pole that had eaten a space hopper. Fixing my hair hole would be like trying to improve the overall appearance of the Elephant Man by cutting his fingernails.

There's no doubt that for some people cosmetic surgery is important. It can be used to boost self-confidence and it can certainly help if you've been trapped in the cockpit of a burning Hurricane. Plus, in the world of celebrity, where long lenses can pick out a spot of cellulite from half a mile away, it is handy, too.

My eldest daughter came into the world looking like the lion from *Daktari*. The poor little mite had to spend the first three years of her life staring at nothing but the ends of both her noses. So she had cosmetic surgery, the squint was corrected, and nobody would have denied her that.

For sure, I wouldn't want a doctor to fill my lips with collagen because it's made from the skin of a bison, but there's no doubt that the full Steve Tyler does make a girl prettier. And I'm sure Botox is useful if you need to look impassive at all times; in a game of poker, perhaps, or when you are being tortured.

I've sometimes looked down at the vast stomach that hangs over my trousers and thought: 'Well, I could get rid of that by skipping, not drinking anything more exciting than Ribena and eating like a mouse for a year.' But wouldn't it be easier to pop into a hospital and have all the fat hoovered out?

We are forever being told that we spend more in Britain on cosmetic surgery than we do on tea, and that this year more men will go into the vanity cabinet than will join the army.

So what? If you have a wart the size of a melon on your face, or a prolapsed bottom, or teeth that grow out of your forehead, then by all means have the problem sorted and feel not one jot of shame or guilt. These are sophisticated times and you should use whatever science has created to make yourself happy.

However, when it comes to hair, it's best to let nature take its course. I'm not talking about women now. Nobody wants to see what looks like half a pound of Old Holborn poking out of your bikini bottoms. And '99 Red Balloons' was a one-hit wonder for Nena because nobody wanted to see her back on *Top of the Pops* with what appeared to be two guinea pigs peeping out from her armpits. No. I'm talking about men, and specifically the head.

Some chaps think when they go bald that it would be a good idea to grow a beard. Why? It just looks like your face is on upside down.

Others go down the Rooney route and have a transplant, but in my, albeit limited, experience this doesn't work either. Because you end up with hair that grows like conifers on a Scottish hillside. In rows.

Worst of all, though, are chaps who believe they can hold off the ageing process with dye. This is a mind-blowing waste of time. We have been able to determine this by examining Paul McCartney.

By all accounts he is a fairly wealthy man, so we can presume he uses the very best hair-colouring products that Boots can provide. And yet he still looks like a man walking around with a dead red kite on his head.

It's much the same story with Mick Jagger. Does he really think as he flounces down the street with that luxuriant auburn barnet quivering slightly in the breeze that passers-by will mistake him for a seventeen-year-old? Crowning that wind-battered old face with that hair is like crowning York Minster with a heap of solar panels.

And, anyway, what's the point? The only reason a man might choose to cover up his greying temples is to make himself more attractive to the opposite sex. But when you are nudging seventy, I really don't see how this works. Because surely your hair will be writing cheques your gentleman sausage can't cash.

I have a general rule in life, which so far has stood me in reasonably good stead. Never do business with a man who cares about his hair. This is even more important than avoiding a man who goes to the gym or who has a Rolex watch.

Any evidence of layering or product suggests that he is vain and therefore not to be trusted. Certainly do not buy a house from someone who spends more than £25 on a haircut because I can pretty much guarantee it will smell of sewage every time it rains and fall down after six months.

Look at it this way. When England recently drew 2–2 with Switzerland in a lacklustre performance at Wembley, there was one notable absentee from the stands. Wayne Rooney. He didn't even bother to turn up and cheer his mates on, or his country, because he was across town, having his hair transplant.

12 June 2011

We demand our weekends back, Adolf Handlebar

Many thousands of people are not reading this today because they're driving around an unfamiliar village ten miles from where they live, desperately looking for a pair of wilting balloons tied to a gatepost. This will indicate that they've found the right house at which to drop their six-year-old for a party.

Afterwards, they'll have to drive at high speed to a railway station in the vague hope that their fifteen-year-old son has actually woken up on time and caught the train he said he'd catch.

Then, after discovering that he hasn't, and isn't answering his phone and is probably dead in a gutter somewhere, it'll be time to pick up a third child from her sleepover and head back to the unfamiliar little village only to find the balloons have vanished along with the house at which the six-year-old was dropped.

A report out last week said that by the time a child is eighteen, parents will have spent a full year of their lives ferrying it about. An endless round of school trips, social events and sporting fixtures means that you will have driven 23,500 miles. Which is about the same as driving round the fattest part of the world. And you know what? I don't believe it.

Taking my youngest child to and from school clocks up seventy-two miles a day. That's 13,824 miles a year. So that's more than 110,000 miles by the time she is thirteen. And that's before we get to the weekend, when my wife and I have to employ a team of women with long sticks in what we call the map room.

It's their job to vector us in on the postcodes of parties, and to work out which of us is nearer to whichever child has finished one thing and needs taking to something else. We have learnt much from watching the *Battle of Britain*. Some days, we need the Big Wing.

Of course, occasionally we are too hungover to provide this vital role, in which case the kids will be expected to use public transport. They're not very good at this. The eldest has developed an incredibly annoying tactic of volunteering to come home on the train but then ringing from far away to say her credit card is maxed out and that she can't. The boy, meanwhile, reckons that there's a bus stationed in our local town waiting for the rare moments when he has to use it. And he can't understand why sometimes it's not there. The youngest isn't exactly sure what a bus is.

And I don't want to sound like an old person, but it was never like this when I was a kid, because back then I didn't choose friends on the basis that I liked them; I chose them on the basis that they lived within cycling distance.

I had a bicycle at home, which I would ride for fun whenever there was nothing on television, which was – let's think now – almost constantly.

And I had a bicycle at school, which I would use for getting to and from the local girls' school. Which was seventeen miles away. My bicycle was my passport to adulthood. My bike was freedom.

Not any more, of course. A bicycle now is seen as a portal to the Pearly Gates. There's a sense that unless you are dressed up in a spinnaker of luminescence and your head is shrouded in what appear to be five cryogenic bananas, you will definitely be killed within seconds of climbing on board. This takes the fun out of riding.

But it's nonsense. Yes, a friend of mine peeled his face off the other day after falling off, but cycling-related deaths are down by a third since the mid-1990s, and it's probably fair to say there's never been a safer time to go for a ride.

Sadly, though, there's a problem. You see, cycling is seen now not as something that might be exhilarating or even useful but as a frontline propaganda weapon in the war on capitalism, banking, freedom, McDonald's, injustice, Swiss drug companies, rape and progress. Every morning London is chock-full of little individually wrapped Twiglets, their wizened faces contorted with hatred for all that they see. Fat people. Cars. Chain stores. It's all fascism. Fascism, d'you hear?

From what they see as the moral high ground, they sneer at pedestrians, howl at buses, bang on cars, scream at taxi drivers and charge through every convention that defines society with their walnutty bottoms in the air and their stupid legs going nineteen to the dozen.

This sort of thing frightens a child in much the same way that little Norwegian children were frightened when jack-booted Nazis marched through their towns and villages, shouting and generally being scary. Little Olaf, cowering in the cellar, never once thought, 'Ooh, I'd like to be like them when I grow up.'

To address this, we must wage a war on the militants. First, we must make it an offence, punishable by many years in jail, to ride a bicycle in anything other than what I like to call home clothes. Cycling shops selling gel for your bottom crack and outfits with padded gussets will be raided by the police and the owners prosecuted.

This way, cyclists will be stripped of their uniforms and made to look like human beings. They will also be forced to abandon their crash helmets. Nobody in their right mind believes that a bit of yellow polystyrene could possibly keep a head intact should it be run over by the rear wheels of an articulated lorry. So get rid of them.

With the Nazi clobber gone, we shall start to insist that cyclists develop some manners. They should take a leaf out of the horse rider's book, thanking other road users for slowing down rather than shaking their fists because they didn't slow down enough. We need them to recognize that Bob the builder and Roary the racing car have just as much of a right to be out and about as they do.

This way, children will grow up to think that cycling is fun. And as a result of that, parents will be freed at weekends to do what they want, safe in the knowledge that their thin, healthy children are getting the social lives they need without being a bloody nuisance in the process.

19 June 2011

Houston, our spaceships are ugly

Next month the space shuttle *Atlantis* will blast off for the final time, and when it returns, that will be that. America will no longer be capable of getting a man into space. So what, then, will become of the International Space Station (ISS)? For now, the crew in their polo shirts and slacks can be ferried back and forth by the Russians while the Europeans – not us, obviously, or the Greeks – can be relied upon to pop up every now and again to empty their bins.

This is done by what the European Space Agency calls its fleet of space freighters. They take washing-up liquid and other vital supplies into space and are then loaded up with all the rubbish for the journey back to earth. The idea is, of course, that they burn up on re-entry but not every part is destroyed. Indeed, only last week, sailors in the South Pacific were advised to stay in their cabins in case they were hit on the head by bits of just such a ship. Called the ATV *Johannes Kepler*, it did mostly burn up but still dumped various components into the ocean in what can only be described as an act of government-sponsored littering.

There are only three Euro space freighters left, and because the governments that fund the programme are now having to give all their spare cash to Stavros and Mr O'Flaherty to keep them in beer and skittles, there won't be any more.

That means the space station will have to be abandoned. And is that any great loss? We're told that many useful experiments are being conducted up there, but what are they exactly? All the crew seems to do is grow mustard and take pretty pictures of earth. And has anyone thought what will happen to the ISS when the binmen stop coming and the Russians realize they only have a space programme to stop their scientists skipping off to Iran?

Remember Skylab? NASA engineers decided that it could not be kept in orbit forever, so, with their slide rules and their side partings, they decided to bring it down into the sea off South Africa. Unfortunately, they got their sums a bit wrong and most of it crashed into Australia. That time, the American government was hit with a $400 fine for littering. Which it refused to pay.

Boffins, then, may well be reluctant to bring the ISS down in case there is a similar diplomatic incident. But it can't very well be left in space either because of what's called the Kessler syndrome.

At present, there are around 300 million bits of man-made debris orbiting earth at extremely high speed. Some are little flecks of paint or globules of unburnt rocket fuel. But there are also hammers and nuts and bolts. Should one of these things hit the abandoned space station at a closing speed of 35,000mph, there would be many more bits and pieces hurtling around up there, and what an egghead called Donald Kessler worked out is that each time one of these pieces hit another, more smaller bits would result until, eventually, earth would be surrounded by an impenetrable shield of rubbish. Trying to drive a spaceship through it would be like trying to drive a car through a thunderstorm without hitting any of the raindrops.

So here we are, trapped on our own planet by our own mess. We've filled space with junk and littered the oceans with broken-up space freighters and solid rocket boosters and the souls of many dead astronauts. We've spent trillions and all we have to show for it is a bit of useless moon rock and a profound understanding of how to grow mustard when there's no gravity.

What happened to the spirit of the 1960s when John F. Kennedy made his big speech about why we choose to go to the moon and do the other things – what were the other things, by the way? What happened to our dreams? And why am I, a committed fan of the shuttle and the whole nerdy business of space exploration, starting to feel so jaded?

The problem, I think, is aesthetics. Back in the 1950s, futurists would predict what sort of cars we'd be driving in the twenty-first century. But the cars we actually have are better than those that filled their wildest dreams. It's the same story with computers. They never saw the delicious iPad coming, did they? Or Concorde. Or the Gherkin.

But it was very different with space. The film director Stanley Kubrick dreamt up *Discovery One*, a gloriously slender craft with a ball on the front and six big engines at the back. Then we had *Thunderbird* 3. Orange. Jaggedy. Sexy. And the *Eagle* transporter from the television series *Space* 1999. It was very cool. And, while there are words you can use to describe the space shuttle, 'cool' isn't one of them.

Then there's the ISS, which a) is only as far away from earth as Preston is from London and b) looks like a skip full of discarded kitchen appliances.

Mind you, even that's a lot better than the space freighter. In your mind you can probably see a jet-black Mack truck with rockets on the back but I'm afraid in real life it isn't even slightly like that. In fact, it looks like a wheelie bin that's got tangled up in a teenager's crusty bed sheet.

Now, of course, I realize that when you are building a machine for use in space, you don't have to worry about aerodynamics or sleekness. But that's the problem. How many small boys dream of the day when they can go to space in a wheelie bin? How many people think that the freighter's interior, which looks like a *Blue Peter* project, is a worthwhile way of blowing all those taxpayer billions?

To keep the space programme alive, the boffins, and the accountants that fund them, must understand that we don't want practical, bare-minimum engineering. If you're going to call something a space freighter, make it look like the *Nostromo*; make it look impressive. Give it a bit of wow. Equip it with space guns and, most importantly of all, make sure it has a big red self-destruct button so that when you've finished with it, you can vaporize it before it crashes into the Galapagos Islands.

26 June 2011

Look what that little DVD pirate is really doing

In the olden days when we watched movies on video record-ers, we could fast-forward through all the legal and commercial claptrap to the start of the actual film.

Not any more.

Now we are forced by electronic trickery to sit through the endless roll call of production companies, disclaimers and suchlike, until eventually we are presented with a reminder that if we copy the film, we are committing an act of piracy and we will be keelhauled.

I have a deal of sympathy with this argument. Foreign television companies pay a fortune for episodes of *Top Gear* and then transmit them with much trumpeting and brou-haha, only to find that most of the audience is elsewhere, having already watched everything on the internet. A couple of years ago *Top Gear* was the most illegally downloaded show in the world.

Things are even worse for the producers of Hollywood blockbusters. They spend £100 million making an all-action spectacular in which cars are driven at high speed into actual helicopters. And absolutely no one pays to watch the fin-ished result.

Just last week various film companies told the High Court that file-sharing sites on the internet are costing them hun-dreds of millions a year and that firms such as BT and Virgin Media must take action to block them. It's all a total waste of judicial time, partly because if you close down one avenue of access, another will begin immediately somewhere else. But mainly because most of the people who steal films don't really think what they're doing is wrong.

Some argue that if you copy someone's car, it's not theft because the original is still with its rightful owner. But that's legal doublespeak. Most people – and when I say 'people', what I mean is 'teenagers' – have grown up with an internet where everything is free. Phone calls. Facts. Pornography. Nothing costs anything at all.

They go to one site, and a song they want is available for nothing. So why would they go to iTunes and pay 79p? In their silly little heads it makes no sense.

Of course, the idiotic hippie who wrote the song probably thinks it's fair enough, too. But one day, when he's older and wiser and millions of people are stealing his music, he will start to wonder how the concept of theft became so blurred. Perhaps it's always been so.

When I was growing up I would steal rhubarb from the nuns at the local convent. It was their rhubarb. They'd grown it. And they were doubtless looking forward to stewing it and having it for pudding one night with some double cream. I deprived them of that. And yet this was not considered to be burglary. It was called scrumping and, at worst, I could expect a clip round the ear from Constable Plod.

Later, when I was away at school, the council knew that whenever roadworks were necessary in the local village, it could expect to lose pretty well all the cones and most of the flashing amber beacons. Only when we helped ourselves to the temporary traffic lights did it finally come round and make a fuss.

We see similar problems in the workplace. Take a computer home and we all accept that this would be theft. But what about a pen? Nobody's going to mind about that – unless, of course, it's a Montblanc and you took it from the managing director's top pocket.

Hotels are a hotbed of legal fuzziness. I spoke last week to a chap who says his wardrobe at home is stuffed full of dressing gowns he has nicked from various suites around the world. Even though he works in the DVD business, he says that because he has paid many hundreds of pounds for the room he is entitled to take the robe home.

Really? Because on that basis he's also entitled to take the television and the sink. Worse. He can spend £300 on the weekly shop at Waitrose and after settling up he'd be within his rights to swipe half a dozen boxes of Black Magic chocolates.

Shoplifting is an interesting case in point, actually. Obviously, it would be poor form to nick a fridge freezer but a Bounty bar? A gentleman's magazine? I'm a fervent believer that Woolworths went west simply because nobody in the store's history ever actually paid for anything. Every branch was always full of schoolkids with fast hearts, wide eyes and bulging pockets.

And this, I think, is the issue we face with the internet. When a fourteen-year-old downloads the latest collection of noises from JLS it has a known value of 79p. It's a modern-day penny chew, a stalk of rhubarb from the nunnery. It's nothing.

It's the same story with a film. You're nicking something that'll soon be on Sky anyway. And yes, I know, some of you will have read this online, having bypassed the subscription fee. Why not? Rupert Murdoch won't miss a quid.

The trouble is that so long as we continue to believe that theft is only theft if the stolen item is bulky, tangible and expensive, the time will come when Bruce Willis will be forced to hang up his vest and every film made is a tuppence ha'penny slimmed-down version of *The Blair Witch Project*. And the only news you get will be from Twitter. And your book will have been written by someone who actually admits it's worthless.

And you'll have to wade through hours and hours of unimaginable tripe on the music scene before you find a song written by someone who knows what they're doing. A someone who'll eventually hang up their guitar and have to get a proper job so that they can actually get paid.

I don't think there's a damn thing that can be done to stop theft on the internet. It's uncontrollable. But I do think there is something that can be done to change people's perception of illegal downloads. Stop saying that if you nick a film, you are a thief or a pirate. Pirates are cool. Kids have pirate parties and everyone loves Jack Sparrow. Surely it would be better to say that if you nick a film, you are a mugger.

3 July 2011

Dear BBC, why d'ya think Dick Whittington gave Salford a miss?

And in other news last week, Chris Patten, who is chairman of the BBC Trust, said the corporation is too centred on Notting Hill, too bothered about chilli and lemon grass, too Peter Mandelson and completely out of touch with most licence-fee payers, who simply want pies with a splash of chlamydia. Doubtless this tub-thumping rallying call is all part of the BBC's strategy to move various shows and departments from London to a small town called Salford. Which I believe is the stupidest media decision since someone on a tabloid newspaper said: 'Hey, guys. I can listen to Prince William's voicemails.'

A lot of the arguments against the BBC's move have been centred on the expense, but I believe there's a more important problem than money. In short, Salford is up north.

I do not speak now as a trendy southern poof who misses Tony Blair and has angst about sending my kids to private school. A television show found that since 1740 every single person in my family tree was born, married and died within twelve miles of one Yorkshire village. I am therefore a pure-blood northerner, a man who makes Michael Parkinson look like Brian Sewell. Cut me in half and you'd find I run on coal and whippets.

But here's the thing. While I was being raised in the north, my parents would occasionally risk the highwaymen and take me to London on trips. There are photographs that show a six-year-old me looking at an elephant in London Zoo and pointing at a black man on Bayswater Road. I remember trying to make a soldier in a busby blink and gazing in open-mouthed wonderment at the sheer size of the Palace of Westminster. It all seemed so much more exciting somehow than anything I'd ever encountered oop north.

And now, thirty years after I escaped from Yorkshire, that still holds true. I still get a tinkle fizz when the motorway ends and I'm plunged into the labyrinth. I still get a kick out of the BT tower and from hailing a black cab. I absolutely love London. And I'm sorry, but if the BBC now said I had to move back up north, I'd resign in a heartbeat. Many others faced with the same problem have done exactly that.

We are told that too many BBC shows are made by Londoners in London, but that simply is not true. *Top Gear*, the show on which I work, is based in the capital but, so far as I know, every single one of the production team is originally from somewhere else. The producer is from Glossop, in Derbyshire. One of the researchers is from Loughborough, in Leicestershire. Until recently we even employed a Scot. Richard Hammond is from Birmingham. James May is from one of the moons of Jupiter. We are therefore as 'London' as the Chelsea football team . . . when John Terry is ill.

London is full of the cream. The bright. The sharp. The ambitious. People who had the gumption at some point to up sticks and leave the two-bit town in which they were raised and do a Dick Whittington.

You see it as you drive about: cafes rammed full of people reading big newspapers and talking about big things and drinking coffee that people in Salford have never heard of. It's where the shows are. It's where films premiere. It's the nation's Oxbridge. It's the best of the best of the best.

Salford? It's just Salford. A small suburb with a Starbucks and a canal with ducks on it. It's a box that has been ticked. A gentle tousle of the politicians' mop. According to Wikipedia, its only real claim to fame is that a man there was run over by Stephenson's *Rocket*. Oh, and someone once found a head in a bog.

This does not qualify it as a great place to make television shows. Indeed, it's a very bad place. Every week we have to try to entice a guest to our studios, which are in Guildford. Sometimes it's tricky. But it's nowhere near as tricky as it would be if we had to get them up to Manchester. Or as expensive. Every week I'd have to say: 'Ladies and gentlemen, please welcome . . . Stuart Hall. Again.' That might become wearing.

And how could a news programme run from Salford? It's nowhere near any court that matters and nowhere near a single politician.

Furthermore, if we ran the show from Salford, we'd be employing people from Salford. People who were born there and thought, 'Yes. I like this. I see no reason to go anywhere else.' And in the world of television that could be a genuine handicap. Every year we'd end up making a Christmas special from the Dog and Duck or the nearest Arndale centre. A television show needs to be run by worldly people. Not people who are frightened to death of the next town.

And what would be the upside? Who cares where a show is made? Who cares whether the *Blue Peter* garden is in London or not? Who cares whether Simon Mayo is speaking to you from Portland Place or a glass-fronted tower up north? It makes not a jot of difference. At the end of a show now it often says BBC Wales or BBC Scotland. If at the end of *Top Gear* we put up an ident saying BBC England there'd be hell to pay internally. But why? Nobody who'd paid for the joke would give a damn.

The big problem here is that politicians – and they're behind this shift, be in no doubt about that – have got it into their heads that Britain is a big place. But it isn't, really. It's titchy. Moving half the BBC from London to Salford is the same as a parish council moving the table around which it meets from the village hall to the community centre.

Britain is a small place with a whopping great world-class city in its bottom right-hand corner. It therefore makes sense to me that every head office, every government department, every newspaper and, most of all, every television and radio show is based there.

10 July 2011

Okay, I'll come clean on Rebekah and the Chipping Norton plot

A recent piece in Her Majesty's *Daily Telegraph* suggested there is a turning point in the career of all prime ministers after which their place on the scrapheap of history becomes assured.

This is probably true. Tony Blair was doomed from the moment he said to George W.: 'Yes. Let's bomb Iraq.'

John Major had had it after Black Wednesday, and Gordon Brown became a spent force . . . well, when the nurse cut his umbilical cord.

According to Peter Oborne in the *Telegraph*, David Cameron's moment came when he chose to become involved with the Chipping Norton set – 'an incestuous collection of louche, affluent, power-hungry and amoral Londoners' who all have homes near one another in the Cotswolds.

I see. So this pretty little market town, whose most notable resident to date was the famously power-hungry and amoral Ronnie Barker, is actually a haven for the worst excesses of corruption. Behind the hanging baskets and the tea shoppes, the man in the hardware store is let off his VAT bill if he hands Cameron an under-the-counter tin of gloss paint.

It's all rubbish. The fact is that 99 per cent of the population of Chipping Norton are not in the Chipping Norton set, and that 99 per cent of the set don't actually live in Chipping Norton.

According to every single report I've read, Matthew Freud, the PR man who is married to Elisabeth Murdoch, is a leading light and the host of our most glamorous parties. But he lives in Burford, which to most people in Chipping Norton – myself included – is basically France.

Then there's Steve Hilton. Apparently, he's a Tory adviser, but I've never met him. Nor have I met another chap who has been mentioned, Sir Howard Stringer. But that's probably because he lives in Chinnor, which is as far away as Russia. Last weekend the *Mail on Sunday* suggested Nat Rothschild is also involved simply on the basis he once used the M40.

I'll let you into a secret, though. There is a group of Chipping Norton people who do live close to one another and who do meet up most weekends for wine and cheesy things on sticks. I am one of these people. And so is the Blur bassist Alex James, who often brings his children round to swim in our pool.

We have other friends, too. There's Tony and Rita and James and Annabel and Dominic and Caroline. Bored yet? No? Well, that's because I haven't got to Emily and Miles, who have the pub.

Of course, there are some other people in the group who have been in the newspapers recently. There's Cameron and his wife Sam, but we don't see much of them these days, partly because he is jolly busy running the country and partly because Sam is one of those non-smokers who suddenly remembers when she's presented with a smoker like me that what she'd like to do is smoke all my bloody cigarettes. And then send me out to get some more.

Then there's Rebekah Brooks and her husband, Charlie. They actually met over supper in our house one night and are the most fantastically kind and generous people we know. I feel desperately sad that Rebekah has had to resign but the cloud does have a silver lining – I can see more of her. She has been a friend for a long time. She is now. And she always will be.

And now let's get to the meat. The question that has burnt brightly in the *Guardian* for the past six months. The infamous Christmas-time party at Rebekah and Charlie's house. Investigative journalists have established that the Camerons were there but they have not been able to establish what was discussed.

I'm going to tell you everything. I was there with my wife – and that's a story already for the *Mirror*. James Murdoch was there too, with his wife. There were two other couples, neither of whom have even the slightest connection to newspapers, the police force or the government. They were simply neighbours.

We began with a cocktail made from crushed socialists and after we'd discussed how the trade union movement could be smashed and how News Corp should be allowed to take control of the BBC, Rupert Murdoch joined us on a live video feed from his private volcano, stroking a white cat.

Later, I remember vividly, a policeman knocked at the door and Rebekah gave him a wad of cash. Cameron tapped the side of his nose knowingly and went back to his main course – a delicious roast fox.

That's what you want me to say happened, isn't it? But what you're going to get now is the truth. I've kept quiet for six months but I feel the time is right to tell all. What Rebekah and Cameron talked about most of all – and I'm a trained journalist so I understand the need to get things right – is sausage rolls.

We were planning a big walk with all our kids over Christmas and thought it might be a good idea to build a fire in my woods and stop off for a picnic. Rebekah was worried about what we'd eat. Cameron thought sausage rolls would be nice. My wife said she'd get some.

Aha, you cry. But what about evil James Murdoch? Was he

not to be found sticking pins into a waxwork model of Vince Cable?

No, actually. James was sitting opposite me and we spent most of the night arguing about the environment. He likes it and I don't. The row only ended when Samantha Cameron suddenly remembered that what she'd like was 400 of my cigarettes.

In other words, it was much like a million other Christmas-time dinners being held in a million other houses all over the world that day. BSkyB was not mentioned. Nor was phone hacking. And it was the same story the next time we all met. That time, we played tennis. You might call this disgustingly middle class. Going for walks and picnics and tennis. And I won't argue with you. But louche? Amoral? Corrupt? No.

Of course, much has gone wrong in recent years and many will spend the next few years wondering what caused the rot to set in. But I can assure you that the root cause of it all will not be found in Chipping Norton.

17 July 2011

Okay, tontine tango birdie, let's baffle 'em with insider talk

British prisoners of war in some of the more barbaric Japanese camps were not allowed to speak to one another. So, to get round the problem, they developed a new language that featured no Bs, Ms, Ps, Vs or Ws. This meant they could at least whisper, without moving their lips, and thus avoid arousing the suspicion of the guards.

People in certain villages in North Wales perform a similar trick even today: when an English person walks into their local pub, they switch to a version of English in which the A, E, I, O and U are replaced by the letter L.

Then, of course, there were the eighteenth-century plantations where slaves, often from different parts of Africa, conversed in English. But not the sort that their English master would have a hope of understanding. The language has lasted, and now I have literally no idea how the courts work in Barbados since the defendant invariably answers all the questions by speaking in a way that is indecipherable to anyone in a suit. 'Dah you own?', for example, means 'Is that yours?' Not guilty is 'Ah'n do dah'. Which is literally 'I didn't do that'.

So, there have been good reasons in the past for using language as a device for not being understood. But today people seem to mangle language just to make themselves sound more important.

This began in about 1840 with the birth of Cockney rhyming slang and is practised extensively in the world of light aircraft. Instead of speaking to the tower in a manner the passengers can understand, the pilot chooses to say things that make the task look much more difficult than is actually the case. 'Whisky Oscar Tango Squawking on niner niner two decimal seven. Requesting basic service ILS Echo to outer beacon.'

We see a similar problem with the practitioners of business who now talk about 'quantum' instead of money and 'P and L' instead of money and 'piece' instead of money.

It's like footballers coming up with a million new words for 'goal'.

Lawyers are also annoying, never using one word when several thousand will do. And then several thousand more, until the reader has completely lost the point and sometimes the will to live.

You think you have just about got to the end of a sentence but then there's a colon and you know that there's at least a fortnight to go before you get to the next verb. I signed a legal document a while ago, not because I agreed with what it said: I was bored.

So, some people talk strangely to hide what they're saying from eavesdroppers. And some because they want to make a simple job look more difficult. So what excuse, I wonder, do golfists have?

Last week there was a golf tournament in Kent that must have been jolly important because it was the only thing on the news apart from the people who knew the person who once met someone at a party who may or may not have illegally listened to Sienna Miller making a hair appointment.

I'm not kidding. Every half hour on every radio station, we had the phone hacking stuff, and then instead of the collapse of the euro, or the famine in East Africa, all we had was a breathless report about the leaderboard at Sandwich. And I'm sorry, but I couldn't understand what they were on about.

A man, whom I'd never heard of, was four under par behind another man I'd never heard of who needed an eagle and a bogey to win. It was as though the reporter were reading a Scrabble board.

No other sport does this. Even if we are not interested in football, we understand who has won when we are told that Manchester United have scored two and Chelsea have scored three. But in a golf report your car radio needs to have the decoding powers of Bletchley Park or you are left completely in the dark.

Golf fever even spread to the traffic reports. Normally, these begin with Scotland and we all think: 'Oh, do us a favour. They have no idea what a jam is.' But last week they all began with news of hold-ups in Kent, caused, apparently, by people going to the golf match.

That's even more baffling than the leaderboard. I can, if I squint, understand why people play the sport – they don't like their wives – but I cannot understand why anyone would want to watch it, because, so far as I can tell, you choose whether you want to watch a man you've never heard of hit the ball or whether you want to watch the ball land.

Isn't that like being forced in a football match to choose whether you want to watch the man take the penalty, or the other man try to save it? Imagine if the bowler and the batsman in cricket were made to stand three miles apart and you had to choose which one you'd like to see.

Except there is no batsman in golf. A man hits a ball and all you can do if you're at the other end is watch it land. Can you imagine anything in life quite so dreary?

And it was raining. Doesn't that strike you as odd? That you would drive through severe traffic and stand in the rain for hours watching a selection of men in nasty trousers thwack a ball into the clouds. Or, worse, peering into the heavens in the hope that you've selected the right spot to watch it come back down to earth. And you have no idea who's winning because reports of the scores don't make sense.

It's almost like a secret code. Which it is, in a way, since in the early days golf was played almost exclusively by Free-masons. And Freemasons do not make a habit of speaking openly about their activities or their handshakes or their funny words.

Today, of course, most Freemasons are to be found in the police, who don't talk properly either.

24 July 2011

Get on your roof, everyone, and give Biggles an eyeful

In my continuing quest to prove that airport check-in times are fraudulent nonsense, I arrived at Ronaldsway on the Isle of Man the other morning twenty-three minutes before the scheduled departure time.

And made it on to the flight, easily.

I was feeling extremely smug as I cast my eyes over the other passengers. 'Ha,' I thought, 'while I was catching a few more zeds in bed this morning, all you slaves to convention were marooned in the departure lounge, having your hair redone by static electricity from the seats.'

But then the plane took off, and I realized that, unlike everyone else, I hadn't left myself enough time to buy a book or a newspaper.

This meant I had to spend the entire flight looking out of the window. And as we began our descent into London City an hour or so later, I arrived at an interesting conclusion: from the air, England is much too dreary. I realize, of course, that we don't have any Alps and there's no desert – apart from a small one between Birmingham and Coventry – but we do have many towns, and from the air they're all extremely similar and very horrid.

Stoke-on-Trent looks exactly like Stafford. Milton Keynes looks like a retail park. Lichfield appears to serve no purpose at all. And every building you see looks like a prison. Except for all the actual prisons, which look like supermarkets.

There's a very good reason for this. It's because the planning rules were drawn up when only the very tall had an aerial view of anything. Architects therefore concentrated hard on frontal aspects and put all the flotsam and jetsam and the air-conditioning plant on the roof where no one could see it. Now, though, thousands of us can – and do – see it every day.

There's more. Think how much effort is put into a town's ground-level entry points these days. You get a little gate, and some flowerpots, a sign asking you to drive slowly and often a reminder that back in 1996 the Britain in Bloom judges had bestowed upon the council a special commendation. All this effort for a few people in cars.

Whereas people flying overhead are given nothing. It's just a big brown splodge that looks exactly the same as all the other big brown splodges.

So what about a bit of civic advertising. 'You are now flying over Rutland – the best little county by a dam site.' Or 'Mansfield – birthplace of Rebecca Adlington *and* Richard Bacon'. Or 'Chipping Norton – nothing to see here'.

From the air, there seems to be no point at all to Preston. You realize why it was the first town to be given a motorway bypass. There was simply no need to go there. But this was the first British town outside London to be lit by gas. So why not light it up by gas again?

Think of all those eager little American faces, pressed to the windows of their planes, straining in the pre-dawn light to get a better look at Britain's only town to be completely on fire.

Companies, too, could get in on the act. They spend a fortune getting their message across to motorists who have better things to do than look at billboards.

But they spend not a single penny pushing their slogans to the thousands of trapped businessmen who fly over the factories every day.

We know of the story of a man in Wales who became so

fed up with low-level RAF sorties that he put a message on his roof saying 'Piss off Biggles'. Inevitably it backfired because when news broke of his stunt, everyone with a pilot's licence flew over his gaff for a gawp.

But you can see from this story that rooftop advertising has power. Pilots will fly hundreds of miles out of their way, just to be abused. That's how boring Britain is from the air.

As you come in to land at Heathrow, there are thousands of nondescript warehouses on either side of the final approach and I think I'm right in saying that only one owner has had the gumption to festoon his otherwise useless roof space with an advert. That's madness.

At present, escort girls ply for trade by leaving cards in telephone boxes. Why? The only people who use a telephone box these days are people who are desperate for a wee. So why not put a photograph of yourself, a phone number and a brief list of the services you offer on the roof of a warehouse in Hammersmith? One Korean jet and you'd be rushed off your feet, literally, for a month.

It's the same story with Windsor Castle, over which you descend when the wind's blowing from the east. I'm pretty sure that most airline passengers haven't a clue what it is, so why not use a banner to tell them of opening times and ticket prices? Mrs Queen would have enough for a new royal yacht in weeks. And airline passengers would have something to read.

But it's farmers with whom I have the biggest gripe. Who says that crops have to be planted in squares? What's the matter with a good old-fashioned cock and balls?

In Oxfordshire there's an estate on which all the woods were planted in the precise formations of various troops at some battle in the Crimea. The old buffer who did this could not possibly have known that one day people would be able to enjoy the fruits of his imagination. But today, every time I leave Heathrow, I do.

And certainly, if my farm were on a flight path, I'd be doing all sorts of things that would be invisible to arbiters of good taste on the ground but clear as day from 30,000ft in the sky. Some of the things I have in my mind would involve messages, perhaps about Gordon Brown. And if I had some land in Sussex, I'd plant a wood in such a way that Lufthansa's passengers would know that I shared their view of the Greeks.

My plans are good news for everyone. They are good for business, good for tourism, good for civic pride and good for those airline passengers who see the airport as a glorified bus stop. And not a two-hour compulsory shopping trip.

31 July 2011

That's it – one fluffed backhand and I'm broken as a father

As we know, it is much better to lose than to win. First of all, losing requires much less physical exertion. If you want to win a game of tennis or squash, you have to try very hard, which involves a great deal of running and sweat. Whereas if you really couldn't care less, you can spend an enjoyable hour sauntering about, hitting the ball only if it happens to be passing close by.

It's the same story with chess. If you set out to win, you really have to concentrate hard on what you are doing, anticipating all of the moves your opponent could make and deciding how you might respond.

Whereas if you don't mind losing, you can spend the time when it's not your turn drinking martinis and flicking through powerboat magazines. This is much more enjoyable than doing mental maths.

There's another big advantage to being the plucky Brit who comes home second. It's this: if you win, it is almost impossible to get your face right. You have to look pleased but not smug. And you have to walk that tightrope while making magnanimous noises to your opponent. This is tricky.

Whereas if you lose, you can shrug your shoulders and make all sorts of jokes about how useless you are at everything. There is comedy to be had from being a loser, and none at all from being a winner.

That's why I have spent all of my life ensuring that I am no good at anything.

However, there is an exception to all of this. A time when you must risk a heart attack and a seizure to ensure that you wipe your opponent off the board, or the court or the pitch or wherever you might be. This is when your opponent is one of your own children.

I spent some time yesterday with a fifty-three-year-old man who was absolutely charming, until the conversation turned to his fondness for running half marathons, and how he is driven every year on the Great North Run not to just beat, but to humiliate his twenty-seven-year-old son. I understand this very well.

One of the sports at which I don't excel is table tennis. That said, I'm not a complete numpty. Obviously, I won't spend the game standing fifteen yards from the net making stupid spin shots and sweating like an Egyptian burglar. And you can be assured that if you've moved me to the left side of the table and then suddenly sent a shot to the right, I'm not going to risk a coronary running for it. That would be undignified.

However, while playing my son the other day, all of this changed. It was 8-1 to him. A score that was not possible. It's my job as a dad to be better than him and better than all the other dads, too. It's my job to win.

And then it was 10-1. And then 11-1. At this point, I'm ashamed to say, I changed into a pair of training shoes. Then I went outside, took some deep breaths and came back a new man. I may have even been growling a bit.

I sent my serve deep into the bottom corner. It skimmed the very edge of the table, and whooshed under his armpit. 'Yes!!!' I cried, punching the air, my face contorted with determination and rage.

And so it went on until the score was 21-20. To him. He was serving. He took his time. Wondering, perhaps, what the snarling, sweat-soaked monster at the other end of the table had done with his dad. He pulled his hand back, and this was it.

My life hung in the balance. If I messed up, I would have lost to my own son. I focused. The ball came, I sent it back, with some side. He whipped a fast one hard into the left court but I was ready with a chip. Which he reached, sending a short ball back. I smashed a backhand at it. And knew the instant I made the move, it wouldn't work. I was right. The ball sailed into the pile of boxes at the far end of the room and was lost. So was I.

The boy was very kind and said all the right things. He had been lucky. I hadn't been concentrating properly at the beginning. It had been a good game. And so on.

But I knew that what had just passed between us was not a fluffed backhand in a game of table tennis. It was the moment when the line of his ascent to adulthood passed my line of descent into an old people's home.

For fifteen years, I have encouraged my son and taught him things. I have watched him grow and learn, safe in the knowledge that, of course, I will always be faster and cleverer and stronger. And then comes the moment when you are forced to face up to the fact that this just isn't so.

The fluffed backhand was that moment, that pinprick of time when I realized he is now faster and stronger than me, and that one day soon, he will be cleaning up my faeces and holding my hand when I cross the road.

The only good thing, of course, is that despite his new-found strength and agility, he would never have the same level of wisdom. The young bull knows that he can charge into a field of cows and have a couple. The old bull knows that it's better to stroll into the field and have the lot.

So, even when my son is having to wipe my bottom, I will

still be able to offer him advice on the ways of the world – because I will always be thirty-six years older. He will always have thirty-six fewer years to have experienced things. As a result, I will always have the ability to think more strategically than him.

That's why, after I'd smashed my table tennis bat into a million pieces and fed the remains into a wood-chipping machine, I agreed to sit down and play him at chess.

I poured myself a glass of Ribena so that I would go into the match sober. I turned off my telephone. We began.

And he won that, too. I'm now thinking of killing myself.

7 August 2011

French porn and a little software can save our schools

As you are no doubt aware, every single young person in Britain discovered last week that they had passed fifteen GSCE exams with A* grades. This means they are now able to sit their A levels, which they will also pass with flying colours, and pretty soon they will be at university studying, oh, I don't know, 'dance and waste management' or 'Third World development with pop music'. Both of which are real courses, incidentally.

When they have achieved first-class degrees, they will emerge into the workplace fully formed and educated to a higher standard than any other young people in history. Or will they?

Because if you look carefully at the results you will note that many of the successful children passed in subjects such as ceramics, or needlework, or PE. So while the child may be capable of making a flowerpot and doing a forward somersault, he or she may not be able to go to Paris without ending up in Rio de Janeiro.

Some lay the blame for this fairly and squarely at the door of league tables. They argue that to get a tick in the box from the government, each school must ensure that as many kids as possible get as many passes as possible. This means pupils are discouraged from taking an exam in physics, which is hard, and encouraged instead to sit papers on dusting, or using a urinal.

This is undoubtedly true. I know of one girl who insisted on taking various science subjects for her A levels. Her head teacher argued strongly that she should not but she was adamant and scored a C and two Ds. As a result of this – just one pupil – the school fell fifty places in the league tables.

However, league tables are not the only reason for the shift. There's another which comes to light when you note that this year the number of pupils sitting a geography GCSE fell by a whopping 13,800.

When I was at school, geography was a doddle. We learnt about capital cities and American states and then occasionally we were taken on a field trip to the Peak District so we could stand behind millstone grit outcrops, smoking Player's No. 6s. I loved geography and still do.

However, today the geography syllabus has changed beyond all recognition. Instead of learning which countries are next door to Libya, which is interesting and useful, the subject has been hijacked by eco-mentalists.

Yes, there's a bit of interesting stuff on tectonic plates, but mostly it's a non-stop orgy of weird-beard nonsense about man's impact on the ecosystem and why snails are more important than bypasses. Kids are taught to 'appreciate the ways in which people and environments interact and the need to make developments sustainable'. It sounds like a local council pamphlet.

They're also taught about climate change and hazard management, which is another way of saying health and safety. And then, if they are still awake, they are made to sit through hour after interminable hour of the teacher droning on about the green revolution, globalization and how best to manage the world's resources. This isn't education, it's propaganda. And, worse still, it's boring.

We have the same problem with English literature. Instead of getting children to study books such as *Matterhorn* or *Birdsong*, which are exciting and well written, they are still made to read Shakespeare. If I were running the education system, Shakespeare would be banned. His plots are simplistic. His characters are unfathomable. He is only of use to postgraduate dweebs interested in what was going on with the language in the sixteenth century. He should be removed from the curriculum and take Chaucer and bloody Milton with him.

Then there's maths. What in God's name is the point of learning algebra and cosines and long division? Maths is not necessary once you are past the age of four because anything more complicated than adding two and two can be done on a telephone.

To make matters worse, maths is compulsory. Which is almost certainly why so many children choose to spend their days sitting around in an Arndale centre frightening old ladies.

As a country we need a rethink on not only what we teach our children but also how we teach it. Take French. Like geography, it, too, is less popular now than PE and ironing but I know how to reverse that trend. I know how you could make every single child in the land fluent by the time they are fourteen. It's simple. Instead of teaching them that a table is female and how to conjugate verbs, simply play them French – ahem – 'art' films with the subtitles turned off. They'd get the gist pretty quickly.

What's more, when they are in France they will find it much more beneficial if they can say 'My dear, your thighs are exquisite' than if they can only say 'The pen of my aunt'. Just one word of warning. It's probably best not to let children see German 'art' films. Not unless they want to take a GSCE in moustaches.

Let me give you an example of how a change in teaching methods has revolutionized life in my house. Ever since they were old enough to walk, my children have had music lessons.

They've done their scales and learnt to play stupid bits of Bartok and as a result none of them can play an instrument.

But yesterday I was sitting watching television when I heard my youngest daughter sit down at the piano and play 'Clocks' by Coldplay absolutely perfectly. I was so staggered that I went next door to find out how this had been possible.

It turns out she had downloaded the score, which was displayed on an iPad like a Space Invaders game. I had no clue what was going on but, her being twelve, it all made perfect sense. This morning she bashed out the second movement of the 'Moonlight Sonata' so beautifully I thought Beethoven had dropped in for breakfast.

If schools can use technology like this and French pornography and get rid of Shakespeare, the nation will once again be full to the brim with educated people. Rather than people who have a lot of GSCEs.

28 August 2011

Oh, Berbatovs – I've got to learn footballspeak

Back in the 1960s there were many things to occupy the mind of a small boy, many rivalries to be discussed in the playground. There was music, for starters; lots of it and all so very different. There were tunes for mods and rockers and hippies, and there was bubblegum pop for people with pigtails.

Later we would discover Led Zep and the Who and the Stones and I would argue until well into the night about who were best. And this was just the tip of the iceberg. Was *Crime of the Century* better than *Rumours*? Was Mitch Mitchell a better drummer than Nick Mason? Who was better-looking, Christine McVie or Stevie Nicks?

And when we tired of music, there was still a rich seam of debate to be explored. Ferrari versus Lotus. Chelsea versus Leeds. England versus Australia. Communism versus capitalism. America versus Vietnam. The nearest I ever came to an actual schoolboy fistfight was with an idiot who really and truly believed Wrangler made better jeans than Levi's.

Now, though, all this is gone, swept away by the rise and rise of Premier League football. Today, if you listen to children talking, it's not about whether McDonald's does a better fry than Burger King or whether the Taliban have more of a point than Obama. No. There's an occasional discussion – usually among girls – about which *X Factor* contestant is most likely to end up back behind the counter at Asda that week, but mostly it's football.

In our house it's constant. My fifteen-year-old boy is a

fanatical Chelsea supporter and I like to play a game with him: starting the conversation as far away as possible from football and then seeing how long it takes him to get it back to Stamford Bridge. His record is pre-Byzantine architecture to John Terry in three moves.

His fanaticism has even had an effect on me. Until quite recently I saw football as twenty-two overpaid young men with silly hair kicking an inflated sheep's pancreas around a field. Yes, I was able to recite the Chelsea and Leeds teams that played in the 1970 FA Cup final but I only chose to do so, in my head, when I felt I needed to last a little longer in the bedroom department. I would even pray for England to get knocked out of tournaments so that television programming could return to normal and I could get back to discussing the Rubettes and the joy of a pleated Ben Sherman shirt.

Not any more. Last year I flew all the way to South Africa – at my own expense – to watch Holland and Spain play in the World Cup final. Then, last weekend, I voluntarily sat down and watched Tottenham play Manchester City, two teams in which I have absolutely no interest. Because unless I know what's going on these days, I'm useless to my son when I'm at home and in a conversational cul-de-sac when I'm out.

I met a chap last week who drives a Toyota Prius and thinks it's unkind to shoot a pheasant in the face. I was very much looking forward to talking to him about these and other things. But no. We started with football over the prawn cocktail and were still at it as we finished the Black Forest gateau.

It's not just a religion here, either. Premier League football is now screened in more than 200 countries around the world. And we're not talking 'screened' in the same way that Piers Morgan's chat show is 'screened'. I mean watched. And not just casually, but fanatically.

Because the big teams field players from all over the world, pretty well every country has a local hero for whom they can cheer.

Nigerians can support Chelsea because they have John Obi Mikel. Bulgarians can support Manchester United because they have Dimitar Berbatov. Scandinavians have a fondness for Liverpool because the Reds once employed a Nor called John Arne Riise.

This means that wherever we go in the world my son is always first to make friends with the locals. I caught him in earnest conversation with a known Caribbean drug dealer the other day and was very angry, until I realized that they were actually discussing Arsenal's chances this season.

And while it's undoubtedly sad that football now sits in humankind's conversation pit like a gigantic elephant, it's good news that Britain gets to sit in the spotlight every weekend.

There is, however, a problem. According to all the experts, the league will be dominated this year by just two teams: Manchester City and Manchester United. That's not good, because what makes the Premier League so much better than any other in the world is the sheer number of teams that start every season with half a chance. If it's a two-horse race, between the teams from just one city, new boys like me are going to struggle to stay interested.

Which brings me on to an idea suggested by John Timpson, the shoe-repairs magnate, whom I met on holiday last month. He reckons that the Football Association should work out a formula based on a club's finances to determine how big the goalmouths should be.

This is inspired. It would mean that when a rich side such as Manchester City plays a less well-off side such as Norwich, the East Anglians would be aiming at a goal that's about the same size as their home county, while the Mancs would be trying to get the ball through what was basically a letter box.

Obviously it needn't be that pronounced. A few inches either way should be enough to level the playing field. Rich owners could then continue to field great teams playing great football. But the result? Deliciously, it could go either way.

Then – and this is my little twist – if it's 0-0 at half-time, the second half should be played with two balls on the pitch at the same time.

Oh, and finally, this is from my son: anyone appearing for a team with Manchester in the title must play while wearing a bag on his head.

4 September 2011

My daughter and I stepped over the body and into a brothel

There is a terrible famine in East Africa, which is great news if you're a celebrity.

Because it means you can head off to Ethiopia for some nice PR and a spot of late-summer sunshine.

It's a great gig.

All you have to do is walk about on a rubbish tip, looking despondent, and then cuddle a baby with flies in its eyes while pulling your best kid-in-a-wheelchair charity face.

Bang in a couple of shots of you pretending to listen to a starving mum, plaster the finished film with a veneer of 'Everybody Hurts' by REM and it's back to the hotel for a few beers and a sixth-form debate with the charity bigwigs on the injustices of the World Bank, Swiss drug companies, General Motors, climate change, McDonald's and the bloody Tories.

Meanwhile, back at home, everyone is bored to tears. Legend has it that Bonio once told an audience who'd come to hear him sing 'Wiv or Wivout You' that every time he clapped his hands a child in Africa died, prompting one wag in the crowd to shout out: 'Well, stop clapping your hands then.'

Deep down we all feel very sorry for the starving masses but the compassion is buried under the blanket of certainty that Africa is basically screwed. Russell Brand can walk about on a rubbish tip till the cows come home but it'll make no difference to the fact that the leaders are corrupt, violence is a way of life, the Sahara is getting bigger and there's not a damn thing anyone can do about any of it. It's just a question of what wipes them out first: starvation or AIDS.

I've always felt this way. Bob Geldof may have it in his head that I went to Live Aid so that others, less fortunate than me, might have a happier life. Well, I didn't. I went because I wanted to see the Who. And despite constant denials, I've always harboured a deep-down belief that the money I paid for the ticket was used to provide the Ethiopian president's personal bodyguard with a new Kalashnikov.

Anyway, moving on, I have a strict policy with my children about their holidays. They can do their snogging and drinking in the Easter break but in the summer they have to go somewhere a bit more educational. Which is why, last weekend, my eldest daughter and I set off for a mini-break in Uganda.

A few facts. Half the population of this landlocked East African country is fourteen or younger and the gross domestic product is £11 billion or, to put it another way, about a tenth of what Britain spends on the National Health Service alone. It's very poor, but in Entebbe, which is used by the United Nations as a hub, the whole place looks like Surrey. Except for the shops, most of which are named after the baby Jesus. You have the Blessed Lord butchery and the Praise Be to the Almighty banana emporium. You also have a lot of roadside stalls selling double beds. No idea why.

The capital, though, Kampala? That's a different story. I've seen poverty in my travels. I once saw a woman in Bolivia having a tug-of-war with a dog over an empty crisp packet and in Cambodia you get the impression that pretty well everyone has had their legs blown off by landmines. But nothing prepares you for the jaw-dropping horror of a Ugandan slum.

We stepped out of the car, over the body of a man, and

moments later we were surrounded by solid proof that Dante completely miscalculated the number of circles in hell. We'll start with sanitation.

There isn't any. Well, there are a couple of public bogs, but since they cost 200 shillings to use, everyone simply uses what passes for the street. At one point we were taken to a 10ft x 10ft brothel, which in the rainy season floods to a depth of 2ft with raw sewage. This means customers have the opportunity to catch cholera and AIDS in one hit.

You may wonder why anyone goes there. Well, it's simple. In a two-hour walk I didn't see a single girl under the age of eighteen. 'They don't survive,' said our guide. Which, when translated, means they are either raped and then murdered to shut them up or they are beheaded by witch doctors in the daily child sacrifice ceremonies.

Not that most of the boys seem to care very much since almost all of them are completely off their heads on solvents.

They lie there – some of them just three years old – entirely unaware of the fact they're in a puddle of someone else's piss.

You know the cupboard under your stairs? In a Kampala slum this would be considered a luxury house and at night it would sleep seven people. I could not see how this would be possible unless they all stood up. Which, when the rains come, is necessary anyway.

On the upside, we did find a lovely place for lunch. A few miles away from the slum, in the shadow of an amazing new hotel complex owned by the president's wife, was a Belgian restaurant where we had a Nile beer and an excellent beef stew. It cost more than most people in Uganda will earn in a lifetime.

Over coffee, which is delicious in this part of the world, we talked about the Lord's Resistance Army, which runs about in the north of Uganda torturing, mutilating, murdering and raping pretty much anything that hasn't already died of starvation.

Over the obligatory corporate greed and climate change debate on what's to be done, we concluded that Live Aid didn't work. Live 8 didn't work. Nothing's worked. And, yes, while it's good that David Cameron has pledged to keep Britain's foreign aid at similar levels, we shouldn't forget that last year the Ministry of Defence spent £1.7 million on body armour and helmets for the Ugandan army which, honestly, isn't really what most people think of as 'aid'.

All I know is that when you've been there, you feel compelled to do something. Appear in a charity video, walking about on a rubbish tip, wearing a compassionate face? Yup. Count me in.

11 September 2011

Own up, we all had a vile streak long before going online

Every week we are presented with supposedly conclusive proof that Britain is broken. The summer was marked by riots; you get five minutes in jail for murdering a baby; our education system is worse than Slovenia's; and we're told that it's perfectly natural and traditional for travelling people to keep a handful of slaves in the shed. Meanwhile, register offices are full of people who've never met; your village bobby can neither read nor write; your MP is an imbecile; burglaries aren't investigated; the banks are back in cloud cuckoo land; and the rivers are all full of excrement.

Swim down the Thames these days and you really will be 'going through the motions'.

Those who seek to make gloom and doom from all of this say that Britain was much better when everything was in black and white and we had the reassuring spectacle of *Dixon of Dock Green* on the television every week. But this is rubbish. Because back then everyone died of pneumoconiosis when they were twelve, immigrants were routinely poked with sticks, tea was considered exotic and Ronnie and Reggie Kray were running amok in the capital, nailing people's heads to the floor.

If you developed cancer in 1956, you'd had it and would welcome death's cold embrace with open arms because it was a ticket out of the grime and the misery and the unfunny television shows and the soot and the socialism.

The fact, then, is this: life's better now than it has been at any point in human history. It's better than it was ten years ago. It's better than it was yesterday morning. Except for one thing.

You may have read last week about a young man called Sean Duffy, who took it upon himself to post revoltingly unkind internet messages about teenagers who had died. He superimposed the face of one, who had committed suicide by throwing herself in front of a train, on to a video of *Thomas the Tank Engine*. And he put up pictures of the site where another had lost her life in a road smash with the caption: 'Used car for sale, one useless owner.'

It's impossible to conceive how much anguish this caused the families, and that's why you were no doubt delighted to hear that Duffy was given the maximum jail sentence of eighteen weeks.

But hang on a minute: is he so very different from everyone else? Last week one newspaper ran on its website some photos of an actress who had been knocked down by a car. People in their droves left unbelievably unkind comments about her face and her children. There was even worse abuse for Jade Jagger, who had been photographed topless on a beach. She was described as 'ugly', 'fat' and a 'spoilt rude cow'. Elsewhere, Elton John was 'greedy', the Duchess of Cornwall was 'lazy' and Simon Cowell's legs were 'too short'.

If you plunge even more deeply into the darkest corners of cyberspace, you will find websites that show people with severed arms searching for the heads of their loved ones on the hard shoulder. People being eaten by tigers. People after they've jumped from the top of a skyscraper. And each is accompanied by amusing observations from the folks at home. If you die now, you'd better make sure no one has a camera, because if they do, the event is almost certain to end up on the web.

The internet is now just a receptacle for vitriol. It's malice in wonderland. And that's before we get to Facebook – which, let's not forget, was set up as a place where men could go online to make judgements about a girl's appearance – or Twitter.

You may say this is a new phenomenon – another example of the sick society we've created – and that it's caused by the anonymity of the internet. But is it? Long before you had a domain and an email address, you would sit in the safety of your car, muttering abuse at other drivers. Which amounts to exactly the same as muttering cyberspace abuse at Cheryl Cole's hair from the safety of your home or office.

And even before people had windscreens to hide behind they would go home after a hard day down the pit and mumble about the shortcomings of their neighbours, their colleagues, their bosses, the government. This is the way we are. It's just that now the internet lets us grumble in public.

Time and again a mother has presented me with her newborn and I've wanted to say: 'Holy cow. It looks like a smashed ape.' But I've been forced by my frontal lobes to *um* and *ah* until I can find a compliment of some kind. It's usually about the pram.

Once, I was taken backstage after an appalling play to meet the actress who had been simply dreadful in the lead. But, instead of saying she was dire, I cracked my face into a beam and said she'd been 'amazing'. Which was also true. She had.

Then there was the time I interviewed Chuck Yeager, the sound-barrier-breaking former test pilot. I wanted to say afterwards that he had been, without a doubt, the most unpleasant man in the entire world and that he was living, breathing proof that you should never meet your heroes. But instead I thanked him for his time and drove away.

In her latter years my grandmother lost the brake on her brain and would spend her days in the local dress shop, howling with derisive laughter at everyone who came out of the changing rooms. Secretly, I've always wanted to do the same. I bet you have, too.

Well, now the internet lets you. No longer do you have to sit in a fog of impotence during a television show that you dislike. You can get on your phone or computer and let the world know. Last week, for instance, Lily Allen saw a picture of me in the paper and tweeted one word: 'vomit'.

The internet hasn't caused any of this. It isn't, as some would have you believe, another example of Broken Britain and a fractured society. No, the internet is just a tool, which has demonstrated that behind our smiles and our cleverness, human beings, actually, are fairly terrible.

18 September 2011

Down, boy! Fido's fallen in love with the vacuum cleaner

There are many reasons why people choose to own a pet. To stop a daughter's endless nagging; for companionship; as an excuse to take the occasional walk; or because you won it at a fair and it seemed cruel to flush it down the waste disposal unit. Cruel, and difficult, especially if it was a horse.

However, according to a recent survey, 39 per cent of pet owners say they invested in their furry friend to replace a husband or wife. And I'm sorry, but I find this a bit alarming, because how can a pet possibly do that? It can't cook, or iron, or clean the air filter on a 1973 Lotus Elan.

And if you try to use it for a spot of jiggy jiggy, you can be fairly sure the police will want a word.

The trouble is, of course, that we all love animals a lot more than we love people. And the animal we love most of all is the dog. Dogs make us soft in the head.

In the disaster movie 2012, thousands of Chinese people are killed by a tsunami. But that's okay because we are treated to a close-up of the heroine's King Charles spaniel boarding a rescue ship in the nick of time. Then you have *Armageddon*, in which giant meteorites wipe out half of New York. But this is no problem because when the destruction is over, we see that the dog that we thought had been killed is in fact perfectly all right. Phew. It was only people that got flattened and blown up.

Such is our love for the dog that there are now 1.2 million Pakistanis living in Britain, 154,000 Nigerians, about a million Poles and 7.3 million dogs. Many of them live in my house.

On the face of it, it's an excellent idea to keep a pooch. It will bark at burglars and sit by the fire in the evenings, looking all sweet and cuddly. And all it demands in return for its sweetness and its Group 4 policy on security is a handful of biscuits and a bowlful of tinned meat from a company that did somehow work out how to push a horse through a waste disposal unit.

Unfortunately, it doesn't work out like this in reality. Let's take my West Highland terrier as a prime example of the problem. She is very cute and has fully jointed ears that swivel about when she is excited. On the downside, she is very violent. In the past two months alone she has eaten the lady who delivers the papers, the postman and the man who came round to mend my computer. She's like Begbie from *Trainspotting*.

Then there's a labradoodle, which is about the same size as an elephant. This means that no matter how high the shelf on which we put leftover chops and joints of lamb, he can get at them no problem at all. He also manages to look fantastically indignant when you tell him off.

There's also an elderly Labrador, who is now blind, deaf, arthritic and bald. Technically, she isn't really a dog any more. And then there's a young Labrador, who recently had her first period. This drove the labradoodle stark staring mad. He became a sex-crazed elephant-wolf who spent his entire time trying to put his ridiculous dog lipstick into the back of the stricken Lab, until eventually we had to send her away to the kennels.

This made things worse because he was now cut off from the target of his lust. So he began to mount everything else. The dishwasher, the keyhole in the front door, me, my daughter's friends and the exhaust pipe of my bloody car. At one point he attempted to rape the newspaper columnist Jane

Moore's dog and didn't seem to realize that a) it was male and b) he'd accidentally climbed on to the damn thing's face.

We locked him in a fenced-off part of the garden and he tried to eat a metal gate to get out. And then, with blood pouring from the wounds he'd inflicted on himself, he scampered off to the hen house. Nobody in human history has ever thought, 'Hmmm. I fancy a go on that chicken.' But he did.

Meanwhile, the housekeeper's Lab had been similarly affected and had tried to mate with the cat, my wellington boots and the lawnmower. Six months from now I won't be at all surprised if one of my donkeys gives birth to a dog. It's been like living in an inter-species free-love commune. Only with added howling.

You don't think of any of this when you are buying a puppy. You think the worst thing that could happen is that it will unravel the occasional loo roll. Nobody at Battersea Dogs Home ever tells a prospective customer that one day the scampering little mite in which they're interested will try to have sex with the vacuum cleaner.

My wife suggested that we really ought to relieve the pressure by, ahem, giving the maniacal labradoodle a helping hand, but I'm sorry, no: that's up there with morris dancing and incest. And so we took him to the kennels and brought the bitch home.

When she had finished filling the house with what to a doggy nose is Impulse body spray we brought him back and were looking forward to some peace. But no. Because while he was away, he had caught something called kennel cough. It doesn't sound so bad, does it? You think you could live with a coughing dog. Well, you can't, because a more accurate name for the disease would be 'explosive vomiting'.

So now he helps himself to a leg of lamb that we'd stored on top of a pylon, and just a few minutes later it shoots back out of his mouth all over whatever it was he broke last week by trying to have sex with. This upsets the Westie, who decides to bite another visitor, and when you tell him off he has the cheek to look affronted.

This is the reality of dog ownership. Fluids. Mess. Stolen food. Expense. Savaged paper boys. No post. Vets' bills. Broken vacuum cleaners. Ruined washing machines. Chewed shoes. Unravelled bog rolls. Endless barking, and then terrible, aching sadness when they die.

I can understand, therefore, why they make such an ideal substitute for a husband or a wife. There's no real difference.

25 September 2011

Street lights and binmen? Luxuries we just can't afford

So let's see if I've got this straight. If Italy goes belly up, any bank that has lent Mr Berlusconi money will go belly up, too. So will the people whose savings were held there. And all the shops where they used to buy provisions. And the airlines they used to fly with. And the banks from which the airlines had borrowed money. And their customers. And their local shops. If Italy goes, we all go. Plainly, that would be bad.

The experts are sitting around in huddles with their political masters, and the general consensus seems to be that no one has the first clue how to stop this happening. Well, unless I'm being thick, I do.

At present, various bits of British government expenditure are being ring-fenced because, it's claimed, no civilized country can do without them. The National Health Service is an obvious example, but the fact is, we may have been able to afford healthcare for everyone when the most expensive drug on offer was an aspirin and teeth were removed with a hammer; now that we have complex operations and lasers and colonoscopies and people with exotic diseases such as AIDS, we cannot afford it any more.

Nor can we afford an aircraft carrier. Or bypasses. In August alone this country had to borrow £16 billion to meet the gap between what it spent and what it earned. Obviously that's unsustainable.

The problem goes way beyond the big stuff. Because of global warming, or intensive farming, or possibly the satellite that crashed into Canada recently, Britain's waterways are being overrun with blue-green algae that make them extremely pretty. Unfortunately, if you choose to swim in an affected waterway, your skin will itch and you could end up with a poorly tummy.

You can see what's going to happen next. A small boy with freckles and a cute nose is going to end up on a BBC regional news programme all covered in diarrhoea, and his sobbing mum is going to say that someone should have done something about it. To prevent this public relations disaster from unfurling, water companies are being forced to spend millions of pounds clearing it up. That's millions we don't have being spent on some algae. Just so some kid doesn't end up with an itchy botty.

It's absolutely insane. Over the years, my kids have trodden on venomous stonefish and been attacked by jellyfish and battered to pieces by storm-tossed coral. And I don't complain to the authorities in Barbados. It's one of those things. But now, here, it's somehow become a government's job to prevent it from happening. And to provide lavatories for dogs.

In fact we've become used in recent years to the government providing us with everything. We expect it to protect us from algae and take away our rubbish and educate our kids and look after us when we are poorly and have a bobby on the street corner and fight Johnny Taliban and put up park benches and keep the libraries open and stop planes blowing up and build roads and send round an appliance when we've caught fire and make sure the food we eat is delicious and nutritious and lock up vagabonds and house the poor.

Fine, but have you noticed something? All the countries that share this view are now in a complete pickle while countries such as India and China, where shoes are considered a luxury, are doing rather well.

Last weekend the Labour party said that it would solve all our problems by cutting university tuition fees to £6,000. But that's like Dawn French cutting her fingernails to save weight. It's a pointless, meaningless, futile gesture and demonstrates clearly that Ed Miliband must be an imbecile.

We read all the time about people who borrow vast sums to fund their sports cars and speedboats, and we tut and think that they must be very tragic people with many complex problems. The government is behaving in exactly the same way, fearful that if it actually makes the necessary cuts, the country will be cast into poverty and the chance of a second term will be lost. Well, let me make a suggestion. Screw the second term and ask a question instead: what exactly is poverty?

An Eton schoolboy was once asked to write on the subject, and he began thus: 'There was once a very poor family. The father was poor. The mother was poor. The children were poor. Even the butler was poor . . .'

In the olden days you could tell at a glance if someone was existing below the poverty line because they were eight years old and sitting in a gutter with a dirty face, eating a turnip. Now it's more difficult. People claim to be poverty-stricken even when they have mobile phones and a television set and an internet connection. And when you've seen a woman on a Bolivian rubbish tip having a tug-of-war with a dog over an empty crisp packet, it's hard to stop yourself punching people such as this in the middle of their face.

The European Union defines poverty as any household that exists on an income that is less than 60 per cent of the national average. In Monte Carlo that sort of guideline would put Elton John on income support.

Here the average household income is about £35,000 a year and it's said that in the region of one in five exists on less than 60 per cent of this figure. But it's confusing because many pensioners fall way below the threshold in terms of income but own the house in which they are starving to death.

I read one report recently that says poverty should be measured on how poor you 'feel'. Well, I was at a charity fund-raiser the other night and, trust me, among all the Russian oligarchs I felt very poverty-stricken indeed.

The solution is that we all need to be recalibrated. Not just us, but the whole stupid Western world. We all think that street lights and having the bins emptied are essential. We must start to understand that, actually, they're luxuries. And we can't afford them any more.

2 October 2011

Ker-ching! I've got a plan to turn India's pollution into pounds

Over breakfast at a 700-year-old Indian fort that had been lovingly converted into a wonkily wired, no-smoking youth hostel, I met an Englishman who was planning to drive all the way across the subcontinent in an electric Reva G-Wiz. This seemed an especially pointless thing to do.

It turned out that he worked for the British government and was setting up a team to advise the emerging economic superpower on how best to cut its carbon emissions. As you can imagine, I had many questions for him on the matter.

Starting with: right, so you walk into a meeting with Mr Patel and you say . . . what exactly? 'Hello. I come from a country where everyone has musical loo-roll dispensers and patio heaters and enormous televisions, and we recognize you'd like some of that action too. But we feel it would be better for the polar bear and the Amazonian tree frog if you stayed in the Dark Ages.'

I imagine that Mr Patel might not be very sympathetic to this argument. Especially if his next meeting was with a representative from the German government who was going to say exactly the same thing. And doubly especially if he had hosted similar meetings the previous day with the Americans, the Canadians, the French, the Italians and so on.

The idea that Western governments should lecture India on how to conduct itself is absurd. It's like Simon Cowell popping into the terraced home of a lottery winner and telling them it would be better for the planet and their soul if they gave the jackpot to charity.

There's more, too. As we know, the government in Britain is cutting many services as it desperately tries to reduce the nation's debt. The streets are packed with homeless ex-librarians whose places of work have been boarded up in the never-ending quest to save cash. We have the prime minister on the Tube and the mayor of London on a bicycle, the lights are out at Buckingham Palace and BBC2 is showing pretty much what it showed in 1972. We understand that there is a need for all this. It makes sense. And we like to think that, day and night, every single government minister is sitting in a candlelit office, in mittens, desperately thinking up new ways of getting the debt down.

So what in the name of all that's holy are we doing funding a team of people whose job it is to tell the Indians to stick with their oxen? No, really, I mean it. How can we be turning off our street lights and planning to kick-start the Olympics with a pigeon and a box of sparklers when we are running a climate change department in Delhi?

What is Chris Huhne thinking of? I realize that the energy secretary is jolly busy dealing with his speeding ticket and the recent World School Milk Day but I urge him to have a long, hard look at the team in India and think: 'How can I be responsible for putting a million people out of work in Middlesbrough while funding this claptrap on the other side of the world?'

Of course, there are those who think that global warming is the greatest threat to humanity and that if any spending is going to be ring-fenced over the next few years, it must be money used in the war on carbon dioxide. They would abolish the army, the National Health Service, the north and those who live in it if they thought it would keep the polar ice intact. They would even seek to make it a crime to disagree with them. But that hasn't happened yet, so . . .

For sure, the air quality in India is extremely poor. When you come in to land at Delhi airport, it's like descending into a big airborne cloud of HP Sauce. At ground level, life's better – the air is like a consommé – but after a day it still feels as though you've been sucking furiously on a lozenge made from crude oil.

Sadly, though, air you can eat has nothing whatsoever to do with carbon dioxide. If you want to make it go away, you don't send climate change experts. You send mechanics to service the buses properly.

I also recognize that India is committed to reducing its emissions – well, that's what it says in meetings – and that there may be a couple of businesses here that could make a bob or two from popping over there and helping out. But India is a country on the move. And if we in Britain want to make a few quid out of its growth, isn't it better to sell it our jet fighters and our diggers and our bladeless Dyson fans? We should be milking its growth, not trying to stifle it with pious words and Uriah Heep hand-wringing.

It's rare that I actually get cross about something. But I am cross about this. The high commission in India has an important function. It is there to help British nationals who have lost their passports or who have become so incapacitated by diarrhoea that they've just excreted their own spleen.

It is there, too, to promote British business and, most of all, it is there to foster good relations between India and Britain. How are any of these things helped by a team of mean-spirited eco-ists who want to stand on the hose that's fuelling India's growth?

I don't mind that my taxes are used for schools I don't use, street lighting that doesn't shine on my house, hospitals I don't need and a police force that most of the time is a bloody nuisance. I understand that this is how the world works. I pay for a system in which I play no part.

But I really can't get to sleep at night knowing that some of the tax I pay is being used to fund a climate changist to drive across India in a G-Wiz. The only good thing is that it will take him several years, during which time India can choose life, choose a career, choose washing machines, cars, compact-disc players, electrical tin openers, good health, low cholesterol, dental insurance and a nice set of matching luggage.

23 October 2011

Look out, dear, a carbuncle is heading your way

As I'm sure you know, it is very difficult to get planning permission these days. Unless, of course, you are a Free-mason. Even if you want to add a small side extension to your kitchen, the council's inspector will raise all sorts of issues about the neighbour's right to light, the need to pro-tect the original style of the house and what provisions you intend to make for off-street parking.

And even if you cover all these bases, he will usually find a bat in the attic, and that'll be pretty much that.

So imagine how hard life must be if you are a developer and you want to build a 1,000ft skyscraper in the middle of a big city such as London. You'd need to be the Duke of Kent, or at the very least a grand wizard, to stand even half a chance.

And even if you manage to convince the local council your design is sound, that the foundations won't impede progress on the District line and that no bat will need to be rehoused, you will still have to get past the man I met at a dinner last week. The man whose job is to protect 'the look' of London. This must be the hardest job . . . in the world.

Because it's all very well saying now that London is per-fect, but what if someone had done that in 1066? 'I'm sorry, William, but you cannot build a tower on the Thames because it would spoil everyone's view of the inner-city farm on Watling Street.'

It's like those morons who have decided that Britain's countryside was absolutely perfect in about 1910 and that every effort must be made to keep the dry-stone walls and the hedges and the village idiots.

Or, worse, the climate. The temperature has shifted dramatically over the millennia, so which crackpot has decided that it's correct now? Because it absolutely isn't if you live in Sudan.

Then there's the case of Scotland. It began life as part of America, although at the time this was down near the South Pole. Gradually it broke away from Iowa and began its move northwards, until around 400 million years ago, when it sank just off the equator.

What if someone had decided then that the world should be preserved just as it was? We'd have no tarmac. No phones. No penicillin. No Highland bagpipes. No bolshie trade unionists. No Labour party. So, on balance, it wouldn't have been all bad.

Of course, at the other end of the scale, we have the problems of rampant development trampling all over the bedrock of history. Cape Town springs to mind here. From the sea, this used to be one of the world's most attractive cities, but now your eye is drawn to the World Cup stadium that sits in the view like a giant laundry basket.

Then there's Birmingham. Such is the prominence of the Selfridges building that you no longer notice the tumbledown, smoke-stained old factories or the canals full of shopping trolleys.

The history has been obliterated by something that appears to have come from the opening credits of *Doomwatch*.

The man I met at the party wholeheartedly agrees that balance is everything. He knows that new buildings are necessary but has to temper that with various established views and sightlines that should be preserved for the good of our souls.

For example, when you climb up Parliament Hill in the

north of London and turn round, you don't want to be presented with a city that looks like Manhattan. You want the London Eye but you also want to be able to see the things that your forefathers saw. Apparently, it is writ that visitors to Richmond Park in the south-west must be able to look down an avenue of trees and see St Paul's Cathedral in the City. And it doesn't matter how much wizardry developers deploy or how silly their handshakes, that's that.

Here's a good one. As you may know, the Americans decided quite recently that it simply wasn't possible to butcher Grosvenor Square any more and that it was time to move out of their current fortress to a new super-embassy on a five-acre site in Nine Elms, south of the Thames. Everyone was very supportive of this. It would provide many jobs and keep alive the special relationship in which they decide what they'd like to do and we run about wagging our tails, hoping that if we look sweet, they will give us a biscuit. Frankly, if they'd wanted to build their new embassy in the Queen's knicker drawer, we'd all have said, 'Oh yes, Mr Obama. And can we have some more Winalot?'

Happily, however, we have a man in charge of 'the look', who pointed out that if you stood on Vauxhall Bridge, the new embassy would sit slap bang in the sort of view immortalized by Turner. He saw no problems with the building they were proposing but realized that it would undoubtedly have a flag on the roof. So right in the middle of this much-photographed all-English scene would be the Stars and Stripes.

I'm sure the Americans find this objection very petty, and that Mr Cameron has been made to sit on the naughty step, but would they let us fly our flag in between the Capitol building and the Washington Monument? My guess is . . . probably not.

That said, I do wish London were a bit more high-rise. Out in the east there are a few tall buildings shielding us like giant glass leylandii from the views of Essex. But there are nowhere near enough. And there won't be any more because of London City airport and the problems of coming in to land between Barclays' boardroom and the executive fourty-fifth-floor bogs at HSBC.

We need to look elsewhere and find a site where designers and architects can run amok with their gigantic cathedrals to capitalism. A site where there are no snails and where there are no ancient views to worry about. A site where we don't worry about what's been lost, only about what we have gained. And I think I have just the spot: right on top of my ex-wife.

30 October 2011

Oh, the vita is dolce. But the music? Shaddap you face

Perfection varies. One man's dream is another man's gangrenous knee. For some, perfection is a Riva Aquarama and Kristin Scott Thomas and getting ready to go to a party on a warm night with friends. For others, it's a damp hillside and a tent. There is, however, one constant. Everybody is in agreement that while the actors and the scenes and the plot may vary, the location is always the same. The location has to be Italy.

Nearly all my favourite places in the world are in Italy. Lake Como. Capri. Siena. And last week I found another.

It's a little restaurant called Volo in the southern city of Lecce, where you can sit outside in the evening, even in early November, and startle yourself with the swordfish carpaccio and the cheese and the local wine. The owner's almond cakes were the nicest thing I'd ever put in my mouth.

The couples that walked by were dazzlingly beautiful. It was impossibly perfect.

It's in a back street, far from the main squares, but even here the lighting is as carefully considered as if it had been designed for Pink Floyd. Where the narrow street went round a corner, someone had lit a candle. Why? Just to bring a bit of warmth and interest to a small place that would otherwise be lost to the night. That's the Italian way.

I think it's true to say that everyone I've ever met has at some point harboured a secret little dream that one day they will have a house in Umbria, where they will sit under the wisteria eating olives they have bought in the local market that morning. It's one of the things that makes us British: wanting to be Italian. They're everything we're not. And they're everything we want to be. Stylish, unconcerned with petty rules, expressive and well-endowed.

Once, I said that to be born Italian and male was to win first prize in the lottery of life. Nobody argued. Nobody wrote to say: 'No. I wish I were Swedish and gay.'

However, while Italy has many things that we can admire and envy and dream of, there is one big thing wrong with it. It has the worst soundtrack in the world. And I'm not talking about the barking dogs that wake you up every morning. Or the idiot with the strimmer in the next valley, or even the swarms of two-stroke motor scooters. No. I'm talking about the radio stations.

Just as it is everywhere else in the world these days, the dial is rammed full of choice. But actually there is no choice at all because, as with the menu in a TGI Friday's, you don't want any of it.

Music snobs have sneered for years about the awfulness of Europop – and with good reason. It's shocking. Things I'd rather listen to than a Belgian Eurovision wannabe include the sound of my own firing squad. Pop radio is just as bad in France and Spain and Germany – home of the Scorpions – but it reaches the fourteenth circle of hell when you arrive in Rome. I heard one tune on the car radio that was so bad, I felt compelled to find the man who'd written it and cut his head off. So imagine my surprise when the next thirty-six songs were even worse.

How can a country that has given the world so much art and literature and electricity possibly think it is acceptable to drive along listening to home-grown synthpop?

How can a country capable of making an engine sing like the best tenor of all time say that Gabriella Ferri sounds like

Janis Joplin? The only way you could have made Ms Joplin sound remotely similar would have been to plug her into the mains.

You think Italian television is bad, and you're right: it is very bad. But it is a haven of highbrow peace and summer'- s-afternoon tranquillity compared with the non-stop barrage of electronic trash that the radio pumps out. All of the shows are hosted by two people – usually a man and a woman – who argue furiously for a few minutes and then play a noise that sounds like a flock of tomcats being killed with a buzz saw.

And then, just when you think it can't get any worse, some- one starts to sing. And the problem with that is: they are singing in Italian. And while Italian is good when you are making love or ordering lunch or even shouting at another motorist, it really doesn't work in a pop song.

'Yes, sir, I can boogie' becomes 'Si, signor, posso boogie'. Which doesn't sound quite right, somehow. And neither does 'Bambina, puoi guidare la mia macchina', which is Italian for 'Baby, you can drive my car'. Singing anything other than opera in Italian is like mixing cement in a tutu or swimming in a ballgown. Messy and wrong.

Plainly, Silvio Berlusconi knows this, which is why he has chosen to release a CD of love songs. I'm not making that up. He really has. Mr Bunga-Bunga used to be the singer on a cruise ship and . . . oh God, I've just thought of something. What if it was the one that employed John Prescott as a stew- ard? It's hard to think of anything worse than being on a cruise ship, but being stuck out there with a million old people, and two million desperate divorcees, being served by Mr Bolshie and crooned at by Silvio? Honestly, I'd rather fire a nail gun into my testicles.

Anyway, Berlusconi fancies himself as a singer and lyricist, and he has a mate who used to be a traffic warden who fancies himself as a guitarist, and the two of them have battled their way through Italy's increasingly difficult financial problems by staying up late into the night writing a selection of smoochy love songs.

I can give you a taste of the lyrics: 'Listen to these songs. They are for you. Listen to them when you have a thirst for caresses; sing them when you are hungry for tenderness . . .' And now, if you don't mind, I'm going to be sick.

Sadly, the album's release date has been put back because of the eurozone problems, but we are assured it will be out in time for Christmas. It will be the ideal gift for someone you don't like very much.

6 November 2011

Down periscope! I've found an airtight way to quit smoking

Over the years, I've done pretty well all the 100 things you're supposed to do before you die.

I've vomited in a fast jet, met Nelson Mandela.

Broken a bone, been arrested and driven a pick-up truck across the English Channel.

However, there is one piece of the jigsaw missing: I've never been on a nuclear-powered hunter-killer attack submarine.

Most people say that subs are their idea of hell.

Living in a narrow tube, hundreds of feet below the churning sea, pooing in plain view, sharing a bunk that's a bit too small with another man and knowing that your wife is at home porking the postman and that you won't have anything remotely interesting to do until your family and everyone you know has been turned into a whiff of irradiated dust.

Pah! If the balloon were to go up tomorrow, I'd break out my white polo neck and join the submarine service in a heartbeat. I know the Royal Navy once dismissed subs as 'underhand and ungentlemanly' but that's precisely why I like them. You sneak up on an enemy, in big, atomic, softly-softly slippers, flick his ear and then run off and hide. He simply won't know you are there until he has exploded.

And have you ever seen a bad submarine film? *Crimson Tide. Morning Departure. Das Boot.* It is impossible to make an underwater movie dreary. Unless you are the Beatles, of course.

As a result of all this, I was very excited when I was invited recently to spend some time aboard the brand-new HMS *Astute*. I knew that early in its life it had crashed into Scotland and then been hit by the tug that came to rescue it. Really it should have been called HMS *Vulnerable*. But I didn't care. I wanted to spend time on a vessel that is as long as a football pitch but which can barrel along, in reverential silence, at more than thirty knots.

Sadly, the trip was cancelled because of what the navy called a 'technical problem'. This turned out, I think, to be a crew member who had run into the control room and opened fire with an SA80 assault rifle. Maybe a better name would have been HMS *Unlucky*.

No matter. I did not hesitate when another opportunity presented itself. This time, I would join *Astute* as it sailed past Key West in Florida to conduct a test-firing of its missiles. Can you honestly imagine anything you'd like to do more than that? Well, Anne Diamond probably could. And those people on *Loose Women*. But I couldn't and so I packed my little bag and last weekend headed over to Miami.

Unfortunately, by the time I arrived, HMS *Unreliable* had had another 'technical problem'. It had flooded, apparently, and was limping north for repairs. So I spent the night in an airport hotel, watched *The Hunt for Red October* and, with a little tear in my eye, came home again.

It wasn't just the disappointment that made me sad, or the wasted trip to Florida.

No, I was looking forward to spending three days in an environment where smoking is banned and you can't just pop outside when you're desperate.

That trip around the Gulf of Mexico was going to be my cold turkey.

Yes, I admit that the multi-billion-pound HMS *Unlucky* is not the best place for a sixty-a-day man to kick the habit of a lifetime. Not with that nuclear reactor humming away in its bowels and all those cruise missiles in its nose. Perhaps this is why other people choose less extreme methods to give up.

Hypnotism, for example. Well, I tried that and it didn't work because when the man with the half-hunter and the husky voice said, 'Right, you're under now,' I put my hand up and said: 'Er, actually I'm not.' This turned into a heated debate that ended when I tried to leave and he said he needed to bring me round first. I let him go through the motions, then I slipped away.

An alternative is nicotine patches. They work for many people – a point proved by the massive private jet owned by the man who invented them – but they make me itch. And gum is equally ineffective, because it makes you look slovenly and possibly American.

Willpower is obviously the best solution but I have the backbone of a worm and the resolve of a field mouse. The idea of striding purposefully past a newsagent with nothing but my head to stop me going inside and buying a glistening pack of Marlboro is as idiotic as setting a lamb chop in front of a Labrador and asking it not to eat.

However, the fact is that I can do without fags. At the moment, I'm spending about twenty hours a week in aeroplanes and at no point have I ever felt the need to attack the stewardess or murder the fat man in the seat next to me. When I can't smoke, I can cope.

Which is why I was so looking forward to breaking the habit on that sub. However, I do think there is another alternative.

Almost every week, *Country Life* is full of islands off the coast of Scotland that are for sale and it strikes me that these would make ideal getaway hostels for weak-willed, unhypnotizable people like me who want to give up smoking but can't.

There would be no handy branch of WH Smith. No nicotine at all between the shoreline and Glasgow. And the only
visitors would come from out-of-control submarines that
have crashed into the beach. And they wouldn't have any
tabs either.

We could therefore head north and have our withdrawal
tantrums away from our families and loved ones. Furniture
could be provided for us to smash. And Wi-Fi so that we
could do a bit of work.

I even believe the government should fund this idea. We
are forever being told that smoking costs the country £5 billion a year: well, for half that ministers could turn Scotland
from what it is now – a handy storage base for submarines –
into a health farm.

13 November 2011

No more benefits: I'm putting the idle on the bread and sherry line

Put your hand on your heart and answer this question honestly. Do you have the faintest idea what's going on in the eurozone? We are told there's a terrible crisis that has mutated and gone airborne, but it's like the worst kind of bad dream, the sort where you can't actually see what's in the shadows. You're running and you're terrified and now you're on an escalator and, aaaargh, it's going the other way!

Angela Merkel, the German chancellor, likened it last week to the Second World War but I think she's wrong. People knew at the time what caused that and they knew what had to be done to solve it.

The current problems facing Europe are more like the First World War.

There are many historians who have spent their lives trying to work out why millions of young men were forced to die in a bloody, muddy French trench, and the upshot is: no one has a clue. The Serbs wanted a port in Turkey. This enraged the Austrians. And they were enraged even more when a Serbian gang shot one of their royal family. They were so cross in fact that Germany decided to attack Russia.

Then, like your big mate in the playground, it declared war on France and, for no reason at all, thought Belgium ought to be roughed up as well. What the Belgians had to do with a dispute between Serbia and Austria, God only knows, but this was the trigger that brought Britain into the war. And for reasons that are as transparent as concrete, that brought Japan in as well.

Of course, they said it would all be over by Christmas. In the same way as they said the financial crisis was solved when the US insurance giant AIG was rescued. But it wasn't. Millions and millions of people were being killed and this caused the Americans to think: 'You know what? We should send some of our young men over to Europe so they can be killed as well.'

People must have sat about back then thinking, 'What the bloody hell is going on?' in much the way that people are sitting around now trying to get a handle on the eurozone crisis. It is unfathomable, a big potpourri of vested interests, national stereotypes, market reactions, furious students, gormless politicians, petrol bombs, trillion-euro debt and unbelievably complex economics. Trying to sort it out is like trying to untangle the headphone lead to your iPod while blindfold, wearing mittens and being attacked by a bear.

What they seem to be doing is throwing out the concept of democracy by replacing elected leaders with backroom technocrats. And hoping that this will appease the computer that controls the markets.

At times such as this the world should turn to the motor industry for help. In the First World War Henry Ford spent time and money trying to organize a peace conference, and few would disagree that the recent problems in Iraq could have been solved more cheaply and with much less death if every single person in the country had been given a Cadillac. This time round, though, it falls upon me to come up with a solution.

We watched last week a new Greek prime minister being sworn into office and, wow, what an office it was. There were elaborate rugs on the floor, ceilings high enough to stage an air display and furniture so expensive that Andrew Lloyd Webber could only dream about it.

This is a country that's preparing austerity measures that will make 1930s Germany look like Donald Trump's bathroom.

And yet it still owns works of art and buildings that are worth millions. Well, all of it has to go. All of it, d'you hear? Including the Parthenon. Sell it to Coca-Cola, McDonald's, anyone. Just sell it.

Europeans are going to have to get used to the idea that, actually, people in India and Brazil and China have got it right, while we are living a life we cannot afford.

This brings me on to the thrust of my brilliant plan. Benefits. At present you go to the doctor and tell him you have a bad back. He confirms this without looking up and as a result the government gives you a box of money every week that you use to sail across the Atlantic or start up a rock band.

Then you have the Jobseeker's Allowance. If you can show that you spend twelve seconds a week looking for work, you are paid to sit about all day, eating chips, drinking Ace and watching DVDs on the obligatory plasma television to which everyone feels entitled. One woman complained recently that the Jobseeker's Allowance was not big enough to pay for her son's funeral and he was lying on the mortuary slab as a result. Yes. Well, there you go, dear.

Obviously, all of this has to stop, and here's what I suggest. Instead of paying people benefits in cash, why not remove them from the decision-making process and instead give them what they need to live? They go round to the benefits office once a week and are given some bread, some meat, some toothpaste, a schooner of sherry and, at Christmas, one or two wooden toys for their children.

This system would reduce the amount of public drunkenness, because those on benefits would have no cash to spend on beer. It would reduce obesity, because they would be given only healthy food. And it would reduce debt, because they would no longer be able to buy hideous settees using money they have no chance of paying back.

More importantly, it would teach us what the rest of the world already knows: that if you want to watch *The X Factor* from the comfort of a button-backed, reclining La-Z-Boy, you are going to have to work.

That would reduce unemployment, stimulate growth and show our friends in southern Europe that the solution to their woes is not replacing the government, or throwing petrol bombs at policemen, or getting the Germans to attack Russia. No. It shows them that if they want to be part of Europe, they need to get off their arses and get a job. Yours sincerely, Norman Tebbit.

20 November 2011

I walked tall into Savile Row – and left a broken man

For years, short people have blamed hereditary variations for their tragic disorder, but scientists announced last week that, actually, shortness is caused by missing genes and wonky DNA.

And since we know that, genetically speaking, human beings are extremely close to plants and animals, we can deduce that people such as Tom Hollander, star of the hit show *Rev*, Richard Hammond and Ronnie Corbett aren't actually people.

They may have arms and lungs but in fact they are shrubs.

I should imagine that if they are capable of thought they will be very troubled by this. Short people have enough on their plates without being told that they are subhuman. They can't see the action at football matches, they have a bad temper and they cannot play basketball very well. But, speaking as someone who has more genes than usual, and extremely strong DNA, can I just explain that being tall is even worse?

Tall people may be more civilized and cleverer than average but on a clothes-shopping expedition we get some idea of what life must have been like for a black person in South Africa during the time of apartheid. Especially if we are a bit fat as well.

We pick out a garment that we like and then we go through the piles to see if there is one in our size. And even if by some miracle there is an XL, it's still suitable only for a mouse. And now some makers are labelling their clothes XXXL, which I'm afraid is offensive.

How dare some anorexic Italian with his missing genes and his defective DNA call a fine human specimen such as me extra-extra-extra-large? I'm not.

Yes, I have long arms, but they are not so long that people point at me in the street and make baboon noises. However, despite this, shirtmakers, with the notable exception of Thomas Pink, have it in their heads that every single adult male in the world has arms like a T. Rex's.

It's the same story with shoes. If you are a girl and you have size 9 feet, which is not exactly going to get you a job in the circus, you will face a choice. Either you become a hippie and go about your business in bare feet, or you go to a shop that caters for transvestites.

I appreciate, of course, that people who make clothes need to earn money and they will achieve a higher turnover if they cater only for Mr and Mrs Average. But clothing is an international business, and in Holland – home to the tallest people on earth – I'd be the man in the middle. Whereas, in fact, I'm the man on his way to get a suit made to measure.

As you probably know, I am not a fan of the suit. It is fine for newsreaders, but I do not see why the world thinks you are being respectful just because your trousers match your jacket. It's idiotic. But the world does think this way and from time to time my jeans won't cut the mustard.

I have had a suit for some time but just recently I've noticed it has started to shrink. The trousers will no longer do up properly, and the jacket feels very tight. It must have been a fault in the manufacturing process. But, anyway, I decided a new one was in order.

Like all sensible beings, I wish to get my clothes shopping done as quickly as possible, but this is not allowed when you are having something tailored. First of all, the man in the shop will want to measure every single part of your body and

I'm afraid his tape measure is made by the people who make bathroom scales. I don't care what it says: I do not have a 38in waist. Just as I do not weigh 16 stone.

After you have been humiliated, and fondled, you will sit down with a book full of nothing but material. All of it is exactly the same. The tailor can do his best to tell you that some of the fabric is heavier, or warmer, but frankly you can pick one blindfold and it won't make a jot of difference. It'll be grey and fine.

At this point you will be asked to choose a lining and, while you know it doesn't matter, you will feel tempted to go for something a bit mad. You want to present an outward appearance of sober restraint, but you want to know that behind the façade of sobriety beats the heart of a Californian surfer. Lime green was my selection.

Then I was asked how many buttons I'd like on the front and how many I'd like on the cuffs – none isn't an option, for no reason at all – what sort of pockets I'd like, and where they should go, and how far down the heel of my shoe the strides should reach. It was like doing a test in a subject about which I knew absolutely nothing.

However, with that done, there was a sense I could get out of the shop and back to the bothersome business of making a living. But no. You then have to make an appointment to come back for a fitting, and your head is screaming, 'Why?'

You can see short people coming into the shop, selecting a suit that fits just fine and getting out again in five minutes flat. You've been there a year, and now a further day is needed for a fitting. Just because you're tall. It's racism. That's what it is.

Eventually I received a call to say that my new suit was ready. And so, having primed my credit card for what would be a eurozone assault on its core, I made yet another trip to London to collect a garment I didn't really like or agree with.

Then, on Monday last week, I was due at a charity event and felt that my new suit could be given its first outing in public. It fitted very well, it was very grey and it made me look very like an accountant. However, I looked very smart right up to the point where someone threw an ice cream at me.

It hit my jacket square on, and yesterday the dry-cleaner said it was ruined.

27 November 2011

Harry's chopper makes mincemeat of Will's whirlybird

This is a tale of two princes. On the one hand we have Harry, a tanned and muscular Adonis who has just returned from two months in the Wild West of America, where he spent a couple of weeks charging about on a Harley-Davidson motorcycle while learning to fly the fearsome Apache helicopter gunship: an airborne dealer of death with the face of a bulldog and the strike of a stingray.

The gunner, who sits in the front, aims by simply looking at a target and then he chooses how the baddie will go to meet his maker. In the explosion from a tank-busting Hellfire missile, or having been hit between the eyes with a bullet from a 30mm chain gun.

Meanwhile, in the back, we find Prince Harry, who will have learnt how to operate each of his eyes independently. One is used to look at the dashboard while the other is focused on a helmet-mounted monocle that keeps him abreast of combat developments. It's a tricky job, flying at about 150 knots, 50ft from the ground, at night, with each of your eyes doing something different. It's also very glamorous and exciting. Which makes Harry a bit like Robert Shaw in *Battle of Britain*. A skilled and brave killing machine in a white polo neck.

Then we have his brother, William, who is also flying helicopters for a living. But in a very different way. He is sitting on a lump of rock in the Irish Sea, watching his hair fall out and waiting for the fog to lift so he can take to the skies in a lumbering Sea King – a top-loading washing machine that is about as advanced as a Morris Minor's trafficator.

While Harry is learning in the desert sun how to take out underground bunkers, William is clumping about in the heavy, swirling skies of Wales, rescuing idiotic ramblers who have forgotten their shoes and Filipino container ship captains who have driven into the side of Pembrokeshire.

Last year crews at William's remote base rescued 244 people, and I'm sure every single one of them gives thanks on a daily basis that the pilots had the necessary skills to pluck them from the icy-cold jaws of death. But what about the rest of us?

Every year I am invited to be a judge for the *Sun* newspaper's military awards and every year I'm racked with guilt. Because I'm always given four options in each category. Three are always men and women from Afghanistan who have defused a bomb with their teeth or taken out a battalion of Taliban with nothing but a spoon. Then there's the fourth, and it's almost always a search-and-rescue chappie who has saved a kid who had been blown out to sea on his lilo.

And I'm sorry but, with the best will in the world, it's hard to give my vote to the chopper man. It just isn't glamorous enough, somehow.

Yes, I know they must get airborne in fifteen minutes and they are rarely called upon on balmy June days, but no matter how difficult it is to hover above a stricken sailing boat, near an invisible cliff, in a force eight gale, it's not quite as gallant as charging down an enemy machine-gun nest armed with nothing but a square jawline and a sense of moral outrage.

Or, if we are sticking with helicopters, it's not quite as *Boy's Own*, *Commando*-comic heroic as the men who land their monstrous Chinook choppers in a sandstorm, under enemy fire, to rescue one of their mates who has been shot.

Helicopters are glamorous and the people who fly them do so because they love it.

This is true of the men who ferry oil workers out to rigs in the North Sea and the guys who fly photocopier salesmen into Silverstone. It's true, too, of both Prince William and Prince Harry. But when you are landing a Chinook in the middle of a gunfight and you know that you have just become the biggest, juiciest target of them all – well, you need balls like the moons of Jupiter and a heart of gold to do that.

And, frankly, we need more Chinooks and Merlins for the wars we are fighting now and the wars we will undoubtedly fight in future. That's why I'm not really surprised to hear that the navy and RAF's rescue services will soon come to an end. Politicians say we can't afford them. Military bigwigs say neither service was set up to rescue Janet Street-Porter if she trips up and gets a hurty ankle.

I'm afraid I have an objection, too. I don't mind paying for schools and hospitals because a civilized country must help those who cannot afford to help themselves. But why should I fund the rescue of a rambler? He or she chose to go out there in the mountains. He or she knew the risks. And I'm sorry, but if they fall over and get gangrene, they can't furtle around in my wallet for assistance.

And, anyway, we have ambulances for rescuing people who are in trouble on land, and lifeboats for those whose boat has run out of petrol. Maintaining a fleet of ageing Sea Kings, then, seems a luxury we don't need and can't afford.

However, there's a problem. Because the service is not being scrapped. It's being privatized. And how, if you don't mind my asking, is that supposed to work?

Are the pilots going to winch up a fallen climber's credit card before they send down the stretcher? Are drowning Filipinos going to be expected to remember their PIN codes before the man in the immersion suit is allowed to help them on board? Or is this just a bit of creative accounting? Paying a private company to do what the government used to do for itself?

Isn't it better to use sponsorship? I should imagine that large companies would love to have their brand plastered all over a search-and-rescue chopper. They could film the heroics and use them in adverts. And have all the rescue crews dressed up in their corporate livery. Let me leave you with a mental image. Prince William in a Ronald McDonald outfit. Or PC World purple. Tell me that isn't a deal worth millions.

4 December 2011

A *Daily Mail* scoop: I'm a nurse-killing Hitler in blue jeans

Have you ever had one of those nightmares where you can neither see nor feel the monster that's attacking you? But you know it's there all right, and unless you can get away, it's going to gobble you up, burn your house down and sell your children for medical experiments.

Well, let me tell you, such a creature exists in real life. It's called the *Daily Mail*.

Like a Terminator, it doesn't know right from wrong. You can't reason with it.

It has no sense of remorse or humility. It's fuelled by hatred. It hates people who are successful. It hates people who are not. It hates people who are fat just as much as it hates people who are thin. It hates everybody. But for some reason it seems especially to hate me.

So, with hindsight, I should have been a bit more wary when the presenters of *The One Show* asked me a few weeks ago what I thought of the public sector workers who had gone on strike. Knowing that a show such as this, with its skateboarding ducks and neat haircuts, isn't really a platform for serious debate, I gave a wishy-washy *Guardian* answer, saying the walkout had made me all gooey and homesick for the Seventies.

And then I said that because I was on the BBC, I ought to be balanced, so I launched into a right-wing tirade, saying they should all be executed in front of their families. We then moved on to a funny-shaped carrot, and that was that.

But, as you may have noticed, it wasn't. Because someone

took the rabid second part of my answer and put it on YouTube. Someone tweeted it. Someone Facebooked it. And then someone asked one of the trade unions behind the strike what it thought about the madman who had suggested on a fluffy-wuffy early-evening show that teachers and nurses should be shot as their children looked on.

Understandably, it thought I should be sacked. Then it had a rethink and suggested it might call in the police. Yes, it wanted me in jail. And so, out of nowhere, a story was born.

The following morning even the prime minister was asked for his views. Happily, he had gone to the trouble of finding out what I'd actually said and suggested I was just being 'silly'. Downing Street even made a joke, saying: 'Execution is not government policy and we have no plans to make it government policy.'

Sadly, his opposite number from the Labour party – a man called Ed Miliband – hadn't bothered to research the issue so, when he was asked for an opinion, he resorted to the reptilian response of every political nearly-man and said my remarks were 'disgraceful and disgusting'. The story was really burning now.

By this stage almost 5,000 people had complained, so the BBC and I decided we really ought to say sorry.

Sadly, this was like pouring petrol on the flames. Ha-ha. So he really did believe that Florence Nightingale should be tied to a post and machine-gunned in front of her mum. The hysteria became worse.

My house was surrounded by photographers. I was doorstepped by an ITN film crew in Beijing. I was papped constantly in Australia. And in Singapore airport on the way home I was patted on the back by the sort of idiotic right-wing lunatic I'd been mimicking on *The One Show*. I'd become a poster boy for the British National Party. I was Adolf Hitler in Levi's.

And it was all ridiculous. During Wimbledon one year I seem to recall that Terry Wogan said he'd like to take a machine gun to all the people on Henman Hill. No one took him seriously, but me, the two-bit presenter of a poky motoring show on BBC2? Somehow an opinion that wasn't even mine had become the nation's No. 1 topic of conversation.

Apparently I had top billing on that week's *Question Time*. I was front-page news for days. Even Bill Oddie was dragged away from his beavers and asked for an opinion. The worst, though, came from the *Mail*. It said that I was a mental, that my mother had been extremely right wing and that my parents had had little empathy with those less fortunate than themselves. Quite what my poor old mum had done to deserve this after years of unpaid public service, I'm not entirely sure.

But that's the trouble with the *Mail*. There are many creatures on this earth that behave in an unusual way. We can't explain how pigeons find their houses from thousands of miles away or how salmon can find the very spot where they were born. But nothing in the kingdom of nature is quite so unfathomable as a *Mail* reporter.

They look human. They have opposable thumbs and are capable of catching buses. But they don't have the capacity for reason. You can tell them what happened. You can prove it. But it will make no difference.

Here's an example. Last week Mark Thompson, the BBC's director general, was asked by an MP if I was a luxury the corporation could not afford. In the *Daily Mail* this became a statement: 'Jeremy Clarkson is a luxury the BBC cannot afford.' Somehow it had turned a question into a fact. I really do believe that in the whole furore over press standards the wrong newspaper has been closed down.

Anyway, I suppose that while I'm here and there's a little bit of space left, I ought really to set the record straight. So here goes. I absolutely do not think that the public service workers who went on strike should be shot or punished in any way.

But, that said, in these times of great economic uncertainty, when everyone is faced with a need to tighten their belt, it's probably reasonable to take the trade union leaders who organized the strike deep into the Blue John Cavern in Derbyshire and leave them there for a little while.

Clarkson calls for trade union leaders to be buried alive. Read it this week, exclusively, in the *Daily Mail.*

18 December 2011

My RAF training was dull – until I got to bomb Piers Morgan

The Ministry of Defence is said to be worried because the computerized simulations it uses to train squaddies in the art of warfare are not as realistic as the commercially available games that most of their teenage recruits play at home.

Really?

I only ask because I am something of an expert in the *Call of Duty* PlayStation games that allow the player to rush about in various locations around the world shooting down helicopter gunships and planting mines on Russian submarines. I am very good at it.

Sometimes, when I play against my fifteen-year-old son, I can last for three or four seconds before he comes round a corner and stabs me in the heart.

However, this is the problem. After he has stabbed me in the heart, we are treated to a slow-motion replay and then we simply press restart and begin again. That's not how things pan out on a real battlefield, I should imagine.

What's more, when we are playing against computerized enemies, we can be shot with heavy weapons probably seventy times before we are made to go back to the beginning. Hmm. I once shot a railway sleeper with a single round from an AK-47 and it split clean in half. So it stands to reason that if you are hit with seventy rounds from such a weapon, the medical description for your condition would be 'dead'.

Yes, the graphics in the *Call of Duty* games are beyond reproach, but for training to be a soldier, they are about as useful as Lego. I mean it. In my own sitting room, I am an accomplished diver but when I go underwater in a real scuba suit, my ears hurt, my mask fills up with water and I get in a bit of a panic.

It's much the same story when searching house to house for terrorists. In the game, you run into the room, get shot seventy times, and still have the wherewithal to kill the bad guy. In real life – and I've actually done this with proper soldiers – they clipped so many things to my belt that by the time I arrived at the house I was extremely out of breath and my trousers were round my ankles. Then an enormous sergeant threw me out of a window.

Training to be a fighter pilot is rather less tiring. Yes, the equipment used by the RAF on raw recruits is in no way comparable to commercially available computer games. There are no graphics at all. No realistic noises.

In fact you begin your training with a piece of equipment first designed in the Fifties to train London bus drivers. It's made from wood and brass and you have to weave a pointer round a route, taking into account a delay between any input you make and what happens as a result. It's very tricky.

If you can master this, you are allowed on to the next stage. This is very modern. It even uses electricity. In short, you have four dots moving across a screen. When the green one passes behind a green bar, you hit the green button. When the yellow one passes behind the yellow bar, you hit the yellow button, and so on. It's a bit like Space Invaders for the terminally ham-fisted and it's very easy.

However, while you are doing this, a combination of ten letters and numbers flash up in front of you. A few seconds after it disappears, while you are still obliterating dots, four more ten-letter combinations appear and you have to say which matches the one that had flashed up earlier.

That makes the game a bit awkward. But what makes it

absolutely bloody infuriating is that at this stage, the dots are getting a bit faster, the combinations are flashing up constantly and you are being asked multiple-choice general knowledge questions that you have just three seconds to answer. It is nowhere near as much fun as *Call of Duty* and it's nigh on impossible for someone like me to get right. Apparently, only about half of those who take this multitasking test emerge with a pass. Doctors call these people 'women'.

Next up is the centrifuge. You are strapped into a large metal egg that is mounted on the end of an arm in a circular room, and then you are whizzed round and round at extremely high speed until sick starts to come out of your mouth.

Weirdly, I was quite good at this. An extremely fit nineteen-year-old cadet who went before me passed out at 3g whereas I took 4g in my stride, no problem at all. This is because I am what medical experts call a 'smoker'. And that means my arterial route map is so clogged up with fat and nicotine my blood is less likely to pool in either my head or my feet. I am therefore less likely to go unconscious.

Annoyingly, the women who pass the multitasking test usually fall down badly when exposed to g. Because according to one man with whom I chatted, the womb is not fastened in place very well and can, when exposed to sustained g, come detached.

So far, then, your training has been nowhere near as much fun as an afternoon in front of the television shooting Russians. Plus, your womb's come off. But then you get to the Eurofighter simulator. And let me tell you this: there is no game on earth, no fairground ride, nothing, that is half as much fun.

In the middle of a giant dome, you sit in an actual

Eurofighter cockpit and in front is a screen that fills all of your peripheral vision. It is showing Britain in minute detail and your job is to fly under bridges in the Lake District, bomb the houses of people you don't like and shoot down other Eurofighters, which can be given Luftwaffe symbols, if that's what you want.

I spent hours bombing Piers Morgan's house and it was so much fun that I had an idea. Instead of spending a fortune making better graphics for wised-up gamers, the MoD should think about doing things the other way round: making a fortune by licensing its Eurofighter simulator to people who have wombs and a tendency for nausea if they ever had a go in the real thing.

Happy new year to everyone.

1 January 2012

A Commons or garden blunder by the duke of digging

Alan Titchmarsh said last week that he had little time for politics because it was always changing. One minute you have the third way and then it's the big society and it's hard to keep up and stay focused. Gardening, he says, is much more important because it always stays the same.

Now when it comes to deadheading and hoeing, I am not really in a position to argue with the son of Yorkshire. But I will have a go anyway. Because, in truth, gardens have changed hugely even in my lifetime and the main reason for this is – drum roll – Alan Titchmarsh.

Every week for many years he told us that our gardens should incorporate stainless steel and other materials that would have been wholly unfamiliar to Peter Rabbit. Then a woman with no bra would make a water feature and someone with sturdy shoes would put up a pergola. None of these things would have been found in any British garden until 19 September, 1997 – the day *Ground Force* was first broadcast.

I can even give you some numbers. B&Q reported that in 1997 it sold about £5,000-worth of timber decking. After *Ground Force*'s love affair with the stuff, the figure had leapt to £16 million. That's a lot of dug-up lawns. And, after a shower, it's also a lot of sprained ankles. It's a lot of change.

But Mr Titchmarsh goes on undaunted, claiming that, in general, views in the countryside haven't changed all that much in the past 200 years. That may be true if you are the

Duke of Marlborough or Prince Charles, but the rest of us? Once again, Alan, I'm afraid I disagree.

Two hundred years ago Britain was a green and pleasant land because cows lived on a diet of grass. However, a cow that has spent its whole life eating turf doesn't look or taste so good when it's reduced to its component parts and displayed in jigsaw form at the supermarket.

We like fat. Which means feeding our cows on foodstuff made from oilseed rape. And that's why Britain is now, mostly, a yellow and pleasant land full of people sneezing and asthmatics searching their pockets for Ventolin.

Our love of fat has had another effect. When I was growing up, the woods were full of children building dens out of twigs and roasting scrumped apples in bonfires made from stolen wheelchairs. That's what I did, anyway. Now the children are all at home eating fat and sitting in front of computer screens.

All you ever hear in a wood these days is the wind caressing the nearby eco-windmill and the occasional blast from a drunken businessman's twelve-bore.

Not that there are many woods because most trees have died of one disease or another over the centuries, or they've been chopped down and turned into decking to feed the trend started by Alan.

There's more. Two hundred years ago the country was crisscrossed with millions of miles of hawthorn, blackthorn and possibly hazel hedgerow, some of which would have dated back 8,000 years. Then along came the tractor and with it the need for bigger fields. Today the countryside where I live looks like the Nullarbor. Only there's more wildlife in that Australian plain.

Despite the best efforts of Kate Humble to convince us

that Britain's yellow bits are teeming with interesting birds and other animals, the fact of the matter is they aren't.

There's plenty of evidence that woodland creatures live on my farm, but thanks to the way we live today they won't be around for much longer.

The badgers will have to be shot because they are killing all the cows, the squirrels because they ruin the trees, the deer because they eat the saplings, the crayfish because they are like aquatic neutron bombs and the pheasants because they are delicious.

So what of the buildings? Yes, the planners do their best to make sure they are broadly similar to how they were 200 years ago, but it's a lost cause. Because a barn conversion, no matter how sympathetically it is done, never looks like an actual barn.

The biggest change to the countryside is the people who live in it. Two hundred years ago the fields were full of people in smocks with nasty teeth, moulding mud into small mounds. Today the only people you see in fields are ramblers. The teeth are the same but the motives are different: they aren't there to make a living; they are there to make sure someone else can't.

They do this either by tearing up crops with which they have a political issue, or by staking a claim to the land, or by walking up and down on footpaths that haven't been used or needed since the invention of the bus.

Then there are the villages. Back in the time when George III was running around Windsor Castle imagining that he might be a hovercraft or a parsnip, most small settlements in Britain were full mainly of terrible debilitating diseases. Now they are full of investment bankers and lovely children called Sophia. Today the average hen is treated more kindly than most people were in the nineteenth century, and you're more likely to have an SUV than an STD.

Mead has become Mouton Rothschild. Bread has got bits in it. Pigs are pets. People think they are clinging on to the olden days by having an Aga, but in fact this wasn't invented until 1922. There is absolutely not one thing that the people who live in the shires today have in common with the people who lived there 200 years ago. Nothing.

The truth is that Alan Titchmarsh got things the wrong way round. The views from our kitchen windows have changed beyond all recognition in the past couple of centuries. Whereas in politics they still have a black rod, a mace and a room full of men making silly noises. BBC Parliament is where you go for traditional values. The countryside? It's just a patchwork of fads.

8 January 2012

No, Fido, the law says you can eat Raffles – not Postman Pat

If you get a job as a lion tamer or a shark juggler or an Australian, it is reasonable to assume that at some point in your career you will be eaten.

But it turns out that the people most likely to be gobbled up by a savage animal are British postmen.

According to a man called Dave Joyce, who is the health and safety officer for the Communication Workers Union – jobs just don't get better than that – millions of postmen are savaged by dogs every year. One had his arm torn off, and six have lost fingers in the past eight months alone.

How long will it be before there is a fatality? Well, according to American research, probably not that long. Over there 2 per cent of the population is bitten every year and the number of deaths averages out at about twenty-six a year.

In Britain we have the Dangerous Dogs Act, which forces the owners of various types of dog to keep them in a straitjacket whenever they are out and about in public. But now David Cameron is saying this legislation should be changed because it's racist. And he's right.

How dare someone suggest that a dog is going to nick your wallet just because it's a pitbull? Or that it's likely to walk into an airport check-in zone and explode just because it's a Japanese Tosa?

The fact is that the most dangerous and violent dog I've ever encountered is my West Highland terrier. Aesthetically, she is the canine equivalent of a nine-year-old girl in a nativity play. She looks unbelievably cute, and when she pricks up her ears, you are filled with an overwhelming desire to pick her up and give her a damn good tickle.

But I don't recommend this because, despite appearances, she is a weapon dog. So far she has attacked the milkman, the postman, the gasman, the poor old dear who delivers the papers and the man who came to fix my computer.

When she encountered a pack of hounds the other day she dived straight in and all of them were driven away. She will not leave a wood until every creature in it is dead, and there is no point cowering in a burrow far underground because she will dig you out and rip you up.

It could be that she suffers from SDS (small dog syndrome), but, whatever the reason, she makes Begbie from *Trainspotting* look like Miss Jean Brodie, and it's only right and proper that she should be given one of the government's proposed 'dogbos' – canine ASBOS. Although I suspect she would simply trot over to Mr Cameron's house – he lives quite nearby – and shove her ankle bracelet up his bottom.

I realize, of course, that I should try to stop her doing these things, but whenever I remonstrate with her, she looks at me as though she is imagining what I'd look like without a head.

She's terrifying. And anyway, the Dangerous Dogs Act says that a dog is entitled to behave in any way it sees fit at home or in the garden.

And this brings me on to phase two of the government's proposals. Because it has just announced that soon owners who fail to control their dogs, even on their own property, will be committing an offence. In extreme cases the local authority could order that the dog be executed in front of its family.

Doubtless, Postman Pat will welcome this news with open arms – if he has any left. But I'm a bit worried because ministers are expected to ensure that dogs will still be free to attack burglars and protect their owners from violent assault.

So your dog will be expected to know the difference between a man who is bringing your electricity bill and a man who has come to help himself to your wallet. Which amounts to the same thing, really.

How on earth is that possible? We all know that dogs can be trained to sit, lie down, offer up a paw and round up sheep. But how do you train a dog to work out what someone does for a living?

And, what's more, how long would it take the nation's burglars to realize that if they dressed up as postmen, in high-visibility jackets and shorts, their victim's dog would give them nothing more than a good licking as they crept about in the darkness, helping themselves to various knick-knacks and items of jewellery?

I've no doubt Mr Joyce, the health and safety man, would suggest dogs that are prone to violent behaviour should be locked up when visitors arrive at the house. Sounds reasonable, but these days, thanks to internet shopping – and the inability of the utility companies to specify when their men will come round to read the meter – it would mean keeping the dog locked up between nine and one, when the man from Tesco is due, and from one till June, which is when British Gas is sending someone round. In other words, your dog would be locked up constantly.

And how long are you able to do that before someone from the Royal Society for the Prevention of Cruelty to Animals comes round with a warrant, a serious face and a stun gun?

It is probably easier to accept that dogs are animals, and that animals sometimes behave in strange ways. A killer whale will loyally take fish gently from the hand of its trainer for fifteen years and then one day, for no obvious reason, it will bite off her arm instead.

A tiger will be used as a prop in a Las Vegas variety show for decades until one day it decides that it wants to liven things up by killing its owner.

And a dog, even the most mild-mannered Labrador, will occasionally turn into a great white shark with the teeth of a hippo and the morals of a Hellfire missile.

This, of course, provides no comfort for Postman Pat, but I think that on this front we can all do our bit to help. Whenever possible, we should use emails and internet banking so we remove the need to have postmen in the first place.

15 January 2012

Skis on, break a leg . . . and take Sarko to the cleaners

So where are you going skiing this year? Val d'Isère? Val de Shnoss? Schnoss de Val? Schnoss Nosh Losh de Schoss? Actually, scrub that. I'm not interested.

In fact, I have no idea why we always ask people where they're going because the one irrefutable fact about skiing resorts is: they are all identical.

There are high ones. There are low ones. There are big ones. There are little ones. And they're all full of wooden boxes and they all look just the same.

They're all full of slightly drunk English people called Harry getting cross with the hunky Italian, who has just given Sophia a dose of chlamydia, and Hans, who has barged into the bloody lift queue again, and the waiter, for charging £260 for what is nothing more than a dollop of melted cheese on bread.

And with Mrs Harry, for wanting to ski all day with the chiselled François, who has never said anything remotely funny in his life and probably has a tiny penis but makes up for these shortfalls by having eyes the colour of aquamarine and cheekbones that could be used to saw through a horse's saddle.

Over the years, I've been to quite a few skiing resorts around the world, and I've always reckoned that the best is a small one in Germany called Wank. Although there are no lifts, there are many long runs. Plus it's not very far away, it's not Swiss – so coffee doesn't cost 800 quid – and there's another good thing about it too. But I can't for the life of me remember what it is right now.

This year, however, I reckon you'll be better off going to France. It doesn't matter which resort you select because you're not there to look at Roman remains, or frescos. You're there to get up, sit on a ski lift, wish you still smoked, get cross with the Germans, get cross with your wife for going off with Monsieur Pommette-Stupide again, have lunch, get drunk, fall over, go to the doctor's, see a man with a ski pole in his eye, have some cheese on bread, pay the licensed burglar who served it £400, go to bed and try hard not to think about what the chalet girls are doing in their room. And since that's what you'll be doing every day, just choose a snowy French town near Geneva airport. La Clusaz isn't bad.

There are two reasons I'm recommending France. First, I think it will be very enjoyable to laugh openly at its downgraded credit rating, and second, thanks to a selection of ambulance-chasing Alpine lawyers, soon you won't be able to go there any more.

We tend to think that idiotic compensation awards could not possibly happen in France, where people seem to spend most of their time examining the latest American trend and then doing the exact opposite. But there have been two recent court cases involving accidents on the pistes, and in one a woman who was left tetraplegic was awarded £830,000.

The court decided that the Pyrenean resort had failed to warn skiers there was ice ahead and that it had narrowed the piste by installing a half-pipe – a U-shaped structure used to perform stunts – for snowboarders. And I'm sorry, but is this not the most stupid thing you've ever heard of?

Warning someone on a skiing holiday that there may be ice ahead is like warning morning sunbathers in St Tropez that come lunchtime it may get a bit toasty. Of course there's ice. And it's all part of the fun, suddenly hearing that terrible clatter, feeling the sudden lurch and trying not to soil your ski pants.

Then there's the business of providing separate attractions for snowboarders. If it were left up to me, I'd ban them from the slopes completely and confiscate their stupid clothes, but anything that keeps them away from normal people, who are being propelled by gravity rather than a cocktail of crystal meth and exotic weeds, has to be a good thing.

There's more, though, because when you go skiing, you sort of know that an injury is not just possible or even likely, but inevitable. Terrible, blood-curdling injuries and severe pain? It's the price you pay for hurtling down a slope at a million miles an hour. So how can you possibly decide, as you hobble home looking like a Day-Glo version of Tutankhamun, that somehow the injuries you have sustained are the fault of the resort?

Sure, if your boss makes you go up an asbestos chimney without ropes and you fall and your head comes off, then yes, there needs to be redress. But skiing? I just don't get it at all.

And, of course, now that the French courts have decided to take a leaf from the book of Hank J. Silverman, attorney at law, of Aspen, Colorado, the cost of ski passes will rise to cover the increased insurance premiums. Worse, there's talk of making helmets compulsory.

Aaaaaaaaaaaaaaaargh. Nothing fills me with such despair as the sight these days of the piste jammed full of people dressed up as if they're Valentino Rossi. And the idea that someone is going to force me to swap my Doncaster Rovers beanie for what is little more than a plastic colander fills me with rage. Next thing you know, they'll try to stop me skiing in jeans.

I realize, of course, that poor old Natasha Richardson sustained a terrible head injury while skiing and died. And if this worries you, then you are perfectly welcome to dress up like a sperm. Likewise, you may choose to equip your children with hard hats – I do – but the idea that the law will be used to force everyone to follow suit is madness.

The good news, of course, is that it hasn't happened yet. So go to France and ski topless, at high speed, knowing that if you fall, you have a win-win choice. Either you can do the decent thing and accept it was your fault. Or you can sue and win such an enormous amount of damages that, single-handedly, you can reduce Nicolas Sarkozy's credit rating to an even more amusing B minus.

22 January 2012

We've got a million words for sex but not one for best friend

We all learn at a young age that the Eskimos or the Inuit or the indigenous Canadians or whatever it is they like to be called these days have several thousand million words for snow.

But, while I hate to ruin your day, I'm afraid it's a myth. They have the same number of words as we do: one.

However, the Sami people of northern Scandinavia – or Samikins, as they prefer to be called – can choose from hundreds of words to describe what is falling from the sky.

And I'm not surprised. I'm at the top of Sweden as I write and the snow is wondrous in its ability to change from one minute to the next. As I look out of the window now, I'd describe it as 'not see-through'. Earlier today it was 'sideways'. Later I'm going out and it will be 'a bloody nuisance'.

Of course, this is natural. I bet the Timbuktuians have many words for 'sunshine' in the same way as Arabs have several for 'sand' and we in Britain have many for 'rain'. Cats, dogs, drizzle, light, soft, heavy, shower, downpour and so on.

Each person in the world needs to spice up his or her life by having new, intricate ways of talking about things that happen often. It's why I have many ways of describing 'James May'.

It's said that English is fairly easy to learn, chiefly I suppose because, unlike the French, we don't insist that tables are female and that telephones are male. But I'm not sure that this is so, because for every word in the English language there are almost always a thousand or so more that mean pretty much exactly the same thing.

Heroin is a prime example. Even though it is used by only a tiny fraction of the population, it is also known as H, horse, black tar, brown sugar, junk, smack, gear and food. That's like nuclear physicists having a million words for the additive used in the manufacture of fuel rods.

When you say someone is homosexual, it's fairly clear what's meant. So why do we have so many other words that mean exactly the same thing? Furthermore, we have only one word for 'red' but several dozen for 'excrement'.

Army people are particularly good at dreaming up new ways of expressing themselves. Often they use acronyms that take longer to say than the words they have replaced – 'IED', for example, is more of a tongue-twister than 'bomb' or 'mine'. Then they will say they have you 'five by five' when they mean 'I can hear you'. Or 'on point' when they mean 'in front', or 'Your ego is writing cheques your body can't cash' when they mean 'You really are a ghastly little show-off.'

It is of course wonderful, great, marvellous and indeed super that we have so many ways of saying things, emoting and expressing ourselves.

It's especially useful for newspaper sub-editors whose first choice of word won't fit on the page. Famously one tabloid sub shouted across the newsroom: 'Does anyone know another word for Wednesday?'

There isn't one, of course. But strangely, in a language in which there is usually so much choice, there is also only one word for 'friend'.

The person whom you call when your wife has walked out, your car has broken down and you need picking up from Scotland at four in the morning is a friend. Whereas the person who is a good laugh but pretends to be a recorded message when you are in trouble is also a friend.

At work you know plenty of people whom you would see

socially only if there had been some kind of devastating plague and everyone else in the world were dead. Somehow, though, they are all friends, as are the people who clutter up your Facebook page. Even though you have never actually met half of them.

I recognize that we have 'acquaintance' to describe those whom we don't know well. But I'm not talking about that. I'm talking about people whom we do. People whom we see regularly. Having only one word for that wildly disparate group is as daft as having only one word for 'biscuit'.

Of course, you may say that 'mate' does the job of differentiation quite well. But that's not strictly true. I have plenty of good mates but I don't know their phone numbers. So I couldn't call them from Scotland at four a.m. Strangely, the ones I could call are not mates at all. They're something else; something that in the English language cannot be explained.

The sort of loyal, faithful soul who would leap in front of a bullet to save you and sit and listen to your woes for the rest of time, pausing only to make you cups of tea, is like the smell of a dead mouse, or the bit of west London between Wormwood Scrubs and Holland Park, or the noise made by hip-hop musicians.

We've been so busy dreaming up new names for cocaine and Piers Morgan that we have been ignoring the fact that some things in life still don't appear in even the largest dictionary. What, for example, is the word for the cheese-like substance airlines put in their sandwiches?

We have a million words for the act of sex – and we even have one to describe the antics of a dog with worms, dragging itself along while sitting down – but if I asked you for a single word for the sensation of having to be happy with something that actually isn't quite good enough, you'd be stumped. We experience it every day with our phones and our computers and even our houses. But nobody's bothered thinking of a word to describe it.

It's not just us, either. Irish has no word for 'yes'. The Warlpiri Aborigines of Australia cannot count beyond two. And in the Amazonian Amondawa language there's no word for time.

It seems, then, that our language is full to bursting with words we don't need and a bit light when it comes to things we do. And on that note, I'm off to fix the thingumajig on the bottom of my boiler near the whatsit.

29 January 2012

Carry on sniping at the rich, Ed, and I just might steal your seat

Obviously, it is important during times of economic turmoil to keep the Labour party as far away as possible from the purse strings. So, I suspect every right-minded person in the land breathed a massive sigh of relief when the unions rode roughshod over the rank and file and selected the completely unelectable Ed Miliband to be their leader.

'Good,' we all thought. 'The silly little man can flounder about in the background while people who know what they're doing set about rebooting the system.'

Last week he was being particularly stupid, suggesting once again that banks should be forced to get cleaners and postboys to choose how much executives should be paid. Really, Ed? Seriously? Do you think that would work?

I only ask because, years ago, Neil Kinnock was on the BBC's *Question Time* discussing a proposed increase in VAT, when a member of the audience leapt angrily to her feet and said: 'It's all right for you. You must be on £90 or £100 a week.'

She genuinely thought that the then leader of the opposition was earning £5,000 a year. And that this was a fortune. So how would she react today if she were appointed by Barclays to sit on the board and pass judgment on bonuses of five million or ten million quid?

She'd have a fit. They'd end up with a postal order for £2.75. Then they'd move to Frankfurt. And Britain's financial services industry would be finished.

The trouble is that thanks to the hysteria surrounding Fred

Goodwin – why doesn't he just change his name by deed poll to Sir Fred? – and Stephen Hester turning down his £1 million of share options in Royal Bank of Scotland, Miliband genuinely seems to have struck a chord.

People really do believe that other people should not be allowed to earn very large sums of money. I don't understand this. Soon the Facebook chappy Mark Zuckerberg will be worth $28 billion and that's fine by me because it makes absolutely no difference to my life whatsoever.

It's the same story with other high earners, such as the editor of the *Daily Mail*. If his pay were slashed and he had to move into a small house, the only people affected would be him and his immediate family.

And yet, people have got it into their heads that if rich people are paid less, it will somehow make them feel better. That's a hateful state of mind.

It's like a gang of ugly people roaming the streets throwing acid in the faces of those who are beautiful. It's like breaking the legs of those who are good at sport because you are not. It's like having cancer and hoping everyone else develops it as well.

David Cameron is scorned by Miliband and by people who leave comments on newspaper websites for being privileged. They say that because he has never had to burn his furniture to keep warm, he doesn't understand what it's like to be poor.

Well, I've never been to the South Pole but I know it's bloody cold. I've never been burnt at the stake, but I know it would be horrid. I've never been shot either but I know it would hurt. You don't need to have experienced something to understand what it means.

Anyway, it's not like a privileged person can help it. It's something they're born with, whether they like it or not. So how dare Miliband suggest that someone cannot do a job because they came into the world in an elegant pram with a silver spoon in their mouth? It's the same as saying they can't do a job because they were born with one leg, or ginger hair, or a black face. It's obscene and Miliband should be ashamed of himself.

But he isn't. He's consumed with envy and rage and he must be stopped before the stupid and the gullible put him into No. 10. Happily, I have a plan.

Miliband is the MP for Doncaster North and it's hard to see how he has any empathy with this former mining community. His mum is Polish. His dad was born in Belgium. He was born in London and educated at Oxford. He taught for a year at Harvard. It's entirely possible he had not even heard of Doncaster until he was twenty-seven.

So what we need is an independent candidate to stand against him. Someone who was not just born and raised in Donny but someone who can stand up and say, in an authentic Yorkshire accent if need be, that every single person in his family tree, right back to the middle of the eighteenth century, lived and died in the area.

Maybe their grandfather on one side could have been a popular family doctor in Sprotbrough. Maybe his or her grandfather on the other side could have run a pub, such as the Royal Oak in Tickhill. Obviously, whoever takes on the job must be able to say they have some mining stock in their genes.

In other words, we are looking for someone who wasn't just parachuted in to a safe seat but who understands and likes the place. Someone who didn't go to Oxford or Harvard but cut his teeth at a journalism college in Sheffield and later on a local paper in neighbouring Rotherham.

Sadly, the only person I can think of who fulfils all these

requirements is me, and I really don't want to give up my day job. It is more fun to drive across Italy in a Lamborghini than it is to smile while on a sponsored jog to raise money for a new youth centre. And yet . . .

I'm not suggesting for a moment that I could topple Miliband. Doncaster North is a Labour party fortress and the pages of history are littered with the carcasses of idiots from the world of television who thought they'd like to be an MP. And yet . . .

Someone has to do something to keep Miliband away from the nation's important decisions. And wouldn't it be fantastic to watch his little face the moment he realized his party had won the general election. But he had lost his seat.

5 February 2012

Having to sell the family silver – it's comedy gold

According to recent research, the average British Johnny worker takes six and a half days a year off sick. And, plainly, this is ridiculous. Nobody is ill that often. So what is he doing that's more enjoyable and more enriching than going to work?

Obviously, after you've phoned your line manager in the morning and made a selection of coughing noises, you can't very well go shopping or to the pub because you might get rumbled. This means you are confined to your house, alone. And what exactly are you doing in there?

Obviously, if you are under twenty-five, you are playing computer games and looking at pornography on the internet. But the figures suggest that in the past twelve months skiving has become very popular among the over-fifty-fives. Last week I think I found out why.

It started off as a normal cold, a bit of a sniffle, and a general sense that the central heating had gone haywire – one minute roasting the house to the point where the floor polish was melting into puddles and the next turning it into an igloo. Needless to say, all the women I met were very sympathetic. 'I suppose it's man flu. Ha. You should try giving birth. Then you'd understand the meaning of discomfort. My baby came out sideways and I was back at work fifteen minutes later. So get your own soup, and if you want to feel better, chop some logs.'

At first I soldiered on very bravely, and it was only because I talked of nothing else that people realized I was ill at all.

But then something strange happened. Normally a cold turns into a tickly cough and a runny nose, but mine didn't.

All the usual symptoms decided to pool their resources in my right ear. My cochlear nerves developed a cough, my tympanic membrane became inflamed and the gallons of snot and mucus that normally come down a patient's nose were channelled into my Eustachian tube until it felt as if my head would burst. Imagine pumping a trillion gallons of crude oil into a condom and you get the idea of what was going on in there.

I was rendered completely deaf to anything happening in the outside world. All I could hear was things happening in my own mouth. Breathing, the production of saliva and the large quantities of blood seeping from under my teeth. The pain was very bad.

A doctor suggested I perform the trick that you do when a plane is coming in to land. Holding my nose and trying to blow out. Well, I did it so hard, bits of phlegm shot at high speed out of my tear ducts. But my ear remained resolutely blocked.

I went to a chemist and bought every single thing it had. Lemsip. Nasal spray. Gum. Tampons. Cotton buds. Nothing worked.

I went to a hardware shop and bought a plunger, which I used on the side of my head. That didn't work, either.

I thought about trying a small bit of dynamite. The pain at this stage was so bad, I wanted to tear my own eye out to reduce the pressure.

By lying on the floor and screaming, I managed to convince friends that I was in a bad way, so they summoned a specialist, who said that he could drain the fluid but only by cutting a hole in my eardrum. That didn't sound a very good plan so I did the next best thing. For the first time in seventeen years

I phoned in sick and went to bed. And there I discovered a morning television programme called *Cash in the Attic.*

The idea is simple. Each day we are introduced by a woman with lovely diction to an elderly couple who have had a few personal problems. He has trouble with his knees. Her mum's ill. They have regional accents and, unlike those who take part in ITV dating shows, do not have any convictions for aggravated burglary. We therefore like them and feel sorry for them.

They tell us that to cheer themselves up they need £600 for a golden wedding anniversary party or a trip to the seaside or some other activity from the 1950s. To help them realize this dream, an expert descends on their house, snouting about in the loft for bits and bobs that could be converted into money at an auction. Grandad's old pipe. A boyhood collection of cigarette cards. A vase they'd bought together on a long-forgotten holiday in Tenby.

The tension is palpable. You know the couple. You've heard their sob story. You can feel the hope in their hearts as the auction begins. And then the despair as the first lot, a chipped teapot, goes for £1.72. And the next for £3.85. And the third doesn't sell at all.

It's tragic. They are selling the trinkets that bind them together as a couple. They are waving goodbye to their history, and at this rate they won't be able to afford even so much as the bus fare home. After every lot the host asks how they feel, but you already know. 'Very, very sad.'

It's the funniest show I've ever seen and I can quite understand why so many people aged over fifty-five are staying at home to watch it. After half an hour I was still weeping with laughter and had completely forgotten about my illness. I was cured and badly in need of more *Cash in the Attic*, so I went on the internet.

You might imagine that watching someone lose everything was a one-off. But no. It seems that the same thing happens every week. People sell off their things and get almost nothing in return. They'd be better off if they'd been burgled.

Cash in the Attic, then, is a show that proves mostly that you have no cash in the attic – just a lot of broken record players and things without plugs. But it's so addictive that already I'm planning what illness I can develop next week.

Lou Reed told us the perfect day was feeding animals in the zoo. He was wrong. The perfect day is a bowl of chicken soup, a packet of digestive biscuits and the spectacle of a woman in towelling trousers selling her collection of antique thimbles for 65p.

12 February 2012

Listen, officer, that gravy boat is the key to Whitney's death

Of course, we have no idea why Whitney Houston died last weekend. We cannot be certain about her state of mind or what toxins may have been coursing around her arterial route map at the time. All we know for sure is that she was found in a bathtub along with a towel, hair ties and a gravy boat. I suspect that the gravy boat is a clue. Because I had what might be termed a 'session' the other night, and as a result I arrived back at home a little rubbery. My legs wouldn't do quite what they were told and I have a dim recollection of having to repeat – several times – my address to the taxi driver.

Once through the door – this was tricky as there appeared to be many locks, none of which would stand still – I needed many things. Beans on toast was a big priority, along with a can of Coke, or as a friend of mine always calls it, the 'black doctor in the red ambulance'. This, I hoped, would settle my tummy, which appeared to be entirely full of sick.

I also needed my chilled floor tile. This may sound a bit strange but I have kept such a thing in my fridge ever since I realized that when you are in a bad way, it's refreshing and comforting to place your face on a cold floor. The trouble with doing this, of course, is that you usually fall asleep and wake in the morning feeling terrible. That's why I keep a floor tile in the fridge. So I can have the feeling of a cold floor while being in bed.

Ah, bed. That's what I always want most of all when I've had a few. Crisp, cool, cotton sheets, quietness and a sense that soon the spinning and the nausea and the pain will be buried deep under a comforting, numbing cloud of unconsciousness.

At no point have I ever thought, 'Right, what I need now is some gravy.' And even if I did have a hankering for a spot of Bisto, I'm not certain I'd have the gumption to decant it into a boat.

And even if I did, I'm fairly sure I wouldn't then think, 'Mmm. I know. I'll go and eat this in my bath.'

Mainly this is because we know from Jim Morrison that taking a bath when you are the worse for wear is jolly dangerous. You would be better off climbing into a hornets' nest or playing slapsy with a venomous snake. No, really. I have in front of me a chart showing some recent figures of how those who died unexpectedly in America went to meet their maker, and it's surprising.

You might imagine that since the soundtrack of American life is gunfire, that many people die in a hail of bullets, and you'd be right: 230 people were shot by baddies and 270 by the police in the same year. Then there were 55 who were pushed, fell or jumped from a tall building, 185 who died while jogging and 36 who went west as a result of a foreign body entering their being through a 'natural orifice'. In other words, 36 people died with a vacuum cleaner up their bottom.

A predictable 26 were killed by dogs, 395 were electrocuted (not by the state), 9 were killed because their nightclothes melted, and 55 by coming into contact with hot tap water. As you might imagine, the list is long and amusing, but there is one sobering fact: 341 people died in the bath.

Since the bath is warm and relaxing, we have to assume that few of these died from heart attacks. And I presume too that those who decided to share their bath with a toaster or an electric fire would be listed under 'suicides', which means that the vast majority of the 341 must have drowned.

I'm sorry, but how is that possible? It's not like the surface is very far away or that you can become entangled in weeds. Nor are you likely to be swept away from the edge by currents. Unless you are Donald Trump, perhaps.

So how does it happen? Do you fall asleep and slip under the water? I find that hard to believe because most people wake up when their ears hear a rustling outside or their noses detect a funny smell. So it stands to reason we would come to if our lungs noticed that, instead of air, we had suddenly started inhaling water.

Of course, when we are drunk we lose many of our senses. Young girls lying half-naked on the streets of Cardiff on a Saturday night testify to this. But not noticing that your knickers are on display is a far cry from not noticing that your lungs are filling up with soapy water. I suspect, therefore, that to die in the bath you have to be massively drunk. Monumentally out of it. So far gone that you have somehow mistaken a gravy boat for a bar of soap.

We can therefore speculate that Whitney Houston was intoxicated when she climbed into her bath last weekend. And judging by various reports, she was in this sort of state quite often.

Which brings me on to all the things her friends have said since that fateful night. They've all talked, with watery eyes, about how honoured they were to have known her and what good times they had together. And I must say, as I sat through the Grammys, listening to all of them weeping and wailing, I thought, 'Hang on a minute. If she was such a good friend, how come you allowed her to get into such a state that she was bathing with a gravy boat?'

And it's not just Whitney, either. Michael Jackson. Keith Moon. Jim Morrison. John Bonham. Phil Lynott. Elvis Presley. The list of superstars who've died, fat, drunk or alone in a puddle of effluent is enormous.

Nearly as enormous, in fact, as all the people who eulogize about them afterwards. People who claim to have been friends but who simply can't have been. That's the sad truth about superstardom, I guess. You end up with a lot of money and a lot of drugs and a lot of staff. But no one to make sure you're okay.

19 February 2012

Lord Lucan must be dead – no one can escape YouTube

Many years ago I interviewed a conspiracy theorist who maintained that Neil Armstrong could not possibly have walked on the moon. He was extremely convincing. First, he said America was lagging far behind Russia in the space race at the time and, as a result, it needed a public relations coup. And then, with the motive covered, he became technical, explaining that whoever took the famous photograph of Armstrong on what he maintained was a soundstage in Nevada must have been at least 8ft tall, and that cameras couldn't have worked because there was too much radiation, and all the shadows were wrong.

He laid all the evidence before me and, I'll admit, I began to think he might have a point.

Of course, I pointed out to him that the whole world had watched the astronauts climbing down the ladder and on to the lunar surface but he smiled the patronizing smile of a man who is winning and said that, actually, we'd only seen it on TV. We hadn't been there. And neither had they.

All I could do was say, rather hysterically, 'B-b-b-but, they had . . .', and that's no use as an argument when your opponent is talking about how they'd have been killed by the Van Allen radiation belt. This is the key to any great conspiracy theory: have plenty of science at your fingertips and keep calm. Make yourself look reasonable and well read, and make your adversary look ill-informed and mad. Do that well and you could convince half the world no one ever walked on the moon because it's made of cheese.

This, of course, brings us on to Lord Lucan, who, on the evening of 7 November, 1974, re-enacted what sounds like a scene from a game of Cluedo by murdering his children's nanny in the basement, bopping his wife on the head with a piece of lead piping and then disappearing into thin air.

Since then he has been spotted – usually by lunatics – in various parts of the world: Australia, New Zealand, Holland, India and riding through the lost city of Atlantis on a horse that answered to the name of Shergar. Now comes a claim from someone who was close to Lucan, saying that he fled to Africa and that he has seen his children on at least two occasions over the years.

She seems to meet all the requirements of the conspiracy theorist. She has no apparent motive for making the claims: there is no financial reward. She knows more about Lucan than you or I do. And she is calm. However, I think I am in a position to make a counterclaim that makes more sense: Lucan is dead. I don't know how he died, or when, but it was certainly before 11 June, 1997.

It was on this date that a chap called Philippe Kahn took some pictures of his newborn baby on his mobile phone and then wirelessly transmitted them to more than 2,000 friends and family around the world. This is acknowledged to be the birth of instant visual communication.

It has grown so quickly that today it is impossible for anyone to do anything, anywhere, without being found out. There is, for instance, a clip on the net of James May in a forest in Romania, taking a leak. And if you listen carefully, you can hear me saying: 'James. I wouldn't do it there. You'll end up on YouTube.'

Last summer I tried to sneak away to Uganda for a couple of days. It was hopeless because even though most of the locals do not have access to a lavatory or a classroom, almost all have a mobile. Which meant that within five minutes of my leaving Entebbe airport, friends in England were calling to ask why I'd gone to Kampala.

I'm nothing more than the presenter of a motoring show on BBC2 but I've been photographed, Facebooked and tweeted in Syrian market towns, Russian strip clubs, African wildlife parks and Chilean deserts. My family never bother to text to see where I am: they just go online.

There are no secrets any more. BBC reporters may be banned from Iran but those in Tehran who wish to get their message to the World Service can do so with a pay-as-you-go Nokia. I wonder how far the Arab Spring would have got without YouTube. And how much time is spent at GCHQ just looking at online crowd scenes?

Of course, you could argue that Lucan is a peculiarly British story and that the people of a remote African state would not bother to photograph the face of a man with whom they were entirely unfamiliar. True enough. There are no 'Wanted' posters in Mrs Mbutu's post-office window and the local police do not have an e-fit of the errant peer etched on to their craniums.

But this doesn't make a jot of difference. The television show I make is not shown in France but do not think for a moment this means I can walk through the streets of a small Breton town without being spotted. Because on every street corner there's a camera-toting tourist from a country where I am known. Today you can run but you can't hide. And that's why we know Lucan is dead.

It's why we know too that Armstrong walked on the moon. Because 400,000 people were involved in the mission and, if it had been faked, it's inconceivable that one of them wouldn't have put on an electronic veil and gone online to say it was all done with smoke and mirrors just outside Las Vegas.

There's another reason, too. The Van Allen radiation belt. There was a time when, to research this, you would have to get on a plane and go to the Smithsonian Institution in Washington. Now you can find out all you need to know with a couple of clicks. And guess what. It's a band of radiation around the earth that can affect an astronaut's eyesight. So, if Armstrong really had been to the moon, it's reasonable to say his vision would have been damaged.

Well, now let me leave you, calmly, with this little nugget. After returning from space, 33 of the 36 Apollo astronauts who went to the moon developed cataracts.

26 February 2012

Those pesky stars just won't expose themselves any more

Everybody likes Sir Michael Parkinson. Everyone trusts him, too – me most of all. He often pops up in ad breaks to bring news of a life insurance plan that will pay for my funeral with enough left over to provide cash gifts for my family, and even when he's halfway through I'm reaching for the 'Yes, I'll have that' button.

I reckon that at a push he could get me to sign up for a coach tour of North Wales.

But last week we began to see evidence that age had started to eat away at his marbles. Because he wondered out loud and in print why there were no traditional interview shows on television any more, and why, with Jonathan Ross and Graham Norton, it all had to be played for laughs.

That is easy to answer. In the olden days newspapers reported news. They were filled with earnest stories from around the world and weren't interested in the opinions or photographs of those who earned their crust by being in *Are You Being Served?*

So, to keep themselves in the public eye, the people from *Are You Being Served?* had to appear on a chat show. They would beg to appear on *Parkinson* and they would work hard beforehand, thinking up amusing anecdotes and practising their lines. It was important to do this because if people liked them, they would get bigger parts and one day perhaps get a job on *Robin's Nest*. If they were really popular, who knows? They might become David Niven.

If you have been listening to the endless parade of tabloid

newspaper people who have appeared at the Leveson inquiry, you would imagine that this sort of thing still goes on today. And you'd be right. But instead of appearing on chat shows, people who are orange and have no discernible talent employ public relations people to plant pictures in the papers and the glossy magazines of them cuddling African children and giving money to tramps.

That is why, the argument goes, they can hardly complain when they are subsequently photographed fondling an *X Factor* hopeful or vomiting on a homeless person. If you use the press to climb over the parapet and into the public consciousness, then you belong to the press. And it can do what it likes with you.

However, people who are not orange and who rely on their talent to get work, rather than a PR man, are caught in the same net. There is a photographer on every beach, waiting to spot evidence of a bingo wing or orange-peel thighs.

The star takes someone out to dinner and they are snapped. They go home with them afterwards and it's front-page news. They get into a cab and we are told what sort of underwear they've chosen.

I don't know Daniel Craig. Never met him. And yet I know, just from skimming the *Daily Mail*, whom he is married to, where the marriage took place, how many times he had been married before and what he's doing at the moment. It's the same with Brad Pitt. If he'd been around in the Sixties, we'd know what films he'd been in and to whom he was married. But that's it. Today, we know he hasn't seen his granny for years and even what brand of cigarette he smokes. I reckon I know more about Brad – whom I have never met either – than I do about my own children.

So, if I asked him to appear in *Top Gear*'s 'Reasonably Priced Car', he'd think, 'What's the point? I could sit here, in my lovely Los Angeles home, smoking Marlboros and drinking a fruity burgundy with my lovely girlfriend, Angelina. Or I could get on a plane, fly to England, drive a drab little car around an airfield and then have a yellow-toothed buffoon ask me a lot of damn fool questions that are pointless. Because everyone knows the answers already. Because they read OK!'

The only way you can get an even vaguely interesting guest on a chat show these days is if they are on a publicity tour, promoting their new book or film or fitness DVD. They are dragged into the studio in chains, poked into the chair by a film company exec with a cattle prod and nailed in place to make sure they don't wander off or fall asleep.

They don't know who the host is, what the show's about or what country they're in. All they know – because off camera there's a woman with three BlackBerrys and an agitated face tapping her watch – is that they've got only five minutes before they have to catch a flight to Germany to go through the whole rigmarole again. And then on Tuesday it's Uruguay.

Of course, the host could sit back and ask about their relationship with their father – a Parky trick – but there isn't the time. And on the part of the interviewee there isn't the inclination either. Plus, the modern audience isn't interested in a man's soul. Just his manhood and where it has been.

That's why I have such huge respect for Graham Norton and Jonathan Ross. I've tried to do what they do and it's bloody difficult. Seriously. You try keeping the viewers happy and entertained while talking to someone who doesn't want to be there, has nothing to say, feels worn out and is deeply aware that tomorrow the *Daily Express* is going to run pictures of him snogging a horse.

And there's no point being rude or refusing to talk about

their 'important' new project. If you do that, in future the film company will simply book all their big stars on to a rival show. You'll end up with Mr Motivator, Fred West's cleaning lady and Christine Hamilton. If you want the big names, you have to massage their egos, you have to show clips from their new DVD and you have to provide the laughs. Because if you don't, you've had it.

That is what Michael Parkinson has to understand. The talk show is dead. It was killed by OK! and the army of paparazzi who trawl the streets bringing us news of Sienna Miller's underwear.

4 March 2012

Three men go into a bar . . . and I couldn't hear the punchline

Tell someone you suffer from insomnia, and invariably those who do not will reply by saying they never have any trouble getting off to sleep – 'Head hits the pillow and I'm out like a light.'

This is spectacularly cruel because, as Ben Elton once observed, when someone in a wheelchair says they can't walk, you don't reply by saying: 'Crikey. I can. I can also hop and skip and jump.

'And now, if you'll excuse me, I'm going to dance with that pretty girl over there. And maybe later we shall have sex, which I bet you can't do either.'

What we *do* do when we meet someone in a wheelchair is steel ourselves to make absolutely certain that we treat them exactly the same as anyone else. We outstretch an arm in greeting, even though there's a distinct possibility no such gesture will be reciprocated. We ask them how they are, even though it's plain to see they are not well at all, and can't reply anyway because they have tubes coming out of their nose.

We spend ages yabbering away to desperately ill children in vegetative states, assured by their parents that it's all going in, even though there is not one iota of evidence to suggest that's the case. We may not give up our seat to a pregnant woman any more, but we will move heaven and earth to help disabled people go about their business.

We design buses that kneel down. We install ramps outside public buildings. Taxis have bright yellow grab handles so they can be located more easily by those who are hard of seeing. We even host a separate Olympic Games for disabled people. And you know what? A lot of us think it'll be better and more uplifting and more brilliant than the real thing.

But despite all this, despite our big hearts, there are still some disabilities that don't rock our compassion genes at all. Insomnia is just one. Gout is another. So is erectile dysfunction. And people with haemorrhoids? When we watch them walking around like cowboys and wincing when they sit down, we actually find it funny. Well, I do.

We don't laugh when someone has a hideous growth on their face. Not when they're looking, anyway. But when friends say they have piles, I'm gone. Lost in a sea of mirth, and inviting them to play a game of musical chairs.

Then there's deafness. We don't find this funny at all. There'd be no point because the poor soul with the wonky ears wouldn't be able to hear our taunts. Instead – and don't argue with this – we find it annoying.

The voice-activated devices in cars make my point especially well. You ask the electronic woman to set the satellite navigation system for home and she tunes the radio to a hip-hop station. Or says 'Pardon' over and over again. Soon you are seething.

And it's the same story with people. You say something to someone who's hard of hearing and it's deeply exasperating to have to say it again. 'Why? You have ears. I can see them. And maybe if you bothered to remove some of the hair in there, they'd work a bit better, you old bat.'

So we say what we've said again, as if we are Brian Blessed addressing people at the back of the Albert Hall.

Which is the same as picking up someone's wheelchair, with them in it, and hurling it down a flight of stairs because we have been momentarily inconvenienced.

I bring all this up because I've been aware for some time

that my hearing is not quite as good as it was. And how much sympathy do I get from the family? Absolutely none at all. My wife huffs a lot, claiming that I can't hear orders to feed the dogs or do the recycling but can hear someone saying, 'Would you like a glass of wine?' from three miles away. At least that's what I think she's saying. I can't be sure because, as I said, I'm a bit mutton.

Then you have the kids, who speak at 5,000mph, say the television is too loud and turn it down to a point where, to me, every show is basically *The Artist*. Richard Hammond is worse. When I don't hear what he's said – and it's hard sometimes because his mouth is very far below my ears – he just calls me a 'deaf old t***' and moves on to the next story I can't hear either.

And then last month I got a hole in my eardrum, which made everything worse. Well, not everything. Because at least I now can't hear what Vince Cable is on about. But it also means I just have to guess what people sitting to my right are saying. This is slightly awkward when you are at a dinner party, but very tricky indeed when you are hosting the chat-show segment of a TV programme and your guest is Slash, the guitarist formerly of Guns N' Roses.

Despite making loud music, he is very softly spoken, which in my world means he makes about as much noise as a mouse in lambswool slippers tiptoeing across a shag-pile rug. I'd ask him a question and I could see his lips moving but I had literally no idea what he was saying. Occasionally I'd pull a serious face, hoping he wasn't talking about the hilarious occasion when he set Axl Rose's trousers on fire. And sometimes I'd politely titter, praying to God he wasn't chatting away about his mother's funeral. Since he didn't try to punch me, I think I got away with it, but I won't know for sure until I see the interview air this evening.

The worst part of being deaf, though, is you lose your ability to find things funny. You can just about hear the first part of a story – the setup – but, for comic effect, the amusing ending is usually delivered quickly and quietly, which means you don't hear it at all. 'A Pakistani, a Liverpudlian and a Scot walked into a bar. And the Scot said . . .' That's as far as you ever get.

And let me tell you something. Losing your legs or your sight or your ability to sleep is terrible. But losing your ability to laugh? That's the worst thing of all.

11 March 2012

Even James 'Thunder' May couldn't make wind farms work

I predict that thirty years from now there will be just one wind turbine in Britain. It'll have been kept as a reminder of the time when mankind temporarily took leave of its senses and decided wind, waves and lashings of tofu could somehow generate enough electricity for the whole planet.

Schoolchildren will be taken to see it by newly enlightened teachers – in the way that today's children are invited to smirk at the Sinclair C5 – and then afterwards they will be shown a clip from last weekend's episode of the usually brilliant *Countryfile* programme to demonstrate just how silly the human race had become.

The normally trustworthy John Craven said with not a hint of doubt that climate change was fuelled by our love of cars, power, milk and lamb chops. Yup. He told us that cows and sheep produce methane, which is twenty-five times more damaging to the atmosphere than carbon dioxide, and must be fitted with a breathalyser as a result. Well, James May produces a lot of methane. I know because he's sitting next to me right now. Should we fit him with a breathalyser?

Craven also told us not to buy British tomatoes, which are somehow bad for the environment, and to eat instead South American bananas, which somehow are okay. It's all very confusing.

At the moment, you may be ambivalent about wind power. There are probably no plans to erect turbines near your house so you don't care, as long as your kettle works. You may have even heard from a Liberal Democrat energy minister who announced last week that living next to a bird-mincing, noisy monolith was good for you. Though what he meant to say was, 'I like seeing my name in the papers.' Fine, here it is. He's called Ed Idiot. I may have got the spelling a bit wrong but it's something like that.

The fact is that despite what Mr Idiot says, you will soon care very much about wind farms because the government is about to introduce a scheme in which big companies will be charged for emitting carbon dioxide. The idea is to encourage power companies to produce more energy from renewable sources. Of course, the cost of paying to emit all that CO_2 will be passed on to you. The result: your fuel bill is about to sky-rocket. Only last week the executive director of Which? took the unusual step of telling the government it was 'writing a blank cheque' with householders' money. How much money? Oh, about £1.4 billion by 2015–16.

And why? Simply to keep a few lunatics happy. And they really are lunatics. Over in California green enthusiasts are planning to carpet the Mojave desert with solar farms that turn heat into power to feed Wilbur and Myrtle's La-Z-Boy swivel recliner.

Sound good? Well, yes, but now some Native American lunatics have popped up to say, 'How can we make some cash out of this?' Sorry. I don't know why I said that. I'm muddling them up, perhaps, with Australia's Aboriginals, who always announce after every great mineral find that the land has deep religious, spiritual and ecological significance.

Anyway, Hiawatha reckons the solar farms will not only destroy the natural habitat of the desert tortoise and the horny toad but also irritate the gods. He says he wants to use the sun for power but not if it disturbs 'sacred sites, pristine desert, the turtles or the toad'. He then adds that he was placed on earth to be a guardian of 'harmonious equilibrium', and because of that, one green energy company has been forced to spend $22 million (£14 million) – of Wilbur and Myrtle's money – to ensure harmonious equilibrium prevails and the toad can continue to be horny in peace. Of course, this is normal. It is one of the things I enjoy most about members of the loony left. The reason they never get anything done is that they spend most of their lives arguing among themselves. It is hysterically funny and there was a prime example on *Newsnight* recently.

An angry man from the People's Front of Judea argued that climate change was the biggest problem in the world ever, and that we had to embrace nuclear energy if we wished to live beyond next Thursday. Then up popped an even more angry woman from the Judean People's Front, who said that to combat climate change we had to plunge into nature's bountiful larder.

She said at one point that we couldn't use nuclear power because it required too many state subsidies. Forgetting, perhaps, that wind power needs even more. And that uranium is just as 'natural' as wind.

What am I saying? She wasn't forgetting it at all. She wants us to use wind power even if it doesn't work. And perhaps that's what people like her are really after. A world with no electricity. 'What has electricity ever done for us? Apart from light, heat, warmth, better toothbrushes, iron lungs and Mildred's vibrator?'

As far as the Judean People's Front is concerned, a world without electricity will drastically reduce the gap between the rich and the poor. And it may have a point, because in the sixteenth century, before Michael Faraday ruined everything, Henry VIII had a broadly similar lifestyle to the people who mucked out his horses.

The problem with wind power is demonstrated well in

Denmark, which embraced the technology years ago. And as a result not a single conventional power station has been shut down. They're needed for the days when the wind doesn't blow, or blows too strongly. Worse, ramping them up and down all the time uses more energy than keeping them working constantly. So the Danes have paid a fortune to build wind farms that don't work, and, in return, their normal power stations are producing even more CO_2 than they did in the past.

And that's all I've got to say on the subject because I've just remembered I'm doing some shows in Copenhagen later this month and I don't want to be showered in Danish phlegm. It'd be disgusting because, of course, they don't have enough power to charge their electric toothbrushes.

18 March 2012

Smell my cologne: it's called Girlie Tosh pour Homme

Throughout history you were a child, and then you were an adult. You went from 'Baa, Baa, Black Sheep' to Brahms in an instant. But then in the early Sixties the word 'teenager' started to appear in dictionaries and a whole new species was created. A species that had money, but no mortgages to worry about or children to feed or bills to pay.

The creation of the word 'teenager' probably opened up the greatest marketing opportunity since Jesus rose from the dead.

Because now, between 'Baa, Baa, Black Sheep' and Brahms, there was a yawning seven-year gap into which some boogie-woogie could be inserted, along with a burger and Coke and maybe a pair of Levi's.

The trouble is that today every possible way of exploiting a teenager's naivety has been explored. As a result, some bright spark in a pair of thin designer spectacles and a polo-neck jumper has decided that it is time for a new type of customer to be created, a new breed that needs feeding with a whole new range of stuff it didn't know it needed. So he has come up with a concept called 'men'.

Up to now, it has been fairly simple being a man. Eat. Sleep. Mate. The only real complication was knowing which days you were supposed to make a lovely quiche lorraine and which days you were supposed to come home in a bearskin coat and engage in some rough-and-ready grunty-pumpy over the Aga. Certainly you never had to worry about what was written on the waistband of your underpants.

You do now, though. You are also expected to rub mud

into your hair, polish your nails, buy things to make your teeth shiny and white, and join a gymnasium to stay in shape. And gone are the days when you bought a wristwatch so that you could see what time it was.

Open any glossy magazine and it's full of chisel-jawed men advertising watches while doing something heroic and outdoorsy. Wear a Breitling and you are no longer Gareth Cheeseman from accounts. You are Clint Thrust and at weekends you race your Confederate Hellcat round the pylons in the Nevada desert. Wear an IWC and you are a deep-sea diver. Wear an Omega and you are George Clooney.

Arrive at a film premiere these days and some silly little girl with a microphone will ask: 'Who are you wearing?' I'm not wearing anyone, you idiot. I'm wearing what was on the floor next to the bed.

This doesn't work any more, though. A man is expected to be sharp, to know how many buttons he should have on the cuffs of his suit jacket and not to wear a shirt with a breast pocket.

It gets worse. On a recent British Airways flight I plunged into the in-flight shopping magazine, where a note from the editor said that because spring was in the air I should treat myself to a new fragrance. There were many from which to choose.

At work, apparently, I should use Acqua di Parma, which enables me to smell 'clean, fresh and professional'. What!? How can you smell professional? It's not a concept that has any known aroma. It's like smelling shy, or indifferent, or sad.

Then there's Eternity for Men, which is 'ideal' for rugged types as it smells of the sea. What sea? The Mediterranean? The Caspian? Or the little pool outside my holiday cottage? That's full of sea and has the ability to induce nausea from a distance of a thousand yards.

Perhaps we would be better off with 212 VIP Men, which is warm and sweet with sexy notes of vanilla, sandalwood and tonka bean. What is a tonka bean? Well, I've taken the trouble of looking it up and the news is not good. It's banned by America's Food and Drug Administration, it causes liver damage in rodents, it is worshipped by practitioners of the occult, bits of it stop your blood clotting and it is used to flavour tobacco.

You want to wear that to impress the ladies at a nitespot in Peebles? Go right ahead.

But count me out. In fact, count me out of all this tosh. The BA magazine explains that I should layer my fragrances, starting with shower gel and then applying deodorant, aftershave, balm and eau de parfum. I don't have time for that. And I don't need a handy cut-out-'n'-keep guide on the differences between eau de cologne and eau de toilette because I don't want to smell like a German or a bog. I want to smell of whatever I've eaten or done. I'm a man, and scent is for women.

Shopping is for women, and that's what our friend in the thin spectacles seems to have forgotten. I realize, of course, some men like to waste their free time mooching about in town, having their hair cut and buying silly clothes. These people are called footballers, or restaurant critics. They have scrotums but they are not men, really.

A proper man would have to think long and hard if offered the choice between selling his children for medical experiments and going into a cubicle to try on a pair of trousers. Trying on trousers is, without any question or shadow of doubt, the worst thing that can happen in a man's life. It is waterboarding dentistry with added cancer.

Look at a man in a supermarket. He is a fast-forward blur of activity, buying only what he needs at that precise moment, and then getting the hell out of there. Supermarket shopping for a man is like pulling off a plaster – it's best done as quickly as possible.

How many men have you ever seen in the Bicester shopping village in Oxfordshire? None. This place is a little slice of heaven on earth for women, but for me it's one of the circles of hell – a street full of stuff that doesn't fit.

So the marketeers can push as hard as they like with their idea of getting men to waste their time and money on sandalwood and mousse and fabric and handbags. But really they'd be better off targeting dogs. Men will only shop for noise-cancelling headphones. And we have some of those already. So leave us alone.

25 March 2012

A cheap booze ban will just drive your pooch to hooch

Presumably because no one from Foster's or Strongbow has thought to give the Conservative party a suitcase full of money, the government is drawing up plans to end the sale of cheap alcohol. This will make super-strength cider more expensive than petrol, vodka more pricey than myrrh and gin, quite literally, a mother's ruin.

Hilariously, people in V-neck jumpers think this new law is designed to combat the hordes of young girls who go into Cardiff on a Saturday night and wake up in the morning with heart disease, chlamydia, fat thighs and twins. But I'm afraid they've got the wrong end of the stick.

The law is designed primarily to prevent the downtrodden masses from getting so drunk that they fail to turn up for work the next day at the munitions factory. It was always thus. When the breathalyser was introduced here in 1967, an Old Etonian acquaintance of mine was overheard on a pheasant shoot, speaking to his local chief constable. 'It's a bloody good idea,' he said, before adding, in a nudge-nudge way: 'Of course, you won't be stopping anyone in a dinner jacket, will you?'

Frankly, the end of cheap alcohol and two-for-one strong lager offers will do nothing to prevent the passage of the port decanter clockwise around the M25 but it will make life just a little bit more complicated on either side of the M8. Because, unable to afford the traditional passport to inebriation, poor people will simply start making their own booze.

It'll be like prohibition in America, and that's a worry

because have you ever tried moonshine? No, of course not. You wouldn't be sitting there, reading this now. Unlike many other extremely powerful drinks, it is very moreish. And that's a problem because after two sips you start to hallucinate. I had a small glass in North Carolina last year and can report that if it catches on here people will be going to work imagining they are on the bridge of the Battlestar Galactica. I know I did. After another small glass I became convinced Richard Hammond was a Cylon and tried to kill him.

There's another problem, too, which came crashing through my front door last weekend. Our hayloft has no hay in it. Instead, we have vats in which thousands of sloes spend several months being marinaded in gin. Then, last Saturday, while you were out in the garden annoying your neighbours with your new strimmer, we were decanting gallons of the resulting pink refreshment into pretty little bottles we buy from the internet. It's one of the things the *Guardian* has not yet discovered about Chipping Norton: it's twinned with Tennessee.

Anyway, the discarded fruit was deposited on the compost heap, friends were invited over and the drinking began. It was a wonderful night with much laughter and, later, a Chinese takeaway to try to soak up some of the sick. Unfortunately, as we enjoyed life in the kitchen, our dogs were out in the garden, snouting around for tasty treats. A rabbit, perhaps, or their favourite snack – a nugget of horse poo. This time, though, they caught a whiff of something even more interesting and delicious than manure. It was coming from the compost heap, so off they trotted and – joy of joys – it was like the pudding counter at a Harvester. Thousands of wonderful sloes, all gooey and soft. They ate the lot.

Have you ever seen a drunk dog? It is funny beyond belief. A drunk human sort of knows why he can't climb a simple step but a dog does not. A dog cannot understand why its legs have stopped working properly and why it has four noses. You can see the bewilderment in its sad little eyes as it lurches about, leaning on trees for support, walking backwards and wagging its head. I laughed so hard that some of my spleen came out of my ears.

Unfortunately, while you may be tempted at this juncture to fill your dog up with Cointreau to see what happens, I must point out that this is police state Britain and you would be contravening Section 7 of the Animal Welfare Act 2006. A few years ago a Bristol man was given 150 hours' community service and banned from keeping warm-blooded animals for a year after he was found guilty of giving his bull mastiff two-thirds of a can of Stella Artois.

The reasoning's simple. You can take away half your average Brit's liver and three weeks later it'll be as good as new. But dogs are like Native Americans. One sip and you will be faced, as I was, with an invoice from the vet for the use of his stomach-pumping facilities.

The problem, however, is that I did not feed my dogs alcohol. They stole it. And now that cheap alcohol is going to be banned, I suspect that vets will be seeing a lot more of this sort of thing. Because at present beer is either sealed in a tin or sealed in you.

Furthermore, a bottle of gin has a screw top that would defeat the most determined dog. But when people are boiling up sacks of potatoes and every garden shed in the land is a steaming still, booze will not be sealed. It'll be in buckets and bathtubs, an easily reachable treat for the family pet.

So a ban on cheap booze will have several effects. All of them unpalatable. The poor will be forced to stay at home on a Saturday night, drinking potato juice from an oil drum. This means the pubs, kebab shops and nightclubs they used to visit will close. And there'll be no upmarket replacements because the rich won't dare go out in case they're attacked by a drunken dog.

As I've said many times before, it is the job of a government to erect park benches and replace the bulbs in street lamps. If it tries to do anything else, such as deciding who puts what in their mouths on a Saturday night, the moonshine-addled poor will go mad, the rich will be eaten, the country will become peppered with ghost towns and your West Highland terrier will end up with an ASBO.

1 April 2012

Exploding Art Snob – it's the best Hirst masterpiece yet

I've been to church. I've seen *Mamma Mia!*, the musical. I've played Monopoly. I've sat through a double chemistry lesson. I've even been to Lord's. I am therefore an expert on boredom and how deeply it can affect a man's ability to be rational.

Some people are able to fall asleep when they are bored. But in me it triggers a reaction in the liver, which starts to produce bile. This brings on a dull ache in the pit of my stomach, and then, if the boredom doesn't stop, the pain spreads, coursing around my arterial system like a super-heated river of fire.

This is known as impotent rage. Inwardly, I curse at the man who dreamt up the periodic table and the idiot who thought it would be a good idea to turn Abba's songs into a story on the stage. How dare they steal my time from me like this? I am not given to violence as a general rule but when I am bored I can survive the agony only by imagining how the person responsible would look without a head. This is why I am not capable of going on a guided tour of an art gallery.

Once, I went to see the *Mona Lisa* at the Louvre. Then, having seen it, I decided it was time to go to the Zinc cafe for lunch. The guide, however, had other ideas and for thirty minutes talked non-stop about the bloody woman's smile. Then we moved on to the background and why Leonardo da Vinci had made it all wonky. 'Because he wasn't a very good artist?' I suggested. She didn't hear because she was droning on about every single detail of every single thing that ever happened in Italy in the sixteenth century.

I suspect this is why the *Mona Lisa* is guarded by bullet-proof glass. To stop bile-fuelled visitors smashing it up to silence the guides.

I don't mind a bit of art. I once spent an enjoyable thirty seconds looking at Picasso's *Guernica* when it was still at the Prado in Madrid. And a full minute enjoying Turner's *Rain, Steam and Speed*. I must say that Diego M. Rivera's epic mural at the Detroit Institute of Arts is very good. That sustained me for a full five minutes.

What I cannot abide, though, is how art is intellectualized and analysed to the point where I want to club someone to death. Why is the Mona Lisa's smile smudged? Oh for crying out loud. Maybe his brush skidded. What was on Constable's mind when he was painting *The Hay Wain*? Who cares? Being promoted to sergeant, probably.

All of this brings me on to Damien Hirst, whose retrospective exhibition opened in London last week. I quite like his stuff. I have some of his butterflies and I enjoyed his diamond-encrusted skull enormously.

However, those of an artistic disposition plainly don't like Hirst at all. Every report I've seen about him starts off by telling us how much money he has made and how this is disgusting. Why is it disgusting? Who says an artist is not allowed to be successful until after he is dead?

I know the whole country has become infected with a terrible hatred for anyone who is successful, but the loathing reaches new heights when the person is an artist.

'Look at you in your big house, you bastard. Why aren't you in a squat, eating LSD and cutting your ear off? You're not an artist. You're a businessman.'

Arty types also ask whether what Hirst produces is art. I do not know the answer to this but if the experts are reduced to gibbering wrecks by a can of soup or a woman with a smudged smile, then why is a cow's head covered in flies not worthy?

I think *The Hay Wain* is a terrible picture. It may work all right on an old lady's coaster but I'd rather have one of Hirst's chemist shop displays on my wall than a £2-billion Constable Turner greetings card any day of the week. And I'm sorry, but in my mind the Ferrari 275 GTS is an easy match for anything Rembrandt ever did.

Watching serious arts people dismiss popular efforts is like listening to some dismal mouse of a woman who has written about life in a Burmese laundry claiming that what Jilly Cooper does is not literature. It just is.

Then we get to the big issue. How much of Hirst's work is actually Hirst's work? This is the snide aside we are asked to ponder after we've been told the rich bastard is just cashing in on other rich bastards.

Apparently, Hirst has a workshop in which a team of craftsmen – and, I presume, butchers – is called upon to produce his stuff. This is a terrible con, we're told. But is it?

I only ask because, back in the Renaissance, Leonardo started out helping great artists of the time with difficult bits of their work. And when he became a master himself, he also used people to do the stuff that was boring.

Strangely, this brings me on to what many believe was the world's first electronic computer: Colossus, the machine that was used to help break the Nazis' Lorenz code. It was built by an engineer called Tommy Flowers, who worked at the Post Office Research Station in Dollis Hill, London. Heard of him?

No. But I bet you've heard of his fellow codebreaker Alan Turing. Today he is revered as a genius. A bit of the Manchester ring road is named in his honour and some like to believe the Apple logo is a homage to the man who, persecuted for his homosexuality, took his own life by biting into a poisoned Granny Smith. Steve Jobs, Apple's late boss, once said: 'It isn't true but, God, we wish it were.'

This is the thing about Hirst. Did he apply every single diamond to the skull? Did he cut that cow in half himself? Did he kill the shark? Probably not. And does it matter? Does it matter how rich he is? Do you care whether it's art or not? If you like what he dreams up, no.

8 April 2012

Where's the Dunkirk spirit? Doing a runner to Australia

So, would I ever emigrate? Well, if I were given limitless funds, the morals of Silvio Berlusconi, a large house full of lesbians on the Italian lakes, a private jet to shuttle my friends back and forth, some skin that didn't burn every time the sun came up, a sudden effortless gift to speak foreign languages and a capacity to deal with extreme boredom, then, yes, I would be delighted to leave Britain and spend the rest of my days under some wisteria, drinking wine and eating cheese.

However, last week a survey revealed that very nearly half of British people would be willing to up sticks and emigrate with nothing more than what they had in the bank and a stick or two of Ikea furniture.

Frankly, I find this weird. Of course, there are one or two minor irritations with Britain and one big one – the smoking ban – but as a general rule it's a country that works pretty well. We have a climate of such miserableness that we don't spend all day at work wishing we were at the beach, we have free healthcare, our friends are here and, unlike any other nation in the world, apart from South Africa, we have mains sockets that don't zap us every time we want to charge up a mobile phone. Why, then, is 48 per cent of the population either actively planning to emigrate or seriously considering it?

The answer, I think, is to be found on page 141 of a new book called *What It Is Like to Go to War*. It's by a chap called Karl Marlantes, who was educated at Yale and Oxford before joining the US marines. In Vietnam he was awarded the

Navy Cross, the Bronze Star, two navy commendations for valour, two Purple Hearts (some kind of Love Hearts, I presume) and ten air medals. His first novel, *Matterhorn*, is by far the best book I've ever read.

In his latest effort he talks about loyalty, saying he obviously had none for the men under his command since he was asking them to follow idiotic orders to charge a hill. So why did he stand up and say, 'Let's do it'?

He reckons his loyalty was to a mythic projection called the unit. 'It has a thousand specific names,' he says. 'It's the Marine Corps, the legion, the 82nd Airborne, the Gordon Highlanders and the Oxfordshire and Buckinghamshire Light Infantry.' In short, he ordered his men to charge the hill because of 'all those flags, all that history, all that dying'.

I think he makes a very good point. Because we can be sure that, while flying combat missions over Libya last year, Tornado pilots from the famous Dambusters squadron will have wanted to do a good job for the benefit of their senior officers, the Libyan rebels and their political masters.

But I bet that in the back of their minds they mostly wanted to do a good job to honour the ghosts of Guy Gibson and those bomber boys who smashed the Möhne and Eder dams and made the squadron famous.

We don't just see this loyalty to history in war, either. You sense when you watch Wayne Rooney play for Manchester United that he wants to win for the fans, himself, the lovely Coleen . . . and all those who died in the Munich air crash.

When I turn up for work at the BBC, somewhere not quite at the back of my mind is the need to do a good job for the spectre of Lord Reith.

Of course, when you are working, fighting or playing for your 'unit', you need to have a sense of pride about what that unit has done in the past. You don't dwell on its failures.

Rooney does not start every match remembering a far-distant 7-1 drubbing by Accrington Stanley. When I think of the BBC, the first thing that comes to mind is not *Nationwide*'s skateboarding duck.

But this is exactly what we are told to do when we think about Britain. We are a country that raped the world in the name of greed. We sent the Cossacks back to the Soviet Union after the Second World War. We enslaved a continent. We starved the Irish. Every time Tony Blair stood up, it was to apologize on our behalf for some heinous crime of two centuries ago. US marine commanders don't do that. They don't spur their men on by saying, 'We got our bottoms kicked in Vietnam.'

That's what happens here, though. What are the battles that we all remember most clearly? Hastings. The charge of the Light Brigade. The American war of independence. Arnhem. Notice a common thread? They're all battles we lost.

Then there's the whole issue of what it means to be British. For hundreds of years that was the easiest question of them all: we were polite, fair-minded and aloof. We went to work on big red buses, in bowler hats. We had a queen and beefeaters, and when times were hard, we didn't grumble.

What are we now, though? How would you define our 'unit'? It's pretty tricky. We're a nation of bankers, Simon Cowell, football hooligans, royalists, Muslims, tea shops, benefits cheats, Elgar, pearly queens and Polish plumbers.

The French work tirelessly on maintaining their spiritual history and their ways, which is why most people in France are proud of their country. You don't get Nicolas Sarkozy campaigning for re-election by saying, 'We are the surrender capital of the world!' It's the same story in America, where you can be black, white, rich, poor or Donald Trump – it doesn't matter because everyone subscribes to the American way. And as a result, the only American who has ever emigrated is Gwyneth Paltrow.

At the Olympic opening ceremony, I bet you any money there's not a single thing we recognize as being typically British. We don't even know what 'typically British' is any more. We're a unit embarrassed by our past, uncertain about our present and frightened by our future. Which, I presume, is why nearly half of us would rather be Australian.

22 April 2012

Welcome to the fifty-fourth series of *Top Gear*. I'm seventy-seven, you know

Alarming news from the pointy bit of London. According to various financial wizards, millions of fiftysomethings will have to stay at work until their arthritic fingers are bent double and their whole face is one giant liver spot.

Pensions experts say that if you want to enjoy a reasonable standard of living in your retirement, you need an income of around half your gross working wage. For a man thirty years ago, that typically meant keeping your nose on the grindstone until you were sixty-four. Today the average retirement age for men is sixty-five.

But because of all the gloom, analysis suggests that people will soon have to stay at work until they are at least seventy-seven. And at that age what jobs, exactly, are these poor victims of the system expected to do?

Certainly I don't want a surgeon to operate on any member of my family if he arrives in theatre on a mobility scooter, with a worrying wet patch on the front of his trousers. Nor would I put a seventy-five-year-old in charge of a deep-fat fryer. Bomb disposal is right out as well.

The human body is now a longer-lasting item than at any point in history, but by the time it is seventy-seven years old, chances are that there is something wrong with it. And I'm sorry, but how would you feel if your trial judge were suffering from the early stages of Alzheimer's? Or your computer repairman had Parkinson's? Or the ref turned up at Old Trafford with a guide dog?

It is great if a hale and hearty septuagenarian with a fine

mind and bouncy legs wants to work as a lollipop lady, but forcing someone who is tired and ill and a bit mental to go out and earn a crust demonstrates to me that the whole system is properly broken.

After forty years of commuting and dealing with office politics and bringing home the bacon, it's only right and proper that people should be able to put their feet up. I cannot imagine for one moment how horrible it would be for me still to be earning a living by driving round corners too quickly and shouting when I'm seventy-seven. It'll be a young person's job by then, and rightly so.

I have dreamt for some time now of the day when I can wake up without an alarm and spend my hours pottering about in the greenhouse, killing insects and wearing a jumper with holes in it. No more deadlines. No more five a.m. starts. And, best of all, no more James May.

However, today I'm not dreaming about it any more. For reasons that are far too dreary to explain, I'm not actually working at the moment. I'm in a period of temporary retirement. And it is without any question or shadow of doubt the worst thing in the world.

I spend all day inventing things to do, and then inventing reasons why it's better to do all those things tomorrow. I look in the fridge every half an hour to see if by some miracle I missed a plate of cold sausages on my previous sixteen visits. I look at stupid things on the internet. I read instruction manuals. And I thank God for the Leveson inquiry. I've watched it so much I've even developed a crush on the girl who sits over Robert Jay's right shoulder. Each morning I speculate on what she may be wearing that day.

It's not just the boredom, either. It's the expense. Yesterday I thought it would be a good idea to have the interior of my car retrimmed. Then I went out and bought some garden furniture. I spent most of this morning looking at old Mercs on a website, and unless someone gives me something to do soon, I know I'm going to buy one.

Then there's the drinking. If I'm out, I'll have a glass or two of wine with lunch. But I've no one to go out with because they're all working. So I have a glass or two on my own. Then, since there's no reason not to finish off the bottle, I do. Then I go back on the internet and buy something else that I neither want nor need.

It's no good expecting to survive on half your usual earnings when you are retired. You will need ten times more than Bill Gates just to make it through till lunchtime.

Of course, it is possible to keep busy without a chequebook. Mostly this involves going for a walk. And pretending to be interested in all the things that you see. On my last foray into the countryside I spent fifteen minutes examining the latch on a gate. Then I photographed a flower that I'd found so that I could look it up on the internet when I got home. It's just ticking away the moments that make up a dull day, as a wise man once said.

Naturally, for me, this period of inactivity will end and I'll go back to work. But in a real retirement you are simply filling time until a doctor shoves a tube up your nose, looks at his chart and uses the worst word in medicine: 'riddled'.

Retirement may conjure up visions of lemon barley water and grandchildren and a nicely tended garden by the sea, but actually it's a period of catastrophic boredom that has only one ending: death.

You should bear that in mind tomorrow morning when the alarm goes off and you have to trudge through the rain to the bus stop so that you can spend all day dealing with broken photocopiers and emails from people who have electronic diarrhoea.

You may imagine on the way home, when you are forced to sit next to a lunatic on the train, and it's late and you've spilt jam on your suit, that it would be nice to put your feet up one day. Well, mine are up now – and it isn't.

We should therefore rejoice at the economic turmoil that means we now have an excuse to keep at it until we are seventy-seven. Because even if your job is emptying the lavatories at an Indian army base in the tropics, it's better than not having a job at all.

29 April 2012

Heston's grub is great – but so what if your date is ugly?

I'm sure you will be interested to hear that at a glittering ceremony in London last week a herd of food enthusiasts announced with much trumpetry that the best restaurant in the world is a place called Noma in Copenhagen.

Not as far as I'm concerned it isn't, because I went to have lunch there last month and it was shut.

So we ended up at another top restaurant, where, for starters, we were given Kilner jars full of steam. How loony is that?

Another restaurant to feature high up the list of excellence is Mugaritz, in San Sebastian, where, provided you are not blown to pieces by a Basque on the way, you are served 'edible stones'. This is ridiculous. Of course all stones are edible, except perhaps for the ones that you find in Donald Trump's kidneys. But I can't see why you would want to put one in your stomach. Or pay for it.

There is a madness in the world of restauranteering at the moment. I've been a few times to Dinner, Heston's services in Knightsbridge, and while I think the food is absolutely unbe-grigging-lievable and the service even better, it is bonkers to make meat look like a tangerine and to make ice cream with nitrogen.

It's photo-opportunity food, really. Fun once in a while, but it has as much to do with reality as those split-to-the-crotch frocks that actresses wear on the red carpet.

So, to bow down before the genius of Heston Blumenthal, or a man who has the balls to make people pay for steam or stones, is absolutely fine if you are a food enthusiast or a silly rich person, but why publish a list of best restaurants as though it were somehow definitive? Because if you are working on the tills in the Dunfermline branch of Asda, it sort of isn't.

Those who compile the list may turn round at this point and say: 'Aha. But you, Mr so-called Clarkson, work in an industry that spends half its life giving out awards.' You're right. I do. And giving awards for cars is daft, too.

This year's European car of the year is a hybrid called the Vauxhall Ampera, and while I agree that it's a fine and noble choice if you are a climate-change fanatic with no sense of style, it is emphatically not fine if you are Elton John.

Film awards make no sense either. This year the Oscar for best picture went to *The Artist*, which I enjoyed very much indeed. But a fifteen-year-old lout with a fondness for vandalizing headstones and stealing cars would probably describe it as 'a bit boring'.

Every single night of every single year the Grosvenor House hotel in London is filled with Jimmy Carr, who is presenting Geoff Stokes with an award for being the best fertilizer salesman in the north-west. Geoff isn't, though. It's just that his company has bought more advertising that year from the organizers.

BAFTA, or to give it its other name, the Islington Appreciation Society, seems to reckon that *Made in Chelsea* is better than *Downton Abbey*.

But surely that depends on whether you are an elderly snob or a teenage airhead. Choosing between the two is like trying to decide whether you would rather be a petrol pump or a tree.

The fact, then, is this. Apart from the Rose d'Or television festival, which is usually wise with its choices, all awards are a senseless waste of human endeavour. But at least with cars and television shows and films everyone is eligible to chip in with their ten penn'orth. Because we are all exposed to these things every day, we can listen to what the experts say and then make up our own minds.

Eating out, though, is different. Being told that the best restaurant in the world is in Copenhagen is of absolutely no use if you live in Swansea, it's 7.30 p.m. and you're feeling a bit peckish. Then the best restaurant in the world is the kebab joint round the corner.

The food revolution is getting completely out of hand. Steve Hackett is about to start a tour of Britain, which is huge news, but it's lost in the hubbub of chitchat following reports that someone called Ferran Adria, who used to have a caff in Spain, is about to open a tapas bar in London.

Similarly, we are expected to pause for a moment to reflect solemnly on the news that Danny Meyer is thinking of setting up shop in Britain. So what? He's a bloody cook, for crying out loud, and he will probably charge you £400 for a bit of limestone served on a bed of steaming helium.

The problem, I think, is that these days far too much emphasis is placed on the food. I know one well-respected restaurant in London where everything tastes and looks like something else.

You order pigeon because you like pigeon. It arrives at the table in a banana fancy-dress costume and tastes like rabbit. And I want to grab the chef by his swarthy Latin mutton chops and ask him why he has ruined my dinner.

Now I just order something from the menu that I don't like, knowing there's a good chance it'll taste like something I do.

It gets worse. I ate at a restaurant the other day where the menu said, 'Chicken, flattened by a brick.' Seriously now. Do we really need to know how the creature died? 'Pheasant. Shot in the face by a drunken Freemason.' 'Deer. Run over by a Toyota.' Is that what you want?

My point, I suppose, is this. Food is only a small part of what makes a dining experience great. Acoustics are just as important. So is lighting, especially if you have an ugly date. But by far and away the most important thing is the company.

The best restaurant in the world, then? It may be in Denmark. That's what the experts say. But really it's the one where your friends go.

6 May 2012

One hundred lines, Miliband Minor: 'I must not show off in class'

Recently a number of people in suits were summoned to appear in front of a panel of other people in suits in a fantastically expensive and time-consuming attempt to find out exactly who listened to Sienna Miller making her hair appointments and precisely what sort of horse David Cameron prefers.

Interestingly, some of the people in suits said one thing while others said quite the opposite. Which means that a panel of politicians has had to try to work out who has been telling porkies. Fine. But then what?

You may imagine that if you tell a bare-faced lie to members of Her Majesty's elected government, your liver will be removed and your head placed on a spike in the Brent Cross shopping centre. There's even been talk of offenders being locked away for the rest of measurable time in a deafening room under Big Ben. But it doesn't quite work that way.

To find out how you are punished, we need to go back to 1957 – the last time a non-politician faced being reprimanded for contempt of parliament. Inevitably it was a journalist, the fearsome John Junor, who had wondered in his newspaper's editorial why extra petrol was being allocated to politicians during rationing. (To feed the generators in their duck houses, probably.)

And what was his punishment for this heinous crime? Was he hanged? Incarcerated? Deported? Or is that what the famed mace is for? Did they use it to stove in his skull?

No, actually. In fact, he was summoned to the bar of the

House of Commons, which is quite literally a white line across the floor, where he was made to say sorry. I'm not kidding. They took one of the most powerful newspaper people of the time and made him stand on the naughty step. And that makes me wonder. Would the use of primary school punishments work today?

At present there is no way of punishing a banker who has been greedy. We know that what he's done is wrong. And, in the wee small hours, he knows what he's done is wrong. But how can he be made to pay for his sin? At best he can be drummed out of the lodge, made to resign from the golf club and stripped of his knighthood. But that's about it.

We see the same problem in broadcasting. If I make a mistake, can Ofcom take away my children? Fine me? Put me in prison? No. Time and again I read in the *Daily Mail* that I've had my 'knuckles rapped' for 'sparking' some kind of fury. But the truth is, nothing of the sort ever happens. I don't even get a call from the headmaster.

And, who knows, maybe I might be rather more careful if I really did face having my knuckles rapped with a blackboard rubber. Maybe a banker would be a bit less willing to lend money to someone who couldn't pay him back if he thought that he might be forced to stand in Threadneedle Street wearing a dunce's hat.

And then we must move to Greece, where last weekend many people voted for a party that wants to break out the retsina and party like it's 1999. You may think that, in a country that claims to have invented democracy, that's their right.

But since their blinkered stupidity means the rest of the world has been thrown into a state of economic panic, there's no doubt in my mind that they should all be made to stand outside for a while.

I definitely think this kind of school-room justice would work in football. At the moment the yellow card is the premium economy punishment.

A barely noticeable uplift from a straight free kick but a long way from the club-class red. A yellow card doesn't mean anything. But what if the offender were made to go and stand in a corner while sucking his thumb for ten minutes? There would be far fewer late tackles, I bet.

Then we have weather forecasters. They tell us it will be a lovely day tomorrow and then bounce back the following evening showing not a hint of guilt that the picnic you organized on their recommendation was washed into the River Test by hailstones the size of small Toyotas. Would it not be a good idea, if they've made a mistake, to force them to deliver the next evening's bulletin in their school uniform? Certainly I'd like to see ITV's Becky Mantin do this.

It's in public life, though, that the humiliation would work best. All last week Ed Miliband was being foolish, acting up in front of his friends by saying his party had nothing to do with the country's woes and that the current leaders are interested only in millionaires. It was constant party political sound-bite diarrhoea, and there's only one punishment that would work. He needs to be put on silence. And Ed Balls, the fat-faced henchman who sits next to him in the debating society? Make him hold his hand out, palm upwards, and get the serjeant at arms to hit it with a ruler.

And what of the man – he exists somewhere – who chaired a meeting about Britain's naval requirements for the next fifty years and said: 'Yes. I agree. Even though we have no planes to put on the deck, we shall spend £10 billion of someone else's money building two new aircraft carriers'?

Why is he not summoned to the office of Philip Hammond, the defence secretary, and made to write out,

1,000 times: 'I must not order very expensive warships that can't possibly work.'

Other options under my new regime are detention on a Saturday afternoon – I think Theresa May could do with a couple of hours for the Heathrow immigration debacle – and the one thing that used to bring me up short in my school days: the threat of my parents finding out that I'd been smoking while eating in the street, with village boys, in home clothes.

This is what we do with George Osborne. We simply tell him that if he doesn't stop making silly mistakes in class, we shall write to his mum.

13 May 2012

Girls, gongs and JR – if only I'd worn a jockstrap

All awards ceremonies are the same. You sit on an uncomfortable chair for seven hours, watching an endless succession of orange people you don't recognize getting gongs for their contribution to God knows what, and then, when it's your turn, you either have to look pleased that someone else has beaten you, or you have to bound on stage and, through gritted teeth, say that you couldn't have won by yourself. When, in your heart of hearts, you know you could. And indeed have.

The hugely prestigious Rose d'Or festival in Switzerland is different, though. Very different. As different as the petal of a cornflower is from the crankshaft of an American monster truck.

I was there because *Top Gear* had been picked for a gong. And the first indication that the evening might be a bit unusual came when I opened the obligatory goody bag. At this year's Oscars the nominees were given tickets to go on safari in Botswana, a watch, beauty products and a testicular check-up. In Switzerland I was given a tube of toothpaste.

I was then ferried in a smallish Vauxhall to the red carpet, which was a teeming mass of guests, none of whom seemed to have understood the dress code. Either that or in Switzerland 'black tie' means 'anything you fancy, up to and including army boots and a jockstrap'.

Feeling a trifle overdressed, I was ushered by an enthusiastic PR type with a clipboard to a waiting camera crew. The interviewer, a deliciously pretty Swiss girl, plainly had not the first clue who I was. But I'd been presented to her so she had to say something. And what she said was: 'Eeeeerm?'

Since there was no suitable answer to that, I was guided by my elbow to the make-up room, where an enormous German woman pointed to a small pimple on my nose and said to everyone within 500 yards: 'Wow. That is a big spot.' She set to work with a trowel, and fifteen minutes later I was on my way to the green room.

Here I expected to be surrounded by the greats from international television. Simon Cowell. Jay Leno. Piers Morgan. And that madwoman from *Homeland*. But the only two people I recognized were Larry Hagman and Kim Wilde. As we chatted, I was fitted with an earpiece and a microphone and then I was pushed on stage.

It wasn't what I was expecting. Instead of a lectern from where I could deliver my acceptance speech, there was a sofa, adjacent to a massively breasted woman behind a desk. I took the applause from the very large audience, checked out the position of the cameras and sat down.

Now I don't know why, and with hindsight I see it was extremely arrogant, but I assumed the big-breasted woman would speak to me in English. She did not. To my dismay, she addressed me in one of the many languages I don't speak: German.

Happily, a rough translation of what she was saying started filtering through my earpiece. Unhappily, I couldn't make out any of the actual words. So in my right ear I had the Swiss woman speaking in German, and in the left one I had an unseen translator speaking in inaudible tinny English. Small wonder the United Nations is so useless at getting anything done.

Just as I thought things could not get any more confusing, she produced a pair of blacked-out spectacles, told me to put them on and then played Prince singing 'Little Red Corvette'.

You may remember that scene in the movie *Lost in Translation* when Bill Murray appears on a Japanese chat show and has no clue what's going on? Well, that's how I felt.

Mercifully, I was soon allowed to remove my glasses, and there in front of me was an Australian girl from the second *Transformers* film carrying my award. There was applause and then a man with a clipboard took me backstage, past Larry Hagman and back to my seat.

It wasn't over. No sooner had I sat down than that man with a clipboard was back. 'Schnell, schnell!' he said. 'You must go back on stage.' Once there, I was given a massive bunch of flowers and told to stand at the back for reasons that were unclear.

Then they became clear. The big-breasted woman announced the arrival of a newcomer. The audience went wild. And out tottered an elderly gentleman, who began to make a speech. Well, when I say a speech, it wasn't really. A speech has peaks and troughs. It has pauses and moments of light relief. This had none of those things. It was as if he'd been invited on stage to read out every single entry on Wikipedia. Or to count from one to one billion.

After twenty minutes of standing under the hot lights, with my face planted in a hay-fever factory, and wishing I'd opted for the jockstrap rather than my heavy suit, I started to feel quite dizzy. But still the man was droning on. And I know enough about how autocues work to know he wasn't even a third of the way through.

I tried to focus on something important. At first I wondered why the autocue was being projected in widescreen. Then I worked it out. In German, when 'Danube steamship company captain' is one word, you can't have a 4:3 screen or nothing will fit. Having solved this riddle, I started to see if it was possible to will yourself to death.

Luckily, before I succeeded, a woman I did not recognize leapt up from the front row of the audience, thanked the man and took an award from the *Transformers* girl, and that was that.

Afterwards, Larry Hagman was confused. He'd flown all the way from Los Angeles and hadn't won anything. I had, though, so I decided to hit the after-show party. Here a slim and well-dressed Dutchman invited me to spend the night with him 'disco dancing'. I made my excuses and left.

Back in my room I watched Swiss television. It's not like ours in any way. Which is probably why they gave a gong to *Top Gear*.

20 May 2012

I'm desperate to be a German – call me Gunther Good-Loser

You would have thought that after fifty-two years of being absolutely useless at absolutely everything – except perhaps the word game Boggle – I'd have learnt how to be a good loser. And yet I'm deeply ashamed to admit that I haven't.

Vince Lombardi, the famous American football coach, once said, 'Show me a good loser and I will show you a loser.' And that's the trouble. He's right. And I don't want to be a loser. I can't bear it. I can fix something that looks nothing like a smile on my face and I can extend my hand in a show of gracious defeat but, inside, it feels as if I'm on fire.

I lost a close game of table tennis recently to the very tall man in glasses who appears on the television show *Pointless*, and I was gripped in the aftermath by an almost uncontrollable need to stab him in the liver and jump up and down on his bleeding body shouting 'bastard'.

It was much the same story when I watched England lose to South Africa at the Stade de France in Paris five years ago. The etiquette of rugby provides no place for unsportsmanlike behaviour, so when the game ended I dutifully turned to the enormous Boer behind me and said, 'Congratulations.' But, like the 'p' in 'ptarmigan', there was a silent bit. And it was this: 'But I hope when you get home they put a burning tyre around your neck, and the necks of the entire team who have beaten us, you big, thick-necked, southern-hemisphere ape.'

Conversely, when Jonny Wilkinson kicked that last-minute drop goal to clinch the 2003 Rugby World Cup for England,

I spent an hour ringing random numbers in the Sydney phone book and laughing fanatically. This means I'm not a good winner, either. I fear this may be a British disease.

Let us examine the case of Colin Welland, the former *Z Cars* actor. When he won an Oscar for his screenplay for the film *Chariots of Fire*, he held it aloft and told the assembled moguls that 'the British are coming'. Which was inappropriate and, as it turned out, entirely wrong.

Then, later, when he failed to win a Bafta for the same film, he was caught on camera slumping back into his seat and looking as though someone had just launched a surprise sword attack on his scrotum.

When a sporting event finishes, I want close-ups of the losers. I want to enjoy their pain. Sir Ferguson is, we're told, similar to this. Even though he rarely fields the best team in the world, he is a consistent winner, partly because of his capacity for hard work and partly because of his unparalleled experience. Mostly, though, the reason his team win a lot is because the players know that if they lose they will be attacked in the dressing room afterwards. Losing is what defines us. When we think back through our military history, what names leap out of the fog? The American war of independence. The charge of the Light Brigade. Arnhem. In Britain we remember and worship John McEnroe for his tantrums and Paul Gascoigne for his tears. Gore Vidal could have been talking about us when he said, 'Whenever a friend succeeds, a little something in me dies.'

The *Daily Mail*'s website is a massive hit mainly because that is its mantra. In England success and those it envelops are to be ridiculed. Winning is a bad thing.

Was I alone in thoroughly enjoying the last day of the Premier League season? Because we had almost an hour of unbridled joy watching the anguish on the faces of Manchester City fans as they thought the title had gone to Manchester United. And then some icing on the cake when the boys in red realized at the last moment it hadn't.

I'm so unpleasant, in fact, that when a sporting event finishes, I never want to see the winners running around looking happy. I want close-ups of the losers. I want to enjoy their pain. And instead of the winning team being paraded around on an open-top bus, it should be the losers. That would make for much better television.

Unless they are German. The best losers . . . in the world.

It would be easy, and stupid, to suggest that they've had enough practice in recent times but, truth be told, in very recent times they haven't really had any practice at all. Motor racing. Industry. Football. They are alvays ze vinners. They even have the only eurozone economy that's growing.

Last weekend, though, it all went wrong for them. Bayern Munich lost the European footballing crown in a penalty shootout to Chelsea. Which meant that the big German team's fans had to trudge home alongside a joyous army of boys and girls in blue.

I tried – really, I tried – as the game finished, to organize my face into the right shape. It needed to be proud and happy. But not smug or boastful. The effort was wasted, though, because every single German I met was a model of decency und kindness.

Many pointed out the irony of an English team beating a German side at penalties. And how it was quite correct that we should get lucky once in a while. Others shook my hand. Most were quick to say, 'Well done.' And I could see absolutely no evidence that inside they were dying or on fire. There were no balled fists. They were sad to have lost. But happy for us that we'd won.

This is extremely admirable. It's a state of mind I wish

I could achieve in those white-hot moments of despair when the ball goes out, or I pick up a 'Q' at the last moment, or I land on Mayfair, or I get shot in the head by a Nazi zombie.

My inner McEnroe wants to be a Roger Federer, something the Germans seem to have achieved. I don't crave their shorts or their jackets or their moustaches. But I do crave their sportsmanship. I crave their decency. I crave their niceness. I want to be a German.

Because then I could take on the columnist Jane Moore at Boggle. This has not been possible in the past because she is reputedly very good at it. And I fear she would win. And then we'd never be able to speak again. Because she'd be dead.

27 May 2012

Go on, troll me – but leave your name and address

Britain's gold-medal-winning swimmer Rebecca Adlington has announced that during the Olympics she will not be looking at Twitter or any other similar site because she gets upset by remarks about her appearance.

What kind of person looks at a picture of Ms Adlington and thinks, 'I know what I'll do today. I'll go online and let the long-legged, blue-eyed, world-beating blonde know that her conk's a bit on the large side. And then afterwards I'm going to leave a message for Uma Thurman saying she's got thin hair'?

You may think that if this is happening there must be a lunatic on the loose. But you'd be wrong. There are, in fact, tens of thousands of lunatics out there, all of whom spend their days going online to insult a selection of people they've never met.

When a newspaper prints a picture of a pretty girl, comments are invited from readers, all of which follow a pattern. Savagery. Just last week the television presenter Melanie Sykes was described as a 'sleazeball' for finding a boyfriend. Somebody called Hilary Duff was accused of having a 'man's shoulders'. And Keira Knightley was told she looked like a 'famine victim hours from death'.

My wife has been subjected to this as well. She was photographed recently while out running, and you simply wouldn't believe how much bile this prompted. One person was so cruel that I was tempted to go round to her house and cut her in half with a sword. I also wanted to set fire to her photograph albums and boil her pets.

But therein lies the problem. She's anonymous. She's known only as a stupid user name – 'Fluffykins' or some such. She could be in Birmingham or Hobart. She's a microbe in a fog of seven billion particles and she knows it. Which is why, as I write, she's probably telling Bruce Forsyth he looks like a Russian icebreaker. With a moustache!!!!!

Would she walk up to a person in the street and say, 'God, you're fat'? No. And yet she sees nothing wrong with getting the message across just as clearly on the internet. Because that's the sad truth. The only people who read these comments are the people to whom they refer. And they are powerless to reply.

If I say something that offends you, either here or on the television, you know where I am. You can find me. You can shove a pie into my face or throw manure over my garden wall. These things happen and, in a way, it's to be expected.

But the person who ignores Adlington's remarkable achievements in the pool and concentrates only on her nose? She has no idea who they are or where they live.

This has to stop. And we know it's possible from the recent conviction of a Newcastle University student who was given two years' community service for bombarding the football pundit Stan Collymore with racially abusive tweets. This showed that if you are a racialist and you use the n-word, you are not anonymous and the police can find you.

We should be able to do the same. Easily. When people call from blocked numbers in the middle of the night to sing unpleasant songs, I should be able to get their number from Vodafone in a heartbeat. When Adlington is abused for having a daggerboard on the front of her face, she should be able to locate the culprit with a couple of clicks. His name. His address. The name of his boss. The lot.

Fans of the internet boast about its openness but, actually, it isn't open at all. It's a web of secrecy, full of dark corners that can be probed only by government agencies, and sometimes not even then. There are tens of thousands of lunatics out there, and the problem could be solved at a stroke if they were forced to step out from behind their user names and bask in the ice-cold glare of retribution.

This is not just a solution for Adlington. It's a solution for Lord Justice Leveson as well. For what feels like the past 200 years this poor old man has been made to sit in what appears to be *World of Sport*'s old studios, listening to a bombastic man in silly spectacles questioning every single person who has ever been, met or seen a politician, journalist or celebrity.

He is charged, among other things, with trying to recommend a code of conduct to which newspapers must adhere. But whatever he comes up with is pointless because clamping down on newspapers in the digital age is like worrying about a cut finger when you have rabies.

Newspapers are already covered by the laws of libel, which don't affect those on the internet to anything like the same degree. Because even if you can find the online culprit, what's the point of suing a penniless fat man who lives with his mum and spends his day spouting bile from his porn store in the loft? Even if he did turn out to be loaded, you're still up a creek with no boat because the only people who read his bile were you and your immediate family.

Privacy? There's a big debate here, too, but again I must ask why. Why is it not possible for a newspaper to dig around in your dirt when 'Buttcrack775483' can go through your bins and your knicker drawer – even your stools, if it takes his fancy – and describe exactly what he finds on his blog, knowing that he will get away with it?

I'm not suggesting for a moment that you should not be allowed to laugh about the vastness of my stomach. Within certain bounds of reason, you should be entitled to say pretty much what you like about whomsoever you like. But only if you do so in full view.

In short, we need to get rid of web anonymity. And if there's one recommendation I'd make to newspapers, it is this: only accept readers' comments if they are prepared to divulge their name and address. That way, we could choose to visit the person who thinks it's hilarious to make fun of Rebecca Adlington. And give him a comedy nose as well.

3 June 2012

Kaboom! It's my turn to play fantasy climate change

Ray Bradbury died last week. So now the author of *Fahrenheit 451* and *The Martian Chronicles* is up there in the firmament with all the other great science-fiction writers: Jules Verne, H. G. Wells, Isaac Asimov, Douglas Adams and Arthur C. Clarke. There's still a demand for science fiction, of course. *Doctor Who* remains popular among children and *Prometheus* is doing good business at the cinema. But in print? Well, you may imagine, if you spend any time at all in the bookshop, that all anyone seems to write about these days are mentally unstable Scandinavian detectives and women being lightly whipped.

In fact, though, you're wrong. Science fiction is thriving; only today it's all being written by global-warming enthusiasts.

Global warming was invented by Margaret Thatcher as a blunt instrument she could use to bop Arthur Scargill and his sooty miners over the head. But it didn't really catch on until the name was changed from 'global warming', which sounds comforting and pleasant, to 'climate change', which has unstoppable, apocalyptic overtones. With its new handle in place, science fiction had its modern day Martian.

Soon we were reading about how carbon dioxide, an invisible, odourless gas, would cause London to drown in a sea of its own making, turn Italy into a desert and generate flies the size of toasters that would ravage Africa. Al Gore was the new H. G. Wells and your patio heater was a Dalek.

One of the best stories to emerge from the period came

from a chap called Bill McGuire, who is professor of geo-physical and climate hazards at University College London. Back in 1999, he said that one day a volcano on La Palma in the Canary Islands would erupt and that this would cause a rock the size of the Isle of Man to crash into the sea. The immensity of the splash would generate a 500ft tsunami that in a matter of hours would decimate North America's eastern seaboard and wipe all life from the Caribbean. It's happened before, he said. And it will happen again.

Sadly, in 2004, researchers from Southampton University concluded that, if La Palma's volcano does erupt, it'll cause nothing more than a bit of mud to slither into the Atlantic.

Undaunted, Bill started on a new work and last week, at the Hay literary festival, he revealed it to a waiting world. It's a monster. He says that soon, climate change will bring about an age of geological havoc including tsunamis and something he calls 'volcano storms'.

Volcano storms were first charted by Pliny the Younger during the eruption of Vesuvius in AD 79 and were seen most recently when Eyjafjallajokull blew up in Iceland. Few things are as scary, because inside the choking black ash cloud you have a forest of lightning, with jolts of raw power two miles long surging out of the volcano's vents. And this terrifying, end-of-days spectacle, according to McGuire, is coming to Surrey very soon.

Like all the best plots, his theory that global warming can affect the fabric of the planet is based in fact. After the last Ice Age, Sweden literally bounced upwards by 1,000ft and it's still rising by nearly half an inch a year. So it stands to reason that one day the weight of the ice and snow that cover Greenland will diminish to a point where it's no longer sufficient to keep the world's largest island buried in the mud.

When that happens, and it will be sudden, the elasticity of

the earth's crust will cause it to *boing* upwards by perhaps more than half a mile. And you don't need to be a member of D:Ream to know what kind of a mess that will make of the northern hemisphere. A wave of biblical proportions will wipe out not just Iceland and Canada but most of America's eastern seaboard and all of Europe down to the Alps. The Empire State Building will crash into the statue of Jesus in Rio and the Arc de Triomphe will end up on Mont Blanc.

This is fantastic stuff. Scary. Possible. And we haven't even got to the clincher yet, because McGuire says that as all the snow melts, the sea will become heavier and that will cause fault lines to shift all over the world. Japan. Mexico. Chile. All gone. The man is talking here about an extinction-level event. And the word is that when the film rights are sorted, Denzel is earmarked for the lead.

Better still, at Hay, he delivered his cataclysmic view of events to come in much the same way that *The War of the Worlds* was first played on the radio. Seriously, as though it were fact. Very, very clever.

The only problem is that I think his story needs a bit of a lift between the moment when Greenland bounces into the clouds and the last man on earth drops dead. I'm thinking of that audience-pleasing moment in the movie *Deep Impact*, when a small meteorite arrives out of nowhere and flattens Paris.

And I have an idea. Let me run it past you. Like Greenland, Alaska will also bounce upwards when the weight of the ice currently pressing it down into the ooze reaches a critical point. And, as we know from all the recent eco scare stories about fracking, the very rock on which this great state is founded is full of methane and natural gas. That makes it a gigantic bomb. A bomb that will explode thanks entirely to you in your suburban house with your patio heater and your insatiable appetite for turn-on-and-offable gas.

I think you'll agree that this is a scary story. But I think the scariest part is that McGuire is actually employed by the government as an adviser. It actually takes him seriously. Worse – Westminster sorts take me seriously. Only last week, an MP called Ed Miliband quoted something I'd written in this column while making a speech about Scottish independence. On that basis, he will be back on his soap box this week warning citizens not to go to Anchorage because it's about to explode.

10 June 2012

They've read Milton, Mr Gove, now get 'em to rewire a plug

It has been a tense week. With my elder daughter sitting her A levels, the boy facing his GSCEs and the youngest doing common entrance, it's been seven days of American civil rights, worry, tears, the battle of Trafalgar and many heated arguments about the best way to do long multiplication. It's been like living in a never-ending pub quiz.

And to what end? Oh sure, the right results will be a passport to life's next chapter and will help to propel their schools up the league tables. But the awful truth is: none of my children can wire a plug. Nor can they change a wheel, reattach the chain on a bicycle, darn a sock, make a Pimm's, build a bonfire or mend a broken lavatory seat.

Of course, schools have always taught children stuff that doesn't matter, on the basis that parents have always been able to impart information about stuff that does. But parents can't do that any more because we don't know how to reattach a lavatory seat, either. And in my mind a boiler is powered by witchcraft.

This means a generation of children will soon be emerging into the big wide world, blinking in wonderment at all the million billion things that make no sense. Their fresh-faced little heads will spin, and their stomachs will sink in despair as they realize they know absolutely nothing of any relevance.

Will they be able to get a job as a hotel chambermaid? No. Partly because they will want more than the 5p an hour currently being paid to Mrs Borat, but mostly because they are not able to change a set of sheets. Street sweeping requires a rudimentary understanding of how a brush works. And plumbing? Forget it.

Every job I can think of requires a set of skills that no teenager in Britain has. Apart from the media. And by the time they are ready to start earning a living, that avenue will be gone.

Many may decide to go into business, which in the past used to be an easy option. If you had a product that people wanted to buy, and you sold it for more than it cost, then you would be sitting at the top table at the lodge within a matter of months.

It isn't like that any more. Today you start a business not because you want a fountain from which your family can drink. No, you start a business so that one day, as soon as possible, you can sell it.

Again, that sounds simple, but let me assure you that it really isn't. I've spent the past few months negotiating a business deal, and although I am not the most stupid man in the world, I haven't understood a single thing that has been said or done. It has all been gobbledygook, presented in a series of so many acronyms that it sounded as if someone were reading out the model names of every Kawasaki motorcycle ever made.

Each evening I'd call my accountant, who did his best to translate everything into primary school English. It was never any good because eventually it would go dark, and then it would get light and I would be forced by tiredness to say I'd understood when in truth I hadn't.

Are you familiar, for instance, with EBITDA? It sounds as though it might be a character at the bar in *Star Wars* but, in fact, it stands for earnings before interest, taxes, depreciation and amortization. It's critical you understand this in business but you don't, do you? Because you don't know what amortization is. And neither do I.

There's another issue with business that is not made clear on *Dragons' Den*. When you agree terms, you stand up and shake hands.

But then, the next day, the man with whom you did the deal has a completely different version of events in his head. 'No,' he'll say, 'you agreed to sell for 5p and give me your record collection.'

So then you have to employ some suits, who say that you should think more about EBIT rather than EBITDA unless, of course, you choose to use the DCF model. And then it goes quiet and you realize it's your turn to speak and all you can think to say is, 'Would anyone like a cup of tea?'

I haven't even got to the misery of tax yet. Not being Greek or Italian, I fully understand that a percentage of what I earn should go to the government. I recognize that if we want street lighting and a bobby on the beat and prisons, we cannot operate in a river of cash and hope the Germans will pay when our government cannot.

I can even work out how much I need to pay each year. Half of everything I earn. It's a simple sum. However, it turns out that in business, it's not simple at all, and don't ask why because you will then be plunged into a Scrabble bag of acronyms in which time slows down and your internal organs stop working.

To make matters worse, accountancy types actually seem to enjoy sparring with each other using nothing but letters. 'CGT?' one will say. 'Not with this PBT,' will come the snorted retort. After an hour you feel compelled to stand up and say, 'Are you dealing with my business stuff here, or are you playing out-loud Boggle?'

On the next series of Sir Sugar's *The Apprentice*, he should put those gormless marketing-speak idiots in a proper business meeting and then ask them to explain what just went on. It would be hysterical.

It's not hysterical, however, when it's your livelihood. It's bewildering and upsetting. And it's why I shall finish with an idea for Michael Gove, the education secretary, who suggested last week that kids must be able to spell 'appreciate' and do the twelve times table by the time they're nine.

This is all well and good for those who wish to follow the traditional path to university. But wouldn't it be a good idea to have other schools for those who wish to follow a path to somewhere called the world? Plug-wiring at nine a.m. Cook your own pie at lunchtime. And double EBITDA in the afternoon.

17 June 2012

Blow me up, Scotty, before I land on your Manx home

An Isle of Man-based company has stunned the nerd world by announcing that within three years it will be able to offer tourists a trip around the moon, and then onwards into bits of space where no man has gone before.

Passengers will be loaded on board one of four second-hand Russian re-entry capsules, and then blasted to one of two recycled Russian former space stations.

From here they will embark on an eight-month round trip through the final frontier.

Hmmm. Quite a few engineering types, including Sir Branson, are currently engaged in the development of space tourism and I'm not quite sure why, because almost everyone I ever meet says they'd rather spend their holidays in the No. 4 reactor at Fukushima.

They say space flight frightens them because if something goes wrong, there's no air. This, of course, is true but there is also no air in the sea and that doesn't stop anyone snorkelling. Plus space is not full of fish that will stick a spear through your heart, or inject you with a poison, or tear your leg off.

Also, space is not full of currents that will whisk you off to Venus, or people on jet skis who will run you down, or doped-up boatmen who will forget where they dropped you off and leave you out there until your tongue is the size of a marrow and you die a slow, agonizing death. Only a few humans have ever died in space. Plenty, however, have died in the sea.

I will agree that there are a few problems with space tourism. Cost is one. The Isle of Man round trip will be £100 million. And then there's the boredom. For a while the lack of gravity is undoubtedly fun. You can laugh at how everyone's hair is floating about like seaweed and spend an amusing few moments trying to convince your mates that the globule of liquid floating past their faces is tasty orange juice and not a drop of urine that somehow escaped from the lavatory.

But then what? On a cruise ship, you can stop off at the Virgin Islands for 'romantic cocktails'. But you can't do that in space. There's no Jim Davidson, either. You can't even sleep with the captain. You just have to sit there looking out of the window, at nothing at all, for half a million miles, wondering whether a Russian spaceship that's been recycled in the Isle of Man, where they have not invented the diesel locomotive yet, is really the right vehicle for the job.

It certainly sounds preposterous. But, actually, when you spend a few moments sucking the end of your Biro and thinking, you can't help wondering: is it? John F. Kennedy told us back in 1962 that we chose to go to the moon and do the other things, not because they were easy, but because they were hard. No one ever asked what the 'other things' were because they were too busy absorbing the central message: space travel, it's tricky.

I, however, am not so sure that it is. Because NASA showed us in 1970 that it was entirely possible to get a leaking spaceship from the middle of nowhere back to earth, into the atmosphere and gently into the Pacific using nothing more than the electricity needed to power a toaster, a slide rule, some duct tape and the cover of a flight manual.

We were also told that to go into space you needed to be a brave young man with the stamina of an Olympic marathon runner, the reactions of a cobra, the brains of an emeritus maths professor and the ability to hold your breath for seventeen weeks. Humans, they said, need not apply. For space travel you had to be superhuman.

But then in 1998, when the former Mercury astronaut John Glenn was seventy-seven years old, they put him up there without a second thought. And now we often find the International Space Station is full of portly middle-aged men and women who get frightened on a bus and who spend all day in the vast empty ocean, growing lettuces.

So, you don't have to be fit or clever and you don't have to be able to hold your breath for very long because the truth is that if something goes wrong, long before you suffocate, your blood will boil and your eyes will pop out of your head and your brain will burst.

However, there is one problem that does not seem to have been addressed by our friends on Fraggle Rock. It's a big one.

Had you been able to inspect the space shuttle as it sat on its launch pad, you might have noticed that the solid rocket boosters were carrying explosives.

The idea was that if something went wrong in the early stage of the shuttle's ascent and it was heading at several thousand miles an hour for downtown Miami, a man in a bunker at Cape Canaveral – a man who was never allowed to meet any of the people on board – would press a button. And blow it to kingdom come.

This, you see, is the trouble with rockets. Once they are lit, you cannot turn them off again. They run until the fuel is gone. So if something goes wrong with the guidance system and the rocket is heading back down to earth, there's nothing anyone can do. That's why NASA employed a man in a bunker.

If you watch footage of the Challenger disaster, you

will note that after the shuttle disintegrates, both solid rocket boosters spiral off and then explode at precisely the same moment. That's because the button was pressed to destroy them.

The Isle of Man government will have to think about this. And then it will have to employ a man whose only job is to blow up the spaceship and everyone on board. Because that's better than letting it crash into someone's house.

Although, I just have one request for the successful applicant. If it's heading for the headquarters of the Manx rambling association, leave it be.

24 June 2012

And your premium bond prize is . . . a seat in the Lords

If you were put in charge of a brand new country and told to organize a whole new system of government, you probably wouldn't come up with the House of Lords. 'Right. We've got some elected members in the Commons and now, to make sure they don't do anything stupid, we shall have another tier, which we shall fill with religious zealots, chaps whose great-grandads won a battle and various other odds and sods who only ever wake up when their bedsores start to weep.'

However, even though it makes absolutely no sense at all, the House of Lords has worked well for centuries.

It even continued to work when some of the inbreds were replaced by Muslim whales. It works so well, in fact, that Nick Clegg, who is the deputy prime minister, wants to change it. He's even made some suggestions that come straight from paragraph one, page one, chapter one of a book called *How to Let People Know You Are Mad*.

In short, he wants to cut the numbers in the Lords from 826 to 450, most of whom would be elected to represent a specific region. So far, then, he's just come up with a direct copy of the House of Commons. But since the elected representatives won't have the power to make law, what exactly will the job advert say?

'Wanted: a man or a woman – or a whale – to waste their lives listening to adenoidal dullards drone on about waste management on the Isle of Sheppey. The successful applicant must be willing to have his or her private life picked over in microscopic detail by journalists. On the upside, you'll get paid. But not much.'

I know exactly the sort of people who'll sign up for a slice of that. They're the people you find in any large organization, the sort who go to a lot of meetings and when there eat all the biscuits. They're people who never once in their whole joyless, friend-free, celibate lives contribute anything meaningful, constructive, imaginative, daring, fascinating or worthwhile.

They go on marches but half the time have no idea what they're marching for. They get involved in action groups. They wear protest T-shirts over their anoraks so they look stupid. They enjoy regional news. They disagree with shampoo. A lot have cats. All of them are a waste of blood and organs. Many are called Colin. And Nick Clegg wants to put them in the hot seat.

And it gets worse. Because when you've elected your Colin, you're stuck with him for fifteen years, which . . . let's do the maths . . . is pretty much adjacent to forever.

Naturally the costs involved are humungous and, frankly, how many elected representatives do we need? Because if his harebrained scheme goes ahead, we will have to vote for people to sit on a parish council, a borough council, a county council, the House of Commons, the House of Lords and the European parliament. We will be spending most of our lives in polling booths, choosing between candidates who are only united by their utter uselessness.

Suffice to say, I have a better idea. It goes like this. Instead of filling a House of Colins with a bunch of biscuit-eating nonentities, who left to their own devices would struggle to wire a plug, we use the computer that's used to pick premium bond winners to select eight people at random each week from the electoral roll.

Of course, it will be a nuisance for them to take a week off work, but on the upside, they will be brought to London and put up in a swish hotel. And all that will be asked in return is that they have a quick look over the bills being discussed in the House of Commons to make sure none involves reintroducing slavery or invading Portugal.

Humourless people in suits will suggest at this juncture that the second tier of government is rather more complex than that. And they may have a point. But it can't be that difficult because for hundreds of years the House of Lords has been run by a squadron of dribbling infantile buffoons who think they must be right because they talk more loudly than anyone else. And they managed just fine. Many managed even when they were fast asleep, dreaming – and not in a good way – of their old nanny.

Seriously. Who would you rather have doing the job: a man who thinks it's perfectly acceptable to wear a fur scarf on a hot day or your mate Jim from the builder's yard? Quite. We trust randomly selected juries on the important business of a person's liberty so, on the basis that most people can tie up their shoelaces and not get run over while crossing the road, why wouldn't we trust a similar system to apply the checks and balances in government?

A few moments ago I put this idea to Alastair Campbell who popped round for a cup of tea. I know. Strange. And what he said was, 'You're talking about a focus group.' As though this were a bad thing.

It isn't. These days, focus groups choose what we eat, what we drive, what we read, what we watch and how we furnish our houses. Almost nothing makes it on to the market without being presented first to a small group of people selected at random. Occasionally they let something daft through the net, such as cherry-flavoured Coca-Cola and the Toyota

Prius, but for the most part the observations they make are reasonable. Business trusts them. Shareholders trust them. So why shouldn't we?

Certainly I'd rather have a government's ideas checked for idiocy and recklessness by a small, cheap group of ordinary people than by 450 expensive Colins. Although, truth be told, the solution I'd most like to have is the solution we have now.

I understand, of course, why David Cameron allowed his tea boy Clegg to go off and work on House of Lords reform. Because if he's doing that, he's not mucking up something more important. But now that we've seen what Cleggy has in mind, it's probably a good idea to take his mind off it with another idea. Can't he be made to clean the silver or something?

1 July 2012

Cheer up, Mewling Murray, you've made it into *Boohoo's Who*

Last weekend all the tabloid newspapers were full of huge headlines wishing Andy Murray well as he prepared to become the first British man to win Wimbledon for 3,000 years.

This was odd. Normally tabloids are extremely good at judging the mood of the nation but on this occasion they were well wide of the mark. Because I couldn't find a single person, in real life or on Twitter, who wanted the miserablist-in-chief to win. There's a good reason for this. He'd had the bare-faced cheek to plough through the entire tournament playing nothing but tennis.

There had been no hopping, skipping or clowning around of any kind. He was a man with the personality of a vacuum cleaner and in post-match press conferences the sparkle of an old man's brogue. That's why we were all rooting for the man in the monogrammed blazer.

When the final was over and Murray had lost, I was praying he'd express his anger and disappointment by high-fiving his opponent. In the face. With a chair. That's what I'd do if I were ever to lose a game of Boggle. But what he actually did was blub, whimpering and mewling like a hysterical little girl whose puppy dog had gone missing. It was pathetic. And guess what. All of a sudden he became a national hero.

Why? We live on a solid little rock in the north Atlantic. It's cold. It's wet. We admire the bulldog spirit. We keep calm and carry on. We get a grip. Crying? It's like eating a horse. Something foreigners do.

In America a stiff upper lip is something that only ever happens when intimate plastic surgery goes wrong. There is no American word for 'stoic'. Americans cry more often than they don't. The smallest breath of wind and they're all on the news, tears streaming down their blubbery faces as they stand beside their fallen-over wooden houses, explaining between heaving sobs how the good Lord has deserted them.

Even Germans cry, a point that was demonstrated by the enormous and manly Carsten Jancker, who broke down and wept when his side were beaten by Manchester United in the 1999 Champions League final. Finns? Yup. The former racing driver Mika Hakkinen took himself off for a little weep when he thought a mistake had cost him the world championship. And Italian men cry a lot, too. Probably because most of them aren't actually men.

Here, though, things have always been different. A man could come home to find his wife in bed with the plumber, his dog nailed to the front door and his business a smoking ruin, and still he could be relied upon to put on a brave face and think of some suitable understatement to make it all seem not so bad.

It is impossible, for instance, to imagine a tear in the eye of Nobby Stiles or W. G. Grace. I bet Earl Haig had no tear ducts at all. Or Arthur Harris.

And certainly when my father-in-law was surrounded by overwhelming German forces at Arnhem, there is no suggestion that he broke down and wept. He just blew up another tank.

In Britain lachrymosity has always been seen, quite rightly, as a sign that you are not really a proper chap. That you may be someone who bowls from the other end, or a colonial. But, oh dear, that's all changed now.

Every night on the news in recent weeks fat people who've watched far too much American television are to be found standing in front of their moist sofas sobbing as they explain how the flood waters came all the way up to their knees. It's sick-inducing and should be banned from the airwaves. People aren't allowed to bare their breasts on the news. So why should they be allowed to bare their souls?

It gets worse. Nick Faldo wormed his way into the nation's hearts by crying after he won a stupid game of golf. And the only reason we feel sorry for Paul Gascoigne is that he let us see his feminine side during a football match against Germany. Nowadays a little tear on television can win you not just the love of a nation, but also a lucrative advertising deal and a lot of sex with women who think you are all gooey and nice.

Well, that's what they say. They argue that the tear-stained face of a man is a sign that he likes to eat celery and that he gives half of his salary each month to a home for distressed kittens. They say that this is a good thing. They also say they don't want us to come home at night in a bearskin and demand our wicked way. And that isn't true, either. Women want a crybaby in the house in the same way that men want their wives in a pair of Y-fronts.

That said, I can cry. I cried in *Born Free* when Elsa was released into the wild, and I'm told by my mother that I was inconsolable in a film in which Norman Wisdom went to bed with a horse. But as an adult? Well, when our pet Kristin Scott Donkey died I had to go for 'a little walk', and I'm afraid I get quite sniffly in *Educating Rita*. But that's it.

And rightly so. Because, as Britain changes, it is very difficult to think of one single defining national characteristic. We don't wear bowler hats any more. Benny Hill is dead. And our army is now smaller than the Padstow Tufty Club. All we have left is a stiff upper lip.

Which brings me on to the citizen test that all new boys have to pass if they want to become British. At present it's full of irrelevant questions about the number of parliamentary constituencies, what quangos do and who is allowed to vote.

There should be one question only.

When is it acceptable for a grown man to cry in public?

a) Never.

b) Whenever he is upset by something.

Anyone who ticks b) should be taken directly to Heathrow and put on the next flight to abroad.

15 July 2012

We're all running as Team GB, the grim bellyachers

Soon the waiting will be over, and we shall be able to find out whether a Kenyan man we've never heard of can jump further into a sandpit than an American man we've also never heard of. Plus we shall be able to see Russian women with scrotums like tractors hurling hammers about the place. And with a bit of luck, one of the triangular-torsoed diver boys will bash his head on the board. As you may have gathered, I'm no fan of London's forthcoming running and jumping competition, and in recent weeks I've joined in wondering why its officials, among others, should be given one lane of a dual carriageway while 8 million Londoners have to hutch up in the other.

However, even I am now starting to grow weary of the salivatory anticipation that the Olympics will be a soggy festival of incompetence, and that the wall-to-wall television coverage is bound to be ruined by Fearne Cotton saying 'wow' a lot.

When any other Third World country is asked to stage an international event, it doesn't actively hope for it to be a failure: Inner Mongolia, for instance, is hosting this year's Miss World and no one in the local press is saying that all the competitors are sure to get a nasty bout of genital itching.

Here, though, things are rather different. A lone American athlete arrived last week and tweeted to say his first impressions of London weren't good. And somehow this was seen as proof that the whole event was turning into a fiasco.

Of course, what we should have said is, 'Why? What

happened? Were you barked at by a furious immigration official and made to go to the back of a two-hour queue because
you'd accidentally said on your visa waiver form that you had
committed genocide? And then did you climb into a taxi that
had no legroom at all and was being driven by a non-English
speaker who had no idea where he was going? No. Well, shut
up, then, you disgusting little ingrate.'

Then came news that some of the on-site cleaners were
being asked to share a shower. Like everyone who goes to a
£30,000-a-year public school such as Eton. Not that you will
have noticed this little nugget because you were too busy
watching *Twenty Twelve* on your iPlayer.

Meanwhile, a hastily organized select committee was trying to find out why Nick Buckles, the G4S boss, had
announced with just two weeks to go that he'd been unable
to find enough guards to sit at the back of the stadium,
smoking.

But instead, a Labour MP called David Winnick, who
couldn't even do up his tie properly, shouted, 'If I demand
over and over again that you admit it's a humiliating shambles, can I appear on the front of all tomorrow's papers?'

Where was he going with that? And why didn't poor old
Mr Buckles, with his Bay City Rollers haircut, simply tell the
publicity-hungry moron that a much better question would
have been, 'Why did so many of Britain's 2.5 million
unemployed people decide they'd rather stay on benefits
than put on a high-visibility jacket and do a job?'

Whatever. We now get to the hated Olympic lanes, which
have been provided in the hope that visiting journalists are
made to feel so warm and fuzzy that they go home and
encourage business leaders to open an office here.

Do we see it that way? No. What we see instead is one tiny
little mistake on one tiny little road where one lane is for

buses and one is for someone from the *Kampala Gazette*. And for this, apparently, Seb Coe's head must be amputated.

There's more. One woman went to the papers to say that her son hadn't been allowed to wear his expensive training shoes while practising in an east London gym because they hadn't been made by Adidas, one of the Olympic sponsors. Well, yes, I too despair about the commercialization of sport, but the truth is that without Adidas and EDF and BMW, there'd have been no stadium.

Not that we need one, scoffed the cynics, because no tickets at all have been sold for any of the basket-weaving events. And anyway, it's just going to be a white elephant for the rest of time unless Bernie Ecclestone can be persuaded to remove the Monaco race from the grand prix calendar and replace it with an event through the streets of Newham.

By Wednesday last week the hysteria and general sense of impending doom had reached such a pitch that observers were quoting a German magazine that claimed the Games would be a washout because of the weather. And instead of saying, 'Well, yes, but at least the Queen won't storm out if Usain Bolt wins,' we took this as yet more proof that Britain is seen around the world as a useless, wet rock full of tax dodgers, benefit frauds and cheating bankers.

Even Boris Johnson, London's mayor, jumped on the bandwagon, saying that because the swallows were flying backwards and the cotoneaster berries were a little paler than usual, the whole of east London would be soaked for the duration of the Games. Really? Because the weather forecasters say that the jet stream is moving north, that sunny skies are on the way and that as a result the beach volleyball girls will be allowed to perform naked as usual.

I'm not saying the Games are bound to be a triumph, but I am heartily fed up with the mongers of misery who think they'll be a rain-spattered orgy of mud, incompetence, striking bus drivers, disgruntled staff, angry Americans, corporate greed and empty stadiums. And that the army is almost certain to shoot down a patrolling Eurofighter with one of its Fisher-Price ground-to-air missiles.

We need to think positively. We need to imagine that the opening ceremony is rather more than a celebration of diversity and sustainability. We need to picture a bright summer sun glinting off all the gold medals our athletes have won. In short, let's enjoy the hope now and deal with the despair later.

22 July 2012

Stop, or I'll shoot . . . about 100 yards off to your right

Many people in the civilized world were a bit surprised when they heard that the good Christian folk of Denver, Colorado, had responded to the cinema killings by rushing out the next day to stock up on sub-machine guns.

Firearms permit applications were up 40 per cent.

What were they thinking of? 'Right. Good. I have in my belt a Mac-10, so now if I'm interrupted while out for a romantic dinner with my wife, or walking the dog, I shall be able to kill the assailant before he kills me.'

This is extremely unlikely. Gun-toting maniacs tend not to announce their intentions with a shouted warning. Which means that by the time you have located your weapon, withdrawn it from its hiding place, taken off the safety catch, aimed and pulled the trigger, you're already fairly dead.

And even if by some miracle you aren't, have you ever tried to hit a target with a gun? It's pretty much impossible, even if the target is an American. Once I was given a machine gun by a member of the army and asked to hit, quite literally, a barn door from a range of perhaps fifty yards. The first round was successful, but thereafter I was mostly spraying the sky while stumbling backwards with my eyes closed and my face all screwed up as if I were sucking hard on an unripe lemon.

There is no metaphor that quite captures the sheer violence of pulling the trigger on an automatic weapon. One second, it's as still and as silent as a rock. The next, you are attached to a living thing that is trying desperately to break free from your grasp. If you are a trained soldier, you can just about deal with this. If you are an overweight solicitor out for dinner with your wife, you will end up blind, deaf and surrounded by the thirty bodies of all the people you've just shot by mistake.

It's interesting. Since the *Batman* shootings, a handful of teary Democrats have been saying that automatic weapons with large magazines should be banned. In other words, they want to ban baddies from buying precisely the sort of gun that can't actually hit anything.

Mind you, a pistol is not much better. Only recently a deeply worrying man in North Carolina took me to his outdoor shooting range and asked me to 'double tap' one of his Osama bin Laden targets. So, aim carefully at the man's heart, fire and then straight away put the next round in his head. Seen it done in a million films. Simple.

It isn't, actually. The first carefully aimed round grazed Mr bin Laden's shoulder. The next hit a bush several hundred yards to the right.

Americans must know this. Many are descended from cowboys and gunslingers. So they must be at least aware that in the hands of an amateur, in the heat of the moment, a gun is about as useful as a pencil sharpener.

Politicians must know it too. So Mr Barack should simply explain that in the olden days, when there were Indians and Frenchmen and bears rushing about, it was fair enough to keep a Winchester above the fireplace. But today it's ridiculous.

He doesn't say this, though. After the Aurora massacre, instead of announcing an amnesty or a change in the law, he mumbled something about the need to address violence and explained that every day and a half the same number of young Americans are shot to death as died in Denver. It was a presidential shrug.

That's because asking a working-class American male to hand in his gun is like asking him to hand in his penis. Mr Barack knows that Bud and Hank won't vote for him if he takes away their right to have a machine gun. Which gets us back to the question: why would you want one in the first place?

Well, first of all, you grew up in the Cold War. You were taught by your leaders that when the bad guys have intercontinental ballistic missiles, you must have intercontinental ballistic missiles too. Plus the constitution says you can have a gun to defend yourself from the British.

But there's more to it than that. It's because guns are fascinating. If someone came round to your house today with a 9mm Glock, I can pretty much guarantee that if you have a functioning scrotum, you will want to handle it. And if the person in question has some bullets, you will want to go outside and shoot at a tree.

This probably has something to do with mating. When you have a gun in your hand, you are the most powerful person in the room. Which means you're like those birds that appear on natural history programmes with their feathers all puffed out, making themselves look manly and virile in front of all the girl birds.

A gun is also a comfort blanket. You know that if it's just you, with your weedy little arms, versus a bad man with a gun, you stand no chance at all. However, if you too have a gun about your person, there's a slim chance that as you blast away at all the furniture with your eyes closed, he won't stroll over, punch you in the face, take the gun from you and shoot you in the head with it. A gun doesn't level the playing field. But it does tilt it slightly back in your direction.

There's another thing. Guns are fun. I once spent a pleasant evening in the Arizona desert with a man who had a Mack truck filled from floor to ceiling with every kind of weapon you can imagine. He even had two 8,000-round-a-minute mini-guns mounted on his helicopter.

I was especially fond of something called a squad automatic weapon and spent many hours bouncing tracer rounds into the night sky until the desert actually caught fire. There's no reason, in a civilized world, why a member of the public should have this gun. And no reason why anyone should cackle and squeal with joy as they fire it into the void. But I did. And you would too. And that is the problem.

29 July 2012

Listen, Fritz, we'll do the efficiency now – you write the gags

Ben Elton is working on a new television sitcom about a health and safety department. Doubtless it will be full of high-visibility ear defenders and there will be many hilarious consequences. British health and safety is a rich comic vein. Or rather, it was before the Olympics came along.

I gathered with about 200 ocean-going cynics to watch the opening ceremony and as the lights went up on those little black and white children skipping around a maypole, all of us imagined the worst. We'd seen the knuckle-bitingly embarrassing handover in China.

We'd heard about the low-budget sustainable eco-plans for east London and we all knew, deep down in our stone-cold hearts, that Britain is a basketcase. We never get anything right. Only this time we wouldn't get anything right with the whole world watching.

Well, obviously we were wrong. It was a triumph and, as I write, the Games are proving to be a triumph as well. Furthermore, the trains are running on time, there are no strikes at Heathrow and London is quiet. This, I feel, is going to have a profound effect on not just Elton's new comedy but everything else too.

After the last world war, Britain lost its empire and slid into a soot-blackened well of dirt, discontent and despair. People lived in a monochrome world with outside khazis that didn't work, had no job and, as often as not, had a hideous lung disease. And it was here, in the misery pit, that our world-famous sense of humour was forged.

You knew your new Austin Princess wouldn't work properly. You knew the pubs would shut every time you were thirsty. You knew there'd be a power cut very soon and you knew that the little cough you'd developed yesterday was the onset of pneumoconiosis. And the only way to deal with it all was to have a laugh.

Think about it. How much comedy do you find in British literature that was written when we were rich and successful and ran the world? How many laughs are there in *Wuthering Heights* or *The Return of the Native*? Not many. We were known in Victorian times for many things. But being funny wasn't one of them.

However, when unemployment was running at more than 3 million, the miners were all throwing stones at policemen and your rubbish hadn't been collected for a year, Elton was bringing the house down in the Comedy Store and we were all gathered around the television, laughing our heads off at Frankie Howerd. Titter ye not. But titter we did.

When the people of other countries are displeased with their leaders, they chase them into drains or hang them from lamp posts. Us? We employ Ian Hislop to machine gun them with jokes. When John Cleese was unhappy with the service at a dreary seafront hotel, he didn't write an angry letter. No. He wrote *Fawlty Towers*. I spend my working life on TV praying to all the gods that ever there were that James May will catch fire. Because then we can all have a jolly good giggle.

Adversity and hardship are the cradles of comedy, so what are we to do now the Olympics have shown that, actually, Britain can be rather more than Belgium with a bit of drizzle? What if we're all inspired to succeed and everything we do from now on is equally well run and magnificent?

You really do sense this tide of optimism, certainly in London. Most of us watched that opening ceremony, with the inspiring semi-animated rush down the Thames and Kenneth Branagh as Isambard Kingdom Brunel, and we've all plainly decided Britain doesn't need to be rubbish at everything.

People talk about how the achievement will change the way other countries feel about us. Far more important is how it will change the way we feel about ourselves. That's what happened after Barcelona hosted the Games. Basking in a Ready Brek glow of pride, it went from a crummy little fishing port to one of the coolest cities in the world.

That could well happen here. The Olympics have injected us all with a long-forgotten sense of contentment, and who knows what effect this will have?

What if Terminal 2 reopens at Heathrow on time and all the passengers' suitcases end up on the correct planes? What if we build an aircraft carrier that can be used as a launch pad for actual planes? What if the people in charge of parking meters in some London boroughs scrap the pay-by-phone system, which doesn't work, and bring back the coin slot, which does? What if the banks examine what Sebastian Coe has achieved and think, 'Hey, chaps. Why don't we lend money to people who can pay us back?'

Where would that leave *Have I Got News for You*? Paul Merton may still be able to offer up some nugget about a squashed cat, but poor old Hislop would be castrated. And who's going to find Elton's new show funny if health and safety officers start to behave sensibly? Certainly I bet you would have found *Twenty Twelve* far less chucklesome if you'd known then what you know now.

If Britain becomes as well run as Switzerland, we could end up with a Swiss sense of humour. In other words, we'd end up with absolutely no sense of humour at all. You'd have John Bishop and Michael McIntyre and all the other observational comedians walking into empty theatres and saying, 'Have you noticed how all the trains run bang on time . . .'

The only crumb of comfort we can take from all this is that Germany is in a pickle. Thanks to the curious machinations of the European Union, various southern euro states have decided it's best if they sit under an olive tree all day and get Hermann to pay for all their public services.

As a result, Johnny Boche will soon be bankrupt. The country will have strikes and riots, and everyone's Mercedes will break down all the time. This could well mean that in the not-too-distant future, all the world's best comedians will be German.

5 August 2012

Arise, Sir Jeremy – defier of busybody croupiers and barmen

There were calls last week for the Cabinet Office to hand over the honours system to an independent body in the hope that more lollipop ladies could be knighted and more OBEs awarded to those who have done voluntary work in 'the community'.

Of course, this is yet another example of the drive to create a new people-power society in which the fat, the stupid and the toothless are encouraged to lord it over the bright, the thin and the successful. Already we are seeing its effects. A tiny number of morons decided that they would like very much to stroll through my garden, pausing a while to peer through my kitchen window, and now they can.

A noisy minority decided that Jonathan Ross should be driven from the BBC, and he was. And expensive public libraries are now kept open just because an infinitesimal number of internet-phobes from 'the community', chose to dance about outside with placards.

We turn firemen into heroes if they get their trousers wet and treat single mums like round-the-world sailors. David Cameron is an idiot, Boris Johnson is a buffoon, Richard Branson is a spoilt child. But the man who empties your bins is as wise as an owl and must be given a CBE immediately.

Unless this nonsense is stopped, we shall become like America and, having spent a couple of weeks there recently, I can assure you that this would be A Bad Thing.

We begin the shoulder-sagging saga in Las Vegas, six floors below a party that seems to have made the papers. I wanted to show my sixteen-year-old son how blackjack works, but although he was allowed in the casino, he was not allowed to stand near any of the tables.

The croupier had been issued with the power to enforce this law and as a result shouted, 'Back up!' as my son peered over my shoulder. In an attempt to defuse what appeared to be a life-or-death situation, I asked the boy to reverse slowly until he reached a point where the lobster-brained croupier was happy. Quite soon I noticed that he'd reversed perilously close to the table behind him, and I pointed this out to the woman. 'Okay,' she said, realizing the mistake. 'Forwards. Forwards. Forwards a bit more. Stop.' He ended up about nine inches from where he'd started.

Obviously it's a good idea to stop teenage boys gambling but the idea of using a stupid person to enforce this law doesn't work at all. A point that had been made a few days earlier at a hotel near Yosemite. When my eighteen-year-old daughter joined me at the bar for a refreshing Coca-Cola she was told, very loudly, that she needed to be twenty-one to sit there, and that she would have to join the half-hour queue for a table. So let's just get this straight: you can sit at a table and have a Coke but you cannot sit at the bar, even though the two places are 2ft apart?

The shouty barman agreed the law was stupid and that it would be ridiculous to deny a bar stool to, say, a twenty-year-old soldier who had just lost a leg in Afghanistan. But said there was nothing he could do.

Yes, Bud or Hank or Todd, or whatever single-syllable name you have, that's the problem. There is something you can do. You don't spend your evenings peering into the barrel of your Heckler & Koch machine pistol. You don't eat stuff that you know to be poisonous. You have nous. You have at least some initiative. Use it.

When on the balcony of a hotel room in Los Angeles, I was told by a bossy cleaner that she 'needed' me to extinguish my cigarette. Smoking on a balcony in Los Angeles is not allowed. But why? There was no one within 300ft. I was outside. I would place the butt in an empty beer bottle. But logic is a dandelion seed when the hurricane of state law is entrusted to someone with an IQ of four.

We went to an exhibition of Titanic artefacts. For reasons that are entirely unclear, all our cameras had to be left in a locker. But you can't use the lockers unless you can provide the idiotic ticket woman with photo ID. Can you think of a single reason why you need to prove who you are before being allowed to leave one of your own belongings in a locker? Me neither.

There was a similar problem with a zip wire my children wanted to try. Yes, they were tall enough and, yes, my cash money was acceptable. But before they were allowed to have a go I had to give written permission. And for that I needed photo ID.

What would photo ID prove? That my name was Jeremy Clarkson. But would that show I was the children's father? No, because they were not required by state law to prove who they were. The fact is this: ID was required because in totalitarian states such as Soviet Russia and North Korea and America it's important to know who is doing what at all times.

At one hotel we used there were two pools: a family pool that was full mostly of homosexual men, and a European pool where lady guests were allowed to remove their bikini tops. Strangely we weren't allowed to sit round the European pool even though we had photo ID to prove we were actually European.

After two weeks of being told by janitors, night watchmen,

cleaners and passers-by that we couldn't smoke near fruit machines, go barefoot in a shopping mall, park near a fire hydrant, drink in the street, take cameras to the Grand Canyon skywalk or make jokes to anyone in any kind of uniform, we kissed the tarmac at Heathrow and now see Britain in an all-new light.

Yesterday I was overtaken by a man in a sports car who had an unrestrained golden retriever in the passenger seat. And I rejoiced. Then, this morning, I applauded when I saw a cyclist jump a red light. And I have thoroughly enjoyed sitting with my children outside the Plough in Kingham, smoking and drinking and having a nice time. This is what should be meant by people power. The power for people to choose which of the government's petty, silly, pointless laws they want to obey. And which they don't.

2 September 2012

P-p-please open up, Arkwright, I need some t-t-t-trousers

We return this morning to a subject I've talked about before. It's a subject close to every man's heart: the sheer, unadulterated, trudging misery of shopping for clothes.

I buy my shoes at Tod's on Bond Street in London. Its window is always full of many attractive designs, and if I have a few minutes left on the meter I will sometimes pop in to buy a pair. But they never, ever, have anything in a size 11. The lady always comes back from a lengthy trip to the storeroom brandishing a pair of size 5s, asking cheerfully if they will do instead.

Which is a bit like someone in a restaurant ordering the vegetarian option and being asked if a nice, juicy T-bone steak will do instead. No, it won't. And now, thanks to this time-wasting, I have a parking ticket.

Shops never keep shirts in the size I want either, and every single available jacket would only really fit Ziggy Stardust. Trousers? Don't know, because I'm way too big to fit in the overheated postbox the retailer laughingly calls a changing room. However, if by some miracle you do find something in your size that you like, your problems are far from over because you have to pay for it.

When you buy £100-worth of petrol, you put your card in a machine, tap in your code and seconds later walk out with a receipt. When you buy £100-worth of trousers, you must stand at the desk while the sales assistant inputs what feels like the entire works of Dostoevsky into her computer. And then she will want your name and address so that you can be kept abreast of forthcoming clothing lines that won't be available in your size either.

And you can't get round the problem by going somewhere else because these days there is nowhere else.

This is my new beef. Every single high street and every single shopping centre in every single town and city is full of exactly the same shops attempting to sell exactly the same things that you can't buy because they don't keep your size in stock.

A recent trip to San Francisco has demonstrated that it doesn't have to be this way. I took my children to Haight-Ashbury so that I could talk to them about the summer of love and how Janis Joplin was about a billion times better than any of the talentless teenage warblers on their iPods.

At first I was a bit disappointed to find that the whole area had been turned into a vast shopping experience. The kids weren't, though. And soon neither was I.

The first shop was rammed with Sixties clothing and accessories. Purple hippie sunglasses. Vietnam Zippos. Joss sticks and curious-looking chemistry sets. There were posters of Hendrix and CND badges and I bought more in there, in ten minutes, than I've bought in Britain in ten years.

Then I found a shoe shop. It was selling shoes and boots the likes of which you simply would not find anywhere in Britain and it had in stock every single size you could think of. I bought many pairs. Then I bought two jackets that fitted, and then we decided to visit one of the many coffee shops. None of which was Starbucks.

Not a single one of the shops wanted my name or address when I bought anything. They had no intention of sending me exciting product information and they did not expect me to hang around while they updated their stock figures.

You hand over your card, provide the inevitable photo ID, sign your name and leave.

Of course, you may imagine that all of the hundreds of tiny independent shops in the area are being run by free-love people who arrived in San Francisco in June 1967 and who are therefore not interested in profit. You might imagine that as long as you worshipped at the altar of peaceful protest, you could barter for one of the chemistry sets with beans.

There was plenty of evidence to suggest this might be so. One shop was being run by a chap in his sixties. He wore his hair in a ponytail, with a pair of John Lennon glasses, a poncho and a set of groovy loon pants. Later, though, I saw him locking up his shop and climbing into a brand new Cadillac Escalade.

So why, if there's money to be made, have the big boys not moved in? Bloody good question.

Because that's exactly what's happened on the British equivalent of Haight-Ashbury: the King's Road in London. Back in the day this was a mishmash of small shops selling individually made items to Mick Jagger and Johnny Rotten. Now it's WH Smith, HMV, Marks & Spencer. It's exactly the same as Pontefract and Pontypool. Genesis has gone all Phil Collins.

The trouble is that there are only a few streets in London where the big multinational retailers want to be. This means the rents are six times higher on the King's Road than they are on Haight Street in San Francisco. One American chain called Forever 21 paid almost £14 million in key money to HMV to take over its lease on Oxford Street. And against that sort of financial clout, a slightly off-his-head jewellery designer with a fondness for growing beans and a laissez-faire attitude to payment is going to find himself priced out of the market.

The good news is, however, that I'm by no means the only person who shivers with despair at Britain's one-size-fits-nobody attitude to shopping. I'm not the only person who fumes with rage over the sheer length of time it takes to pay. And how the financial pressure to make every square foot count means stock and changing rooms are smaller than most lavatory cisterns.

Which means that one day the Starbucks and the Forever 21s and the Banana Republics will be brought to their knees. And the streets of our towns will be handed back to Ronnie Barker, who'll open all hours, sell us things we like and let us pay at the end of the week. In beads.

9 September 2012

Oh, my head hurts – I've a bad case of hangover envy

As you probably heard, the government announced recently that during the month of what it's calling 'Stoptober', it will run a nationwide campaign designed to make every smoker in the land stub out their last cigarette and quit.

I don't remember that being in the manifesto. And I certainly don't remember giving my permission for the Department of Star Jumps and Push-Ups to spend vast lumps of my money on a series of bossy television advertisements designed to make my life less pleasant. So, in protest, I decided to give up drinking.

Most nights, like many people of my age, I drink a bottle of wine, and this means that most mornings I have a bit of clutch slip until after I've had some coffee, a couple of Nurofen and some quiet time with the papers.

I'm comfortable with that. But I'm not really comfortable with the effects the booze has had on my stomach. Visually, it's a bit silly. It looks like I have the actual moon in my shirt. It's so vast that when I bend over to tie up my shoelaces, it squashes into my lungs so firmly that I can't breathe.

And when I run, it turns into a giant pendulum, sloshing from side to side so vigorously that sometimes I get the impression it may actually break free from its moorings. I needed to get rid of it, and if in the process I could stick a finger in the eye of a hectoring government, so much the better. I therefore decided to give up booze.

So the first night. I felt no need for wine. I'm not an alcoholic in the true sense of the word. But my hands felt a bit fidgety, like they'd been made redundant. They wanted something to do. They wanted a glass of something to nurture but what could I put in it?

Milk? Lovely. My favourite drink in the whole wide world. But even more fattening than wine and at seven p.m. it seemed wrong. Water? No. The stupidest idea in the world. It's just liquefied air. Something fizzy? Too carcinogenic. I thought about tea but I'm not old enough yet, and then discounted tomato juice on the basis that its primary function in life is to cure what I wouldn't be suffering from any more.

I went to the supermarket, where I discovered that all of the non-alcoholic 'beverages' are aimed either at people who want to stay awake, or who are four years old. It's row after row of idiotic lime-green labelling and contents that appear to have come from the props department of *Doctor Who*.

I was in despair until, at the last moment, I discovered a bottle of Robinsons lemon barley water. The taste of my childhood; Dan Maskell in a bottle. I took it home and it was like drinking the sound of a wood pigeon and a distant tractor. I was very happy.

The second night, I was going out and it transpires that no bar or restaurant stocks Robinsons barley water. So I had to think of something else.

I was still thinking several hours later, by which time my friends were unsteady on their feet and very garrulous.

And suddenly I discovered the biggest problem of not drinking in a society that does. When everyone else is drunk, they look stupid, they sound stupid, they laugh at things that aren't funny, such as a fart, and you start to hate them on a cellular level.

You begin to wonder what they would look like without heads, and because you are sober, the imagery is frighteningly clear.

Turning up in polite society and asking for a soft drink is like turning up and sobbing. It puts a damper on proceedings.

A meeting of friends is supposed to be light and filled with laughter. The last thing a group of happy people wants is one person sitting in the middle talking about the trauma of Syria.

If I was going to keep this non-drinking lark up, there is no doubt that the moon in my shirt would start to shrink. But, on the downside, I would lose all my friends and I would have to come to terms with the fact that never again would I have a great night out. No, really, I mean it. Can you think of a single memorable evening you've ever had when you weren't absolutely blasted? Nope. Neither can I.

In fact, you won't really have a night out at all because such is the pressure to drink, to join the herd, to find a fart funny, that it's a thousand times easier to decline the invitation and stay at home. Which is why for the next four nights I did just that, with my barley water, watching television and enriching my life not one bit.

I learnt something else as well. It is possible to suffer from hangover envy. In a morning, as you're doing a bit of light skipping, you see your friends clinging on to trees and street furniture, looking like a pile of laundry, with faces the colour of ostrich eggs.

This should be uplifting. It should make you feel good as you *boing* along the street with a zip in your step and sparkling eyes. But, in fact, it makes you crestfallen. Because at four a.m., when you were asleep, which is the same as being dead, they were very much alive. They were making memories in police cells and on inappropriate girls, and you were at home snoring the snore of a dullard. Waking up feeling fresh is like dying with a clear conscience and a healthy bank balance. It means you've wasted your life.

So here we are, ten days into my non-drinking regime. It's nine p.m., I have a glass of wine by the laptop and some friends have just invited me over – I'm going and I don't plan to be home till two. So when *Top Gear* returns to your screen, know this: yes, it will look like I've got a planet in my shirt, but I will be smiling the smile of a man who's happy with his life. I will be smiling the smile of a man who's had a drink.

16 September 2012

If breasts are no big deal, girls, don't get them reupholstered

In the past week I've been mildly startled by the attitude of many women, who've said they cannot understand why someone would take photographs of a girl sunbathing topless, why a magazine would pay money for the right to publish them and why Buckingham Palace should have used the courts to try to prevent further images from reaching a wider audience. All have said the same thing: 'Breasts are no big deal.'

On the face of it, that's true. How can they be a big deal when half the world has them? Well, I'll tell you how. Because the other half can't really ever think of anything else.

In a list of stuff that matters most to a man, breasts appear at No. 4, between oxygen and food.

Breasts fascinate us. We cannot imagine why women don't spend all day at home playing with them, because if we had them, that's what we'd do. It's why we were all so keen to have a look at what sort the future queen has. Would they be angry, sad, milky or pointy? Would they look like deflated zeppelins or dried fish? Or would they not really be there at all?

Often we are told by women that when at work or out socializing, they are heartily fed up with men who talk to their chest rather than their face. Well, I would like to say here and now that men do not do that. I would like to. But I cannot. Because on occasion we do. We can't help it.

In the same way that women could not help having a quiet moment with their laptop if they thought the internet was hosting a full-frontal picture of George Clooney.

Of course, since the invention of clothing there have been many attempts to desexualize the breast. In the 1960s, *National Geographic* magazine was undoubtedly seen as a weighty and learned tome full of many interesting facts about the world and its people. Not to me, it wasn't. It was a girlie mag.

Later, women's liberationists argued that by burning their bras they were freeing themselves from the shackles of history and propelling themselves through the glass ceiling. And this received a great deal of support from male observers, all of whom were equally keen for bra-less women to be seen anywhere.

Today new mothers are often to be found in crowded places breastfeeding their infants. They could go behind a tree or to a quiet spot, but by popping one out in public they send a clear message: This is not a sex toy. It's a food dispensary unit, so stop staring.

Yeah, right. Telling us to stop staring at a breast is like telling us not to stare at a burning airliner. It isn't possible.

The Duchess of Cambridge is probably fearful that she is the first senior royal to be seen in public in such a state of undress.

Not so. Queen Mary II was painted topless, and in France, scene of the current brouhaha, Charles VII's mistress would constantly swan around court with her breasts on show. It was the fashion then.

You might like to think that things changed in Victorian times but evidently not. The Victorians were idiotically prudish and got it into their tiny minds that the ankle and the shoulder should be concealed beneath many layers of velvet, steel and wood. Despite this, it was absolutely fine to turn up at a Brunellian reception for the monarch herself in the sort of top that even Kate Moss would find 'too revealing'.

So men have been exposed to breasts for centuries. Many of us were brought up on them. We see them every day in the nation's bestselling newspaper, on the internet and on even the coldest Saturday night in Newcastle. We see them on the beach when we go on holiday and in the office on a hot day. Breasts are simply everywhere. They should be about as sexual as moths. But they aren't.

Let me pose a delicate question. In the sort of exotic South Sea societies that used to appear in the *National Geographic* magazine, it is still completely normal for women to be top-less as they go about their daily business. So does this mean that during lovemaking sessions, their boyfriends and hus-bands treat their breasts like their noses and ignore them? It's possible, I suppose, but I very much doubt it.

What's more, if breasts are no big deal, why do women buy bras that lift and separate and do all sorts of other things besides? Why queue round the block to have your breasts reupholstered?

It's because you know that, in fact, your breasts are a big deal. Mrs Mountbatten-Windsor knows it too and that's why she was so mortified to find them in the press and plastered all over the internet.

Those pictures should not have been taken and they should not have been published. And it is stupid to claim that she's to blame because she was in full view of the public road. Because that's only true if you were looking at her through a two-million-millimetre telephoto lens.

Happily, though, the argument brings me on to a solution. Doubtless one day the photographer who took the offending snaps will be identified, and when that happens he will become a public figure. According to his rules, that will make him fair game.

So someone should wait for him to go to the lavatory and

then snap away. If he chooses to complain about having a private moment appear on the internet, then we will simply argue that, at the time, he was clearly visible to anyone who happened to be on a stepladder peering over the top of the cubicle. And that he should have known better.

23 September 2012

Call me Comrade Clarkson, liberator of the jobsworths

In the past couple of weeks everyone in the country, except me, seems to have decided that Andrew Mitchell, the government chief whip, is a potty-mouthed snob who goes through life gorging on swan, goosing his housekeeper and shooting poor people for sport.

Last week the police released details of exactly what was said between officers and Mr Mitchell after he'd been told he couldn't ride his bicycle through the main gates at Downing Street. Mr Mitchell demanded that he be allowed to exit through the main gate whereupon it was explained to him this was not possible.

A police officer on duty said: 'I am more than happy to open the side pedestrian gate for you, sir, but it is policy that we are not to allow cycles through the main vehicle gate.'

At this point Mr Mitchell seems to have become angry, telling the officers they had best learn their effing place, that they were effing plebs and that they hadn't heard the last of the matter.

Hmmm. While his choice of abuse seems a bit weak, I sympathize with his sentiments absolutely. Because what petty-minded pen-pusher made this policy and why? What possible difference can it make which gate people use when leaving work? Why should bicycles use one gate and cars another?

These are the questions that matter. Except, of course, we already know the answers. 'It's security, sir.' Or maybe: 'It's health and safety, sir.' These are the catch-all responses from anyone in a uniform who thinks if he uses the word 'sir' as often as possible, we won't notice he's being a complete arse.

Only very recently I arrived at a department of the BBC, where I engaged in the usual good-natured banter with a security guard I've known for many years. I asked how he was. He asked after my family. We chatted momentarily about the weather and then, after I explained that I'd accidentally left my pass at home, he said he couldn't let me in. 'Security policy,' he said, with the good-natured shrug of a small cog that has never asked a bigger cog: 'Why?'

I felt it immediately: a hotness surging into my head and threatening to sever my tongue from its mountings, leaving it free to call the blithering idiot many cruel and unusual names. I began to imagine what he might look like without a head. And the noises he'd make if I staked him out in the desert with no eyelids.

This happens all the time. With traffic wardens who somehow can't see that I only popped into the tobacconist's for a moment; with airport security guards who think my youngest daughter is a dead ringer for Abu Hamza; and most recently in America with a moron who wanted photo ID before I could rent a luggage locker.

Then you have the imbeciles at the post office and various other large organizations who explain their company's stupid policy and, when they see you're about to boil over, point at a sign on their desk that says: 'The company will not tolerate physical or verbal abuse directed at our employees.' In other words: 'If you complain about our small-minded idiocy you will go to prison.'

So you stand there and you say, as calmly as you can: 'Why can you not deliver my parcel/fridge/important document?' And invariably you are told it is for security reasons. Or health and safety.

Actually, neither of those things is the reason. No. The reason the police officers in Downing Street, the nation's traffic wardens and the counter staff at the post office do not bend the rules even when they can see you're making sense is simple: they fear for their jobs. They've been told by their line manager what the policy is and they know that if they bend it even a little bit, just once, they will be sacked.

Things are different in Italy. Last week I flew back to Britain through Milan's Linate airport. And it was plainly obvious that the X-ray arch machine had been set to such a level it could detect tiny fragments of zinc in a lady's vajazzle, or bits of nickel in those hard bits at the end of a man's shoelaces.

We see this a lot with airport scanners these days and we know what the response will be. You'll be sent back to take off yet another item of clothing until you are butt naked. And even then, thanks to the cardamom in the chicken casserole you ate the night before, a man will want to rub his wand over your genitals. It's humiliating and disgusting.

In Milan, however, they do things rather differently. Someone would walk through the machine. It would beep. The security guard would note that it was a businessman or an old lady and would simply wave them through. I beeped. He looked at me. Saw no beard. Saw I had hands rather than hooks. And that was that.

Of course, he will have been told loudly, and usually by the Americans, that every single person getting on every single airliner is likely to explode at any moment, but Luigi uses his nous. And he has obviously worked out that if a terrorist organization is going to go to all the bother of blowing up a plane, it probably won't be the 11.30 a.m. commuter shuttle from Milan to London.

So why is Luigi allowed to use the power of reason when

Mr Patel at Heathrow is not? Simple. Because Luigi cannot be sacked.

Well, he can, but under the terms of Italian employment law, his employer must continue to pay his wages, his mortgage, his children's school fees and the grocery bill of his descendants forever.

I have no doubt at all that Mr Mitchell, a Tory, would fight tooth and nail to stop such communist laws being introduced in Britain. Which is why he will continue to be told by knees-knocking policemen that they can't let him cycle through the vehicle gate because using their common sense is more than their job's worth.

Simple solution. Introduce a system where it becomes less than their job's worth.

30 September 2012

If foreigners weren't watching, we'd be lynching bell-ringers

While on a tour of a factory in South America recently, David Cameron appeased the nation's meat-eaters by saying that at some point in the next parliament there might possibly be a referendum on whether Britain stayed in the European Union.

Isolationism is very popular at the moment. Not just with middle England but with the Scotch, too, and the Corns — everyone. If you gave people in Leicester the chance to form their own government and their own state, I bet you any money a majority would say, 'Ooh, yes please.'

Certainly the idea of Chipping Norton breaking free from the shackles of Westminster and Brussels is very appealing. There is little crime, so we wouldn't need a police force. Or an army. Many people own guns, so we'd easily be able to hold out should we be attacked by Stow-on-the-Wold or Moreton-in-Marsh. We have meat, trout and vegetables. We could trade jam for oil. And we have wind for power.

Taxes would be very low, since we would only really need a school, two doctors and a fire station. And we could introduce some new laws relevant to our way of life. We could make it illegal to be Piers Morgan or to harbour a badger. Campanology would be outlawed, too, along with motorcycles. On the face of it, then, life would be peachy.

To understand where all of this might end, you need to go back to the 1850s in what at the time was known as 'darkest Africa'. British explorers stumbled on a tribe living on the tranquil northern shores of Lake Victoria. People had been living there for tens of thousands of years, assuming that they were the only people on earth. They had never met anyone from another tribe, let alone an Arab or a white man. And it was interesting to see how their society had developed.

They had not invented the wheel or the plough. But they had invented beer. And they could carry it around in vessels woven exquisitely from reeds. They also had fine cloth and knew to wash their hands in the lake before eating. They had also come up with the idea of extreme violence.

If a child was making too much noise over lunch, it would be beheaded. If it got up without clearing its plate? That was a beheading offence, too. Beheading was their society's equivalent of the naughty step. It was also a cure for snoring, nagging or looking at someone in a funny way.

It could be worse, though. You could have ended up as one of the king's wives. They were kept bound on the floor and forced to drink milk for eight hours a day, non-stop.

This ensured that when the head honcho fancied a spot of rumpy-pumpy, the girl he selected would be nice and fat. Kate Moss? She would have been beheaded before she'd reached puberty.

Now remember, this was the middle of the nineteenth century. Elsewhere in the world there were steam engines and ladies with parasols taking tea in the park. People in India wore clothes made in Huddersfield. People in Louisiana drank tea from Ceylon. And yet in the middle of it all was a civilization in which you could be beheaded for talking with your mouth full.

What stopped it was the arrival of other people. People who said, 'Yes, cutting your daughter's head off is certainly one way of teaching her not to use her fingers at meal times. But have you tried a stern word, or a smacked bottom, because where we come from that works quite well, too?'

This argument is still relevant today. What do you think stops American police forces waterboarding pretty much everyone they take into custody? The answer has nothing to do with the inner goodness of a man's soul. It's the sure-fire knowledge that other people are watching.

Why do you think Robert Mugabe is such a monster? Because Zimbabwe is cut off. He can do as he pleases because he doesn't have people from other places raising an eyebrow and saying, 'Are you sure?'

Closer to home we have the Isle of Man. Because it's not really in the EU and not really part of the UK and because people from abroad are viewed by locals as Romulan stormtroopers, it was 1992 before they stopped birching homosexuals in front of a baying mob. And why? Because that's when satellite TV from other countries showed them that homosexuality wasn't a lifestyle choice and that birching was a bit last week. Maybe one day soon its idiotic government will also learn that it can't just go around confiscating people's gardens.

Most governments in the civilized world are constitutionally bound by checks and balances to ensure they don't do something idiotic. And what are those checks and balances? They usually have fancy names but, actually, they all boil down to the same thing: other people.

In Britain every single poll on the death penalty suggests that the vast majority of us would like to see the gallows reintroduced. And, of course, if we weren't in the EU, a government would be free to bring it back.

But what for? At first, it would be for premeditated murder and rape. However, with no one looking, how long would it be before we were hanging people for having a beard, or for shouting at meal times, or for being Peter Mandelson? How long before disaffected Muslim youths started disappearing?

And before child molesters and bell-ringers were hung from lamp posts by lynch mobs?

Take the case of Abu Hamza. Every fibre of your being wanted him gone and you didn't really care where. If he'd ended up becoming part of a new flyover on the M6, you'd have been relieved. But would that have been a good thing? Really?

We need to be in Europe, to trade with the Germans and holiday in France. We need to be Spain's checks and Sweden's balances. For the sake of decency and the advancement of science, we need to share ideas, to compromise, to be a team. We need to look after one another. Not the Greeks, though. They can get lost.

7 October 2012

Take another step, Simba, and you'll feel my foldaway spoon

When I was growing up I used to go on a great many bicycle rides and they were great fun. But, of course, you can't do that any more because today cycling has been hijacked by thin-spectacled men from the marketing department, and as a result it's become a 'lifestyle choice'.

This means you can't just buy a bicycle. You need lots of other paraphernalia as well.

You need what's called 'kit'. A helmet with a built-in camera, brakes made from materials that aren't even on the periodic table, some sideburns, a carbon-fibre boot mount for your car, some ridiculous energy bars and half a pint of special gel to keep your gentleman's area zesty and fresh.

And then, when you have all this, you will meet other people who've made the same lifestyle choice and they'll explain that their gel is better than your gel and that their energy bars are more energetic. So you'll have to throw all your stuff away and upgrade immediately.

It's the same story with fishing. Gone are the days when you could splosh about, netting sticklebacks. Now, you have titanium rods and a range of neoprene waders. If you want to hold your head up on the river, you'll be forced by your bank manager to sell all the natty golf-bag attachments you bought during your recent flirtation with the men of Pringle.

All you need to shoot a pheasant is a gun and some cartridges. But, of course, that's not true because today you need to turn up looking like a cross between King Edward

VII and Pablo Escobar. And in addition to the fancy-dress costume you'll need noise-cancelling headphones, leather wellies, some care-in-the-community fingerless gloves, a pair of yellow sunglasses, a Range Rover and the ability to talk for hours about the weight of the shot in your cartridges. This means the cost of each pheasant you bring down is approximately £1 million.

It doesn't seem to matter, though. For many men nowadays the thrill of buying a new hobby-related gadget far outweighs the thrill of actually doing the hobby. And absolutely nothing proves this more than a trip to see the big five in Africa.

I've just spent a couple of weeks over there with a handful of colleagues who I know from experience travel the world armed only with jeans and T-shirts. Unless they're in the Arctic Circle, in which case it's jeans, T-shirts and an anorak.

When they go to China none of them feels the need to dress up like Chairman Mao. When they're in Japan they don't wear kimonos and slippers. And in France none of them comes down to breakfast wearing a beret. But in Africa they all take leave of their senses and turn up dressed like the zipped and Velcroed love children of Bear Grylls and Joy Adamson. And that's before we get to the kit.

One night a hippopotamus came into the camp, and like any sentient being I was mesmerized by the stupidity of its ears and the idiocy of its noises. But no one else even looked up because they were all engrossed in Richard Hammond's new torch.

When it comes to holding my attention, a torch is right up there with a knitting needle or some lettuce.

But this one was somehow amazing because it had come from an African adventurer's kit shop. Along with Hammond's trousers, which had many pockets for his foldaway cutlery, his compass and, bizarrely, his massive knife.

Now I can see why you might need a knife when you are carving the Sunday joint or chopping vegetables. But why would you need such a thing in Africa? Do people really imagine that they will be attacked by a lion? It's nonsense because a) lions are too busy sleeping or having sex to attack people, and b) even if one did, do you think you'd have the presence of mind to unzip your special knife pocket, retrieve the blade and stick it into a bit of the beast that might somehow make a difference?

Hammond was not the only one to have succumbed to the marketing man's spell. Our minicam operator had plainly overdosed on the gullible pills because he arrived with a head torch that shone a red light.

'It doesn't attract insects,' he said from inside what looked like a beehive.

His other new toy was a hammock that featured a shaped bottom section and a ribbed mosquito net on the top. It had probably cost about £2,000 and looked very sleek and impressive. But as he climbed inside on the first night, he discovered as the rain started that while it kept the flies away, it was not waterproof.

Shoes were another big thing among the chaps. It seems that people in the outdoor pursuits industry have it in their minds that in Africa there is very little gravity, so to anchor yourself in place you need to be sporting footwear that weighs the same as a small house.

Plus, because they've also decided there is almost no friction in Africa, the soles must be made from chunky grooved rubber that appears to have come from the tyres of an earth mover.

Americans are very easily conned by the outdoor leisure

industry's marketing powers, which is why they turn up at every hippo watering hole looking as though they've just stepped off the set of *Daktari*. I realize, of course, that American tourists are always more interesting than whatever they're looking at, but in Africa's game reserves they are absolutely hysterical. I saw one with a canvas drinking canteen. What use would that be on a holiday where you are never more than 30ft from a fridge?

I'm not saying that all hobby-related kit is useless. Obviously you can't jump from a balloon in outer space wearing a blazer and slacks, and you can't dive to the bottom of the deepest trench in the ocean in a suit and tie. Sometimes equipment is necessary. But if you are going for a walk, or going on holiday, or going for a bicycle ride, trust me on this: it isn't.

21 October 2012

So, the Scouts came to earth in a reptilian space plane, right?

Many state-educated people have it in their heads that life for those in Britain's public schools is a deeply weird potpourri of silly uniforms, brutal sport and endless lessons about tax avoidance and the benefits of offshore slavery. In Latin.

I sympathize with all this, of course.

You see those Eton boys poncing about in their frilly shirts and their frock coats and because you have no idea what goes on behind the closed doors, you're bound to think they're all a bit mad, bad and dangerous.

It's the same story with Scientology. We have a vague idea that if you follow its principles, you will be able to fly an F-14 upside down and sleep with Kelly McGillis. On the downside, however, you have to believe that humans were transported to earth millions of years ago in a DC-8-like craft by a tyrant ruler of the galactic confederacy. This is hard to swallow, of course, because the DC-8 was a jet. And jets don't work in space.

At this point we should move on to Mitt Romney. I am told that it is not possible to take anything he says seriously because he is a Mormon and, of course, I nod sagely even though – if I'm honest – I really don't have a clue what Mormons do. Are they the ones who can have nine wives but no blood transfusions? Or is that the Jehovah's Witnesses?

You see the problem. We get snippets of information about these organizations and they worry us. Ignorance makes us afraid. That's why I have a morbid fear of the Freemasons. As I understand it, you may not progress beyond the rank of constable in the police unless you are a member. Which means that every single senior officer has to really believe that if he explains the secrets of the handshake, his tongue will be torn from its mountings and thrown in the sea.

This is why when I'm talking to a sergeant I'm always a bit frightened. Because, thanks to the small amount of knowledge I have about his lodge meetings, I think he is a loony.

But I reserve my greatest fear and trepidation for people who are, or who have been, Scouts. In the olden days, Scouting was very obviously a harmless pursuit. You'd see them in the woods from time to time, tying knots and rubbing sticks together, and then once a year they'd emerge from the treeline and offer to rub grit into your car in exchange for a shilling.

Now, though, we never see them at all. However, like the ebola virus, they're still out there in their millions. And we have scant idea of what they're up to . . .

Their leader in Britain is a man called Bear Grylls, a survival expert who stays in hotels and likes to be attacked at night by friends and colleagues in wildlife costumes.

More importantly, we heard last week that Scouts are no longer permitted to use nicknames. That is very sinister. Scout chiefs say that nicknames can lead to bullying and argue that this is in some way a bad thing. I disagree.

Bullying gives a man a spine. It forces him to address his issues and work out what he's doing wrong. I was bullied for two straight years at school and I like to think it toughened me up and made me realize that you can't go through life being a hopeless, quivery-bottom-lipped, unfunny prig.

In the early days this is what Scouting was all about. It prepared boys for life as adults. It made them strong and practical. They knew what to do when they were attacked by a fox. They knew that if they worked they would be rewarded.

They also knew how to keep Scout masters out of the tent at night. So when you left the Scouting movement you were more of a man than if you'd never joined.

But now that your comrades are no longer allowed to call you 'Chubby' or 'Ginger' or 'Slob Boy', you will be weak and unprepared to deal on your own with life's little crises, so you will have to rely on the authorities to settle your disputes.

There's more. Jews, Muslims and Buddhists are all welcome but you are not allowed to join if you are an agnostic or an atheist. How mad is that? The movement's leaders argue that this is in the sprit of Robert Baden-Powell's demand that members believe in a higher power.

Hmm. So why are gays allowed in? I can't imagine he'd have approved of that. He didn't even like foreigners very much.

This is the big problem for Scouts. We hear about the hypocrisy and the nonsense. But other than that we know very little. So we fill in the blanks ourselves, assuming that in America it's a front for the neo-Nazis and that in Britain it's a division of the Liberal Democrats, only with more on-message sustainability and inclusivity.

Happily, however, I have a solution. Twenty years ago the Scouts' bob-a-job week was abandoned for fear that little Johnnie – known until then as Fatso – might fall foul of health and safety legislation or get sued by a little old lady for fire-hosing her cat to death.

There was an attempt earlier this year to bring it back. It was called 'community week' and it saw Scouts planting wild flowers and retrieving shopping trolleys from canals. But, I'm sorry, to take the mystery out of Scouting it's not good enough to have members in a faraway lock, doing what prisoners should be doing.

We need them at our doors, with pockets full of scrumped

apples, offering to clean our shoes and sweep the chimney for 5p. We need to encounter Scouts in our daily lives, helping old ladies across the road and petting guide dogs.

It's the same story, in fact, with all the world's esoteric organizations. Opus Dei, the Masons, UKIP, Tom and John at the Scientologists, Eton, the European Union, the Salvation Army. All of you. Come round this evening and clean my shoes. Not the Jehovah's Witnesses, though. I've had enough of you already. You can stay at home.

28 October 2012

This lanky git will call you what he wants, ref – you blind idiot

For the sake of English football Manchester United always need to win. Which is probably why, in last weekend's top-of-the-table clash, the referee set about sending the entire Chelsea team off for wearing blue clothes. And then, when that didn't work, he awarded a goal to a player who was so offside he might as well have been standing in Bristol.

As a Chelsea supporter I was very cross about all this. Indeed I spent most of the game wondering what the ref in question would look like without a head.

Today, though, I feel rather sorry for the stupid, blind idiot because it has been alleged that during the game he made derogatory remarks about John Obi Mikel. It was also suggested earlier in the week that he had called Juan Mata a 'Spanish t***'. (Clue: not 'twit'.)

I would imagine that this sort of thing has been going on in football since someone inflated a sheep's pancreas and discovered that jumpers could be used for goalposts. But suddenly it isn't allowed any more. So the ref has been suspended and is being investigated for a racially aggravated offence by Plod. In other words, the sharp-elbowed group hug of inclusivity has now landed in the middle of a football pitch.

Football is not croquet. The stands are visceral and ugly places full of rage and hatred. And standing in the middle of it all, trying to keep order, is the referee. Until 2001 he was an unhappily married amateur called Keith who used a Saturday-afternoon kickabout to get back at everyone who had made his working week so dreary and miserable. I do not know a football referee. I've never even met one. And I bet you haven't, either.

Today Premier League refs are professionals on more than £70,000 a year. But, I'm sorry, that's not enough.

Dentistry is bad. You live in a fog of halitosis waiting for the day when you accidentally catch AIDS. And I can't imagine it's much fun being a North Sea trawlerman either. You spend all day in a fish-scented cloud of diesel smoke, vomiting, and when you get home a bureaucrat tells you to throw the six cod you caught back into the sea.

But worse than both these things – worse even than being a dentist on a trawler – is the job of a Premier League referee. No. 1) you have to wear shorts. No. 2) there is a very great deal of running about. And No. 3) every single person in the entire world would like to eviscerate you, in front of your family, on the internet.

Can you imagine what life would be like for a surgeon if he had to go through his working day with his assistants, his nurses and even his patient telling him loudly and constantly that he was useless, that he was bent and that he worshipped at the altar of onanism? 'Call that an incision, you effing w*****?'

Then there's the business of making mistakes. We all do that. I make millions, and so do surgeons, even when they are in a warm room, wearing long trousers and listening to the calming strains of Pachelbel's Canon.

A football referee, on the other hand, is not listening to classical music. He can't sit back in a comfy chair to ruminate over a steaming mug of tea on what he should do next. He is running at top speed, often in the rain, trying to keep on top of the action in a game that is played 20 per cent faster now than it was just five years ago. He is being told to eff off at every turn.

And then he thinks he sees something happen and must react without a moment's pause. I think I would be useless. I think you would be, too.

But Premier League refs are not. Because more than 92 per cent of the decisions they make are subsequently proved by slow-motion replays to be correct.

To achieve this level of accuracy, they train hard. Not just so they're as fit as the players they're monitoring but also so they can see like a bird. Seriously. They do eye exercises to improve both their peripheral vision and their ability to spot, through a fast-moving pack of tangled limbs twenty yards away, who's doing what to whom.

In short, then, the man in black must have the stamina of an athlete, the eyesight of a pigeon, the reactions of a king-fisher, the legs of a male model and an autistic indifference to the opinions of other people. And now, on top of all this, he must also behave like a vicar.

Last weekend Mark Clattenburg, the ref at the Chelsea game, was having an off day. He must have known this because 35,000 people, including my son, were reminding him very loudly, and with uprooted chairs. It is entirely pos-sible that Juan Mata was reminding him also. So what's wrong with saying, 'Shut it, you Spanish t***'?

When Richard Hammond is being annoying, which is when he's awake, I refer to him as a 'Brummie t***'. He, in turn, often calls me a 'lanky t***', and both of us regularly call James May a 'boring t***'. No harm is meant by any of it.

But we are now reaching the point where, even on a foot-ball pitch during a vital game between the two best teams in the country, people are expected to address one another like promenading ladies on a Victorian pier. It's absurd.

And, of course, it's all the fault of a man called Ed Mili-band who runs the Labour party. He is leading the charge to make it impossible to tease anyone because of their colour, their facial disfigurements, their religion, their size, the colour of their hair, their sexual orientation, the country of their birth or their sex. Only last week he added a new one: we can no longer poke fun at those who suffer from mental illnesses.

Of course we can't go around tipping people out of wheelchairs and hounding fatties to death. But there should be a distinction between genuinely unpleasant behaviour and harmless banter. Otherwise we end up with a situation where I can't call Miliband an 'adenoidal t***', but I can call him a 't***'. Which is why I just did.

4 November 2012

Chew on a Big Mac with fibs before you answer a survey

I think it was the much-missed Keith Waterhouse who invented the 'I have never' game. The rules are simple. You tell a group of friends something that you have never done in your whole life and those that have done it give you 10p.

Keith's sure-fire winner was 'I have never taken a dog for a walk'. But I could always retort with the incredible but true 'I have never bought anything from Marks & Spencer'.

And there are other nuggets in my repertoire. I have never seen a single moment of *EastEnders*. I have never seen any of the *Godfather* movies. I've never smoked a joint. And I've never been on a London bus.

The only problem with the game is that after about five minutes people are struggling to think of mundane things that they alone have never done. So things become sexual. And embarrassing, as ten people around a bottle-strewn table try to claim that they too have never had intercourse in a public place or by themselves in front of a computer.

Once, having been cleaned out by a chap who had never been to Scotland, I was so desperate I came up with, 'I have never used a tampon', knowing that half the table would have to cough up. Amazingly one man gave me 10p, though obviously I won't mention his name here – only that it begins with a J and ends in Ames May. Apparently he uses them to clean hard-to-reach parts of his cooker.

Anyway, a survey revealed last week that the smuttiness and tampon admissions are unnecessary because millions of people in Britain have never done anything mundane at all.

Some of the findings are not surprising: 37 per cent have never read anything by Shakespeare, 68 per cent have never been skiing and 36 per cent have never been to a football match.

But most of it is just too amazing for words: 23 per cent of the nation – that's more than 14 million souls – have never been on an aeroplane while an equal number haven't even been to France. Also 17 per cent have never wired a plug; 6 per cent have never used a mobile phone; 16 per cent have never sent an email; and 30 per cent have never ordered a takeaway cup of coffee. But for me the biggest surprise is this one: 19 per cent have never eaten anything from McDonald's.

Of course, we all know the problem that lurks behind Ronald's cheery grin. McDonald's is fundamentally evil. We don't know why we know this, but we do. Which is why whenever three or four protesters are gathered together, they head immediately for the golden arches.

It doesn't matter whether they are fathers fighting for justice, or anti-G8 communists, or students campaigning on behalf of Brian May's badger; all of them feel certain that their cause will be strengthened if they go and kick a hole through Ronald's windows.

It has been argued in the past that no two countries where McDonald's operates have ever gone to war with each other. And that's true. Apart from when America invaded Panama. And when NATO bombed Serbia. And Libya, obviously. And Russia bombed Georgia. And so on. 'You see,' scream the protesters. 'Evil!!!'

Then you have the comedian Robin Williams, who once said of his new son: 'I have a dream where one day he is saying, "I would like to thank the Nobel academy." And a nightmare where he is saying, "Do you want fries with that?"'

My children have had Big Macs in the past but now they are full of righteous teenage anger they would not have one again. This is partly because they know for sure that McDonald's is pouring acid into the sea and partly because company executives like to unwind after a busy day by clubbing puppy dogs to death.

Mostly, though, it's because they know as a fact that McDonald's has bulldozed the entire Brazilian rainforest to create pasture for its beef herds. Yes, that's right. It has severed the world's lungs to increase its filthy profits. This is the level of evil we are talking about here. Top baddies such as Blofeld and Osama bin Laden pale into obscurity alongside the corporate savagery emanating on a day-by-day basis from the company's Illinois headquarters.

And that's before we get to the damage done by its products. A Big Mac is a heart attack in a bun. A Quarter Pounder has exactly the same effect on your well-being as licking the debris at Fukushima. And a McNugget is basically a piece of battered excrement. Eat any of this stuff and you will swell up until you are the size of a Buick. And then you will burst, showering everyone within 400 yards with thick, yellow fat, and spiders.

However, the problem is that after a night out, when you are weary and hungover, there is nothing that hits the spot quite so well as a Big Mac and fries.

I have tried everything in these circumstances: pills; hairs of every dog I can think of; worcestershire sauce with a splash of tomato juice; and once an injection of vitamin B. All of them work – the injection works brilliantly, in fact – but none works quite as well as a Big Mac.

It's as comforting as your childhood teddy bear, and as tasty as the tastiest thing you ever put in your mouth. And when you've finished, and it's down there in your stomach, absorbing the sick, you know that despite everything your head may be saying, all will soon be right with the world once more.

I am plainly not alone in thinking this because in Britain McDonald's serves 2.5 million customers every day. Around the world it serves more than 75 burgers every second. To date it has sold more than 245 billion and that means, all on its own, the company has a bigger economy than Ecuador.

So when I read that almost one in five British people claims to have never had a Big Mac, I draw a simple conclusion. Either many millions of people are missing out on one of life's greatest pleasures, or Britain is home to a great many liars.

11 November 2012

Yes, siree – count me in for genocide and conservatory-building

Twenty years ago I would land at Heathrow after every trip to America and kiss the tarmac, thanking every god I could think of that I was back in the land of the free.

Back then in Britain we were allowed to smoke and smack our children and rush about the countryside on horseback.

Footballers could call one another names, children could cycle in home clothes, we could drink irresponsibly and park on a yellow line while we popped into the shop for some milk. We could use cameras to film school sports days, abuse useless counter staff and get on a plane with our toothpaste. It was nice.

America, meanwhile, was drowning in a thunderstorm of petty bureaucracy that meant every janitor was armed with a walkie-talkie and a gun and encouraged to shoot anyone who broke any of the laws, no matter how bonkers they may have been.

You had to wear shoes while shopping. It was illegal to deface signs telling you it was illegal to deface signs. You were not allowed to swim in the pool if you'd had a tummy upset within the past fourteen days. Drinking in the street was prohibited. And you were not permitted to take any smoking material on to federal property. You couldn't even use a police car park if there was a cigarette lighter in your vehicle. It was madness.

In Soviet Russia you were allowed to do everything but vote. Whereas in America twenty years ago you could vote. But do nothing else. And it's still bad today. In the summer my daughter was carted off by the police for smoking near a fruit machine while under the age of twenty-one. And we had to produce photo ID before being allowed to rent a locker. It was almost as though they'd studied the ancient British laws governing London taxi drivers and high sheriffs and thought, 'Ooh. They look good. Let's insist New York cabbies carry a bale of hay in the boot, and ban people from taking fish into a cinema in Colorado.'

And it's even worse if you are part of a television crew because you'll need a permit before you film anything. And even when you get a permit, there will be a problem. An example: you can get permission to film on Wall Street. But it does not entitle you to film any of the buildings. And have you tried to take a picture in this concrete canyon without any office block appearing in the back of the shot? It's pretty tricky.

Another example: you can close a street in Detroit but you must give every single business whose door opens on to the street in question several weeks' notice of the closure.

And if you don't, an angry policeman will arrive to tell you the mayor has chewed the district attorney's bottom and that the DA has chewed his bottom and that now he's going to chew yours.

However, I was in America last week and I have some good news. Because while the fools in state and federal government continue to cut away at every basic human freedom, people are starting to find ways round the nonsense.

There's a bar in Los Angeles where the roof does not quite meet in the middle. This means that, technically, it's open to the air and that means you can smoke. And at the fabulous Roosevelt hotel in Los Angeles, there is no smoking allowed anywhere. But no one stops you if you do. In fact, they'll even bring you a saucer, saying you can use it as an ashtray.

It gets better. Because although we were forced to have a highway patrol officer in attendance while filming on the road, he was empowered to let us do what we wanted. Which meant that last Saturday I went past him on State Route 111 in southern California doing 186mph.

So to sum up: they've made a law that requires me to have a policeman on site, and by doing so have enabled me to break the law he's supposedly there to enforce.

But it gets even better. We also wanted to film some aeroplanes that needed to be flying at 300mph about six inches off the ground. To make sure that didn't happen, the authorities sent along an aviation inspector, who turned up and promptly moved heaven and earth to make sure that it did.

Everywhere we went it was the same thing. Normally if you make one little mistake on your visa waiver form you are sent to the back of a three-hour queue. This time I'd made lots. I couldn't be bothered to rummage around in the overhead locker to find out what my passport number was so I'd made one up. I said I was staying at a Premier Inn. And that I had been on a farm, and in Africa and that I had done a bit of genocide. None of which bothered the Homeland Security chap one bit.

Plainly, then, everyone is becoming content to let the politicians huff and puff and introduce silly laws to appease tiny but very noisy minorities. Just so long as the people employed to enforce those laws don't. This is very cheery news because, of course, what happens in America happens here shortly afterwards.

At present we are in a mess. You couldn't shoot a badger. Then you could, but only if your shot was monitored by a government official. And then you couldn't shoot a badger again.

You couldn't build a conservatory on the end of your

house. Then you could, so long as it was less than 27ft long. And then you could build a chemical plant as well, and your neighbours weren't allowed to object four times – only twice. Provided they weren't smoking at the time, or under arrest for hugging a teenage fan thirty years ago, or for taking make-up samples home from work just before the police arrived to search the building for evidence of a crime they said hadn't happened.

It's time we started to behave like modern-day Americans and used our nous. These badgers are killing my cows. I shall shoot them. No one will be inconvenienced if I stop here for a moment to buy stamps. And if I'm warned by someone's employer that I face prosecution for telling counter staff they are morons, I shall write back saying they are morons too.

25 November 2012

Coming soon, *I'm a Terrorist . . . Make Me Lick Nadine's Toes*

Every so often someone with too much time on their hands works out how much of our lives we spend at work, or eating, or looking for cooking utensils that we haven't used for a while.

Well, last week, while waiting for yet another flight, I worked out that I spend, on average, twenty hours a month sitting around in airports. That's ten days of my year spent in a cloud of idiotic perfume, looking at watches and trying to make the Wi-Fi work. Simply so that I can get on what is basically a bus. And there's no point complaining to the authorities, because it's 'security, sir'.

This is the problem. So long as there is one man out there with a grudge and a stick of dynamite, governments have a perfect excuse to stick their fingers in your bottom, look at pictures of you naked and rummage around in your handbag. You can shout as much as you like, but it will make absolutely no difference.

If you abuse the staff, they won't let you on the plane. If you refuse to let them look in your underpants, they won't let you on the plane. If you ask them not to take photographs of your breasts with their X-ray cameras, they won't let you on the plane. It makes my teeth itch with rage. But happily, last weekend, I came up with a solution. We simply get rid of terrorism.

In the early seventeenth century the world was troubled by religious division. I know, I know. Hard to believe, but there you are. Anyway, some Catholic Brummies felt they were being persecuted by King James I of England and decided it would be best if he, his family and all his Protestant muckers were killed. They decided, therefore, to blow up the House of Lords during the state opening of parliament. And the Gunpowder Plot was hatched.

Unfortunately, from their point of view, there was much plague around at the time and, as a result, the state opening was delayed for more than six months, by which time the gunpowder had spoilt. So they went off to buy some more, and while this was happening one of the group accidentally told some of the king's men what they were up to.

The House of Lords was searched and in the undercroft soldiers found Guy Fawkes standing next to a big pile of wood. He claimed he was a servant and they went away. But the next day they went back and the idiot was there again. So they looked under his wood and found all the gunpowder, and that was the end of that.

Fawkes, then, was a terrible terrorist. Such a moron, in fact, that today people of all faiths celebrate his subsequent execution by burning his effigy, eating sausage rolls and keeping the neighbours awake with various loud noises. In short, our forefathers turned him into a figure of ridicule and as a result we've had a Protestant monarch ever since.

Today, though, things have changed. We put Che Guevara on a T-shirt and think he looked rather cool. People say that Osama bin Laden had kind eyes. We've dug up poor old Yasser Arafat to see if he was murdered. And in Northern Ireland former enthusiasts of terror are allowed to take up serious positions in the government.

This is all wrong. Instead we should rename Guantanamo Bay as the Che Correctional Institute because that would annoy him. Every year on 2 May – the anniversary of bin Laden's death – the free world should be invited to go round to one another's houses for a piss-up. And all those IRA boys should be put on floats, dressed as clowns and paraded around town centres so we can laugh at them and their failure.

Nobody would ever dream of giving a failed terrorist community service. But that's exactly the sort of humiliation I'm after. I'd very much like to see the shoe bomber cutting all the grass in Hyde Park. With nail scissors. And it'd be a hoot to make the underwear bomber clean all the stained glass in Westminster Abbey. With his tongue.

We could even bring back *It's a Knockout* and howl with Stuart Hall-style laughter as two teams from, say, the Real IRA and al-Qaeda splosh about the streets of Corby in yellow onesies and big shoes. We could then see them for what they are. Not ogres. Not heroes. Just sad, pathetic, misguided losers whose big idea ended in capture.

At present we see terrorists as swivel-eyed, hook-handed madmen with hearts of stone and nitroglycerine for blood. Wrong. The authorities should show us pictures of them naked. Crying. Begging for their mums. We need to see what they really are. Humans who've gone a bit wrong.

There's another advantage too. At present, Muslim extremists are told that if they explode in a shopping centre they will have a jolly happy afterlife full of many good things. This means that from their perspective there's no downside. But if the bomb fails to go off and they end up as part of an insect-based bushtucker trial on *I'm a Celebrity . . . Get Me Out of Here!*, they may well think twice about putting on the vest.

When you are a serious, religious, committed zealot, you do not want to spend the rest of your days sucking worms from between the toes of Nadine Dorries. Or working out how long we spend on the lavatory. And you certainly won't want to be remembered every year as an excuse to get bladdered on mulled wine. Ask Guy Fawkes about that.

I realize, of course, that none of my ideas will be taken seriously, which is why I have devised a back-up plan. All Western governments abolish, immediately, all security screening at all airports. Because nothing tells a terrorist he's failed more than a show of complete lack of interest.

Sadly, though, this won't be adopted, either. Because governments are interested in the contents of your bottom. Obama Barack wants to look inside your handbag. And airports like it too. Because the longer you have to wait, the greater the chances you'll end up buying a tin of horrible shortbread with a picture of Windsor Castle on the lid.

2 December 2012

Write in now, eel fanciers, and claim your million quid

It's very rare that we ever catch a glimpse of a newspaper editor. But last week there they all were, suited and booted and strolling down Downing Street in a scene that in their minds probably looked like a publicity poster from *Reservoir Dogs*.

Unfortunately, in my mind they looked like the sixth form on their way to be beaten by the headmaster. You had the speccy Potter boy from the *Guardian*, the one who looks like a young farmer from *The Times*, the rather suave one from the *Sunday Times* [Ed: Christmas bonus for you, Jeremy] and a diminutive urchin from the *Sun*.

The school bully – the man from the *Daily Mail* – was missing because he had a note from his mum.

Inside No. 10 they were told, more in sorrow than anger, that they must come up with a tough new set of rules for themselves or the headmaster would be forced to introduce even tougher ones himself.

In short, they were informed that they must set up an independent body that could a) hand out fines of up to a million quid and b) force them to write lines on the front page of their homework when they got their facts wrong: 'I must stop calling people murderers when they are not.'

To Grant and Clegg, the smaller boys in the school, this probably seems a good idea, but in reality there are going to be some serious problems. Because these guys are not sixth-formers. They are the editors of national institutions. And now they face being neutered by one of the biggest scourges of modern society – the pressure group.

Every single thing you can think of is represented by a pressure group. Trees. Haulage contractors. Bats. Shrubs. People with big ears. The Welsh. Great crested grebes. Oil companies. The royal family. I bet you there's even one for women who have supernumerary nipples.

At present an editor is free to place letters from such organizations in the bin. But when they threaten to go to the new independent body, and that body is able to hand out million-quid fines and force him to print humiliating front-page apologies, he is going to have to take them seriously. And that – from my experience at the BBC – is an absolute nightmare.

When I get a complaint letter from an individual, it is fair enough. They are entitled to their opinion and are allowed to express it. But when that individual has some official-looking headed notepaper and a website, he is a pressure group. And he is not expressing an opinion. He is expressing what he sees as a fact.

And he cares. Boy, does he care. He cares so much that once he has his teeth into your ankles, he will not let go until you are sacked and dead. And to make matters worse, he knows what to say in his complaint letters and to whom they must be addressed. He knows – because he is a pressure group and it is therefore his job – how to get any independent body to sit up and pay attention.

This means I have to go through life with a thousand tractor tyres on my back, spending 10 per cent of my day doing my job and 90 per cent dealing with someone from the Incontinent Society who was offended because the previous week on television I said I'd driven so fast I'd wet myself.

Several years ago a pressure group called Transport 2000 contacted the BBC saying that either *Top Gear* had to be pulled from the schedules or a new pro-bus eco-car show must be commissioned as balance.

Now if you wrote to the editor of the *Daily Mail* ordering him either to stop printing stories about the Duchess of Cambridge's pregnancy or to set up an anti-monarchist newspaper to provide readers with an alternative point of view, you'd either get no reply at all or a two-liner inviting you to go and boil your head.

But because the BBC is governed and monitored by precisely the sort of independent body that Lord Justice Leveson wants, Transport 2000 – despite its out-of-date name and its communistic outlook – had to be taken seriously. Very seriously. So for months, hundreds of man hours were wasted on analysing and studying its stupid suggestions. Before sense finally prevailed and they were rejected.

This is what the editors are going to face. Legally savvy nutcases with time on their hands, using every trick in the book in an attempt to force newspapers to toe a line, no matter how idiotic that line might be.

Yesterday I blew up an eel. No big deal, you might think. It was only going to be eaten by a Cockney, anyway. But next year, when the scene is shown on television, we can be absolutely sure that someone from the Eel Preservation Society will start the complaint ball rolling.

And even if that person is just one madman, living in his mother's loft, it will be considered by all the organizations that have been set up to make sure no one at the BBC ever upsets anyone ever. The editorial-compliance people. Ofcom. The BBC Trust. They'll pore over the complaint. They'll study the explosion in slow motion. They'll contact experts from other pressure groups to see if the creature suffered in any way. (Yes. It died.) And afterwards they'll write to me to say that I've just issued an 'unreserved' apology. Because a 'sincere' apology or a 'profound' apology won't do.

It's this constant pressure that explains why, with the notable exceptions of Harry & Paul, there are now no edgy comedians on the BBC. I spoke to one last week, who said, 'It just isn't worth it any more.'

And don't, for heaven's sake, think the committee set up to monitor and fine newspapers will be staffed by people such as you and me; people who'll strive to keep the pressure groups at bay and the fun ball rolling. Because that won't happen.

Instead it'll be run by hopeless do-gooders who in their ridiculous quest for fair play will ensure that there's no play at all. Which means that this time next year, no matter what paper you buy, it will be the *Guardian*.

9 December 2012

Of all the towns in all the world, Cold, Wet and Closed is best

Soon the nation's experts will settle down to decide what's been the best of everything in 2012. Best sports personality. Best frock. Best dog. And best moment.

Actually, scrub that. The best moment's easy. It was when those five rings of what appeared to be molten steel were lowered into the Olympic stadium and the whole country, as one, suddenly decided that it wasn't so bad to be British after all.

I've already named my best car; AA Gill will soon be revealing which chef did the best job of disguising the bodily fluids in his food; and you, in the meantime, will be in a frilly dinner shirt at a crappy hotel on Park Lane as a comedian with a vaguely familiar face presents some drunken halfwit with the award for 2012's best new packaging solution.

Rough Guides, meanwhile, has announced the ten best places to visit in all of the world. And No. 1 is Northern Cyprus, apparently.

Of course, this is nonsense. Northern Cyprus is just southern Cyprus, only with more soldiers and cheaper carpets. As a travel destination, it is in no way a match for Hue in Vietnam, or New York, neither of which is in the Rough Guides top-ten list.

Puerto Rico is, but that's madness. Unless you like staying in a hotel where the lifeguard has a sub-machine gun.

I'm not sure that north-eastern Iceland should be there either. Because if what you want is peace and quiet and rugged volcanic splendour, you can find that twenty minutes from Keflavik airport. Driving six hours to find something even better is like spending a day rummaging around in a box of Lego, looking for a more impressive yellow brick.

And I'm sorry, but Dresden? This is the world's fifth-best place in the same way that Angela Merkel is the world's fifth-best-looking woman. There are some fabulous towns in eastern Germany but Dresden isn't one of them. Yes, you get some beautifully restored cobbles but you also get a lot of bitter old men who hate you very much and wish the communists would come back.

However, the entry on the Rough Guides list that seems to have surprised most people is to be found at No. 7. It's the only place in all of the British Isles to get a mention: Margate.

Even the locals seem to have been taken aback, with one saying the town centre is full of yobs and amusement arcades and boarded-up shops. And there's more too: Margate is in Kent and, frankly, that's the least accessible place on earth. If you live anywhere else in Britain, it's easier to get to Yukon. Not that I'd recommend that either, unless you enjoy being bitten by mosquitoes.

However, I can see the logic of Rough Guides with Margate. Sure, it's not as visually impressive as Sydney or Hong Kong. And I am certain San Francisco has more restaurants. But put yourself in the mind of a visitor coming to Britain.

When we go abroad on holiday, we like to annoy our children by taking them to see the 'real' country. We like to find the restaurants where the menus aren't also printed in English and we want to drink the local wine. Even though we would get the same taste sensation by sucking on one of the blue tablets at the bottom of the urinals.

It stands to reason, then, that many people coming here would want to see the 'real' Britain. So where should we send them? Once, I sent some particularly nasal Americans to Loughborough, telling them they couldn't get more British than that. But what if you were taking it seriously?

A seaside town makes sense. Fish. Chips. Vinegar. Endless afternoons in the Cafe de Formica, rubbing condensation from the windows and kidding yourself that the sky is definitely getting brighter. Walks on the gritty sand in the drizzle. A mug of tea. And then off to an amusement arcade to shoot an alien.

There is simply nowhere else on earth where people do that to get away from it all. So I'd say to any visiting American: once you've done Stratford-upon-Avon and an open-top bus tour of Warwick Castle, and you are fed up with how Britain was, get a taste of how it is now with a trip to the seaside.

Margate would do nicely, for sure, but if you want somewhere that's a bit easier to reach from your overheated, Polish-run central London hotel, I think you can do better. Tenby, for instance. Or north Cornwall. Or East Yorkshire.

All of these places are still dripping with echoes of the past. You have hints of fishing and roll-out-the-barrel revelry. But most now also have hotels run by people who've been to London and know that nylon is no longer an acceptable bedding solution.

Back in the summer I spent a few days in Whitby and it was perfect. Cold. Wet. And mostly shut. I bought fish and chips and I ate them on a bench overlooking a forlorn-looking trawler. It plainly hadn't been out for months, because all you can catch in Whitby these days is chlamydia.

I loved it. I loved the wiggly little streets and the old cottages and the sea air. I loved the sound of the gulls and of the rigging in the sail boats, flapping about in the biting wind. I also loved the hotel I found just north of the town, a little bit of Knightsbridge wedged between the bleak moors and the rocky shoreline where I spent a couple of idyllic hours looking for sea creatures in slippery ponds.

We've all spent time in a seaside town such as Whitby. It's one of the few bonds that we all share. France has its cheese. America has its proms. Rwanda has days when the whole country goes out on the streets to clear up litter. And we have our seaside. It's our glue.

So, yes, since millions of foreign visitors come here every year wanting to know who we really are, it makes sense that one of the world's ten best places to visit is a town on the British coast. For me, that'd be Whitby.

16 December 2012

Help, I've lost track of world affairs in Bradley's barnet

When a televisual quiz show finds its feet and becomes popular, its producers get it into their heads that the audience would be much happier if the ordinary contestants with their terrible shoes and their ghastly jumpers were replaced by 'celebrities'.

So instead of Brian standing there, sweating slightly as he tries to win enough cash for some new decking or a short cruise, we have a bright orange woman whose name we can't quite remember trying to win money for injured rabbits and various other charities no one's heard of.

Shows to have gone down this route in the past include *Mr & Mrs*, *Who Wants to Be a Millionaire?*, *Weakest Link* and *University Challenge*. Most recently, we've been treated to a star-studded version of the rather brilliant *Pointless*. Which ended up being called *Pointless Celebrities*. And so it turned out to be.

One team was made up of two extremely enthusiastic young people who may have been in a soap opera, or one of Simon Cowell's singing contests, or perhaps a sex tape. But anyway, it quickly became obvious that they had put a great deal of effort into their appearance but none whatsoever into any sort of research.

Luckily, however, the topic that would take them through to the next round was easy: David Cameron. All they had to do was correctly answer just one of the following questions. Which famous public school did he attend? What's the name of his baby daughter? What's his constituency? What's his wife called? And for which former chancellor was he a special adviser?

Amid staccato bursts of shallow, forced, embarrassed laughter, they had to admit that, actually, they didn't know any of the answers, but that they were prepared to hazard a guess at the name of the public school he'd attended. 'Oxford,' they said nervously.

Now if I'd been the host, I'd have fixed them with a steely glare and wondered out loud what on earth had possessed them to appear on a quiz show when neither of them even knew the difference between a school and a university. Perhaps this is why I'm not the host of a quiz show.

But here's the thing. While I knew all the answers to the questions about Mr Cameron, I would make an equally enormous fool of myself if I were in their shoes and I was asked questions about *EastEnders*, which I have never seen, or musicals, which I studiously avoid, or Chaucer, the one man from history whom I'd most like to murder.

In the fairly recent past, it was not hard to be knowledgeable. So long as you had read a couple of Shakespeare's plays and you spent an hour each morning reading *The Times*, you were pretty well placed to hold your head high at even the most sophisticated dinner party.

Not any more. I spoke last night to an extremely bright girl. She was eloquent and fully up to speed with how pigs are farmed in Chile, but when it came to recent problems with the press, she had it in her head that journalists had paid the police to hack Milly Dowler's phone.

I encounter similar problems at work because when I introduce the Stig, I usually include a sideways reference to some report from the papers that day. And afterwards, we have to dub on the laughter because almost no one in the audience gets it. That's why you always hear people laughing so hard it sounds like their spleens are coming out of their noses. And yet the people in the back of shot look like they've just been told a theory about particle physics, in Latin.

The problem is that in the olden days, news was roughly divided in two. You had news about ragamuffins who had appeared in court. And you had news of natives being brought to heel in some far-flung corner of the empire.

Nowadays there's so much information coming from so many different places, we cannot possibly keep abreast of it. Syria, for example. I was really concentrating hard on the complexities of the civil war and what its effects on the region might be when, all of a sudden, *The X Factor* finished and suddenly I felt compelled to read up on the winner.

But before I even had a chance to discover his or her name, I found myself embroiled in a heated late-night debate on the American constitution and the rights and wrongs of being permitted to bear arms. Hard when your head is full of Alex Reid's sexuality. And Bradley Wiggins's haircut. And whether Aston Martin will do a deal with Mercedes.

Today the news agenda is so vast you don't absorb information. You simply skim along its surface. I read a fair bit about the plight of soldiers in Afghanistan and I was fairly clear on one thing: lots of them were being shot by local soldiers they'd helped to train.

But then at a recent military function I spoke to some chaps who'd actually been there and they assured me that this was complete rubbish. So how do I check this out? In the past you would turn to the BBC or the papers but almost no one does that any more. Which is why we end up with a head full of misconceptions, half-truths and flimflam about Kelly Brook's breasts.

Some have argued that Twitter would be the answer to all our prayers; that it would provide a balance of real-time information from people who are actually on the spot. You'd have news from the rebels in Syria and news too from President Bashar al-Assad. But the truth is that you can't really condense the complexities of the Middle East into a *Very Hungry Caterpillar*-sized crucible of just 140 characters.

And anyway, these days, if you speak your mind on Twitter or any other social networking site, you will wake at five the next morning to find half a dozen policemen ripping up your floorboards.

But the worst thing about any ether-based news delivery system is that no one's on hand to decide on our behalf what matters and what doesn't. Which is why we have two pointless celebrities going on television to demonstrate that, actually, they don't know anything at all.

And neither do I, if I'm honest. Except that it's Christmas this week. Have a happy time and see you on the flip side.

23 December 2012

Stand by, Earth, to boldly look where there's no point looking

As we speak, British boffins are busy building a remotely operated telescope high in Chile's Atacama Desert.

The optics have come from Austria, the mounts from America and the housing from a company in Cornwall that makes cat flaps.

When it is finished, it will be pointed at a randomly selected star to see if the light dims from time to time. If it does, they will know that orbiting planets are passing in front of it. And then they will get to work, measuring how much the light dims.

This will tell them if the planet in question has an atmosphere, and even what sort of atmosphere that might be. A lot of oxygen suggests it may be host to all sorts of plants and photosynthetic bacteria. If there is water vapour as well, then there might also be water on the ground and that could mean it is capable of supporting life.

There are, however, one or two slight issues with all of this. First of all, there are 125 billion galaxies. And there are probably 300 billion stars in each one. So the chances that our new telescope is looking at the right one at the right time are quite remote.

Second, we know that the earth is home to a great deal of oxygen and water but we keep being told by Prince Charles that it's the delicate balance of other things – such as the Ferrybridge power stations and the Dog and Duck's smoker-friendly patio heaters – that provide the conditions for life to flourish.

So even if the new telescope does spot a likely-looking planet, it may well be it has no ozone or a tiny bit too much methane and, as a result, the only life there is a walrus or a version of Esther Rantzen that has two heads and can only say 'wibble'.

It gets worse because even if the life in question does have digital sound and non-stick frying pans, it's very unlikely that its inhabitants speak English. Or even French. Over the years, scientists have pondered this problem, with many suggesting that maths would be the only way of conversing.

They've been wasting their time, though, because even the nearest star – apart from the sun – is about 25 trillion miles away and it would take 81,000 years to get there.

And there's no point using the radio to transmit all our prime numbers and theories about pi because the message would still take more than four years to arrive. And if there was anyone on the other end, they'd just think, 'Oh Christ, we've had a call from James May.' And not bother replying.

To sum up, then. There is only an infinitesimal chance that our telescope will find a planet capable of supporting intelligent life, and even if it does, we can't speak to the inhabitants. As a result, the whole exercise is a complete waste of everyone's time.

Except it isn't, and here's why. Back in the day, a bunch of Vikings set off across a seemingly endless ocean to seek out new worlds and new civilizations that they could rape. After 500 miles they must have thought, 'This is pointless.' After 1,000 miles one of the rowers must have stood up and said to the captain, 'Look, sir, I'm sorry, but I really want to give up.'

But they didn't give up. And after nearly 2,000 miles of rowing and sweat and toil, they bumped into America. Where there was no intelligent life, so they went back to Oslo.

More recently, Victorian explorers stomped about in

Africa being eaten by lions and catching malaria simply so they could find the source of the Nile. Before then you had Captain Cook who went off to find Australia, even though the world knew it wasn't there.

A Dutch explorer called Abel Tasman had been to the region in 1642. He had found Tasmania, New Zealand and later the Fiji islands, but many doubted there was any other large land mass. So Cook's mission was pointless and stupid. Except, of course, it wasn't.

Exploration against all the odds is still going on today. For the past few months, Russian, American and British scientists have been engaged in a race to explore a recently discovered sub-glacial lake in Antarctica. Though, sadly, the British team had to pull out over the Christmas period because its generators ran out of fuel.

Undaunted, the others are soldiering on in the belief that 52 million years ago the region was home to a giant rainforest and that some strange life forms have survived. I have to say that this is unlikely because the lake in question is buried under a slab of ice that's two miles thick. Which means there's no air and no sunlight.

'Unlikely', however, is not a good enough reason for quitting. Nor is 'pointless'.

Many years ago I was on board a plane that sort of crash-landed at a remote airstrip in the Sahara. It could have been in Libya or it could have been in Chad. The pilot didn't know because he was a bit drunk.

Anyway, we would be stuck for a while, so I decided to sit under the plane's port wing. After an hour or so, this became boring, so I switched to the starboard wing. And when this became dreary I set off on foot to have a look over the nearest horizon. Even though I knew for sure, because I'd already seen from the air, that I'd find nothing of any use at all.

Human beings like checking stuff out. When a child says he wants to go into the woods to 'explore', no parent says, 'What's the point? All you're going to find are nettles.' And it was the same when John F. Kennedy said America would send a spaceship to the moon. Everyone knew it was just a big dusty golf ball and that no good would come of it; but they went anyway, and who now thinks it was a bad idea?

I don't expect our new telescope will find a damn thing. I really don't. But let me conclude with this: many years ago, a friend lost his signet ring while swimming off Pampelonne beach in the south of France. The next day he set off on a completely pointless mission to find it. And he did.

13 January 2013

Dim staff and no stock: the key to hanging on in the high street

Three more teeth have been smashed out of the high street this month. Jessops, the camera people, went belly up and HMV, the purveyor of tunes and action films, called in the administrator, before Blockbuster, which wanted you to rent the same films from it, followed suit.

We're told they were casualties of the nation's new-found love affair with online shopping and renting. And this seems to make sense. Figures just out reveal that 9 per cent of all business in Britain is done on the internet. That's the highest proportion in the world.

It doesn't include me because I find online shopping a bit sinister. I have it in my mind that the moment I feed the details of my credit card into the system, someone in California will use them to buy a light aircraft. I know this is irrational but it's what I believe, and as a result I have never bought anything from someone I can't see.

There are other reasons too. If you buy online, your goods have to be delivered. Which means the streets of suburbia are now full of dithering van drivers getting lost and doing three-point turns and generally getting in everyone's way. This annoys me.

Plus, if your groceries are being delivered, you have to be in when they arrive. And if you also have to be in to receive your kids' birthday presents, your replacement toaster, your copy of *Madagascar* 3, your new shoes, a sex toy, a dog blanket and three hats, you will never find the time to go out. Which means you will become friendless and lonely.

And cross. Because, from what I can gather, supermarkets guess at what might make a suitable replacement if what you ordered isn't in stock. And usually they get it spectacularly wrong. Duraglit, for example, cannot be used to power a torch. And you can't make a salad with advocaat. Plus, as I like to point out to American barmen, I'll only accept that Pepsi is a substitute for Coca-Cola if they accept that Monopoly money is a substitute for cash.

Anyway, as you can see, there are many good reasons I choose not to shop online. But I must say that shopping for real is becoming increasingly difficult these days. Because most shops never have a single thing in stock, ever.

Shopping for shoes in Tod's, for instance, is like being stuck in Monty Python's cheese shop. Loafers? Nope. Brogues? Nope. Wellies? Nope. Lace-ups? Nope. Slip-ons? No, sir. Not today. I'm convinced the storeroom is full of nothing but sales assistants making coffee while pretending to look for the size you need.

Then you have Sony. I went there last week to buy a television and a PlayStation. The first branch I tried had closed down, and the second had neither in stock. How can Sony not stock a Sony PlayStation? Apple? Yes, it had the iPhone I needed, but no way of taking the data from the previous model and putting it on the new version.

So, after a wasted half-hour, we cancelled the credit-card transaction and I left empty-handed.

You will find this everywhere you go – shops that carry just enough goods to fill the window display and that's it. You want to actually buy something? Well, they ask a lot of damn-fool questions about where you live and whether you're transsexual, and then the gormless imbecile on the till tells you that what you wanted is still in its component parts, in Hamburg.

That said, there was one notable exception to all of this, one shop that carried a selection of goods and was staffed with extremely enthusiastic, knowledgeable and delightful staff. Its name was Jessops.

We are used, these days, to shop assistants being one step removed from plankton. Many have not mastered the art of speech, know nothing about what they're selling and would much rather you died of a heart attack than bought anything. Not in Jessops, though.

Let's be brutally honest. The sort of people who are keen on cameras and photography are deeply suspect. I imagine that most are mainly interested in pornography. But even when the Jessops people were presented with a man who plainly wanted a camera to take up-skirt shots of women in the super-market, they remained as bubbly and as helpful as ever.

They were knowledgeable too. I went to the company's Westfield branch in west London on several occasions over the past couple of years – my kids do photography at school, in case you were wondering – and whoever served me could always explain whether one of the submenus on a Canon was better than that on a Nikon. They knew about f-stops and aperture priority. They knew about focal length and could advise on toughness. They had plainly been trained well and they were brilliant. And they always had whatever I selected in stock.

And where did the former chief executive of this fine chain of shops end up? Yup. HMV. Another well-organized shop, if I'm honest.

Now, I don't know anything about retailing, but I can see a pattern here. Run a shop well and it will go out of business. Run it on a shoestring with no stock and staff who can only just about manage to walk on two legs and you'll hang on in there. Just. But not for long.

Some say this is a good thing; that when all the chain stores have gone, the high street will once again become home to lots of little shops selling home-made biscuits. But in a world that worships cheapness and convenience, it's more likely that the high street will become home to nothing more than charity shops, pizza takeaway joints and *Daily Mail* photographers, prowling around looking for a drunk girl in a short skirt.

Eventually, Amazon and eBay will turn Stow-on-the-Wold into downtown Detroit and cause Hartlepool to drown in a sea of vomit.

Still, it's not completely the end of the world. Because many of the Jessops sales staff are now posting pictures of themselves and contact details in the windows of the shops where they used to work. They are, in short, selling themselves. And, frankly, they are probably the best things you can buy on the high street right now.

20 January 2013

Forget the cat and the pension, wrinklies, a gap year beckons

Round about now your teenage child will be queuing at the check-in desk for an airline you have never heard of, and flying off to a part of the world you have never visited, to spend a few months doing stuff you don't understand. It's called a gap year. And it sounds fun.

Now, when I grew up in South Yorkshire there was no such thing as a gap year. You left school at three o'clock in the afternoon and by quarter to four you were down the pit. Besides, 'abroad' was Nottingham, and 'university' . . . it was a place of learning for hoity-toity homosexuals. So it was on nobody's radar in Doncaster.

It certainly wasn't on mine. I left school, rather earlier than I'd planned, on a Thursday and by Monday morning I was starting work, on a picket line, outside the *Rotherham Advertiser*. And I spent the short gap in between buying a coat and a notebook.

Things seem to have changed, though, because most of my friends' children are currently cycling round Mexico before taking a trip to Cambodia via space. They're all turning their geography lessons into reality, in Israel, New Zealand and Canada. And it all seems to have been funded by light babysitting, occasional bar work and a one-off payment from some long-forgotten godparent.

Last weekend my daughter outlined her gap-year plans. She announced that she'll go to Cape Town, do a spot of work, buy a car and then drive it via various countries beginning with Z to Uganda. It would be the tip of Africa to the equator, the trip of a lifetime. And the total cost, so far as I can see, is about £7.50.

When she had finished outlining the route, where she would stay and what she would see, a deathly hush descended like a snowy blanket on the adults in the room. Sure, we had arranged our faces to suggest we were thinking of pitfalls she might not have considered and titbits that we, in our wisdom, could pass on.

But I know everyone in that room was thinking the exact same thing. And it had nothing to do with my daughter's wellbeing. It was this: 'Goddamn. I would kill someone's small dog to make a trip like that.' And it got me thinking. Maybe in society's haste to create a gap year, we've put it in the wrong place.

Eighteen-year-olds are vibrant and their brains are tuned beautifully to receive and disseminate even the most complex information. So it stands to reason that at this age they should be at work, dreaming up new ideas and making the world a better place.

It's stupid that they spend the sharpest year of their lives catching chlamydia on a beach in Thailand when they could be inventing batteries that rejuvenate themselves, and corkscrews that actually work.

Gap years, I think, would work better for older people. Now I'm not suggesting for a moment that you get up from the breakfast table and, after a brief trip to the cash machine, set off like the hero in a Leslie Thomas book, on an odyssey of beach bars, sultry girls, mad jobs, endless starry nights and no real sense of what the next day will bring. That would be absurd. You have a job in accountancy and responsibilities to your children and your family. So you can't just set off and drift about the world in a two-legged demonstration of Brownian motion.

Besides, you have a lodge meeting at the civic centre on Thursday so you can't very well be in Laos that day, lying on a hammock, drinking an ice-cold beer with an Australian girl called Sarah who's wearing a white, Flake-advert gypsy dress and not much else.

No. I'm not suggesting that a gap year would work at all well for people in their forties and fifties. But what about when you're sixty-five? What about a gap year between the drudgery of work and the mind-numbing tedium of retirement?

In the olden days you retired because you were simply too old and feeble to carry the coal to the surface any more. But today people pack in the day job with forty years of life left in their bones. And then what? They spend half their savings on a lousy cruise on a lousy ship round a lousy bit of coastline of what we used to call the eastern bloc. And then they come home to the floral-print conservatory and an eternity of watering plants and praying one of the children will ring that day.

They won't. They've got their own kids to worry about, and all the responsibilities of moving on and moving up. Listen to Harry Chapin's song 'Cat's in the Cradle' and forget about them. And forget about your savings, too. Leave them where they are. Hitch a lift to the ferry port in Dover and see what happens next.

At sixty-five you're showroom-fresh. You can play tennis and ski and scuba dive. So why don't you just bugger off and spend twelve months doing what you can while it's all still possible?

You know by that age what you haven't seen and what you want to see. You know what you haven't done. So go and do it. Bungee jump into the Grand Canyon and make love on a Tahitian beach. I know what you're thinking. What about the cat? How would I carry all my things?

Well, stop it. Kick the cat out. It'll be fine, and when it comes to luggage, take a leaf out of the teenagers' book. It doesn't matter whether my son is going skiing for a week, going to a party at the other end of the country or pheasant shooting in Outer Mongolia, he only ever travels with what he's wearing, a phone and a credit card.

And what's wrong with that? Someone always has a phone charger and a jumper you can borrow. And if you need a new pair of pants, which you will after you've worn them back to front on day two, inside out on day three and both on day four, get a job for a couple of days.

Or you could get an allotment, I suppose, and have Betty round for a sherry a week on Tuesday.

27 January 2013

Your next HS2 service is the 3.15 to Victorian England

As I see it, there are two clearly defined camps in the debate about the proposed high-speed rail link.

You have those who live more than five miles from the proposed route. They say it will be a wonderful piece of engineering, that it will make the nation proud and that it will bring untold riches to the north. And then you have those who live less than five miles away. They say it is stupid and wrong-headed and a complete waste of money.

Interestingly, both sides are wrong.

I have a great deal of sympathy with people who will soon have trains charging at 225mph through their kitchens. You sign up for a quiet life in the countryside and then you are told that soon your life will be ruined and your house value-less. Nimbyism is much criticized but it is an understandable reaction at times such as this.

Certainly if someone said they were going to locate the town tip in my back garden, or build a footpath right past my bedroom window, I'd fight like a savage dog to make the problem go away.

However, if we'd always put the needs of the few above the needs of the many, we'd still be in smocks, herding oxen. When Isambard Kingdom Brunel announced plans for his Great Western Railway, he faced a staggering level of resistance. But today we thank God he prevailed, or Bristol would still be ten minutes behind London and you'd have to travel between the two on a horse.

It was the same story with the M1. The chief engineer

spent months touring the proposed route, being shouted at by farmers and red-faced lords. But again we are grateful today that he was able to win them round. Or Leeds would be as inaccessible as space.

I like big engineering projects. They make my tummy do backflips. Often, when I'm on my way to Hull – it doesn't happen too often – I'll pull over and spend a few moments admiring the Humber Bridge. When it was proposed, it was considered stupid to spend millions linking Barton and Hessle, two settlements no one had heard of. And it probably was. But we ended up with what, to my mind, is the most beautiful bridge in the world. And that makes me feel all warm and gooey.

Which brings me on to the other side of the argument about HS2. The people who say it's a wonderful piece of engineering. Because is it? Really?

No French or Japanese person I've met lists the railway network as a reason for visiting their country. A big dam, yes. That would be tremendous. Or an elegant viaduct. But some track nailed to some sleepers and laid on a bed of cinders? My boat's unfloated, I'm afraid.

Part of the problem is that trains are a bit Victorian. Tub-thumping and puffing your chest up about a new railway line is like tub-thumping and sticking your chest out about a new steamship. Or a new woollen mill.

We're told that no one can know what life will be like when HS2 opens for business in 2026. Absolutely. But we can make an educated guess that the electronic revolution will have turned our lives completely upside down and that in all probability there will be no need to travel at all.

Which brings us on to the biggest problem with HS2. David Cameron quite rightly acknowledges that the north-south divide in Britain is getting so wide that unless something is done, we really will end up with two countries. I'm troubled by this as well but I fail to see how a railway line connecting the haves and the have-nots will help.

Last month I climbed on board a train in London and after just two chapters of my Jack Reacher book I was arriving in a northern town where there was some drizzle and a bit of graffiti. One chapter after that, I was in Liverpool. It was seriously quick.

But here's the thing. Even if HS2 shaves an extra thirty or so minutes off the journey, I wonder how many people in Kensington and Chelsea will wake up and say, 'You know what? Since Liverpool is only ninety minutes away, we shall move to the Wirral.'

It's even more bonkers when you view the situation from the other side of the coin. Because does anyone honestly think that Scousers continue to live and work in Liverpool simply because the current train ride to London takes too long?

At this point politicians tell us that a faster rail link would be good for business. Right. I see. But hang on a minute. What business?

One of the stations will be located at Sheffield's vast out-of-town Meadowhall shopping centre. So are we expected to believe that because Yorkshire is only seventy-five minutes away, people in Notting Hill will decide to forgo a trip to Portobello Road on a Saturday morning and spend all their hard-earned City bonuses up north instead? I'm struggling with that concept, if I'm honest.

And I also struggle to imagine that life will become any easier for those running the BBC's new northern headquarters in Salford. Today, even though staff in London are being offered up to £90,000 to relocate, many are refusing to move away from their friends, their families and their children's schools. And those who do go are finding that booking guests for their shows is difficult. Tom Cruise, for example, would travel to west London to promote his new film. But Manchester? Not a chance. And I can't see the situation changing just because the journey time is an hour faster.

And in the big scheme of things, what's the journey time got to do with it, anyway? People don't choose to live in Liverpool or Sheffield because of how near they are to London. It's just not relevant.

Most northern people I know hate London and care about its proximity only when their football team are playing Arsenal or Chelsea. If you live in Rotherham, you eat, socialize, drink and mate in Rotherham. What many don't do, however, is work. Because there are very few jobs. And I'm afraid to say that problem won't be solved by a big, noisy Victorian throwback.

3 February 2013

Oh, waiter, can I pay with this microchipped finger?

We have been informed by the government that we have three years to microchip our dogs. And that if we fail to comply, we will be fined up to £500. This is normally the sort of bullying nonsense that makes me want to spit tacks and vandalize a bus shelter.

But I've read the details and I'm alarmed to say that the new law seems to make sense.

At present more than 100,000 dogs a year are either dumped or lost, and these days the police are too busy investigating dead disc jockeys to cycle around the parish comparing those out-of-focus 'missing' posters on lamp posts with the forlorn collection of pooches they have in the station kennels.

We can hardly expect the RSPCA to help out, either. Well, we can, but sadly this once great charity is now little more than a branch of the Communist party, which would rather spend its money prosecuting people for living near David Cameron than help a little girl to find her lost Labrador.

In fact, the RSPCA seems to have rather missed the point of the chipping scheme, with a spokesman saying it will do little to prevent dogs from biting other animals such as hedgehogs, badgers or, horror of horrors, possibly even one of the charity's beloved foxes. This is true. Other things it will not prevent include barking at postmen and urinating.

However, those of us who are not mainly interested in resurrecting the ghost of Stalin can see there is one big advantage. The chip containing your details is inserted into a small glass cylinder the size of a grain of rice that is then injected into your dog's back.

So, if it's lost, the dog can be scanned in the same way that you scan vegetables at the supermarket and, hey presto, it'll be back in its own bed, drinking warm milk by nightfall. Brilliant. And, at the moment, it can be done free. It's so brilliant, in fact, that I started to wonder why, for instance, you could not insert a similar chip in your laptop and your phone or even your children.

You may argue, of course, that if a lost child is subsequently found, a chip is not necessary, because they are capable of telling their rescuers what their name is and where they live. But what if they're not found?

As we all know, your mobile phone is constantly telling anyone who cares to look where you are. So long as the battery is connected, it's a non-stop homing beacon. So why do Apple and BlackBerry not start selling parents the technology that can do this? Insert it into a child's back and when they wander off at the supermarket you can wave goodbye to the misery of spinning round and round in pointless circles and in just a few moments find out exactly where they've gone.

Naturally, it gets better. Because later in life, when they are sixteen and they say they are popping out to the library to catch up on some physics homework, you can determine whether this is true, or whether, in reality, they are doing 90mph in a mate's Vauxhall Corsa, on their way to the Duck and Sick Bag.

Indeed, as I lay in the bath last night, considering all the advantages of chipping children, I hit upon an even bigger brainwave: chipping myself.

I bet the government has already had many meetings about this. Because if every single person in the country were chipped, they'd know where we'd been, who we'd been with and how fast we'd driven home. Such a scheme would free up so much police time, they'd be able to investigate even more dead DJs.

But, of course, there's the pesky question of human rights. We don't necessarily want Mr Cameron to know where we were last night, so we may be reluctant to provide him with a means of finding out. And we may remain reluctant right up to the point where we realize the advantages.

For many years boffins have inserted electronic devices into our bodies to regulate the beat of our heart and alter our mood and even bring about orgasm. But this, I feel, is just the start.

Look at that tiny chip in your credit card. Why does it have to be mounted in a bit of plastic that one day, as sure as eggs are eggs, you will lose? Why can it not be sewn into the palm of your hand, which, unless you go shoplifting in Saudi Arabia, you will not?

There are other advantages, too. There's no reason why, when you pick up a product at the supermarket, its sensors cannot read your chip and automatically deduct its cost from your bank account. This would mean no more queuing at the checkout tills.

It's the same story at airports because the electronic chip in a modern passport would easily fit into your earlobe. You just walk past a scanner and – ping. You're in. And, of course, your other earlobe could contain details of your driving licence, which would cut the time it takes to rent a car from the current average of around sixteen hours to just a few seconds.

Pub landlords would also welcome the idea because at present they have to serve a six-year-old child with six double vodkas simply because they have produced a scrap of

ID, written in crayon, that says they're actually eighteen. But with chipping, he'd know.

You could have an electronic ignition key for your car sewn into one thumb and a complex laptop password sewn into the other. And never again would you forget to withdraw your card from the cash dispenser because you wouldn't need one. Simply insert your wedding ring finger into the slot and seconds later bundles of delicious money will pour forth.

You could even have a chip containing your medical records sewn into your genitals so that on one-night stands your partner would be able to determine whether you were suffering from anything they would rather not catch. The possibilities are quite literally endless.

It's been said for many years that your body is a temple. And that's fine. But I'd quite like mine to be a mobile phone and a credit card as well.

10 February 2013

Hello, sailor. Show me what Britain is really made of

As we know, everything run by the dull, penny-pinching hand of government is a bit rubbish. Walk through Heathrow and when you get to the customs hall, all the equipment is scuffed and the tables are held together with duct tape.

In a hospital the front-of-house staff may be cheery and the shop may sell all kinds of succulent-looking fruit but peep into the spaces where the public are not allowed and it's like peering into Eeyore's Gloomy Place. It's like nobody cares. And that's the trouble, really. Nobody does.

It's the same story with the police. Elsewhere in the world, they get snazzy costumes, flash cars and cool sunglasses. Here they rock up in a Vauxhall Astra, sporting a pair of trousers that have plainly been designed to fit someone else.

You just know that if the government had built the Shard it would have been quite a lot shorter and that the lifts wouldn't work. The government doesn't do fabulous. It does woeful. A point that was well made by the Royal Navy Lynx helicopter that recently came to pick me up in Stavanger in Norway.

To keep this ancient design even vaguely relevant, it has been retro-fitted with all sorts of radar equipment so now it looks like it's caught a terrible warty skin disease. But it took off, nevertheless, and half an hour later deposited me on the navy frigate HMS *Westminster*.

It's a little bit shorter than Roman Abramovich's latest yacht. And cost slightly less to build. And from the outside, it's not hard to see why. There's a bucket for fag ends, and a principal armament of just one 4.5in artillery piece. Or as a Second World War admiral would say, 'one peashooter'.

There are, however, several health and safety notices advising crew members on how not to get hurt. Which seemed to be a bit incongruous on a warship. But this is a government vessel. So what do you expect? Four functioning diesels, perhaps? Nope. Sorry. One of them was broken. Oh, and the previous evening it had sprung a leak. It might as well have been called HMS *Vulnerable*.

You could say that of the whole service because, if you exclude training vessels, the minesweepers and various other odds and sods, the number of Royal Navy frontline surface ships stands at eighteen. That's eighteen vessels – frigates and destroyers – you would recognize as a warship.

To put that in perspective, the number of surface ships sent to give the gauchos a thick ear in 1982 – and I'm not including the subs or the transporters or the service vessels, just the main warship flotilla – was twenty-five.

At the outbreak of the Second World War the Royal Navy had 317 surface ships. At the Battle of Jutland in 1916 it lost fourteen warships and 6,784 men in just one encounter. And still came home saying, 'We won'.

All of which makes you think, with only eighteen ships currently ready for duty, we couldn't even defend ourselves against Belgium. Or could we? Because unlike any other government-run operation, HMS *Westminster* is much better than first appearances would have you believe. First of all, there's the crew. One was just back from a spell with NASA. Another, who had a regional accent, could mend a gas turbine with his eyelashes. Sailors? Yes. But everyone who I spoke to was a top-class engineer as well.

And you should see how they operate on the bridge. Quietly. Like components in a brand-new laptop. Orders are spoken. They are repeated. Something happens. Have you ever been in a really busy restaurant in Turin? Well, this ship is the exact opposite of that.

And then you have the toys. What you can't see from the outside is the astonishing array of missile launchers. The 4.5in gun is only there to frighten a Somalian pirate. The real hardware is the Sea Wolf and Harpoon missiles, and the torpedoes. It's a smorgasbord of guided ordnance designed to make Johnny Baddie have a surprisingly bad day.

But they are nothing compared with what you find in the bowels of HMS *Westminster*. You go down and then down some more, through tiny hatches that feature standard-issue military-sharp edges, until you arrive in a below-the-waterline room that looks like an air-traffic-control centre. But it's no such thing. Because it's not designed to land planes safely. It's designed to land them quickly and at very high speed in the sea.

Then you move into the submarine-detection area. Same deal. It's a room built specifically to make the enemy submariner all wet and uncomfortable. And yet, like the bridge, it's as quiet down there as a chess tournament. Even at full speed. I know this because we went there. And Holy Mother of God . . .

Have you ever rented a jet ski while on holiday? Feels fast, doesn't it? Well, the *Westminster* is faster still. And then, as we approached 30 knots and we were playing Moses, the captain ordered a sharp turn to port. You'd imagine a ship this size would respond like an elderly dog. But no. One second we were heading north and then we were heading west and I was standing on the aft deck, wondering out loud how the bloody thing hadn't capsized.

You often see books that tell a man what he must do before he dies. Well, I've landed on a Nimitz-class aircraft carrier and flown an F-15 and been shot at while flying over Basra but I can tell you that the No. 1 must-have experience is a Type 23 frigate turning hard to port at almost 30 knots. It is absolutely hysterical.

As night began to fall, it was time to make port in Bergen. The sentries put on body armour and manned the machine guns, in case the Norwegians got any silly ideas. And we were nudged to a standstill by a local tug. When you have only eighteen warships in total, you can't risk dinging one in a parking accident.

As I disembarked, I couldn't help turning round for one last look. It may be a government vessel in a government navy. But I can tell you this. It does something no other government operation does: it makes you achingly proud to be British.

17 February 2013

Work on the accent, Brum, and Tom Cruise will be in for a balti

If I may be permitted to liken Britain to the human body, then Scotland is the brain, East Anglia is the stomach, North and East Yorkshire are the breasts and London is the heart that pumps vital nutrients and oxygen to the fingernails and the ears and Preston. Which leaves us with the garden shed we built years ago when we decided to take up metalworking: that's Birmingham.

In recent years it's been tidied up. Earnest locals have fitted funky new lighting and a bar. They've polished the lathe, too, and turned the vice into an amusing beer pump.

But still nobody's interested. We don't do metalwork any more. So, neat though it now may be, the shed remains rather unloved.

Early last week there were many big news stories to titillate the nation. A meteorite had crashed into Russia, a film had been made about Tom Cruise visiting a curry house last August in St Albans and people were very interested in the dramatic downfall of Oscar Pistorius. But even so, the eighth-most-read story on the BBC website was: 'Why does everyone hate Birmingham?'

Twenty years ago it was very probably the worst place on earth. If you fancied eating something that wasn't a curry, you'd set off on a long and fruitless walk that would culminate in you being vomited on. And then stabbed, for daring to get in the way of someone's sick.

There was only one hotel where you had even half a chance of not catching lice and only one nightclub where you wouldn't necessarily be glassed. Not that you could find either because a few years earlier someone had decided the city should have a series of underpasses. Unfortunately they'd got a bit carried away, so that visitors would turn off the M6, disappear immediately into a hole and not emerge until they were past Kidderminster. Birmingham, then, was difficult to find and horrible if, by some miracle, you succeeded.

The reasons for going? Well, Brummies were keen to point out that they had more canals than Venice. By which I think they meant more shopping trolleys in their canals than Venice. And, er, that's it. Birmingham was just an industrial city that had no industry any more.

Today, though, everything's changed. There are bars and nightclubs and Selfridges. And all the old industrial buildings have been turned into loft apartments for thrusting young executives. So why do we still have a problem with it? I realize, of course, that it takes a while for people to notice there's been a change. We still, for instance, think of Stella Artois as reassuringly expensive rather than a drink that causes you to beat up your wife.

But continuing to think of Birmingham as a wart is as daft as continuing to imagine that York is full of oxen. You simply can't not like the city any more. And it's hard to dislike the people either. Chiefly because they are usually more British than we'll ever be.

Show a Brummie a spectacular house and after he's arranged his face to register a complete and absolute lack of interest, he will say, 'I wouldn't want to hoover a sitting room that big.' Show him an amazing garden and he will say, 'I bet that takes a lot of digging.' Put his wife in a pretty frock and he will wonder what happens when she spills her balti on it. In short, a Birmingham person is born with an inability to say, 'That is amazing.'

The British have a global reputation for keeping their emotions hidden. But Brummies have taken this to a level that would flabbergast even the Duke of Marlborough. Their emotions are not just hidden. They are locked in a safe and buried under twenty tons of concrete, in a well, at the bottom of the garden.

You know Michaela Strachan? The bubbly, enthusiastic former children's TV presenter? She's not from Birmingham. We know this because she released a video called *Wild About Baby Animals*. If she'd been a Brummie, it would have been called *Not Bothered Either Away About Baby Animals*.

Of course, this refusal to find anything wondrous can be rather irritating. Especially when you are with a Brummie at the Grand Canyon and he's facing the other way, checking his text messages. I'm not saying who that was. Only that his name begins with R and ends with ichard Hammond.

However, when you see a party of Americans whooping and high-fiving one another about something as trivial as a tropical sunset, you crave the company of a Brummie, who'll wilfully face east and tell you he'd rather be in Moseley.

I'd be happy in the trenches with a Brummie too. Because the upside of his downbeat nature is that he doesn't find things spectacularly bad either. You get the impression a Brummie would be capable of sitting there watching a rat eat his gangrenous foot without moaning anywhere near as much as, say, me.

So. We go back to the original question. Why, if the city's improved and the people are stoic, does the rest of the country have such a problem with the place? Well, there's no easy way of saying this. But, um, it's the accent.

In the complex world of advertising, a Yorkshire twang is perceived to be honest. Which is why Sean Bean is used to promote every single thing. It's the same story with the

Scotch. *Gavin & Stacey* has made the Welsh accent funny and likeable, and now that Cilla Black has taken her mocking tones into retirement, posh is okay as well.

A Birmingham accent, however, makes you sound thick. If Einstein had been from King's Heath, no one would have taken the theory of relativity seriously. If Churchill had been a Brummie, we'd have lost the war. And if you don't believe me, just get someone from Castle Bromwich to read out the 'We shall fight on the beaches' speech.

That's why people hate Birmingham. It's because they think everyone who lives there is a bit daft. Happily, though, I have a solution. If the council really wants its city to thrive after the second phase of HS2 has turned it into an oxbow lake, it needs to stop giving the locals more bars. And send them for elocution lessons instead.

24 February 2013

As Russians say, manners maketh the British late

Time. It's now so precious that we will happily spend an absolute fortune making all the things we do faster, simply so we have time to do more things.

A decade or more ago, if you were suddenly consumed with a need to watch some online footage of a cat falling over, it took about a minute for your internet to load the film. This was a minute none of us could spare. Then we got the idea of watching it on the go. Luckily a conglomerate of international mobile phone companies had paid the British government £22 billion for something called 3G. This meant people had to wait only five seconds to see a cat falling over, and for a while we were all very happy.

But then we realized that in the modern world five seconds is far too long. So now phone companies have paid a further £2.3 billion for 4G, a service that delivers hilarious animal-related accidents almost instantaneously.

We see the same thing going on in lifts. We need a button that closes the doors when we're ready to go because we simply cannot wait four seconds for them to close by themselves. Rightly so. Two lift journeys a day could waste eight seconds. Which in a working week is forty seconds. In a time frame that vast we could have watched six cats falling over. And an amusing helicopter crash.

It's the same at our favourite supermarket. If the queues are too long, we will go elsewhere. Even if we know the next shop fills its burgers with horses, toenails and bits of mashed bat.

I know I'm more pathological than most about wasting time, but surely you too must froth at the mouth when you sit down to watch a DVD and you are electronically prevented from fast-forwarding through the legal disclaimers that precede it. This is lawyers stealing our lives. And we hate it.

It's strange, though. We fume in traffic jams and curse when people on pavements walk too slowly, yet we are prepared to waste hours and hours of every day gurning and engaging in idle chitchat with people we don't know.

The British middle-class obsession with good manners means we feel obliged to discuss the weather with our postman and our holidays with our hairdresser. We write ridiculously long thank-you letters to people we've already thanked verbally. In business emails we use words that aren't necessary simply because we feel the need to be polite, and if we want directions we always start out by saying, 'Excuse me. I hate to be a bother but . . .'

Been on a flight recently? The obsequiousness is now so rampant that it takes half an hour to make every announcement. 'Any bread items for yourself at all today, sir?'

I bring all of this up because I've just spent a week in Russia where manners don't seem to have been invented. When a hotel receptionist needs your passport, she doesn't say, 'Would it be possible to see your passport for a moment, sir, if it isn't too much trouble?' She says, 'Passport.' And if you can't find it within three seconds, she says, 'Now!'

When you order a dish from a menu that isn't available, there's no tiresome hand-wringing explanation from the waiter. He just says, 'It's off.' And if you are struggling to get your luggage through a revolving door, no one waits patiently until you've sorted the problem out. They repeatedly shove the handles until everything in your suitcase is smashed and your fingers have been severed.